BELIEVE ME

ALSO BY TAHEREH MAFI

SHATTER ME SERIES:

Shatter Me

Unravel Me

Ignite Me

RESTORE ME SERIES:

Restore Me

Defy Me

Imagine Me

NOVELLA COLLECTIONS:

Unite Me (Destroy Me & Fracture Me)

Find Me (Shadow Me & Reveal Me)

A Very Large Expanse of Sea

An Emotion of Great Delight

This Woven Kingdom

These Infinite Threads

BELIEVE ME

TAHEREH MAFI

DEAN

DEAN

First published in Great Britain 2021 by Electric Monkey, part of Farshore
This edition published 2023 by Dean, part of Farshore
An imprint of HarperCollins*Publishers*
1 London Bridge Street, London SE1 9GF
www.farshore.co.uk

HarperCollins*Publishers*
Macken House, 39/40 Mayor Street Upper,
Dublin 1, D01 C9W8, Ireland

Text copyright © 2021 Tahereh Mafi

ISBN 978 0 0086 0668 8
Printed and Bound in the UK using 100% Renewable Electricity
at CPI Group (UK) Ltd
005

A CIP catalogue record for this title is available from the British Library.

All rights reserved. No part of this publication may be reproduced,
stored in a retrieval system, or transmitted, in any form or by any means,
electronic, mechanical, photocopying, recording or otherwise, without
the prior permission of the publisher and copyright owner.

Stay safe online. Farshore is not responsible for content hosted by third parties.

This book is produced from independently certified FSC™ paper
to ensure responsible forest management.

For more information visit: www.harpercollins.co.uk/green

ONE

The wall is unusually white.

More white than is usual. Most people think white walls are true white, but the truth is, they only seem white and are not actually white. Most shades of white are mixed in with a bit of yellow, which helps soften the harsh edges of a pure white, making it more of an ecru, or ivory. Various shades of cream. Egg white, even. True white is practically intolerable as a color, so white it's nearly blue.

This wall, in particular, is not so white as to be offensive, but a sharp enough shade of white to pique my curiosity, which is nothing short of a miracle, really, because I've been staring at it for the greater part of an hour. Thirty-seven minutes, to be exact.

I am being held hostage by custom. Formality.

"Five more minutes," she says. "I promise."

I hear the rustle of fabric. Zippers. A shudder of—

"Is that tulle?"

"You're not supposed to be listening!"

"You know, love, it occurs to me now that I've lived through hostage situations less torturous than this."

"Okay, okay, it's off. Packed away. I just need a second to put on my cl—"

"That won't be necessary," I say, turning around. "Surely this part, I should be allowed to watch."

I lean against the unusually white wall, studying her as she frowns at me, her lips still parted around the shape of a word she seems to have forgotten.

"Please continue," I say, gesturing with a nod. "Whatever you were doing before."

She holds on to her frown for a moment longer than is honest, her eyes narrowing in a show of frustration that is pure fraud. She compounds this farce by clutching an article of clothing to her chest, feigning modesty.

I do not mind, not one single bit.

I drink her in, her soft curves, her smooth skin. Her hair is beautiful at any length, but it's been longer lately. Long and rich, silky against her skin, and—when I'm lucky—against mine.

Slowly, she drops the shirt.

I stand up straighter.

"I'm supposed to wear this under the dress," she says, her fake anger already forgotten. She fidgets with the boning of a cream-colored corset, her fingers lingering along the garter belt, the lace-trimmed stockings. She can't meet my eyes. She's gone shy, and this time, it's real.

Do you like it?

The unspoken question.

I assumed, when she invited me into this dressing room, that it was for reasons beyond me staring at the color variations in an unusually white wall. I assumed she wanted me here to see something.

To see her.

I see now that I was correct.

"You are so beautiful," I say, unable to shed the awe in my voice. I hear it, the childish wonder in my tone, and it embarrasses me more than it should. I know I shouldn't be ashamed to feel deeply. To be moved.

Still, I feel awkward.

Young.

Quietly, she says, "I feel like I just spoiled the surprise. You're not supposed to see any of this until the wedding night."

My heart actually stops for a moment.

The wedding night.

She closes the distance between us and twines her arms around me, freeing me from my momentary paralysis. My heart beats faster with her here, so close. And though I don't know how she knew that I suddenly required the reassurance of her touch, I'm grateful. I exhale, pulling her fully against me, our bodies relaxing, remembering each other.

I press my face into her hair, breathe in the sweet scent of her shampoo, her skin. It's only been two weeks. Two weeks since the end of an old world. The beginning of a new one.

She still feels like a dream to me.

"Is this really happening?" I whisper.

A sharp knock at the door startles my spine straight.

Ella frowns at the sound. "Yes?"

"So sorry to bother you right now, miss, but there's a gentleman here wishing to speak with Mr. Warner."

Ella and I lock eyes.

"Okay," she says quickly. "Don't be mad."

"Why would I be mad?"

Ella pulls away to better look me in the eye. Her own eyes are bright, beautiful. Full of concern. "It's Kenji."

I force down a spike of anger so violent I think I give myself a stroke. "What is he doing here?" I manage to get out. "How did he know how to find us?"

She bites her lip. "We took Amir and Olivier with us."

"I see." We took extra guards along, which means our outing was posted to the public security bulletin. Of course.

Ella nods. "He found me just before we left. He was worried—he wanted to know why we were heading back into the old regulated lands."

I try to say something then, to marvel aloud at Kenji's inability to make a simple deduction despite the abundance of contextual clues right before his eyes—but she holds up a finger.

"I told him," she says, "that we were looking for replacement outfits and reminded him that, for now, the Supply Centers are still the only places to shop for food or clothing or"—she waves a hand, frowns—"anything, at the moment. Anyway, he said he'd try to meet us here. He said he wanted to help."

My eyes widen slightly. I feel another stroke incoming.

"He said he wanted to *help*."

She nods.

"Astonishing." A muscle ticks in my jaw. "And funny, too, because he's already helped so much—just last night he helped us both a great deal by destroying my suit and your dress, forcing us to now purchase clothing from a"—I look around, gesture at nothing—"a *store* on the very day we're supposed to get married."

"Aaron," she whispers. She steps closer again. Places a hand on my chest. "He feels terrible about it."

"And you?" I say, studying her face, her feelings. "Don't *you* feel terrible about it? Alia and Winston worked so hard to make you something beautiful, something designed precisely for you—"

"I don't mind." She shrugs. "It's just a dress."

"But it was your wedding dress," I say, my voice failing me now.

She sighs, and in the sound I hear her heart break, more for me than for herself. She turns around and unzips the massive garment bag hanging on a hook above her head.

"You're not supposed to see this," she says, tugging yards of tulle out of the bag, "but I think it might mean more to you than it does to me, so"—she turns back, smiles—"I'll let you help me decide what to wear tonight."

I nearly groan aloud at the reminder.

A nighttime wedding. Who on earth is married at night? Only the hapless. The unfortunate. Though I suppose we now count among their ranks.

Rather than reschedule the entire thing, we pushed it a few hours so that we'd have time to purchase new clothes. Well, I have clothes. My clothes don't matter as much.

But her dress. He destroyed her dress the night before our wedding. Like a monster.

I'm going to murder him.

"You can't murder him," she says, still pulling handfuls of fabric out of the bag.

"I'm certain I said no such thing out loud."

"No," she says, "but you were thinking it, weren't you?"

"Wholeheartedly."

"You can't murder him," she says simply. "Not now. Not ever."

I sigh.

She's still struggling to unearth the gown.

"Forgive me, love, but if all this"—I nod at the garment bag, the explosion of tulle—"is for a single dress, I'm afraid I already know how I feel about it."

She stops tugging. Turns around, eyes wide. "You don't like it? You haven't even seen it yet."

"I've seen enough to know that whatever this is, it's not a gown. This is a haphazard layering of polyester." I lean around her, pinching the fabric between my fingers. "Do they not carry silk tulle in this store? Perhaps we can speak to the seamstress."

"They don't have a seamstress here."

"This is a clothing store," I say. I turn the bodice inside out, frowning at the stitches. "Surely there must be a seamstress. Not a very good one, clearly, but—"

"These dresses are made in a factory," she says to me. "Mostly by machine."

I straighten.

"You know, most people didn't grow up with private tailors at their disposal," she says, a smile playing at her lips. "The rest of us had to buy clothes off the rack. Premade. Ill-fitting."

"Yes," I say stiffly. I feel suddenly stupid. "Of course. Forgive me. The dress is very nice. Perhaps I should wait for you to try it on. I gave my opinion too hastily."

For some reason, my response only makes things worse.

She groans, shooting me a single, defeated look before folding herself into the little dressing room chair.

My heart plummets.

She drops her face in her hands. "It really is a disaster, isn't it?"

Another swift knock at the door. "Sir? The gentleman seems very eager t—"

"He's certainly not a gentleman," I say sharply. "Tell him to wait."

A moment of hesitation. Then, quietly: "Yes, sir."

"Aaron."

I don't need to look up to know that she's unhappy with my rudeness. The owners of this particular Supply Center shut down their entire store for us, and they've been excruciatingly kind. I know I'm being an ass. At present, I can't seem to help it.

"Aaron."

"Today is your wedding day," I say, unable to meet her eyes. "He has ruined your wedding day. Our wedding day."

She gets to her feet. I feel her frustration fade. Transform. Shuffle through sadness, happiness, hope, fear, and finally—

Resignation.

One of the worst possible feelings on what should be a joyous day. Resignation is worse than frustration. Far worse.

My anger calcifies.

"He hasn't ruined it," she says finally. "We can still make this work."

"You're right," I say, pulling her into my arms. "Of course you're right. It doesn't matter, really. None of it does."

"But it's my wedding day," she says. "And I have nothing to wear."

"You're right." I kiss the top of her head. "I'm going to kill him."

A sudden pounding at the door.

I stiffen. Spin around.

"Hey, guys?" More pounding. "I know you're super pissed at me, but I have good news, I swear. I'm going to fix this. I'm going to make it up to you."

I'm just about to respond when Ella tugs at my hand, silencing my scathing retort with a single motion. She shoots me a look that plainly says—

Give him a chance.

I sigh as the anger settles inside my body, my shoulders dropping with the weight of it. Reluctantly, I step aside to allow her to deal with this idiot in the manner she prefers.

It is her wedding day, after all.

Ella steps closer to the door. Points at it, jabbing her finger at the unusually white paint as she speaks. "This better be good, Kenji, or Warner is going to kill you, and I'm going to help him do it."

And then, just like that—

I'm smiling again.

TWO

We're driven back to the Sanctuary the same way we're driven everywhere these days—in a black, all-terrain, bulletproof SUV—but the car and its heavily tinted windows only make us more conspicuous, which I find worrisome. But then, as Castle likes to point out, I have no ready solution for the problem, so we remain at an impasse.

I try to hide my reaction as we drive up through the wooded area just outside the Sanctuary, but I can't help my grimace or the way my body locks down, preparing for a fight. After the fall of The Reestablishment, most rebel groups emerged from hiding to rejoin the world—

But not us.

Just last week we cleared this dirt path for the SUV, enabling it to now get as close as possible to the unmarked entrance, but I'm not sure it's doing much to help. A mob of people has already crowded in so tightly around us that we're moving no more than an inch at a time. Most of them are well-meaning, but they scream and pound at the car with the enthusiasm of a belligerent crowd, and every time we endure this circus I have to physically force myself to remain calm. To sit quietly in my seat and ignore the urge to remove the gun from its holster beneath my jacket.

Difficult.

I know Ella can protect herself—she's proven this fact a thousand times over—but still, I can't help but worry. She's become notorious to a near-terrifying degree. To some extent, we all have. But Juliette Ferrars, as she's known around the world, can go nowhere and do nothing without drawing a crowd.

They say they love her.

Even so, we remain cautious. There are still many around the globe who would love to bring back to life the emaciated remains of The Reestablishment, and assassinating a beloved hero would be the most effective start to such a scheme. Though we have unprecedented levels of privacy in the Sanctuary, where Nouria's sight and sound protections around the grounds grant us freedoms we enjoy nowhere else, we've been unable to hide our precise location. People know, generally, where to find us, and that small bit of information has been feeding them for weeks. The civilians wait here—thousands and thousands of them—every single day.

For no more than a glimpse.

We've had to put barricades in place. We've had to hire extra security, recruiting armed soldiers from the local sectors. This area is unrecognizable from what it was a month ago. It's a different world already. And I feel my body go solid as we approach the entrance. Nearly there now.

I look up, ready to say something—

"Don't worry." Kenji locks eyes with me. "Nouria upped

the security. There should be a team of people waiting for us."

"I don't know why all this is necessary," Ella says, still staring out the window. "Why can't I just stop for a minute and talk to them?"

"Because the last time you did that you were nearly trampled," Kenji says, exasperated.

"Just the one time."

Kenji's eyes go wide with outrage, and on this point, he and I are in full agreement. I sit back and watch as he counts off on his fingers. "The same day you were nearly trampled, someone tried to cut off your hair. Another day a bunch of people tried to kiss you. People literally throw their newborn babies at you. I've already counted six people who've peed their pants in your presence, which, I have to add, is not only upsetting but unsanitary, especially when they try to hug you while they're still wetting themselves." He shakes his head. "The mobs are too big, princess. Too strong. Too passionate. Everyone screams in your face, fights to put their hands on you. And half the time we can't protect you."

"But—"

"I know that most of these people are well intentioned," I say, taking her hand. She turns in her seat, meets my eyes. "They are, for the most part, kind. Curious. Overwhelmed with gratitude and desperate to put a face to their freedom.

"I know this," I say, "because I always check the crowds, searching their energy for anger or violence. And though the vast majority of them are good"—I sigh, shake my head—"sweetheart, you've just made a lot of enemies. These massive, unfiltered crowds are not safe. Not yet. Maybe not ever."

She takes a deep breath, lets it out slowly. "I know you're right," she says quietly. "But somehow it feels wrong not to be able to talk to the people we've been fighting for. I want them to know how I feel. I want them to know much we care—and how much we're still planning on doing to rebuild, to get things right."

"You will," I say. "I'll make sure you have the chance to say all those things. But it's only been two weeks, love. We don't have the necessary infrastructure to make that happen."

"But we're working on it, right?"

"We're working on it," Kenji says. "Which, actually—not that I'm making excuses or anything—but if you hadn't asked me to prioritize the reconstruction committee, I probably wouldn't have issued orders to knock down a series of unsafe buildings, one of which included Winston and Alia's studio, which"—he holds up his hands—"for the record, I didn't know was their studio. And again, not that I'm making excuses for my reprehensible behavior or anything—but how the hell was I supposed to know it was an art studio? It was officially listed in the books as unsafe, marked for demolition—"

"They didn't know it was marked for demolition," Ella says, a hint of impatience in her voice. "They made it into their studio precisely because no one was using it."

"Yes," Kenji says, pointing at her. "Right. But, see, I didn't know that."

"Winston and Alia are your friends," I say unkindly. "Isn't it your business to know things like that?"

"Listen, man, it's been a really hectic two weeks since the world fell apart, okay? I've been busy."

"We've all been busy."

"Okay, enough," Ella says, holding up a hand. She's looking out the window, frowning. "Someone is coming."

Kent.

"What's Adam doing here?" Ella asks. She turns back to look at Kenji. "Did you know he was coming?"

If Kenji responds, I don't hear him. I'm peering out of the very-tinted windows at the scene outside, watching Adam push his way through the crowd toward the car. He appears to be unarmed. He shouts something into the sea of people, but they won't be quieted right away. A few more tries—and they settle down. Thousands of faces turn to stare at him.

I struggle to make out his words.

And then, slowly, he stands back as ten heavily armed men and women approach our car. Their bodies form a barricade between the vehicle and the entrance into the Sanctuary, and Kenji jumps out first, going invisible and leading the way. He projects his power to protect Ella, and I steal his stealth for myself. The three of us—our bodies invisible—move cautiously toward the entrance.

Only once we're on the other side, safely within the boundaries of the Sanctuary, do I finally relax.

A little.

I glance back, the way I always do, at the crowd gathered just beyond the invisible barrier that protects our camp. Some days I just stand here and study their faces, searching for something. Anything. A threat still unknown, unnamed.

"Hey—awesome," Winston says, his unexpected voice shaking me out of my reverie.

I turn to look at him, discovering him sweaty and out of breath.

"So glad you guys are back," he says. "Do any of you happen to know anything about fixing pipes? We've got a kind of sewage problem in one of the tents, and it's all hands on deck."

Our return to reality is swift.

And humbling.

But Ella steps forward, already reaching for the—dear God, is it wet?—wrench in Winston's hand, and I almost can't believe it. I wrap an arm around her waist, tugging her back. "Please, love. Not today. Any other day, maybe. But not today."

"What?" She glances back. "Why not? I'm really good with a wrench. Hey, by the way," she says, turning to the others, "did you know that Ian is secretly good at woodworking?"

Winston laughs.

"It's only been a secret to you, princess," Kenji says.

She frowns. "Well, we were fixing one of the more savable buildings the other day, and he taught me how to use everything in his toolbox. I helped him build a wall," she says, beaming.

"That's a strange justification for spending the hours before your wedding digging feces out of a toilet." Kent again. He's laughing.

My brother.

So strange.

He saunters up to us, a happier, healthier version of him than I've ever seen before. He took a week to recover after we got him back here, but when he regained consciousness and we told him what happened—and assured him that James was safe—he fainted.

And didn't wake up for another two days.

He's become an entirely different person in the days since. Practically jubilant. Happy for everyone. A darkness still clings to all of us—will probably cling to all of us forever—

But Adam seems undeniably changed.

"Just a heads-up," he says, "that we're doing a new thing now. Nouria wants me to go out there and do a general deactivation before anyone enters or exits the grounds. Just as a precaution." He looks at Ella. "Juliette, is that okay with you?"

Juliette.

So many things changed when we came home, and this was one of them. She took back her name. Reclaimed it. She said that by erasing Juliette from her life she feared she was giving the ghost of my father too much power over her. She realized she didn't want to forget her years as Juliette—or to diminish the young woman she was, fighting against all odds to survive. Juliette Ferrars is who she was when she was made known to the world, and she wants it to remain that way.

I'm the only one allowed to call her Ella now.

It's just for us. A tether to our shared history, a nod to our past, to the love I've always felt for her, no matter her name.

I watch her as she laughs with her friends, as she pulls a hammer free from Winston's tool belt and pretends to hit Kenji with it—no doubt for something he deserves. Lily and Nazeera come out of nowhere, Lily carrying a small bundle of a dog she and Ian saved from an abandoned building nearby. Ella drops the hammer with a sudden cry and Adam jumps back in alarm. She takes the filthy beast into her arms, smothering it with kisses even as it barks at her with a wild ferocity. And then she turns to look at me, the animal still yipping in her ear, and I realize there are tears in her eyes. She is crying over a dog.

Juliette Ferrars, one of the most feared, most lauded heroes of our known world, is crying over a dog. Perhaps no one else would understand, but I know that this is the first time she's ever held one. Without hesitation, without fear, without danger of causing an innocent creature any harm. For her, this is true joy.

To the world, she is formidable.

To me?

She is the world.

So when she dumps the creature into my reluctant arms, I hold it steady, uncomplaining when the beast licks my face with the same tongue it used, no doubt, to clean its hindquarters. I remain steady, betraying nothing even when warm drool drips down my neck. I hold still as its grimy feet dig into my coat, nails catching at the wool. I am so still, in fact, that eventually the creature quiets, its anxious limbs settling against my chest. It whines as it stares at me, whines until I finally lift a hand, drag it over its head.

When I hear her laugh, I am happy.

THREE

"Warner?"

"Mr. Warner?"

The invocation of my name in stereo nearly startles me; I absorb this surprise with practiced calm, carefully releasing the dog to the ground. I begin to turn in the direction of the familiar voices, but the liberated creature decides to do nothing with its freedom, instead lifting a paw to my trousers as it whines, yet again, its upturned face imploring me to do something.

Feed it? Pet it?

It barks then, and I spare it a single sharp look, after which it quiets, eyes cast down as its mangy body slumps to the ground, head resting on its paws. The dog settles so close to me its little black snout bumps my boot. I sigh.

"Mr. Warner?" Castle, again.

He and his daughter, Nouria, are staring at me, the latter breaking eye contact only to shoot her father a nearly imperceptible look of frustration.

I glance between them. Clearly, the two still haven't fully settled the specifics of their roles around here.

"Yes?" I say, even as a feeling of unease blooms in my chest.

Castle and Nouria have come to collect me for a private conversation; I can sense this right away. That my mind reaches for anger in response is irrational—I understand this even as it happens—for they cannot know the fear I experience when I leave Ella behind. I have a sudden need to search for her eyes then, to reach for her hand, and I crush the impulse even as my heart rate climbs, a symptom of the new panic lately born in my body. These reactions began shortly after we returned to the Sanctuary; when, to the soundtrack of horrified screams, Ella's limp figure was carted off the plane and planted in the medical tent, where she lived and slept for ten of the fourteen days we've been back. It has been, in a word—*difficult*. And now, whenever I can't see her, my brain tries to convince me she's dead.

Castle says, "Could we steal you for a brief window? Something urgent has come up, and w—"

Nouria presses pause on this statement with a gentle touch to her father's forearm. Her smile is forced.

"I'll need only a few minutes of your time," she says, glancing briefly at someone—Ella, probably—before meeting my eyes again. "I promise it won't take long."

I want to say no.

Instead, I say, "Of course," and finally compel myself to look at Ella, whose steady gaze I have been avoiding. I smile at her as my brain attempts to override its own instincts, to do the calculus necessary to prove my fears a manifestation of an imaginary threat. Every day that Ella remains alive and well is a victory, a concrete set of numbers to add to a column, all of which make it easier for me to do this math; I'm able to process the panic a bit faster now than I did those first few nights. Still—despite my efforts to keep this from her—I have felt Ella watch me. Worry.

Even now, my smile has not convinced her.

She scrutinizes my eyes as she presses a bouquet of newly acquired tools—screwdrivers?—into Kenji's arms. She walks over to me and promptly takes my hand and I'm dealt the blow of an emotional eye roll from our audience. It is a miracle, then, that Ella's love is louder; and I'm so grateful for the reassurance of her touch it pierces me through the chest.

"What's going on?" she says to Nouria. "Maybe I can help."

I catch a note of worry from Nouria then, and, impressive: it never touches her features. She grins when she says, "I think you have enough to do today. Warner and I just have some things we need to discuss. *Privately.*"

She says this last bit in a teasing way, the implication that our discussion might have something to do with the wedding. I stare intently at Nouria, who will not now meet my eyes.

Ella squeezes my hand and I turn to face her.

You okay? she seems to say.

She's done this a lot lately, speaking to me with her thoughts, her emotions.

For a moment, I can only stare at her. A riot of feeling seems to have fused inside me, fear and joy and love and terror now indistinguishable from one another. I lean down, kiss her gently on the cheek. Her skin is so soft I'm tempted to linger, even as the emotional disgust of our audience ratchets only higher.

I've been afraid to touch her lately.

In fact, I've done little more than hold her since we fled Oceania. She nearly died on the flight home. She was already weak when we found Emmaline, having spent most of her energy fighting to kill the poisonous program overriding her mind; worse, she'd torn the tech free from her arm, leaving behind a gaping, gruesome wound. She was still bleeding from her ears, her nose, her eyes, and her teeth when she tore through Max's light, stripping the flesh from her fingers in the process. She was so drained by this point that even with Evie's reinforcements her body was failing. She landed badly and snapped her femur when she fell loose from Max's holding chamber, and then used what little strength she had left to first kill her own sister and then set fire to the capital of Oceania.

When the adrenaline wore off and I saw, for the first time, the edge of severed bone jutting through her pant leg—

The memory is not worth describing.

The next several hours were grim; we had no healers on the flight home, no sufficient pain medication, nothing more than a basic first aid kit. Ella had lost so much blood—and was in such excruciating pain—that she soon fell unconscious. I had no doubt she would die before we touched ground. That she survived that horrific plane ride was its own miracle.

When we finally arrived on base Sonya and Sara did everything they could to help Ella, but they made no promises; even as Ella's physical injuries healed, she was unresponsive. She was incapable of even opening her eyes.

For days, I wasn't sure she would make it.

"Aaron—"

"*Secrets*," I whisper, forcing myself to draw away. "Nothing to worry about."

She studies my eyes. I feel her quietly wage war, happiness and doubt fighting for dominance.

"Good secrets?" she asks hopefully.

My heart lurches at the softness in her voice, the smile that lights up her eyes. I never cease wondering at how skillfully she compartmentalizes her emotions, even in the wake of so much brutality.

Ella is strong where I have forever been weak.

I lost faith in people—in the world—long ago. But no matter how much bloodshed and darkness she experiences, Ella never seems to lose hope in humanity. She is always striving to build a better future. She is always gentle and kind with those she loves.

It is still so strange to me that I am one of those people.

I feel the hum of Castle and Nouria's increasing impatience, and my resentment grows only larger; I generate a fresh smile for Ella and walk away as I do, having left her question unanswered. I don't know what Nouria needs from me, but I fear her news is bleak; no doubt Ella's life is at risk in some new way we'd not anticipated.

The thought alone fills me with dread.

Unbidden, I feel my hands tremble; I shove them in my pockets as I go. The hesitant bark of a mangy dog is soon followed by the sound of its paws tapping the ground, the little beast picking up speed as it hurries to keep pace with me. Briefly, I close my eyes.

This place is a zoo.

Even as I recognize the importance of our work, there remains a regrettably large portion of my mind that finds everyone here detestable—*everything* here detestable.

I am tired.

I want nothing more than to escape this noise with Ella. I want, above all else, for her to be safe. I want people to stop trying to kill her. I want, for the first time in my life, to live in peace, undisturbed; I want to be required by no one but my wife.

These, I realize, are unattainable fantasies.

Castle and Nouria both nod at me as I approach, indicating that I should follow their lead as they turn down the path. I already know they're headed to Nouria and Sam's office—affectionately labeled *the war room*—where we've had many similar meetings.

I glance back just once, hoping to catch a final glimpse of Ella's face, and instead home in on Kenji, whose thoughts are so loud they're impossible to ignore. I experience a flash of anger; I know he's going to follow me even before he moves in my direction.

Between him and the dog trailing me, I'd choose the dog.

Still, both creatures are on my heels now, and I hear Adam laugh as he says something unintelligible to Winston, the two of them no doubt enjoying the spectacle that is my life.

"What?" I say sharply.

The approaching shadow soon evolves into flesh beside me, Kenji matching my strides down the overgrown path, our boots crushing aggressive weeds underfoot. Figures dot the periphery of my vision, their feelings assaulting me as I go. Some of them still think I'm some kind of hero, and are consumed as a result by an idiotic devotion to a warped perception of my identity. My face. My body.

I find these interactions suffocating. Just now, Kenji's anger toward me is so audible I feel it giving me a headache. Still—better anger, I think, than grief.

The collective grief of a crowd is nearly unbearable.

"You know, I really thought you'd be less of an asshole once we got J home," he says flatly. "I see nothing has changed. I see all the efforts I made to defend your shitty behavior were for nothing."

The dog barks. I hear it panting.

It barks again.

"So you're just going to ignore me?" Kenji exhales, irritated. "Why? Why are you like this? Why are you always such a dick?"

Sometimes I'm so desperate for quiet I think I might

commit murder for a moment of silence. Instead, I shut down incrementally, tuning out as many voices as I'm able. It wasn't so bad before I was forced to join this peace cult. In my previous life at Sector 45 I was left alone. At Omega Point, I spent most of my time in solitary confinement. When we later took over 45, I retained the privacy of my rooms.

Here, I am losing my mind.

I am bombarded, en masse, by the emotional downloads of others. There is no reprieve from the pandemonium. Ella likes spending time with these people, and these people do everything in crowds. Meals are taken in a massive dining tent. End-of-day mingling is done communally, in the quiet tent, where it is never quiet. Many of the cabins were damaged or destroyed in the battle, which means everyone is currently sharing space—or sleeping in common areas—while we rebuild. Nouria and Sam did us a kindness by repurposing Ella's room in the medical tent; it seemed the only alternative to bunking with everyone else in a makeshift barracks. Still, our room smells always of antiseptic and death. There is only one narrow hospital bed, over which Ella and I argue each night. She insists, despite my unassailable protests, that I take the bed while she sleeps on the floor.

It's the only time I ever get upset with her.

I don't mind the cold floor. I don't mind physical discomfort. No, what I hate is lying awake every night listening to the pain and grief of others still recovering. I hate being reminded constantly of the ten days I spent standing in the corner of our room watching Ella struggle to come back to life.

My need for silence has grown debilitating. Sometimes I think if I could kill this part of me, I would.

"*Don't touch me*," I say suddenly, sensing Kenji's intention to make contact with me—to tap my shoulder or grab my arm—before it happens. It takes a great deal of self-control not to physically respond.

"Why do you have to say it like that?" he says, wounded. "Why do you make it sound like I was going to *enjoy* touching you? I'm just trying to get your attention."

"What do you need, Kishimoto?" I ask unkindly. "I'm not interested in your company."

His responding pain is loud; it glances off my chest, leaving a vague impression. This pathetic new development fills me with shame. I desperately don't want to care, and yet—

Ella adores this idiot.

I come to a sudden stop on the path. The dog bumps my legs, wagging its tail violently before barking again. I take a deep breath, stare at a tree in the distance.

"What is it you need?" I ask again, this time gently.

I feel him frown as he processes his feelings. He doesn't look at me when he says, "I just wanted to tell you that I got it."

I stiffen at that, my body activating with awareness. I pivot fully to face him. Suddenly, Kenji Kishimoto appears to me vividly rendered: his tired eyes, his tanned skin, his heavy, sharp black brows—and his hair, in desperate need of a cut. There's a bruise fading along his temple, his left hand wrapped in gauze. I hear the rattle of leaves and spot a squirrel, darting into a bush. The dog goes berserk.

"You got what?" I say carefully.

"Oh, now you're interested?" He meets my eyes, his own narrowed in anger. "Now you're going to look at me like I'm a human being? You know what? Fuck this. I don't even know why I do shit for you."

"You didn't do it for me."

Kenji makes a sound of disbelief, looking away before looking back at me. "Yeah, well, she deserves to have a nice ring, doesn't she? You miserable piece of shit. Who proposes to a girl without a ring?"

"I might remind you that you are in no position to exercise moral superiority," I say, my voice growing lethal even as I will myself to remain calm. "Having *destroyed* her wedding dress."

"That was an accident!" he cries. "Yours was an oversight!"

"Your very existence is an oversight."

"Oh, wow." He throws up his hands. "Ha ha. Very mature comeback."

"Do you have it or not?"

"Yeah. I do." He shoves his hands in his pockets. "But, you know, now I'm thinking I should just give it to her myself. After all, I was the one who did all of this for you. I was the one who asked Winston to sketch your design.

I was the one who found someone to make the goddamn thing—"

"*I was not going to leave the grounds while she was lying in a hospital bed,*" I say, so close to shouting that Kenji visibly startles. He steps back, studies me a moment.

I neutralize my expression, but too late.

Kenji loses his anger as he stands there, softening as he stares at me. I experience nothing but rage in response.

He never seems to understand. It's his constant pity—his sympathy, not his stupidity—that makes me want to kill him.

I take a step forward, lower my voice. "If you are idiotic enough to think I will allow you to be the one to give her this wedding ring, you have clearly underestimated me. I might not be able to kill you, Kishimoto, but I will devote my life to making yours a palpable, never-ending hellscape."

He cracks a smile. "I'm not going to give her the ring, man. I wouldn't do that. I was just messing with you."

I stare at him. I can hardly speak for wanting to throttle him. "You were just *messing* with me? That was your idea of a joke?"

"Yeah, okay, listen, you are way too intense," he says, making a face. "Juliette would've thought that was funny."

"You clearly don't know her very well if you think so."

"Whatever." Kenji crosses his arms. "I've known her longer than you have, asshole."

At this, I experience an anger so acute I think I might actually kill him. Kenji must see this, because he backpedals.

"No—you're right," he says, pointing at me. "My bad, bro. I forgot about all the memory-wiping stuff. I didn't mean that. I only meant, like— I know her, too, you know?"

"I'm going to give you five seconds to get to your point."

"See? Who says stuff like that?" Kenji's brows furrow; his anger is back. "What does that even mean? What are you going to do to me in five seconds? What if I don't even have a point? No—you know what, I do have a point. My point is that I'm sick of this. I'm sick of your attitude. I'm sick of making excuses for your crappy behavior. I really thought you'd try to be cool for J's sake, especially now, after everything she's been through—"

"I know what she's been through," I say darkly.

"Oh, really?" Kenji says, feigning surprise. "So then maybe you already know this, too"—he makes a dramatic gesture with his hands—"*news flash*: she's, like, a genuinely nice person. She actually gives a shit about other people. She doesn't threaten to murder people all the time. *And she likes my jokes.*"

"She's very charitable, I know."

Kenji exhales angrily and looks around, searching the sky for inspiration. "You know, I've tried, I really have, but I just don't know what she sees in you. She's like—she's like sunshine. And you're a dark, violent rain cloud. Sun and rain don't—"

Kenji cuts himself off, blinking.

I walk away before the realization hits him. Nothing is worth listening to him finish that sentence.

"Oh my God," he says, his voice carrying. *"Oh my God."*

I pick up speed.

"Hey— Don't walk away from me when I'm about to say something awesome—"

"Don't you dare say it—"

"I'm going to say it, man. I have to say it," Kenji says, jumping ahead of me on the path. He's walking backward now, grinning like an idiot.

"I was wrong," he says, making a crude heart shape with his hands. "Sun and rain make a rainbow."

I come to a sudden halt. For a moment, I close my eyes.

"I want to throw up now," Kenji says, still smiling. "Really. Actual vomit. You disgust me."

I'm able to manufacture only mild anger in response to this slew of insults, as the feeling dissipates in the face of irrefutable evidence: Kenji's words belie his emotions. He's genuinely happy for us; I can feel it.

He's happy for Ella, in particular.

I experience a pang at that, at the love and devotion she's inspired in others. It's a rare thing to find even a single person who desires your unqualified joy; she has found many.

She's built her own family.

I exist on the outskirts of this phenomenon: hyperaware that I eclipse her light with my darkness, worried always that she will find me wanting. These relationships mean a great deal to her; I have long known this, and I have tried, for her sake, to be more social. To be nicer to her friends.

I don't protest when she asks to gather with the others; I no longer suggest that we take our meals alone together. I follow her around, sitting quietly beside her as she talks and laughs with people whose names I struggle to remember. I watch her bloom in the company of those she cares about, all while I try to drown out their voices, to kill the noise in my head. I worry, constantly, that despite my efforts, I will not be able to be what she wants.

It's true; I am insufferable.

I wonder whether it is only a matter of time before Ella discovers this fact for herself.

Subdued, the fight leaves my body.

"Either give me the ring or leave me alone," I say, hearing the exhaustion in my voice. "Nouria and Castle are waiting for me."

Kenji registers the change in my tone and switches gears, activating in himself a rarely witnessed solemnity. He looks at me for longer than I am comfortable before reaching into his pocket, from which he withdraws a dark blue velvet box.

This, he holds out to me.

I experience an unsettling spike of nerves as I study the box, and collect the object with trepidation, closing my fingers around its soft contours while staring into the distance, trying to collect myself.

I was not expecting to feel like this.

My heart is hammering in my chest. I feel like a nervous child. I wish Kenji were not here to witness this moment, and I wish I cared less about the contents of this box than I actually do, which is impossible.

It's desperately important to me that Ella love it.

Very slowly, I force myself to open the lid, the delicate objects inside catching the light before I've even had a chance to examine them. The rings glitter in the sun, refracting color everywhere. I don't dare remove them from their case, choosing instead only to stare, heart pounding as I do.

I couldn't decide between the two.

Kenji told me it was stupid to get two rings, but as I seldom care for Kenji's opinions, I'd ignored him. Now, as I stare at the set, I wonder if she will think me absurd. One is meant to be an engagement ring, and the other a wedding band—but they are both equally stunning, each in their own way.

The engagement ring is more traditional; the gold band is ultrathin, simple and elegant. There is a single center stone—repurposed from an antique—and though it's quite large, it seemed to me a study in contrasts that reflected how I saw Ella: both powerful and gentle. The jeweler had sent me a selection of stones, each extracted from rings salvaged from different eras. I'd been fascinated by the unusual faceting of an old mine cut diamond. It had been forged by hand a very, very long time ago and was, as a result, slightly imperfect, but I liked that it wasn't machine-made. The tedious, painful honing of a dull but unbreakable stone into a state of dazzling brilliance—it seemed appropriate.

Kenji had assured me there was such a thing as a *princess*-cut diamond, which he thought would be a hilarious choice for Ella, as it recalls his ridiculous nickname for her. I told him I had no interest in choosing a ring based on a joke; neither did I want my wife's wedding ring reminding her of another man. Besides, when I saw the shape of the stone in question, it felt wrong. The square was too sharp—all hard edges. It didn't remind me of Ella at all.

I asked that the antique stone be placed in a lightly filigreed, brushed-gold setting, the whisper-thin band of which I wanted to resemble an organic, delicate twig. This design is matched in the wedding band: a fine, curving branch rendered in gold, bare but for two tiny emerald leaves growing on opposite sides of the same path.

"It's really beautiful, man. She's going to love it."

I snap the box shut, returning to the present moment with a disorienting jolt. I look up to discover a contemplative Kenji has been watching me too closely; and I feel so suddenly uncomfortable in his presence that I fantasize, for a moment, about disappearing.

Then, I do.

"*Son of a bitch*," Kenji says angrily. He runs both hands through his hair, glaring at the place I stood. I tuck the velvet box into my pocket and turn down the path.

The dog barks twice.

"That's real mature, bro," Kenji shouts in my direction. "Very nice." Then—acidly—"And *you're welcome*, by the way. Dickhead."

The dog, still barking, haunts me all the way to the war room.

FOUR

The unvarnished wooden table has been worn smooth over the years, its raw edges buffed into submission by the calloused hands of rebels and revolutionaries. I run my fingers along the natural grooves, the faded age lines of a long-dead tree. The soft tick of a hanging clock signals what I already know to be true: that I have been here too long, and that every passing second costs me more of my sanity.

"Warner—"

"Absolutely not," I say quietly.

"We've hardly even discussed it. Don't dismiss the idea outright," Nouria says, her flat tone doing little to hide her true frustration, simmering too close to the surface. But then, Nouria is seldom able to hide how much she dislikes me.

I shove away from the table, my chair scraping against wood. It should probably concern me how easily my mind turns to murder for a solution to my problems, but I cannot now dissect these thoughts.

They separated me from Ella for *this*.

"You already know my position on the matter," I say, staring at the exit. "And it's not changing."

"I understand that. I know you're worried about her

safety—we're all worried about her safety—but we need help around here. We have to be able to bend the rules a little."

I meet Nouria's eyes then, my own bright with anger. The room shifts out of focus around her and still I see it: dark walls, old maps, a feeble bookshelf stocked with a collection of chipped coffee mugs. The air smells stale. It's depressing in here, shafts of sunlight slicing us all in half.

Things have been far from easy since we took power.

Those who lived well under the reign of The Reestablishment continue to cause us trouble—disobeying missives, refusing to leave their posts, continuing to rule their fiefdoms as if The Reestablishment were still at large. We don't have enough resources quite yet to track all of them down—most of whom know they will be promptly arrested and prosecuted for their crimes—and while some are bold enough to remain at their posts, others have been smart enough to go into hiding, from where they've been hiring mercenaries to carry out all manner of espionage—and inevitably, assassinations. These ex-officials are convening, recruiting ex-supreme soldiers to their side, and attempting to infiltrate our ranks in order to break us from within. They are perhaps the greatest threat to all that we are struggling to become.

I am deeply concerned.

I say little about this to Ella, as she's only just come back to herself in recent days, but our grasp on the world is tenuous at best. History has taught us that revolutions often fail—even after they've won—for fighters and rebels are often unequipped to handle the crushing weight of all they've fought for, and worse: they make for terrible politicians. This is the problem I've always had with Castle, and now with Nouria and Sam.

Revolutionaries are naive.

They don't seem to understand how the world really works, or how difficult it is to sate the whims and wishes of so many. It's a struggle every day to hold on to our lead, and I lose a great deal of sleep thinking about the havoc our enemies will inevitably wreak, the fear and anger they will foment against us.

Still, my own allies refuse to trust me.

"I know we need help," I say coldly. "I'm not blind. But bending the rules means putting Juliette's life at risk. We cannot afford to start bringing in civilians—"

"You won't even let us bring in soldiers!"

"That is patently untrue," I say, bristling. "I never objected to you bringing in extra soldiers to secure the grounds."

"To secure the exterior, yes, but you refused to let us bring them inside the Sanctuary—"

"I didn't *refuse* anything. I'm not the one telling you what to do, Nouria. Lest you forget, those orders came from Juliette—"

"With all due respect, Mr. Warner," Castle interjects, clearing his throat. "We're all aware how much Ms. Ferrars values your opinion. We're hoping you might be able to convince her to change her mind."

I pivot to face him, taking in his graying locs, his weathered brown skin. Castle has aged several years in a short time; these past months have taken their toll on all of us. "You would have me convince her to put her own life at risk? Have you lost your mind?"

"*Hey*," Nouria barks at me. "Watch your tone."

I feel myself stiffen in response; old impulses dare me to reach for my gun. It is a miracle that I am able to speak at all when I say: "Your first offense was separating me from my fiancée on my wedding day. That you would then ask me to allow unvetted persons to enter the only safe space she is allowed in the *entire known world*—"

"They wouldn't be unvetted!" Nouria cries, getting to her feet as she loses her temper. She glows a bit when she's mad, I've noticed, the preternatural light making her dark skin luminous.

"*You* would be there to vet them," she says, gesturing at me from across the table. "You could tell us whether they're safe. That's the whole point of this conversation—to get your cooperation."

"You expect me to follow these people around, then? Twenty-four hours a day? Or did you think it was as simple as making a single deduction and being done with it?"

"It wouldn't be twenty-four hours," she says. "They wouldn't live here—we'd have teams come inside to complete projects, during the day—"

"We've only been in power a matter of weeks. You really

think it wise to start bringing strangers into our inner sanctum? My powers are not infallible. People can hide their true feelings from me," I point out, my voice hardening, "and have done so in the past. I am, therefore, entirely capable of making mistakes, which means you cannot depend on me to be a foolproof defense against unknown entities, which means your plan is faulty."

Nouria sighs. "I will acknowledge that there is a very, very small chance that you might miss something, but I really feel that it might be wor—"

"Absolutely not."

"Mr. Warner." Castle, this time. Softer. "We know this is a lot to ask. We're not trying to put undue pressure on you. Your position here, among us, is critical. None of us know the intricacies of The Reestablishment as well as you do—none of us is as equipped to dismantle, from the inside, the North American system better than you are. We value what you bring to our team, son. We value your opinions. But you have to see that we're running out of options. The situation is dire, and we need your support."

"And this was your plan?" I ask, almost tempted to laugh. "You really thought you could sway me with a bit of good cop, bad cop?" I look at Nouria. "And I take it you're the bad cop?"

"We have more to do than ever before," Nouria says angrily. "We can hardly get our own cabins rebuilt. People need privacy, and proper places to sleep. We need to get the schools running again for the children. We need to stop living off generators and automat dinners." She gesticulates wildly with her arm, accidentally knocking a stack of papers to the floor. "We're struggling to take care of our own people—how can we be expected to take care of the people of 241, or the sectors beyond that?"

She drops her emotional armor for only a second, but I feel it: the weight of her grief is profound.

"We're drowning," she says quietly, running a hand down her face. "We need help. We lost too many of our own in the battle. The Sanctuary is falling apart, and we don't have time to rebuild slowly. The whole world is watching us now. We need more hands on deck, more crews to come in and help us do the work. If we don't, we're going to fail before we've even had a chance to start."

For a moment, I'm silent.

Nouria's not wrong; the Sanctuary is a disaster. So, too, is the planet. I've already sent Haider and Stephan and Lena and the twins back to their respective continents; we needed capable proxies on the ground assessing the current situation abroad—neutralizing chaos wherever possible—and no one was better suited. Nazeera is the only one who stayed behind, claiming that Haider would be fine on his own, that she wanted to stick around for my wedding. I might've been flattered by this nonsense if I didn't know she was lying.

She wanted to stay here to be with Kenji.

Still, I've been grateful for her presence. Nazeera is smart and resourceful and has been an immense help these last couple of weeks. The Sanctuary had enough to do when it was trying only to keep its own people alive; now the entire world is looking to us for direction.

Looking to *Ella* for direction.

What they don't know, of course, is that she's been conscious for only four days. When she finally woke up there was so much for her to do—the world had been waiting for proof that Juliette Ferrars had survived—and despite my many, many protests, she agreed to make limited appearances, to issue statements, to begin discussing what the future might look like for the people. She insisted that we get started right away, that we put together a committee responsible for designing the world's largest public works project—rebuilding towns, schools, hospitals. Investing in infrastructure. Creating jobs, remapping cities.

On a global scale.

Even so, there's hardly been time to think about these things. I spent most of the last two weeks doing what I could to keep Ella alive while trying to put out as many fires as possible. In a moment of honesty I might even be willing to admit that Kenji's mistake—knocking down the wrong building—was almost inevitable. There is an infinite number of things to do and never enough people to do it, or to oversee the details.

Which means we're often making mistakes.

On a micro level, we're also required to pitch in, rebuild our cabins. Cut the grass. Cook the food. Wash the dishes. Ella dragged me into the kitchen as soon as she was able, slapping a pair of questionable rubber gloves against my chest before tugging on a grimy pair of her own, all the while grinning at the gluey bottom of an oatmeal-encrusted cauldron like it was a gift. If Ella were a house, she would be a grand home, one with many rooms and doors, all of which were easily unlocked, flung open.

If I were a house, I would be haunted.

"*And I would remind you,*" Nouria says, her brittle voice returning me to the present, "that you are not the only person on earth ever to have been married. I'm sorry you can't bear to be separated from your fiancée long enough to have a single vital discussion about our failing world, but the rest of us must continue to move, Warner, even if it means deprioritizing your personal happiness."

Her words strike a raw nerve.

"Too true," I say quietly. "There are few, indeed, who've ever prioritized my personal happiness. I wouldn't expect you to be the exception."

I regret the words the moment they've left my mouth.

I steel myself as Nouria reels, processing my uncomfortable moment of honesty. She looks away, guilt flickering, fighting with irritation. Her anger ultimately wins the battle, but when she meets my eyes again, there's a note of regret there, in her gaze, and I realize only then that I have been tricked.

There is more.

I take an imperceptible breath; the true purpose of this meeting is only now about to be revealed to me.

"While we're on the subject," Nouria says, sparing her father an anxious glance. "I—well. I'm really sorry, Warner, but we're going to have to postpone the wedding."

I stare at her.

My body goes slowly solid, a dull panic working its way through my nervous system. I feel multiple things at once— anger, grief, confusion. A strange sort of resignation rises up above them all, crowning a familiar pain, a familiar fear: that joy, like dew, evaporates from my life the moment I begin to trust the sun.

This is it, then. Par for the course.

"Postpone the wedding," I say, hollow.

"Today is just turning out to be a bad day for everyone," she says, rushing to get the words out. "There's too much going on. There's a major sewage problem we need to get under control, which is using up most of our manpower at the moment, and everyone else is knee-deep in other projects. We don't have enough hands to set up or break things down—and we tried, we really tried to make it work, but we just can't spare the generator tonight. Our electricity has been touch and go, and the temperatures are supposed to be brutal tonight; we can't let the kids freeze in their beds."

"I don't understand. I spoke with Brendan, he offered—"

"Brendan is drained. We've been relying on him too much lately. Winston has already threatened to kill me if we don't let him sleep tonight."

"I see." I stare at the table, then my hands. I have turned

to stone, even as my heart races in my chest. "We'd need the generator for only an hour."

"An hour?" Nouria laughs, but she seems unnerved. "Have you ever been to a wedding? Outside? At night? You'd need lights and heat and music. Not to mention all that we'd have to do to get the kitchen going that late, and distributing food— We never got around to making a cake—"

"I don't need a wedding," I say, cutting her off. I sound strange even to myself, nervous. "I just need an officiant. It doesn't have to be a big deal."

"I think it might be a big deal to Juliette."

I look up at that.

I have no worthy response; I can't speak for Ella. I'd never deny her a real wedding if it's what she wants.

The whole thing feels suddenly doomed. The day after I proposed to Ella, she was attacked by her sister, after which she fell into a coma and came home to me nearly dead. We were supposed to have been married this morning, except that her dress was destroyed, and now—

"Postpone until when?"

"I'm not sure, if I'm being honest." Nouria's nerves and apprehension are growing louder now. I try to meet her eyes, but she keeps glancing at Castle, who only shakes his head. "I was hoping maybe we could look at the calendar," she says to me, "think about planning something when things are less crazy around here—"

"You can't be serious."

"Of course I'm serious."

"You know as well as I do," I say angrily, "that there is no guarantee things will ever calm down around here, or that we'll ever be able to get this situation under control—"

"Well, *right now* is a bad time, okay?" She crosses her arms. "It's just a bad time."

I look away. My heart seems to be racing in my head now, pounding against my skull. I feel myself dissociating—detaching from the moment—and struggle to remain present.

"Is this some kind of perverse revenge?" I ask. "Are you trying to prevent my wedding because I won't let you bring in civilians? Because I refuse to put Juliette's life in jeopardy?"

Nouria is quiet for so long I'm forced to look up, to return my mind to itself. She's staring at me with the strangest look in her eyes, something like guilt—or regret—washing her out completely.

"Warner," she says quietly. "It was Juliette's idea."

FIVE

The small velvet box weighs heavy in my pocket, the right angles of which dig into my thigh as I sit here, at the edge of a short cliff, staring down at our very own graveyard. This area was built shortly after the battle—a memorial to all the lives lost.

It's become an unexpected refuge for me.

Few people come through here anymore; for some, the pain is still too fresh, for others, the demands on their time too many. Either way, I'm grateful for the quiet. It was one of the only places to escape while Ella was in recovery, which meant I spent quite a bit of time acquainting myself with this view, and with my seat: a smooth, flat stretch of a massive boulder. The view from this rock is surprisingly peaceful.

Today, it fails to calm me.

I hear a sound then; a distant, faded trill my mind can only describe as birdsong. The dog lifts its head and barks.

I stare at the animal.

The dirty little creature waited for me outside the war room only to follow me here. I've done nothing to inspire its loyalty. I don't know how to get rid of him. Or her.

As if sensing the direction of my thoughts, the dog turns

to face me, panting lightly now, looking for all the world as if it might be smiling. I've hardly had a chance to digest this before it jerks away to bark once more at the sky.

That oddly familiar chirp, again.

I've heard birdsong more often lately; we all have. Castle, who's always insisted all was not lost, claims even now that the animals had not died out entirely. He said that traditionally, birds hide during severe weather, not unlike humans. They seek shelter when experiencing illness, too, during what they believe to be the last moments of their life. He argues that the birds went into mass hiding—either from fear, or from sickness—and that now, with Emmaline's weather manipulations gone, what's left of them have come out of hiding. It's not a foolproof theory, but lately it's grown harder to deny. Even I find myself searching the sky these days, hoping for a glimpse of the impossible creature.

A cold wind barrels through the valley then, pushing through my hair, snapping against my skin. It is with some regret that I realize I left my coat in the war room. The dog whimpers, nudging my leg with its nose. Reluctantly, I rest my hand on what is no doubt its flea-infested head, and the dog quiets. Its thin body curls into a tight ball at my feet, tail tapping the ground.

I sigh.

The day had dawned bright this morning, the sun unencumbered in the sky, but each passing hour has brought with it heavier clouds and an inescapable chill.

Nouria was right; this night will be brutal.

Anxious as I always am to be apart from Ella, my impulses were blunted after meeting with Castle and Nouria. Confused. I wanted nothing more than to seek out Ella; I wanted nothing more than to be alone. I ended up here, in the end—my feet carrying me when my head made no decision—staring into a valley of death, circling the drain of my mind. This morning had been agitating but rewarding; full of irritation but hope, too. I hadn't resented the ticking clock against which I'd been marking time.

In the end, the afternoon has proven empty.

My evening, cleared.

Save the myriad domestic and international disasters that remain unresolved, I've no reason to hurry anymore. I'd thought I was getting married tonight.

As it turns out, I'm not.

I tug free the velvet box from my pocket, clutching it in my fist a moment before taking a sharp breath, then carefully opening the lid. I stare at the glittering contents not unlike a child witnessing fire for the first time. *Naive.*

It's strange: of all the reprehensible things I've known myself to be, I'd never thought I was stupid.

I snap the lid closed, tuck the box back into my pocket.

Nouria didn't lie when she said my wedding wouldn't happen tonight. She didn't lie when she told me it was Ella's idea to postpone. What I don't understand is why Ella never mentioned this to me—or why she said nothing this morning at the dress shop. Perhaps most confusing of all: I've felt no hesitation from her on the matter. Surely, if she didn't want to marry me, I'd have known.

I clench my jaw against the cold.

Somehow, despite the howling wind, the dog appears to have fallen asleep, its body vibrating like a small motor at my feet. I take a moment to study its patchy brown fur, noticing, for the first time, that there's a piece missing from one of its ears.

I exhale, slowly, and rest my elbows on my knees, drop my head into my hands. The small box digs deeper into my flesh.

I'm trying to convince myself to get going—to return to work—when I feel Ella approach. I stiffen, then straighten.

My pulse picks up.

I sense her long before I see her, and when she finally comes into view my heart reacts, contracting in my chest even as my body remains motionless. She lifts a hand when she sees me, the single moment of distraction costing her a fight with a bramble. This area, like so many others, is carpeted in half-dead brush, ripe for a wildfire. Ella struggles to disentangle herself, yanking hard to free her shirt—and promptly frowns when she's released. She studies what appears to be the torn edge of her sweater before looking up at me. She shrugs.

I didn't really care about this sweater anyway, she seems to say, and I can't help but smile.

Ella laughs.

She is windswept. The gusts are growing more aggressive, whipping her hair so that it wraps around her face as she heads in my direction. I can hardly see her eyes; only glimpses of her lips and cheeks, pink with exertion. She swipes at her dark hair with one hand, pushing at overgrown weeds with the other. She is gently rendered in this light, soft in a nondescript sweater the color of moss. Dark jeans. Tennis shoes.

The light changes as she moves, the clouds fighting to hide the sun and occasionally failing. It makes the scene feel dreamlike. She looks so much like herself in this moment that it startles me; it's almost as if she's stepped out of some of my favorite memories.

"I've been looking for you everywhere," she says breathlessly, laughing as she collapses beside me on the boulder. She smells like apricot—it's a new shampoo—and the scent of it fills my head.

She pokes me in the stomach. "Where've you been?"

"Here."

"Very funny," she says, but her smile fades as she studies my face. I find it difficult to meet her gaze.

"Hey," she says softly.

"Hi," I say.

"What's wrong?"

I shake my head slowly. "Nothing."

"Liar," she whispers.

I close my eyes.

I feel myself change when she's near me; the effect is powerful. My body unclenches, my limbs grow heavy. All the tension I carry seems to melt away, taking with it my resolve; I become almost lethargic with relief.

I take a shallow breath.

"Hey," she says again, touching her cool fingers to my face, grazing my cheek. "Who do I have to kill?"

I pull away, smiling faintly at the ground when I say, "Did you tell Nouria you wanted to postpone our wedding?"

Ella's horror is immediate.

She sits back and stares at me, fear and shock and anger coalescing into a single, indistinguishable mass of feeling. I avert my eyes as she processes my question, but her reaction does quite a bit to ameliorate my headspace. Just until she says—

"Yes."

I go unnaturally still.

"But Nouria wasn't supposed to tell you that."

I look up at her then. Ella is trying to hide her panic from me. She looks away, looks into her hands. I don't understand what's happening, and I say this out loud.

Ella can't stop shaking her head. She clasps her hands tight. "Nouria wasn't supposed to tell you that. That wasn't—she wasn't—"

"But it's true."

Ella meets my eyes. "It's technically true, yes, but she shouldn't have— She shouldn't have been the one to say that to you. Nouria and I discussed this a couple of days ago. I'd said that if we couldn't—if we couldn't pull things together in time, that maybe, maybe we could wait—"

"Oh." I squint up into the sky, searching for the sun.

"I was going to tell you myself," she says, more quietly now. "I was just waiting to know . . . more. About how today might turn out. There were some unexpected setbacks this morning, which cost us a lot of time, but I was still hoping we'd be able to figure everything out. Everyone has been working really hard—Kenji told me there was a chance we could still pull it all together today, but if Nouria—"

"I see." I push a hand through my hair, drag it down my neck. "So you discussed this with everyone? Everyone but me."

"Aaron. I'm so sorry. This sounds horrible. I hear it—I hear myself saying it, and I hear how horrible it sounds."

I take a deep, shaky breath. I don't know what to do with my arms, or my legs. They feel prickly suddenly; all pins and needles. I want to tear them off my body.

I'm staring at the ground when I say, "Have you changed your mind? About marrying me?"

"*No*," she says, the word and the emotional force behind it so potent I'm compelled to look up. I see the anguish in her eyes, and I feel it, too; she seems racked with guilt and resignation, an unusual combination of feelings I can't parse. But her love for me is palpable. She takes my hands and the feeling magnifies, flooding my body with a relief so acute I want to lie down.

Something seems to unclench in my chest.

"I love you," she whispers. "I love you so much. I just want to do this right—for both of us. I want you to have a beautiful wedding. I think it matters more to you than you think."

"It doesn't," I say, shaking my head. "I don't care, love. I don't care about any of it. I just want you. I want you to be my family."

She doesn't argue with me. Instead, she squeezes my fingers as her emotions spiral, compound. I close my eyes against the force of it. When I finally look up again, her eyes are shining with unshed tears.

The sight drives a stake into my heart.

"No," I whisper, brushing the backs of my fingers along her jaw, the skin there cold and silken. "Postpone the wedding for as long as you want. We can get married whenever you want, I don't care."

"Aaron—"

I move slowly at first, kissing her cheek and lingering there, pressing my face to the softness of her skin. There's no one here but us. No thoughts but hers and mine. She touches my chest in response, sighing softly as she trails a hand up the back of my neck, into my hair.

My body responds before my mind has had a chance to catch up.

I take her face in my hands and kiss her like I've wanted to for days. *Weeks*. I nudge her mouth open and taste her, running my hands down her body now, drawing her closer.

Her desires consume me as they evolve, leaving me slightly intoxicated. It's always a heady cocktail, experiencing her like this, feeling her emotions in real time. The harder I kiss her the more she wants, the more desperate her needs become. It's dangerous; it makes it hard to think straight, to remember where we are.

She makes a sound when I kiss her neck, a soft moan followed by the whisper of my name, and the combination incites a riot in my body. My hands are under her sweater now, grazing the satin of her skin, the clasp of her bra, and she's reaching for me, for the button of my pants, and I can hear, but choose to ignore, the distant voice in my head telling me that there has to be a better place for this— somewhere warmer, somewhere softer, somewhere that isn't a *graveyard*—

The dog barks loudly, and Ella breaks away from me with a startled cry.

"*Oh my God*," she says, clutching a hand to her chest. "I didn't— Oh my God. Has the dog been here this whole time?"

I struggle to catch my breath. My heart is pounding in my chest. "Yes," I say, still staring at her.

I pull her back into my arms, claiming her mouth with a single-minded focus that renders the moment surreal, even for me. She's surprised for only a second before she goes soft in my arms, breaking open, kissing me back. I haven't touched her like this in so long—we haven't been together like this in so long—

Something registers in the back of my mind.

I break away, struggling once more to breathe, hoping the muted warning bell in my head was a mistake.

"What's wrong?" Ella says, her hands going to my face.

She's still languid with pleasure, her thoughts undiluted by the noise that plagues me always. She kisses my throat, soft and slow. My eyes close.

"Nothing," I whisper, wishing more than ever that we had a bedroom—or even a proper bed. "Nothing. I just thought I heard—"

"Oh my God. *This* is where you guys have been hiding?"

I go suddenly solid, ice chasing away the heat in my veins so fast I almost shudder.

"*Crap*," Ella whispers.

"You two have no shame, huh? You were just going to desecrate a graveyard? Can't even keep your clothes on in this freezing weather?"

"Kenji," Ella says quietly. The word is a warning.

"What?" He crosses his arms. "I've said it before and I'll say it again: *gross*. I think I need to go bleach my eyes."

I help Ella to her feet, drawing an arm around her waist. "What do you want?" I say to Kenji, entirely unable to rein in my anger.

"Nothing from you, buddy, thanks. I'm here because I need Juliette."

"Why?" Ella and I ask at the same time.

Kenji blows out a breath, looking away once before looking back at Ella. Cryptically, he says, "I just need you to come with me, okay?"

"Oh." Her eyes widen a fraction. "Okay."

"What's wrong?" I ask. "Do you need help?"

Ella shakes her head. I feel her apprehension, but she

pastes on a smile. "No, it's nothing—just boring stuff out on unregulated turf. We actually managed to track down one of the pre-Reestablishment city planners in this area, and he's coming by to discuss our ideas."

"Oh," I say.

Ella is hiding something.

I can feel it—can feel that she's not being entirely truthful. The realization provokes a sinking feeling in my gut that scares me.

"You won't miss me, right?" Her smile is strained. "I know you always have a ton of stuff to do."

"Yes." I look away. "There's always a great deal to accomplish."

A pause. "So—I'll see you tonight?"

"Tonight?" I glance at Ella, then the sun.

There are still hours left before nightfall, which means she intends to be gone for all of them. My mind is overrun with doubt. First our wedding, now this. I don't understand why Ella isn't being honest with me. I want to say something to her, to ask her a direct question, but not here, not in front of Kenji—

Ella's emotions take a sudden turn.

I look up to find her staring at me now with concern, with a palpable fear—for *me*.

"Or I can stay here," she says more quietly. "I don't have to go anywhere."

"Uh, yes, princess, you do—"

"Be quiet, Kenji."

"We need you out there," he insists, throwing his arms wide. "You have to be there—we can't just deci—"

"Aaron," Ella says, placing a hand on my chest. "Are you going to be okay?"

I stiffen, then step back.

The question inspires in me a reaction I do not admire. I bristle at the sympathy in her voice, at the thought that she might think me incapable of surviving a few hours on my own.

Understanding hits me with the force of a sledgehammer:

Ella thinks I am broken.

"I'll be fine," I say, unable to meet her eyes. "I have, as you said, a great deal to do."

"Oh," she says carefully. "Okay."

I can still feel her studying me, and though I don't know what she sees in my face, my expression appears to have convinced her that I won't turn to dust in her absence. An approximation of the truth.

A tense silence stretches out between us.

"All right, great," Ella finally says, all false brightness. "So, I'll see you tonight? Or sooner— I mean, depending on how quickly I can—"

Kenji makes a sound; something like a choked laugh. "Yeah, if I were you, I'd clear my schedule."

"Love," I say quietly. "Are you sure everything is okay?"

"Absolutely," she says, straining to smile wider. She squeezes my hand, kissing me briefly before pulling away.

"I promise. I'll be back as soon as I can."

Ella is still lying. It hits me like a blow.

"Hey, sorry about the wedding, man," Kenji says, making a face. "Who knew the downside of overthrowing a corrupt government was that we'd have absolutely no free time?"

I swallow, hard, ignoring the fresh vise around my chest. "I see everyone already knows about that."

"Yeah, I mean, it was J's idea to postpone. There's just so much to do, and trying to have the wedding at night was going to be really complicated, and she thought it would be better to jus—"

"*Kenji,*" she says sharply. She shoots him a look I can't entirely decipher, but her anger surprises me.

"My bad, princess." Kenji holds up both hands. "My bad. I didn't realize it was controversial to let the groom know what was happening with his own wedding, but I guess I just don't know how weddings work, do I?" He says that last part with an edge, irritation souring his expression.

I have no idea what's going on between them.

Ella rolls her eyes, more frustrated with Kenji than I've ever seen her. She practically stomps toward him, hugging herself against the cold. I hear her mutter, "You're going to pay for that," before they're off, the two of them disappearing into the distance without a backward glance.

Without me.

I stand there for so long after they're gone that the sun finally moves toward the horizon, taking with it any lingering warmth. I shiver slightly as the temperatures plummet, but I can ignore the cold. I cannot, however, seem to ignore the dull ache in my chest.

When I woke up this morning I'd thought this would be the happiest day of my life. Instead, as the day approaches dusk—

I feel hollow.

The dog barks suddenly, a series of sharp yaps in a row. When I turn to face the creature it makes an altogether different sound, something like a growl, and jumps up enthusiastically, lifting its paws to my pant leg. I give the animal a firm look, indicating with my index finger that it should disengage immediately. It sinks, slowly, back onto its feet, tail wagging.

Another bark.

I sigh at the sight of its eager, upturned face. "I suppose I shouldn't be ungrateful. You seem to be the only one interested in my company today."

A bark.

"Very well. You may come with me."

The dog rises up onto all four legs, panting, tail wagging harder.

"But if you defecate on any interior surface—or chew up my boots, or urinate on my clothes—I will put you right back outside. You will hold your bowel movements until you are a considerable distance away from me. Is that clear?"

Another responding bark.

"Good," I say, and walk away.

The dog chases after me so quickly its snout bumps my

heels. I listen to the sound of its paws hitting the ground; I can hear it breathing, sniffing the earth.

"First," I tell it, "someone needs to give you a bath. Not me, obviously. But someone."

The dog gives an aggressive, eager yap at that, and I realize with a start that I'm able to get a bead on its emotions. The reading, however, is imprecise; the creature doesn't always understand what I'm saying, so its emotional responses are inconsistent. But I see now that the dog understands essential truths.

For some inexplicable reason, this animal trusts me. More perplexing: my earlier declaration made it happy.

I don't know much about dogs, but I've never heard of one that enjoyed being bathed. Though it occurs to me then that if the animal understood the word *bath*, it must once have had an owner.

I come to a sudden stop, turning to study the creature: its matted brown fur, its half-eaten ear. It pauses when I do, lifting a leg to scratch behind its head in an undignified manner.

I see now that it's a boy.

Otherwise, I have no idea what kind of dog this is; I wouldn't even know how to begin classifying his species. He's obviously some kind of mutt, and he's either young, or naturally small. He has no collar. He's clearly underfed. And yet, a single glance at its nether regions confirmed that the animal had been neutered. He must've once had a proper home. A family. Though he likely lost his owner some time ago to have been reduced to this half-feral state.

I'm compelled to wonder, then, what happened.

I meet the dog's deep, dark eyes. We're both quiet, assessing each other. "You mean to tell me that you *like* the idea of taking a bath?"

Another happy bark.

"How strange," I say, turning once more down the path. "So do I."

SIX

By the time I step foot in the dining tent, it's already nine o'clock. Ella has been gone several hours now, and I have succeeded only a little in distracting myself from this fact. I know, intellectually, that she is not in danger; but then, my mind has always been my fiercest adversary. All the day's compounding uncertainties have led to a mounting apprehension in my body, the experience of which recalls the sensation of sandpaper against my skin.

The worst uncertainties are the ones I cannot kill or control.

In the absence of action I am forced instead to marinate in these thoughts, the anxiety abrading me more in every minute, corroding my nerves. So thorough is this excoriation that my entire body is rendered an open wound in the aftermath, so raw that even a metaphorical breeze feels like an attack. The mental exertion necessary to withstand these simple blows leaves me worse than irritable, and quick to anger. More than anything, these exhausting efforts make me want to be alone.

I don't know what's happening anymore.

I scan the dining tent as I head toward the unusually short serving line, searching for familiar faces. The interior space isn't nearly as large as it once was; a great portion of it has been sectioned off to use for temporary sleeping arrangements. Still, the room is emptier than I expect. There are only a few people occupying the scattered dining tables, none of whom I know personally—save one.

Sam.

She's sitting alone with a stack of papers and a mug of coffee, fully absorbed in her reading.

I make my way through the tables to stand in the short serving line, accepting, after a brief wait, my foil bowl of food. I choose a seat for myself in a far corner of the room, sitting down with some reluctance. I waited as long as I could to have this meal with Ella, and eating alone feels a bit like admitting defeat. It is perhaps maudlin to ruminate on this fact, to imagine myself abandoned. Still, it's how I feel.

Even the dog is gone.

It disturbs me to I think I might trade the relative quiet of this room for its regular chaos if only to have Ella by my side. It's an unnerving thought, one that does nothing but magnify my childish longing.

I tear back the foil lid and stare at its contents: a single gelatinous mass of something resembling stir-fry. I set my plastic fork on the table, sit back in my seat. Nouria was right about one thing, at least.

This is unsustainable.

After finding someone to take the dog, I spent the afternoon catching up on digital correspondence, most of which required fielding calls and perusing reports from the supreme kids, all of whom are dealing with different—and equally concerning—dilemmas. Luckily, Nazeera helped us set up a more sophisticated network here at the Sanctuary, which has since made it easier to be in touch with our international counterparts. The Sanctuary has been great for many things, but there has been, since the beginning, a dearth of accessible technology. Omega Point, by comparison, was home to formidable, futuristic tech that was impressive even by The Reestablishment's standards. This quality of tech, I realized, was something I'd taken for granted; as it turns out, not all rebel headquarters are built equally.

When I realized the Sanctuary was to be our new, permanent home, I insisted we make changes. This was when Nouria and I first discovered the depth of our mutual dislike.

Unlike Sam, Nouria is quick to wound; she is injured too easily by perceived slights against her camp—and her leadership—which has made it difficult to push for change. Progress.

Still, I pushed.

We took as much hardware from the local military headquarters as we were able, sacrificing what was once the elementary school tent to piece together a functioning command center, the capabilities of which were entirely unfamiliar to both Nouria and Sam, who still refuse to learn more than its most basic functions.

Lucky for them, I don't need assistance.

I do my work most days surrounded by the ancient

hieroglyphics of sticky children; crayon drawings of indecipherable creatures are thumbtacked to the wall above my desk; crudely formed bees and butterflies flutter from the ceiling. I hang my jacket on a rack painted in colors of the rainbow, slinging my gun holster around the back of a small yellow chair decorated with handprints.

The disturbing dichotomy is not lost on me.

Still, between Nazeera and Castle—who surprised me by revealing he was the mastermind behind most of Omega Point's innovative tech—we're close to designing an interface that would rival what we'd built at Sector 45.

I buried myself in work for hours, hardly coming up for air, not even to eat. In addition to all else, I've been designing a plan—a safer plan—that would help us bring in the assistance we need while mitigating our risk of exposure. Ella's, most of all. Usually, this kind of work is enough to hold my focus. But today, of all days—a day my mind continues to remind me was meant to be my wedding day—

It doesn't matter what I do; I am distracted.

I sigh, resting my hands on my thighs, too uncomfortably aware of the little velvet box still tucked into my pocket.

I clench, unclench my fists.

I scan the dining room again, restless with nervous energy. It's still surprising to me how easily I shed my solitude for the privilege of Ella's company. The truth is, I learned to enjoy the mechanics of life with her by my side; her presence renders my world brighter, the details richer.

It is impossible not to feel the difference when she is gone.

Still, this has been a strange and difficult day.

I know Ella loves me—and I know she means it when she says she wants to be with me—but today has been ripe not merely with disappointment but also concerning obfuscations. Ella is hiding something from me, and I have been waiting all day for her to return so that I might ask her, privately, a single clarifying question that might resolve this incertitude. Until then, it's hard to know how to feel, or what to believe.

More simply: I miss her.

I regret even relinquishing the dog.

Upon my return from the gravesite, I searched the grounds for a familiar face—to find someone to take him—and despite my efforts, I couldn't find anyone I recognized. There's a great deal of work to do in the previously unregulated areas outside the Sanctuary, so it's not surprising to see people gone; I was only surprised to find myself disappointed. All I've wanted for so long was a single moment of quiet, and now that I have it in abundance, I'm not sure I want it.

The realization has quietly shocked me.

Regardless, I was about to abandon the idea of bathing the animal when a nervous young woman approached me, her face as red as her hair as she stammered aloud a suspicion that I might need help.

I appreciated the effort on her part, but the conversation was far from ideal.

The girl turned out to be a part of a persistent, ridiculous subsection of people here at the Sanctuary, a lingering group of men and women who still insist on treating me like I'm some kind of a hero. I fought off my father's supreme soldiers in a failed attempt at protecting Ella, and these well-meaning fools have somehow idealized this failure; one of the worst days of my life now fossilized in their memories as a day that should be celebrated.

It makes me ill.

They've romanticized me in their minds, these people, romanticized the very idea of my existence, and often objectify me in the process. Every time I looked this young woman in the eye she would visibly tremble, her feelings both indecent and sincere, the mixture of which was almost too uncomfortable to recount.

I thought she might be more at ease if I stared at the animal as I spoke, which I did, and which seemed to calm her. I told her about the dog—explaining that he needed a bath, and food—and which she generously offered to take into her care. As I sensed no actual danger from the girl, I accepted her overture.

"Does he have a name?" she'd asked.

"He is a dog," I'd said, frowning as I looked up. "You may call him a dog."

The young woman froze at that, at our sudden eye contact. I watched her pupils dilate as she grappled with an emotional combination too often flung in my direction: abject terror and desire. It confirmed for me then what I've always known to be true—that most people are disappointing and should be avoided.

She said nothing to me after that, only scooping up the reluctant, whining animal into her trembling arms and shuffling away. I've not seen either of them since.

It would not be an exaggeration to say that this day has been a thorough disappointment.

I push back my chair and get to my feet, taking the foil bowl to go; I plan to save the food-adjacent mass for the dog, should I ever see him again. I glance up at the large clock on the wall, noting that I managed only to kill another thirty minutes.

Quietly, I acknowledge I should accept this day for the nonevent it turned out to be—and, as it appears unlikely I will see Ella tonight, I should go to bed. Still, I'm demoralized by this turn of events; so much so that it takes me a moment to realize Sam is calling my name.

I pivot in her direction.

She's waving me over, but I have no interest in a conversation right now. I want nothing more than to retreat, fester in my wounds. Instead, I force myself to clear the short distance between us, unable to generate even a modicum of warmth as I approach.

I stare at her by way of hello.

Sam is even more exhausted than I first assumed, her eyes held up by lavender half-moons. Her skin is grayer than I've ever seen it, her short blond hair limp, falling into her face.

She spares no time for formalities, either.

"Have you read the recent incident reports from"—she

looks down at her papers, rubbing one eye with the palm of her hand—"18, 22, 36, 37, 142 through 223, and 305?"

"Yes."

"Have you noticed what they all have in common?"

I sigh, feeling my body tense anew when I say, "Yes."

Sam folds her arms atop her stack of papers, peering up at me from her seat. "Great. Then you'll understand why we need Juliette to tour the continent. She has to make appearances—physical appearances—"

"No."

"They are rioting in the streets, Warner." Sam's voice is unusually hard. "Against *us*. Not against The Reestablishment—against *us*!"

"People are impatient and ungrateful," I say sharply. "Worse: they are stupid. They don't understand that change takes time. Clearly they assumed that the fall of The Reestablishment would bring instant peace and prosperity to the world, and in the two weeks since we've been in power, they can't understand why their lives haven't miraculously improved."

"Yes, okay, but the solution isn't in ignoring them. These people need hope—they need to see her face—"

"She's done televised broadcasts. She's made a couple of local appearances—"

"*It's not enough*," Sam says, cutting me off. "Listen. We all know the only reason Juliette isn't doing more is because of you. You're so worried about keeping *her* safe that you're putting our entire movement in jeopardy. She did this,

Warner. It was her choice to take on The Reestablishment—it was her choice to carry this burden. The world needs her now, which means you have to get your shit together. You have to be braver than this."

I stiffen at that, at the surgical precision of her blade.

I say nothing.

Sam exhales in the wake of my silence, something like a laugh. "You think I don't understand what it's like to be with someone whose life is constantly in danger? You think I don't understand how terrifying it is to watch them step foot out the door every day? Do you have any idea how many attempts have been made on Nouria's life?"

Still, I say nothing.

"It's really fucking hard," she says angrily, surprising me with her language. Sam pushes both hands through her hair before rubbing her eyes again. "It's really, really, *really* hard."

"Yes," I say quietly.

She meets my eyes then. "Look. I know you're not doing this on purpose. I know you only want the best for her. But you're holding her back. You're holding all of us back. I don't know exactly what you two have been through—whatever it was, it must've been serious, because Juliette's clearly more worried for you than she is for herself, but—"

"What?" I frown. "That's not—"

"Trust me. She and I have had a lot of conversations about this. Juliette doesn't want to do anything to scare you. She thinks you're processing something right now—she wouldn't tell me what—and she's adamant that she won't do anything risky until she's sure you can handle it. Which means I need you to handle it. Now."

"I'm doing *fine*," I say, my jaw clenching.

"Wonderful." Sam generates a smile. "If you're doing fine, go ahead and tell her that. Encourage Juliette to go on an international tour—or at minimum, a national one. Juliette knows how to talk to crowds; when she's looking people in the eye they *believe* her. I know you've seen it. In fact, you probably know better than anyone that no one cares more about these people than she does. She genuinely cares about their families, their futures—and right now, the world needs a reminder. They need reassurance. Which means you have to let her do her job."

I feel my heart rate spike. "I would never keep her from doing her job. I just want her to be safe."

"Yes—you prioritize her safety above all else, to the detriment of the world. You're making decisions from a place of fear, Warner. You can't help heal the planet if you're only thinking about what's best for one person—"

"I never got into this to heal the planet," I say sharply. "I have never pretended to care about the future of our pathetic civilization, and if you ever took me for a revolutionary, that was your mistake. I see now that I have to make something clear, so remember this: I would happily watch the world go up in flames if anything happened to her, and if that's not enough for you, you can go to hell."

Sam shoves back her chair so fast it makes a piercing, skin-crawling screech that echoes around the near-empty dining tent. She's on her feet now, boring a hole in the floor with the heat of her anger. The few faces still dotting the room turn to look at us; I feel their surprise, their mounting curiosity. Sam is diminutive in stature, but fierce when she chooses to be, and right now she looks as if she's considering killing me with her bare hands.

"You are not special," she says. "You are not the only one of us who's ever suffered. You're not the only one who lies awake at night worrying for the safety of their loved ones. I have no sympathy for your pain, or your problems."

"Good," I say, more than matching her anger. "As long as we understand each other."

Sam shakes her head and throws up her hands, looking for a moment like she might laugh. Or cry. "What on earth does she see in you? You're nothing but a callous, coldhearted narcissist. You don't care about anyone but yourself. I hope you know how lucky you are that Juliette tolerates your presence. You wouldn't even be here if it weren't for her. I sure as hell wouldn't vouch for you."

I lower my eyes, absorbing these blows with studied indifference. My body is not unlike the moon, cratered so thoroughly by brutality it's hard to imagine it untouched by violence.

"Good night," I say quietly, and turn to leave.

I hear Sam sigh, her regret building as I walk away. "Warner, wait," she says, calling after me. "I'm sorry—that was over the line— It's been a long day, I didn't mean—"

I don't look back.

SEVEN

I'm sandwiched between two thin blankets on the frozen floor of this hospital room, eyes closed, pretending to sleep, when I hear the soft whine of the door, Ella's familiar presence entering the room.

It's hours past midnight.

She brings with her the faint smell of something slightly chemical, which confuses me, but more important: I feel her fear as she tiptoes into the space, all displaced by a sudden relief when she catches sight, no doubt, of my prone body.

Relief.

I don't understand.

She is relieved to discover me asleep. She is relieved she doesn't have to speak with me.

The pressure in my chest intensifies.

I listen to the sounds of her shedding her shoes and clothes in the dark, wondering how best I might shatter the silence, bracing myself for her surprise—then disappointment—to discover I am awake. I give her a moment, hearing the familiar sounds of sheets rustling. I'm imagining her climbing into the narrow hospital bed, tucking herself under the covers, when her emotions pivot without warning: she experiences a sharp, stunning wave of happiness.

Somehow, this only scares me more.

Ella is not merely relieved, then, but *happy* to have evaded me. She's happy to be going to sleep without being disturbed.

My heart races faster, dread multiplying. I'm almost afraid to say anything now, knowing that the sound of my voice would only prompt the demolition of her joy. Still, I have to speak with her. I need to know what's happening between us—and I'm preparing to say as much when I hear her breathing change.

She is already asleep.

I have been lying awake fully clothed, sinking into darkness for hours. Ella has fallen asleep in moments.

I feel frozen. Fastened to this cold floor by fear, familiar pins and needles sparking to life in my limbs.

My eyes fly open; I can't seem to breathe.

I hadn't known what to do with the jewelry box in my pocket. I was afraid to leave it somewhere, worried it might be misplaced, or discovered. It remains with me instead, branding my leg with its presence, reminding me of all that feels suddenly and terrifyingly lost.

Unconsciously, I reach for an altogether different piece of jewelry, my fingers finding the smooth stone of the jade ring in the dark, the piece so much a part of me now that I can't remember what my hand looks like without it. I spin the cold band around my pinkie finger in a familiar, repetitive motion, wondering whether it has been a mistake, all these years, to keep this token of grief so close to my skin.

The ring had been a gift from my mother; it was the only present I'd ever received as a child. And yet, the memories associated with this object are so dark and painful—reminders in every moment of my father's tyranny, my mother's suffering, my grandfather's betrayal—

I have often wanted to lock away this memento of my tortured childhood. Touching it even now reminds me of versions of myself—six years old, then seven, eight, nine, and on and on—that once clutched it desperately even as I screamed, explosive pain branching across my back, over and over.

For a long time, I hadn't wanted to forget. The ring reminded me always of my father's brutality, of the hatred that motivated me to stay alive if only to spite him.

More than that, it is all I have left of my mother.

And yet, perhaps this ring has tethered me to my own darkness, this symbol of infinite repetition fated to conjure, forever, the agonies of my past.

Sometimes I fear I will be trapped forever in this cycle: incapable of happiness, inseparable from my demons.

I close my eyes, scenes from the day replaying as if on an automatic loop. I seem doomed to relive the events in perpetuity, combing them for answers, for evidence of anything that might explain what's happening to my life. And despite my best efforts to shut them out, I recall Sam's voice, then Kenji's—

You're nothing but a callous, coldhearted narcissist.

I hope you know how lucky you are that Juliette tolerates your presence.
I'm sick of your attitude.
I'm sick of making excuses for your crappy behavior.
I just don't know what she sees in you.
What on earth does she see in you?

EIGHT

When I open my eyes, the light is filtering through the half-closed curtains, blinding me. I can tell just by its position in the room that the sun is new; the morning is young.

I don't know when I fell asleep; I don't even know how I managed to accomplish this feat except through sheer exhaustion. My body succumbed to the need even as my mind refused, protesting this decision with a series of nightmares that begin to replay as I sit up, closing my eyes against the glare.

I spent the night outrunning an indecipherable natural disaster. It was that vintage of vague dream-element that makes sense only in the dream and none at all upon waking.

I couldn't stop running.

I had no choice but to keep moving for fear of being decimated by the impending calamity, searching all the while for Ella, from whom I had been separated. When I finally heard her voice it was from high above: Ella was sitting in a tree, far from danger, staring happily at the clouds as I ran for my life. The disaster—something like a tornado or tsunami or both—increased in intensity, and I picked up speed, unable to slow down long enough to speak with her, or even to climb the tree, whose trunk was so impossibly tall I couldn't understand how she'd scaled it.

In a desperate effort I called her name, but she didn't hear me; she was turned away, laughing, and I realized then that Kenji was sitting in the tree with her. So was Nazeera, who'd no doubt flew them both to safety.

I screamed Ella's name once more, and this time she turned at the sound of my voice, meeting my eyes with a kind smile. I finally stopped then, falling to my knees from overexertion.

Ella waved at me just as I was pulled under.

A sharp knock at the hospital door has me upright in a moment, my mind on a delay even as my instincts sharpen. I notice only then that Ella is not here. Her rumpled hospital sheets are the only evidence she ever was.

I drag a hand down my face as I head for the door, faintly aware that I'm still in the clothes I was wearing yesterday. My eyes are dry, my stomach empty, my body exhausted.

I am wrung out.

I open the door, so surprised to see Winston's face that I take a step back. I seldom—if ever—speak with Winston. I've never had any specific reason to dislike him, but then, he and I are ill-acquainted. I don't even know if I've ever seen his face from so close a distance.

"Wow," he says, blinking at me. "You look like shit."

"Good morning."

"Right. Yeah. Good morning." He takes a deep breath and attempts a smile, adjusting his black glasses for no reason but nerves.

Winston, I'm baffled to discover, is *very* nervous to be near me.

"Sorry, I was just surprised," he says, rushing his words. "You're usually really—you know, like, put together. Anyway you might want to take a shower before we get going."

I'm so unable to process the absurdity—or the audacity—of this request, that I close the door in his face. Turn the lock.

The pounding begins immediately after. "Hey," he says, shouting to be heard. "I'm serious— I'm supposed to take you to breakfast this morning, but I really th—"

"I don't need a chaperone," I say, pulling off my sweater. This hospital room is one of the larger ones, with an en suite, industrial bathroom/shower combination. "And I don't need you to remind me to bathe."

"I didn't mean it as an insult! Damn." A nervous laugh. "Literally everyone tried to warn me that you were hard to deal with, but I thought maybe they were exaggerating, at least a little. That was my mistake. Listen, you look fine. You don't smell or anything. I just think you'll want to take a shower—"

"Again, I don't need your advice on this matter." I'm stepping out of my pants, folding them carefully to contain the small box still trapped in the pocket. "Leave."

I turn on the shower, the sound of which distorts Winston's voice. "Come on, man, don't make this difficult. I was the only one willing to come get you this morning. Everyone else was too afraid. Even Kenji said he was too tired today to deal with your shit."

I hesitate then.

I abandon the bathroom, returning to the closed door in only my boxer briefs. "Come get me for what?"

I feel Winston startle at the sound of my voice, so close. He equivocates, saying only: "Um, yeah, I can't actually tell you."

A terrifying unease moves through me at that. Winston's guilt and fear is palpable, his anxiety growing.

Something is wrong.

I glance one last time at Ella's empty bed before unlatching the lock. I'm only dimly aware of my appearance, that I'm opening the door in my underwear. I'm reminded swiftly of this fact when Winston does an exaggerated double take upon seeing me.

He quickly averts his eyes.

"Fucking hell—why did you have to take off your clothes?"

"What is going on?" I ask coldly. "Where is Juliette?"

"What? I don't know." Winston is turned away entirely now, pinching the bridge of his nose between his thumb and index finger. "And I'm not allowed to tell you what's going on."

"Why not?"

He looks up at that, meeting my eyes for only a nanosecond before turning sharply away; a mottled heat rushes up his neck, burns his ears. "Please, for the love of God," he says, yanking off his glasses to rub at his face. "Put on some clothes. I can't talk to you like this."

"Then leave."

Winston only shakes his head, crossing his arms against his chest. "I can't. And I can't tell you what's going on, because it's supposed to be a surprise."

The fight leaves my body in a single gust, leaving me light-headed. "A surprise?"

"Can you please go take a shower? I'll wait for you outside the MT. Just—just show up with your clothes on. *Please.*"

I let the door slam shut between us, then stare at it, my heart pounding wildly in my chest. There's a wave of relief from Winston, then a flicker of happiness.

He seems—excited.

I finally walk away, stepping out of my underwear and tossing it into a nearby laundry bin before entering the quickly steaming bathroom. I catch my reflection in the floor-length mirror affixed to the wall, my face and body being devoured slowly by steam.

It's supposed to be a surprise.

For a protracted moment, I can't seem to move. My eyes, I notice, are dilated in this dim light—darker. I look slightly different to myself, my body hardening by degrees every day. I've always been toned, but this is different. My face has lost any lingering softness. My chest is broader, my legs more firmly planted. These slight changes in muscle definition, in vascularity—

I can see myself getting older.

Our research for The Reestablishment indicated that there was once a time when the *twenties* were considered the prime years of youth. I always struggled to visualize this world, one wherein teenagers were treated like children, where those in their twenties felt young and carefree, their futures boundless.

It sounded like fiction.

And yet—I have often played this game in the privacy of my mind. *In another world, I might live in a house with my parents.* In another world, I might not even be expected to have a job. In another world, I might not know the weight of death, might never have held a gun, shot a bullet, killed so many. The thoughts register as absurd even as I think them: that in an alternate universe I might be considered some kind of adolescent, free from responsibility.

Strange.

Was there ever truly a world wherein parents did the job expected of them? Was there ever a reality in which the adults were not murdered merely for resisting fascism, leaving their young children behind to raise themselves?

Here, we are nearly all of us a contingent of orphans roaming—then running—this broken planet.

I often imagine what it would be like to step into such an alternate reality. I wonder what it would be like to set down the weight of darkness in exchange for a family, a home, a refuge.

I abandon my reflection to step under the hot water.

I never thought I'd come close to touching such a dream;

I never thought I'd be able to trust, or love, or find peace. I've been searching for so long for a pocket of quiet to inhabit, a place to exist unencumbered. I always wanted a door I might close—for even a moment—against the violence of the world. I didn't understand then that a home is not always a place. Sometimes, it's a person.

I would sleep on the cold floor of our hospital room for the rest of my life if it meant staying by Ella's side. I can forgo quiet. I can compartmentalize my need for space. My desire for privacy.

But to lose *her*—

I close my eyes against the water pressure, the jet forging tributaries against my face, my body. The heat is a balm, welcome against my skin. I want to burn off the residue of yesterday. I want an explanation for all that happened—or even to forget it altogether. When things are out of alignment between myself and Ella, I can't focus. The world seems colorless; my bones too large for my body. All I want, more than anything else, is to bridge the distance between us.

I want this uncertainty gone.

I turn my face up toward the jet, closing my eyes as the water pelts my face. I breathe deep, drawing in water and steam, trying to steady my heartbeat.

I know better than to be optimistic, but even as I forbid myself to think it, I cannot help but reflect that the word *surprise* is seldom associated with something negative.

It might've been a poor choice of words on Winston's part, but his moment of excitement seemed to confirm this choice; he might've chosen a more pejorative term had he wished to manage my expectations of disappointment.

Despite my every silent protest, hope takes hold of me, forces from me the dregs of my composure. I lean my forehead against the cool tile, the water beating the scars on my back. I can hardly feel it, the sensations there dulled from nerve damage. Scar tissue.

I straighten at a sudden sound.

I turn, heart racing, at the soft shudder of the bathroom door opening. I already know it's her. I always feel her before I can see her, and when I see her—when she opens the bathroom door and stands there, smiling at me—

My relief is so acute I reach for the wall, bracing myself against the cold tile. Ella is holding two mugs of coffee, dressed the way she often is: in a soft sweater and jeans, her dark brown hair so long now it skims her elbows. She grins at me, then disappears into the outer room, and I start to follow her, nearly slipping in my haste. I catch the doorframe to steady myself, watching as she rests the coffee mugs on a nearby table. She slips off her tennis shoes. Tugs off her socks.

When she pulls her sweater over her head, I have a minor heart attack. She's facing away from me, but her back is bare. She's not wearing a bra.

"You were sound asleep this morning," she says, glancing over her shoulder at me as she unbuttons her jeans. "I was afraid to wake you up. I went out to get us some coffee, but the line at breakfast was really long. I'm sorry I wasn't here."

She shimmies out of her jeans then, tugging them down over her hips. She's wearing a scrap of lace masquerading as underwear, and I watch, immobilized, as she bends over to yank off the last of the jeans, pulling her feet free.

When she turns around, I'm struggling to breathe.

She's so beautiful I can hardly look at her; I feel as if I've stepped into some strange dream, the debilitating fears that gripped me yesterday somehow forgotten in a moment. Heat courses through me at a dangerous speed, my mind unable to grasp what my body clearly understands. There's so much I still need to say to her—so much I remember wanting to ask her. But when she steps out of her underwear and walks through the open bathroom door, into the shower, and then directly into my arms, I remember nothing.

My brain shuts down.

Her soft, naked body is pressed against every hard inch of mine, and suddenly I want nothing, nothing but this. The need is so great it actually feels like it might break me.

"Hey, handsome," she says, peering up at me. She runs her hands down my back, then lower. I can hear her smile. "You look too good in here to be all by yourself."

I can't speak.

She takes my hand, still smiling, and rests it against her breast before slowly guiding it down her body; she's showing me exactly what she wants from me. How she wants it.

But I already know.

I know where she wants my hands. I know where she wants my mouth. I know where she wants me most of all.

I take her into my arms, hitching her leg around my thigh before I kiss her, breaking her open. She's so soft, slick, and eager in my arms, kissing me back with an urgency that drives me wild. I tilt her head back as I break away, kissing her neck, then lower; slowly, carefully, replacing my hands with my mouth everywhere on her body. Her desperate, anguished sounds send shock waves of pleasure through me, setting me on fire. She reaches behind her, searching for purchase against the tile wall, her back arching with pleasure.

I love the way she loses herself with me, the way she lets go, trusting me completely with her needs, her pleasure. I never feel closer to her than when we're so entwined, when there's nothing but openness and love between us.

She touches me then, gently wraps her hand around me, and I squeeze my eyes shut, hardly able to contain the sound I make, low in my throat. All I can think in this moment is that I don't want this to be over; I want to be trapped in here for hours, her slick body against mine, her voice in my ear begging me, as she is now, to make love to her.

"Please," she says, still touching me. "Aaron—"

I sink down, without warning, onto my knees. Ella steps back, confused for all of a second before her eyes widen with understanding.

"Come here, love."

Ella is hesitant at first. I feel her sudden shyness, desire, and self-consciousness colliding, and I study her as she stands there, the sheen of her wet curves in this light, her long dark hair painted to her skin. Hot drops of water race down her breasts, skim her navel. She's dripping wet, so gorgeous I hardly know what to do with myself.

She makes her way over to me slowly, her cheeks pink with heat, her eyes dark with need. I intercept her once she's standing in front of me, planting my hands around her hips. I look up at her in time to see her blush, a moment of self-consciousness gone in seconds. She's soon gasping my name, her hands in my hair, at the back of my neck. She's already so wet, so ready for me; the sight of her—the taste of her—it's too much. I feel like I'm detaching from my mind as I watch her lose herself. I can feel her legs shaking as she cries out for more, for *me*, and when she comes she stifles her scream in my hair. I'm on my feet a moment later, capturing the last of her cries with my mouth, kissing her as she trembles in my arms, her harsh breaths slowing down. Ella reaches for me even then, touches me until I'm blind with pleasure. She pushes me, gently, up against the wall, kissing my throat, running her hands down my chest, my torso, and then she sinks to her knees in front of me, taking me into her mouth—

I make a tortured sound, grasping at the wall, hardly able to breathe. The pleasure is white-hot; all-encompassing. I can't think around it. I can hardly see straight. And for a moment I think I've actually lost my mind, separated from my body.

"Ella," I gasp.

"I want you," she says, breaking away, her words hot against my skin. "Please—now—"

My heart still pounding in my chest, I step aside.

Turn off the shower.

Ella startles, surprised even as she gets to her feet. I step past her to grab a towel for each of us and she accepts hers with some confusion, refusing to dry herself off.

"But—"

I scoop her up without a word and she squeaks, half laughing as I carry her over to the single bed in our room. I lay her down carefully, and she looks up at me, eyes wide with wonder, her wet hair plastered to her skin, water dripping everywhere. I couldn't care less if we flooded this room.

I join her on the bed, carefully straddling her damp, gleaming body before leaning down to kiss her, this need so brutal it's almost indistinguishable from anguish. I touch her while I kiss her, stroking her slowly at first, then deeper, more urgent. She whimpers against my mouth, urging me closer, lifting her hips.

I move inside her with painstaking slowness, the pleasure so profound it seems to sever my connection to reality.

"God, you feel so good," I say, hardly recognizing the ragged sound of my own voice. "I can't believe you're mine."

She only moans my name in response, her arms wrapped tight around my neck as she pulls me closer.

I can feel her growing torment, her need for release as great as my own. We find a rhythm as we move. Ella hooks her legs around my waist, and she doesn't stop kissing me; my mouth, my cheeks, my jaw—any part of me she can reach—her feverish touches interrupted only by desperate pleas begging me for more—faster, harder—

"I love you," she says desperately. "I love you so much—"

I let go when I feel her come apart, losing myself in the moment with a stifled cry, my body seizing as it succumbs to this, the most acute form of pleasure.

I bury my face in her chest, listening to the sound of her racing heart for only a moment before disengaging myself, for fear of crushing her. Somehow the two of us manage, just barely, to squeeze in together on the narrow bed.

Ella tucks herself into my side, pressing her face against my neck, and I reach for the insubstantial covers, drawing them up around us. She grazes my chest with the tips of her fingers, drawing patterns, and this single action ignites a low heat deep inside me.

I could do this all day.

I don't care what happened yesterday. I don't need an explanation. None of it seems to matter anymore, not when she's here with me. Not when her naked body is wrapped up in mine, not when she draws her hands along my skin, touching me with a tenderness that tells me everything I need to know.

All I want is this. Her.

Us.

I don't even realize I've fallen asleep until her voice startles me awake.

"Aaron," she whispers.

It takes me a moment to open my eyes, to find my voice. I turn toward her as if in a dream, pressing a soft kiss to her forehead. "Yes, love?"

"There's something I want to show you."

NINE

The morning is cool and serene, everything limned in golden light. Touches of dew dot leaves and grass, the sun still stretching itself into the sky. The air is fresh with scents I cannot adequately describe; it's an amalgam of early morning fragrances, the familiar smell of the world shuddering awake. That I notice these things at all is unusual; it is clear, even to me, that my mood is greatly improved.

Ella is holding my hand.

She's been buoyant this morning. She got dressed even more quickly than I did, tugging me out the door with an enthusiasm that almost made me laugh.

Winston, who we discover waiting for us just outside the medical tent, possesses a range of emotions diametrically opposed. He says nothing when Ella and I approach, first taking in the two of us, then glancing at his watch.

"Hey, Winston," Ella says, still beaming. "What are you doing here?"

"Who, me?" He points at himself, feigning shock. "Oh, nothing. Just waiting out here for this jackass"—he shoots me a dark look—"for over an hour."

"What? Why?" Ella frowns. "And don't call him a jackass."

I process this exchange with some confusion. I'd not realized until just that moment how much I'd been hoping Winston's appearance at my door had something to do with Ella.

I see now that it does not.

"Winston came to our room this morning," I explain to her. "He told me he had . . . a surprise for me."

Ella's frown deepens. "A surprise?"

"*An hour ago*," Winston adds angrily.

"Yes," I say, meeting his eyes. "An hour ago."

He visibly clenches his jaw. "You really are the worst, you know that? I mean, everyone is always telling me that you're the worst—not that I've ever doubted it—but wow, this morning has just proven to me how completely self-absorbed you are. I can't believe I even offered to come get—"

"Winston." Ella's voice is quiet, carefully controlled, but her anger is loud. I turn to look at her, not surprised, exactly, but—

Yes, surprised.

I'm still unfamiliar with this dynamic. I'm still not used to someone taking my side.

"Look," she says. "Warner might be too nice to say anything when you talk to him like that—"

Winston sounds for a moment like he's choking.

"—but I'm not. So don't. Not only because it's awful, but because you're wrong."

Winston is still staring at Ella, dumbfounded. "I'm sorry— You think he's *too nice* to say anything? You think the reason Warner gets all quiet and gives people death stares is because he's *too nice*? To say anything?" Winston glances at me. "*Him?*"

I am smiling.

Ella is indignant, Winston is furious, and I am smiling. Very nearly laughing.

"Yes," Ella says, refusing to back down. "You guys are too comfortable bullying him."

Winston looks around himself a moment, for all the world as if he's entered some alternate universe. He opens his mouth to say something, looks at me, looks away, and then crosses his arms.

"You heard what he was like, right?" he finally says to Ella. "When you were gone? You heard all the stories about how h—"

"Yes," she says, her voice darker now. "I heard exactly what happened."

"And? So you know about all the people he murdered and how horrible he was to everyone and how he made a ton of people here cry and how Nouria nearly shot him for it—and you think *we* are the ones bullying *him*? That's what you think is happening here?"

"Clearly."

"And you," Winston says, turning to face me, his eyes narrowing with barely suppressed anger. "You agree with this assessment of your character?"

I smile wider. "Yes."

"Wow, you really are an asshole."

"Winston—"

"He made me wait out here for an *hour*! And this was after I told him I had a surprise for him, and after he slammed the door in my face—multiple times." Winston shakes his head. "You should've heard him. He's so scathing—so rude—"

"Hey, what the hell is going on over here?" Kenji is stalking toward us. "And where have *you* been?" he says to Ella. "We're all waiting for you guys!"

"Waiting for us?" I ask. "For what?"

Kenji throws up his arms in frustration. "Oh my God. You haven't told him yet?" he says to Ella. "What are you waiting for? Listen, I thought this idea was dumb to begin with, but now it's just getting ridiculous—"

"I was going to tell him this morning," she says, tensing. "I just haven't had a chance yet. We've been busy—"

"I bet you were, princess," Kenji says, a muscle ticking in his jaw. "Why is your hair wet?"

"I took a shower."

"You took a shower," he says, eyes narrowing. "Really."

"Okay— What is going on?" I ask, glancing between Ella and the others as a familiar dread moves up my spine. "Is this about the surprise?"

"The surprise?" Kenji is confused only a moment before understanding alights in his eyes. He looks at Winston. "Wait—I thought we sent you to go get him an *hour* ago?"

Winston explodes. *"This is exactly what I've been trying to say—* This son of a bitch made me wait outside the MT for an hour, even though I was perfectly nice to him, despite my better judgment—"

"Fucking hell," Kenji mutters angrily, pushing his hands through his hair. "As if we didn't have enough going on today." He turns to me. "You made Winston wait an entire hour just to give you the damn dog?"

"The dog?" I frown. "*The dog* is the surprise? How is it a surprise if I already know it exists?"

"Wait, what dog?" Ella looks at me, then at the others. "You mean the dog from yesterday?"

"Yeah." Kenji sighs. "Yara took the dog last night. She gave him a bath, scrubbed him up. She got him a collar and everything. She really wanted it to be a surprise for Warner and made us promise not to say anything about it. The dog is wearing a stupid bow on his head right now."

Ella has stiffened beside me. "Who's Yara?"

Her faint, almost undetectable note of jealousy—*possessiveness*—only cements my smile in place.

"You know Yara," Kenji says to Ella. "Redhead? Tall? Runs the school group? You've talked to her—"

Kenji catches sight of my face and cuts himself off.

"And what the hell are you smiling about? You've messed up our entire schedule, dickhead. We're an hour behind on everything now, all becau—"

"*Stop*," Ella says angrily. "Stop calling him names. He's not a dickhead. He's not a jackass. He's not self-absorbed. I don't know why you guys think it's okay to just say whatever terrible things you want about him—to his face—as if he's made of stone. You all do it. You all insult him over and over again and he just takes it—he doesn't even say anything—and somehow you've convinced yourselves it's okay. Why? He's a real, flesh-and-blood person. Why don't you care? Why don't you think he has feelings? What the hell is wrong with you?"

My smile is gone in an instant.

I experience a strange pain then, a sensation not unlike dissolving slowly from the inside. This feeling sharpens to a point, piercing me.

I turn to look at Ella.

She seems to sense the change in me; for a moment, they all do.

I feel a vague mortification at that, at the realization that I've somehow exposed myself. The proceeding silence is brief but torturous, and when Ella wraps her arms around my waist, hugging me close even in the midst of all this, I hear Winston clear his throat.

Tentatively, I lift a hand to her head, drawing it slowly down her hair. I worry, sometimes, that my love for her will expand beyond the limitations of my body, that it will one day kill me with its heft.

Kenji averts his eyes.

He is subdued when he says, "Yeah. Um, anyway, last I checked, the dog was in the dining tent, eating breakfast with everyone."

Another awkward beat, and Winston sighs. "Should I go get Yara? Do we even have time?"

"I don't think so," Kenji says. "I think we should tell her

to keep the dog until after."

"After what?" I ask, trying to read the maelstrom of emotions around me and failing. "What's going on?"

Kenji blows out a breath. He looks exhausted. "J, you have to tell him."

She pulls away from me, panicked in an instant. "But I had a plan—I was going to take him there first—"

"We don't have time for this, princess. You waited too long, and now it's officially a problem. Tell him what's happening."

"Right now? While you're standing here?"

"Yes."

"No way." She shakes her head. "You have to at least give us some privacy."

"Absolutely not." Kenji crosses his arms. "I've given you tons of privacy, and you've proven you can't be trusted. If I leave you two alone together you'll either end up in bed or accomplish nothing, neither of which are conducive to our goals."

"Was that really necessary?" I say, irritated. "Did you really feel the need to comment on our private life?"

"When it costs us an hour of our lives, *yes*," Winston says, moving, in an act of solidarity, to stand next to Kenji. He even crosses his arms against his chest, matching Kenji's stance.

"Go ahead." He nods at Ella. "Tell him."

Ella looks nervous.

Winston and Kenji are an irritated, impatient audience;

they stare us down, unrelenting, and I don't even know whether to be angry about it—because the truth is, I want to know what's going on, too. I want Ella to tell me what's happening.

I look from her to them, my heart pounding in my chest. I have no idea what she's about to say. No idea whether this revelation will be good or bad—though her nerves seem to indicate something is wrong. I brace myself as I watch her take a deep breath.

"Okay," she says, exhaling. "Okay." Another quick breath and she remembers to look at me, this time pasting an anxious smile on her face. "So—I didn't want to tell you like this, but I'd been thinking for a little while about how to do this in the best possible way, because I wanted everything to be *right*, you know? Right for both of us—and also, I didn't want it be anticlimactic. I didn't want this big thing to happen and then it was just, like, we go back to the status quo—I wanted it to feel special—like something was going to change—and I'm sorry I didn't tell you sooner, it was supposed to be a surprise, but it just wasn't ready in time, and if I'd told you about it, it wouldn't have been a surprise anymore, and Kenji kept insisting that I tell you anyway but I just—I'm sorry about yesterday, by the way, and I'm sorry about Nouria—I've been planning this whole thing with her since I woke up, practically, but she wasn't supposed to say anything to you, and she *knows* she wasn't supposed to say anything to you, because she and I had an agreement that I was supposed to tell you what was going on but yesterday

I didn't know exactly what was going to happen and I was waiting for more information because we were still trying really hard to make everything work in time but I know how important it is to you t—"

"Jesus fucking Christ," Winston mutters.

Kenji shouts: *"You two are getting married today."*

I turn sharply, stunned, to look at them.

"Kenji, what the hell—"

"You were taking too long—"

"We're getting married today?" I turn back to meet Ella's eyes, my heart pounding now for an entirely new reason. A better reason. *"We're getting married today?"*

"Yes," she says, blushing fiercely. "I mean—only if you want to."

I smile at her then, smile so wide I start laughing, disbelief rendering me foreign even to myself.

I hardly recognize this sound.

The sensations moving through my body right now—it's hard to explain. The relief flooding my veins is intoxicating; I feel as if someone punched a hole through my chest in the best possible way. This is some kind of madness.

I'm trying, but I can't stop laughing.

"Huh," says Winston quietly. "I didn't even know his face could do that."

"Yeah," Kenji says. "It's super weird the first time you see it."

"I can't look away. I'm trying to look away and I can't. It's like if a baby was born with a full set of teeth."

"Yes! *Exactly*. It's exactly like that!"

"But nice, too."

"Yeah." Kenji sighs. "Nice, too."

"Hey, did you know he had dimples? I didn't know he had dimples."

"C'mon, man, that's old news—"

"Could you two just—please—*be quiet* for a second?" Ella says, squeezing her eyes shut. "Just for one second?"

Kenji and Winston mime zipping their mouths shut before taking a step back, holding their hands up in surrender.

Ella bites her lip before meeting my eyes.

"So," she says. "What do you think?" She clasps, unclasps her hands. "Are you busy this morning? There's still something I want to show you—something I've been working on for the last few—"

I take her in my arms and she laughs, breathlessly, just until she meets my eyes. Her smile is soon replaced by a look—a softness in her expression that likely mirrors my own. I can still feel the outline of that little velvet box against my leg; I've been carrying it with me everywhere, too afraid to leave it behind, too afraid to lose hope.

"I love you," I whisper.

When I kiss her I breathe her in, inhaling the scent of her skin as I draw my hands down her back, pulling her tighter. Her response is immediate; her small hands move up my chest to claim my face, holding me close as she deepens the kiss, standing on tiptoe as she slowly twines her arms around my neck.

The pilot light in my body catches fire.

I break away reluctantly, and only because I remember we have an audience. Still, I press my forehead to hers, keeping her close.

I'm smiling again. Like a common idiot.

"Okay, well, that took a gross turn."

"Is it over yet?" Kenji asks. "I had to close my eyes."

"I don't know. I think it might be over, but if I were you I'd keep my eyes shut for another minute just in case—"

"Can you two keep your commentary to yourselves?" I say, pivoting to face them. "Is it so impossible for you to just be happy for—"

The words die in my throat.

Winston and Kenji are both bright-eyed and beaming, the two of them failing to fight back enormous smiles.

"Congratulations, man," Kenji says softly.

His sincerity is so unexpected it strikes me before I've had a chance to armor myself, and the consequences leave me reeling.

An unfamiliar, overwhelming heat erupts in my head, in my chest, pricking the whites of my eyes.

Ella takes my hand.

I can't help but study Kenji's face; I'm astonished by the kindness there, the happiness he does nothing to hide. It becomes more obvious by the moment that he's played a larger role in executing Ella's plans than I might've suspected, and I experience the truth then—feel it clearly, for the first time—the realization like a physical jolt.

Kenji genuinely wants me to be happy.

"Thank you," I say to him.

He smiles, but it's only a flicker of movement. Everything else is in his expression, in the tight nod he gives me by way of response.

"Anytime," he says quietly.

There's a beat of silence, broken only by the sound of Winston sniffing.

"All right, okay, that was a really beautiful moment, but you guys need to knock it off before I start crying," he says, laughing even as he tugs off his glasses to rub at his eyes. "Besides, we still have a shit ton of work to do."

"Work," I say, searching the sky for the sun. "Of course." It can't be much later than eight in the morning, but I'm usually at my desk much earlier. "I'll need to make a quick stop at the command center. How long do you think we'll be gone today? I have to reschedule some calls. There are time-sensitive materials I'm supposed to deliver today, and if I—"

"Not that kind of work," Kenji says, a strange smile on his face. "You don't need to worry about that today. It's all been taken care of."

"Taken care of?" I frown. "How?"

"Juliette already notified everyone last night. Obviously we can't check out of work completely, but we've divvied up today's responsibilities. We're all going to take shifts." He hesitates. "Not you, two, obviously. Both your schedules have been cleared for the day."

Somehow, this is a greater surprise than everything else.

If our schedules have been cleared, that means today wasn't some spur-of-the-moment decision. It means things didn't just serendipitously align in time to make it happen.

This was orchestrated. Premeditated.

"I don't think I understand," I say slowly. "As much as I appreciate the time off, this shouldn't take much more than an hour. We only need an officiant and a couple of witnesses. Ella doesn't even have a dress. Nouria said there was no time to make food, or a cake, or even to spare people to help set up, so it won't—"

Ella squeezes my hand, and I meet her eyes.

"I know we'd agreed to do something really small," she says softly. "I know you weren't expecting much. But I thought you might like this better."

I stare at her, dumbfounded. "Like *what* better?"

As if on cue, Brendan pops his white-blond head around a corner. "Morning, everyone! All right to bring everyone through? Or do you lot need another minute?"

Winston lights up at the sight of him, assuring Brendan that we need just a few more minutes.

Brendan says, "Roger that," and promptly disappears.

I turn to Ella, my mind whirring.

Save the birthday cake she surprised me with last month, I have very little in my life to offer me a frame of reference for this experience. My brain is at war with itself, understanding—while incapable of understanding—what now seems obvious. Ella has organized something elaborate.

In secret.

All of her earlier evasiveness, her half-truths and missing explanations—my fear that she'd been hiding something from me—

Suddenly everything makes sense.

"How long have you been planning this?" I ask, and Ella visibly tenses with excitement, emanating the kind of joy I've only ever felt in the presence of small children.

It nearly takes my breath away.

She wraps her arms around my waist, peering up at me. "Do you remember when we were on the plane ride home," she says, "and the adrenaline wore off, and I started kind of losing my mind? And I kept looking at the bone sticking out my leg and screaming?"

Of all things, this was not what I was expecting her to say.

"Yes," I say carefully. I have no interest in recalling the events of that plane ride. Or discussing them. "I remember."

"And do you remember what I said to you?"

I look away, sighing as I stare at a point in the distance. "You said you couldn't wear a wedding dress with part of your bone sticking out."

"Yeah," she says, and laughs. "Wow. I was pretty out of it."

"It's not funny," I whisper.

"No," she says, drawing her hands up my back. "No, it's not funny. But it was strange, how nothing was really making sense in my head. We'd just been through hell, but all I could think as I stared at myself was how impractical it was to be bleeding so much. I told you I couldn't marry you if the bleeding didn't stop, because then I'd get blood all over my dress, and your suit, and then we'd both just be covered in blood, and everything we touched would get bloody. And you"—she takes a deep breath—"you said you'd marry me right then. You said you'd marry me with my bleeding teeth, with a visibly broken leg, with dried blood on my face, with blood dripping from my ears."

I flinch at that, at the memory of what my father put her through. What her own parents did to her. Ella suffered and sacrificed so much for this world—all to bring The Reestablishment to its knees. All because she cared so much about this planet, and the people in it.

I feel suddenly ill.

What I hate, perhaps more than anything else, is that it doesn't stop. The demands on her body never stop. It doesn't seem to matter what side of history we're on; good or evil, everyone asks for more of her. Even now, after the fall of The Reestablishment, the people and their leaders *still* want more from her. They don't seem to care that she's only one person, or that she's already given so much. The more she gives, the more they require, and the quicker their gratitude shrivels up, the desiccated remains of which become something else altogether: expectation. If it were up to them, they'd keep taking from her until they've bled her dry—and I will never allow that to happen.

"Aaron."

Finally, I meet her eyes. "I meant what I said, love."

"I was hideous."

"You have never been hideous."

"I was a monster." She smiles as she says this. "I had that huge gash in my arm, the skin on my hands had split open, my nose wouldn't stop bleeding, my eyes wouldn't stop bleeding. I even had a freshly sutured finger. I was Frankenstein's monster. You remember? From that book—"

"Ella—please— We don't have to talk about this—"

"And I couldn't stop screaming," she says. "I was in so much pain, and I was so upset that I wouldn't stop bleeding, and I kept saying the craziest things, and you just sat next to me and listened. You answered every ridiculous question I asked like I wasn't completely out of my mind. *For hours.* I still remember, Aaron. I remember everything you said to me. Even after I passed out I heard you, on a loop, in my dreams. It was like your voice got caught in my head." She pauses. "I can only imagine what that experience must've been like for you."

I shake my head. "It wasn't about me. My experience doesn't matter—"

"Of course it does. It matters to *me*. You don't get to be the only one who worries about the person you love. I get to do that, too," she says, breaking away to better look me in the eye. "You spend so much time thinking about what's best for me. You're always worried about my safety and my happiness and the things I might need. Why don't I get to do that for you? Why don't I get to think about your happiness?"

"I am happy, love," I say quietly. "You make me happy."

She looks away at that, but when she meets my eyes again, she's fighting tears. "But if you could marry me however you wanted, you'd choose to do it differently, wouldn't you?"

"Ella," I whisper, tugging her back into my arms. "Sweetheart, why are you crying? I don't care about having a wedding. It doesn't matter to me. I'll marry you as you are right now, in the clothes we're wearing, right where we're standing."

"But if you *could* do it however you wanted, you'd do it differently," she says, looking up at me. "You'd do it better than that, wouldn't you?"

"Well— Yes—" I falter. "I mean, if it were a different world, maybe. If things were different for us, if we had more time, or more resources. And maybe one day we'll have a chance to do it over again, but right now all I—"

"No." She shakes her head. "I don't want to do it over again. I don't want you to look back on our wedding day as a placeholder for something else, or for what might've been. I want us to do it right the first time. I want to walk down an aisle to reach you. I want you to see me in a pretty dress. I want someone to take our picture. I want you to have that. You deserve to have that."

"But—how—"

I look up, distracted by the sounds of movement, voices. A crowd of people is swarming, moving toward us. Nazeera and Brendan lead the charge; Lily and Ian and Alia and Adam and James and Castle and Nouria and Sam and dozens of others—

They're all holding things: bouquets of flowers and covered trays of food and colorful boxes and folded linens and—

My blood pressure seems to plummet at the sight, leaving me dangerously light-headed. I take a sharp breath, try to clear my head. When I speak, I hardly recognize my voice.

"Ella, what did you do?"

She only smiles at me, eyes shining with feeling.

"How did you find so many flowers? Where—"

"All right," Winston says, holding up his hands. He sniffs, twice, and I see then that his eyes are red. "No more divulging secrets. We're done here."

Kenji, I notice, is looking determinedly away from all of us.

He clears his throat then, still staring at the sky when he says, "For what it's worth, bro, I tried to get her to tell you. I don't approve of this whole surprise-wedding nonsense. I told her—I said, if it were me, I'd want to know." Finally, Kenji meets my eyes. "But she wouldn't listen. She said it had to be a surprise. I said, *You're going to go back to your room tonight smelling like paint, and he's going to know! The man is not an idiot!* And she was like blah blah blah he's not going to know, blah blah blah, I'm the queen of the world, blah blah—"

"KENJI."

"What?"

Ella's fists are clenched. She looks like she might punch him in the face. "Please. Stop speaking."

"Why?" Kenji looks around. "What'd I say?"

"Paint," I say, frowning as I remember. "Of course. I thought you smelled like something faintly chemical last night. I wasn't sure what it was, though."

"What?" Ella says, crestfallen. "How? I thought you were asleep."

I shake my head, smiling now, though mostly for her benefit. Ella's guilt is palpable, and multiplying quickly.

"What was the paint for?" I ask.

"Nope!" Winston claps his hands together. "We're not doing that right now! You guys ready to get started? Good. Kenji and I will lead the way."

TEN

Ella is holding my hand like a lifeline, grinning as we forge an unfamiliar path through the Sanctuary. Her happiness is so electric it's contagious. I feel heavy with it, overwhelmed by it. I don't even think my body knows what to do with this much of it.

But seeing her like this—

It's impossible to describe what it does to me to see her so happy, smiling so wide she can hardly speak. I only know that I never want to do anything to make it stop.

We're following Kenji and Winston, both of whom were quickly joined by their counterparts, Nazeera and Brendan, while the rest of the crowd follows close behind. I seem to be the only one of us who doesn't know where we're going, and Ella still refuses to tell me anything more about our destination.

"Will you at least tell me whether we're leaving the Sanctuary?" I ask.

She smiles up at me. "Yes and no."

I frown. "Are we going somewhere to see the thing you wanted to show me? Or is this something else?"

Her smile grows bigger. "Yes and no."

"I see," I say, squinting into the distance. "So you're

torturing me on purpose."

"Yes," she says, poking me in the stomach. "And no."

I shake my head, laughing a little, and she pokes me in the stomach again.

"Ow," I say quietly.

Ella beams before wrapping her arms around my waist, hugging me as we walk, not seeming to care at all that she stumbles every few steps. I'm so incomprehensibly happy I seem to have misplaced most of my brain cells. I can hardly gather my thoughts.

After a moment, Ella says, "You know, it's not much fun to poke you in the stomach. It's not even possible, really, to poke hard muscle." She slides her hand up under my shirt, then slowly down my torso. "This whole thing would work much better if you had some body fat."

I take a steadying breath. "I'm sorry to disappoint you."

"I never said I was disappointed," she says, still smiling. "I love your body."

Her words conjure a simmering heat somewhere deep inside me. I tense as she draws patterns along my skin, her fingers grazing my navel before moving slowly up again, tracing lines with excruciating care.

I finally cover her hand with my own.

"That," I say, "is very distracting."

"What is?" She's not even looking at the path ahead anymore. One of her arms is wrapped around my waist, and the other is tucked unabashedly under my shirt. "This?" She drags her hand across my abs, moving steadily downward.

"Is this distracting?"

I inhale. "Yes."

"What about this?" she says, staring up at me, the picture of innocence as her free hand travels lower, then slips just underneath my waistband. "Is this distracting?"

"Ella."

"Yes?"

I laugh, but the sound is breathless. Nervous. It's a struggle to maintain the control necessary to keep my body from announcing to everyone exactly what I would rather be doing right now.

"Do you want me to stop?" she asks.

"No."

She smiles wider. "Good, because—"

"If you two are going to be disgusting on your wedding day," Kenji says over his shoulder, "could you at least *whisper*? It's close quarters in this crowd, okay? No one wants to hear your filthy conversations."

"Yeah," Nazeera says, turning to look at us. "No cute talk, either. Cute talk is highly discouraged on any day, but especially on your wedding day."

Ella's hand is gone from my body in an instant.

She turns to face them, the moment all but forgotten; I, on the other hand, need a minute. The effect she has on my nerves takes longer to dissipate.

I exhale slowly.

"I'm starting to think you two might be turning into the same person," Ella says. "And I'm not sure I mean that as a compliment."

Kenji and Nazeera laugh at that, Kenji drawing an arm around Nazeera's waist as they walk, pulling her closer. She leans into him, planting a brief kiss at the base of his jaw.

Kenji's provocations have grown innocuous in recent weeks. His bite is more habit than harmful, as he's in no position to criticize. He and Nazeera are as inseparable as is possible these days, the two of them ensconced in darkened corners at every available opportunity. To be fair, we're all lacking in privacy right now; very few people have their own rooms at the moment, which means we're not the only ones engaging in public displays of affection.

Kenji and Nazeera seem truly happy, though.

I've not known Kenji a particularly long time, but Nazeera—I never thought I'd see her like this.

I suppose she might say the same about me.

"You know, technically, you two shouldn't even be together right now," Winston says, swiveling to face us. He walks backward as he says, "The bride and groom can't just hang out together on their wedding day. Tradition frowns upon it."

"Excellent point," Brendan adds. "And as they're both such pure, innocent souls, we wouldn't want them to risk accidental, indecent skin-to-skin contact."

"Yeah, I think it might be too late for that," Kenji says.

"Seriously?" Brendan and Nazeera say at the same time.

Brendan laughs, but Nazeera turns sharply around to look at Ella, whose responding blush all but confirms their suspicions.

"Wow," Nazeera says after a moment, nodding. "Nice. You have interesting priorities."

"*Oh my God*," Ella says, covering her face with her hand. "Sometimes I really hate you guys."

I decide to change the subject.

"Will we be arriving at this mysterious destination soon?" I ask. "We've been walking for so long I'm beginning to wonder whether I'll need international clearance."

"Is this guy serious?" Winston calls back, exasperated. "It's been *maybe* five minutes."

"Sprinting two miles—uphill, in the heat, in a suit—and he doesn't break a sweat," Kenji says. "Wouldn't even let me rest for thirty-seconds. But *this*—yeah, this is too much for him. Makes sense."

"Okay, you can ignore them," Ella says, taking my hand again. "We're pretty close now." I feel her enthusiasm building anew, her eyes brightening as she peers ahead.

"So—what changed yesterday?" I ask her. "To make all this happen?"

Ella looks up. "What do you mean?"

"Yesterday Nouria told me that, for a number of different reasons, it was basically out of the question for us to have a wedding. But today"—I glance around us, at the mass of people sacrificing hours of their work and life to help organize this event—"those issues no longer seem to be relevant."

"Oh," Ella says, and sighs. "Yeah. Yesterday was a mess.

I really didn't want to postpone things, but there were just so many different disasters to deal with. Losing our clothes was one obstacle, but trying to host the wedding at night was proving a logistical nightmare. I realized we could either get married last night and have to compromise on almost everything, or push it by a day, and *maybe*, just maybe, be able to do it right—"

"A day?" I frown. "Nouria made it seem like it might be months before we could reschedule. She made it sound functionally impossible."

"*Months?*" Ella stiffens. "Why would she say that?"

"You must've really pissed her off," Kenji says, his laughter echoing. "Nouria knew Juliette wouldn't have postponed the wedding that long. She was probably just torturing you."

"*Really.*" The revelation makes me scowl. Between her and Sam, I seem to have made two very powerful enemies.

"Hey—I'm sorry she said that to you," Ella says softly, hugging me from the side as we walk. I wrap my arm around her shoulders, holding her tight against me.

"I think Nouria leaned a little too hard into the cover story," she says. "I had no idea you thought we might be postponing the wedding that far into the future. I'm only now realizing that yesterday must've been pretty rough for you."

"It wasn't," I lie, gently cupping the back of her head, my fingers threading through the silk of her hair. I study her face as she stares up at me, noticing then how the sun changes her eyes; her irises look more green in the light. Blue in the dark. "It was fine."

Ella doesn't buy this.

Her hands graze my hips as she draws away, lingering before she lets go. "I was so busy trying to make everything work that I didn't even—"

She cuts herself off, her emotions changing without warning.

"Hey," she says. "What's this?"

"What's what?"

"This," she says, gently prodding my pant leg in a manner that would disturb Kenji for weeks. "This box."

"*Oh*."

I come to a sudden and complete stop, heart pounding as the crowd surges around us, several of them calling out congratulations as they pass. Someone sticks a homemade tiara on Ella's head at one point, which she accepts with a gracious nod before discreetly tugging it out of her hair.

They seem to know better than to touch me.

In the distance, I hear Winston clap his hands. "All right, everyone, we're basically here. Juliette, will you and Warner pl— Wait, where's Juliette?"

"I'm back here!"

"Why the hell are you back there?" Kenji cries.

I hear faint grumbling from Winston, more exasperated words from Kenji; all this is followed by soothing sounds made by their partners. The sequence would be comical if I were in any mood to laugh.

Instead, I have turned to stone.

"We'll be right there!" Ella reassures them. "You can start setting up without us!"

"*Set up without you?* If I find out this was your plan all along, princess, Nazeera is going to kick your ass."

"I absolutely won't," she calls out cheerfully. "In fact, I fully support the two of you tearing off each other's clothes, if that's what you've got planned!"

"Oh my God, Nazeera—"

"What?"

"*Don't encourage them,*" Kenji and Winston shout at the same time.

"Why not?" Brendan says. "I think it's romantic."

They bicker a bit more while my mind spins. I feel the outline of the box against my leg more acutely than ever, a square spot of heat against my skin.

This is happening out of order.

I manage to comfort myself with the reminder that everything about us has unfolded in an unconventional way; I shouldn't be too surprised to discover that, here, too, things are not going to plan.

Then again, I didn't really have a plan.

In an ideal scenario, I would've proposed to her with the ring; she should've already had it on her finger. Instead, we are now fast approaching our actual wedding and I've yet to give it to her. And while it occurs to me that I could find a way to evade her curiosity right now, I'm not sure there's any point in prolonging it. I have no idea where we're going.

I don't know what's going to happen next.

I might not even have time later to do this properly.

I swallow, hard, trying to force back my apprehension. I don't know why I'm so nervous.

That's not true.

I know why I'm nervous. I'm worried she's going to hate it, and I don't know what I'll do if she hates it. I suppose I'll have to return it. I'll have to marry her without a ring, acknowledging all the while that I am an idiot of astronomical proportions, one who couldn't even manage to pick out a decent ring for his fiancée.

This imagining inspires in me a wave of dread so severe I close my eyes against the force of it.

"Aaron," Ella says, and my eyes fly open, bringing me back to the present.

She is smiling at me.

Ella, I realize, already knows what's in the box.

Somehow, this makes me more nervous. I look around myself, searching for calm, and register a beat too late that we're all alone. The crowd has dispersed into the distance beyond us, and as I watch them disappear—their bodies growing smaller by the second—I recognize only then that I have no idea where we are.

I take stock of our surroundings: there are paved roads and sidewalks not far away, wilting trees planted at regular intervals. The air smells different—sharper—and the sun seems brighter, unencumbered by dense woods. I hear that familiar trill of birdsong and search the sky again, trying to orient myself. My mind searches itself for maps, blueprints, old information. This area looks less wild than the Sanctuary, stripped back. I feel quite certain we must be encroaching upon old, unregulated territory, but as we still appear to be within the boundary of Nouria's protections, that can't be possible. The lights that delineate our space from the outside world are clearly visible.

"Where are we?" I ask. For a moment, my nerves are forgotten. "This isn't—"

"We can get to that in just a second," Ella says, still smiling. She drops the homemade tiara to the ground and steps forward, drawing her hand slowly up my thigh, tracing a faint circle around the impression of the box. "But first, I feel like I have no choice but to make a terrible joke about finding something hard in your pants."

I drag a hand down my face, vaguely mortified. "Please don't."

Ella fights to be serious, biting her lip to keep from smiling. She mimes locking her mouth, tossing the key.

I actually laugh then, after which I sigh, staring for a moment into the distance.

"So. What's in the box?" she asks, her joy so bright it's blinding. "Is it for me?"

"Yes."

When I make no move to procure the object, she frowns. "Can I . . . have it?"

With great reluctance, I tug free the little velvet box from my pocket, clenching it tight for so long she finally reaches for my hand. Gently, she wraps her small fingers around my fist.

"Aaron," she says. "What's wrong?"

"Nothing." I take a deep breath. "Nothing is wrong. I just—" I force myself to open my palm to her, heart still pounding. "I really hope you like it."

She smiles as she takes the box. "I'm sure I'm going to love it."

"It's okay if you don't. You don't have to love it. If you hate it I can always get you something else—"

"You know, I'm not used to seeing you nervous like this." She tilts her head at me. "It's kind of adorable."

"I feel like an idiot," I say, trying and failing to smile. "Though I'm glad you find it entertaining."

She opens the box as I say this, giving me no time to brace myself before she gasps, her eyes widening in astonishment. She covers her mouth with one hand, her emotions so unrestrained I can hardly read them. There's too much all at once: shock, happiness, confusion—

The effort to say nothing nearly costs me my sanity.

"Where did you get this?" she says, finally dropping her hand away from her face. Carefully, she tugs the engagement ring free from its setting, examining it closely before staring up at me. "I've never seen anything like this."

"I had it made," I manage to say, my body still so tense it's difficult to speak. She hasn't said whether she likes it, which means the vise around my chest refuses to disengage.

Still, I force myself to retrieve the glittering piece from

her, taking her left hand in mine with great care. My own hands are miraculously steady as I slide the ring into place on her fourth finger.

The fit, as I knew it would be, is perfect.

I took the necessary measurements while she was heavily asleep, still recovering in the medical tent.

"You had it *made?*" Ella is staring at her hand, the ring refracting the light, shattering color everywhere. The center stone is large, but not garishly so, and suits her beautifully.

I think so, anyway.

I watch her as she studies the ring, turning her hand left and right. "How did you get it made?" she asks. "*When?* I thought there'd be a simple wedding band inside, I didn't think—"

"There is a wedding band inside. There are two rings."

She looks up at me then, and I see, for the first time, that her eyes are bright with tears. The sight cuts me straight through the heart but brings with it the hope of relief. It might be the only time in my life I've ever been happy to see her cry.

With great trepidation, Ella reopens the velvet box, slowly retrieving from its depths the wedding band.

She holds it up to the sky with a trembling hand, staring at its detail. The brushed gold band resembles a twig, so delicate it looks almost as if it were forged from thread. It glints in the sun, the two emerald leaves bright against the infinite branch.

She slips it onto her finger, gasping softly when it

settles into place. It was designed to fit perfectly against the engagement ring.

"The leaves—are supposed to be—like us," I say, hearing how stupid it sounds when I say it out loud. How perfectly pedestrian.

I suddenly hate myself.

Still, Ella says nothing, and I can't hold the question in any longer. "Do you like it? If you don't like it I can always—"

She snaps the box shut and throws her arms around my neck, hugging me so tight I feel the damp press of her cheek against my jaw. She pulls back to pepper my face with kisses, half laughing as she does, swiping at her tears with shaking hands.

"How can you even ask me that?" she says. "I've never owned anything so beautiful in my whole life. I love these rings. I love them so much. And I know you probably didn't think about this when you had them made—because you wouldn't—but the emeralds remind me of your eyes. They're stunning."

I blink at that, surprised. "My eyes?"

"Yes," she says quietly, her expression softening. "And you're right. They *are* like us. We've been growing toward each other from the opposite sides of the same path since the beginning, haven't we?"

Relief hits me like an opiate.

I pull her into my arms, burying my face in her neck before I kiss her—softly at first—and our slow, searing touches quickly change into something else altogether. Ella is drawing her hand under my shirt again, my skin heating under her touch.

"I love you," she whispers, kissing my throat, my jaw, my chin, my lips. "And I never want to take these off." Her words are accompanied by a passion so profound I can hardly breathe around it. I close my eyes as the sensations build and spiral; the cold graze of her rings against my chest striking my skin like a match.

Desire soon shuts down my mind.

When we break apart I'm breathing hard, molten heat coursing through my veins. I'm imagining scenarios far too impractical to execute. Being with Ella this morning was like breaking a dam; I'd been so afraid to touch her while she was in recovery, and then terrified to overwhelm her in the days after. I'd wanted to make sure she was okay, that she took her time getting back to normal, at her own pace, without anyone crowding her personal space.

But now—

Now that she's ready—now that my body remembers this—it's suddenly impossible to get enough.

"I'm so glad you like the rings, love," I whisper against her mouth. "But I'm going to need to take back the band."

"What?" she says, pulling away. She stares at her hand, heartbroken in an instant. "Why?"

"Those are the rules." I'm still smiling when I touch her face, grazing her cheek with my knuckles. "I promise, after I give this ring to you today, I'll never ask for it back."

When still she makes no move, I reach, without looking,

for the box clenched in her right fist.

She relinquishes the item with great reluctance, sighing as she steps back to slip the wedding band off her finger. I open the recovered box, presenting it to her, and after she settles the ring back into its nest I snap the lid shut, tucking the object safely back into my pocket.

My heart has grown ten sizes in the last several minutes.

"We should probably get going if you want to get this back," I say, touching her waist, then tugging her close. My lips are at her ear when I whisper: "I'm going to marry you today. And then I'm going to make love to you until you can't remember your name."

Ella makes a startled, breathless sound, her hands tightening in my shirt. She pulls me closer and kisses me, nipping my bottom lip before claiming my mouth, touching me now with a new desperation; a hunger still unmet. She presses her body against me, hard and soft soldered together, and I lose myself in it, in the intoxication of knowing just how much she wants this.

Me.

Her mouth is hot and sweet, her limbs heavy with pleasure. She drags her hand down the front of my pants and I make an anguished sound somewhere deep in my chest. I take her face in my hands as she touches me, kissing her deeper, harder, still unable to find relief. She seems to be torturing me on purpose—torturing both of us—knowing there's nothing we can do here, knowing there are people waiting for us—

"Ella," I gasp, the word practically a plea as I break away, trying and failing to cool my head, my thoughts. I can't walk back into a crowd right now, looking like this. I can't even think straight.

My thoughts are wild.

I want nothing more than to strip her bare. I want to fall to my knees and taste her, make her lose her mind with pleasure. I want her to beg before I make her come, right here, in the middle of nowhere.

"I really don't think you understand what you do to me, love," I say, trying to steady myself. "You have no idea how badly I want you. You have no idea what I want to do to you right now."

My words do not have the intended effect. Ella is not deterred.

Her desire seems to intensify, more in every second. That she could ever want me like this—that I could ever inspire in her the kind of need she inspires in me—

It still seems impossible.

And it's addicting.

"*You* have no idea," she says softly, "how you make me feel when you look at me like that."

I take a deep, unsteady breath when she touches me again, dragging my hands down her body before sliding a hand under her sweater, up the curve of her rib cage. She gasps as I skim the soft, heavy swell of her breasts, her body responding in an instant to my touch.

Her skin here, like everywhere, is like satin.

"God," I breathe. "I can never get enough of you."

Ella shakes her head even as she closes her eyes, surrendering to my hands. "Kenji was right," she says breathlessly. "We can't be left alone together."

I kiss her neck slowly, tasting her there until she moans, not enough to leave a mark. She reaches for me then, her own hands grasping for the button of my pants. In my delirium I let it happen, forgetting for a moment where we are or what we need to be doing until I feel her soft fingers wrap around me—a cool hand against my feverish skin—and my head nearly catches fire.

I'm moments away from losing my mind. I want to strip off her sweater. I want to unhook her bra. I want her to undress in front of me before I—

This is madness.

Common sense is returned to me only through a brutal, agonizing reclamation of self-control, just enough for me to place a hand over hers, forcing myself to breathe slowly.

"We can't do this here," I say, hating myself even as I say it. "Not here. Not now."

She looks around herself then as if emerging from a dream, the real world coming back into focus by degrees. I take advantage of her distraction to put myself to rights, stunned to realize I was only moments away from doing something reckless.

Ella's disappointment is palpable.

"I need to take you to bed, love," I say, my voice still rough with desire. "I need hours. Days. Alone with you."

She nods, her ring catching the light as she reaches for me, collapsing against my chest. "Yes. Please. I really hope you're not planning on falling asleep tonight."

I laugh at that, the sound still a bit shaky. "One day we'll have a proper bed," I say, kissing her forehead. "And then I doubt I will ever sleep again."

Ella jerks back suddenly.

Her eyes widen with something like comprehension, then delight. She nearly bounces up and down before taking my hand, and with only a sharp exclamation of excitement, she tugs me forward.

"Wait— Ella—"

"I still have something to show you!" she cries, and breaks off into a run.

I have no choice but to chase after her.

ELEVEN

At first, I hear only Ella's laughter, the effortless joy of a carefree moment. Her hair whips around her as she runs, streaming in the sun. I enjoy this sight more than I know how to explain; she runs through the several remaining feet of undeveloped land into the center of an abandoned street, all with the uninhibitedness of a child. I'm so entranced by this scene that it's a moment before I register the distant scream of an ungreased hinge: the repetition of steel abrading itself. My feet finally hit pavement as I follow her down the neglected road, the impact of my boots on the ground signifying the sudden change in place with hard, definitive thuds. The sun bears down on me as I run, surprising me with its severity, the light undiminished by cloud or tree cover. I slow down as the distant whine grows louder, and when the source of this keening finally comes into view, I skid to a sudden stop.

A playground.

Rusted and abandoned, a set of swings screeching as the wind pushes around their empty seats.

I've seen such things before; playgrounds were common in a time before The Reestablishment; I saw a great deal of them on my tours of old unregulated territory. They were built most often in areas where there existed large groupings of homes. Neighborhoods.

Playgrounds were not known to be found at random near densely forested areas like the Sanctuary, nor were they built for no reason in the middle of nowhere.

Not for the first time, I'm desperate to understand where we are.

I wander closer to the rusting structure, surprised to feel a distinct lack of resistance when I step onto the haunted play area. The playground is built atop material that gives a bit when I walk; it seems to be made from something like rubber, surrounded otherwise by concrete pavers anchored by metal benches, paint peeling in sharp ribbons. There are long stretches of dirt beyond the borders, where no doubt grass and trees once thrived.

I frown.

This couldn't possibly be any part of the Sanctuary—and yet there's no question at all that we're still within Nouria's jurisdiction.

I look around then, searching for Ella.

I catch a glimpse of her before she disappears down yet another poorly paved road—the asphalt ancient and cracked—and silently berate myself for falling behind. I'm about to cross what appears to be the remains of an intersection when suddenly she's back, her distant figure rushing into view before coming to a halt.

She noticed I was gone.

It's a small gesture—I realize this even as I react to

it—but it makes me smile nonetheless. I watch her as she spins around, searching the street for me, and I lift a hand to let her know where I am. When our eyes finally meet she jumps up and down, waving me forward.

"Hurry," she cries, cupping her mouth with her hands.

I clear the distance between us, analyzing my surroundings as I do. The old street signs have been vandalized so completely they're now rendered meaningless, but there remain a few traffic lights still hung at intervals. Relics of the old speaker system installed in the early days of The Reestablishment have survived as well, the ominous black boxes still affixed to lampposts.

People used to live here, then.

When I finally reach Ella, I take her hand, and she immediately tugs me forward, even as she's slightly out of breath. Running has always been harder for Ella than it is for me. Still, I resist her effort to drag me along.

"Love," I say. "Where are we?"

"I'm not going to tell you," she says, beaming. "Even though I have a feeling you've already figured it out."

"This is unregulated territory."

"Yes." She smiles brighter, then dims. "Well, sort of."

"But how—"

She shakes her head before attempting to pull me forward again, now with greater difficulty. "No explanations yet! Come on, we're almost there!"

Her energy is so effervescent it makes me laugh. I watch her a moment as she struggles to move me, her effort not unlike that of a cartoon character. I imagine it must frustrate her not to be able to use her powers on me, but then I remind myself that Ella would never do something like that even if she could; she'd never overpower me just to get what she wanted. That's not who she is.

She is, and always has been, a better person than I will ever be.

I take her in then, her eyes glinting in the sun, the wind tousling her hair. She is a vision of loveliness, her cheeks flushed with feeling and exertion.

"*Aaron*," she says, pretending to be mad. I don't think it productive to tell her, but I find this adorable. When she finally lets go of my hand, she throws up her arms in defeat.

I'm smiling as I tuck a windblown hair behind her ear; her pretend anger dissipates quickly.

"You really don't want to tell me anything about where we're going?" I ask. "Not a single thing? I'm not allowed to ask even one clarifying question?"

She shakes her head.

"I see. And is there any particular reason why our destination is such a highly guarded secret?"

"That was a question!"

"Right." I frown, squinting into the distance. "Yes."

Ella puts her hands on her hips. "You're going to ask me another question, aren't you?"

"I just want to know how Nouria managed to draw unregulated territory into her protection. I'd also like to know why no one told me she had plans to do such a thing.

And why—"

"No, no, I can't answer those questions without spoiling the surprise." Ella blows out a breath, thinking. "What if I promise to explain everything when we get there?"

"How much longer until we get there?"

"Aaron."

"Okay," I say, fighting back a laugh. "Okay. No more questions."

"You swear?"

"I swear."

She makes an exclamation of delight before kissing me quickly on the cheek, and then takes my hand again. This time, I let her drag me forward, following her, without another word, onto an unmarked road.

The street curves as we go, unwilling even now to reveal our destination. We ignore the sidewalks, as cars aren't to be expected here, but it still feels strange to be walking down the center of a street, our feet following the faded yellow lines of another world, avoiding potholes as we go.

There are more trees here than I expected, more green leaves and patches of living grass than I thought we'd find. These are vestiges of another time, still managing to survive, somehow, despite everything. The limp greenery seems to multiply the farther we walk, the half-bare trees planted on either side of the pockmarked road clasping branches overhead to form an eerie tunnel around us. Sunlight shatters through the wooden webbing above, casting a kaleidoscope of light and shadow across our bodies.

I know we must be getting close to our destination when Ella's energy changes, her emotions a jumble of joy and nerves. It's not long before the dead road finally opens up onto an expansive view—and I come to a violent halt.

This is a residential street.

Just under a dozen houses, each several feet apart, separated by dead, square lawns. My heart pounds wildly in my chest, but this is nothing I haven't seen before. It's a vision of a bygone era; these homes, like so many others on unregulated turf, are in various states of decay, succumbing to time and weather and neglect. Roofs collapsing, walls boarded up, windows broken, front doors hanging from their hinges, all of them half-destroyed. It's like so many other neighborhoods around the continent, save one extraordinary difference.

In the center is a home.

Not a house—not a building—but a *home*, salvaged from the wreckage. It's been painted a simple, tasteful shade of white—not too white—its walls and roof repaired, the front door and shutters a pale sage green. The sight gives me déjà vu; I'm reminded at once of another house of a different vintage, in a different place. *Robin's-egg blue.*

The difference between them, however, is somehow palpable.

My parents' old house was little more than a graveyard, a museum of darkness. This house is bright with possibility, the windows big and brilliant, and beyond them: people. Familiar faces and bodies, crowding together in the front room. If I strain, I can hear their muted voices.

This must be some kind of dream.

The lawn is in desperate need of water, the single tree in the front yard withering slowly in the sun. There's a duo of rusty garbage bins visible in a side alley, where a surprise street cat languishes in a streak of sunlight. I can't recall the last time I saw a cat. I feel as if I've stepped into a time machine, into a vision of a future I was told I'd never have.

"Ella," I whisper. "What did you do?"

She squeezes my hand; I hear her laugh.

I turn slowly to face her, a wealth of feeling rising up inside me with a force so great it scares me.

"What is this?" I ask, hardly able to speak. "What am I looking at?"

Ella takes a deep breath, exhaling as she clasps her hands together. She's nervous, I realize.

This astonishes me.

"I had the idea a long time ago," she says, "but it wasn't workable back then. I always wanted us to be able to reclaim these old neighborhoods; it always seemed like such a waste to lose them altogether. We're still going to have to demolish most of them, because the majority are too far gone for repair, but that means we can redesign better, too—and it means we can tie it all into the new infrastructure package, creating jobs for people.

"I've been in talks with our newly contracted city planner, by the way." She smiles tightly. "I never got to tell you about that yesterday. We're hoping to rebuild these areas in phases, prioritizing the transplantation of the disabled and the elderly and those with special needs. The Reestablishment did everything it could to throw anyone they deemed *unfit* into the asylums, which means none of the compounds they built made provisions for the old or infirm or all the orphans—which, I mean—of course, you already know all this." She looks sharply away at that, hugging herself tightly. When she looks up again I'm struck by the potency of her grief and gratitude.

"I really don't think I've said thank you enough for all that you've done," she says, her voice breaking as she speaks. "You have no idea how much it meant to me. Thank you. *So much.*"

She throws herself into my arms, and I hold her tight, still stunned into silence. I feel all her emotions at once, love and pain and fear, I realize, for the future. My heart is jackhammering in my chest.

Ella has always been deeply concerned with the well-being of the asylum inmates. After reclaiming Sector 45, she and I would talk late into the night about her dreams for change; she often said the first thing she'd do after the fall of The Reestablishment would be to find a way to reopen and staff the old hospitals—in anticipation of the immediate transfer of asylum residents.

While Ella was in recovery, I launched this initiative personally.

We've begun staffing the newly open hospitals not only with reclaimed doctors and nurses from the compounds but with supplies and soldiers from local sector headquarters all across the continent. The plan is to assess each asylum victim before deciding whether they need continued medical treatment and/or physical rehabilitation. Any healthy and able among them will be released back into the care of their living relatives, or else found safe accommodations.

Ella has thanked me for doing this a thousand times, and each time I've assured her that my efforts were nominal at best.

Still, she refuses to believe me.

"There's no one in the whole world like you," she says, and I can practically feel her heart beating between us. "I'm so grateful for you."

These words cause me an acute pain, a kind of pleasure that makes it hard to breathe. "I am nothing," I say to her. "If I manage to be anything, it is only because of you."

"Don't say that," she says, hugging me tighter. "Don't talk about yourself like that."

"It's true."

I never would've been able to get things done so quickly for her if Ella hadn't already won over the military contingent, a feat managed almost entirely through rumor and gossip regarding her treatment of the soldiers from my old sector.

During her brief tenure in 45, Ella gave soldiers leave to reunite with their families, allocated those with children larger rations, and removed execution as a punishment for any infraction, minor or major. She regularly shrugs off these changes as if they were nothing. To her, they were casual declarations made over a meal, a young woman waving a fork around as she raged against the fundamental dignities denied our soldiers.

But these changes were radical.

Her effortless compassion toward even the lowest foot soldiers gained Ella loyalty across the continent. It took little work, in the end, to convince our North American infantrymen and -women to take orders from Juliette Ferrars; they moved quickly when I bade them to do so on her behalf.

Their superiors, however, have proven an altogether different struggle.

Even so, Ella doesn't see yet just how much power she wields, or how significantly her point of view changes the lives of so many. She refuses herself, as a result, any claim to credit; attributing her decisions to what she calls "a basic grasp of human decency." I tell her, over and over again, how rare it is to find any among us who've retained such decency. Even fewer remain who can look beyond their own struggles long enough to bear witness to the suffering of others; fewer still, who would do anything about it.

That Juliette Ferrars is incapable of seeing herself as an exception is part of what makes her extraordinary.

I take a deep, steadying breath as I hold her, still studying the house in the distance. I hear the muted sound of laughter, the bustle of movement. A door opens somewhere, then slams shut, unleashing sound and clamor, voices growing louder.

"Where do you want these chairs?" I hear someone shout, the proceeding answer too quiet to be intelligible.

Emotional tremors continue to wreck me.

They are setting up for our wedding, I realize.

In our house.

"No," Ella whispers against my chest. "It's not true. You deserve every good thing in the world, Aaron. I love you more every single day, and I didn't even think that was possible."

This declaration nearly kills me.

Ella pulls back to look me in the eye, now fighting tears, and I can hardly look at her for fear I might do the same.

"You never complain when I want to eat every meal with everyone. You never complain when we spend hours in the Q in the evening. You never complain about sleeping on the floor of our hospital room, which you've done every single night for the last fourteen nights. But I know you. I know it must be killing you." She takes a sharp breath, and suddenly she can't meet my eyes.

"You need quiet," she says. "You need space, and privacy. I want you to know that I know that—that I see you. I appreciate everything you do for me, and I see it, I see it every single time you sacrifice your comfort for mine. But I want to take care of you, too. I want to give you peace. I want to give you a home. With me."

There's a terrifying heat behind my eyes, a feeling I force myself always to kill at all costs, and which today I am unable to defeat entirely. It's too much; I feel too full; I am too many things. I look away and take a sharp breath, but my exhalation is unsteady, my body unsteady, my heart wild.

Ella looks up, slowly at first, her expression softening at the sight of my face.

I wonder what she sees in me then. I wonder whether she's able to see right through me even now, and then I surprise myself for wondering. Ella is the only one who's ever bothered to wonder whether I'm more than I appear.

Still, I can only shake my head, not trusting myself to speak.

Ella experiences a sharp stab of fear in the intervening silence, and bites her lip before asking: "Was I wrong? Do you hate it?"

"Hate it?" I break away from her entirely at that, finding my voice only as a strange panic seizes me, making it hard for me to breathe. "Ella, I don't . . . I've done *nothing* to deserve you. The way you make me feel—the things you say to me— It's terrifying. I keep thinking the world will realize, any second now, how completely unworthy I am. I keep waiting for something horrible to happen, something to reset the scales and return me to hell, where I belong, and then all of this will just disappear. You'll just disappear. God, just thinking about it—"

Ella is shaking her head. "You and I— Aaron, people like us think good things will disappear because that's how it's always been. Good things have never lasted in our lives;

happiness has never lasted. And somehow we can only expect what we've experienced."

I'm sustaining full-blown anxiety now, my traitorous body shutting down, and Ella takes my hands, anchoring me.

I look into her eyes even as my heart races.

"But do you know what I've realized?" she says. "I've realized that we have the power to break these cycles. We can choose happiness for ourselves and for each other, and if we do it often enough, it'll become our new normal, displacing the past. Happiness will stop feeling strange if we see it every day."

"Ella—"

"I love you," she says. "I've always loved you. I'm not going anywhere."

I take her into my arms then, pulling her tightly against me, breathing in the familiar scent of her. When she's here, *right here*, it's so much easier to breathe. She's real when she's in my arms.

"I don't even know how to thank you for this," I whisper into her hair, closing my eyes against the heat in my head, in my chest. "You have no idea what it means to me, love. It's the greatest gift anyone has ever given me."

She laughs then, soft and gentle.

"Don't thank me yet," she says, peering up. "The house still needs a lot of work. The exterior is in pretty good shape now, but the inside is still kind of a disaster. We were only able to get one of the rooms ready in time, but it was—"

"*We?*" I lean back, frowning.

Ella laughs out loud at the look on my face. "Of course *we*," she says. "Did you think I did this all on my own? Everyone helped. They all gave up so much of their time to make this happen for you."

I shake my head. "If people helped, they did it for you," I point out. "Not me."

"They care about you, too, Aaron."

"That is a very generous lie," I say, smiling now.

"It's not a lie."

"It's possibly the biggest lie you've ever told."

"It's not! Even Ian helped. He taught me how to frame a wall—and he was so patient—and you know how he feels about me. Even Nouria helped. Well, especially Nouria. We couldn't have done any of this without Nouria."

I find this especially surprising, given her undisguised loathing of my existence. "She pulled this area into her protection? Just for me?"

Ella nods, then frowns. "Well. Yes. I mean, sort of. It's also part of a larger plan."

I smile wider at that. "Really," I say.

Nouria's involvement—and the involvement of the others—makes a great deal more sense if this project is in fact one small part of a broader initiative, though I keep this to myself. Ella seems incapable of believing how much everyone here hates me, and I don't relish disabusing her of this notion.

"We're going to build a campus for the Sanctuary," she explains, "and this is the first phase. We had scouts do a ton of site visits beforehand; these are the best and most functional homes in the surrounding area, because some of them were used in various capacities by the local sector CCR and her subordinates."

I raise my eyebrows, fascinated.

Ella never told me about this. She's clearly been hiding this project from me for days—which is both concerning and not. Part of me is relieved to finally understand the distance I've felt between us, while the other part of me wishes I'd been involved.

"So, yeah, we've reclaimed several dozen acres of unregulated territory here," she says. "All of which, up until a couple of weeks ago, were under military control. I figured that, as long as we need absolute security—which might be a while—we can't live like we're in prison. We're going to need to expand the Sanctuary, and give our people here a real, viable life.

"It's going to be a long road to recovery," Ella adds with a sigh. "The work is going to be brutal. The least I can do is give proper shelter, privacy, and amenities to those dedicating their lives to its reconstruction. I want to rebuild all the houses in this area first. Then I want to build schools, and a proper hospital. We can safeguard some of the original undeveloped land, turning it into parks. I'm hoping it'll one day become a private campus—a new capital—as we rebuild the world. And then, maybe one day when things are safer, we can let down our walls and reunite with the general public."

"Wow."

I detach from her a moment to look up and down the street, then into the distance. What she's describing is an enormous undertaking. I can't believe how much space they were already able to reclaim. "This is a remarkable idea, Ella. Truly. It's brilliant." I look back at her, forcing a smile. "I only wish I could've helped."

"I really, really wanted to tell you about it," she says, her brows knitting together. "But I couldn't say anything because I knew you'd want to come see the area, and then you would've noticed all the building materials, and then you would've wanted to know why so many people were working so hard on this one house, and then you would've wanted to know who was going to live in it—"

"I wouldn't have asked that many questions."

She shoots me a hard look.

"No, you're right." I nod. "I would've ruined the surprise."

"HEY!"

I spin around at the sound of the familiar voice. Kenji is coming around the side yard of the house. He's holding a folding chair in one hand, and waving what appears to be a sprig of some kind of flower in the other. "You two coming in or what? Brendan is complaining about losing the light or some shit—he says the sun will be directly overhead in a couple of hours, which is apparently really bad for photos? Anyway, Nazeera is getting impatient, too; she says J needs to start getting ready soon."

I stare at Kenji, then Ella, dumbfounded. She already looks perfect. "Get ready how?"

"I have to put on my dress," she says, and laughs.

"And makeup," Kenji shouts from across the street. "Nazeera and Alia say they need to do her makeup. And something about her hair."

I stiffen. "You have a dress? But I thought—"

Ella kisses me on the cheek, cutting me off. "Okay, there might be a few more surprises left in the day."

"I'm not sure my heart can handle any more surprises, love."

"How's this for a surprise?" Kenji says, leaning against the folding chair. "This beautiful piece of shit right here?" He gestures at the dilapidated house next door. "This one's mine."

That wipes the smile off my face.

"That's right, buddy." Kenji is grinning now. "We're going to be neighbors."

TWELVE

Ella is soon whisked away by a tornado of women—Nazeera, Alia, and Lily—who come charging out the door in a swarm, enveloping her in their depths before I've even had a chance to say a proper goodbye.

There's little more than a faint squeak from Ella—

And she's gone.

I find myself standing alone in front of what I'm still processing as *my own home*, my mind spinning, heart racing, when Kenji walks over to me.

"C'mon, man," he says, still smiling. "You've got stuff to do, too."

I look at him. "What kind of stuff?"

"Well, first of all, this is for you," he says, offering me the small sprig I noticed in his hand earlier. "It's for your lapel. It's like a, you know—like a—a—"

"I know what a boutonniere is," I say stiffly. I accept the small spray, examining it now with surprise. It's a single gardenia nestled against a tasteful arrangement of its own glossy leaves, the stems tied up with a bit of black ribbon, struck through with a pin. The bundle is elegant and shockingly fragrant. Gardenias are in fact one of my favorite flowers.

I look up at Kenji then, unable to hide my confusion.

He shrugs. "Don't look at me, bro. I have no idea what kind of flower that is. J just told me what she wanted."

"Wait." I frown at that, more confused by the moment. "*You* did this?"

"I just did what she asked me to do, okay?" he says, putting up his hands. "So if you hate the flower you should talk to your fiancée, because it's not my fault—"

"But where did this flower come from? I saw people with flowers earlier, too, and I didn't understand where—"

"Oh." Kenji drops his hands. He stares at me a moment before saying, "The old sector headquarters. You remember how you guys always had these rare flower arrangements at 45? We never knew where or how they were being sourced, but everyone always thought it was strange that the HQ could get fancy orchids or whatever, while civilians couldn't get their hands on much more than dandelions. Anyway it was Juliette's idea, actually. She recommended we track down the flower guy who used to carry out orders for The Reestablishment in this area. He helped us get everything we needed—but the flowers weren't delivered until late last night. Another reason why J wanted to postpone."

"Right." I'm stunned. "Of course."

My astonishment has nothing to do with discovering that Ella is just as impressive and resourceful as I've always known her to be; no, I'm simply incapable of believing anyone would go to such lengths for *me*.

I'm still reeling a bit as I attempt to pin the flower to my sweater, when Kenji holds up a hand again.

"Uh, don't do that just yet," he says. "Come on."

"Why?"

"Because, man, we still have things to do."

He turns as if to go, but I remain rooted to the ground.

"What kinds of things?" I ask.

"You know." He makes an indecipherable gesture, frowning at me. "Wedding things?"

I feel myself tense. "If the purpose of my question has not yet been made evident to you, Kishimoto, allow me to be crystal clear now: I am asking you to be specific."

He laughs at that. "Do you ever do anything anyone asks you to do without first asking a million questions?"

"No."

"Right." He laughs again. "Okay. Well, J is probably going to be getting her hair and makeup done for a little while, which means you can help us finish setting up in the backyard. But first, Winston has a surprise for you."

"No, thank you."

Kenji blinks. "What do you mean, *no, thank you*?"

"I don't want any more surprises," I say, my chest constricting at the very thought. "I can't take any more surprises."

"Listen, I can honestly understand what you might be feeling right now." He sighs. "Your head is probably spinning. I tried to tell her—I told her it wasn't a good idea to spring a wedding on a person, but whatever. She just does her own thing. Anyway, this is a good surprise, I promise.

Plus, I can give you a little tour of your new place."

It's this last line that uproots me from where I stand.

There's a short set of steps leading up to the house, and I take them slowly, my heart pounding nervously as I look around. There's a sizable front porch with freshly painted beams and railings, a decent area to set up a table and chairs when the weather's nice. The large windows flanking the front door are accented with what appear to be functioning, pale-sage-green shutters, the front door painted to match. Slowly, I push open this door—which has been left ajar—crossing the threshold now with even greater trepidation. The wood floor underfoot creaks as I step into the front hall, the clamor and commotion of the room coming to a sudden, eerie halt as I enter.

Everyone turns to look at me.

The drumbeat in my chest pounds harder, and I feel, for a moment, afloat in this sea of uncertainty. I'm lost for words, having never been prepared, in all my life, to deal with such a strange scenario.

I try to think, then, of what Ella would do.

"Thank you," I say into the silence. "For everything."

The crowd erupts into whoops and cheers at that, the tension gone in an instant. People shout congratulations into the din, and as my nerves begin to relax, I'm better able to make out their individual faces—some I recognize; others I don't. Adam is the first to wave at me from a distant corner, and I notice then that he's got his free arm wrapped around the waist of a young woman with blond hair.

Alia.

I remember her name. She's a painfully quiet girl, one of the troupe who collected Ella earlier—and one of Winston's friends. Today she seems unusually bright and happy.

So does Adam.

I nod at him in response, and he smiles before turning away to whisper something in Alia's ear. James appears then, almost out of nowhere, tapping Adam on the arm aggressively, after which the three of them engage in a brief, quiet discussion that ends with Alia nodding fervently. She kisses Adam on the cheek before disappearing into a room just down the hall, and I stare at the door of this room long after she's closed it.

Ella must be in there.

For what feels like a dangerously long time I feel paralyzed in place, studying the imperfect walls and windows of a home that is mine, that will be mine today, tonight, tomorrow.

I can't believe it.

I could kiss its rotting floor.

"Follow me," Kenji says, his voice stirring me from my stupor. He leads me through the small house as if he's walked these paths a hundred times—and I realize then that he has.

All these days he's been working on this project. For Ella. For me.

I experience a sharp, distracting stab of guilt.

"Hello?" Kenji waves a hand in front of my face. "You

want to see the kitchen, or no? I mean, I don't really recommend it, because the kitchen probably needs the most work, but hey, it's your house."

"I don't need to see the kitchen."

"Great, then we'll just get right to it. Winston first, then the backyard. Sound good? You never seem to have a problem working in a suit, so I don't think it'll be a problem for you today, either."

I sigh. "I have no problem assisting with manual labor, Kishimoto. In fact, I would've been happy to do so earlier."

"Great, well, that's what we like to hear." Kenji slaps me on the back, and I grit my teeth to keep from killing him.

"All right," he says. "So, I'm not going to torture you with any more unknowns, because I don't think you actually like surprises. I also think you're probably the kind of guy who likes to be able to pre-visualize stuff—helps manage the anxiety of not knowing things—so I'm going to walk you through this step-by-step. Sound good?"

I come to a sudden stop, staring at Kenji like I've never seen him before. "What?"

"What do you mean, *what*?"

"How did you know that I don't like surprises?"

"Bro, you're forgetting that I watched you have an actual panic attack." He taps his head. "I know some things, okay?"

I narrow my eyes at him.

"Okay, well"—he clears his throat—"there's also this doctor we're working with now—one of the ladies leading the exit evaluations for the asylum residents—and she's, like, crazy smart. She's got all kinds of interesting things to say about these patients, and everything they've been through. Anyway, you should talk to her. We had a patient who was cleared—healthy, fine, totally normal—to be returned to their relatives, but this dude couldn't get on a plane without having a major panic attack. The doctor was explaining to Sam that, for some people, getting on a plane is terrifying because they have to be able to trust the pilot to control the plane—and some people just can't trust like that. They can't cede control. Anyway, it made me think of you."

I deeply loathe this comparison, and I tell him as much. "I am perfectly capable of getting on planes," I point out.

"Yeah, I know, but—you know what I mean, right? Generally?"

"No."

Kenji sighs. "I'm just saying that I think it probably helps you to know exactly what's going to happen next. You like being in control. You don't like not knowing things. You probably like to imagine things in your head before they happen."

"You had a single conversation with a doctor and now you think you're capable of psychoanalyzing me?"

"I'm not—" Kenji throws up his arms. "You know what, whatever. Let's go. Winston's waiting."

"Wait."

Kenji looks up at me, irritation written all over his features. "What?"

"There might be a small grain of truth in what you said. A very, very small grain."

"*I knew it,*" he says, pointing at me. "I told her, too, I was like, wow, you should really talk to this one guy we know, he could use a lot of help working through some—"

"You didn't." A muscle jumps in my jaw. "Tell me you didn't actually say that to her."

"I did too say that to her. She was a smart lady, and I think she might have some really interesting things to say to you. She was talking about some of these inmates and the problems they were facing and I was like, oh my God, you could be describing Warner right now."

"I see," I say, and nod. "I should just kill you here, shouldn't I? In my own house. On my wedding day. It could be your gift to me."

"*This*, right here!" He throws out his arms. "This is a perfect example! You don't know how to problem solve without resorting to murder! How do you not see this as an issue?" He shakes his head. "I don't know, man, you really might want to consider—"

I take a sharp breath, staring up at the ceiling. "For the love of God, Kishimoto. Where is Winston, and what does he want with me?"

"Did someone say my name?" Winston pops his head out of a door in the corridor ahead. "Come on in. I'm all ready for you."

I shoot Kenji a scathing look before retreating down the hall, peering into the new room with some concern. It appears to be some kind of a bedroom, though it's in desperate need of work. And paint. Winston has set up what appears to be a small command center—a dingy folding table displaying an artfully arranged selection of ties, bow ties, cuff links, and socks. I stare at it, beginning to understand, but I'm distracted by a strange, pungent odor that only seems to strengthen the longer I stand here.

"What on earth is that smell?" I ask, frowning at the old wood paneling.

"Yeah," Winston says, shrugging. "We don't know. We think maybe there's a dead rat in the wall. Or maybe a couple of dead rats."

"What?" I look at him sharply.

"Or!" Kenji says brightly. "Or, it's just mold!"

"A delightful alternative."

"Okay." Winston claps his hands together, beaming. "We can talk about the rats tomorrow. You ready to see your suit?"

"What suit?"

"Your wedding suit," Winston says, staring at me now with a strange expression on his face. "You didn't really think you were getting married today in the clothes you're wearing, did you?"

"Not they aren't nice clothes," Kenji adds. "To be fair."

I meet Winston's eyes. "I haven't been able to predict a single thing that was going to happen to me today. How was I supposed to know that you'd managed to salvage my wedding suit from the wreckage? No one told me."

"We didn't salvage it from the wreckage," Winston says, laughing. "I made you a new one."

This leaves me briefly speechless. I stare at Winston, then Kenji. "You made me a new suit? How? Why? *When?*"

"What do you mean?" Winston is still smiling. "We couldn't let you get married without a proper suit."

"But how did you find the time? You must've—"

"Been up all night?" Brendan ducks his head into the room, then steps fully inside. "Finishing most of the work by hand? Yes, Winston was up all night on your behalf. Hardly slept at all. Which is why it wasn't very nice of you to be so rude to him this morning."

I glance from Brendan to Winston to Kenji.

I have no idea what to say, and I'm just thinking of how to respond when Adam and James show up at the door, two sets of knuckles knocking a rapid staccato on the frame.

"Hi!" James says, abandoning the door and his brother to invade my personal space. "Did they tell you I'm the only kid allowed at the wedding?"

"No."

"Well, I am. I'm the only kid allowed at the wedding. My friends are super jealous right now because they're all stuck in class."

"And was there any particular reason," I ask carefully, "why they made an exception for you?"

James rolls his eyes and lunges at me, hugging me right around the middle in a show of unprecedented self-assurance that shocks me, briefly, into paralysis.

"Congratulations," he says against my sweater. "I'm really happy for you guys."

I have to remind myself that James is not only—biologically—my brother, but also a child, and undeserving of rejection. I pat him on the head in a single, wooden movement that startles a laugh out of Kenji, a gasp from Winston, stunned silence from Brendan, and slack-jawed astonishment from Adam.

I clear my throat, disengaging from James as gently as I can.

"Thank you," I say to him.

"You're welcome," he says, beaming. "Thanks for inviting me."

"I didn't invi—"

"So!" Adam cuts me off, trying and failing now to fight a smile. "We, um, we just came by to check in with you on a couple of details." He glances at James. "Right, buddy?"

James nods. "Right."

"First of all: Did anyone talk to you about your vows? Do you want to go traditional, or do you plan on saying something—"

"He's going traditional," Kenji says, answering for me before I've had a chance to respond. "I already told Castle." He turns to face me. "Castle is doing the ceremony, by the way—you know that, right?"

"No," I say, staring at him. "I did not know that. But what makes you think I don't want to write my own vows?"

He shrugs. "You don't strike me as the kind of guy who

likes to get up in front of a crowd and shoot from the heart. But I'm happy to be wrong," he says. "If you want to write your own vows, stand in front of a ton of people—most of whom you hardly know—and tell Juliette her face reminds you of a sunrise, no problem. Castle is flexible."

"I would rather impale myself on a pike."

"Yeah." Kenji grins. "That's what I thought."

Kenji turns away to ask Adam a question, something about ceremony logistics, and I study the back of his head, confused.

How? I want to ask. *How did you know?*

Winston unfolds a garment bag, hangs it on a nearby door, and unzips the length of it while Brendan unearths a box of shoes from a dingy closet.

Adam says, "Okay, I still have a few questions for Warner, but I need to confirm with Castle about the vows, so we'll be right back—and I'll find out about the music—"

And I feel as if I've stepped into a strange, alternate reality, into a world where I didn't think I'd ever belong. I could never have anticipated that somehow, somewhere along this tumultuous path—

I'd acquired friends.

THIRTEEN

The backyard is a modest rectangle of scorched land, the sparse and parched grass nicely obscured by a selection of time-worn wooden folding chairs, the arrangement parted down the middle by an artificial aisle, all of which face a hand-wrought wedding arch. Two thick, ten-foot cylindrical wooden stakes have been hammered into the ground, the five feet of empty space between them bridged at the top by a raw, severed tree limb, the joints bound together by rope. This crudely constructed bower is decorated with a robust selection of colorful wildflowers; leaves and petals flutter in the gentle breeze, infusing the early-morning air with their combined fragrance.

The scene is at once simple and breathtaking, and I am immobilized by the sight of it.

I am in a perfectly tailored, dark green, three-piece suit with a white shirt and black tie. My original suit was black, by request; Winston told me he decided to go with this deep shade of green because he thought it would suit my eyes and offset my gold hair. I wanted to argue with him except that I was genuinely impressed with the quality of his work, and did not protest when he handed me a pair of black, patent leather shoes to match. Absently, I touch the gardenia affixed to my lapel, feeling the always-present weight of the velvet box against my thigh.

There are folding tables arranged along the opposite end of the yard still waiting for their tablecloths, and I have been assigned the task of dressing them. I have also been ordered to see to the tables and chairs that need to be arranged inside the as-yet-unfurnished living and dining rooms, where the reception is meant to take place later this evening after a break post-ceremony, during which our guests will change work shifts, see to things back at the base, and Ella and I will have a chance to take pictures.

This all sounds so perfectly human as to render me ill.

I have, as a result, done none of things requested of me. I've been unable to move from this spot, staring at the wedding arch where I will soon be expected to stand and wait.

I clutch the back of a chair, holding on for dear life as the weight of the day's revelations inhale me, drowning me in their depths. Kenji is right; I don't enjoy surprises. This is fundamentally true, and yet—I would like to be the kind of person who enjoys surprises. I want to live a life like this, to be able to withstand unexpected moments of kindness delivered by the person I love most in the world. It's only that I don't know what to do with these experiences; my body doesn't know how to accept or digest them.

I am so happy it's physically uncomfortable; I am so full of hope it seems to depress my chest, forcing the air from my lungs.

I draw in a sharp breath against this feeling, forcing myself to be calm while doing, over and over, the mental gymnastics necessary to remind myself that my fears are irrational, when I feel the approach of a familiar nervous energy.

I turn around carefully to meet her, surprised she's sought me out at all.

"Hey," Sam says, trying to smile. She's dressed up; she even appears to have attempted something like makeup, her eyelids shimmering in the soft light of the morning. "Big day."

"Yes."

"Listen, I'm sorry." She sighs. "I didn't mean to lash out at you like that last night. Really, I didn't."

I nod, then look away, staring into the distance. This yard is separated from its neighbor's by only a short, shabby wooden fence. Kenji will no doubt spend the rest of our lives tormenting me from over top of it.

Sam sighs again, louder this time. "I know you and I don't always see eye to eye," she says, "but I'm hoping maybe—if we get to know each other better—that'll change."

I look up at that, analyzing Sam now.

She is being sincere, but I find her suggestion unlikely. I notice Nouria in my periphery then, huddled up with her father and three others, and shift my gaze in her direction. She's wearing a simple sheath dress in a shade of chartreuse that compliments her dark skin. She appears to be happy at the moment—smiling—which even I realize is rare for

Nouria these days.

Sam follows my line of sight, seeming to understand where my thoughts have gone. "I know she's a little hard on you sometimes, but she's been under crazy amounts of pressure lately. She's never had to oversee so many people, or so many details, and The Reestablishment has been a lot harder to deconstruct than we'd thought—you can't even imagine—"

"Can't I?" I almost smile, even as my jaw tenses. "You think me incapable of understanding the weight of the burden we shoulder now?"

Sam looks away. "I didn't say that. That's not what I meant."

"Our position is worse than precarious," I say to her. "And whatever you think of me—whatever you think you understand about me—I am only trying to help."

For the third time, Sam sighs.

Now, more than ever, those of us at the Sanctuary should be allied, but Sam and Nouria have grown to detest me over the last couple of weeks because I challenge them at every turn, refusing to agree with their tactics or ideology when I find it lacking—and unwilling to acquiesce merely to get along.

They find this fundamentally infuriating, and I don't care.

I refuse to do anything that would put Ella's life in jeopardy, and letting our movement fail would be doing exactly that.

"I want us to try again," Sam says, steely now as she meets my eyes. "I want us to start over. We've been fighting a lot lately, and I think you would agree with me that it's not sustainable. We should be united right now."

"United? Nouria deliberately made me think I couldn't get married. She willfully manipulated the truth to make the situation seem dire, simply to wound me. How can such petty machinations form any foundation for unity?"

"She wasn't trying to wound you. She was trying to protect you."

"In what alternate reality could that possibly be true?"

Sam's anger flares. "You know what your problem is?"

"Yes. The list is long."

"*Oh my God,*" she says, her irritation building. "This, *this* is exactly your problem. You think you know everything. You're uncooperative, you're uncompromising, and you've already decided you've figured everything out. You don't know how to be part of a *team*—"

"You and Nouria don't know how to take constructive criticism."

"Constructive criticism?" Sam gapes at me. "You call your criticism *constructive?*"

"You're free to call it whatever you like," I say unkindly. "But I refuse to remain silent when I believe you and Nouria are making the wrong choices. You regularly forget that I was raised within The Reestablishment, from its infancy, and that there is a great deal I understand about the mechanics of our enemies' minds—more than you are even willing to consider—"

"All okay over here?" Castle asks, striding toward us. His smile is uncertain. "We're not talking about work right now, are we?"

"Oh, everything is fine," Sam says too brightly. "I was just reminding Warner here how much Nouria has done to keep him and Juliette safe on their wedding day. An event I think we all agree would render them both most vulnerable to an outside threat."

I go suddenly still.

"Well—yes," Castle says, confused. "Of course. You already know that, though, don't you, Mr. Warner? News of your impending nuptials was beginning to spread, and we feared the possible repercussions for both you and Ms. Ferrars on such a joyous day."

I'm still staring at Sam when I say quietly: "That's why you all lied to me yesterday?"

"Nouria thought it was imperative that we convince *you*," Sam says stiffly, "more than anyone else, that you wouldn't be getting married today. The supreme kids knew about the wedding before they left, and Nouria worried that even a whiff of an exchange on the subject yesterday might be intercepted in your daily communications, which we wanted to make certain you carried out as normal. The notifications Juliette sent out last night were done in code."

"I see," I say, glancing again at Nouria, who's now deep in conversation with the girls—Sonya and Sara—both of whom are holding what appear to be small black suitcases.

I should be touched by this gesture of protection, but the fact that they felt I couldn't be trusted with such a plan does little to improve my mood.

"You do realize you could've simply asked me to say nothing, don't you? I'm perfectly capable of discretion—"

"What is going on between you two?" Castle frowns. "This is not the energy I expected from either of you on—"

"Sir?" Ian is standing at the sliding screen door—the only access point into the house from the backyard—and motioning Castle forward with an agitated wave. "Can you come here, please? Now?"

Castle frowns, then glances between myself and Sam. "There will be plenty of time to discuss unpleasant matters later, do you understand? Today is a day of celebration. *For all of us.*"

"Oh, don't worry," Sam says to Castle. "Everything will be fine—right, Warner?"

"Perhaps," I say, holding her gaze.

Sam and I say nothing else, and Castle shakes his head before stalking off, leaving the two of us alone to enjoy an uncomfortable moment of silence.

Sam takes a sudden deep breath.

"Anyway," she says loudly, looking around now for an exit. "Exciting day. Best wishes and everything."

My jaw clenches. I'm saved the need to respond to this limp performance of civility by the abrupt, sharp bark of a dog, accompanied by the timid admonishment of a human.

Sam and I both spin around toward the sounds.

An animal I hardly recognize is scratching wildly at the screen door, yapping—at me, specifically—from several feet away. Its once mangy, matted fur is now a healthy brown, with an unexpected smattering of white; this accomplishment is undermined by its bright red collar and ridiculous, matching headband, the undignified accessory crowned with a large crimson bow, which sits atop the animal's head. The perpetrator of this crime is standing just beyond the dog, a tall, redheaded young woman desperately begging the pup to be calm.

Kenji had said her name was Yara.

She struggles in vain; the creature pays her no mind as he barks over and over, all the while pawing anxiously at the screen door—*my screen door*—which he will no doubt destroy if he does not soon desist.

"Let him out," I say to her, my voice carrying.

The young woman startles at that, quickly fumbling now to unlatch the screen door. When she finally manages to slide the panel open, the animal all but lunges through the doorway, yanking her along with him.

Beside me, Sam makes a poorly muffled sound of disgust.

"I didn't realize you hated animals," I say without looking at her.

"Oh, I love animals. Animals are better at being human than people are."

"I don't disagree."

"Shocking."

I turn to face her, surprised. "Why are you so angry?"

Sam sighs and nods discreetly at Yara, who waves enthusiastically even as she's dragged along in our direction.

I raise my eyebrows at Sam.

"Oh, don't look at me like that," she says, irritated. "You have no idea what Nouria and I have had to deal with since you arrived. It got a hundred times worse after everyone decided you were some kind of a hero. It was a really low moment for us, realizing that so many people we respected were shockingly shallow."

"If it makes you feel any better," I say, taking a breath as I lift a hand in Yara's direction, "I don't like it, either."

"Bullshit," Sam says automatically, but I sense her flicker of uncertainty.

I lower my voice as Yara closes in on us. "Would you enjoy being reduced to nothing but your physical footprint, forced all the while to absorb the weight of strangers' indecent emotions as they assess and undress you?"

Sam stiffens beside me. She turns to look at me, her feelings scattered and confused. I feel her reexamining me.

"Hi!" Yara says, coming to a stop in front of us.

She is an objectively kind young woman; I recognize this even as I fight back a wave of revulsion. Yara has done the animal—and me, by extension—a great courtesy, which she needn't have done for a stranger on such short notice. Still, her feelings are both generous and disconcerting, some of them loud enough to make me physically uncomfortable.

The dog is wise enough to halt at my feet.

He lifts a tentative paw as if to touch me, and I give him a sharp look, after which the paw retreats. In the intervening silence, the dog stares up at me with big, dark eyes, his tail wagging furiously.

"It was kind of you to wash the animal," I say to Yara, still staring at the dog. "He looks much better now."

"Oh, it was my pleasure," she says, hesitating before adding: "You look—you look really, really nice today."

My smile is tight.

I don't want to feel what she's feeling right now. I don't want to know these things—not ever—but especially not on my wedding day.

I bend down to look the dog in the eye and draw a gentle hand over his head, into which he eagerly leans. He sniffs me, nosing the palm of my hand, and I pull away before the beast decides to lick me. I decide instead to check his collar; there is a single metal coin hanging from the red strap, and I pinch it between two fingers, the better to examine it.

It reads: DOG.

"That's what you said you wanted to call him, right?" Yara is still smiling. "*Dog?*"

I look up at her then, meeting the young woman's eyes against my better judgment, and her smile trembles.

Sam stifles a laugh.

"Yes," I say slowly. "I suppose I did say something like that."

Yara beams. "Well, he's all yours now. Happy wedding and everything."

I stand up sharply. "What?"

"Oh, and it looks like he's already been neutered, so I think he's had a family before. You made a great choice. I'm not sure what kind of dog he is—he's definitely some kind of mixed breed—but he's not totally wild, and I think he'll be a good—

"I'm afraid you've gravely misunderstood the situation. I don't want a dog. I merely wanted you to wash the animal, and maybe feed it—"

Sam is laughing openly now, and I pivot to face her.

"You think this is funny? What am I supposed to do with a dog?"

"Um, I don't know"—she shoots me an incredulous look—"give it a loving home?"

"Don't be ridiculous."

"I'm—I'm so sorry," Yara says, her eyes widening now with panic. "I thought he was *your* dog—I didn't think he was— I mean he doesn't obey anyone else, and he seems really attached to you—"

"Don't worry, Yara," Sam says gently. "You did great. Warner just wasn't expecting you to be so generous, and he's kind of, um, overwhelmed with gratitude right now. Isn't that right, Warner?" She turns to me. "Yara was so kind to get . . . *Dog* here all washed and ready for your wedding day. Wasn't she?"

"Very kind," I say, my jaw tensing.

Yara looks nervously in my direction. "Really?"

Briefly, I meet her eyes. "Really."

She flushes.

"Yara, why don't you hold on to"—she fights back a smile—"*Dog* until the end of the ceremony? Maybe make sure he gets something to eat."

"Oh, sure." Yara shoots me one last furtive look before tugging gently on the animal's leash. The dog whines at that, then barks as she coaxes him, one foot at a time, back toward the house.

I turn my eyes skyward. "This is unforgivable."

"Why?" I can hear practically hear Sam smile. "I bet Juliette would love to have a dog."

I look at Sam. "Did you know, I once watched a dog vomit—and then proceed to *eat* its own vomit."

"Okay, but—"

"And then vomit. Again."

Sam crosses her arms. "That was one dog."

"Another dog once defecated right in front of me while I was patrolling a compound."

"That's perfectly norm—"

"After which it promptly ate its own feces."

Sam crosses her arms. "All right. Well. That's still better than the awful things I've seen humans do."

I'm prevented from responding by a sudden swell of commotion. People are starting to rush around, pushing past us to scatter wildflowers in the grassy aisle. Sonya and Sara, clad in identical green gowns, take positions adjacent to the wedding arch, their black suitcases gone. In their hands they hold matching violins and bows, the sight of which paralyzes me anew. I feel that familiar pain in my chest, something like fear.

It's beginning.

"You're right, though," I say quietly to Sam, wondering, for the hundredth time, what Ella might be doing inside the house. "She'd love to have a dog."

"Wait— I'm sorry, did you just say I was *right* about something?"

I release a sharp breath. It sounds almost like a laugh.

"You know," Sam says thoughtfully. "I think this might be the most pleasant conversation you and I have ever had."

"Your standards are very low, then."

"When it comes to you, Warner, my standards have to be low."

I manage to smile at that, but I'm still distracted. Castle is walking toward the arch now, a small leather-bound notebook in his hand, a sprig of lavender pinned to his lapel. He nods at me as he goes, and I can only stare, feeling suddenly like I can't breathe.

"I've seen her, by the way," Sam says softly.

I turn to face her.

"Juliette." Sam smiles. "She looks beautiful."

I'm struggling to formulate a response to this when I sense the approach of a familiar presence; his hand lands on my arm, and for the first time, I don't flinch.

"Hey, man," Kenji says, materializing at my side in a surprisingly sharp suit. "You ready? There's not much of a wedding party, so we're not doing a processional, which means J will be walking down the aisle pretty soon. Nazeera just gave us the ten-minute . . ."

Kenji trails off, distracted as if on cue, by Nazeera herself. She saunters toward the wedding arch, tall and steady in a gauzy, blush-colored gown. She grins at Castle, who acknowledges her with a smile of his own; Nazeera takes a position just off to the side of the arch, adjusting her skirts as she settles in place.

It becomes terrifyingly clear to me then exactly where Ella is expected to soon stand. Where *I* am expected to soon stand.

"But I haven't finished with the tablecloths," I say, "or the seating inside—"

"Yeah. I noticed." Kenji takes a sharp breath, tearing his gaze away from Nazeera to look me in the eye. "Anyway, don't worry. We took care of it. You seemed really busy standing still for half an hour, staring at nothing. We didn't want to interrupt."

"All right, I think I should get going," Sam says, offering me a real, genuine smile. "Nouria is saving me a seat. Good luck out there."

I nod at her as she goes, surprised to discover that, despite the long road ahead, there might be hope of a truce between us after all.

"Okay." Kenji claps his hands together. "First things first: do you need to go to the bathroom or anything before we start? Personally, I think you should go even if you don't think you have to, because it would be really awkward if you suddenly had t—"

"Stop."

"Oh—right!" Kenji says, slapping his hand to his forehead. "My bad, bro, I forgot—you never have to use the bathroom, do you?"

"No."

"No, of course not. Because that would be human, and we both know you're secretly a robot."

I sigh, resisting the urge to run my hands through my hair.

"Seriously, though—anything you need to do before you go up there? You've got the ring, right?"

"No." My heart is pounding furiously in my chest now. "And yes."

"Okay, then." Kenji nods toward the wedding arch. "Go ahead and get into position under that flower thing. Castle will show you exactly where to stand—"

I turn sharply to face him. "You're not coming with me?"

Kenji goes stock-still at that, his mouth slightly agape. I realize, a moment too late, exactly what I've just suggested—and still I can't bring myself to retract the question, and I can't explain why.

Right now, it doesn't seem to matter.

Right now, I can't quite feel my legs.

Kenji, to his credit, does not laugh in my face. Instead, his expression relaxes by micrometers, his dark eyes assessing me in that careful way I detest.

"Yeah," he says finally. "Of course I'm coming with you."

FOURTEEN

Sunlight glances off my eyes, the glare shifting, flickering through a webbing of bare branches as a gentle breeze moves through the yard, fluttering leaves and skirts and flower petals. The scent of the gardenia affixed to my lapel wafts upward, filling my head with a heady perfume as the sharp collar of my shirt scrapes against my neck, my tie too tight; I clasp my hands in front of me to keep from adjusting it, my palms brushing against the wool of my suit, the fabric soft and lightweight and still somehow abrasive, suffocating me as I stand here in stiff shoes sinking slowly into dead grass, staring out at a sea of people come to bear witness to what might be one of the most publicly vulnerable moments of my life.

I can't seem to breathe.

I can't seem to make out their faces, but I can feel them, the individual emotional capsules that make up the members of this audience, the collective frenzy of their thoughts and feelings overwhelming me in a breathtaking crush that crowds my already chaotic thoughts. I feel myself begin to panic—my heart rate increasing rapidly—as I try to digest this noise, to tune out the barrage of other people's nervousness and excitement. It's a struggle even to hear myself think, to unearth my own consciousness. I try, desperately, to find an anchor in this madness.

It is nearly impossible.

Sonya and Sara lift their violins, sharing a glance before one of the sisters, Sonya, takes the lead, launching into the opening of Pachelbel's Canon in D. Sara soon accompanies her, and the evocative, heart-wrenching notes fill the air, igniting in my chest a flare of emotion that only intensifies my apprehension, pulling my nerves taut to a painful degree. I swallow, hard, my pulse racing dangerously fast. My hands seem to spark and fade with feeling, prickling hot and cold, and I flex them into fists.

"Hey, man," Kenji whispers beside me. "You all right?"

I shake my head an inch.

"What's wrong?"

I can feel Kenji studying my face.

"Oh—*shit*—are you having a panic attack?"

"Not yet," I manage to say. I close my eyes, try to breathe. "It's too loud in here."

"The music?"

"*The people.*"

"Okay. Okay. Shit. So you can, like, feel everything they're feeling right now? Right. *Shit*. Of course you can. Okay. All right, what should I do? You want me to talk to you? How about I just talk to you? Why don't you just focus on me, on the sound of my voice. Fade everything else out."

"I don't know if that will work," I say, taking a shaky breath. "But I can try."

"Cool. Okay. First of all, open your eyes. Juliette is going to walk out in a couple of minutes, and you won't want to miss it. Her dress is awesome." He whispers this, his voice altered just enough that I can tell he's trying not to move his lips. "I'm not supposed to tell you anything about it, because, you know, it's supposed to be a surprise, but whatever, we're throwing surprises out the window right now because this is an emergency, and I have a feeling that once you see her your brain will do that creepy super-focus thing it always does—you know, like when you ignore literally everyone around you—and then you'll start feeling better because, um, yeah"—he laughs, nervously—"you know what? I'm beginning to realize only right this second that, uh, when she's around you don't even seem to notice other people, so, um—until then I can—yeah, I'm just going to describe her to you, because, like I said, she's going to look great. Her dress is, like, really, really pretty, and I don't even know anything about dresses, so that should tell you something."

The sound of his voice is a strange lifeline.

The more he speaks, filling my head with easily digestible nonsense, I feel my heart rate start to slow, the iron fist around my lungs beginning, slowly, to unclench.

I force my eyes open, and the scene briefly blurs in and out of focus, the pounding of my heart still loud in my head. I glance at Kenji, who is staring straight ahead, his face at rest as if nothing is amiss. This helps ground me, somehow, and I manage to pull myself together long enough to look down the petal-dusted aisle.

"So Juliette's dress is, um, like, really glittery, but also really soft-looking? Winston and Alia had to come up with a new design on such short notice," Kenji explains, "but they were able to repurpose some gown you guys got at the Supply Center yesterday. There was lots of, like, sheer fluffy fabric, I don't know what it's call—"

"Tulle."

"Yes. Tulle. Yes. Whatever. Anyway Alia spent all night, like, first of all, making it nicer, and then sewing these little glittery beads all over it—but, like, in a nice way. It's really nice. And it's got, like, these little tulle sleeves that aren't really sleeves—they sort of fall off the shoulder— Hey, is this helping?"

"Yes," I say, drawing in a full breath for the first time in minutes.

"Great, so—nice sleeves, and, and um, you know, it's got a long fluffy skirt— Okay, yeah, I'm sorry, bro, but I'm kind of out of descriptions for Juliette's dress, but— Oh, hey, here's a fun fact: Did you know that Sonya and Sara used to be, like, young virtuosos, way back in the day, pre-Reestablishment?"

"No."

"Yeah—yeah, so they started playing violin when they were fresh out of diapers. Pretty cool, huh? Nazeera helped us confiscate the violins they're using today from old Reestablishment holdings. They're playing this song from *memory*. I don't know what it's called, but I'm pretty sure it's something fancy, from some old dead dude—"

"Of course you know what it's called," I say, still staring straight ahead. "Everyone knows it."

"Well *I* don't know it."

"This is the work of German composer Johann Pachelbel," I explain, struggling not to frown. "It's often called Pachelbel's Canon in D, because it was meant to be played in the key of D major. Do you know nothing about music?"

"Yeah, I don't even know what the hell you just said."

"How can y—"

"All right, shut up, no one cares—the music is changing, do you hear that? When it goes high like that? That means she's going to come out any second now—"

The audience rises almost at once, a rush of breaths and bodies clambering to their feet, craning their necks, and for a moment, I can't see her at all.

And then, suddenly, I do.

Relief hits me like a gust, leaving me so suddenly unsteady I worry, for a moment, that I might not make it.

Ella looks spun from gossamer, glowing as she glitters in the soft light. Her gown has a corseted, glimmering bodice that flows into a soft, decadent skirt, her arms bare save delicate, off-the-shoulder scraps of tulle that graze her skin.

She is luminous.

I've never seen her wear makeup, and I have no idea what they've done to her face, except that she is now so beautiful as to be unreal, her hair in an elegant arrangement atop her head, a long veil gracing her shoulders, flowing with her as she walks.

She does not look like she belongs in this world, or in this dingy backyard, or in this dilapidated neighborhood, or on this crumbling planet. She is above it. Above us all. A spark of light separated from the sun.

A dangerous heat builds behind my eyes and I force myself to fight it back, to remain calm, but when she sees me, she smiles—and I nearly lose the fight.

"I told you it was a nice dress," Kenji whispers.

"Kenji."

"Yes?"

"Thank you," I say, still staring at Ella. "For everything."

"Anytime," he says, his voice more subdued than before. "This is the beginning of a new chapter for all of us, man. For the whole world. This wedding is making history right now. You know that, right? Nothing is ever going to be the same."

Ella glides toward me, nearly within reach. I feel my heart pounding in my chest, happiness threatening to destroy me. I'm smiling now, smiling like the most ordinary of men, staring at the most extraordinary woman I've ever known.

"Believe me," I whisper. "I do."

Keep reading for a sneak peek at

THIS WOVEN KINGDOM,

the first book in Tahereh Mafi's stunning fantasy series!

ONE

ALIZEH STITCHED IN THE KITCHEN by the light of star and fire, sitting, as she often did, curled up inside the hearth. Soot stained her skin and skirts in haphazard streaks: smudges along the crest of a cheek, a dusting of yet more darkness above one eye. She didn't seem to notice.

Alizeh was cold. No, she was *freezing*.

She often wished she were a body with hinges, that she might throw open a door in her chest and fill its cavity with coal, then kerosene. Strike a match.

Alas.

She tugged up her skirts and shifted nearer the fire, careful lest she destroy the garment she still owed the illegitimate daughter of the Lojjan ambassador. The intricate, glittering piece was her only order this month, but Alizeh nursed a secret hope that the gown would conjure clients on its own, for such fashionable commissions were, after all, the direct result of an envy born only in a ballroom, around a dinner table. So long as the kingdom remained at peace, the royal elite—legitimate and illegitimate alike—would continue to host parties and incur debt, which meant Alizeh might yet find ways to extract coin from their embroidered pockets.

She shivered violently then, nearly missing a stitch, nearly toppling into the fire. As a toddling child Alizeh had once been so desperately cold she'd crawled onto the searing hearth on purpose. Of course it had never occurred to her that she might be consumed by the blaze; she'd been but a babe following an instinct to seek warmth. Alizeh couldn't have known then the singularity of her affliction, for so rare was the frost that grew inside her body that she stood in stark relief even among her own people, who were thought to be strange indeed.

A miracle, then, that the fire had only disintegrated her clothes and clogged the small house with a smoke that singed her eyes. A subsequent scream, however, signaled to the snug tot that her scheme was at an end. Frustrated by a body that would not warm, she'd wept frigid tears as she was collected from the flames, her mother sustaining terrible burns in the process, the scars of which Alizeh would study for years to come.

"*Her eyes*," the trembling woman had cried to her husband, who'd come running at the sounds of distress. "See what's happened to her eyes— They will kill her for this—"

Alizeh rubbed her eyes now and coughed.

Surely she'd been too young to remember the precise words her parents had spoken; no doubt Alizeh's was a memory merely of a story oft-repeated, one so thoroughly worn into her mind she only imagined she could recall her mother's voice.

She swallowed.

Soot had stuck in her throat. Her fingers had gone numb. Exhausted, she exhaled her worries into the hearth, the action disturbing to life another flurry of soot.

Alizeh coughed for the second time then, this time so hard she stabbed the stitching needle into her small finger. She absorbed the shock of pain with preternatural calm, carefully dislodging the bit before inspecting the injury.

The puncture was deep.

Slowly, almost one at a time, her fingers closed around the gown still clutched in her hand, the finest silk stanching the trickle of her blood. After a few moments—during which she stared blankly up, into the chimney, for the sixteenth time that night—she released the gown, cut the thread with her teeth, and tossed the gem-encrusted novelty onto a nearby chair.

Never fear; Alizeh knew her blood would not stain. Still, it was a good excuse to cede defeat, to set aside the gown. She appraised it now, sprawled as it was across the seat. The bodice had collapsed, bowing over the skirt much like a child might slump in a chair. Silk pooled around the wooden legs, beadwork catching the light. A weak breeze rattled a poorly latched window and a single candle blew out, taking with it the remaining composure of the commission. The gown slid farther down the chair, one heavy sleeve releasing itself with a hush, its glittering cuff grazing the sooty floor.

Alizeh sighed.

This gown, like all the others, was far from beautiful. She thought the design trite, the construction only passably good. She dreamed of unleashing her mind, of freeing her hands to create without hesitation—but the roar of Alizeh's imagination was quieted, always, by an unfortunate need for self-preservation.

It was only during her grandmother's lifetime that the Fire Accords had been established, unprecedented peace agreements that allowed Jinn and humans to mix freely for the first time in nearly a millennia. Though superficially identical, Jinn bodies had been forged from the essence of fire, imbuing in them certain physical advantages; while humans, whose beginnings were established in dirt and water, had long been labeled *Clay*. Jinn had conceded to the establishment of the Accords with a variegated relief, for the two races had been locked in bloodshed for eons, and though the enmity between them remained unresolved, all had tired of death.

The streets had been gilded with liquid sun to usher in the era of this tenuous peacetime, the empire's flag and coin reimagined in triumph. Every royal article was stamped with the maxim of a new age:

MERAS
May Equality Reign Always Supreme

Equality, as it turned out, had meant Jinn were to lower themselves to the weakness of humans, denying at all times the inherent powers of their race, the speed and strength and elective evanescence born unto their bodies. They were to cease at once what the king had declared "such supernatural operations" or face certain death, and Clay, who had exposed themselves as an insecure sort of creature, were only too willing to cry cheat no matter the context. Alizeh could still hear the screams, the riots in the streets—

She stared now at the mediocre gown.

Always she struggled not to design an article too exquisite, for extraordinary work came under harsher scrutiny, and was only too quickly denounced as the result of a preternatural trick.

Only once, having grown increasingly desperate to earn a decent living, had Alizeh thought to impress a customer not with style, but with craftsmanship. Not only was the quality of her work many orders of magnitude higher than that of the local modiste, but Alizeh could fashion an elegant morning gown in a quarter of the time, and had been willing to charge half as much.

The oversight had sent her to the gallows.

It had not been the happy customer, but the rival dressmaker who'd reported Alizeh to the magistrates. Miracle of miracles, she'd managed to evade their attempt to drag her away in the night, and fled the familiar countryside of her childhood for the anonymity of the city, hoping to be lost among the masses.

Would that she might slough off the burdens she carried with her always, but Alizeh knew an abundance of reasons to keep to the shadows, chief among them the reminder that her parents had forfeited their lives in the interest of her quiet survival, and to comport herself carelessly now would be to dishonor their efforts.

No, Alizeh had learned the hard way to relinquish her commissions long before she grew to love them.

She stood and a cloud of soot stood with her, billowing

around her skirts. She'd need to clean the kitchen hearth before Mrs. Amina came down in the morning or she'd likely be out on the street again. Despite her best efforts, Alizeh had been turned out onto the street more times than she could count. She'd always supposed it took little encouragement to dispose of that which was already seen as disposable, but these thoughts had done little to calm her.

Alizeh collected a broom, flinching a little as the fire died. It was late; very late. The steady *tick tick* of the clock wound something in her heart, made her anxious. Alizeh had a natural aversion to the dark, a rooted fear she could not fully articulate. She'd have rather worked a needle and thread by the light of the sun, but she spent her days doing the work that really mattered: scrubbing the rooms and latrines of Baz House, the grand estate of Her Grace, the Duchess Jamilah of Fetrous.

Alizeh had never met the duchess, only seen the glittering older woman from afar. Alizeh's meetings were with Mrs. Amina, the housekeeper, who'd hired Alizeh on a trial basis only, as she'd arrived with no references. As a result, Alizeh was not yet permitted to interact with the other servants, nor was she allotted a proper room in the servants' wing. Instead, she'd been given a rotting closet in the attic, wherein she'd discovered a cot, its moth-eaten mattress, and half a candle.

Alizeh had lain awake in her narrow bed that first night, so overcome she could hardly breathe. She minded neither the rotting attic nor its moth-eaten mattress, for Alizeh knew herself to be in possession of great fortune. That any grand house was willing to employ a Jinn was shocking enough, but that she'd been given a room—a respite from the winter streets—

True, Alizeh had found stretches of work since her parents' deaths, and often she'd been granted leave to sleep indoors, or in the hayloft; but never had she been given a space of her own. This was the first time in years she had privacy, a door she might close; and Alizeh had felt so thoroughly saturated with happiness she feared she might sink through the floor. Her body shook as she stared up at the wooden beams that night, at the thicket of cobwebs that crowded her head. A large spider had unspooled a length of thread, lowering itself to look her in the eye, and Alizeh had only smiled, clutching a skin of water to her chest.

The water had been her single request.

"A skin of water?" Mrs. Amina had frowned at her, frowned as if she'd asked to eat the woman's child. "You can fetch your own water, girl."

"Forgive me, I would," Alizeh had said, eyes on her shoes, on the torn leather around the toe she'd not yet mended. "But I'm still new to the city, and I've found it difficult to access fresh water so far from home. There's no reliable cistern nearby, and I cannot yet afford the glass water in the market—"

Mrs. Amina roared with laughter.

Alizeh went silent, heat rising up her neck. She did not know why the woman laughed at her.

"Can you read, child?"

Alizeh looked up without meaning to, registering the

familiar, fearful gasp before she'd even locked eyes with the woman. Mrs. Amina stepped back, lost her smile.

"Yes," said Alizeh. "I can read."

"Then you must try to forget."

Alizeh started. "I beg your pardon?"

"Don't be daft." Mrs. Amina's eyes narrowed. "No one wants a servant who can read. You ruin your own prospects with that tongue. Where did you say you were from?"

Alizeh had frozen solid.

She couldn't tell whether this woman was being cruel or kind. It was the first time anyone had suggested her intelligence might present a problem to the position, and Alizeh wondered then whether it wasn't true: perhaps it *had* been her head, too full as it was, that kept landing her in the street. Perhaps, if she was careful, she might finally manage to keep a position for longer than a few weeks. No doubt she could feign stupidity in exchange for safety.

"I'm from the north, ma'am," she'd said quietly.

"Your accent isn't northern."

Alizeh nearly admitted aloud that she'd been raised in relative isolation, that she'd learned to speak as her tutors had taught her; but then she remembered herself, remembered her station, and said nothing.

"As I suspected," Mrs. Amina had said into the silence. "Rid yourself of that ridiculous accent. You sound like an idiot, pretending to be some kind of toff. Better yet, say nothing at all. If you can manage that, you may prove useful to me. I've heard your kind don't tire out so easily, and I expect your work to satisfy such rumors, else I'll not scruple to toss you back into the street. Have I made myself clear?"

"Yes, ma'am."

"You may have your skin of water."

"Thank you, ma'am." Alizeh curtsied, turned to go.

"Oh—and one more thing—"

Alizeh turned back. "Yes, ma'am?"

"Get yourself a snoda as soon as possible. I never want to see your face again."

TWO

,,

ALIZEH HAD ONLY JUST PULLED open the door to her closet when she felt it, felt *him* as if she'd pushed her arms through the sleeves of a winter coat. She hesitated, heart pounding, and stood framed in the doorway.

Foolish.

Alizeh shook her head to clear it. She was imagining things, and no surprise: she was in desperate need of sleep. After sweeping the hearth, she'd had to scrub clean her sooty hands and face, too, and it had all taken much longer than she'd hoped; her weary mind could hardly be held responsible for its delirious thoughts at this hour.

With a sigh, Alizeh dipped a single foot into the inky depths of her room, feeling blindly for the match and candle she kept always near the door. Mrs. Amina had not allowed Alizeh a second taper to carry upstairs in the evenings, for she could neither fathom the indulgence nor the possibility that the girl might still be working long after the gas lamps had been extinguished. Even so, the housekeeper's lack of imagination did nothing to alter the facts as they were: this high up in so large an estate it was near impossible for distant light to penetrate. Save the occasional slant of the moon through a mingy corridor window, the attic presented opaque in the night; black as tar.

Were it not for the glimmer of the night sky to help her navigate the many flights to her closet, Alizeh might not have found her way, for she experienced a fear so paralyzing in the company of perfect darkness that, when faced with such a fate, she held an illogical preference for death.

Her single candle quickly found, the sought after match was promptly struck, a tear of air and the wick lit. A warm glow illuminated a sphere in the center of her room, and for the first time that day, Alizeh relaxed.

Quietly she pulled closed the closet door behind her, stepping fully into a room hardly big enough to hold her cot.

Just so, she loved it.

She'd scrubbed the filthy closet until her knuckles had bled, until her knees had throbbed. In these ancient, beautiful estates, most everything was once built to perfection, and buried under layers of mold, cobwebs, and caked-on grime, Alizeh had discovered elegant herringbone floors, solid wood beams in the ceiling. When she'd finished with it, the room positively gleamed.

Mrs. Amina had not, naturally, been to visit the old storage closet since it'd been handed over to the help, but Alizeh often wondered what the housekeeper might say if she saw the space now, for the room was unrecognizable. But then, Alizeh had long ago learned to be resourceful.

She removed her snoda, unwinding the delicate sheet of tulle from around her eyes. The silk was required of all those who worked in service, the mask marking its wearer as a member of the lower classes. The textile was designed for hard work, woven loosely enough to blur her features without obscuring necessary vision. Alizeh had chosen this profession with great forethought, and clung every day to the anonymity her position provided, rarely removing her snoda even outside of her room; for though most people did not understand the strangeness they saw in her eyes, she feared that one day the wrong person might.

She breathed deeply now, pressing the tips of her fingers against her cheeks and temples, gently massaging the face she'd not seen in what felt like years. Alizeh did not own a looking glass, and her occasional glances at the mirrors in Baz House revealed only the bottom third of her face: lips, chin, the column of her neck. She was otherwise a faceless servant, one of dozens, and had only vague memories of what she looked like—or what she'd once been told she looked like. It was the whisper of her mother's voice in her ear, the feel of her father's calloused hand against her cheek.

You are the finest of us all, he'd once said.

Alizeh closed her mind to the memory as she took off her shoes, set the boots in their corner. Over the years Alizeh had collected enough scraps from old commissions to stitch herself the quilt and matching pillow currently laid atop her mattress. Her clothes she hung from old nails wrapped meticulously in colorful thread; all other personal affects she'd arranged inside an apple crate she'd found discarded in one of the chicken coops.

She rolled off her stockings now and hung them—to air them out—from a taut bit of twine. Her dress went to one of the colorful hooks, her corset to another, her snoda to the last. Everything Alizeh owned, everything she touched, was clean and orderly, for she had learned long ago that when a home was not found, it was forged; indeed it could be fashioned even from nothing.

Clad only in her shift, she yawned, yawned as she sat on her cot, as the mattress sank, as she pulled the pins from her hair. The day—and her long, heavy curls—crashed down around her shoulders.

Her thoughts had begun to slur.

With great reluctance she blew out the candle, pulled her legs against her chest, and fell over like a poorly weighted insect. The illogic of her phobia was consistent only in perplexing her, for when she was abed and her eyes closed, Alizeh imagined she could more easily conquer the dark, and even as she trembled with a familiar chill, she succumbed quickly to sleep. She reached for her soft quilt and drew it up over her shoulders, trying not to think about how cold she was, trying not to think at all. In fact she shivered so violently she hardly noticed when he sat down, his weight depressing the mattress at the foot of her bed.

Alizeh bit back a scream.

Her eyes flew open, tired pupils fighting to widen their aperture. Frantically, Alizeh patted down her quilt, her pillow, her threadbare mattress. There was no body on her bed. No one in her room.

Had she been hallucinating? She fumbled for her candle and dropped it, her hands shaking.

Surely, she'd been dreaming.

The mattress groaned—the weight shifting—and Alizeh experienced a fear so violent she saw sparks. She pushed backward, knocking her head against the wall, and somehow the pain focused her panic.

A sharp snap and a flame caught between his barely there fingers, illuminated the contours of his face.

Alizeh dared not breathe.

Even in silhouette she couldn't see him, not properly, but then—it was not his face, but his voice, that had made the devil notorious.

Alizeh knew this better than most.

Seldom did the devil present himself in some approximation of flesh; rare were his clear and memorable communications. Indeed, the creature was not as powerful as his legacy insisted, for he'd been denied the right to speak as another might, doomed forever to hold forth in riddles, and allowed permission only to persuade a person to ruin, never to command.

It was not usual, then, for one to claim an acquaintance with the devil, nor was it with any conviction that a person might speak of his methods, for the presence of such evil was experienced most often only through a provoking of sensation.

Alizeh did not like to be the exception.

Indeed it was with some pain that she acknowledged the circumstances of her birth: that it had been the devil to first offer congratulations at her cradle, his unwelcome ciphers as inescapable as the wet of rain. Alizeh's parents had tried, desperately, to banish such a beast from their home, but he had returned again and again, forever embroidering the tapestry of her life with ominous forebodings, in what seemed a promise of destruction she could not outmaneuver.

Even now she felt the devil's voice, felt it like a breath loosed inside her body, an exhale against her bones.

There once was a man, he whispered.

"No," she nearly shouted, panicking. "Not another riddle—please—"

There once was a man, he whispered, *who bore a snake on each shoulder.*

Alizeh clapped both hands over her ears and shook her head; she'd never wanted so badly to cry.

"Please," she said, "please don't—"

Again:

There once was a man
who bore a snake on each shoulder.
If the snakes were well-fed
their master ceased growing older.

Alizeh squeezed her eyes shut, pulled her knees to her chest. He wouldn't stop. She couldn't shut him out.

What they ate no one knew, even as the children—

"Please," she said, begging now. "Please, I don't want to know—"

What they ate no one knew,
even as the children were found
with brains shucked from their skulls,
bodies splayed on the ground.

She inhaled sharply and he was gone, gone, the devil's voice torn free from her bones. The room suddenly shuddered around her, shadows lifting and stretching—and in the warped light a strange, hazy face peered back at her. Alizeh bit her lip so hard she tasted blood.

It was a young man staring at her now, one she did not recognize.

That he was human, Alizeh had no doubt—but something about him seemed different from the others. In the dim light the young man seemed carved not from clay, but marble, his face trapped in hard lines, centered by a soft mouth. The longer she stared at him the harder her heart raced. Was this the man with the snakes? Why did it even matter? Why would she ever believe a single word spoken by the devil?

Ah, but she already knew the answer to the latter.

Alizeh was losing her calm. Her mind screamed at her to look away from the conjured face, screamed that this was all madness—and yet.

Heat crept up her neck.

Alizeh was unaccustomed to staring too long at any face,

and this one was violently handsome. He had noble features, all straight lines and hollows, easy arrogance at rest. He tilted his head as he took her in, unflinching as he studied her eyes. All his unwavering attention stoked a forgotten flame inside her, startling her tired mind.

And then, a hand.

His hand, conjured from a curl of darkness. He was looking straight into her eyes when he dragged a vanishing finger across her lips.

She screamed.

KEEP READING FOR A SNEAK PEEK AT

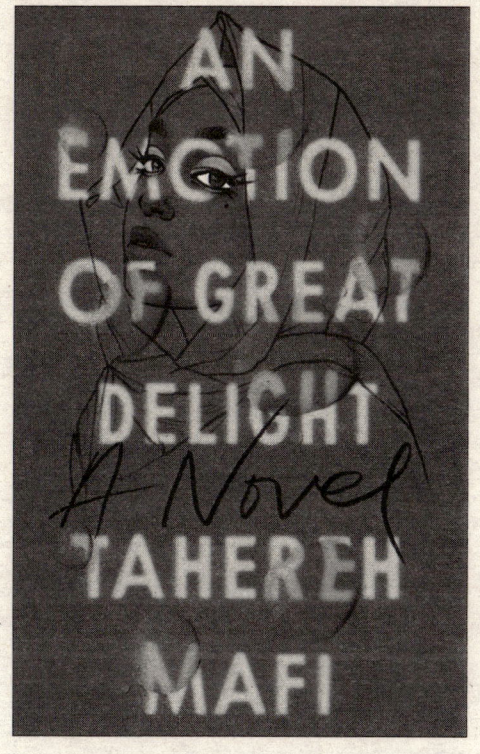

"A bluntly powerful read that shouldn't be missed."
—ALA *Booklist* (starred review)

DECEMBER
2003

ONE

The sunlight was heavy today, fingers of heat forming sweaty hands that braced my face, dared me to flinch. I was stone, still as I stared up into the eye of an unblinking sun, hoping to be blinded. I loved it, loved the blistering heat, loved the way it seared my lips.

It felt good to be touched.

It was a perfect summer day out of place in the fall, the stagnant heat disturbed only by a brief, fragrant breeze I couldn't source. A dog barked; I pitied it. Airplanes droned overhead, and I envied them. Cars rushed by and I heard only their engines, filthy metal bodies leaving their excrement behind and yet—

Deep, I took a deep breath and held it, the smell of diesel in my lungs, on my tongue. It tasted like memory, of movement. Of a promise to go somewhere, I released the breath, anywhere.

I, I was going nowhere.

There was nothing to smile about and still I smiled, the tremble in my lips an almost certain indication of oncoming hysteria. I was comfortably blind now, the sun having burned so deeply into my retinas that I saw little more than glowing orbs, shimmering darkness. I laid backward on dusty asphalt, so hot it stuck to my skin.

I pictured my father again.

His gleaming head, two tufts of dark hair perched atop his ears like poorly placed headphones. His reassuring smile that everything would be fine. The dizzying glare of fluorescent lights.

My father was nearly dead again, but all I could think about was how if he died I didn't know how long I'd have to spend pretending to be sad about it. Or worse, so much worse: how if he died I might not have to pretend to be sad about it. I swallowed back a sudden, unwelcome knot of emotion in my throat. I felt the telltale burn of tears and squeezed my eyes shut, willing myself to get up. Stand up.

Walk.

When I opened my eyes again a ten-thousand-foot-tall police officer was looming over me. Babble on his walkie-talkie. Heavy boots, a metallic swish of something as he adjusted his weight.

I blinked and backed up, crab-like, and evolved from legless snake to upright human, startled and confused.

"This yours?" he said, holding up a dingy, pale blue backpack.

"Yes," I said, reaching for it. "Yeah."

He dropped the bag as I touched it, and the weight of it nearly toppled me forward. I'd ditched the bloated carcass for a reason. Among other things, it contained four massive textbooks, three binders, three notebooks, and two worn paperbacks I still had to read for English. The after-school pickup was near a patch of grass I too-optimistically frequented, too often hoping someone in my family would remember I existed and spare me the walk home. Today, no such luck. I'd abandoned the bag and the grass for the empty parking lot.

Static on the walkie-talkie. More voices, garbled.

I looked up.

Up, up a cloven chin and thin lips, nose and sparse lashes, flashes of bright blue eyes. The officer wore a hat. I could not see his hair.

"Got a call," he said, still peering at me. "You go to school here?" A crow swooped low and cawed, minding my business.

"Yeah," I said. My heart had begun to race. "Yes."

He tilted his head at me. "What were you doing on the ground?"

"What?"

"Were you praying or something?"

My racing heart began to slow. Sink. I was not devoid of a brain, two eyes, the ability to read the news, a room, this man stripping my face for parts. I knew anger, but fear and I were better acquainted.

"No," I said quietly. "I was just lying in the sun."

The officer didn't seem to buy this. His eyes traveled over my face again, at the scarf I wore around my head. "Aren't you hot in that thing?"

"Right now, yes."

He almost smiled. Instead he turned away, scanned the empty parking lot. "Where are your parents?"

"I don't know."

A single eyebrow went up.

"They forget about me," I said.

Both eyebrows. "They forget about you?"

"I always hope someone will show up," I explained. "If not, I walk home."

The officer looked at me for a long time. Finally, he sighed.

"All right." He backhanded the sky. "All right, get going. But don't do this again," he said sharply. "This is public property. Do your prayers at home."

I was shaking my head. "I wasn't—" I tried to say. *I wasn't*, I wanted to scream. *I wasn't*.

But he was already walking away.

TWO

It took a full three minutes for the fire in my bones to die out.

In the increasing quiet, I looked up. The once-white clouds had grown fat and gray; the gentle breeze was now a chilling gust. The drunk December day had sobered with a suddenness that bordered on extreme and I frowned at the scene, at its burnt edges, at the crow still circling above my head, its caw caw a constant refrain. Thunder roared, suddenly, in the distance.

The officer was mostly memory now.

What was left of him was marching off into the fading light, his boots heavy, his gait uneven; I watched him smile as he murmured into his radio. Lightning tore the sky in two and I shivered, jerkily, as if electrocuted.

I did not have an umbrella.

I reached under my shirt and tugged free the folded newspaper from where I'd stashed it in my waistband, flush against my torso, and tucked it under my arm. The air was heavy with the promise of a storm, the wind shuddering through the trees. I didn't really think a newspaper would hold up against the rain, but it was all I had.

These days, it was what I always had.

There was a newspaper vending machine around the corner from my house, and a few months ago, on a whim, I'd purchased a copy of the *New York Times*. I'd been curious about Adults Reading the Newspaper, curious about the articles therein that sparked the conversations that seemed to be shaping my life, my identity, the bombing of my friends' families in the Middle East. After two years of panic and mourning post-9/11, our country had decided on aggressive political action: we had declared war on Iraq.

The coverage was relentless.

The television offered a glaring, violent dissemination of information on the subject, the kind I could seldom stomach. But the slow, quiet business of reading a newspaper suited me. Even better, it filled the holes in my free time.

I'd started shoving quarters in my pocket every day, purchasing copies of the newspaper on my way to school. I perused the articles as I walked the single mile, the exercise of mind and body elevating my blood pressure to dangerous heights. By the time I reached first period I'd lost both my appetite and my focus. I was growing sick on the news, sick of it, heedlessly gorging myself on the pain, searching in vain for an antidote in the poison. Even now my thumb moved slowly over the worn ink of old stories, back and forth, caressing my addiction.

I stared up at the sky.

The lone crow overhead would not cease its staring, the weight of its presence seeming to depress the air from my lungs. I forced myself to move, to shutter the windows in my mind as I went. Silence was too welcoming of unwanted thoughts; I listened instead to the sounds of passing cars, to the wind sharpening against their metal bodies. There were two people in particular I did not want to think about. Neither did I want to think about looming college applications, the police officer, or the newspaper still clenched in my fist, and yet—

I stopped, unfurled the paper, smoothed its corners.

Afghan Villagers Torn by Grief After US Raid Kills 9 Children

My phone rang.

I retrieved it from my pocket, going still as I scanned the flashing number on the screen. A blade of feeling impaled me—and then, just as suddenly, withdrew. *Different number.* Heady relief nearly prompted me to laugh, the sensation held at bay only by the dull ache in my chest. It felt as if actual steel had been buried between my lungs.

I flipped open the phone.

"Hello?"

Silence.

A voice finally broke through, a mere half word emerging

from a mess of static. I glanced at the screen, at my dying battery, my single bar of reception. When I flipped the phone shut, a prickle of fear moved down my spine.

I thought of my mother.

My mother, my optimistic mother who thought that if she locked herself in her closet I wouldn't hear her sobs.

A single, fat drop of water landed on my head.

I looked up.

I thought of my father, six feet of dying man swaddled in a hospital bed, staring into the middle distance. I thought of my sister.

A second drop of rain fell in my eye.

The sky ruptured with a sudden *crack* and in the intervening second—in the heartbeat before the deluge—I contemplated stillness. I considered lying down in the middle of the road, lying there forever.

But then, rain.

It arrived in a hurry, battering my face, blackening my clothes, pooling in the folds of my backpack. The newspaper I lifted over my head endured all of four seconds before succumbing to the wet, and I hastily tucked it away, this time in my bag. I squinted into the downpour, readjusted the demon on my back, and pulled my thin jacket more tightly around my body.

Walked.

LAST YEAR

PART I

Two sharp knocks at my door and I groaned, pulled the blanket over my head. I'd been up late last night memorizing equations for my physics class, and I'd gotten maybe four hours of sleep as a result. The very idea of getting out of bed made me want to weep.

Another hard knock.

"It's too early," I said, my voice muffled by the blanket. "Go away."

"Pasho," I heard my mother say. *Get up*.

"Nemikham," I called back. *I don't want to*.

"Pasho."

"Actually, I don't think I can go to school today. I think I have tuberculosis."

I heard the soft *shh* of the door pushing open against carpet, and I curled away instinctively, a nautilus in its shell.

I made a pitiful sound as I waited for what seemed inevitable—for my mother to drag me, bodily, out of bed, or, at the very least, to rip off the covers.

Instead, she sat on me.

I nearly screamed at the unexpected weight. It was excruciating to be sat upon while curled in the fetal position; somehow my stacked bones made me more vulnerable to damage. I thrashed around, shouted at her to get off me, and she just laughed, pinched my leg.

I cried out.

"Goftam pasho." *I said get up*.

"How am I supposed to get up now?" I asked, batting away the sheets from my face. "You've broken all my bones."

"Eh?" She raised her eyebrows. "You say that to me? Your mother"—she said all this in Farsi—"is so heavy she could break all your bones? Is that what you're saying?"

"Yes."

She gasped, her eyes wide. "Ay, bacheyeh bad." *Oh, you bad child*. And with a slight bounce, she sat more heavily on my thighs.

I let out a strangled cry. "Okay okay I'll get up I'll get up oh my God—"

"Maman? Are you up here?"

At the sound of my sister's voice, my mom got to her feet. She whipped the covers off my bed and said, "In here!" Then, to me, with narrowed eyes: "Pasho."

"I'm pasho-ing, I'm pasho-ing," I grumbled.

I got to my feet and glanced, out of habit, at the alarm clock I'd already silenced a half dozen times, and nearly had a stroke when I saw the hour. "I'm going to be late!"

"Man keh behet goftam," my mom said with a shrug. *I told you.*

"You told me nothing." I turned, eyes wide. "You never told me what time it was."

"I did tell you. Maybe your tuberculosis made you deaf."

"Wow." I shook my head as I stalked past her. "Hilarious."

"I know, I know, I'm heelareeus," she said with a flourish of her hand. She switched back to Farsi. "By the way, I can't take you to school today. I have a dentist appointment. Shayda is taking you instead."

"No I'm not," my sister called, her voice growing louder as she approached. She popped her head inside my room. "I have to leave right now, and Shadi isn't even dressed."

"No— Wait—" I startled scrambling. "I can be dressed in five minutes—"

"No you can't."

"Yes I can!" I was already across the hall in our shared bathroom, applying toothpaste to my toothbrush like a crazy person. "Just wait, okay, just—"

"No way. I'm not going to be late because of you."

"Shayda, what the hell—"

"You can walk."

"It'll take me forty-five minutes!"

"Then ask Mehdi."

"Mehdi is still asleep!"

"Did someone say my name?"

I heard my brother coming up the stairs, his words a little rounder than usual, like maybe he was eating something as he spoke. My heart gave a sudden leap.

I spat toothpaste into the sink, ran into the hall. "I need a ride to school," I cried, toothbrush still clenched in my fist. "Can you take me?"

"Never mind. I've gone suddenly deaf." He barreled back down the stairs.

"Oh my God. What is wrong with everyone in this family?"

My dad's voice boomed upward. "Man raftam! Khodafez!" *I'm leaving! Bye!*

"Khodafez!" the four of us shouted in unison.

I heard the front door slam shut as I flew to the banister, caught sight of Mehdi on the landing below.

"Wait," I said, "please, please—"

Mehdi looked up at me and smiled his signature, devastating smile, the kind I knew had already ruined a few lives. His hazel eyes glittered in the early-morning light. "Sorry," he said. "I've got plans."

"How do you have plans at seven thirty in the morning?"

"Sorry," he said again, his lean form disappearing from view. "Busy day."

My mom patted me on the shoulder. "Mikhasti zoodtar pashi." *You could've woken up earlier.*

"An excellent point," Shayda said, swinging her backpack over one shoulder. "Bye."

"No!" I ran back into the bathroom, rinsed my mouth, splashed water on my face. "I'm almost ready! Two more minutes!"

"Shadi, you're not even wearing pants."

"What?" I looked down. I was wearing an oversize T-shirt. No pants. "Wait— Shayda—"

But she was already moving down the stairs.

"Manam bayad beram," my mom said. *I have to go, too*. She shot me a sympathetic glance. "I'll pick you up after school, okay?"

I acknowledged this with a distracted goodbye and darted back into my room. I changed into jeans and a thermal at breakneck speed, nearly stumbling over myself as I grabbed socks, a hair tie, my scarf, and my half-zipped backpack. I flew downstairs like a maniac, screaming Shayda's name.

"Wait," I cried. "Wait, I'm ready! Thirty seconds!"

I hopped on one foot as I pulled on my socks, slipped on my shoes. I tied back my hair, knotted my scarf à la Jackie O— or, you know, a lot of Persian ladies—and bolted out the door. Shayda was at the curb, unlocking her car, and my mom was settling into her minivan, still parked in the driveway. I waved at her, breathless as I shouted—

"I made it!"

My mom smiled and flashed me a thumbs-up, both of which I promptly reciprocated. I then turned the wattage of my smile on Shayda, who only rolled her eyes and, with a heavy sigh, granted me passage in her ancient Toyota Camry.

I was euphoric.

I waved another goodbye at my mom—who'd just turned on her car—before depositing my unwieldy bag in Shayda's back seat. My sister was still buckling herself into the driver's side, arranging her things, placing her coffee mug in the cup holder, et cetera, and I leaned against the passenger side door, taking advantage of the moment to both catch my breath and enjoy my victory.

Too late, I realized I was freezing.

It was the end of September, the beginning of fall, and I hadn't yet adjusted to the new season. The weather was inconsistent, the days plagued by both hot and cold stretches, and I wasn't sure it was worth risking Shayda's wrath to run upstairs and grab my jacket.

My sister seemed to read my mind.

"Hey," she barked at me from inside the car. "Don't even think about it. If you go back in the house, I'm leaving."

My mom, who was also a mind reader, suddenly hit the brakes on her minivan, rolled down the window.

"Bea," she called. *Here.* "Catch."

I held out my hands as she tossed a balled-up sweatshirt in my direction. I caught it, assessed it, held it up to the sky. It was a standard-issue black hoodie, the kind you pulled over your head. Its only distinguishing features were the drawstrings, which were a vibrant blue.

"Whose is this?" I asked.

My mom shrugged. "It must be Mehdi's," she said in Farsi. "It's been in the car for a long time."

"A long time?" I frowned. "How long is a long time?"

My mom shrugged again, put on her sunglasses.

I gave the cotton a suspicious sniff, but it must not have been abandoned in our car for too long, because the sweater still smelled nice. Something like cologne. Something that made my skin hum with awareness.

My frown deepened.

I pulled the sweatshirt over my head, watched my mom disappear down the drive. The hoodie was soft and warm and way too big for me in the best way, but this close to my skin that faint, pleasant scent was suddenly overwhelming. My thoughts had begun to race, my mind working too hard to answer a simple question.

Shayda honked the horn. I nearly had a heart attack.

"Get in right now," she shouted, "or I'm running you over."

The brand new YA fantasy romance series from the author of
TikTok sensation, **Shatter Me**

IMAGINE ME

ALSO BY TAHEREH MAFI

SHATTER ME SERIES:
Shatter Me

Unravel Me

Ignite Me

Restore Me

Defy Me

Imagine Me

NOVELLA COLLECTIONS
Unite Me (Destroy Me & Fracture Me)

Find Me (Shadow Me & Reveal Me)

Believe Me

A Very Large Expanse of Sea

An Emotion of Great Delight

This Woven Kingdom

These Infinite Threads

IMAGINE ME

TAHEREH MAFI

DEAN

DEAN

First published in the USA 2020 by HarperCollins Children's Books
First published in Great Britain 2020 by Electric Monkey, part of Farshore
This edition published 2023 by Dean, part of Farshore
An imprint of HarperCollins*Publishers*
1 London Bridge Street, London SE1 9GF
www.farshore.co.uk

HarperCollins*Publishers*
Macken House, 39/40 Mayor Street Upper,
Dublin 1, D01 C9W8, Ireland

Published by arrangement with HarperCollins Children's Books,
a division of HarperCollins Publishers, New York, New York, USA

Text copyright © 2020 Tahereh Mafi

ISBN 978 0 0086 0664 0
Printed and Bound in the UK using 100% Renewable Electricity
at CPI Group (UK) Ltd
005

A CIP catalogue record for this title is available from the British Library.

All rights reserved. No part of this publication may be reproduced, stored in a retrieval system, or transmitted, in any form or by any means, electronic, mechanical, photocopying, recording or otherwise, without the prior permission of the publisher and copyright owner.

Stay safe online. Farshore is not responsible for content hosted by third parties.

This book is produced from independently certified FSC™ paper
to ensure responsible forest management.

For more information visit: www.harpercollins.co.uk/green

~~ELLA~~ JULIETTE

In the dead of night, I hear birds.

I hear them, I see them, I close my eyes and feel them, feathers shuddering in the air, bending the wind, wings grazing my shoulders when they ascend, when they alight. Discordant shrieks ring and echo, ring and echo—

How many?

Hundreds.

White birds, white with streaks of gold, like crowns atop their heads. They fly. They soar through the sky with strong, steady wings, masters of their destinies. They used to make me hope.

Never again.

I turn my face into the pillow, digging fingers into cotton flesh as the memories crash into me.

"Do you like them?" she says.

We're in a big, wide room that smells like dirt. There are trees everywhere, so tall they nearly touch the pipes and beams of the open ceiling. Birds, dozens of them, screech as they stretch their wings. Their calls are loud. A little scary. I try not to flinch as one of the large white birds swoops past me. It wears a bright, neon-green bracelet around one leg. They all do.

This doesn't make sense.

I remind myself that we're indoors—the white walls, the concrete floor under my feet—and I look up at my mother, confused.

I've never seen Mum smile so much. Mostly she smiles when Dad is around, or when she and Dad are off in the corner, whispering together, but right now it's just me and Mum and a bunch of birds and she's so happy I decide to ignore the funny feeling in my stomach. Things are better when Mum is in a good mood.

"Yes," I lie. "I like them a lot."

Her eyes brighten. "I knew you would. Emmaline didn't care for them, but you—you've always been a bit too fond of things, haven't you, darling? Not at all like your sister." Somehow, her words come out mean. They don't seem *mean, but they* sound *mean.*

I frown.

I'm still trying to figure out what's happening when she says—

"I had one as a pet when I was about your age. Back then, they were so common we could never be rid of them." She laughs, and I watch her as she watches a bird, midflight. "One of them lived in a tree near my house, and it called my name whenever I walked past. Can you imagine?" Her smile fades as she asks the question.

Finally, she turns to look at me.

"They're very nearly extinct now. You understand why I couldn't let that happen."

"Of course," I say, but I'm lying again. There is little I understand about Mum.

She nods. "These are a special sort of creature. Intelligent. They can speak, dance. And each of them wears a crown." She turns away again, staring at the birds the way she stares at all the things she makes for work: with joy. "The sulphur-crested cockatoo mates for life," she says. "Just like me and your father."

The sulphur-crested cockatoo.

I shiver, suddenly, at the unexpected sensation of a warm hand on my back, fingers trailing lightly along my spine.

"Love," he says, "are you all right?"

When I say nothing he shifts, the sheets rustling, and he tucks me into his hollows, his body curving around mine. He's warm and strong and as his hand slides down my torso I cant my head toward him, finding peace in his presence, in the safety of his arms. His lips touch my skin, a graze against my neck so subtle it sparks, hot and cold, right down to my toes.

"Is it happening again?" he whispers.

My mother was born in Australia.

I know this because she once told me so, and because now, despite my desperation to resist many of the memories now returned to me, I can't forget. She once told me that the sulphur-crested cockatoo was native to Australia. It was introduced to New Zealand in the nineteenth century, but Evie, my mother, didn't discover them there. She fell in love with the birds back home, as a child, when one of them, she claims, saved her life.

These were the birds that once haunted my dreams.

These birds, kept and bred by a crazy woman. I feel embarrassed to realize I'd held fast to nonsense, to the faded, disfigured impressions of old memories poorly discarded. I'd hoped for more. Dreamed of more. Disappointment lodges in my throat, a cold stone I'm unable to swallow.

And then

again

I feel it

I stiffen against the nausea that precedes a vision, the sudden punch to the gut that means there's more, there's more, there's always more.

Aaron pulls me closer, holds me tighter against his chest.

"Breathe," he whispers. "I'm right here, love. I'll be right here."

I cling to him, squeezing my eyes shut as my head swims. These memories were a gift from my sister, Emmaline. The sister I only just discovered, only just recovered.

And only because she fought to find me.

Despite my parents' relentless efforts to rid our minds of the lingering proof of their atrocities, Emmaline prevailed. She used her psychokinetic powers to return to me what was stolen from my memories. She gave me this gift—this gift of remembering—to help me save myself. To save *her*. To stop our parents.

To fix the world.

But now, in the wake of a narrow escape, this gift has become a curse. Every hour my mind is reborn. Altered. The memories keep coming.

And my dead mother refuses to be silenced.

"Little bird," she whispers, tucking a stray hair behind my ear. *"It's time for you to fly away now."*

"But I don't want to go," I say, fear making my voice shake. *"I want to stay here, with you and Dad and Emmaline. I still don't understand why I have to leave."*

"You don't have to understand," she says gently.

I go uncomfortably still.

Mum doesn't yell. She's never yelled. My whole life, she's never raised a hand to me, never shouted or called me names. Not like Aaron's dad. But Mum doesn't need to yell. Sometimes she just says things, things like you don't have to understand *and there's a warning there, a finality in her words that's always scared me.*

I feel tears forming, burning the whites of my eyes, and—

"No crying," she says. *"You're far too old for that now."*

I sniff, hard, fighting back the tears. But my hands won't stop shaking.

Mum looks up, nods at someone behind me. I turn around just in time to spot Paris, Mr. Anderson, waiting with my suitcase. There's no kindness in his eyes. No warmth at all. He turns away from me, looks at Mum. He doesn't say hello.

He says: "Has Max settled in yet?"

"Oh, he's been ready for days." Mum glances at her watch, distracted. *"You know Max,"* she says, smiling faintly. *"Always a perfectionist."*

"Only when it comes to your wishes," says Mr. Anderson. *"I've never seen a grown man so besotted with his wife."*

Mum smiles wider. She seems about to say something, but I cut her off.

"Are you talking about Dad?" I ask, my heart racing. "Will Dad be there?"

My mother turns to me, surprised, like she'd forgotten I was there. She turns back to Mr. Anderson. "How's Leila doing, by the way?"

"Fine," he says. But he sounds irritated.

"Mum?" Tears threaten again. "Am I going to stay with Dad?"

But Mum doesn't seem to hear me. She's talking to Mr. Anderson when she says, "Max will walk you through everything when you arrive, and he'll be able to answer most of your questions. If there's something he can't answer, it's likely beyond your clearance."

Mr. Anderson looks suddenly annoyed, but he says nothing. Mum says nothing.

I can't stand it.

Tears are spilling down my face now, my body shaking so hard it makes my breaths rattle. "Mum?" I whisper. "Mum, please a-answer me—"

Mum clamps a cold, hard hand around my shoulder and I go instantly still. Quiet. She's not looking at me. She won't look at me. "You'll handle this, too," she says. "Won't you, Paris?"

Mr. Anderson meets my eyes then. So blue. So cold. "Of course."

A flash of heat courses through me. A rage so sudden it briefly replaces my terror.

I hate him.

I hate him so much that it does something to me when I look at him—and the abrupt surge of emotion makes me feel brave.

I turn back to Mum. Try again.

"Why does Emmaline get to stay?" I ask, wiping angrily at my *wet cheeks. "If I have to go, can't we at least go toge—"*

I cut myself off when I spot her.

My sister, Emmaline, is peeking out at me from behind the mostly closed door. She's not supposed to be here. Mum said so.

Emmaline is supposed to be doing her swimming lessons.

But she's here, her wet hair dripping on the floor, and she's staring at me, eyes wide as plates. She's trying to say something, but her lips move too fast for me to follow. And then, out of nowhere, a bolt of electricity runs up my spine and I hear her voice, sharp and strange—

Liars.
LIARS.
KILL THEM ALL

My eyes fly open and I can't catch my breath, my chest heaving, heart pounding. Warner holds me, making soothing sounds as he runs a reassuring hand up and down my arm.

Tears spill down my face and I swipe at them, hands shaking.

"I hate this," I whisper, horrified at the tremble in my voice. "I hate this so much. I hate that it keeps happening. I hate what it does to me," I say. "*I hate it.*"

~~Warner~~ Aaron presses his cheek against my shoulder with a sigh, his breath teasing my skin.

"I hate it, too," he says softly.

I turn, carefully, in the cradle of his arms, and press my forehead to his bare chest.

It's been less than two days since we escaped Oceania. Two days since I killed my own mother. Two days since I met the residue of my sister, Emmaline. Only two days since my entire life was upended yet again, which feels impossible.

Two days and already things are on fire around us.

This is our second night here, at the Sanctuary, the locus of the rebel group run by Nouria—Castle's daughter—and her wife, Sam. We're supposed to be safe here. We're supposed to be able to breathe and regroup after the hell of the last few weeks, but my body refuses to settle. My mind is overrun, under attack. I thought the rush of new memories would eventually gutter out, but these last twenty-four hours have been an unusually brutal assault, and I seem to be the only one struggling.

Emmaline gifted all of us—all the children of the supreme commanders—with memories stolen by our parents. One by one we were awoken to the truths our parents had buried, and one by one we were returned to normal lives.

All but me.

The others have since moved on, reconciled their timelines, made sense of the betrayal. My mind, on the other hand, continues to falter. Spin. But then, none of the others lost as much as I did; they don't have as much to remember. Even Warner—*Aaron*—isn't experiencing so thorough a reimagining of his life.

It's beginning to scare me.

I feel as though my history is being rewritten, infinite paragraphs scratched out and hastily revised. Old and new images—memories—layer atop each other until the ink runs, rupturing the scenes into something new, something incomprehensible. Occasionally my thoughts feel like disturbing hallucinations, and the onslaught is so invasive I fear it's doing irreparable damage.

Because something is changing.

Every new memory is delivered with an emotional violence that drives into me, reorders my mind. I'd been feeling this pain in flickers—the sickness, the nausea, the disorientation—but I haven't wanted to question it too deeply. I haven't wanted to look too closely. The truth is, I didn't want to believe my own fears. But the truth is: I am a punctured tire. Every injection of air leaves me both fuller and flatter.

I am forgetting.

"Ella?"

Terror bubbles up inside of me, bleeds through my open eyes. It takes me a moment to remember that I am ~~Juliette~~ Ella. Each time, it takes me a moment longer.

Hysteria threatens—

I force it down.

"Yes," I say, forcing air into my lungs. "Yes."

~~Warner~~ Aaron stiffens. "Love, what's wrong?"

"Nothing," I lie. My heart is pounding fast, too fast. I don't know why I'm lying. It's a fruitless effort; he can sense everything I'm feeling. I should just tell him. ~~I don't know why I'm not telling him.~~ I know why I'm not telling him.

I'm waiting.

I'm waiting to see if this will pass, if the lapses in my memory are only glitches waiting to be repaired. Saying it out loud makes it too real, and it's too soon to say these thoughts aloud, to give in to the fear. After all, it's only been a day since it started. It only occurred to me yesterday that something was truly wrong.

It occurred to me because I made a mistake.

Mistakes.

We were sitting outside, staring at the stars. I couldn't remember ever seeing the stars like that—sharp, clear. It was late, so late it wasn't night but infant morning, and the view was dizzying. I was freezing. A brave wind stole through a copse nearby, filling the air with steady sound. I was full of cake. Warner smelled like sugar, like decadence. I felt drunk on joy.

I don't want to wait, he said, taking my hand. Squeezing it. *Let's not wait.*

I blinked up at him. *For what?*

For what?

For what?

How did I forget what had happened just hours earlier? How did I forget the moment he asked me to marry him?

It was a glitch. It felt like a glitch. Where there was once a memory was suddenly a vacancy, a cavity held empty only until nudged into realignment.

I recovered, remembered. Warner laughed.

I did not.

I forgot the name of Castle's daughter. I forgot how we landed at the Sanctuary. I forgot, for a full two minutes, how I ever escaped Oceania. But my errors were temporary; they seemed like natural delays. I experienced only confusion as my mind buffered, hesitation as the memories resurfaced, waterlogged and vague. I thought maybe I was tired. Overwhelmed. I took none of it seriously, not until I was sitting under the stars and couldn't remember promising to spend the rest of my life with someone.

Mortification.

Mortification so acute I thought I'd expire from the full force of it. Even now fresh heat floods my face, and I find I'm relieved Warner can't see in the dark.

Aaron, not Warner.

Aaron.

"I can't tell just now whether you're afraid or embarrassed," he says, and exhales softly. It sounds almost like a laugh. "Are you worried about Kenji? About the others?"

I grab on to this half-truth with my whole heart.

"Yes," I say. "*Kenji.* James. Adam."

Kenji has been sick in bed since very early this morning. I squint at the slant of moon through our window and remember that it's long past midnight, which would mean that, technically, Kenji got sick yesterday morning.

Regardless, it was terrifying for all of us.

The drugs Nazeera forced into Kenji on their international flight from Sector 45 to Oceania were a dose too strong, and he's been reeling ever since. He finally collapsed—the twins, Sonya and Sara, have checked in on him and say he's going to be just fine—but not before we learned that Anderson has been rounding up the children of the supreme commanders.

Adam and James and Lena and Valentina and Nicolás are all in Anderson's custody.

James is in his custody.

It's been a devastating, awful couple of days. It's been a devastating, awful couple of weeks.

Months, really.

Years.

Some days, no matter how far back I go, I can't seem to find the good times. Some days, the occasional happiness I've known feels like a bizarre dream. An error. Hyperreal and unfocused, the colors too bright and the sounds too strong.

Figments of my imagination.

It was just days ago that clarity came to me, bearing gifts. Just days ago that the worst seemed behind me, that the world seemed full of potential, that my body was stronger than ever, my mind fuller, sharper, more capable than I'd ever known it.

But now

But now

But now I feel like I'm clinging to the blurring edges of

sanity, that elusive, fair-weather friend always breaking my heart.

Aaron pulls me close and I melt into him, grateful for his warmth, for the steadiness of his arms around me. I take a deep, shuddering breath and let it all go, exhaling against him. I inhale the rich, heady scent of his skin, the faint aroma of gardenias he somehow carries with him always. Seconds pass in perfect silence and we listen to each other breathe.

Slowly, my heart rate steadies.

The tears dry up. The fears take five. Terror is distracted by a passing butterfly and sadness takes a nap.

For a little while it's just me and him and us and everything is untarnished, untouched by darkness.

I knew I loved ~~Warner~~ Aaron before all this—before we were captured by The Reestablishment, before we were ripped apart, before we learned of our shared history—but that love was new, green, its depths uncharted, untested. In that brief, glimmering window during which the gaping holes in my memory felt fully accounted for, things between us changed. *Everything* between us changed. Even now, even with the noise in my head, I feel it.

Here.

This.

My bones against his bones. This is my home.

I feel him suddenly stiffen and I pull back, concerned. I can't see much of him in this perfect darkness, but I feel the delicate rise of goose bumps along his arms when he says, "What are you thinking about?"

My eyes widen, comprehension dethroning concern. "I was thinking about you."

"Me?"

I close the gap between us again. Nod against his chest.

He says nothing, but I can hear his heart, racing in the quiet, and eventually I hear him exhale. It's a heavy, uneven sound, like he might've been holding his breath for too long. I wish I could see his face. No matter how much time we spend together, I still forget how much he can feel my emotions, especially at times like this, when our bodies are pressed together.

Gently, I run my hand down his back. "I was thinking about how much I love you," I say.

He goes uncommonly still, but only for a moment. And then he touches my hair, his fingers slowly combing the strands.

"Did you feel it?" I ask.

When he doesn't answer, I pull back again. I blink against the black until I'm able to make out the glint of his eyes, the shadow of his mouth.

"Aaron?"

"Yes," he says, but he sounds a little breathless.

"Yes, you felt it?"

"Yes," he says again.

"What does it feel like?"

He sighs. Rolls onto his back. He's quiet for so long that, for a while, I'm not sure he's going to answer. Then, softly, he says:

"It's hard to describe. It's a pleasure so close to pain I sometimes can't tell the two apart."

"That sounds awful."

"No," he says. "It's exquisite."

"I love you."

A sharp intake of breath. Even in this darkness I see the strain in his jaw—the tension there—as he stares at the ceiling.

I sit straight up, surprised.

Aaron's reaction is so unstudied I don't know how I never noticed it before. But then, maybe this is new. Maybe something really has changed between us. Maybe I never loved him this much before. That would make sense, I suppose. Because when I think about it, when I really think about how much I love him now, after everything we've—

Another sudden, sharp breath. And then he laughs, nervously.

"*Wow*," I say.

He claps a hand over his eyes. "This is vaguely mortifying."

I'm smiling now, very nearly laughing. "Hey. It's—"

My body seizes.

A violent shudder rushes up my skin and my spine goes rigid, my bones held in place by invisible pins, my mouth frozen open and trying to draw breath.

Heat fills my vision.

I hear nothing but static, grand rapids, white water, ferocious wind. Feel nothing. Think nothing. Am nothing.

I am, for the most infinitesimal moment—
Free.

My eyelids flutter open *closed* open *closed* open *closed* I am a wing, two wings, a swinging door, five birds

Fire climbs inside of me, explodes.

Ella?

The voice appears in my mind with swift strength, sharp, like darts to the brain. Dully, I realize that I'm in pain— my jaw aches, my body still suspended in an unnatural position—but I ignore it. The voice tries again:

Juliette?

Realization strikes, a knife to the knees. Images of my sister fill my mind: bones and melted skin, webbed fingers, sodden mouth, no eyes. Her body suspended underwater, long brown hair like a swarm of eels. Her strange, disembodied voice pierces through me. And so I say, without speaking:

Emmaline?

Emotion drives into me, fingers digging in my flesh, sensation scraping across my skin. Her relief is tangible. I can taste it. She's relieved, relieved I recognized her, relieved she found me, relieved relieved relieved—

What happened? I ask.

A deluge of images floods my brain until it sinks, I sink. Her memories drown my senses, clog lungs. I choke as the feelings crash into me. I see Max, my father, inconsolable in the wake of his wife's murder; I see Supreme Commander Ibrahim, frantic and furious, demanding Anderson gather the other children before it's too late; I see Emmaline, briefly abandoned, seizing an opportunity—

I gasp.

Evie made it so that only she or Max could control Emmaline's powers, and with Evie dead, the fail-safes implemented were suddenly weakened. Emmaline realized that in the wake of our mother's death there would be a brief window of opportunity—a brief window during which she might be able to wrest back control of her own mind before Max remade the algorithms.

But Evie's work was too good, and Max's reaction too prompt. Emmaline was only partly successful.

Dying, she says to me.
Dying.

Every flash of her emotion is accompanied by torturous assault. My flesh feels bruised. My spine seems liquid, my eyes blind, searing. I feel Emmaline—her voice, her feelings, her visions—more strongly than before, because *she's* stronger than before. That she managed to regain enough power to find me is proof alone that she is at least partly untethered, unrestrained. Max and Evie had been experimenting on Emmaline to a reckless degree in the last several months, trying to make her stronger even as her body withered. This, *this*, is the consequence.

Being this close to her is nothing short of excruciating.

I think I've screamed.

Have I screamed?

Everything about Emmaline is heightened to a fever pitch; her presence is wild, breathtaking, and it shudders to life inside my nerves. Sound and sensation streak across my vision, barrel through me violently. I hear a spider scuttle across the wooden floor. Tired moths drag their wings along the wall. A mouse startles, settles, in its sleep. Dust motes fracture against a window, shrapnel skidding across the glass.

My eyes skitter, unhinged in my skull.

I feel the oppressive weight of my hair, my limbs, my flesh wrapped around me like cellophane, a leather casket. My tongue, my tongue is a dead lizard perched in my mouth, rough and heavy. The fine hairs on my arms stand and sway, stand and sway. My fists are so tightly clenched my fingernails pierce the soft flesh of my palms.

I feel a hand on me. Where? Am I?

Lonely, she says.

She shows me.

A vision of us, back in the laboratory where I first saw her, where I killed our mother. I see myself from Emmaline's point of view and it's startling. She can't see much more than a blur, but she can feel my presence, can make out the shape of my form, the heat emanating from my body. And then my words, my own words, hurled back into my brain—

there has to be another way
you don't have to die
we can get through this together
please
i want my sister back
i want you to live
Emmaline
i won't let you die here
Emmaline Emmaline
we can get through this together
we can get through this together
we can get through this
together

A cold, metallic sensation begins to bloom in my chest. It moves through me, up my arms, down my throat, pushes into my gut. My teeth throb. Emmaline's pain claws and slithers, clings with a ferocity I can't bear. Her tenderness, too, is desperate, terrifying in its sincerity. She's overcome by emotion, hot and cold, fueled by rage and devastation.

She's been looking for me, all this time.

In these last couple of days Emmaline has been searching the conscious world for my mind, trying to find safe harbor, a place to rest.

A place to die.

Emmaline, I say. *Please—*

Sister.

Something tightens in my mind, squeezes. Fear propels through me, punctures organs. I'm wheezing. I smell earth and damp, decomposing leaves and I feel the stars staring at my skin, wind pushing through darkness like an anxious parent. My mouth is open, catching moths. I am on the ground.

Where?

No longer in my bed, I realize, no longer in my tent, I realize, no longer protected.

But when did I walk?

Who moved my feet? Who pushed my body?

How far?

I try to look around but I'm blind, my head trapped in a vise, my neck reduced to fraying sinew. My breaths fill my ears, harsh and loud, harsh and loud, rough rough gasping efforts my head

swings

My fists unclench, nails scraping as my fingers uncurl,

palms flattening, I smell heat, taste wind, hear dirt.

Dirt under my hands, in my mouth, under my fingernails. I'm screaming, I realize. Someone is touching me and I'm screaming.

Stop, I scream. *Please, Emmaline— Please don't do this—*

Lonely, she says.

l o n e l y

And with a sudden, ferocious agony—
I am displaced.

KENJI

It feels weird to call it luck.

It feels weird, but in some perverse, twisted way, this is luck. Luck that I'm standing in the middle of damp, freezing woodlands before the sun's bothered to lift its head. Luck that my bare upper body is half-numb from cold.

Luck that Nazeera's with me.

We pulled on our invisibility almost instantly, so she and I are at least temporarily safe here, in the half-mile stretch of untouched wilderness between regulated and unregulated territories. The Sanctuary was built on a couple of acres of unregulated land not far from where I'm standing, and it's masterfully hidden in plain sight only because of Nouria's unnatural talent for bending and manipulating light. Within Nouria's jurisdiction, the climate is somehow more temperate, the weather more predictable. But out here in the wild, the winds are relentless and combative. The temperatures are dangerous.

Still— We're lucky to be here at all.

Nazeera and I had been out of bed for a while, racing through the dark in an attempt at murdering one another. In the end it all turned out to be a complicated misunderstanding, but it was also a kind of kismet: If Nazeera hadn't snuck into my room at three o'clock in the morning and nearly killed me, I wouldn't have chased her through the forest, beyond the sight and soundproof protections of the Sanctuary. If we hadn't been so far from the Sanctuary, we never would've heard the distant, echoing screams of citizens crying out in terror. If we hadn't heard those cries, we never would've rushed toward the source. And if we hadn't done any of that, I never would've seen my best friend screaming her way into dawn.

I would've missed this. This:

J on her knees in the cold dirt, Warner crouched down beside her, both of them looking like death while the clouds literally melt out of the sky above them. The two of them are parked right outside the entrance to the Sanctuary, straddling the untouched stretch of forest that serves as a buffer between our camp and the heart of the nearest sector, number 241.

Why?

I froze when I saw them there, two broken figures entwined, limbs planted in the ground. I was paralyzed by confusion, then fear, then disbelief, all while the trees bent sideways and the wind snapped at my body, cruelly reminding me that I'd never had a chance to put on a shirt.

If my night had gone differently, I might've had that chance.

If my night had gone differently, I might've enjoyed, for the first time in my life, a romantic sunrise and an overdue reconciliation with a beautiful girl. Nazeera and I would've laughed about how she'd kicked me in the back and almost killed me, and how afterward I almost shot her for it. After that I would've taken a long shower, slept until noon, and eaten my weight in breakfast foods.

I had a plan for today: take it easy.

I wanted a little more time to heal after my most recent near-death experience, and I didn't think I was asking for much. I thought that, maybe, after everything I'd been through, the world might finally cut me some slack. Let me breathe between tragedies.

Nah.

Instead, I'm here, dying of frostbite and horror, watching the world fall to pieces around me. The sky, swinging wildly between horizontal and vertical horizons. The air, puncturing at random. Trees, sinking into the ground. Leaves, tap-dancing around me. I'm seeing it—I'm actively witnessing it—and still I can't believe it.

But I'm choosing to call it luck.

Luck that I'm seeing this, luck that I feel like I might throw up, luck that I ran all this way in my still-ill, injured body just in time to score a front-row seat to the end of the world.

Luck, fate, coincidence, serendipity—

I'll call this sick, sinking feeling in my gut a fucking magic trick if it'll help me keep my eyes open long enough to bear witness. To figure out how to help.

Because no one else is here.

No one but me and Nazeera, which seems crazy to an

improbable degree. The Sanctuary is supposed to have security on patrol at all times, but I see no sentries, and no sign of incoming aid. No soldiers from the nearby sector, either. Not even curious, hysterical civilians. Nothing.

It's like we're standing in a vacuum, on an invisible plane of existence. I don't know how J and Warner made it this far without being spotted. The two of them look like they were literally dragged through the dirt; I have no idea how they escaped notice. And though it's possible J only just started screaming, I still have a thousand unanswered questions.

They'll have to wait.

I glance at Nazeera out of habit, forgetting for a moment that she and I are invisible. But then I feel her step closer, and I breathe a sigh of relief as her hand slips into mine. She squeezes my fingers. I return the pressure.

Lucky, I remind myself.

It's lucky that we're here right now, because if I'd been in bed where I should've been, I wouldn't have even known J was in trouble. I would've missed the tremble in my friend's voice as she cried out, begging for mercy. I would've missed the shattering colors of a twisted sunrise, a peacock in the middle of hell. I would've missed the way J clamped her head between her hands and sobbed. I would've missed the sharp scents of pine and sulfur in the wind, would've missed the dry ache in my throat, the tremor moving through my body. I would've missed the moment J mentioned her sister by name. I wouldn't have heard J *specifically* ask her sister not to do something.

Yeah, this is definitely luck.

Because if I hadn't heard any of that, I wouldn't have known who to blame.

Emmaline.

ELLA

~~JULIETTE~~

I have eyes, two, feel them, rolling back and forth, around and around in my skull I have lips, two, feel them, wet and and heavy, pry them open have teeth, many, tongue, one and fingers, ten, count them

    onetwothreefourfive, again on the other side strange, ssstrange to have a tongue, sstrange it's a sssstrange ssort of thing, a strange ssssssssssortofthing

loneliness

    it creeps up on you
quiet
    and
still,
sits by your side in the dark, strokes your hair as you sleep wrapssitself around your bones squeezing sotightyoualmostcan't breathe almost can't hear the pulse racing in your blood as it rush, rushes up your

skin

touches its lips to the soft hairs at the back of your

neck

loneliness is a strangesortof thinga sstrangesortofthing an old friend standing beside you in the mirror screaming you're notenoughneverenough never ever enough

ssssometimes it just
                won't

let

    go

KENJI

I sidestep an eruption in the ground and duck just in time to avoid a cluster of vines growing in midair. A distant rock balloons to an astronomical size, and the moment it starts barreling in our direction I tighten my hold on Nazeera's hand and dive for cover.

The sky is ripping apart. The ground is fracturing beneath my feet. The sun flickers, strobing darkness, strobing light, everything stilted. And the clouds— There's something newly wrong with the clouds.

They're *disintegrating*.

Trees can't decide whether to stand up or lie down, gusts of wind shoot up from the ground with terrifying power, and suddenly the sky is full of birds. Full of fucking *birds*.

Emmaline is out of control.

We knew that her telekinetic and psychokinetic powers were godlike—beyond anything we've ever known—and we knew that The Reestablishment built Emmaline to control our experience of the world. But that was all, and that was just talk. Theory.

We'd never seen her like this.

Wild.

She's clearly doing something to J right now, ravaging

her mind while lashing out at the world around us, because the acid trip I'm staring at is only getting worse.

"Go back," I cry out over the din. "Get help—bring the girls!"

A single shout of agreement and Nazeera's hand slips free from mine, her heavy boots on the ground my only indication that she's bolting toward the Sanctuary. But even now—especially now—her swift, certain actions fill me with no small measure of relief.

It feels good to have a capable partner.

I claw my way across the sparse forest, grateful to have avoided the worst of the obstacles, and when I'm finally close enough to properly discern Warner's face, I pull back my invisibility.

I'm shaking with exhaustion.

I'd only barely recovered from being drugged nearly to death, and yet here I am, already about to die again. But when I look up, half-bent, hands on my knees and trying to breathe, I realize I have no right to complain.

Warner looks even worse than l expected.

Raw, clenched, a vein straining at his temple. He's on his knees holding on to J like he's trying to hold back a riot, and I didn't realize until just this second that he might be here for more than just emotional support.

The whole thing is surreal: they're both practically naked, in the dirt, on their knees—J with her hands pressed flat against her ears—and I can't help but wonder what kind of hell brought them to this moment.

I thought I was the one having a weird night.

Something slams suddenly into my gut and I double over, hitting the ground hard. Arms shaking, I push up onto all fours and scan the immediate area for the culprit. When I spot it, I gag.

A dead bird, a couple feet away.

Jesus.

J is still screaming.

I shove my way through a sudden, violent gust of wind—and just when I've regained my balance, ready to clear the last fifty feet toward my friends—the world goes mute.

Sound, off.

No howling winds, no tortured screams, no coughs, no sneezes. This is not ordinary quiet. It's not stillness, not silence.

It's more than that.

It's nothing at all.

I blink, blink, my head turning in slow, excruciating motion as I scan the distance for answers, willing the explanations to appear. Hoping the sheer force of my mind is enough to sprout reason from the ground.

It isn't.

I've gone deaf.

Nazeera is no longer here, J and Warner are still fifty feet away, and I've gone deaf. Deaf to the sound of the wind, to the shuddering trees. Deaf to my own labored breathing, to the cries of citizens in the compounds beyond. I try to clench my fists and it takes forever, like the air has grown dense. Thick.

Something is wrong with me.

I'm slow, slower than I've ever been, like I'm running underwater. Something is purposely keeping me back, physically pushing me away from Juliette—and suddenly, it all makes sense. My earlier confusion dissolves. Of course no one else is here. Of course no one else has come to help.

Emmaline would never allow it.

Maybe I got this far only because she was too busy to notice me right away—to sense me here, in my invisible state. It makes me wonder what else she's done to keep this area clear of trespassers.

It makes me wonder if I'll survive.

It's growing harder to think. It takes forever to fuse thoughts. Takes forever to move my arms. To lift my head. To look around. By the time I manage to pry open my mouth, I've forgotten that my voice makes no sound.

A flash of gold in the distance.

I spot Warner, shifting so slowly I wonder whether we're both suffering from the same affliction. He's fighting desperately to sit up next to J—J who's still on her knees, bent forward, mouth open. Her eyes are squeezed shut in concentration, but if she's screaming, I can't hear it.

I'd be lying if I said I wasn't terrified.

I'm close enough to Warner and J to be able to make out their expressions, but it's no good; I have no idea whether they're injured, so I don't know the extent of what we're dealing with. I have to get closer, somehow. But when I take a single, painful step forward, a sharp keening explodes in my ears.

I cry out soundlessly, clapping my hands to my head as the silence is suddenly—*viciously*—compounded by pressure. The knifelike pain needles into me, pressure building in my ears with an intensity that threatens to crush me from the inside. It's like someone has overfilled my head with helium, like any minute now the balloon that is my brain will explode. And just when I think the pressure might kill me, just when I think I can't bear the pain any longer, the ground begins to rumble. Tremble.

There's a seismic *crack*—

And sound comes back online. Sound so violent it rips open something inside of me, and when I finally tear my hands away from my ears they're red, dripping. I stagger as my head pounds. Rings. Rings.

I wipe my bloody hands on my bare torso and my vision swims. I lunge forward in a stupor and land badly, my still-damp palms hitting the earth so hard the force of it shudders up my bones. The dirt beneath my feet has gone slick. Wet. I look up, squinting at the sky and the sudden, torrential rain. My head continues to swing on a well-oiled hinge. A single drop of blood drips down my ear, lands on my shoulder. A second drop of blood drips down my ear, lands on my shoulder. A third drop of blood drips down my—

Name.

Someone calls my name.

The sound is large, aggressive. The word careens dizzily

in my head, expanding and contracting. I can't pin it down.

Kenji

I turn around and my head rings, rings.

K e n j i

I blink and it takes days, revolutions around the sun.

Trusted

friend

Something is touching me, under me, hauling me up, but it's no good. I don't move.

Too

heavy

I try to speak but can't. I say nothing, do nothing as my mind is broken open, as cold fingers reach inside my skull and disconnect the circuitry within. I stand still. Stiffen. The voice echoes to life in the blackness behind my eyes, speaking words that feel more like memory than conversation, words I don't know, don't understand *the pain I carry, the fears I should've left behind. I sag under the weight of loneliness, the chains of disappointment. My heart alone weighs a thousand pounds. I'm so heavy I can no longer be lifted away from the earth. I'm so heavy I have no choice now but to be buried beneath it. I'm so heavy, too heavy*

I exhale as I go down.

My knees crack as they hit the ground. My body slumps forward. Dirt kisses my face, welcomes me home.

The world goes suddenly dark.

Brave

My eyes flicker. Sound hums in my ears, something like dull, steady electricity. Everything is plunged into darkness. A blackout, a blackout in the natural world. Fear clings to my skin. Covers me.

but

w e a k

Knives bore holes into my bones that fill quickly with sorrow, sorrow so acute it takes my breath away.

I've never been so hopeful to cease existing.

I am floating.

Weightless and yet—weighted down, destined to sink forever. Dim light fractures the blackness behind my eyes and in the light, I see water. My sun and moon are the sea, my mountains the ocean. I live in liquid I never drink, drowning steadily in marbled, milky waters. My breathing is heavy, automatic, mechanic. I am forced to inhale, forced to exhale. The harsh, shuddering rasp of my own breath is my constant reminder of the grave that is my home.

I hear something.

It reverberates through the tank, dull metal against dull metal, arriving at my ears as if from outer space. I squint at the fresh set of shapes and colors, blurred forms. I clench my fists but my flesh is soft, my bones like fresh dough, my skin peeling in moist flakes. I'm surrounded by water but my thirst is insatiable and my anger—

My anger—

Something snaps. My head. My mind. My neck.

My eyes are wide, my breathing panicked. I'm on my knees, my forehead pressed into the dirt, my hands buried in wet earth.

I sit straight up and back, my head spinning.

"What the *fuck*?" I'm still trying to breathe. I look around. My heart is racing. "What— What—"

I was digging my own grave.

Slithering, terrifying horror moves through my body as I understand: Emmaline was in my head. She wanted to see if she could get me to kill myself.

And even as I think it—even as I look down at the miserable attempt I made to bury myself alive—I feel a dull, stabbing sympathy for Emmaline. Because I felt her pain, and it wasn't cruel.

It was desperate.

Like she was hoping that if I killed myself while she was in my head, somehow I'd be able to kill her, too.

J is screaming again.

I stagger to my feet, heart in my throat as the skies wrench open, releasing their wrath upon me. I'm not sure why Emmaline gave the inside of my head a shot—*brave but weak*—but I know enough to understand that whatever the hell is happening here is more than I can handle on my own. Right now, I can only hope that everyone in the Sanctuary is okay—and that Nazeera gets back here soon. Until then, my broken body will have to do its best.

I push forward.

Even as old, cold blood dries in my ears, across my chest, I push forward, steeling myself against the increasingly volatile weather conditions. The steady succession of earthquakes. The lightning strikes. The raging thunderstorm growing quickly into a hurricane.

Once I'm finally close enough, Warner looks up.

He seems stunned.

It occurs to me then that he's only just seeing me—after all this—he's only just realizing I'm here. A flicker of relief flashes through his eyes, too quickly replaced by pain.

And then he calls out two words—two words I never

thought I'd inspire him to say:

"*Help me.*"

The sentence is carried off in the wind, but the agony in his eyes remains. And from this vantage point, I finally understand the depth of what he's endured. At first I'd thought Warner was only holding her steady, trying to be supportive.

I was wrong.

J is vibrating with power, and Warner is only barely hanging on to her. Holding her still. Something—*someone*—is physically animating Juliette's body, articulating her limbs, trying to force her upright and possibly away from here, and it's only because of Warner that Emmaline hasn't succeeded.

I have no idea how he's doing it.

J's skin has gone translucent, veins bright and freakish in her pale face. She's nearly blue, ready to crack. A low-level hum emanates from her body, the crackle of energy, the buzz of power. I grab on to her arm and in the half second Warner shifts to distribute her weight between us, the three of us are flung forward. We hit the ground so hard I can hardly breathe, and when I'm finally able to lift my head I look at Warner, my own eyes wide with unmasked terror.

"Emmaline is doing this," I say, shouting the words at him.

He nods, his face grim.

"What can we do?" I cry. "How can she just keep screaming like this?"

Warner only looks at me.

He just *looks* at me, and the tortured expression in his eyes tells me everything I need to know. J *can't* keep screaming like this. She can't just be here on her knees screaming for a century. This shit is going to kill her. Jesus Christ. I knew it was bad, but for some reason I didn't think it was this bad.

J looks like she's going to die.

"Should we try to pick her up?" I don't even know why I ask. I doubt I could lift her arm above my head, much less her whole body. My own body is still shaking, so much so that I can barely do my part to keep this girl from lifting directly off the ground. I have no idea what kind of crazy shit is pumping through her veins right now, but J is on another planet. She looks half-alive, mostly alien. Her eyes are squeezed shut, her jaw unhinged. She's *radiating* energy. It's fucking terrifying.

And I can barely keep up.

The ache in my arms has begun to creep up my shoulders and down my back and I shiver, violently, when a sharp wind strikes my bare, overheated skin.

"Let's try," Warner says.

I nod.

Take a deep breath.

Beg myself to be stronger than I am.

I don't know how I do it, but through nothing short of a miracle, I make it to my feet. Warner and I manage to bind Juliette between us, and when I look over at him, I'm at least relieved to discover that he looks like he's struggling, too. I've never seen Warner struggle, not really, and I'm pretty sure I've never seen him sweat. But as much as I'd love to laugh a little right now, the sight of him straining so hard just to hold on to her only sends a fresh wave of fear through me. I have no idea how long he's been trying to restrain her all by himself. I have no idea what would've happened to her if he hadn't been there to hold on. And I have no idea what would happen to her right now, if we were to let go.

Something about that realization gives me renewed strength. It takes choice out of the situation. J needs us right now, period.

Which means I have to be stronger.

Standing upright like this has made us an easy target in all this madness, and I call out a warning as a piece of debris flies toward us. I pivot sharply to protect J, but take a hit to my spine, the pain so breathtaking I'm seeing stars. My back was already injured earlier tonight, and the bruises are bound to be worse now. But when Warner locks eyes with me in a sudden, terrified panic, I nod, letting him know I'm okay. I've got her.

Inch by agonizing inch, we move back toward the Sanctuary.

We're dragging J like she's Jesus between us, her head flung backward, feet dragging across the ground. She's finally stopped screaming, but now she's convulsing, her body seizing uncontrollably, and Warner looks like he's hanging on to his sanity by a single, fraying thread.

It feels like centuries pass before we see Nazeera again, but the rational part of my brain suspects it must've been only twenty, thirty minutes. Who knows. I'm sure she was trying her best to get back here with people who could help, but it feels like we're too late. Everything feels too late.

I have no idea what the hell is happening anymore.

Yesterday, this morning—an hour ago—I was worried about James and Adam. I thought our problems were simple and straightforward: get the kids back, kill the supreme commanders, have a nice lunch.

But now—

Nazeera and Castle and Brendan and Nouria rush to a sudden stop before us. They look between us.

They look beyond us.

Their eyes go round, their lips parting as they gasp. I crane my neck to see what they're seeing and realize that there's a tidal wave of fire headed straight toward us.

I think I'm going to collapse.

My body is worse than unsteady. By this point, my legs are made of rubber. I can barely support my own weight, and it's a miracle I'm holding on to J at all. In fact, a quick glance at Warner's clenched, insanely tense body is all it takes to realize that he's probably doing most of the work right now.

I don't know how any of us are going to survive this. I can't *move*. I sure as hell can't outrun a wave of fire.

And I don't really understand everything that happens next.

I hear an inhuman cry, and Stephan is suddenly rushing toward us. *Stephan.* He's suddenly in front of us, suddenly between us. He picks J up and into his arms like she might be a rag doll, and starts shouting at all of us to run. Castle hangs back to redirect water from a nearby well, and though his efforts at dousing the flames aren't entirely successful, it's enough to give us the edge we need to escape. Warner and I drag ourselves back to camp with the others, and the minute we cross the threshold into the Sanctuary, we're met with a frantic sea of faces. Countless figures surge forward, their shouts and cries and hysterical commotion fusing into a single, unbroken soundstorm. Logically, I understand why people are out here, worried, crying, shouting unanswered questions at each other—but right now I just want them all to get the hell out of my way.

Nouria and Sam seem to read my mind.

They bark orders into the crowd and the nameless bodies begin to clear out. Stephan is no longer running, but walking briskly, elbowing people out of his way as necessary, and I'm grateful. But when Sonya and Sara come sprinting toward us, shouting for us to follow them to the medical tent, I nearly launch myself forward and kiss them both.

I don't.

Instead, I take a moment to search for Castle, wondering if he made it out okay. But when I look back, scanning our stretch of protected land, I experience a sudden, sobering moment of realization. The disparity between *in here* and *out there* is unreal.

In here, the sky is clear.

The weather, settled. The ground seems to have sutured itself back together. The wall of fire that tried to chase us all the way back to the Sanctuary is now nothing but fading smoke. The trees are in their upright positions; the hurricane is little more than a fine mist. The morning looks almost pretty. For a second I could've sworn I heard a bird chirping.

I'm probably out of my mind.

I collapse in the middle of a well-worn path leading back to our tents, my face thudding against wet grass. The smell of fresh, damp earth fills my head and I breathe it in, all of it. It's a balm. A miracle. *Maybe*, I think. Maybe we're going to be okay. Maybe I can close my eyes. Take a moment.

Warner stalks past my prone body, his motions so intense I'm startled upright, into a sitting position.

I have no idea how he's still moving.

He's not even wearing shoes. No shirt, no socks, no shoes. Just a pair of sweatpants. I notice for the first time that he's got a huge gash across his chest. Several cuts on his arms. A nasty scratch on his neck. Blood is dripping slowly down his torso, and Warner doesn't even seem to notice. Scars all over his back, blood smeared across his front. He looks insane. But he's still moving, his eyes hot with rage and something else— Something that scares the shit out of me.

He catches up to Stephan, who's still holding J—who's

still having seizures—and I crawl toward a tree, using the trunk to hoist myself off the ground. I drag myself after them, flinching involuntarily at a sudden breeze. I turn too fast, scanning the open woods for debris or a flying boulder, and find only Nazeera, who rests a hand on my arm.

"Don't worry," she says. "We're safe within the borders of the Sanctuary."

I blink at her. And then around, at the familiar white tents that cloak every solid, freestanding structure on the glorified campsite that is this place of refuge.

Nazeera nods. "Yeah—that's what the tents are for. Nouria enhanced all of her light protections with some kind of antidote that makes us immune to the illusions Emmaline creates. Both acres of land are protected, and the reflective material covering the tents provides more assured protection indoors."

"How do you know all of that?"

"I asked."

I blink at her again. I feel dumb. Numb. Like I broke something deep inside my brain. Deep inside my body.

"Juliette," I say.

It's the only word I've got right now, and Nazeera doesn't even bother to correct me, to tell me her real name is Ella. She just takes my hand and squeezes.

ELLA

~~JULIETTE~~

When I dream, I dream of sound.

Rain, taking its time, softly popping against concrete. Rain, gathering, drumming, until sound turns into static. Rain, so sudden, so strong, it startles itself. I dream of water dripping down lips and tips of noses, rain falling off branches into shallow, murky pools. I hear death when puddles shatter, assaulted by heavy feet.

I hear leaves—

Leaves, shuddering under the weight of resignation, yoked to branches too easily bent, broken. I dream of wind, lengths of it. Yards of wind, acres of wind, infinite whispers fusing to create a single breeze. I hear wind comb the wild grass of distant mountains, I hear wind howling confessions in empty, lonely plains. I hear the *sh sh sh* of desperate rivers trying to hush the world in a fruitless effort to hush itself.

But

> buried

in the din

is a single scream so steady it goes every day unheard. We see, but do not understand the way it stutters hearts, clenches jaws, curls fingers into fists. It's a surprise, always a surprise, when it finally stops screaming long enough to

speak.
    Fingers tremble.
    Flowers die.
    The sun flinches, the stars expire.
    You are in a room, a closet, a vault, no key—
    Just a single voice that says

    Kill me

KENJI

J is sleeping.

She seems so close to death I can hardly look at her. Skin so white it's blue. Lips so blue they're purple. Somehow, in the last couple of hours, she lost weight. She looks like a little bird, young and small and fragile. Her long hair is fanned around her face and she's motionless, a little blue doll with her face pointed straight up at the ceiling. She looks like she could be lying in a casket.

I don't say any of this out loud, of course.

Warner seems pretty close to death himself. He looks pale, disoriented. Sickly.

And he's become impossible to talk to.

These past months of forced camaraderie nearly had me brainwashed; I'd almost forgotten what Warner used to be like.

Cold. Cutting. Eerily quiet.

He seems like an echo of himself right now, sitting stiffly in a chair next to her bed. We dragged J back here hours ago and he still won't really look at anyone. The cut on his chest looks even worse now, but he does nothing about it. He disappeared at one point, but only for a couple of minutes, and returned wearing his boots. He didn't bother to wipe the blood off his body. Didn't stop long enough to put on a shirt. He could easily steal Sonya's and Sara's powers to heal himself, but he makes no effort. He refuses to be touched. He refuses to eat. The few words out of his mouth were so scathing he made three different people cry. Nouria finally told him that if he didn't stop attacking her teammates she'd take him out back and shoot him. I think it was Warner's lack of protest that kept her from following through.

He's nothing but thorns.

Old Kenji would've shrugged it off and rolled his eyes. Old Kenji would've thrown a dart at Dickhead Warner and, honestly, would've probably been happy to see him suffer like this.

But I'm not that guy anymore.

I know Warner too well now. I know how much he loves J. I know he'd turn his skin inside out just to make her happy. He wanted to marry her, for God's sake. And I just watched him nearly kill himself to save her, suffering for hours through the worst levels of hell just to keep her alive.

Almost two hours, to be exact.

Warner said he'd been out there with J for nearly an hour before I showed up, and it was at least another forty-five minutes before the girls were able to stabilize her. He spent nearly two hours physically fighting to keep Juliette from harm, protecting her with his own body as he was lashed by fallen trees, flying rocks, errant debris, and violent winds. The girls said they could tell just by looking at him that he had at least two broken ribs. A fracture in his right arm. A dislocated shoulder. Probably internal bleeding. They raged at him so much that he finally sat down in a chair, wrapped his good hand around the wrist of his injured arm, and pulled his own shoulder back in place. The only proof of his pain was a single, sharp breath.

Sonya screamed, rushing forward, too late to stop him.

And then he broke open the seam at the ankle of his sweatpants, tore off a length of cotton, and made a sling for his freshly socketed arm. Only after that did he finally look up at the girls.

"Now leave me alone," he said darkly.

Sonya and Sara looked so frustrated—their eyes blazing with rare anger—I almost didn't recognize them.

I know he's being an asshole.

I know he's being stubborn and stupid and cruel. But I can't find the strength to be mad at him right now. I can't.

My heart is breaking for the guy.

We're all standing around J's bed, just staring at her. A monitor beeps softly in the corner. The room smells like chemicals. Sonya and Sara had to inject J with serious tranquilizers in order to get her body to settle, but it seemed to help: the moment she slowed down, the world outside did, too.

The Reestablishment was quick on the uptake, doing such seamless damage control I almost couldn't believe it. They capitalized on the problem, claiming that what happened this morning was a taste of future devastation. They claimed that they managed to get it under control before it got any worse, and they reminded the people to be grateful for the protections provided by The Reestablishment; that, without them, the world would be a lot worse. It fairly scared the shit out of everyone. Things feel a lot quieter now. The civilians seem subdued in a way they weren't before. It's stunning, really, how The Reestablishment managed to convince people that the sky collapsing while the sun just *disappeared* for a full minute were normal things that could happen in the world.

It's unbelievable that they feed people that kind of bullshit, and it's unbelievable that people eat it up.

But when I'm being super honest with myself, I'll admit that what scares me the most is that, if I didn't know any better, I might've eaten that shit up, too.

I sigh, hard. Drag a hand down my face.

This morning feels like a weird dream.

Surreal, like one of those melting clock paintings The Reestablishment destroyed. And I'm so wrung out, so tired, I don't even have the energy to be angry. I've only got enough energy to be sad.

We're all just really, really sad.

The few of us who could squeeze into this room: me, Castle, Nouria, Sam, Superman (my new nickname for Stephan), Haider, Nazeera, Brendan, Winston, Warner. All of us, sad, sorry sacks. Sonya and Sara left for a bit, but they'll be coming back soon, and when they do, they'll be sad, too.

Ian and Lily wanted to be here, but Warner kicked them out. He just straight up told them to get out, for reasons he didn't offer to disclose. He didn't raise his voice. Didn't even look at Ian. Just told him to turn around and leave. Brendan was so stunned his eyes nearly fell out of his head. But all of us were too afraid of Warner to say anything.

A small, guilty part of me wondered if maybe Warner knew that Ian talked shit about him that one time, that Warner knew (who knows how) that Ian didn't want to make the effort to go after him and J when we lost them at the symposium.

I don't know. It's just a theory. But it's obvious Warner is done playing the game. He's done with courtesy, done with patience, done with giving a single shit about anyone but J. Which means the tension in here is insane right now. Even Castle seems a little nervous around Warner, like he's not sure about him anymore.

The problem is, we all got too comfortable.

For a couple of months we forgot that Warner was scary. He smiled like four and a half times and we decided to forget that he was basically a psychopath with a long history of ruthless murder. We thought he'd been reformed. Gone soft. We forgot that he was only tolerating any of us because of Juliette.

And now, without her—

He no longer seems to belong.

Without her, we're fracturing. The energy in this room has palpably changed. We don't really feel like a team anymore, and it's scary how quickly it happened. If only Warner weren't so determined to be a dickhead. If only he weren't so eager to put on his old skin, to alienate everyone in this room. If only he'd muster the smallest bit of goodwill, we could turn this whole thing around.

Seems unlikely.

I'm not as terrified as the others, but I'm not stupid, either. I know his threats of violence aren't a bluff. The only people unperturbed are the supreme kids. They look right at home with this version of him. Haider, maybe most of all. That dude always seemed on edge, like he had no idea who Warner had turned into and he didn't know how to process the change. But now? No problem. Super comfortable with psycho Warner. Old pals.

Nouria finally breaks the silence.

Gently, she clears her throat. A couple of people lift their heads. Warner glares at the floor.

"Kenji," she says softly, "can I talk to you for a minute? Outside?"

My body stiffens.

I look around, uncertain, like she's got me confused with someone else. Castle and Nazeera turn sharply in my direction, surprise widening their eyes. Sam, on the other hand, is staring at her wife, struggling to hide her frustration.

"Um"—I scratch my head—"maybe we should talk in here," I say. "As a group?"

"Outside, Kishimoto." Nouria is on her feet, the softness gone from her voice, her face. "Now, please."

Reluctantly, I get to my feet.

I lock eyes with Nazeera, wondering if she has an opinion on the situation, but her expression is unreadable.

Nouria calls my name again.

I shake my head but follow her out the door. She leads me around a corner, into a narrow hallway.

It smells overwhelmingly like bleach.

J is posted up inside the *MT*—an obvious nickname for their medical tent—which feels like a misnomer, actually, because the tent element is entirely superficial. The inside of the building is a lot more like a proper hospital, with individual suites and operating rooms. It blew my mind a little the first time I first walked through here, because this space is super different from what we had at Omega Point and Sector 45. But then, before Sonya and Sara showed up, the Sanctuary had no healers. Their medical work was a lot more traditional: practiced by a handful of self-taught doctors and surgeons. There's something about their old-fashioned, life-threatening medical practices that makes this place feel a lot more like a relic of our old world. A building full of fear.

Out here, in the main corridor, I can hear more clearly the standard sounds of a hospital—machines beeping, carts rolling, occasional moans, shouts, pages over an intercom. I flatten myself against the wall as a team of people barrels past, pushing a gurney down the hallway. Its occupant is an elderly man hooked up to an IV, an oxygen mask on his face. When he sees Nouria, he lifts his hand in a weak wave.

Attempts a smile.

Nouria gives him a bright smile in return, holding it steady until the man is wheeled into another room. The moment he's out of sight, she corners me. Her eyes flash, her dark brown skin glowing in the dim light like a warning. My spine straightens.

Nouria is surprisingly terrifying.

"What the hell happened out there?" she says. "What did you do?"

"Okay, first of all"—I hold up both hands—"I didn't *do* anything. And I already told you guys exactly what happened—"

"You never told me that Emmaline tried to access your mind."

That stops me up. "What? Yes I did. I literally told you that. I used those exact words."

"But you didn't provide the necessary details," she says. "How did it start? What did it feel like? Why did she let go?"

"I don't know," I say, frowning. "I don't understand what happened—all I've got are guesses."

"Then *guess*," she says, narrowing her eyes. "Unless— She's not still in your head, is she?"

"What? No."

Nouria sighs, more irritation than relief. She touches her fingers to her temples in a show of resignation. "This doesn't make sense," she says, almost to herself. "Why would she try so hard to infiltrate Ella's mind? Why *yours*? I thought she was fighting against The Reestablishment. This feels more like she's working for them."

I shake my head. "I don't think so. When Emmaline was in my head it felt more to me like a desperate, last-ditch effort—like she was worried J wouldn't have the heart to kill her, and she was hoping I'd get it done faster. She called me brave, but weak. Like, I don't know, maybe this sounds crazy, but it felt almost like Emmaline thought—for a second—that if I'd made it that far in her presence, I might've been strong enough to contain her. But then she jumped in my head and realized she was wrong. I wasn't strong enough to hold her mind, and definitely not strong enough to kill her." I shrug. "So she bailed."

Nouria straightens. When she looks at me, she looks stunned. "You think she's really that desperate to die? You think she wouldn't put up a fight if someone tried to kill her?"

"Yeah, it's awful," I say, looking away. "Emmaline's in a really bad place."

"But she can exist, at least partially, in Ella's body." Nouria frowns. "Both consciousnesses in one person. How?"

"I don't know." I shrug again. "J said that Evie did a bunch of work on her muscles and bones and stuff while she was in Oceania—priming her for Operation Synthesis—to basically become Emmaline's new body. So I think, ultimately, J playing host to Emmaline is what Evie had planned all along."

"And Emmaline must've known," Nouria says quietly.

It's my turn to frown. "What are you getting at?"

"I don't know, exactly. But this situation complicates things. Because if our goal was to kill Emmaline, and Emmaline is now living in Ella's body—"

"Wait." My stomach does a terrifying flip. "Is that why we're out here? Is this why you're being so secretive?"

"Lower your voice," Nouria says sharply, glancing at something behind me.

"I will not lower my fucking voice," I say. "What the hell are you thinking? What are you— Wait, what do you keep looking at?" I crane my neck but see only a blank wall behind my head. My heart is racing, my mind working too fast. I whip back around to face her.

"Tell me the truth," I demand. "Is this why you cornered me? Because you're trying to figure out if we can kill J while she's got Emmaline inside of her? Is that it? *Are you insane?*"

Nouria glares at me. "Is it insane to want to save the world? Emmaline is at the center of everything wrong with our universe right now, and she's trapped inside a body lying in a room just down the *hall*. Do you know how long we've been waiting for a moment like this? Don't get me wrong, I don't love this line of thinking, Kishimoto, but I'm not—"

"Nouria."

At the sound of her wife's voice, Nouria goes visibly still. She takes a step back from me, and I finally relax. A little.

We both turn around.

Sam's not alone. Castle is standing next to her, both of

them looking more than a little pissed.

"Leave him alone," Castle says. "Kenji's been through enough already. He needs time to recuperate."

Nouria tries to respond, but Sam cuts her off. "How many times are we going to talk about this?" she says. "You can't just shut me out when you're stressed. You can't just go off on your own without telling me." Her blond hair falls into her eyes and, frustrated, she shoves the strands out of her face. "I'm your *partner*. This is our Sanctuary. Our life. We built it together, remember?"

"Sam." Nouria sighs, squeezing her eyes closed. "You know I'm not trying to shut you out. You know that's not—"

"You are literally shutting me out. You literally shut the door."

My eyebrows fly up my forehead. Castle and I connect glances: we seem to have walked into a private argument.

Good.

"Hey, Sam," I say, "did you know that your wife wants to kill Juliette?"

Castle gasps.

Sam's body goes slack. She stares at Nouria, stunned.

"Yeah," I say, nodding. "Nouria wants to murder her right now, actually, while she's still comatose. What do you think?" I tilt my head at Sam. "Good idea? Bad idea? Maybe sleep on it?"

"That can't be true," Sam says, still staring at her wife. "Tell me he's joking."

"It's not that simple," says Nouria, who shoots me a

look so venomous I almost feel bad for being petty. I don't actually want Nouria and Sam to fight, but whatever. She can't casually suggest murdering my best friend and expect me to be nice about it. "I was just pointing out th—"

"Okay, enough."

I look up at the sound of Nazeera's voice. I have no idea when she showed up, but she's suddenly in front of us, arms crossed against her chest. "We're not doing this. No side conversations. No subgroups. We all need to talk about the impending shitstorm headed our way, and if we're going to have any chance of figuring out how to fight it, we have to stick together."

"Which impending shitstorm?" I ask. "Please be specific."

"I agree with Nazeera," Sam says, her eyes narrowing at her wife. "Let's all go back inside the room and talk. To each other. At the same time."

"Sam," Nouria tries again. "I'm not—"

"Bloody hell." Stephan stops short at the sight of us, his shoes squeaking on the tile. He seems to tower over our group, looking too polished and civilized to belong here. "What on earth are you lot doing out here?"

Then, quietly, to Nazeera: "And why've you left us alone with him? He's being a proper ass. Nearly made Haider cry just now."

Nazeera sighs, closing her eyes as she pinches the bridge of her nose. "Haider does this to himself. I don't understand why he's deluded himself into thinking Warner is his best friend."

"That, he might well be," Stephan says, frowning. "The bar is quite low, as you know."

Nazeera sighs again.

"If it makes Haider feel any better, Warner's being equally horrible to just about everyone," Sam says. She looks at Nouria. "Amir still won't tell me what Warner said to him, by the way."

"Amir?" Castle frowns. "The young man who oversees the patrol unit?"

Sam nods. "He quit this morning."

"No." Nouria blinks, stunned. "You're kidding."

"I wish I were. I had to give his job to Jenna."

"This is crazy." Nouria shakes her head. "It's only been three days and already we're falling apart."

"Three days?" says Stephan. "Three days since *we* arrived, is that it? That's not a very nice thing to say."

"We are not falling apart," Nazeera says suddenly. Angrily. "We can't afford to fall apart. Not right now. Not with The Reestablishment about to appear at our doorstep."

"Wait—what?" Sam frowns. "The Reestablishment has no idea where we—"

"God, this is so depressing," I groan, running both hands through my hair. "Why are we all at each other's throats right now? If Juliette were awake, she'd be so pissed at all of us. And she'd be super pissed at Warner for acting like this, for pushing us apart. Doesn't he realize that?"

"No," Castle says quietly. "Of course he doesn't."

A sharp *knock knock*—

And we all look up.

Winston and Brendan are peering around the corner at us, Brendan's closed fist held aloft an inch from the wall. He knocks once more against the plaster.

Nouria exhales loudly. "Can we help you?"

They march over to us, their expressions so different it's almost—*almost*—funny. Like light and dark, these two.

"Hello, everyone," Brendan says, smiling brightly.

Winston yanks the glasses off his face. Glowers. "What the hell is going on? Why are you all having a conference out here on your own? And why did you leave us alone with him?"

"We didn't," I try to say.

"We're not," Sam and Nazeera say at the same time.

Winston rolls his eyes. Shoves his glasses back on. "I'm getting too fucking old for this."

"You just need some coffee," Brendan says, gently patting Winston's shoulder. "Winston doesn't sleep very well at night," he explains to the rest of us.

Winston perks up. Goes instantly pink.

I smile.

I swear, it's all I do. I just smile, and in a fraction of a second Winston's locked eyes with me, his death stare screaming, *Shut your mouth, Kishimoto*, and I don't even have a chance to be offended before he turns abruptly away, his ears bright red.

An uncomfortable silence descends.

I wonder, for the first time, if it's really possible that Brendan has no idea how Winston feels about him. He seems oblivious, but who knows. It's definitely not a secret to the rest of us.

"Well." Castle takes a sharp breath, claps his hands together. "We were about to go back inside the room to have a proper discussion. So if you gentlemen"—he nods at Winston and Brendan—"wouldn't mind turning back the way you came? We're getting a bit cramped in the hall."

"Right." Brendan glances quickly behind him. "But, um, do you think we might wait another minute or so? Haider was crying, you see, and I think he'd appreciate the privacy."

"Oh, for the love of God," I groan.

"What happened?" Nazeera asks, concern creasing her forehead. "Should I go in there?"

Brendan shrugs, his extremely white face glowing almost neon in this dark corridor. "He said something to Warner in Arabic, I believe. And I don't know exactly what Warner said back to him, but I'm pretty sure he told Haider to sod off, in one way or another."

"Asshole," Winston mutters.

"It's true, unfortunately." Brendan frowns.

I shake my head. "All right, okay, I know he's being a dick, but I think we can cut Warner a little slack, right? He's devastated. Let's not forget the hell he went through this morning."

"Pass." Winston crosses his arms, anger seeming to lift him out of embarrassment. "Haider is *crying*. Haider

Ibrahim. Son of the supreme commander of Asia. He's sitting in a hospital chair *crying* because Warner hurt his feelings. I don't know how you can defend that."

"To be fair," Stephan interjects, "Haider's always been a bit delicate."

"Listen, I'm not defending Warner, I'm just—"

"*Enough.*" Castle's voice is loud. Sharp. "That is quite enough." Something tugs gently at my neck, startling me, and I notice Castle's hands are up in the air. Like he just physically turned our heads to face him. He points back down the hall, toward J's recovery room. I feel a slight push at my back.

"Back inside. All of you. Now."

Haider doesn't seem any different when we step back inside the room. No evidence of tears. He's standing in a corner, alone, staring into the middle distance. Warner is in exactly the same position we left him in, sitting stiffly beside J.

Staring at her.

Staring at her like he might be able to will her back into consciousness.

Nazeera claps her hands together, hard. "All right," she says, "no more interruptions. We need to talk about strategy before we do anything else."

Sam frowns. "Strategy for what? Right now, we need to discuss Emmaline. We need to understand the events of the morning before we can even think about discussing the next steps forward."

"We *are* going to talk about Emmaline, and the events of the morning," Nazeera says. "But in order to discuss the Emmaline situation, we'll need to talk about the Ella situation, which will necessitate a conversation about a larger, overarching strategy—one that will dovetail neatly with a plan to get the supreme kids back."

Castle stares at her, looking just as confused as Sam. "You want to discuss the supreme kids right now? Isn't it better if we star—"

"Idiots," Haider mutters under his breath.

We ignore him.

Well, most of us. Nazeera is shaking her head, giving the room at large that same look she gives me so often—the one that expresses her general exhaustion at being surrounded by idiots.

"How are you so unable to see how these things connect? The Reestablishment is looking for us. More specifically, they're looking for Ella. We were supposed to be in hiding, remember? But Emmaline's egregious display this morning just blew the cover on our location. We all saw the news— you all read the emergency reports. The Reestablishment did serious damage control to subdue the citizens. That means they know what happened here."

Again, more blank stares.

"Emmaline just led them directly to Ella," she says. She says this last sentence really slowly, like she fears for our collective intelligence. "Whether on purpose or by accident, The Reestablishment now has an approximate idea of our location."

Nouria looks stricken.

"Which means," Haider says, drawing the words out with his own irritating condescension, "they're much closer to finding us now than they were a few hours ago."

Everyone sits up straighter in their chairs. The air is suddenly different, intense in a new way. Nouria and Sam exchange worried glances.

It's Nouria who says, "You really think they know where we are?"

"I knew this would happen," Sam says, shaking her head.

Castle stiffens. "What's that supposed to mean?"

Sam bristles, but her words are calm when she says: "We took an enormous risk letting your team stay here. We risked our livelihood and the safety of our own men and women to allow you to take shelter among us. You're here for three days and already you've managed to disclose our location to the world."

"We haven't disclosed anything— And what happened today was no one's fault—"

Nouria lifts a hand. "Stop," she says, shooting a look at Sam, a look so brief I almost miss it. "We're losing our focus again. Nazeera was right when she said we were all in this together. In fact, we came together for the express purpose of defeating The Reestablishment. It's what we've always been working toward. We were never meant to live forever in self-made cages and communities."

"I understand that," Sam says, her steady voice belying the anger in her eyes. "But if they really know which sector to search, we could be discovered in a matter of days. The Reestablishment will be increasing their military presence within the hour, if they haven't done so already."

"They have done," Stephan says, looking just as exasperated as Nazeera. "Of course they have."

"So naive, these people," Haider says, shooting a dark look at his sister.

Nazeera sighs.

Winston swears.

Sam shakes her head.

"So what do you propose?" Winston says, but he's not looking at Nouria or Sam or Castle. He's looking at Nazeera.

Nazeera doesn't hesitate.

"We wait. We wait for Ella to wake up," she says. "We need to know as much as we can about what happened to her, and we need to prioritize her security above all else. There's a reason why Anderson wants her so desperately, and we need to find out what that reason is before we take any next steps."

"But what about a plan for getting the other kids back?" Winston asks. "If we wait for Ella to wake up before making a move to save them, we could be too late."

Nazeera shakes her head. "The plan for the other kids has to be tied up in the plan to save Ella," she says. "I'm certain that Anderson is using the kidnapping of the supreme kids as bait. A bullshit lure designed to draw us out into the open. Plus, he designed that scheme before he had any idea we'd accidentally out ourselves, which only further supports my theory that this was a bullshit lure. He was only hoping we'd step outside of our protections just long enough to give away our approximate location."

"Which we've now done," Brendan says, quietly horrified.

I drop my head in my hands. *Shit.*

"It seems clear that Anderson wasn't planning on doing any kind of honest trade for the hostages," Nazeera says. "How could he possibly? He never told us where he was. Never told us where to meet him. And most interestingly: he didn't even ask for the rest of the supreme kids. Whatever his plans are, he doesn't seem to require the full set of us. He didn't want Warner or me or Haider or Stephan. All he wanted was Ella, right?" She glances at Nouria. "That's what you said. That he only wanted Ella?"

"Yes," Nouria says. "That's true— But I still don't think I understand. You just laid out all the reasons for us to go to war, but your plan of attack involves doing nothing."

Nazeera can't hide her irritation. "We should still be making plans to fight," she says. "We'll need a plan to find the kids, steal them back, and then, eventually, murder our parents. But I'm proposing we wait for Ella until we make any moves. I'm suggesting we do a full and complete lockdown here at the Sanctuary until Ella is conscious. No going in or out until she wakes up. If you need emergency supplies, Kenji and I can use our stealth to go on discreet missions to find what you need. The Reestablishment will have soldiers posted up everywhere, monitoring every movement in this area, but as long as we remain isolated, we should be able to buy ourselves some time."

"But we have no idea how long it'll take for Ella to wake up," Sam says. "It could be weeks—it could be *never*—"

"Our mission," Nazeera says, cutting her off, "has to be about protecting Ella at all costs. If we lose her, we lose everything. That's it. That's the whole plan right now. Keeping Ella alive and safe is the priority. Saving the kids is secondary. Besides, the kids will be fine. Most of us have been through worse in basic training simulations."

Haider laughs.

Stephan makes an amused sound of agreement.

"But what about James?" I protest. "What about Adam? They're not like you guys. They've never been prepared for this shit. For God's sake, James is only ten years old."

Nazeera looks at me then, and for a moment, she falters. "We'll do our best," she says. And though her words sound genuinely sympathetic, that's all she gives me. *Our best.*

That's it.

I feel my heart rate begin to spike.

"So we're just supposed to risk letting them die?" Winston asks. "We're just supposed to gamble on a ten-year-old's life? Let him remain imprisoned and tortured at the hands of a sociopath and hope for the best? Are you serious?"

"Sometimes sacrifices are necessary," Stephan says.

Haider merely shrugs.

"No way, no way," I say, panicking. "We need another plan. A better plan. A plan that saves everyone, and quickly."

Nazeera looks at me like she feels sorry for me.

That's enough to straighten my spine.

I spin around, my panic transforming quickly into anger. I home in on Warner, sitting in the corner like a useless sack of meat. "What about you?" I say to him. "What do you think about this? You're okay with letting your own brothers die?"

The silence is suddenly suffocating.

Warner doesn't answer me for a long time, and the room is too stunned at my stupidity to interfere. I just broke a tacit agreement to pretend Warner doesn't exist, but now that I've provoked the beast, everyone wants to see what happens next.

Eventually, Warner sighs.

It's not a calm, relaxing sound. It's a harsh, angry sound that only seems to leave him more tightly wound. He doesn't even lift his head when he says, "I'm okay with a lot of things, Kishimoto."

But I'm too far gone to turn back now.

"That's bullshit," I say, my fists clenching. "That's bullshit, and you know it. You're better than this."

Warner says nothing. He doesn't move a muscle, doesn't stop staring at the same spot on the floor. And I know I shouldn't antagonize him—I *know* he's in a fragile state right now—but I can't help it. I can't let this go, not like this.

"So that's it? After everything—that's it? You're just going to let James die?" My heart is pounding, hard and heavy in my chest. I feel my frustration peaking, spiraling.

"What do you think J would say right now, huh? How do you think she'd feel about you letting someone murder a child?"

Warner stands up.

Fast, too fast. Warner is on his feet and I'm suddenly sorry. I was feeling a little brave but now I'm feeling nothing but regret. I take an uncertain step back. Warner follows. Suddenly he's standing in front of me, studying my eyes, but it turns out I can't hold his gaze for longer than a second. His eyes are such a pale green they're disorienting to look at on his good days. But today— Right now—

He looks insane.

I notice, when I turn away, that he's still got blood on his fingers. Blood smeared across his throat. Blood streaking through his gold hair.

"*Look at me*," he says.

"Um, no thanks."

"Look at me," he says again, quietly this time.

I don't know why I do it. I don't know why I give in. I don't know why there's still a part of me that believes in Warner and hopes to see something human in his eyes. But when I finally look up, I lose that hope. Warner looks cold. Detached. All wrong.

I don't understand it.

I mean, I'm devastated, too. I'm upset, *too*, but I didn't turn into a completely different person. And right now, Warner seems like a completely different person. Where's the guy who was going to propose to my best friend? Where's the guy having a panic attack on his bedroom floor? Where's the guy who laughed so hard his cheeks dimpled? Where's the guy I thought was my friend?

"What happened to you, man?" I whisper. "Where'd you go?"

"Hell," he says. "I've finally found hell."

ELLA
~~JULIETTE~~

I wake in waves, consciousness bathing me slowly. I break the surface of sleep, gasping for air before I'm pulled under
  another current
  another current
  another

Memories wrap around me, bind my bones. I sleep. When I sleep, I dream I am sleeping. In those dreams, I dream I am dead. I can't tell real from fiction, can't tell dreams from truth, can't tell time anymore it might've been days or years who knows who knows I begin to
  s
   t
    i
  r

I dream even as I wake, dream of red lips and slender fingers, dream of eyes, hundreds of eyes, I dream of air and anger and death.

I dream Emmaline's dreams.

She's here.

She went quiet once she settled here, in my mind. She stilled, retreated. Hid from me, from the world. I feel heavy with her presence but she does not speak, she only decays, her mind decomposing slowly, leaving compost in its wake. I am heavy with it, heavy with her refuse. I am incapable of carrying this weight, no matter how strong Evie made me I am incapable, incompatible. I am not enough to hold our minds, combined. Emmaline's powers are too much. I drown in it, I drown in it, I

gasp

when my head breaks the surface again.

I drag air into my lungs, beg my eyes to open and they laugh. Eyes laughing at lungs gasping at pain ricocheting up my spine.

Today, there is a boy.

Not one of the regular boys. Not Aaron or Stephan or Haider. This is a new boy, a boy I've never met before.

I can tell, just by standing next to him, that he's terrified.

We stand in the big, wide room filled with trees. We stare at the white birds, the birds with the yellow streaks and the crowns on their heads. The boy stares at the birds like he's never seen anything like them. He stares at everything with surprise. Or fear. Or worry. It makes me realize that he doesn't know how to hide his emotions. Whenever Mr. Anderson looks at him, he sucks in his breath. Whenever I look at him, he goes bright red. Whenever Mum speaks to him, he stutters.

"What do you think?" Mr. Anderson says to Mum. He tries to whisper, but this room is so big it echoes a little.

Mum tilts her head at the boy. Studies him. "He's what, six years old now?" But she doesn't wait for him to answer. Mum just shakes her head and sighs. "Has it really been that long?"

Mr. Anderson looks at the boy. "Unfortunately."

I glance at him, at the boy standing next to me, and watch as he stiffens. Tears spring to his eyes, and it hurts to watch. It hurts so much. I hate Mr. Anderson so much. I don't know why Mum likes him. I don't know why anyone likes him. Mr. Anderson is an awful person, and he hurts Aaron all the time. In fact— Now that I think about it, there's something about this boy that reminds me of Aaron. Something about his eyes.

"Hey," I whisper, and turn to face him.

He swallows, hard. Wipes at his tears with the edge of his sleeve.

"Hey," I try again. "I'm Ella. What's your name?"

The boy looks up, then. His eyes are a deep, dark blue. He's the saddest boy I've ever met, and it makes me sad just to look at him.

"I'm A-Adam," he says quietly. He turns red again.

I take his hand in mine. Smile at him. "We're going to be friends, okay? Don't worry about Mr. Anderson. No one likes him. He's mean to all of us, I promise."

Adam laughs, but his eyes are still red. His hand trembles in mine, but he doesn't let go.

"I don't know," he whispers. "He's pretty mean to me."

I squeeze his hand. "Don't worry," I say. "I'll protect you."

Adam smiles at me then. Smiles a real smile. But when we finally look up again, Mr. Anderson is staring at us.

He looks angry.

There's a buzzing building inside of me, a mass of sound that consumes thought, devours conversation.

We are flies—gathering, swarming—bulging eyes and fragile bones flittering nervously toward imagined destinies. We hurl our bodies at the panes of tantalizing windows, aching for the world promised on the other side. Day after day we drag injured wings and eyes and organs around the same four walls; open or closed, the exits elude us. We hope to be rescued by a breeze, hoping for a chance to see the sun.

Decades pass. Centuries stack together.

Our bruised bodies still careen through the air. We continue to hurl ourselves at promises. There is madness in the repetition, in the repetition, in the repetition that underscores our lives. It is only in the desperate seconds before death that we realize the windows against which we broke our bodies were only mirrors, all along.

KENJI

It's been four days.

Four days of nothing. J is still sleeping. The twins are calling it a coma, but I'm calling it sleeping. I'm choosing to believe J is just really, really tired. She just needs to sleep off some stress and she'll be fine. This is what I keep telling everyone.

She'll be fine.

"She's just tired," I say to Brendan. "And when she wakes up she'll be glad we waited for her to go get James. It'll be fine."

We're in the Q, which is short for the quiet tent, which is stupid because it's never quiet in here. The Q is the default common room. It's a gathering space slash game room where people at the Sanctuary get together in the evenings and relax. I'm in the kitchen area, leaning against the insubstantial counter. Brendan and Winston and Ian and I are waiting for the electric kettle to boil.

Tea.

This was Brendan's idea, of course. For some reason, we could never get our hands on tea back at Omega Point. We only had coffee, and it was seriously rationed. Only after we moved onto base in Sector 45 did Brendan realize we could get our hands on tea, but even then he wasn't so militant about it.

But here—

Brendan's made it his mission to force hot tea down our throats every night. He doesn't even need the caffeine—his ability to manipulate electricity always keeps his body charged—but he says he likes it because he finds the ritual soothing. So, whatever. Now we gather in the evenings and drink tea. Brendan puts milk in his tea. Winston adds whiskey. Ian and I drink it black.

"Right?" I say, when no one answers me. "I mean, a coma is basically just a really long nap. J will be fine. The girls will get her better, and then she'll be fine, and everything will be fine. And James and Adam will be fine, obviously, because Sam's seen them and she says they're fine."

"Sam saw them and said they were unconscious," Ian says, opening and closing cabinets. When he finds what he's looking for—a sleeve of cookies—he rips the package open. He doesn't even have a chance to pull one free before Winston's swiped it.

"Those cookies are for our tea," he says sharply.

Ian glowers.

We all glance at Brendan, who seems oblivious to the sacrifices being made in his honor. "Yes, Sam said that they were unconscious," he says, collecting small spoons from a drawer. "But she also said they looked stable. Alive."

"Exactly," I say, pointing at Brendan. "Thank you. *Stable. Alive.* These are the critical words."

Brendan takes the rescued sleeve of cookies from Winston's proffered hand, and begins arranging dishes and flatware with a confidence that baffles us all. He doesn't look up when he says, "It's really kind of amazing, isn't it?"

Winston and I share a confused look.

"I wouldn't call it amazing," Ian says, plucking a spoon from the tray. He examines it. "But I guess forks and shit are pretty cool, as far as inventions go."

Brendan frowns. Looks up. "I'm talking about Sam. Her ability to see across long distances." He retrieves the spoon from Ian's hand and replaces it on the tray. "What a remarkable skill."

Sam's preternatural ability to see across long distances was what convinced us of Anderson's threats to begin with. Several days ago—when we first got the news about the kidnapping—she'd used both data and sheer determination to pinpoint Anderson's location to our old base at Sector 45. She'd spent a straight fourteen hours searching, and though she hadn't been able to get a visual on the other supreme kids, she'd been able to see flickers of James and Adam, who are the only ones I care about anyway. Those flickers of life—unconscious, but alive and stable—aren't much in the way of assurances, but I'm willing to take anything at this point.

"Anyway, yeah. Sam is great," I say, stretching out against the counter. "Which brings me back to my original point: Adam and James are going to be fine. And J is going to wake up soon and be fine. The world owes me at least that much, right?"

Brendan and Ian exchange glances. Winston takes off his glasses and cleans them, slowly, with the hem of his shirt.

The electric kettle pops and steams. Brendan drops a couple of tea bags into a proper teapot and fills its porcelain belly with the hot water from the kettle. He then wraps the teapot in a towel and hands it to Winston, and the two of them carry everything over to the little corner of the room we've been claiming for ourselves lately. It's nothing major, just a cluster of seats with a couple of low tables in the middle. The rest of the room is abuzz with activity. Lots of talking and mingling.

Nouria and Sam are alone in a corner, deep in conversation. Castle is talking quietly with the girls, Sonya and Sara. We've all been spending a lot of time here—pretty much everyone has—ever since the Sanctuary was declared officially on lockdown. We're all in this weird limbo right now; there's so much happening, but we're not allowed to leave the grounds. We can't go anywhere or do anything about anything. Not yet, anyway. Just waiting for J to wake up.

Any minute now.

There are a ton of other people here, too—but only some I'm beginning to recognize. I nod hello to a couple of people I know only by name, and drop into a soft, well-worn armchair. It smells like coffee and old wood in here, but I'm starting to like it. It's becoming a familiar routine. Brendan, as usual, finishes setting everything up on the coffee table.

Teacups, spoons, little plates and triangle napkins. A little pitcher for milk. He's really, really into this whole thing. He readjusts the cookies he'd already arranged on a plate, and smooths out the paper napkins. Ian stares at him with the same expression every night—like Brendan is crazy.

"Hey," Winston says sharply. "Knock it off."

"Knock what off?" Ian says, incredulous. "Come on, man, you don't think this is a little weird? Having tea parties every night?"

Winston lowers his voice to a whisper. "I'll kill you if you ruin this for him."

"All right, enough. I'm not deaf, you know." Brendan narrows his eyes at Ian. "And I don't care if you lot think it's weird. I've little left of England, save this."

That shuts us up.

I stare at the teapot. Brendan says it's steeping.

And then, suddenly, he claps his hands together. He stares straight at me, his ice-blue eyes and white-blond hair giving me Warner vibes. But somehow, even with all his bright, white, cold hues, Brendan is the opposite of Warner. Unlike Warner, Brendan glows. He's warm. Kind. Naturally hopeful and super smiley.

Poor Winston.

Winston, who's secretly in love with Brendan and too afraid of ruining their friendship to say anything about it. Winston thinks he's too old for Brendan, but the thing is— he's not getting any younger, either. I keep telling Winston that if he wants to make a move, he should do it now, while he's still got his original hips, and he says, *Ha ha I'll murder you, asshole*, and reminds me he's waiting for the right moment. But I don't know. Sometimes I think he'll keep it inside forever. And I'm worried it might kill him.

"So, listen," Brendan says carefully. "We wanted to talk to you."

I blink, refocusing. "Who? Me?"

I glance around at their faces. Suddenly, they all look serious. Too serious. I try to laugh when I ask, "What's going on? Is this some kind of intervention?"

"Yes," Brendan says. "Sort of."

I go suddenly stiff.

Brendan sighs.

Winston scratches a spot on his forehead.

Ian says, "Juliette is probably going to die, you know that, right?"

Relief and irritation flood through me simultaneously. I manage to roll my eyes and shake my head at the same time. "Stop doing this, Sanchez. Don't be that guy. It's not funny anymore."

"I'm not trying to be funny."

I roll my eyes again, this time looking to Winston for support, but he just shakes his head at me. His eyebrows furrow so hard his glasses slip down his nose. He tugs them off his face.

"This is serious," he says. "She's not okay. And even if she does wake up again— I mean, whatever happened to her—"

"She's not going to be the same," Brendan finishes for him.

"Says who?" I frown. "The girls said—"

"Bro, the girls said that something about her chemistry changed. They've been running tests on her for days. Emmaline did something weird to her—something that's, like, physically altered her DNA. Plus, her brain is fried."

"I know what they said," I snap, irritated. "I was there when they said it. But the girls were just being cautious. They think it's *possible* that whatever happened to her might've left some damage, but—this is Sonya and Sara we're talking about. They can heal anything. All we need to do is wait for J to wake up."

Winston shakes his head again. "They wouldn't be able to heal something like that," he says. "The girls can't repair that kind of neurological devastation. They might be able to keep her alive, but I'm not sure they'll be able t—"

"She might not even wake up," Ian says, cutting him off. "Like, ever. Or, best-case scenario, she could be in a coma for *years*. Listen, the point here is that we need to start making plans without her. If we're going to save James and Adam, we need to go now. I know Sam's been checking on them, and I know she says they're stable for now, but we can't wait anymore. Anderson doesn't know what happened to Juliette, which means he's still waiting for us to give her up. Which means Adam and James are still at risk— Which means we're running out of time. And, for once," he says, taking a breath, "I'm not the only one who feels this way."

I sit back, stunned. "You're messing with me, right?"

Brendan pours tea.

Winston pulls a flask out of his pocket and weighs it in his hand before holding it out to me. "Maybe you should have this tonight," he says.

I glare at him.

He shrugs, and empties half the flask into his teacup.

"Listen," Brendan says gently. "Ian is a beast with no bedside manner, but he's not wrong. It's time to think of a new plan. We all still love Juliette, it's just—" He cuts himself off, frowns. "Wait, is it Juliette or Ella? Was there ever a consensus?"

I'm still scowling when I say, "I'm calling her Juliette."

"But I thought she wanted to be called Ella," Winston says.

"She's in a fucking coma," Ian says, and takes a loud sip of tea. "She doesn't care what you call her."

"Don't be such a brute," Brendan says. "She's our friend."

"*Your* friend," he mutters.

"Wait— Is that what this is about?" I sit forward. "Are you jealous she never best-friended you, Sanchez?"

Ian rolls his eyes, looks away.

Winston is watching with fascinated interest.

"All right, drink your tea," Brendan says, biting into a biscuit. He gestures at me with the half-eaten cookie. "It's getting cold."

I shoot him a tired look, but I take an obligatory sip and nearly choke. It tastes weird tonight. And I'm about to push it away when I realize Brendan is still staring at me, so I take a long, disgusting pull of the dark liquid before replacing the cup in the saucer. I try not to gag.

"Okay," I say, slamming my palms down on my thighs. "Let's put it to a vote: Who here thinks Ian is annoyed that J didn't fall in love with him when she showed up at Point?"

Winston and Brendan share a look. Slowly, they both lift their hands.

Ian rolls his eyes again. *"Pendejos,"* he mutters.

"The theory holds at least a little water," Winston says.

"I have a girlfriend, dumbasses." And as if on cue, Lily looks up from across the room, locks eyes with Ian. She's sitting with Alia and some other girl I don't recognize.

Lily waves.

Ian waves back.

"Yes, but you're used to a certain level of attention," Winston says, reaching for a biscuit. He looks up, scans the room. "Like those girls, right over there," he says, gesturing with his head. "They've been staring at you since you walked in."

"They have not," Ian says, but he can't help but glance over.

"It's true." Brendan shrugs. "You're a handsome guy."

Winston chokes on his tea.

"Okay, enough." Ian holds up his hands. "I know you guys think this is hilarious, but I'm being serious. At the end of the day, Juliette is *your* friend. Not mine."

I exhale dramatically.

Ian shoots me a look. "When she first showed up at

Point, I tried reaching out to her, to offer her my friendship, and she never followed up. And even after we were taken hostage by Anderson"—he nods an acknowledgment at Brendan and Winston—"she took her sweet time trying to get information out of Warner. She never gave a shit about the rest of us, and all we've ever done is put everything on the line to protect her."

"Hey, that's not fair," Winston says, shaking his head. "She was in an awful position—"

"Whatever," Ian mutters. He looks down, into his tea. "This whole situation is some kind of bullshit."

"Cheers to that," Brendan says, refilling his cup. "Now have more tea."

Ian mutters a quiet, angry thank-you, and lifts the cup to his lips. Suddenly, he stiffens. "And then there's this," he says, raising an eyebrow. As if all that weren't enough, we have to deal with *this* douche bag." Ian gestures, with the teacup, toward the entrance.

Shit.

Warner is here.

"She brought him here," Ian is saying, but he has the sense, at least, to keep his voice down. "It's because of her that we have to tolerate this asshole."

"To be fair, that was originally Castle's idea," I point out.

Ian flips me off.

"What's he doing here?" Brendan asks quietly.

I shake my head and take another unconscious sip of my disgusting tea. There's something about the grossness that's beginning to feel familiar, but I can't put my finger on it.

I look up again.

I haven't spoken a word to Warner since that first day— The day J got attacked by Emmaline. He's been a ghost since then. No one has really seen him, no one but the supreme kids, I think.

He went straight back to his roots.

It looks like he finally took a shower, though. No blood. And I'm guessing he healed himself, though there's no way to be sure, because he's fully clothed, wearing an outfit I can only assume was borrowed from Haider. A lot of leather.

I watch, for only a few seconds, as he stalks clear across the room—straight through people and conversations and apologizing to no one—toward Sonya and Sara, who are still talking to Castle.

Whatever.

Dude doesn't even look at me anymore. Doesn't even acknowledge my existence. Not that I care. It's not like we were actually friends.

At least, that's what I keep telling myself.

Somehow I've already drained my teacup, because Brendan's refilled it. I throw back the fresh cup in a couple of quick gulps and shove a dry biscuit in my mouth. And then I shake my head. "All right, we're getting distracted," I say, and the words feel just a little too loud, even to my own ears. "Focus, please."

"Right," Winston says. "Focus. What are we focusing on?"

"New mission," Ian says, sitting back in his chair. He counts off on his fingers: "Save Adam and James. Kill the other supreme commanders. Finally get some sleep."

"Nice and easy," Brendan says. "I like it."

"You know what?" I say. "I think I should go talk to him."

Winston raises an eyebrow. "Talk to who?"

"Warner, obviously." My brain feels warm. A little fuzzy. "I should go talk to him. No one talks to him. Why are we just letting him revert back into an asshole? I should talk to him."

"That's a great idea," Ian says, smiling as he sits forward. "Go for it."

"Don't you dare listen to him," Winston says, shoving Ian back into his chair. "Ian just wants to watch you get murdered."

"Fucking rude, Sanchez."

Ian shrugs.

"On an unrelated note," Winston says to me. "How does your head feel?"

I frown, gingerly touching my fingers to my skull. "What do you mean?"

"I mean," Winston says, "that this is probably a good time to tell you I've been pouring whiskey in your tea all night."

"What the hell?" I sit up too fast. Bad idea. "Why?"

"You seemed stressed."

"I'm not stressed."

Everyone stares at me.

"All right, whatever," I say. "I'm stressed. But I'm not drunk."

"No." He peers at me. "But you probably need all the brain cells you can spare if you're going to talk to Warner. I would. I'm not too proud to admit that I find him genuinely terrifying."

Ian rolls his eyes. "There's nothing terrifying about that guy. His only problem is that he's an arrogant son of a *puta* with his own head stuck so far up his ass he ca—"

"Wait," I say, blinking. "Where'd he go?"

Everyone spins around, looking for him.

I swear, five seconds ago he was standing right there. I swivel my head back and forth like a cartoon character, understanding only vaguely that I'm moving both a little too fast and a little too slow due to Winston, number one idiot slash well-meaning friend. But in the process of scanning the room for Warner, I spot the one person I'd been making an effort to avoid:

Nazeera.

I fling myself back down in my chair too hard, nearly knocking myself out. I hunch over, breathing a little funny, and then, for no rational reason, I start laughing. Winston, Ian, and Brendan are all staring at me like I'm insane, and I don't blame them. I don't know what the hell is wrong with me. I don't even know why I'm hiding from Nazeera. There's nothing scary about her, not exactly. Nothing more scary than the fact that we haven't really discussed the last emotional conversation we had, shortly after she kicked me in the back and I nearly murdered her for it.

She told me I was her first kiss.

And then the sky melted and Juliette was possessed by her sister and the romantic moment was forever interrupted. It's been about five days since she and I had that conversation, and ever since then it's just been super stress and work and more stress and Anderson is an asshole and James and Adam are being held hostage.

Also: I've been pissed at her.

There's a part of me that would really, really like to just carry her away to a private corner somewhere, but there's another part of me that won't allow it. Because I'm mad at her. She knew how much it meant to me to go after James, and she just shrugged it off with little to no sympathy. A little sympathy, I guess. But not much. Anyway, am I thinking too much? I think I'm thinking too much.

"What the hell is wrong with you?" Ian is staring at me, stunned.

"Nazeera is here."

"So?"

"So, I don't know, Nazeera is here," I say, keeping my voice low. "And I don't want to talk to her."

"Why not?"

"Because my head is stupid right now, that's why not." I glare at Winston. "You did this to me. You made my head stupid, and now I have to avoid Nazeera, because if I don't,

I will almost certainly do and or say something extremely stupid and fuck everything up. So I need to hide."

"Damn," Ian says, and shrugs. "That's too bad, because she's heading straight here."

I stiffen. Stare at him. And then, to Brendan: "Is he lying?"

Brendan shakes his head. "I'm afraid not, mate."

"Shit. Shit. Shit shit shit."

"It's nice to see you, too, Kenji."

I look up. She's smiling.

Ugh, so pretty.

"Hi," I say. "How are you?"

She looks around. Fights back a laugh. "I'm good," she says. "How . . . are you?"

"Fine. Fine. Thanks for asking. It was nice seeing you."

Nazeera glances from me to the other guys and back again. "I know you hate it when I ask you this, but— Are you drunk?"

"No," I say too loudly. I slump down farther in my seat. "Not drunk. Just a little . . . fuzzy." The whiskey is starting to settle now, warm, liquid fingers reaching up around my brain and squeezing.

She raises an eyebrow.

"Winston did it," I say, and point.

He shakes his head and sighs.

"All right," Nazeera says, but I can hear the mild irritation in her voice. "Well, this is not the ideal situation, but I'm going to need you on your feet."

"What?" I crane my head. Look at her. "Why?"

"There's been a development with Ella."

"What kind of development?" I sit straight up, feeling suddenly sober. "Is she awake?"

Nazeera tilts her head. "Not exactly," she says.

"Then what?"

"You should come see for yourself."

ELLA

~~JULIETTE~~

Adam feels close.

I can almost see him in my mind, a blurred form, watercolors bleeding through membrane, staining the whites of my eyes. He is a flooded river, blues in lakes so dark, water in oceans so heavy I sag, surrendering to the heft of the sea.

I take a deep breath and fill my lungs with tears, feathers of strange birds fluttering against my closed eyes. I see a flash of dirty-blond hair and darkness and stone I see blue and green and

Warmth, suddenly, an exhalation in my veins—

Emmaline.

Still here, still swimming.

She has grown quiet of late, the fire of her presence reduced to glowing embers. She is sorry for taking me from myself. Sorry for the inconvenience. Sorry to have disturbed my world so deeply. Still, she does not want to leave. She likes it here, likes stretching out inside my bones. She likes the dry air and the taste of real oxygen. She likes the shape of my fingers, the sharpness of my teeth. She is sorry, but not sorry enough to go back, so she is trying to be very small and very quiet. She hopes to make it up to me by taking up as little space as possible.

I don't know how I understand this so clearly, except that her mind seems to have fused with mine. Conversation is no longer necessary. Explanations, redundant.

In the beginning, she inhaled everything.

Excited, eager—she took it all. New skin. Eyes and mouth. I felt her marvel at my anatomy, at the systems drawing in air through my nose. I seemed to exist here almost as an afterthought, blood pumping through an organ beating merely to pass the time. I was little more than a passenger in my own body, doing nothing as she explored and decayed in starts and sparks, steel scraping against itself, stunning contractions of pain like claws digging, digging. It's better now that she's settled, but her presence has faded to all but an aching sadness. She seems desperate to find purchase as she disintegrates, unwittingly taking with her bits and pieces of my mind. Some days are better than others. Some days the fire of her existence is so acute I forget to draw breath.

But most days I am an idea, and nothing more.

I am foam and smoke moonlighting as skin. Dandelions gather in my rib cage, moss growing steadily along my spine. Rainwater floods my eyes, pools in my open mouth, dribbles down the hinges holding together my lips.

    I

        continue

        to

        sink.

And then—

    why now?

    suddenly
  surprisingly
      chest heaving, lungs working, fists clenching, knees bending, pulse racing, blood pumping

    I float

"Ms. Ferrars— That is, Ella—"

"Her name is Juliette. Just call her Juliette, for God's sake."

"Why don't we call her what she *wants* to be called?"

"Right. Exactly."

"But I thought she wanted to be called Ella."

"There was never a consensus. Was there a consensus?"

Slowly, my eyelids flutter open.

Silence explodes, coating mouths and walls and doors and dust motes. It hangs in the air, cloaking everything, for all of two seconds.

Then

Shouts, screams, a million sounds. I try to count them all and my head spins, swims. My heart is pounding hard and fast in my chest, recklessly shaking me, shaking my hands, ringing my skull. I look around fast, too fast, head whipping back and forth and everything swings around and around and

So many faces, blurred and strange.

I'm breathing too hard, spots dotting my vision, and I place two hands down on the—I look down—bed below me and squeeze my eyes shut

What am I
Who am I
Where am I

Silence again, swift and complete, like magic, magic, a hush falls over everyone, everything, and I exhale, panic draining out of me and I sit back, soaking in the dregs when

Warm hands
touch mine.

Familiar.

I go suddenly still. My eyes stay closed. Feeling moves through me like a wildfire, flames devouring the dust in my chest, the kindling in my bones. Hands become arms around me and the fire blazes. My own hands are caught between us and I feel the hard lines of his body through the soft cotton of his shirt.

A face appears, disappears, behind my eyes.

There's something so safe here in the feel of him, in the scent of him—something entirely his own. Being near him does something to me, something I can't even explain, can't control. I know I shouldn't, know I shouldn't, but I can't help but drag the tips of my fingers down the perfect lines of his torso.

I hear his breath catch.

Flames leap through me, jump up my lungs and I inhale, dragging oxygen into my body that only fans the flames further. One of his hands clasps the back of my head, the other grasps at my waist. A flash of heat roars up my spine, reaches into my skull. His lips are at my ear whispering, whispering

Come back to life, love
I'll be here when you wake up

My eyes fly open.

The heat is merciless. Confusing. Consuming. It calms

me, settles my raging heart. His hands move along my body, light touches along my arms, the sides of my torso. I claw my way back to him by memory, my shaking hands tracing the familiar shape of his back, my cheek still pressed against the familiar beat of his heart. The scent of him, so familiar, so familiar, and then I look up—

His eyes, something about his eyes

Please, he says, *please don't shoot me for this*

The room comes into focus by degrees, my head settling onto my neck, my skin settling onto my bones, my eyes staring into the very desperately green eyes that seem to know too much, too well. Aaron Warner Anderson is bent over me, his worried eyes inspecting me, his hand caught in the air like he might've been about to touch me.

He jerks back.

He stares, unblinking, chest rising and falling.

"Good morning," I assume. I'm unsure of my voice, of the hour and this day, of these words leaving my lips and this body that contains me.

His smile looks like it hurts.

"Something's wrong," he whispers. He touches my cheek. Soft, so soft, like he's not sure if I'm real, like he's afraid if he gets too close I'll just oh, look she's gone, she's just disappeared. His four fingers graze the side of my face, slowly, so slowly before they slip behind my head, caught in that in-between spot just above my neck. His thumb brushes the apple of my cheek.

My heart implodes.

He keeps looking at me, looking into my eyes for help, for guidance, for some sign of a protest like he's so sure I'm going to start screaming or crying or running away but I won't. I don't think I could even if I wanted to because I don't want to. I want to stay here. Right here. I want to be paralyzed by this moment.

He moves closer, just an inch. His free hand reaches up to cup the other side of my face.

He's holding me like I'm made of feathers. Like I'm a bird. White with streaks of gold like a crown atop its head.

I will fly.

A soft, shuddering breath leaves his body.

"Something's wrong," he says again, but distantly, like he might be talking to someone else. "Her energy is different. Tainted."

The sound of his voice coils through me, spirals around my spine. I feel myself straighten even as I feel strange, jet-lagged, like I've traveled through time. I pull myself into a seated position and Warner shifts to accommodate me. I'm tired and weak from hunger, but other than a few general aches, I seem to be fine. I'm alive. I'm breathing and blinking and feeling human and I know exactly why.

I meet his eyes. "You saved my life."

He tilts his head at me.

He's still studying me, his gaze so intense I flush, confused, and turn away. The moment I do, I nearly jump out of my skin. Castle and Kenji and Winston and Brendan and a ton of other people I don't recognize are all staring at me, at Warner's hands on me, and I'm suddenly so mortified I don't even know what to do with myself.

"Hey, princess." Kenji waves. "You okay?"

I try to stand and Warner tries to help me and the moment his skin brushes mine another sudden, destabilizing bolt of feeling runs me over. I stumble, sideways, into his arms and he pulls me in, his heat setting fire to my body all over again. I'm trembling, heart pounding, nervous pleasure pulsing through me.

I don't understand.

I'm overcome by a sudden, inexplicable need to touch him, to press my skin against his skin until the friction sets fire to us both. Because there's something about him—there's *always* been something about him that's intrigued me and I don't understand it. I pull away, startled by the intensity of my own thoughts, but his fingers catch me under the chin. He tilts my face toward him.

I look up.

His eyes are such a strange shade of green: bright, crystal clear, piercing in the most alarming way. His hair is thick, the richest slice of gold. Everything about him is meticulous. Pristine. His breath is cool and fresh. I can feel it on my face.

My eyes close automatically. I breathe him in, feeling suddenly giddy. A bubble of laughter escapes my lips.

"Something's definitely wrong," someone says.

"Yeah, she doesn't look like she's okay." Someone else.

"Oh, okay, so we're all just saying really obvious things out loud? Is that what we're doing?" Kenji.

Warner says nothing. I feel his arms tighten around me and my eyes flicker open. His gaze is fixed on mine, his eyes green flames that will not extinguish and his chest is rising and falling so fast, so fast, so fast. His lips are there, right there above mine.

"Ella?" he whispers.

I frown.

My eyes flick up, to his eyes, then down, to his lips.

"Love, do you hear me?"

When I don't answer, his face changes.

"Juliette," he says softly, "can you hear me?"

I blink at him. I blink and blink and blink at him and find I'm still fascinated by his eyes. Such a startling shade of green.

"We're going to need everyone to clear the room," someone says suddenly. Loudly. "We need to begin running tests immediately."

The girls, I realize. It's the girls. They're here. They're trying to get him away from me, trying to get him to break away from me. But Warner's arms are like steel bands around my body.

He refuses.

"Not yet," he says urgently. "Not just yet."

And for some reason they listen.

Maybe they see something in him, see something in

his face, in his features. Maybe they see what I see from this disjointed, foggy perspective. The desperation in his expression, the anguish carved into his features, the way he looks at me, like he might die if I do.

Tentatively, I reach up, touch my fingers to his face. His skin is smooth and cold. Porcelain. He doesn't seem real.

"What's wrong?" I say. "What happened?"

Impossibly, Warner goes paler. He shakes his head and presses his face to my cheek. "Please," he whispers. "Come back to me, love."

"Aaron?"

I hear the small hitch in his breath. The hesitation. It's the first time I've used his name so casually.

"Yes?"

"I want you to know," I tell him, "that I don't think you're crazy."

"What?" He startles.

"I don't think you're crazy," I say. "And I don't think you're a psychopath. I don't think you're a heartless murderer. I don't care what anyone else says about you. I think you're a good person."

Warner is blinking fast now. I can hear him breathing.

In and out.

Unevenly.

A flash of stunning, searing pain, and my body goes suddenly slack. I see the glint of metal. I feel the burn of the syringe. My head begins to swim and all the sounds begin to melt together.

"Come on, son," Castle says, his voice expanding, slowing down, "I know this is hard, but we need you to step back. We have t—"

An abrupt, violent sound gives me a sudden moment of clarity.

A man I don't recognize is at the door, one hand on the doorframe, gasping for breath. "They're here," he says. "They've found us. They're here. Jenna is dead."

KENJI

The guy gasping at the doorframe is still finishing his sentence when everyone jumps into action. Nouria and Sam rush past him into the hall, shouting orders and commands—something about initiating protocol for System Z, something about gathering the children, the elderly, and the sick. Sonya and Sara press something into Warner's hands, glance one last time at J's limp, unconscious figure, and chase Nouria and Sam out the door.

Castle crouches to the ground, closing his eyes as he flattens his hands against the floor, listening. Feeling.

"Eleven—no twelve, bodies. About five hundred feet out. I'd guess we have about two minutes before they reach us. I'll do my best to slow them down until we can clear out of here." He looks up. "Mr. Ibrahim?"

I don't even realize Haider is here with us until he says, "That's more than enough time."

He stalks across the room to the wall opposite Juliette's bed, running his hands along the smooth surface, ripping down picture frames and monitors as he goes. Glass and wood shatter in a heap on the floor. Nazeera gasps, goes suddenly still. I turn, terrified, to face her and she says—

"I need to tell Stephan."

She dashes out the door.

Warner is unhooking Juliette from the bed, removing her needles, bandaging her wounds. Once she's free, he wraps her sleeping body in the soft blue robe hanging nearby, and at nearly the exact same moment, I hear the telltale ticking of a bomb.

I glance back, at the wall where Haider still stands. Two carefully spaced explosives are now affixed to the plaster, and I hardly even have time to digest this before Haider bellows at us to move out into the hall. Warner is already halfway out the door, holding the carefully wrapped bundle of J in his arms. I hear Castle's voice—a sudden cry—and my own body is lifted and thrown out the door, too.

The room explodes.

The walls shake so hard it rattles my teeth, but when the tremors settle, I rush back into the room.

Haider blew off a single wall.

A perfect, exact rectangle of wall. Gone. I didn't even know such a feat was possible. Pieces of brick and wood and drywall are scattered on the open ground beyond J's room, and cold night winds rush in, slapping me awake. The moon is excessively full and bright tonight, a spotlight shining directly into my eyes.

I'm stunned.

Haider explains without prompting: "The hospital is too big, too complicated—we needed an efficient exit. The Reestablishment won't care about collateral damage when they come for us—in fact, they might be craving it—but if we're to have any hope of sparing innocent lives, we have to remove ourselves as far from the central buildings and common spaces as possible. Now move out," he shouts. "Let's go."

But I'm reeling.

I blink at Haider, still recovering from the blast, the lingering whisper of whiskey in my brain, and now this:

Proof that Haider Ibrahim has a conscience.

He and Warner stalk past me, through the open wall, and start running into the gleaming woods, Warner with J in his arms. Neither of them bothers to explain what they're thinking. Where they're going. What the hell is going to happen next.

Well, actually, I think that last part is obvious.

What's going to happen next is that Anderson is going to show up and try to murder us.

Castle and I lock eyes—we're the last people still standing in what remains of J's hospital room—and we chase after Warner and Haider toward a clearing at the far end of the Sanctuary, as far away from the tents as possible. At one point Warner breaks off from our group, disappearing down a path so dark I can't see the end of it. When I move to follow, Haider barks at me to leave him alone. I don't know what Warner does with Juliette, but when he rejoins us, she's no longer in his arms. He says something, briefly, to Haider, but it sounds like French. Not Arabic. *French.*

Whatever. I don't have time to think about it.

It's already been five minutes, by my estimate. Five

minutes, which means they should be here any second now. There are twelve bodies incoming. There are only four of us here.

Me, Haider, Castle, Warner.

I'm freezing.

We're standing quietly in the darkness, waiting for death, and the individual seconds seem to tick by with excruciating slowness. The smell of wet earth and decaying vegetation fills my head and I look down, feeling but not seeing the thick pile of leaves underfoot. They're soft and slightly damp, rustling a little when I shift my weight.

I try not to move.

Every sound unnerves me. A sudden shudder of branches. An innocent breeze. My own ragged breaths.

It's too dark.

Even the bright, robust moon isn't enough to properly penetrate these woods. I don't know how we're going to fight anyone if we can't see what's coming. The light is uneven, scattering through branches, shattering across the soft earth. I look down, examining a narrow shaft of light illuminating the tops of my boots, and watch as a spider scuttles up and around the obstacle of my feet.

My heart is pounding.

There's no time. If only we had more time.

It's all I can think. Over and over again. They caught us off guard, we weren't prepared, it didn't have to go down like this. My head is spinning with *what-ifs* and *maybes* and *it could've beens* even as I face down the reality right in front of me. Even as I stare straight into the black hole devouring my future, I can't help but wonder if we could've done this differently.

The seconds build. Minutes pass.

Nothing.

The rapid beating of my heart slows into a sick stutter of dread. I've lost perspective—my sense of time is warped in the dark—but I swear it feels like we've been here for too long.

"Something is wrong," Warner says.

I hear a sharp intake of breath. Haider.

Warner says softly, "We miscalculated."

"No," Castle cries.

That's when I hear the screams.

We run without hesitation, all four of us, hurtling ourselves toward the sounds. We tear through branches, sprain ankles on overgrown roots, propel ourselves into the darkness with the force of pure, undiluted panic. *Rage.*

Sobs rend the sky. Violent cries echo into the distance. Inarticulate voices, guttural moans, goose bumps rising along my flesh. We are sprinting toward death.

I know we're close when I see the light.

Nouria.

She's cast an ethereal glow above the scene, bringing the remains of a battlefield into sharp focus.

We slow down.

Time seems to expand, fracturing apart as I bear witness to a massacre. Anderson and his men made a detour. We hoped they'd come straight for Warner, straight for Juliette. We hoped. We tried. We took a gamble.

We bet wrong.

And we know The Reestablishment well enough to understand that they were punishing these innocent people for harboring us. Slaughtering entire families for providing us aid and relief. Nausea hits me with the force of a blade, stunning me, knocking me sideways. I slump against a tree. I can feel my mind disconnecting, threatening unconsciousness, and somehow I force myself not to pass out from horror. Terror. Heartbreak.

I keep my eyes open.

Sam and Nouria are on their knees, holding broken, bleeding bodies close to their chests, their tortured cries piercing the strange half night. Castle stands beside me, his body slack. I hear his half-choked sob.

We knew it was possible—Haider said they might do this—but somehow I still can't believe my eyes. I desperately want this to be a nightmare. I would cut off my right arm for a nightmare. But reality persists.

The Sanctuary is little more than a graveyard.

Unarmed men and women mowed down. From where I'm standing I count six children, dead. Eyes open, mouths agape, fresh blood still dripping down limp bodies. Ian is on his knees, vomiting. Winston stumbles backward, hits a tree. His glasses slide down his face and he only remembers to catch them at the last moment. Only the supreme kids still seem to have their heads on straight, and there's something about that realization that strikes fear into my heart. Nazeera, Haider, Warner, Stephan. They walk calmly through the wreckage, faces unchanged and solemn. I don't know what they've seen—what they've been a part of—that makes them able to stand here, still relatively cool in the face of so much human devastation, and I don't think I want to know.

I offer Castle my hand and he takes it, steadies himself. We exchange a single glance before diving into the fray.

Anderson is easy to spot, standing tall in the midst of hell, but hard to reach. His Supreme Guard swarms us, weapons drawn. Still, we move closer. No matter what comes next, we fight to the death. That was always the plan, from the first. And it's what we'll do now.

Round two.

The still-living fighters on the field straighten at our approach, at the scene forming, and steal glances at one another. We're surrounded by firepower, that's true, but nearly everyone here has a supernatural gift. There's no reason we shouldn't be able to put up a fight. A crowd gathers slowly around us—half Sanctuary, half Point—hale bodies breaking away from the wreckage to form a new battalion. I feel the fresh hope moving through the air. The tantalizing *maybe*. Carefully, I pull free a gun from my side holster.

And just as I'm about to make a move—

"Don't."

Anderson's voice is loud. Clear. He breaks through his

wall of soldiers, stalking toward us casually, looking as polished as always. I don't understand, at first, why so many people gasp at his approach. I don't see it. I don't notice the body he's dragging with him, and when I finally notice the body, I don't recognize it. Not right away.

It's not until Anderson jerks the small figure upright, nudging his head back with a gun, that I feel the blood exit my heart. Anderson presses the gun to James's throat, and my knees nearly give out.

"This is very simple," Anderson says. "You will hand over the girl, and in return, I won't execute the boy."

We're all frozen.

"I should clarify, however, that this is not an exchange. I'm not offering to return him to you. I'm only offering not to murder him here, on the spot. But if you hand over the girl now, without a fight, I will consider letting most of you disappear into the shadows."

"Most of us?" I say.

Anderson's eyes glance off my face and the faces of several others. "Yes, most of you," he says, his gaze lingering on Haider. "Your father is very disappointed in you, young man."

A single gunshot explodes without warning, ripping open a hole in Anderson's throat. He grabs at his neck and falls, with a choked cry, on one knee, looking around for his assailant.

Nazeera.

She materializes in front of him just in time to jump up,

into the sky. The supreme soldiers start shooting upward, releasing round after round with impunity, and though I'm terrified for Nazeera, I realize she took that risk for me. For James.

We'll do our best, she'd said. I didn't realize her best included risking her life for that kid. For *me*. God, I fucking love her.

I go invisible.

Anderson is struggling to stanch the flow of blood at his throat while keeping his grip on James, who appears to be unconscious.

Two guards remain at his side.

I fire two shots.

They both go down, crying out and clutching limbs, and Anderson nearly roars. He starts clawing at the air in front of him, then fumbles for his gun with one red hand, blood still seeping from his lips. I take that opportunity to punch him in the face.

He rears back, more surprised than injured, but Brendan moves in quickly, clapping his hands together to create a twisting, crackling bolt of electricity he wraps around Anderson's legs, temporarily paralyzing him.

Anderson drops James.

I catch him before he hits the floor, and bolt toward Lily, who's waiting just outside of Nouria's ring of light. I unload his unconscious body into her arms and Brendan builds an electric shield around their bodies. A beat later, they're gone.

Relief floods through me.

Too quickly. It unsteadies me. My invisibility falters for less than a second, and in less than a second I'm attacked from behind.

I hit the ground, hard, air leaving my lungs. I struggle to flip over, to stand up, but a supreme soldier is already pointing a rifle at my face. He shoots.

Castle comes out of nowhere, knocking the soldier off his feet, stopping the bullets with a single gesture. He redirects the ammunition meant for my body, and I don't even realize what's happened until I see the dude drop to his knees. He's a human sieve, bleeding out the last of his life right in front of me, and it all feels suddenly surreal.

I drag myself up, my head pounding in my throat. Castle is already moving, ripping a tree from its roots as he goes. Stephan is using his superstrength to pummel as many soldiers as he can, but they won't stop shooting, and he's moving slowly, blood staining nearly every inch of his clothing. I watch him sway. I run toward him, try to shout a warning, but my voice gets lost in the din, and my legs won't move fast enough. Another soldier charges at him, unloading rounds, and this time, I scream.

Haider comes running.

He dives in front of his friend with a cry, knocking Stephan to the ground, protecting his body with his own, throwing something into the air as he goes.

It explodes.

I'm thrown backward, my skull ringing. I lift my head,

delirious, and spot Nazeera and Warner, each locked in hand-to-hand combat. I hear a bloodcurdling scream and force myself up, toward the sound.

It's Sam.

Nouria beats me to her, falling to her knees to lift her wife's body off the ground. She wraps blinding bands of light around the two of them, the protective spirals so bright they're excruciating to look at. A nearby soldier throws his arm over his eyes as he shoots, crying out and holding steady even as the force of Nouria's light begins to melt the flesh off his hands.

I put a bullet through his teeth.

Five more guards appear out of nowhere, coming at me from all sides, and for half a second I can't help but be surprised. Castle said there were only twelve bodies, two of which belonged to Anderson and James, and I thought we'd taken out at least several of the others by now. I glance around the battlefield, at the dozens of soldiers still actively attacking our team, and then back again, at the five heading my way.

My head swims with confusion.

And then, when they all begin to shoot—terror.

I go invisible, stealing through the single foot of space between two of them, turning back just long enough to open fire. A couple of my shots find their marks; the others are wasted. I reload the clip, tossing the now-empty one to the ground, and just as I'm about to shoot again, I hear her voice.

"Hang on," she whispers.

Nazeera wraps her arms around my waist and jumps.

Up.

A bullet whizzes past my calf. I feel the burn as it grazes skin, but the night sky is cool and bracing, and I allow myself to take a steadying breath, to close my eyes for a full and complete second. Up here, the screams are muted, the blood could be water, the screams could be laughter.

The dream lasts for only a moment.

Our feet touch the ground again and my ears refill with the sounds of war. I squeeze Nazeera's hand by way of thanks, and we split up. I charge toward a group of men and women I only vaguely recognize—people from the Sanctuary—and throw myself into the bloodshed, urging one of the injured fighters to pull back and take shelter. I'm soon lost in the motions of battle, defending and attacking, guns firing. Guttural moaning. I don't even think to look up until I feel the ground shake beneath my feet.

Castle.

His arms are pointed upward, toward a nearby building. The structure begins to shake violently, nails flying, windows shuddering. A cluster of supreme guards reaches for their guns but stop short at the sound of Anderson's voice. I can't hear what he says, but he seems to be nearly himself again, and his command appears to be shocking enough to inspire a moment of hesitation in his soldiers. For no reason I can fathom, the guards I'd been fighting suddenly slink away.

Too late.

The roof of the nearby building collapses with a scream,

and with a final, violent shove, Castle tears off a wall. With one arm he shoves aside the few of our teammates standing in harm's way, and with the other he drops the ton of wall to the ground, where it lands with an explosive crash. Glass flies everywhere, wooden beams groaning as they buckle and break. A few supreme soldiers escape, diving for cover, but at least three of them get caught under the rubble. We all brace for a retaliatory attack—

But Anderson holds up a single arm.

His soldiers go instantly still, weapons going slack in their hands. Almost in unison, they stand at attention.

Waiting.

I glance at Castle for a directive, but he's got eyes on Anderson just like the rest of us. Everyone seems paralyzed by a delirious hope that this war might be over. I watch Castle turn and lock eyes with Nouria, who's still cradling Sam to her chest. A moment later, Castle raises his arm. A temporary standstill.

I don't trust it.

Silence coats the night as Anderson staggers forward, his lips a violent, liquid red, his hand casually holding a handkerchief to his neck. We'd heard about this, of course—about his ability to heal himself—but seeing it actually happen in real time is something else altogether. It's *wild*.

When he speaks, his voice shatters the quiet. Breaks the spell. "Enough," he says. "Where is my son?"

Murmurs move through the crowd of bloodied fighters, a red sea slowly parting at his approach. It's not long before

Warner appears, striding forward in the silence, his face spattered in red. A machine gun is locked in his right hand.

He looks up at his father. He says nothing.

"What did you do with her?" Anderson says softly, and spits blood on the ground. He wipes his lips with the same cloth he's using to contain the open wound on his neck. The whole scene is disgusting.

Warner continues to say nothing.

I don't think any of us know where he hid her. J seems to have *disappeared*, I realize.

Seconds pass in a silence so intense we all begin to worry about the fate of our standstill. I see a few of the supreme soldiers lift their guns in Warner's direction, and not a second later a single lightning bolt fractures the sky above us.

Brendan.

I glance at him, then at Castle, but Anderson once again lifts his arm to stall his soldiers. Once again, they stand down.

"I will only ask you one more time," Anderson says to his son, his voice trembling as it grows louder. *"What did you do with her?"*

Still, Warner stares impassively.

He's spattered in unknown blood, holding a machine gun like it might be a briefcase, and staring at his father like he might be staring at the ceiling. Anderson can't control his temper the way Warner can—and it's obvious to everyone that this is a battle of wills he's going to lose.

Anderson already looks half out of his mind.

His hair is matted and sticking up in places. Blood is congealing on his face, his eyes shot through with red. He looks so deranged—so unlike himself—that I honestly have no idea what's going to happen next.

And then he lunges for Warner.

He's like a belligerent drunk, wild and angry, unhinged in a way I've never seen before. His swings are wild but strong, unsteady but studied. He reminds me, in a sudden, frightening flash of understanding, of the father Adam so often described to me. A violent drunk fueled by rage.

Except that Anderson doesn't appear to be drunk at the moment. No. This is pure, unadulterated anger.

Anderson seems to have lost his mind.

He doesn't just want to shoot Warner. He doesn't want someone else to shoot Warner. He wants to beat him to a pulp. He wants physical satisfaction. He wants to break bones and rupture organs with his own hands. Anderson wants the pleasure of knowing that he and he alone was able to destroy his own son.

But Warner isn't giving him that satisfaction.

He meets Anderson blow for blow in fluid, precise movements, ducking and sidestepping and twisting and defending. He never misses a beat.

It's almost like he can read Anderson's mind.

I'm not the only one who's stunned. I've never seen Warner move like this, and I almost can't believe I've never seen it before. I feel a sudden, unbidden surge of respect for him as I watch him block attack after attack. I keep waiting for him to knock the dude out, but Warner makes no effort to hit Anderson; he only defends. And only when I see the increasing fury on Anderson's face do I realize that Warner is doing this on purpose.

He's not fighting back because he knows it's what Anderson wants. The cool, emotionless expression on Warner's face is driving Anderson insane. And the more he fails to rattle his son, the more enraged Anderson gets. Blood still trickles, slowly, from the half-healed wound on his neck when he cries out, angrily, and pulls free a gun from inside his jacket pocket.

"*Enough*," he shouts. "That is enough."

Warner takes a careful step back.

"Give me the girl, Aaron. Give me the girl and I will spare the rest of these idiots. I only want the girl."

Warner is an immovable object.

"Fine," Anderson says angrily. "Seize him."

Six supreme guards begin advancing on Warner, and he doesn't so much as flinch. I exchange glances with Winston and it's enough; I throw my invisibility over Winston just as he throws his arms out, his ability to stretch his limbs knocking three of them to the ground. In the same moment, Haider pulls a machete from somewhere inside the bloodied chain mail he's wearing under his coat, and tosses it to Warner, who drops the machine gun and catches the blade by the hilt without even looking.

A fucking *machete*.

Castle is on his knees, arms toward the sky as he breaks off more pieces of the half-devastated building, but this time Anderson's men don't give him the chance. I run forward, too late to help as Castle is knocked out from behind, and still I throw myself into the fight, battling for ownership of the soldier's gun with skills I developed as a teenager: a single, solid punch to the nose. A clean uppercut. A hard kick to the chest. A good old-fashioned strangulation.

I look up, gasping for breath, hoping for good news—

And do a double take.

Ten men have closed in on Warner, and I don't understand where they came from. I thought we were down to three or four. I spin around, confused, turning back just in time to watch Warner drop to one knee and swing up with the machete in a sudden, perfect arc, gutting the man like a fish. Warner turns, another strong swing slicing through the guy on his left, disconnecting the dude's spine in a move so horrific I have to look away. In the second it takes me to turn back, another guard has already charged forward. Warner pivots sharply, shoving the blade directly up the guy's throat and into his open, screaming mouth. With a final tug, Warner pulls the blade free, and the man falls to the ground with a single, soft thud.

The remaining members of the Supreme Guard hesitate.

I realize then, that—whoever these new soldiers are—they've been given specific orders to attack Warner, and no one else. The rest of us are suddenly without an obvious task, free to sink into the ground, disappear into exhaustion.

Tempting.

I search for Castle, wanting to make sure he's okay, and realize he looks stricken.

He's staring at Warner.

Warner, who's staring at the blood pooling beneath his feet, his chest heaving, his fist still clenched around the shank of the machete. All this time, Castle really thought Warner was just a nice boy who'd made some simple mistakes. The kind of kid he could bring back from the brink.

Not today.

Warner looks up at his father, his face more blood than skin, his body shaking with rage.

"Is this what you wanted?" he cries.

But even Anderson seems surprised.

Another guard moves forward so silently I don't even see the gun he's aimed in Warner's direction until the soldier screams and collapses to the ground. His eyes bulge as he clutches at his throat, where a shard of glass the size of my hand is caught in his jugular.

I whip my head around to face Warner. He's still staring at Anderson, but his free hand is now dripping blood.

Jesus Christ.

"Take me, instead," Warner says, his voice piercing the quiet.

Anderson seems to come back to himself. "What?"

"Leave her. Leave them all. Give me your word that you will leave her alone, and I will come back with you."

I go suddenly still. And then I look around, eyes wild, for

any indication that we're going to stop this idiot from doing something reckless, but no one meets my eyes. Everyone is riveted.

Terrified.

But when I feel a familiar presence suddenly materialize beside me, relief floods through my body. I reach for her hand at the same time she reaches for mine, squeezing her fingers once before breaking the brief connection. Right now, it's enough to know she's here, standing next to me.

Nazeera is okay.

We all wait in silence for the scene to change, hoping for something we don't even know how to name.

It doesn't come.

"I wish it were that simple," Anderson says finally. "I really do. But I'm afraid we need the girl. She is not so easily replaced."

"You said that Emmaline's body was deteriorating." Warner's voice is low, but clear. Miraculously steady. "You said that without a strong enough body to contain her, she'd become volatile."

Anderson visibly stiffens.

"You need a replacement," Warner says. "A new body. Someone to help you complete Operation Synthesis."

"No," Castle cries. "No— Don't do this—"

"Take me," Warner says. "I will be your surrogate."

Anderson's eyes go cold.

He sounds almost convincingly calm when he says, "You would be willing to sacrifice yourself—your youth and your health and your entire life—to let that damaged, deranged girl continue to walk the earth?" Anderson's voice begins to rise in pitch. He seems suddenly on the verge of another breakdown.

"Do you even understand what you're saying? You have every opportunity—all the potential—and you'd be willing to throw it all away? In exchange for *what*?" he cries. "Do you even know the kind of life to which you'd be sentencing yourself?"

A dark look passes over Warner's face. "I think I would know better than most."

Anderson pales. "Why would you do this?"

It becomes clear to me then that even now, despite everything, Anderson doesn't actually want to lose Warner. Not like this.

But Warner is unmoved.

He says nothing. Betrays nothing. He only blinks as someone else's blood drips down his face.

"Give me your word," Warner finally says. "Your word that you will leave her alone forever. I want you to let her disappear. I want you to stop tracking her every move. I want you to forget she ever existed." He pauses. "In exchange, you can have what's left of my life."

Nazeera gasps.

Haider takes a sudden, angry step forward and Stephan grabs his arm, somehow still strong enough to restrain Haider even as his own body bleeds out. "This is his choice," Stephan gasps, wrapping his free arm around a tree for support. "Leave him."

"This is a stupid choice," Haider cries. "You can't do this, *habibi*. Don't be an idiot."

But Warner doesn't seem to hear anyone anymore. He stares only at Anderson, who seems genuinely distraught.

"I will stop fighting you," Warner says. "I will do exactly as you ask. Whatever you want. Just let her live."

Anderson is silent for so long it sends a chill through me. Then:

"No."

Without warning, Anderson raises his arm and fires two shots. The first, at Nazeera, hitting her square in the chest. The second—

At me.

Several people scream. I stumble, then sway, before collapsing.

Shit.

"Find her," Anderson says, his voice booming. "Burn the whole place to the ground if you have to."

The pain is blinding.

It moves through me in waves, electric and searing. Someone is touching me, moving my body. *I'm okay*, I try to say. I'm okay. I'm okay. But the words don't come. He's hit me in my shoulder, I think. Just shy of my chest. I'm not sure. But Nazeera— Someone needs to get to Nazeera.

"I had a feeling you'd do something like this," I hear Anderson say. "And I know you used one of these two"—I imagine him pointing to my prone body, to Nazeera's—"in order to make it happen."

Silence.

"Oh, I see," Anderson says. "You thought you were clever. You thought I didn't know you had any powers at all." Anderson's voice seems suddenly loud, too loud. He laughs. "You thought *I* didn't know? As if you could hide something like that from me. I knew it the day I found you in her holding cell. You were sixteen. You think I didn't have you tested after that? You think I haven't known, all these years, what you yourself didn't realize until six months ago?"

A fresh wave of fear washes over me.

Anderson seems too pleased and Warner's gone quiet again, and I don't know what any of that means for us. But just as I'm beginning to experience full-blown panic, I hear a familiar cry.

It's a sound of such horrific agony I can't help but try to see what's happening, even as flashes of white blur my vision.

I catch a mottled glimpse:

Warner standing over Anderson's body, his right hand clenched around the handle of the machete he's buried in his father's chest. He plants his right foot on his father's gut, and, roughly, pulls out the blade.

Anderson's moan is so animal, so pathetic I almost feel sorry for him. Warner wipes the blade on the grass, and tosses it back to Haider, who catches it easily by the hilt even as he stands there, stunned, staring at—*me*, I realize.

Me and Nazeera. I've never seen him so unmasked. He seems paralyzed by fear.

"Watch him," Warner shouts to someone. He examines a gun he stole from his father, and, satisfied, he's off, running after the Supreme Guard. Shots ring out in the distance.

My vision begins to go spotty.

Sounds bleed together, shifting focus. For moments at a time all I hear is the sound of my own breathing, my heart beating. At least, I hope that's the sound of my heart beating. Everything smells sharp, like rust and steel. I realize then, in a sudden, startling moment, that I can't feel my fingers.

Finally I hear the muffled sounds of nearby movement, of hands on my body, trying to move me.

"Kenji?" Someone shakes me. "Kenji, can you hear me?" Winston.

I make a sound in my throat. My lips seem fused together.

"Kenji?" More shaking. "Are you okay?"

With great difficulty, I pry my lips apart, but my mouth makes no sound. Then, all at once: "Heyyyyybuddy."

Weird.

"He's conscious," Winston says, "but disoriented. "We don't have much time. I'll carry these two. See if you can find a way to transport the others. Where are the girls?"

Someone says something back to him, and I don't catch it. I reach out suddenly with my good hand, clamping down on Winston's forearm.

"Don't let them get J," I try to say. "Don't let—"

~~ELLA~~
~~JULIETTE~~

When I open my eyes, I feel steel.

Strapped and molded across my body, thick, silver stripes pressed against my pale skin. I'm in a cage the exact size and shape of my silhouette. I can't move. Can hardly part my lips or bat an eyelash; I only know what I look like because I can see my reflection in the stainless steel of the ceiling.

Anderson is here.

I see him right away, standing in a corner of the room, staring at the wall like he's both pleased and angry, a strange sneer plastered to his face. There's a woman here, too, someone I've never seen before. Blond, very blond. Tall and freckled and willowy. She reminds me of someone I've seen before, someone I can't presently remember.

And then, suddenly—

My mind catches up to me with a ferociousness that's nearly paralyzing. James and Adam, kidnapped by Anderson. Kenji, falling ill. New memories from my own life, continuing to assault my mind and taking with them, bits and pieces of me.

And then, Emmaline.

Emmaline, stealing into my consciousness. Emmaline, her presence so overwhelming I was forced into near oblivion, coaxed to sleep. I remember waking, eventually, but my recollection of that moment is vague. I remember confusion, mostly. Distorted reels.

I take a moment to check in with myself. My limbs. My heart. My mind. Intact?

I don't know.

Despite a bit of disorientation, I feel almost fully myself. I can still sense pockets of darkness in my memories, but I feel like I've finally broken the surface of my own consciousness. And it's only then that I realize I no longer feel even a whisper of Emmaline.

Quickly, I close my eyes again. I feel around for my sister in my head, seeking her out with a desperate panic that surprises me.

Emmaline? Are you still here?

In response, a gentle warmth rushes through me. A single, soft shudder of life. She must be close to the end, I realize.

Nearly gone.

Pain shoots through my heart.

My love for Emmaline is at once new and ancient, so complicated I don't even know how to properly articulate my feelings about it. I only know that I have nothing but compassion for her. For her pain, her sacrifices, her broken spirit, her longing for all that her life could've been. I feel no anger or resentment toward her for infiltrating my mind, for violently disrupting my world to make room for herself in my skin. Somehow I understand that the brutality of her act was nothing more than a desperate plea for companionship in the last days of her life.

She wants to die knowing she was loved.

And I, I love her.

I was able to see, when our minds were fused, that Emmaline had found a way to split her consciousness, leaving a necessary bit of it behind to play her role in Oceania. The small part of her that broke off to find me—that was the small part of her that still felt human, that felt the world acutely. And now, it seems, that human piece of her is beginning to fade away.

The callused fingers of grief curve around my throat.

My thoughts are interrupted by the sharp staccato of heels against stone. Someone is moving toward me. I'm careful not to flinch.

"She should've been awake by now," the female voice says. "This is odd."

"Perhaps the sedative you gave her was stronger than you thought." Anderson.

"I'm going to assume your head is still full of morphine, Paris, which is the only reason I'm going to overlook that statement."

Anderson sighs. Stiffly, he says: "I'm sure she'll be awake any minute now."

Fear trips the alarms in my head.

What's happening? I ask Emmaline. *Where are we?*

The dregs of a gentle warmth become a searing heat that blazes up my arms. Goose bumps rise along my skin.

Emmaline is afraid.

Show me where we are, I say.

It takes longer than I'm used to, but very slowly Emmaline fills my head with images of my room, of steel walls and glittering glass, long tables laid out with all manner of tools and blades, surgical equipment. Microscopes as tall as the wall. Geometric patterns in the ceiling glow with warm, bright light. And then there's me.

I am mummified in metal.

I'm lying supine on a gleaming table, thick horizontal stripes holding me in place. I am naked but for the carefully placed restraints keeping me from full exposure.

Realization dawns with painful speed.

I recognize these rooms, these tools, these walls. Even the smell—stale air, synthetic lemon, bleach and rust. Dread creeps through me slowly at first, and then all at once.

I am back on base in Oceania.

I feel suddenly ill.

I am a world away. An international flight away from my chosen family, back again in the house of horrors I grew up in. I have no recollection of how I got here, and I don't know what devastation Anderson left in my wake. I don't know where my friends are. I don't know what's become of Warner. I can't remember anything useful. I only know that something must be terribly, terribly wrong.

Even so, my fear feels different.

My captors—Anderson? This woman?—have obviously done something to me, because I can't feel my powers the way I normally do, but there's something about this horrible, familiar pattern that's almost comforting. I've woken up in chains more times than I can remember, and every time, I've found my way out. I'll find my way out of this, too.

And at least this time, I'm not alone.

Emmaline is here. As far as I'm aware, Anderson has no idea she's with me, and it gives me hope.

The silence is broken by a long-suffering sigh.

"Why do we need her to be awake, anyway?" the woman says. "Why can't we perform the procedure while she's asleep?"

"They're not my rules, Tatiana. You know as well as I do that Evie set this all in motion. Protocol states that the subject must be awake when the transfer is initiated."

I take it back.

I take it back.

Pure, unadulterated terror spikes through me, dispelling my earlier confidence with a single blow. It should've occurred to me right away that they'd try to do to me what Evie didn't get right the first time. Of course they would.

My sudden panic nearly gives me away.

"Two daughters with the exact same DNA fingerprint," Tatiana says suddenly. "Anyone else would think it was a wild coincidence. But Evie was always careful about having a backup plan, wasn't she?"

"From the very beginning," Anderson says quietly. "She made sure there was a spare."

The words are a blow I couldn't have anticipated.

A spare.

That's all I ever was, I realize. A spare part kept in captivity. A backup weapon in the case that all else failed.

Shatter me.

Break glass in case of emergency.

It takes everything I've got to remain still, to fight back the urge to swallow the sudden swell of emotion in my throat. Even now, even from the grave, my mother manages to wound me.

"How lucky for us," the woman says.

"Indeed," Anderson says, but there's tension in his voice. Tension I'm only just beginning to notice.

Tatiana starts rambling.

She begins talking about how clever Evie was to realize that someone had interfered with her work, how clever she was to have realized right away that Emmaline was the one who'd tampered with the results of the procedure she'd performed on me. Evie always knew, Tatiana is saying, that there was a risk in bringing me back to base in Oceania—and the risk, she says, was Emmaline's physical closeness.

"After all," Tatiana says, "the two girls hadn't been in such close proximity in nearly a decade. Evie was worried Emmaline would try to make contact with her sister." A pause. "And she did."

"What is your point?"

"My point," Tatiana says slowly, like she's talking to a child, "is that this seems dangerous. Don't you think it's more than a little unwise to put the two girls under the same roof again? After what happened last time? Doesn't this seem a little . . . reckless?"

Stupid hope blooms in my chest.

Of course.

Emmaline's body is nearby. Maybe Emmaline's voice disappearing from my mind has nothing to do with her impending death—maybe she feels farther away simply because she *moved*. It's possible that upon reentry to Oceania the two parts of her consciousness reconnected. Maybe Emmaline feels distant now only because she's reaching out to me from her tank—the way she did the last time I was here.

Sharp, searing heat flashes behind my eyes, and my heart leaps at her response.

I am not alone, I say to her. *You are not alone.*

"You know as well as I do that this was the only way," Anderson says to Tatiana. "I needed Max's help. My injuries were too serious."

"You seem to be needing Max's help quite a lot these days," she says coldly. "And I'm not the only one who thinks your needs are becoming liabilities."

"Don't push me," he says quietly. "This isn't the day."

"I don't care. You know as well as I do that it would've

been safer to initiate this transfer back at Sector 45, thousands of miles away from Emmaline. We had to transport the boy, too, remember? Extremely inconvenient. That you so desperately needed Max to assist with your vanity is an altogether different issue, one that concerns both your failings and your ineptitude."

Silence falls, heavy and thick.

I have no idea what's happening above my head, but I can only imagine the two of them are glaring each other into the ground.

"Evie had a soft spot for you," Tatiana says finally. "We all know that. We all know how willing she was to overlook your mistakes. But Evie is dead now, isn't she? And her daughter would be two for two if it weren't for Max's constant efforts to keep you alive. The rest of us are running out of patience."

Before Anderson has a chance to respond, a door slams open.

"Well?" A new voice. "Is it done?"

For the first time, Tatiana seems subdued. "She's not yet awake, I'm afraid."

"Then wake her up," the voice demands. "We're out of time. All the children have been tainted. We still have to get the rest of them under control and clear their minds as soon as possible."

"But not before we figure out what they know," Anderson says quickly, "and who they might've told."

Heavy footsteps move into the room, fast and hard. I hear a rustle of movement, a sudden brief gasp. "Haider told me something interesting when your men dragged him back here," the man says quietly. "He says you shot my daughter."

"It was a practical decision," Anderson says. "She and Kishimoto were possible targets. I had no choice but to take them both out."

It takes every ounce of my self-control to keep from screaming.

Kenji.

Anderson shot Kenji.

Kenji, and this man's daughter. He must be talking about Nazeera. Oh my God. Anderson shot Kenji and Nazeera. Which would make this man—

"Ibrahim, it was for the best." Tatiana's heels click against the floor. "I'm sure she's fine. They've got those healer girls, you know."

Supreme Commander Ibrahim ignores her.

"If my daughter is not returned to me alive," he says angrily, "I will personally remove your brain from your skull."

The door slams shut behind him.

"Wake her up," Anderson says.

"It's not that simple— There's a process—"

"I won't say it again, Tatiana." Anderson is shouting now, his temperature spiking without warning. "Wake her up now. I want this over with."

"Paris, you have to calm d—"

"I tried to kill her *months* ago." Metal slams against metal.

"I told all of you to finish the job. If we're in this position right now—if Evie is dead—it's because no one listened to me when they should have."

"You are unbelievable." Tatiana laughs, but the sound is flat. "That you ever assumed you had the authority to murder Evie's daughter tells me everything I need to know about you, Paris. You're an idiot."

"Get out," he says, seething. "I don't need you breathing down my neck. Go check in on your own insipid daughter. I'll take care of this one."

"Feeling fatherly?"

"Get. Out."

Tatiana says nothing more. I hear the sound of a door opening and closing. The soft, distant clangs and chimes of metal and glass. I have no idea what Anderson is doing, but my heart is beating wildly. Angry, indignant Anderson is nothing to take lightly.

I would know.

And when I feel a sudden, ruthless spike of pain, I scream. Panic forces my eyes open.

"I had a feeling you were faking it," he says.

Roughly, he yanks the scalpel out of my thigh. I choke back another scream. I've hardly had a chance to catch my breath when, again, he buries the scalpel in my flesh—deeper this time. I cry out in agony, my lungs constricting. When he finally wrenches the tool free I nearly pass out from the pain. I'm making labored, gasping sounds, my chest so tightly bound I can't breathe properly.

"I was hoping you'd hear that conversation," Anderson says calmly, pausing to wipe the scalpel on his lab coat. The blood is dark. Thick. My vision fades in and out. "I wanted you to know that your mother wasn't stupid. I wanted you to know that she was aware that something had gone wrong. She didn't know the exact failings of the procedure—but she suspected the injections hadn't done everything they were meant to do. And when she suspected foul play, she made a contingency plan."

I'm still gasping for air, my head spinning. The pain in my leg is searing, clouding my mind.

"You didn't think she was that stupid, did you? Evie Sommers?" Anderson almost laughs. "Evie Sommers hasn't been stupid a day in her life. Even on the day she died, she died with a plan in place to save The Reestablishment, because she'd dedicated her life to this cause. This was it," he says, prodding at my wound. "You.

"You and your sister. You were her life's work, and she wasn't about to let it all go up in flames without a fight."

I don't understand, I try to say.

"I know you don't understand," he says. "Of course you don't understand. You never did inherit your mother's genius, did you? You never had her mind. No, you were only ever meant to be a tool, from the very beginning. So here's everything you need to understand: you now belong to me."

"No," I gasp. I struggle, uselessly, against the restraints. "No—"

I feel the sting and the fire at the same time. Anderson has stuck me with something, something that blazes through me with a pain so excruciating my heart hardly remembers to beat. My skin breaks out in an all-consuming sweat. My hair begins to stick to my face. I feel at once paralyzed and as if I'm falling, free-falling, sinking into the coldest depths of hell.

Emmaline, I cry.

My eyelids flutter. I see Anderson, flashes of Anderson, his eyes dark and troubled. He looks at me like he's finally got me exactly where he wants me, where he's always wanted me, and I understand then, without understanding why, exactly, that he's excited. I sense his happiness. I don't know how I know. I can just tell from the way he stands, the way he stares. He's feeling joyous.

It terrifies me.

My body makes another effort to move but the action is futile. There's no point in moving, no point in struggle.

This is over, something tells me.

I have lost.

I've lost the battle and the war. I've lost the boy. I've lost my friends. I've lost my will to live, the voice says to me.

And then I understand: Anderson is in my head.

My eyes are not open. My eyes might never again open. Wherever I am is not in my control. I belong to Anderson now. I belong to The Reestablishment, where I've always belonged, *where you've always belonged,* he says to me, *where you will remain forever. I've been waiting for this moment for a very, very long time,* he says to me, *and now, finally, there's nothing you can do about it.*

Nothing.

Even then, I don't understand. Not right away. I don't understand even as I hear the machines roar to life. I don't understand even as I see the flash of light behind my eyelids. I hear my own breath, loud and strange and reverberating in my skull. I can feel my hands shaking. I can feel the metal sinking into the soft flesh of my body. I am here, strapped into steel against my will and there is no one to save me.

Emmaline, I cry.

A whisper of heat moves through me in response, a whisper so subtle, so quickly extinguished, I fear I might've imagined it.

Emmaline is nearly dead, Anderson says. *Once her body is removed from the tank, you will take her place. Until then, this is where you'll live. Until then, this is where you'll exist. This is all you were ever meant for,* he says to me.

This is all you will ever be.

KENJI

No one comes to the funeral.

It took two days to bury all the bodies. Castle tired his mind nearly to sickness digging up so much dirt. The rest of us used shovels. But there weren't many of us to do the work then, and there aren't enough of us to attend a funeral now.

Still, I sit here at dawn, perched atop a boulder, sitting high above the valley where we buried our friends. Teammates. My left arm is in a sling, my head hurts like a bitch, my heart is permanently broken.

I'm okay, otherwise.

Alia comes up behind me, so quiet I hardly even notice her. I hardly *ever* notice her. But there are too few bodies for her to hide behind now. I scoot over on the rock and she settles down beside me, the two of us staring out at the sea of graves below. She's holding two dandelions. Offers one to me. I take it.

Together, we drop the flowers, watching them as they float gently into the chasm. Alia sighs.

"You okay?" I ask her.

"No."

"Yeah." I nod.

Seconds pass. A gentle breeze pushes the hair out of my

face. I stare directly into the newborn sun, daring it to burn my eyes out.

"Kenji?"

"Yeah?"

"Where's Adam?"

I shake my head. Shrug.

"Do you think we'll find him?" she asks, her voice practically a whisper.

I look up.

There's a yearning there—something more than general concern in her tone. I turn fully to meet her eyes, but she won't look at me.

She's suddenly blushing.

"I don't know," I say to her. "I hope so."

"Me too," she says softly.

She rests her head on my shoulder. We stare out, into the distance. Let the silence devour our bodies.

"You did an amazing job, by the way." I nod at the valley below. "This is beautiful."

Alia really outdid herself. She and Winston.

The monuments they designed are simple and elegant, made from stone sourced from the land itself.

And there are two.

One for the lives lost here, at the Sanctuary, two days ago. The other for the lives lost *there*, at Omega Point, two months ago. The list of names is long. The injustice of it all roars through me.

Alia takes my hand. Squeezes.

I realize I'm crying.

I turn away, feeling stupid, and Alia lets go, gives me space to pull myself together. I wipe at my eyes with excessive force, angry with myself for falling apart. Angry with myself for being disappointed. Angry with myself for ever allowing hope.

We lost J.

We're not even sure exactly how it happened. Warner has been virtually comatose since that day, and getting information out of him has been near impossible. But it sounds like we never really stood a chance, in the end. One of Anderson's men had the preternatural ability to clone himself, and it took us too long to figure it out. We couldn't understand why their defense would suddenly double and triple just as we thought we were wearing them down. But it turns out Anderson had an inexhaustible supply of dummy soldiers. Warner couldn't get over it. It was the one thing he kept repeating, over and over—

I should've known, I should've known

—and despite the fact that Warner's been killing himself for the oversight, Castle says it was precisely because of Warner that any of us are still alive.

There weren't supposed to be *any* survivors. That was Anderson's decree. The command he gave after I went down.

Warner figured out the trick just in time.

His ability to harness the soldier's powers and use it against him was our one saving grace, apparently, and when the dude realized he had competition, he took what he could get and ran.

Which means he managed to snag an unconscious Haider and Stephan. It means Anderson escaped.

And J, of course.

It means they got J.

"Should we head back?" Alia says quietly. "Castle was awake when I left. He said he wanted to talk to you."

"Yeah." I nod, get to my feet. Pull myself together. "Any update on James, by the way? Is he cleared for visitors yet?"

Alia shakes her head. Stands up, too. "Not yet," she says. "But he'll be awake soon. The girls are optimistic. Between his healing powers and theirs, they feel certain they'll be able to get him through it."

"Yeah," I say, taking a deep breath. "I'm sure you're right."

Wrong.

I'm not sure of anything.

The wreckage left in the wake of Anderson's attack has laid all of us low. Sonya and Sara are working around the clock. Sam was severely injured. Nazeera is still unconscious. Castle is weak. Hundreds of others are trying to heal.

A serious darkness has descended upon us all.

We fought hard, but we took too many hits. We were too few to begin with. There was only so much any of us could do.

These are the things I keep telling myself, anyway.

We start walking.

"This feels worse, doesn't it?" Alia says. "Worse than

last time." She stops, suddenly, and I follow her line of sight, study the scene before us. The torn-down buildings, the detritus along the paths. We did our best to clean up the worst of it, but if I look in the wrong place at the wrong time, I can still find blood on broken tree branches. Shards of glass.

"Yeah," I say. "Somehow, this is so much worse."

Maybe because the stakes were higher. Maybe because we've never lost J before. Maybe because I've never seen Warner this lost or this broken. Angry Warner was better than this. At least angry Warner had some fight left in him.

Alia and I part ways when we enter the dining tent. She's been volunteering her time, going from cot to cot to check on people, offering food and water where necessary, and this dining tent is currently her place of work. The massive space has been made into a sort of convalescent home. Sonya and Sara are prioritizing major injuries; minor wounds are being treated the traditional way, by what's left of the original staff of doctors and nurses. This room is stacked, end to end, with those of us who are either healing from minor injuries, or resting after major intervention.

Nazeera is here, but she's sleeping.

I drop down in a seat next to her cot, checking up on her the way I do every hour. Nothing's changed. She's still lying here, still as stone, the only proof of life coming from a nearby monitor and the gentle movements of her breathing. Her wound was a lot worse than mine. The girls say she's going to be okay, but they think she'll be asleep until at least tomorrow. Even so, it kills me to look at her. Watching that girl go down was one of the hardest things I've ever had to witness.

I sigh, dragging a hand down my face. I still feel like shit, but at least I'm awake. Few of us are.

Warner is one of them.

He's still covered in dry blood, refusing to be helped. He's conscious, but he's been lying on his back, staring at the ceiling since the day he was dragged in here. If I didn't know any better, I'd think he was a corpse. I've been checking, too, every once in a while—making sure I caught that gentle rise and fall of his chest—just to be certain he was still breathing.

I think he's in shock.

Apparently, once he realized J was gone, he tore the remaining soldiers to pieces with his bare hands.

Apparently.

I don't buy it, of course, because the story sounds just a little to the left of what I consider credible, but then, I've been hearing all kinds of shit about Warner these last couple of days. He went from being only relatively consequential to becoming genuinely terrifying to assuming superhero status—in thirty-six hours. In a plot twist I never could've expected, people here are suddenly obsessed with him.

They think he saved our lives.

One of the volunteers checking my wound yesterday told me that she heard someone else say that they saw Warner uproot an entire tree with only one hand.

Translation: He probably broke off a tree branch.

Someone else told me that they'd heard from a friend that some girl had seen him save a cluster of children from friendly fire.

Translation: He probably shoved a bunch of kids to the ground.

Another person told me that Warner had single-handedly murdered nearly all the supreme soldiers.

Translation—

Okay, that last one is kind of true.

But I know Warner wasn't trying to do anyone around here a favor. He doesn't give a shit about being a hero.

He was only trying to save J's life.

"You should talk to him," Castle says, and I startle so badly he jumps back, freaking out for a second, too.

"Sorry, sir," I say, trying to slow my heart rate. "I didn't see you there."

"That's quite all right," Castle says. He's smiling, but his eyes are sad. Exhausted. "How are you doing?"

"As well as can be expected," I say. "How's Sam?"

"As well as can be expected," he says. "Nouria is struggling, of course, but Sam should be able to make a full recovery. The girls say it was mostly a flesh wound. Her skull was fractured, but they're confident they can get it nearly back to the way it was." He sighs. "They'll be all right, both of them. In time."

I study him for a moment, suddenly seeing him like I've

never seen him before:

Old.

Castle's dreads are untied, hanging loose about his face, and something about the break from his usual style—locs tied neatly at the base of his neck—makes me notice things I'd never seen before. New gray hairs. New creases around his eyes, his forehead. It takes him a little longer to stand up straight like he used to. He seems worn out. Looking like he's been kicked down one too many times.

Kind of like the rest of us.

"I hate that this is the thing that seems to have conquered the distance between us," he says after a stretch of silence. "But now Nouria and I—both resistance leaders—have each suffered great losses. The whole thing has been hard for her, just as it was for me. She needs more time to recover."

I take a sharp breath.

Even the mention of that dark time inspires an ache in my heart. I don't allow myself to dwell for too long on the husk of a person Castle became after we lost Omega Point. If I do, the feelings overwhelm me so completely I pivot straight to anger. I know he was hurting. I know there was so much else going on. I know it was hard for everyone. But for me, losing Castle like that—however temporarily—was worse than losing everyone else. I needed him, and it felt like he'd abandoned me.

"I don't know," I say, clearing my throat. "It's not really the same thing, is it? What we lost— I mean, we lost literally everything in the bombing. Not only our people and our home, but years of research. Priceless equipment. Personal treasures." I hesitate, try to be delicate. "Nouria and Sam only lost half of their people, and their base is still standing. This loss isn't nearly as great."

Castle turns, surprised. "It's not as if it's a competition."

"I know that," I say. "It's just th—"

"And I wouldn't want my daughter to know the kind of grief we've experienced. You have no idea the depth of what she's already suffered in her young life. She certainly doesn't need to experience more pain to be deserving of your compassion."

"I didn't mean it like that," I say quickly, shaking my head. "I'm only trying to point out th—"

"Have you seen James yet?"

I gape at him, my mouth still shaped around an unspoken word. Castle just changed the subject so quickly it nearly gave me whiplash. This isn't like him. This isn't like *us*.

Castle and I never used to have trouble talking. We never avoided hard topics and sensitive conversations. But things have felt off for a little while now, if I'm being honest. Maybe ever since I realized Castle had been lying to me, all these years, about J. Maybe I've been a little less respectful lately. Crossed lines. Maybe all this tension is coming from me— maybe I'm the one pushing him away without realizing it.

I don't know.

I want to fix whatever is happening between us, but right now, I'm just too wrung out. Between J and Warner and James and unconscious Nazeera— My head is in such a weird place I'm not sure I have the bandwidth for much else.

So I let it go.

"No, I haven't seen James," I say, trying to sound upbeat. "Still waiting on that green light." Last I checked, James was in the medical tent with Sonya and Sara. James has his own healing abilities, so he should be fine, physically—I know that—but he's been through so much lately. The girls wanted to make sure he was fully rested and fed and hydrated before he had any visitors.

Castle nods.

"Warner is gone," he says after a moment, a non sequitur if there ever was one.

"What? No I just saw him. He—" I cut myself off as I glance up, expecting to find the familiar sight of him lying on his cot like a carcass. But Castle's right. He's gone.

I whip my head around, scanning the room for his retreating figure. I get nothing.

"I still think you should talk to him," Castle says, returning to his opening statement.

I bristle.

"You're the adult," I point out. "You're the one who wanted him to take refuge among us. You're the one who believed he could change. Maybe you should be the one to talk to him."

"That's not what he needs, and you know it." Castle sighs. Glances across the room. "Why is everyone so afraid of him? Why are *you* so afraid of him?"

"Me?" My eyes widen. "I'm not afraid of him. Or, I mean, whatever, I'm not the only one afraid of him. Though let's be real," I mutter, "anyone with two brain cells to rub together should be afraid of him."

Castle raises an eyebrow.

"Except for you, of course," I add hastily. "What reason would you have to be afraid of Warner? He's such a nice guy. Loves children. Big talker. Oh, and bonus: He no longer murders people professionally. No, now murdering people is just a fulfilling hobby."

Castle sighs, visibly annoyed.

I crack a smile. "Sir, all I'm saying is that we don't really know him, right? When Juliette was around—"

"Ella. Her name is Ella."

"Uh-huh. When she was around, Warner was tolerable. Barely. But now she's not around, and he's acting just like the guy I remember when I enlisted, the guy he was when he was working for his dad and running Sector 45. What reason does he have to be loyal or kind to the rest of us?"

Castle opens his mouth to respond, but just then arrives my salvation: lunch.

A smiling volunteer comes by, handing out simple salads in bowls of foil. I take the proffered food and plastic silverware with an overenthusiastic *thanks*, and promptly rip the lid off the container.

"Warner has been dealt a punishing blow," Castle says. "He needs us now more than ever."

I glance up at Castle. Shove a forkful of salad in my

mouth. I chew slowly, still deciding how to respond, when I'm distracted by movement in the distance.

I look up.

Brendan and Winston and Ian and Lily are in the corner gathered around a small, makeshift table, all of them holding tinfoil lunch bowls. They're waving us over.

I gesture with a forkful of salad. Speak with my mouth full. "You want to join us?"

Castle sighs even as he stands, smoothing out invisible wrinkles in his black pants. I glance over at Nazeera's sleeping figure as I collect my things. I know, rationally, that she's going to be fine, but she's recovering from a full blow to the chest—not unlike J once did—and it hurts to see her so vulnerable. Especially for a girl who once laughed in my face at the prospect of ever being overpowered.

It scares me.

"Coming?" Castle says, glancing over his shoulder. He's already a few steps away, and I have no idea how long I've been standing here, staring at Nazeera.

"Oh, yeah," I say. "Right behind you."

The minute we sit down at their table, I know something is off. Brendan and Winston are sitting stiffly, side by side, and Ian doesn't do more than glance at me when I sit down. I find this reception especially strange, considering the fact that *they* flagged *me* down. You'd think they'd be happy to see me.

After a few minutes of uncomfortable silence, Castle

speaks. "I was just telling Kenji," he says, "that he should be the one to talk to Warner."

Brendan looks up. "That's a great idea."

I shoot him a dark look.

"No, really," he says, carefully choosing a piece of potato to spear. Wait—where did they get potatoes? All I got was salad. "Someone definitely needs to talk to him."

"*Someone* definitely does," I say, irritated. I narrow my eyes at Brendan's potatoes. "Where'd you get those?"

"This is just what they gave me," Brendan says, looking up in surprise. "Of course, I'm happy to share."

I move quickly, jumping out of my seat to spear a chunk of potato from his bowl. I shove the whole piece in my mouth before I even sit back down, and I'm still chewing when I thank him.

He looks mildly repulsed.

I guess I am a bit of a caveman when Warner isn't around to keep me decent.

"Anyway, Castle's right," Lily says. "You should talk to him, and soon. I think he's kind of a loose cannon right now."

I stab a piece of lettuce, roll my eyes. "Can I maybe eat my lunch before everyone starts jumping down my throat? This is the first real meal I've had since I got shot."

"No one is jumping down your throat." Castle frowns. "And I thought Nouria said the normal dining hours went back into effect yesterday morning."

"They did," I say.

"But you were shot three days ago," Winston says. "Which means—"

"All right, okay, calm down, Detective Winston. Can we change the subject, please?" I take another bite of lettuce. "I don't like this one."

Brendan puts down his knife and fork. Hard.

I straighten.

"Go talk to him," he says again, this time with an air of finality that surprises me.

I swallow my food. Too fast. Nearly choke.

"I'm serious," Brendan says, frowning as I cough up a lung. "This is a wretched time for all of us, and you've more of a connection with him than anyone else here. Which means you have a moral responsibility to find out what he's thinking."

"A moral responsibility?" My cough turns into a laugh.

"Yes. A moral responsibility. And Winston agrees with me."

I look up, raising my eyebrows at Winston. "I bet he does. I bet Winston agrees with you all the time."

Winston adjusts his glasses. He stabs blindly at his food and mutters, "I hate you," under his breath.

"Oh yeah?" I gesture between Winston and Brendan with my fork. "What the hell is going on here? This energy is super weird."

When no one answers me I kick Winston under the table. He turns away, mumbling nonsense before taking a long pull from his water glass.

"Okay," I say slowly. I pick up my own water glass. Take a sip. "Seriously. What's going on? You two playing footsie under the table or someshit?"

Winston goes full tomato.

Brendan picks up his utensils and, looking down at his plate, says, "Go ahead. Tell him."

"Tell me what?" I say, glancing between the two of them. When no one responds, I look over at Ian like, *What the hell?*

Ian only shrugs.

Ian's been quieter than usual. He and Lily have been spending a lot more time together lately, which is understandable, but it also means I haven't really seen him much in the last couple of days.

Castle suddenly stands.

He claps me on the back. "Talk to Mr. Warner," he says. "He's vulnerable right now, and he needs his friends."

"Are you—?" I make a show of looking around, over my shoulders. "I'm sorry, which friends are you referring to? Because as far as I know, Warner doesn't have any."

Castle narrows his eyes at me. "Don't do this," he says. "Don't deny your own emotional intelligence in favor of petty grievances. You know better. Be better. If you care about him at all, you will sacrifice your pride to reach out to him. Make sure he's okay."

"Why do you have to make it sound so dramatic?" I say, looking away. "It's not that big of a deal. He'll survive."

Castle rests his hand on my shoulder. Forces me to meet his eyes. "No," he says to me. "He might not."

I wait until Castle is gone before I finally set down my fork. I'm irritated, but I know he's right. I mumble a general good-bye to my friends as I push away from the table, but not before I notice Brendan smiling triumphantly in my direction. I'm about to give him shit for it, but then I notice, with a start, that Winston has turned a shade of pink so magnificent you could probably see it from space.

And then, there it is: Brendan is holding Winston's hand under the table.

I gasp, audibly.

"Shut up," Winston says. "I don't want to hear it."

My enthusiasm withers. "You don't want to hear me say congratulations?"

"No, I don't want to hear you say *I told you so*."

"Yes, but I did fucking tell you so, didn't I?" A wave of happiness moves through me, conjures a smile. I didn't know I still had it in me.

Joy.

"I'm so happy for you guys," I say. "Truly. You just made this shitty day so much better."

Winston looks up, suspicious. But Brendan beams at me.

I stab a finger in their direction. "But if you two turn into Adam and Juliette clones I swear to God I will lose my mind."

Brendan's eyes go wide. Winston turns purple.

"Kidding!" I say. "I'm just kidding! Obviously I'm super happy for you two!" After a dead beat, I clear my throat. "No but seriously, though."

"Fuck off, Kenji."

"Yup." I shoot a finger gun at Winston. "You got it."

"*Kenji*," I hear Castle call out. "Language."

I swivel around, surprised. I thought Castle was gone. "It wasn't me!" I shout back. "For the first time, I swear, it wasn't me!"

I see only the back of Castle's head as he turns away, but somehow, I can tell he's still annoyed.

I shake my head. I can't stop smiling.

It's time to regroup.

Pick up the pieces. Keep going. Find J. Find Adam. Tear down The Reestablishment, once and for all. And the truth is—we're going to need Warner's help. Which means Castle is right, I need to talk to Warner. Shit.

I look back at my friends.

Lily's got her head on Ian's shoulder, and he's trying to hide his smile. Winston flips me off, but he's laughing. Brendan pops another piece of potato in his mouth and shoos me away.

"Go on, then."

"All right, all right," I say. But just as I'm about to take the necessary steps forward, I'm saved yet again.

Alia comes running toward me, her face lit in an expression of happiness I rarely see on her. It's transformative. Hell, she's glowing. It's easy to lose track of Alia, who's quiet in both voice and presence. But when she smiles like that—

She looks beautiful.

"James is awake," she says, nearly out of breath. She's squeezing my arm so hard it's cutting off my circulation.

I don't care.

I'd been carrying this tension for almost two weeks now. Worrying, all this time, about James and whether he was okay. When I saw him for the first time the other day, bound and gagged by Anderson, I felt my knees give out. We had no idea how he was doing or what kind of trauma he'd sustained. But if the girls are letting him have visitors—

That's got to be a good sign.

I send up silent thanks to anyone who might be listening. Mom. Dad. Ghosts. I'm grateful.

Alia is half dragging me down the hall, and even though her physical effort isn't necessary, I let her do it. She seems so excited I don't have the heart to stop her.

"James is officially up and ready for visitors," she says, "and he asked to see *you*."

~~ELLA~~
JULIETTE

When I wake, I am cold.

I dress in the dark, pulling on crisp fatigues and polished boots. I pull my hair back in a tight ponytail and perform a series of efficient ablutions at the small sink in my chamber.

Teeth brushed. Face washed.

After three days of rigorous training, I was selected as a candidate for supreme soldier, honored with the prospect of serving our North American commander. Today is my opportunity to prove I deserve the position.

I lace my boots, knotting them twice.

Satisfied, I pull the release latch. The lock exhales as it comes open, and the seam around my door lets through a ring of light that cuts straight across my vision. I turn away from the glare only to be met by my own reflection in a small mirror above the sink. I blink, focusing.

Pale skin, dark hair, odd eyes.

I blink again.

A flash of light catches my eye in the mirror. I turn. The monitor adjacent to my sleep pod has been dark all night, but now it flashes with information:

Juliette Ferrars, report

Juliette Ferrars, report

My hand vibrates.

I glance down, palm up, as a soft blue light beams through the thin skin at my wrist.

report

I push open the door.

Cool morning air rushes in, shuddering against my face. The sun is still rising. Golden light bathes everything, briefly distorting my vision. Birds chirp as I climb my way up the side of the steep hill that protects my private chamber against the howling winds. I haul myself over the edge.

Immediately, I spot the compound in the distance.

Mountains stagger across the sky. A massive lake glitters nearby. I push against tangles of wild, ferocious gusts of wind as I hike toward base. For no reason at all, a butterfly lands on my shoulder.

I come to a halt.

I pluck the insect off my shirt, pinching its wings between my fingers. It flutters desperately as I study it, scrutinizing its hideous body as I turn it over in my hand. Slowly, I increase the intensity of my touch, and its flutters grow more desperate, wings snapping against my skin.

I blink. The butterfly thrashes.

A low hum drums up from its insect body, a soft buzz that passes for a scream. I wait, patiently, for the creature to die, but it only beats its wings harder, resisting the inevitable. Irritated, I close my fingers, crushing it in my fist. I wipe its remains against an overgrown stalk of wheat and soldier on.

It's the fifth of May.

This is technically fall weather in Oceania, but the temperatures are erratic, inconsistent. Today the winds are particularly angry, which makes it unseasonably cold. My nose grows numb as I forge my way through the field; when I find a paltry slant of sunlight I lean into it, warming under its rays. Every morning and evening, I make this two-mile hike to base. My commander says it's necessary.

He did not explain why.

When I finally reach headquarters, the sun has shifted in the sky. I glance up at the dying star as I push open the front door, and the moment I step foot in the entry, I'm assaulted by the scent of burnt coffee. Quietly, I make my way down the hall, ignoring the sounds and stares of workers and armed soldiers.

Once outside his office, I stop. It's only a couple of seconds before the door slides open.

Supreme Commander Anderson looks up at me from his desk.

He smiles.

I salute.

"Step inside, soldier."

I do.

"How are you adjusting?" he says, closing a folder on his

desk. He does not ask me to sit down. "It's been a few days since your transfer from 241."

"Yes, sir."

"And?" He leans forward, clasps his hands in front of him. "How are you feeling?"

"Sir?"

He tilts his head at me. Picks up a mug of coffee. The acrid scent of the dark liquid burns my nose. I watch him take a sip and the simple action conjures a stutter of emotion inside of me. Feeling presses against my mind in flashes of memory: a bed, a green sweater, a pair of black glasses, then nothing. Flint failing to spark a flame.

"Are you missing your family?" he asks.

"I have no family, sir."

"Friends? A boyfriend?"

Vague irritation rises up inside of me; I push it aside. "None, sir."

He relaxes in his chair, his smile growing wider. "It's better that way, of course. Easier."

"Yes, sir."

He gets to his feet. "Your work these past couple of days has been remarkable. Your training has been even more successful than we expected." He glances up at me then, waiting for a reaction.

I merely stare.

He takes another sip of the coffee before setting the cup down beside a sheaf of papers. He walks around the desk and stands in front of me, assessing. One step closer and the smell of coffee overwhelms me. I inhale the bitter, nutty scent and it floods my senses, leaving me vaguely nauseated. Still, I stare straight ahead.

The closer he gets, the more aware of him I become.

His physical presence is solid. Categorically male. He's a wall of muscle standing before me, and even the suit he wears can't hide the subtle, sculpted curves of his arms and legs. His face is hard, the line of his jaw so sharp I can see it even out of focus. He smells like coffee and something else, something clean and fragrant. It's unexpectedly pleasant; it fills my head.

"Juliette," he says.

A needle of unease pierces my mind. It is more than unusual for the supreme commander to call me by my first name.

"Look at me."

I obey, lifting my head to meet his eyes.

He stares down at me, his expression fiery. His eyes are a strange, stark shade of blue, and there's something about him—his heavy brow, his sharp nose—that stirs up ancient feelings inside my chest. Silence gathers around us, unspoken curiosities pulling us together. He searches my face for so long that I begin to search him, too. Somehow I know that this is rare; that he might never again give me the opportunity to look at him like this.

I seize it.

I catalog the faint lines creasing his forehead, the starbursts around his eyes. I'm so close I can see the grain of his skin, rough but not yet leathery, his most recent shave evidenced in a microscopic nick at the base of his jaw. His brown hair is full and thick, his cheekbones high and his lips a dusky shade of pink.

He touches a finger to my chin, tilts up my face. "Your beauty is excessive," he says. "I don't know what your mother was thinking."

Surprise and confusion flare through me, but it does not presently occur to me to be afraid. I do not feel threatened by him. His words seem perfunctory. When he speaks, I catch a glimpse of a slight chip on his bottom incisor.

"Today," he says. "Things will change. You will shadow me from here on out. Your duty is to protect and serve my interests, and mine alone."

"Yes, sir."

His lips curve, just slightly. There's something there behind his eyes, something more, something else. "You understand," he says, "that you belong to me now."

"Yes, sir."

"My rule is your law. You will obey no other."

"Yes, sir."

He steps forward. His irises are so blue. A lock of dark hair curves across his eyes. "I am your master," he says.

"Yes, sir."

He's so close I can feel his breath against my skin. Coffee and mint and something else, something subtle, fermented. Alcohol, I realize.

He steps back. "Get on your knees."

I stare at him, frozen. The command was clear enough, but it feels like an error. "Sir?"

"On your knees, soldier. Now."

Carefully, I comply. The floor is hard and cold and my uniform is too stiff to make this position comfortable. Still, I remain on my knees for so long that a curious spider scuttles forward, peering at me from underneath a chair. I stare at Anderson's polished boots, the muscled curves of his calves noticeable even through his pants. The floor smells like bleach and lemon and dust.

When he commands me to, I look up.

"Now say it," he says softly.

I blink at him. "Sir?"

"Tell me that I am your master."

My mind goes blank.

A dull, warm sensation washes over me, a searching paralysis that locks my tongue, jams my mind. Fear propels through me, drowning me, and I fight to break the surface, clawing my way back to the moment.

I meet his eyes.

"You are my master," I say.

His stiff smile bends, curves. Joy catches fire in his eyes. "Good," he says softly. "Very good. How strange that you might turn out to be my favorite yet."

KENJI

I stop short at the door.

Warner is here.

Warner and James, together.

James was given his own private section of the MT—which is otherwise full and cramped—and the two of them are here, Warner sitting in a chair beside James's bed, James propped up against a stack of pillows. I'm so relieved to see him looking okay. His dirty-blond hair is a little too long, but his light, bright blue eyes are open and animated. Still, he looks more than a little tired, which probably explains the IV hooked up to his body.

Under normal circumstances, James should be able to heal himself, but if his body is drained, it makes the job harder. He must've arrived malnourished and dehydrated. The girls are probably doing what they can to help speed up the recovery process. I feel a rush of relief.

James will be better soon. He's such a strong kid. After everything he's been through—

He'll get through this, too. And he won't be alone.

I glance again at Warner, who looks only marginally better than the last time I saw him. He really needs to wash that blood off his body. It's not like Warner to overlook basic rules of hygiene—which should be proof enough that the guy is close to a full-on breakdown—but for now, at least, he seems okay. He and James appear to be deep in conversation.

I remain at the door, eavesdropping. It only belatedly occurs to me that I should give them privacy, but by then I'm too invested to walk away. I'm almost positive Anderson told James the truth about Warner. Or, I don't know, exactly. I can't actually imagine a scenario in which Anderson would gleefully reveal to James that Warner is his brother, or that Anderson is his dad. But somehow I can just tell that James knows. *Someone* told him. I can tell by the look on his face.

This is the come-to-Jesus moment.

This is the moment where Warner and James finally come face-to-face not as strangers, but as brothers. Surreal.

But they're speaking quietly, and I can only catch bits and pieces of their conversation, so I decide to do something truly reprehensible: I go invisible, and step farther into the room.

The moment I do, Warner stiffens.

Shit.

I see him glance around, his eyes alert. His senses are too sharp.

Quietly, I back up a few steps.

"You're not answering my question," James says, poking Warner in the arm. Warner shakes him off, his eyes narrowed at a spot a mere foot from where I'm standing.

"Warner?"

Reluctantly, Warner turns to face the ten-year-old. "Yes,"

he says, distracted. "I mean— What were you saying?"

"Why didn't you ever tell me?" James says, sitting up straighter. The bedsheets fall down, puddle in his lap. "Why didn't you say anything to me before? That whole time we lived together—"

"I didn't want to scare you."

"Why would I be scared?"

Warner sighs, stares out the window when he says, quietly, "Because I'm not known for my charm."

"That's not fair," James says. He looks genuinely upset, but his visible exhaustion is keeping him from reacting too strongly. "I've seen a lot worse than you."

"Yes. I realize that now."

"And *no one* told me. I can't believe no one told me. Not even Adam. I've been so mad at him." James hesitates. "Did everyone know? Did Kenji know?"

I stiffen.

Warner turns again, this time staring precisely in my direction when he says, "Why don't you ask him yourself?"

"Son of a bitch," I mutter, my invisibility melting away.

Warner almost smiles. James's eyes go wide.

This was not the reunion I was hoping for.

Still, James's face breaks into the biggest smile, which— I'm not going to lie—does wonders for my self-esteem. He throws off the covers and tries to jump out of bed, barefoot and oblivious to the needle stuck in his arm, and in those two and a half seconds I manage to experience both joy and terror.

I shout a warning, rushing forward to stop him from ripping open the flesh of his forearm, but Warner beats me to it. He's already on his feet, not so gently pushing the kid back down.

"Oh." James blushes. "Sorry."

I tackle him anyway, pulling him in for a long, excessive hug, and the way he clings to me makes me think I'm the first to do it. I try to fight back a rush of anger, but I'm unsuccessful. He's a ten-year-old kid, for God's sake. He's been through hell. How has no one given him the physical reassurance he almost certainly needs right now?

When we finally break apart, James has tears in his eyes. He wipes at his face and I turn away, trying to give him privacy, but when I take a seat at the foot of James's bed I catch a flash of pain steal in and out of Warner's eyes. It lasts for only half a second, but it's enough to make me feel bad for the guy. And it's enough to make me think he might be human again.

"Hey," I say, speaking to Warner directly for the first time. "So what, uh— What are you doing here?"

Warner looks at me like I'm an insect. His signature look. "What do you think I'm doing here?"

"Really?" I say, unable to hide my surprise. "That's so decent of you. I didn't think you'd be so . . . emotionally . . . responsible." I clear my throat. Smile at James. He's studying us curiously. "But I'm happy to be wrong, bro. And I'm sorry I misjudged you."

"I'm here to gather information," Warner says coldly.

"James is one of the only people who might be able to tell us where my father is located."

My compassion quickly turns to dust.

Catches fire.

Turns to rage.

"You're here to interrogate him?" I say, nearly shouting. "Are you insane? The kid has only barely recovered from unbelievable trauma, and you're here trying to mine him for information? He was probably *tortured*. He's a freaking *child*. What the hell is wrong with you?"

Warner is unmoved by my theatrics. "He was not tortured."

That stops me cold.

I turn to James. "You weren't?"

James shakes his head. "Not exactly."

"Huh." I frown. "I mean, don't get me wrong—I'm thrilled—but if he didn't torture you, what did Anderson do with you?"

James shrugs. "He mostly left me in solitary confinement. They didn't beat me," he says, rubbing absently at his ribs, "but the guards were pretty rough. And they didn't feed me much." He shrugs again. "But honestly, the worst part was not seeing Adam."

I pull James into my arms again, hold him tight. "I'm so sorry," I say gently. "That sounds horrible. And they wouldn't let you see Adam at all? Not even once?" I pull back. Look him in the eye. "I'm so, so sorry. I'm sure he's okay, little man. We'll find him. Don't worry."

Warner makes a sound. A sound that seems almost like a laugh.

I spin around angrily. "What the hell is wrong with you?" I say. "This isn't funny."

"Isn't it? I find the situation hilarious."

I'm about to say something to Warner I really shouldn't say in front of a ten-year-old, but when I glance back at James, I pull up short. James is rapidly shaking his head at me, his bottom lip trembling. He looks like he's about to cry again.

I turn back to Warner. "Okay, what is going on?"

Warner almost smiles when he says, "They weren't kidnapped."

My eyebrows fly up my forehead. "Say what now?"

"They weren't kidnapped."

"I don't understand."

"Of course you don't."

"This is not the time, bro. Tell me what's going on."

"Kent tracked down Anderson on his own," Warner says, his gaze shifting to James. "He offered his allegiance in exchange for protection."

My entire body goes slack. I nearly fall off the bed.

Warner goes on: "Kent wasn't lying when he said he would try for amnesty. But he left out the part about being a traitor."

"No. No way. No fucking way."

"There was never an abduction," Warner says. "No kidnapping. Kent bartered himself in exchange for James's protection."

This time, I actually fall off the bed. "Barter himself—how?" I manage to drag myself up off the floor, stumbling to my feet. "What does Adam even have to barter with? Anderson already knows all our secrets."

It's James who says quietly, "He gave them his power."

I stare at the kid, blinking like an idiot.

"I don't understand," I say. "How can you give someone your power? You can't just give someone your power. Right? It's not like a pair of pants you can just take off and hand over."

"No," Warner says. "But it's something The Reestablishment knows how to harvest. How else do you think my father took Sonya's and Sara's healing powers?"

"Adam told them what he can d-do," James says, his voice breaking. "He told them that he can use his power to turn other people's powers off. He thought it m-might be useful to them."

"Imagine the possibilities," Warner says, affecting awe. "Imagine how they might weaponize a power like that for global use—how they could make such a thing so powerful they could effectively shut down every single rebel group in the world. Reduce their *Unnatural* opposition to zero."

"Jesus fucking Christ."

I think I'm going to pass out. I actually feel faint. Dizzy. Like I can't breathe. Like this is impossible. "No way," I'm saying. I'm practically breathing the words. "No way. Not possible."

"I once said that Kent's ability was useless," Warner says

quietly. "But I see now that I was a fool."

"He didn't want to do it," James says. He's actively crying now, the silent tears moving down his face. "I swear he only did it to save me. He offered the only thing he had—the only thing he thought they'd want—to keep me safe. I know he didn't want to do it. He was just desperate. He thought he was doing the right thing. He kept telling me he was going to keep me safe."

"By running into the arms of the man who abused him his whole life?" I'm clutching my hair in my hands. "This doesn't make any sense. How does this— *How*—? *How?*"

I look up suddenly, realizing.

"And then look what he did," I say, stunned. "After everything, Anderson still used you as bait. He brought you here as leverage. He would've *killed* you, even after everything Adam gave up."

"Kent was a desperate idiot," Warner says. "That he was ever willing to trust my father with James's well-being tells you exactly how far gone he was."

"He was desperate, but he's not an idiot," James says angrily, his eyes refilling with tears. "He loves me and he was just trying to keep me safe. I'm so worried about him. I'm so scared something happened to him. And I'm so scared Anderson did something awful to him." James swallows, hard. "What are we going to do now? How are we going to get Adam and Juliette back?"

I squeeze my eyes shut, try to take deep breaths. "Listen, don't stress about this, okay? We're going to get them back.

And when we do, I'm going to murder Adam myself."

James gasps.

"Ignore him," Warner says. "He doesn't mean it."

"Yes, I damn well do mean it."

Warner pretends not to hear me. "According to the information I gathered just moments before you barged in here," he says calmly, "it sounds like my father was holding court back in Sector 45, just as Sam predicated. But he won't be there now, of that I'm certain."

"How can you be certain of *anything* right now?"

"Because I know my father," he says. "I know what matters most to him. And I know that when he left here, he was severely, gruesomely injured. There's only one place he'd go in a state like that."

I blink at him. "Where?"

"Oceania. Back to Maximillian Sommers, the only person capable of piecing him back together."

That stops me dead. "*Oceania?* Please tell me you're joking. We have to go back to Oceania?" I groan. "Dammit. That means we have to steal another plane."

"*We*," he says, irritated, "aren't doing anything."

"Of course we—"

Just then, the girls walk in. They come up short at the sight of me and Warner. Two sets of eyes blink at us.

"What are you doing here?" they ask at the same time.

Warner is on his feet in an instant. "I was just leaving."

"I think you mean *we* were just leaving," I say sharply.

Warner ignores me, nods at James, and heads for the

door. I'm following him out of the room before I remember, suddenly—

"James," I say, spinning around. "You're going to be okay, you know that, right? We're going to find Adam and bring him home and make all of this okay. Your job from here on out is to relax and eat chocolate and sleep. All right? Don't worry about anything. Do you understand?"

James blinks at me. He nods.

"Good." I step forward to plant a kiss on the top of his head. "Good," I say again. "You're going to be just fine. Everything is going to be fine. I'm going to make sure everything is fine, okay?"

James stares up at me. "Okay," he says, wiping away the last of his tears.

"Good," I say for the third time, and nod, still staring at his small, innocent face. "Okay, I'm going to go make that happen now. Cool?"

Finally, James smiles. "Cool."

I smile back, giving him everything I've got, and then dart out the door, hoping to catch Warner before he tries to rescue J without me.

ELLA JULIETTE

It is a relief not to speak.

Something changed between us this morning, something broke. Anderson seems relaxed in front of me in a way that seems unorthodox, but it's not my business to question him. I'm honored to have this position, to be his most trusted supreme soldier, and that's all that matters. Today is my first official day of work, and I'm happy to be here, even when he ignores me completely.

In fact, I enjoy it.

I find comfort in pretending to disappear. I exist only to shadow him as he moves from one task to another. I stand aside, staring straight ahead. I do not watch him as he works, but I feel him, constantly. He takes up all available space. I am attuned to his every movement, his every sound. It is my job now to know him completely, to anticipate his needs and fears, to protect him with my life, and to serve his interests entirely.

So I listen, for hours, to the details.

The creak of his chair as he leans back, considering. The sighs that escape him as he types. Leather chair and wool pants meeting, shifting. The dull thud of a ceramic mug hitting the surface of a wooden desk. The tinkle of crystal, the quick pour of bourbon. The sharp, sweet scent of tobacco and the rustle of tissue-thin paper. Keystrokes. A pen scratching. The sudden tear and fizz of a match. Sulfur. Keystrokes. A snap of a rubber band. Smoke, making my eyes tear. A stack of papers slapping together like a settling deck of cards. His voice, deep and melodic on a series of phone calls so brief I can't tell them apart. Keystrokes. He never seems to require use of the bathroom. I do not think about my own needs, and he does not ask. Keystrokes. Occasionally he looks up at me, studying me, and I keep my eyes straight ahead. Somehow, I can feel his smile.

I am a ghost.

I wait.

I hear little. I learn little.

Finally—

"Come."

He's on his feet and out the door and I hasten to follow. We're up high, on the top floor of the compound. The hallways circle around an interior courtyard, in the center of which is a large tree, branches heavy with orange and red leaves. Fall colors. I glance, without moving my head, outside one of the many tall windows gracing the halls, and my mind registers the incongruence of the two images. Outside, things are a strange mix of green and desolate. Inside, this tree is warm and rosy-hued. Perfect autumn foliage.

I shake off the thought.

I have to walk twice as fast to keep up with Anderson's

long strides. He stops for no one. Men and women in lab coats jump aside as we approach, mumbling apologies in our wake, and I'm surprised by the giddy sensation that rises up inside of me. I like their fear. I enjoy this power, this feeling of unapologetic dominion.

Dopamine floods my brain.

I pick up speed, still hurrying to keep up. It occurs to me then that Anderson never looks back to make sure I'm following him, and it makes me wonder what he'd do if he discovered I was missing. And then, just as quickly, the thought strikes me as bizarre. He has no reason to look back. I would never go missing.

The compound feels busier than usual today. Announcements blare through the speakers and the air around me fills with fervor. Names are called; demands made. People come and go.

We take the stairs.

Anderson never stops, never seems out of breath. He moves with the strength of a younger man but with the kind of confidence acquired only by age. He carries himself with a certainty both terrifying and aspirational. Faces pale at the sight of him. Most look away. Some can't help but stare. One woman nearly faints when his body brushes against hers, and Anderson doesn't even break his stride when she causes a scene.

I am fascinated.

The speakers crackle. A smooth, robotic female voice announces a code-green situation so calmly I can't help but be surprised by the collective reaction. I witness something akin to chaos as doors slam open around the building. It all seems to happen in sync, a domino effect echoing along corridors from top to bottom of the compound. Men and women in lab coats surge and swarm all levels, jamming the walkways as they scuttle along.

Still, Anderson does not stop. The world revolves around him, makes room for him. Slows when he speeds up. He does not accommodate anyone. Anything.

I am taking notes.

Finally, we reach a door. Anderson presses his hand against the biometric scanner, then peers into a camera that reads his eyes.

The door fissures open.

I smell something sterile, like antiseptic, and the moment we step into the room the scent burns my nose, causing my eyes to tear. The entrance is unusual; a short hallway that hides the rest of the room from immediate view. As we approach, I hear three monitors beep at three different decibel levels. When we round the corner, the room quadruples in size. The space is vast and bright, natural light combining with the searing white glow of artificial bulbs overhead.

There's little else here but a single bed and the figure strapped into it. The beeping is coming not from three machines, but seven, all of which seem to be affixed to the unconscious body of a boy. I don't know him, but he can't be much older than I am. His hair is cropped close to his scalp, a soft buzz of brown interrupted only by the wires drilled into his skull. There's a sheet pulled up to his neck, so I can't see much more than his resting face, but the sight of him there, strapped down like that, reminds me of something.

A flash of memory flares through me.

It's vague, distorted. I try to peel back the hazy layers, but when I manage a glimpse of something—a cave, a tall black man, a tank full of water—I feel a sharp, electrifying sting of rage that leaves my hands shaking. It unmoors me.

I take a jerky step back and shake my head a fraction of an inch, trying to compose myself, but my mind feels foggy, confused. When I finally pull myself together, I realize Anderson is watching me.

Slowly, he takes a step forward, his eyes narrowed in my direction. He says nothing, but I feel, without knowing why, exactly, that I'm not allowed to look away. I'm supposed to maintain eye contact for as long as he wants. It's brutal.

"You felt something when you walked in here," he says.

It's not a question. I'm not sure it requires an answer. Still—

"Nothing of consequence, sir."

"Consequence," he says, a hint of a smile playing at his lips. He takes a few steps toward one of the massive windows, clasps his hands behind his back. For a while, he's silent.

"So interesting," he says finally. "That we never did discuss consequences."

Fear slithers, creeps up my spine.

He's still staring out the window when he says softly, "You will not withhold anything from me. Everything you feel, every emotion you experience—it belongs to me. Do you understand?"

"Yes, sir."

"You felt something when you walked in here," he says again. This time, his voice is heavy with something, something dark and terrifying.

"Yes, sir."

"And what was it?"

"I felt anger, sir."

He turns around at that. Raises his eyebrows.

"After anger, I felt confusion."

"But anger," he says, stepping toward me. "Why anger?"

"I don't know, sir."

"Do you recognize this boy?" he says, pointing at the prone body without even looking at it.

"No, sir."

"No." His jaw clenches. "But he reminds you of someone."

I hesitate. Tremors threaten, and I will them away. Anderson's gaze is so intense I can hardly meet his eyes.

I glance again at the boy's sleeping face.

"Yes, sir."

Anderson's eyes narrow. He waits for more.

"Sir," I say quietly. "He reminds me of you."

Unexpectedly, Anderson goes still. Surprise rearranges his expression and suddenly, startlingly—

He laughs.

It's a laugh so genuine it seems to shock him even more than it shocks me. Eventually, the laughter settles into a smile. Anderson shoves his hands in his pockets and leans against the window frame. He stares at me with something resembling fascination, and it's such a pure moment, a moment so untainted by malice that he strikes me, suddenly, as beautiful.

More than that.

The sight of him—something about his eyes, something about the way he moves, the way he smiles— The sight of him suddenly stirs something in my heart. Ancient heat. A kaleidoscope of dead butterflies kicked up by a brief, dry gust of wind.

It leaves me feeling sick.

The stony look returns to his face. "That. Right there." He draws a circle in the air with his index finger. "That look on your face. What was that?"

My eyes widen. Unease floods through me, heating my cheeks.

For the first time, I falter.

He moves swiftly, charging toward me so angrily I wonder at my ability to remain steady. Roughly, he takes my chin in his hand, tilts up my face. There are no secrets here, this close to him. I can hide nothing.

"Now," he says, his voice low. Angry. "Tell me now."

I break eye contact, trying desperately to gather my thoughts, and he barks at me to look at him.

I force myself to meet his eyes. And then I hate myself,

hate my mouth for betraying my mind. Hate my mind for thinking at all.

"You— You are extremely handsome, sir."

Anderson drops his hand like he's been burned. He backs away, looking, for the first time—

Uncomfortable.

"Are you—" He stops, frowns. And then, too soon, anger clouds his expression. His voice is practically a growl when he says, "You are lying to me."

"No, sir." I hate the sound of my voice, the breathy panic.

His eyes sharpen. He must see something in my expression that gives him pause, because the anger evaporates from his face.

He blinks at me.

Then, carefully, he says: "In the middle of all of this"—he waves around the room, at the sleeping figure hooked up to the machines—"of all the things that could be going through your mind, you were thinking . . . that you find me attractive."

A traitorous heat floods my face. "Yes, sir."

Anderson frowns.

He seems about to say something, and then hesitates. For the first time, he seems unmoored.

A few seconds of tortured silence stretch between us, and I'm not sure how best to proceed.

"This is unsettling," Anderson finally says, and mostly to himself. He presses two fingers to the inside of his wrist, and lifts his wrist to his mouth.

"Yes," he says quietly. "Tell Max there's been an unusual development. I need to see him at once."

Anderson spares me a brief glance before dismissing, with a single shake of his head, the entire mortifying exchange.

He stalks toward the boy strapped down on the bed and says, "This young man is part of an ongoing experiment."

I'm not sure what to say, so I say nothing.

Anderson bends over the boy, toying with various wires, and then stiffens, suddenly. Looks up at me out of the corner of his eye. "Can you imagine why this boy is part of an experiment?"

"No sir."

"He has a gift," Anderson says, straightening. "He came to me voluntarily and offered to share it with me."

I blink, still uncertain how to respond.

"But there are many of you—*Unnaturals*—running wild on this planet," Anderson says. "So many powers. So many different abilities. Our asylums are teeming with them, overrun with power. I have access to nearly anything I want. So what makes him special, hmm?" He tilts his head at me. "What power could he possibly have that would be greater than yours? More useful?"

Again, I say nothing.

"Do you want to know?" he asks, a hint of a smile touching his lips.

This feels like a trick. I consider my options.

Finally, I say, "I want to know only if you want to tell me, sir."

Anderson's smile blooms. White teeth. Genuine pleasure.

I feel my chest warm at his quiet praise. Pride straightens my shoulders. I avert my eyes, staring quietly at the wall.

Still, I see Anderson turn away again, appraising the boy with another single, careful look. "These powers were wasted on him anyway."

He removes the touchpad slotted into a compartment of the boy's bed and begins tapping the digital screen, scrolling and scanning for information. He looks up, once, at the monitors beeping out various vitals, and frowns. Finally, he sighs, dragging a hand through his perfectly arranged hair. I think it looks better for being mussed. Warmer. Softer. Familiar.

The observation frightens me.

I turn away sharply and glance out the window, wondering, suddenly, if I will ever be allowed to use the bathroom.

"Juliette."

The angry timbre of his voice sends my heart racing. I straighten in an instant. Look straight ahead.

"Yes, sir," I say, sounding a little breathless.

I realize then that he's not even looking at me. He's still typing something into the touchpad when he says, calmly, "Were you daydreaming?"

"No, sir."

He returns the touchpad to its compartment, the pieces connecting with a satisfying metallic *click*.

He looks up.

"This is growing tiresome," he says quietly. "I'm already losing patience with you, and we haven't even come to the end of your first day." He hesitates. "Do you want to know what happens when I lose patience with you, Juliette?"

My fingers tremble; I clench them into fists. "No, sir."

He holds out his hand. "Then give me what belongs to me."

I take an uncertain step forward and his outstretched hand flies up, palm out, stopping me in place. His jaw clenches.

"I am referring to your mind," he says. "I want to know what you were thinking when you lost your head long enough to gaze out the window. I want to know what you are thinking right now. I will always want to know what you're thinking," he says sharply. "In every moment. I want every word, every detail, every emotion. Every single loose, fluttering thought that passes through your head, I want it," he says, stalking toward me. "Do you understand? It's mine. You are *mine*."

He comes to a halt just inches from my face.

"Yes, sir," I say, my voice failing me.

"I will only ask this once more," he says, making an effort to moderate his voice. "And if you ever make me work this hard again to get the answers I need, you will be punished. Is that clear?"

"Yes, sir."

A muscle jumps in his jaw. His eyes narrow. "What were you daydreaming about?"

I swallow. Look at him. Look away.

Quietly, I say:

"I was wondering, sir, if you would ever let me use the bathroom."

Anderson's face goes suddenly blank.

He seems stunned. He regards me a moment longer before saying, flatly: "You were wondering if you could use the bathroom."

"Yes, sir." My face heats.

Anderson crosses his arms across his chest. "That's all?"

I feel suddenly compelled to tell him what I thought about his hair, but I fight against the urge. Guilt floods through me at the indulgence, but my mind is soothed by a strange, familiar warmth, and suddenly I feel no guilt at all for being only partly truthful.

"Yes, sir. That's all."

Anderson tilts his head at me. "No new surges of anger? No questions about what we're doing here? No concerns over the well-being of the boy"—he points—"or the powers he might have?"

"No, sir."

"I see," he says.

I stare.

Anderson takes a deep breath and undoes a button of his blazer. He pushes both hands through his hair. Begins to pace.

He's becoming flustered, I realize, and I don't know what to do about it.

"It's almost funny," he says. "This is exactly what I wanted, and yet, somehow, I'm disappointed."

He takes a deep, sharp breath, and spins around.

Studies me.

"What would you do," he says, nodding his head an inch to his left, "if I asked you to throw yourself out that window?"

I turn, examining the large window looming over us both.

It's a massive, circular stained glass window that takes up half the wall. Colors scatter across the ground, creating a beautiful, distracted work of art over the polished concrete floors. I walk over to window, run my fingers along the ornate panes of glass. I peer down at the expanse of green below. We're at least five hundred feet above the ground, but the distance doesn't inspire my fear. I could make that jump easily, without injury.

I look up. "I would do it with pleasure, sir."

He takes a step closer. "What if I asked you to do it without using your powers? What if it was simply my desire that you throw yourself out the window?"

A wave of searing, blistering heat moves through me, seals shut my mouth. Binds my arms. I can't pry my own mouth open against the terrifying assault, but I can only imagine it's part of this challenge.

Anderson must be trying to test my allegiance.

He must be trying to trap me into a moment of disobedience. Which means I need to prove myself. My loyalty.

It takes an extraordinary amount of my own supernatural strength to fight back the invisible forces clamping my mouth shut, but I manage it. And when I can finally speak, I say,

"I would do it with pleasure, sir."

Anderson takes yet another step closer, his eyes glittering with something— Something brand-new. Something akin to wonder.

"Would you, really?" he says softly.

"Yes, sir."

"Would you do anything I asked you to do? Anything at all?"

"Yes, sir."

Anderson's still holding my gaze when he lifts his wrist to his mouth again and says quietly:

"Come in here. Now."

He drops his hand.

My heart begins to pound. Anderson refuses to look away from me, his eyes growing bluer and brighter by the second. It's almost like he knows that his eyes alone are enough to upset my equilibrium. And then, without warning, he grabs my wrist. I realize too late that he's checking my pulse.

"So fast," he says softly. "Like a little bird. Tell me, Juliette. Are you afraid?"

"No, sir."

"Are you excited?"

"I— I don't know, sir."

The door slides open and Anderson drops my wrist. For

the first time in minutes, Anderson looks away from me, finally breaking some painful, invisible connection between us. My body goes slack with relief and, remembering myself, I quickly straighten.

A man walks in.

Dark hair, dark eyes, pale skin. He's young, younger than Anderson, I think, but older than me. He wears a headset. He looks uncertain.

"Juliette," Anderson says, "this is Darius."

I turn to face Darius.

Darius says nothing. He looks paralyzed.

"I won't be requiring Darius's services anymore," Anderson says, glancing in my direction.

Darius blanches. Even from where I'm standing, I can see his body begin to tremble.

"Sir?" I say, confused.

"Isn't it obvious?" Anderson says. "I would like you to dispose of him."

Understanding dawns. "Certainly, sir."

The moment I turn in Darius's direction, he screams; it's a sharp, bloodcurdling sound that irritates my ears. He makes a run for the door and I pivot quickly, throwing out my arm to stop him. The force of my power sends him flying the rest of the way to the exit, his body slamming hard against the steel wall.

He slumps, with a soft moan, to the ground.

I open my palm. He screams.

Power surges through me, filling my blood with fire. The

feeling is intoxicating. Delicious.

I lift my hand and Darius's body lifts off the floor, his head thrown back in agony, his body run through by invisible rods. He continues to scream and the sound fills my ears, floods my body with endorphins. My skin hums with his energy. I close my eyes.

Then I close my fist.

Fresh screams pierce the silence, echoing around the vast, cavernous space. I feel a smile tugging at my lips and I lose myself in the feeling, in the freedom of my own power. There's a joy in this, in using my strength so freely, in finally letting go.

Bliss.

My eyes flutter open but I feel drugged, deliriously happy as I watch his seized, suspended body begin to convulse. Blood spurts from his nose, bubbles up inside his open, gasping mouth. He's choking. Nearly dead. And I'm just beginning t—

The fire leaves my body so suddenly it sends me stumbling backward.

Darius falls, with a bone-cracking thud, to the floor.

A desperate emptiness burns through me, leaves me feeling faint. I hold my hands up as if in prayer, trying to figure out what happened, feeling suddenly close to tears. I spin around, trying to understand—

Anderson is pointing a weapon at me.

I drop my hands.

Anderson drops his weapon.

Power surges through me once more and I take a deep, grateful breath, finding relief in the feeling as it floods my senses, refilling my veins. I blink several times, trying to clear my head, but it's Darius's pathetic, agonized whimpers that bring me back to the present moment. I stare at his broken body, the shallow pools of blood on the floor. I feel vaguely annoyed.

"Incredible."

I turn around.

Anderson is staring at me with unvarnished amazement. "Incredible," he says again. "That was incredible."

I stare at him, uncertain.

"How do you feel?" he asks.

"Disappointed, sir."

His eyebrows pull together. "Why disappointed?"

I glance at Darius. "Because he's still alive, sir. I didn't complete the task."

Anderson's face breaks into a smile so wide it electrifies his features. He looks young. He looks kind. He looks wonderful.

"My God," he says softly. "You're perfect."

KENJI

"Hey," I call out. "Wait up!"

I'm still sprinting after Warner and, in a move that surprises absolutely no one, he doesn't wait. He doesn't even slow down. In fact, I'm pretty sure he speeds up.

I realize, as I pick up the pace, that I haven't felt fresh air in a couple of days. I look around as I go, trying to take in the details. The sky is bluer than I've ever seen it. There's no cloud in sight for miles. I don't know if this weather is unique to the geographical location of Sector 241, or if it's just regular climate change. Regardless, I take a deep breath. Air feels good.

I was getting claustrophobic in the dining hall, spending endless hours with the ill and injured. The colors of the room had begun to bleed together, all the linen and ash-colored cots and the too-bright, unnatural light. The smells were intense, too. Blood and bleach. Antiseptic. It was making my head swim. I woke up with a massive headache this morning—though, to be fair, I wake up with a massive headache almost every morning—but being outside is beginning to soothe the ache.

Who knew.

It's nice out here, even if it's a little hot in this outfit. I'm wearing a pair of old fatigues I found in my room. Sam and Nouria made sure from the start that we had everything we needed—even now, even after the battle. We have toiletries. Clean clothes.

Warner, on the other hand—

I squint at his retreating figure. I can't believe he still hasn't taken a shower. He's still wearing Haider's leather jacket, but it's practically destroyed. His black pants are torn, his face still smudged with what I can only imagine is a combination of blood and dirt. His hair is wild. His boots are dull. And somehow—*somehow*—he still manages to look put together. I don't get it.

I slow my pace when I pull up next to him, but I'm still power walking. Breathing hard. Beginning to sweat.

"Hey," I say, pinching my shirt away from my chest, where it's starting to stick. The weather is getting weirder; it's suddenly sweltering. I wince upward, toward the sun.

Here, within the Sanctuary, I've been getting a better idea of the state of our world. News flash: The earth is still basically going to shit. The Reestablishment has just been taking advantage of the aforementioned shit, making things seem irreparably bad.

The truth, on the other hand, is that they're only reparably bad.

Ha.

"Hey," I say again, this time clapping Warner on the shoulder. He shoves off my hand with so much enthusiasm I nearly stumble.

"Okay, listen, I know you're upset, but—"

Warner suddenly disappears.

"Hey, where the hell are you going?" I shout, my voice ringing out. "Are you heading back to your room? Should I just meet you there?"

A couple of people turn to stare at me.

The normally busy paths are pretty empty right now because so many of us are still convalescing, but the few people lingering in the bright sun shoot me dirty looks.

Like I'm the weirdo.

"Leave him alone," someone hisses at me. "He's grieving."

I roll my eyes.

"Hey—*douche bag*," I shout, hoping Warner's still close enough to hear me. "I know you love her, but so do I, and I'm—"

Warner reappears so close to my face I nearly scream. I take a sudden, terrified step backward.

"If you value your life," he says, "don't come near me."

I'm about to point out that he's being dramatic, but he cuts me off.

"I didn't say that to be dramatic. I didn't even say it to scare you. I'm saying it out of respect for Ella, because I know she'd rather I didn't kill you."

I'm quiet for a full second. And then I frown.

"Are you fucking with me right now? You're definitely fucking with me right now. Right?"

Warner's eyes go flinty. Electric. That scary kind of crazy.

"Every single time you claim to understand even a fraction of what I'm feeling, I want to disembowel you. I want to sever your carotid artery. I want to rip out your vertebrae, one by one. You have no idea what it is to love her," he says angrily. "You couldn't even begin to imagine. So stop trying to understand."

Wow, sometimes I really hate this guy.

I have to literally clench my jaw to keep myself from saying what I'm really thinking right now, which is that I want to put my fist through his skull. (I actually imagine it for a moment, imagine what it'd be like to crush his head like a walnut. It's oddly satisfying.) But then I remember that we need this asshole, and that J's life is on the line. The fate of the world is on the line.

So I fight back my anger and try again.

"Listen," I say, making an effort to gentle my voice. "I know what you guys have is special. I know that I can't really understand that kind of love. I mean, hell, I know you were even thinking about proposing to her—and that must've—"

"I did propose to her."

I suddenly stiffen.

I can tell just by the sound of his voice that he's not joking. And I can tell by the look on his face—the infinitesimal flash of misery in his eyes—that this is my opening. This is the data I've been missing. This is the source of the agony that's been drowning him.

I scan the immediate area for eavesdroppers. Yep. Too many new members of the Warner fan club clutching their hearts.

"Come on," I say to him. "I'm taking you to lunch."

Warner blinks, confusion temporarily clearing his anger. And then, sharply: "I'm not hungry."

"That's obviously bullshit." I look him up and down. He looks good—he always looks good, the asshole—but he looks hungry. Not just the regular kind of hungry, either, but that desperate hunger that's so hungry it doesn't even feel like hunger anymore.

"You haven't eaten anything in days," I say to him. "And you know better than I do that you'll be useless on a rescue mission if you pass out before you even get there."

He glares at me.

"Come on, bro. You want J to come home to skin and bones? The way you're going, she'll take one look at you and run screaming in the opposite direction. This is not a good look. All these muscles need to eat." I poke at his bicep. "Feed your children."

Warner jerks away from me and takes a long, irritated breath. The sound of it almost makes me smile. Feels like old times.

I think I'm making progress.

Because this time, when I tell him to follow me, he doesn't fight.

~~ELLA~~
JULIETTE

Anderson takes me to meet Max.

I follow him down into the bowels of the compound, through winding, circuitous paths. Anderson's steps echo along the stone and steel walkways, the lights flickering as we go. The occasional, overly bright lights cast stark shadows in strange shapes. I feel my skin prickle.

My mind wanders.

A flash of Darius's limp body blazes in my mind, carrying with it a sharp twinge that twists my gut. I fight against an impulse to vomit, even as I feel the contents of my meager breakfast coming up my throat. With effort, I force back the bile. Sweat beads along my forehead, the back of my neck.

My body is screaming to stop moving. My lungs want to expand, collect air. I allow neither.

I force myself to keep walking.

I wick away the images, expunging thoughts of Darius from my mind. The churning in my stomach begins to slow, but in its wake my skin takes on a damp, clammy sensation. I struggle to recount the things I ate this morning. I must've eaten poorly; something isn't agreeing with my stomach. I feel feverish.

I blink.

I blink again, but this time for too long and I see a flash of blood, bubbling up inside Darius's open mouth. The nausea returns with a swiftness that scares me. I suck in a breath, my fingers fluttering, desperate to press against my stomach. Somehow, I hold steady. I keep my eyes open, widening them to the point of pain. My heart starts pounding. I try desperately to maintain control over my spiraling thoughts, but my skin begins to crawl. I clench my fists. Nothing helps. Nothing helps. *Nothing*, I think.

nothing

nothing

nothing

I begin to count the lights we pass.

I count my fingers. I count my breaths. I count my footsteps, measuring the force of every footfall that thunders up my legs, reverberates around my hips.

I remember that Darius is still alive.

He was carried away, ostensibly to be patched up and returned to his former position. Anderson didn't seem to mind that Darius was still alive. Anderson was only testing me, I realized. Testing me, once again, to make sure that I was obedient to him and him alone.

I take in a deep, fortifying breath.

I focus on Anderson's retreating figure. For reasons I can't explain, staring at him steadies me. Slows my pulse. Settles my stomach. And from this vantage point, I can't help but admire the way he moves. He has an impressive, muscular frame—broad shoulders, narrow waist, strong legs—but I marvel most at the way he carries himself. He has a confident stride. He walks tall, with smooth, effortless efficiency. As I watch him, a familiar feeling flutters through me. It gathers in my stomach, sparking dim heat that sends a brief shock to my heart.

I don't fight it.

There's something about him. Something about his face. His carriage. I find myself moving unconsciously closer to him, watching him almost too intently. I've noticed that he wears no jewelry, not even a watch. He has a faded scar between his right thumb and index finger. His hands are rough and callused. His dark hair is shot through with silver, the extent of which is only visible up close. His eyes are the blue-green of shallow, turquoise waters. Unusual.

Aquamarine.

He has long brown lashes and laugh lines. Full, curving lips. His skin grows rougher as the day wears on, the shadow of facial hair hinting at a version of him I try and fail to imagine.

I realize I'm beginning to like him. Trust him.

Suddenly, he stops. We're standing outside a steel door, next to which is a keypad and biometric scanner.

He brings his wrist to his mouth. "Yes." A pause. "I'm outside."

I feel my own wrist vibrate. I look down, surprised, at the blue light flashing through the skin at my pulse.

I'm being summoned.

This is strange. Anderson is standing right next to me;

I thought he was the only one with the authority to summon me.

"Sir?" I say.

He glances back, his eyebrows raised as if to say— *Yes?* And something that feels like happiness blooms to life inside of me. I know it's unwise to make so much of so little, but his movements and expressions feel suddenly softer now, more casual. It's clear that he's begun to trust me, too.

I lift my wrist to show him the message. He frowns.

He steps closer to me, taking my flashing arm in his hands. The tips of his fingers press against my skin as he gently bends back the joint, his eyes narrowing as he studies the summons. I go unnaturally still. He makes a sound of irritation and exhales, his breath skittering across my skin.

A bolt of sensation moves through me.

He's still holding my arm when he speaks into his own wrist. "Tell Ibrahim to back off. I have it under control."

In the silence, Anderson tilts his head, listening on an earpiece that isn't readily visible. I can only watch. Wait.

"I don't care," he says angrily, his fingers closing unconsciously around my wrist. I gasp, surprised, and he turns, our eyes meeting, clashing.

Anderson frowns.

His pleasant, masculine scent fills my head and I breathe him in almost without meaning to. Being this close to him is difficult. Strange. My head is swimming with confusion.

Broken images flood my mind—a flash of golden hair, fingers grazing bare skin—and then nausea. Dizziness.

It nearly knocks me over.

I look away just as Anderson tugs my arm up, toward a floodlight, squinting to get a better look. Our bodies nearly touch, and I'm suddenly so close I can see the edges of a tattoo, dark and curving, creeping up the edge of his collarbone.

My eyes widen in surprise. Anderson lets go of my wrist.

"I already know it was him," he says, speaking quickly, his eyes darting at and away from me. "His code is in the timestamp." A pause. "Just clear the summons. And then remind him that she reports only to me. I decide if and when he gets to talk to her."

He drops his wrist. Touches a finger to his temple.

And then, narrows his eyes at me.

My heart jumps. I straighten. I no longer wait to be prompted. When he looks at me like that, I know it's my cue to confess.

"You have a tattoo, sir. I was surprised. I wondered what it was."

Anderson raises an eyebrow at me.

He seems about to speak when, finally, the steel door exhales open. A curl of steam escapes the doorway, behind which emerges a man. He's tall, taller than Anderson, with wavy brown hair, light brown skin, and light, bright eyes the color of which aren't immediately obvious. He wears a white lab coat. Tall rubber boots. A face mask hangs around his neck, and a dozen pens have been shoved into the pocket of his coat. He makes no effort to move forward or to step aside; he only stands in the doorway, seemingly undecided.

"What's going on?" Anderson says. "I sent you a message an hour ago and you never showed up. Then I come to your door and you make me wait."

The man—Anderson told me his name was Max—says nothing. Instead, he appraises me, his eyes moving up and down my body in a show of undisguised hatred. I'm not sure how to process his reaction.

Anderson sighs, grasping something that isn't obvious to me.

"Max," he says quietly. "You can't be serious."

Max shoots Anderson a sharp look. "Unlike you, we're not all made of stone." And then, looking away: "At least not entirely."

I'm surprised to discover that Max has an accent, one not unlike the citizens of Oceania. Max must originate from this region.

Anderson sighs again.

"All right," Max says coolly. "What did you want to discuss?" He pulls a pen out of his pocket, uncapping it with his teeth. He reaches into his other pocket and pulls free a notebook. Flips it open.

I go suddenly blind.

In the span of a single instant darkness floods my vision. Clears. Hazy images reappear, time speeding up and slowing down in fits and starts. Colors streak across my eyes, dilate my pupils. Stars explode, lights flashing, sparking. I hear voices. A single voice. A whisper—

I am a thief

The tape rewinds. Plays back. The file corrupts.

I am
I am
I I I
am
a thief
a thief I stole
I stole this notebook andthispenfromoneofthedoctors

"Of course you did."

Anderson's sharp voice brings me back to the present moment. My heart is beating in my throat. Fear presses against my skin, conjuring goose bumps along my arms. My eyes move too quickly, darting around in distress until they rest, finally, on Anderson's familiar face.

He's not looking at me. He's not even speaking to me.

Quiet relief floods through me at the realization. My interlude lasted but a moment, which means I haven't missed much more than a couple of exchanged words. Max turns to me, studying me curiously.

"Come inside," he says, and disappears through the door.

I follow Anderson through the entryway, and as soon as I cross the threshold, a blast of icy air sends a shiver up my skin. I don't make it much farther than the entrance before I'm distracted.

Amazed.

Steel and glass are responsible for most of the structures in the space—massive screens and monitors; microscopes; long glass tables littered with beakers and half-filled test tubes. Accordion pipes sever vertical space around the room, connecting tabletops and ceilings. Blocks of artificial light fixtures are suspended in midair, humming steadily. The light temperature in here is so blue I don't know how Max can stand it.

I follow Max and Anderson over to a crescent-shaped desk that looks more like a command center. Papers are stacked on one side of the steel top, screens flickering above. More pens are stuffed into a chipped coffee mug sitting atop a thick book.

A *book*.

I haven't seen a relic like that in a long time.

Max takes his seat. He gestures at a stool tucked under a nearby table, and Anderson shakes his head.

I continue to stand.

"All right, then, go on," Max says, his eyes flickering in my direction. "You said there was a problem."

Anderson looks suddenly uncomfortable. He says nothing for so long that, eventually, Max smiles.

"Out with it," Max says, gesturing with his pen. "What did you do wrong this time?"

"I didn't do anything wrong," Anderson says sharply. Then he frowns. "I don't think so, anyway."

"Then what is it?"

Anderson takes a deep breath. Finally: "She says that she's . . . attracted to me."

Max's eyes widen. He glances from Anderson to me and then back again. And then, suddenly—

He laughs.

My face heats. I stare straight ahead, studying the strange equipment stacked on shelves against the far wall.

Out of the corner of my eye, I see Max scribbling in a notepad. All this modern technology, but he still seems to enjoy writing by hand. The observation strikes me as odd. I file the information away, not really understanding why.

"Fascinating," Max says, still smiling. He gives his head a quick shake. "Makes perfect sense, of course."

"I'm glad you think this is funny," Anderson says, visibly irritated. "But I don't like it."

Max laughs again. He leans back in his chair, his legs outstretched, crossed at the ankles. He's clearly intrigued—excited, even—by the development, and it's causing his earlier iciness to thaw. He bites down on the pen cap, considering Anderson. There's a glint in his eye.

"Do mine eyes deceive me," he says, "or does the great Paris Anderson admit to having a conscience? Or perhaps: a sense of morality?"

"You know better than anyone that I've never owned either, so I'm afraid I wouldn't know what it feels like."

"Touché."

"Anyway—"

"I'm sorry," Max says, his smile widening. "But I need

another moment with this revelation. Can you blame me for being fascinated? Considering the uncontested fact of your being one of the most depraved human beings I've ever known—and among our social circles, that's saying a lot—"

"Ha ha," Anderson says flatly.

"—I think I'm just surprised. Why is *this* too much? Why is this the line you won't cross? Of all the things . . ."

"Max, be serious."

"I am being serious."

"Aside from the obvious reasons why this situation should be disturbing to anyone— The girl's not even eighteen. Even I am not as depraved as that."

Max shakes his head. Holds up his pen. "Actually, she's been eighteen for four months."

Anderson seems about to argue, and then—

"Of course," he says. "I was remembering the wrong paperwork." He glances at me as he says it, and I feel my face grow hotter.

I am simultaneously confused and mortified.

Curious.

Horrified.

"Either way," Anderson says sharply, "I don't like it. Can you fix it?"

Max sits forward, crosses his arms. "Can I *fix* it? Can I fix the fact that she can't help but be attracted to the man who spawned the two faces she's known most intimately?" He shakes his head. Laughs again. "That kind of wiring isn't undone without incurring serious repercussions. Repercussions that would set us back."

"What kind of repercussions? Set us back how?"

Max glances at me. Glances at Anderson.

Anderson sighs. "Juliette," he barks.

"Yes, sir."

"Leave us."

"Yes, sir."

I pivot sharply and head for the exit. The door slides open in anticipation of my approach, but I hesitate, just a few feet away, when I hear Max laugh again.

I know I shouldn't eavesdrop. I know it's wrong. I know I'd be punished if I were caught. I know this.

Still, I can't seem to move.

My body is revolting, screaming at me to cross the threshold, but a pervasive heat has begun to seep into my mind, dulling the compulsion. I'm still frozen in front of the open door, trying to decide what to do, when their voices carry over.

"She clearly has a type," Max is saying. "At this point, it's practically written in her DNA."

Anderson says something I don't hear.

"Is it really such a bad thing?" Max says. "Perhaps her affection for you could work out in your favor. Take advantage of it."

"You think I'm so desperate for companionship—or so completely incompetent—that I'd need to result to seduction in order to get what I want out of the girl?"

Max barks out a laugh. "We both know you've never been desperate for companionship. But as to your competence . . ."

"I don't know why I even bother with you."

"It's been thirty years, Paris, and I'm still waiting for you to develop a sense of humor."

"It's been thirty years, Max, and you'd think I'd have found some new friends by now. Better ones."

"You know, your kids aren't funny, either," Max says, ignoring him. "Interesting how that works, isn't it?"

Anderson groans.

Max only laughs louder.

I frown.

I stand there, trying and failing to process their interactions. Max just insulted a supreme commander of The Reestablishment—multiple times. As Anderson's subordinate, he should be punished for speaking so disrespectfully. He should be fired, at the very least. Executed, if Anderson deems it preferable.

But when I hear the distant sound of Anderson's laughter, I realize that he and Max are laughing *together*. It's a realization that both startles and stuns me:

That they must be friends.

One of the overhead lights pops and hums, startling me out of my reverie. I give my head a quick shake and head out the door.

KENJI

I'm suddenly a big fan of the Warner groupies.

On our way back to my tent, I told only a couple of people I spotted on the path that Warner was hungry—but still not feeling well enough to join everyone in the dining hall—and they've been delivering packages of food to my room ever since. The problem is, all this kindness comes with a price. Six different girls (and two guys) have shown up so far, each one of them expecting payment for their generosity in the form of a conversation with Warner, which—obviously—never happens. But they usually settle for a good long look at him.

It's weird.

I mean, even I know, objectively, that Warner's not disgusting to look at, but this whole production of unabashed flirtation is really starting to feel weird. I'm not used to being in an environment where people openly admit to liking anything about Warner. Back at Omega Point—and even on base in Sector 45—everyone seemed to agree that he was a monster. No one denied their fear or disgust long enough to treat him like the kind of guy at whom they might bat their eyelashes.

But what's funny is: I'm the only one getting irritated.

Every time the doorbell rings I'm like, this is it, this is the time Warner is finally going to lose his mind and shoot someone, but he never even seems to notice. Of all the things that piss him off, gawking men and women don't appear to be on the list.

"So is this, like, normal for you, or what?" I'm still arranging food on plates in the little dining area of my room. Warner is standing stiffly in a random spot by the window. He chose that random spot when we walked in and he's just been standing there, staring at nothing, ever since.

"Is what normal for me?"

"All these people," I say, gesturing at the door. "Coming in here pretending they're not imagining you without your clothes on. Is that just, like, a normal day for you?"

"I think you're forgetting," he says quietly, "that I've been able to sense emotions for most of my life."

I raise my eyebrows. "So this *is* just a normal day for you."

He sighs. Stares out the window again.

"You're not even going to pretend it's not true?" I rip open a foil container. More potatoes. "You won't even pretend you don't know that the entire world finds you attractive?"

"Was that a confession?"

"You wish, dickhead."

"I find it boring," Warner says. "Besides, if I paid attention to every single person who found me attractive I'd never have time for anything else."

I nearly drop the potatoes.

I wait for him to crack a smile, to tell me he's joking, and when he doesn't, I shake my head, stunned.

"Wow," I say. "Your humility is a fucking inspiration."

He shrugs.

"Hey," I say, "speaking of things that disgust me— Do you maybe want to, like, wash a little bit of the blood off your face before we eat?"

Warner glares at me in response.

I hold up my hands. "Okay. Cool. That's fine." I point at him. "Actually, I heard that blood's good for you. You know—organic. Antioxidants and shit. Very popular with vampires."

"Are you able to hear the things you say out loud? Do you not realize how perfectly idiotic you sound?"

I roll my eyes. "All right, beauty queen, food's ready."

"I'm serious," he says. "Does it never occur to you to think things through before you speak? Does it never occur to you to cease speaking altogether? If it doesn't, it should."

"Come on, asswipe. Sit down."

Reluctantly, Warner makes his way over. He sits down and stares, blankly, at the meal in front of him.

I give him a few seconds of this before I say—

"Do you still remember how to do this? Or did you need me to feed you?" I stab a piece of tofu and point it in his direction. "Say *ah*. The tofu choo choo is coming."

"One more joke, Kishimoto, and I will remove your spine."

"You're right." I put down the fork. "I get it. I'm cranky when I'm hungry, too."

He looks up sharply.

"That wasn't a joke!" I say. "I'm being serious."

Warner sighs. Picks up his utensils. Looks longingly at the door.

I don't push my luck.

I keep my face on my food—I'm genuinely excited to be getting a second lunch—and wait until he takes several bites before I go for the jugular.

"So," I finally say. "You proposed, huh?"

Warner stops chewing and looks up. He strikes me, suddenly, as a young guy. Aside from the obvious need for a shower and a change of clothes, he looks like he's finally beginning to shed the tiniest, tiniest bit of tension. And I can tell by the way he's holding his knife and fork now—with a little more gusto—that I was right.

He was hungry.

I wonder what he would've done if I hadn't dragged him in here and sat him down. Forced him to eat.

Would he have just driven himself into the ground?

Accidentally died of hunger on his way to save Juliette?

He seems to have no real care for his physical self. No care for his own needs. It strikes me, suddenly, as bizarre. And concerning.

"Yes," he says quietly. "I proposed."

I'm seized by a knee-jerk reaction to tease him—to suggest that his bad mood makes sense now, that she probably turned him down—but even I know better than that. Whatever is happening in Warner's head right now is dark. Serious. And I need to handle this part of the conversation with care.

So I tread carefully. "I'm guessing she said yes."

Warner doesn't meet my eyes.

I take a deep breath, let it out slowly. It's all beginning to make sense now.

In the early days after Castle took me in, my guard was up so high I couldn't even see over the top of it. I trusted no one. I believed nothing. I was always waiting for the other shoe to drop. I let anger rock me to sleep at night because being angry was far less scary than having faith in people—or in the future.

I kept waiting for things to fall apart.

I was so sure this happiness and safety wouldn't last, that Castle would turn me out, or that he'd turn out to be a piece of shit. Abusive. Some kind of monster.

I couldn't relax.

It took me *years* before I truly believed that I had a family. It took me years to accept, without hesitation, that Castle really loved me, or that good things could last. That I could be happy again without fear of repercussion.

That's why losing Omega Point was so cataclysmic.

It was the amalgamation of nearly all my fears. So many people I loved had been wiped out overnight. My home. My family. My refuge. And the devastation had taken Castle, too. Castle, who'd been my rock and my role model; in the aftermath, he was a ghost. Unrecognizable. I didn't know how anything would shake out after that. I didn't know how we'd survive. Didn't know where we'd go.

It was Juliette who pulled us through.

Those were the days when she and I got really close. That was when I realized I could not only trust her and open up to her, but that I could *depend* on her. I never knew just how strong she was until I saw her take charge, rising up and rallying us all when we were at our lowest, when even Castle was too broken too stand.

J made magic out of tragedy.

She found us safety and hope. Unified us with Sector 45— with Warner and Delalieu—even in the face of opposition, at the risk of losing Adam. She didn't sit around waiting for Castle to take the reins like the rest of us did; there was no time for that. Instead, she dove right into the middle of hell, completely inexperienced and unprepared, because she was determined to save us. And to sacrifice herself in the process, if that was the cost. If it weren't for her—if it weren't for what she did, for all of us—I don't know where we'd be.

She saved our lives.

She saved my life, that's for sure. Reached out a hand in the darkness. Pulled me out.

But none of it would've hurt as much if I'd lost Omega Point during my early years there. It wouldn't have taken me so long to recover, and I wouldn't have needed so much help to get through the pain. It hurt like that because I'd finally let my guard down. I'd finally allowed myself to believe that things were going to be okay. I'd begun to hope. To dream.

To *relax*.

I'd finally walked away from my own pessimism, and the moment I did, life stuck a knife in my back.

It's easy, during those moments, to throw in the towel. To shrug off humanity. To tell yourself that you tried to be happy, and look what happened: more pain. Worse pain. Betrayed by the world. You realize then that anger is safer than kindness, that isolation is safer than community. You shut everything out. Everyone. But some days, no matter what you do, the pain gets so bad you'd bury yourself alive just to make it stop.

I would know. I've been there.

And I'm looking at Warner right now and I see the same deadness behind his eyes. The torture that chases hope. That specific flavor of self-hatred experienced only after being dealt a tragic blow in response to optimism.

I'm looking at him and I'm remembering the look on his face when he blew out his birthday candles. I'm remembering him and J afterward, cuddled up in the corner of the dining tent. I'm remembering how angry he was when I showed up at their room at the asscrack of dawn, determined to drag J out of bed on the morning of his birthday.

I'm thinking—

"*Fuck.*" I throw down my fork. The plastic hits the foil plate with a surprising thud. "You two were engaged?"

Warner is staring at his food. He seems calm, but when he says, "Yes," the word is a whisper so sad it drags a knife through my heart.

I shake my head. "I'm so sorry, man. I really am. You have no idea."

Warner's eyes flick up in surprise, but only for a moment. Eventually, he stabs a piece of broccoli. Stares at it. "This is disgusting," he says.

Which I realize is code for *Thank you*.

"Yeah," I say. "It is."

Which is code for *No worries, bro. I'm here for you*.

Warner sighs. He puts down his utensils. Stares out the window. I can tell he's about to say something when, abruptly, the doorbell rings.

I swear under my breath.

I shove away from the table to answer the door, but this time, I only open it a crack. A girl about my age peers back at me, standing there with a tinfoil package in her arms.

She smiles.

I open the door a bit more.

"I brought this for Warner," she says, stage-whispering. "I heard he was hungry." Her smile is so big you could probably see it from Mars. I have to make a real effort not to roll my eyes.

"Thanks. I'll take th—"

"Oh," she says, jerking the package out of reach. "I thought I could deliver it to him personally. You know, just to be sure it's being delivered to the right person." She beams.

This time, I actually roll my eyes.

Reluctantly, I pull open the door, stepping aside to let

her enter. I turn to tell Warner that another member of his fan club is here to take a long look at his green eyes, but in the second it takes me to move, I hear her scream. The container of food crashes to the ground, spaghetti noodles and red sauce spilling everywhere.

I spin around, stunned.

Warner has the girl pinned to the wall, his hand around her throat. "Who sent you here?" he says.

She struggles to break free, her feet kicking hard against the wall, her cries choked and desperate.

My head is spinning.

I blink and Warner's got her on the floor, on her knees. His boot is planted in the middle of her back, both of her arms bent backward, locked in his grip. He twists. She cries out.

"Who sent you here?"

"I don't know what you're talking about," she says, gasping for breath.

My heart is pounding like crazy.

I have no idea what the hell just happened, but I know better than to ask questions. I remove the Glock tucked inside my waistband and aim it in her direction. And then, just as I'm beginning to wrap my head around the fact that this is an ambush—and likely from someone here, from inside the Sanctuary—I notice the food begin to move.

Three massive scorpions begin to scuttle out from underneath the noodles, and the sight is so disturbing I nearly throw up and pass out at the same time. I've never seen scorpions in real life.

Breaking news: they're *horrifying*.

I thought I wasn't afraid of spiders, but this is like if spiders were on crack, like if spiders were very, very large and kind of see-through and wore armor and had huge, venomous stingers on one end just primed and ready to murder you. The creatures make a sharp turn, and all three of them head straight for Warner.

I let out a panicked gasp of breath. "Uh, bro—not to, um, freak you out or anything, but there are, like, three scorpions headed straight toward y—"

Suddenly, the scorpions freeze in place.

Warner drops the girl's arms and she scrambles away so fast her back slams against the wall. Warner stares at the scorpions. The girl stares, too.

The two of them are having a battle of wills, I realize, and it's easy for me to figure out who's going to win. So when the scorpions begin to move again—this time, toward her—I try not to pump my fist in the air.

The girl jumps to her feet, her eyes wild.

"Who sent you?" Warner asks again.

She's breathing hard now, still staring at the scorpions as she backs farther into a corner. They're climbing up her shoes now.

"Who?" Warner demands.

"Your father sent me," she says breathlessly. Shins. Knees. Scorpions on her knees. Oh my God, scorpions on her knees. "Anderson sent me here, okay? Call them off!"

"Liar."

"It was him, I swear!"

"You were sent here by a fool," Warner says, "if you were led to believe you could lie to me repeatedly without repercussion. And you are yourself a fool if you believe I will be anything close to merciful."

The creatures are moving up her torso now. Climbing up her chest. She gasps. Locks eyes with him.

"I see," he says, tilting his head at her. "Someone lied to you."

Her eyes widen.

"You were misled," he says, holding her gaze. "I am not kind. I am not forgiving. I do not care about your life."

As he speaks, the scorpions creep farther up her body. They're sitting near her collarbone now, just waiting, venomous stingers hovering below her face. And then, slowly, the scorpions' stingers begin curving toward the soft skin at her throat.

"Call them off!" she cries.

"This is your last chance," Warner says. "Tell me what you're doing here."

She's breathing so hard now that her chest heaves, her nostrils flaring. Her eyes dart around the room in a wild panic. The scorpions' stingers press closer to her throat. She flattens against the wall, a broken gasp escaping her lips.

"Tragic," Warner says.

She moves fast. Lightning fast. Pulls a gun from somewhere inside her shirt and aims it in Warner's direction and I don't even think, I just react.

I shoot.

The sound echoes, expands—it seems violently loud—but it's a perfect shot. A clean hole through the neck. The girl goes comically still and then slumps, slowly, to the ground.

Blood and scorpions pool around our feet. The body of a dead girl is splayed on my floor, just inches from the bed I woke up in, her limbs bent at awkward angles.

The scene is surreal.

I look up. Warner and I lock eyes.

"I'm coming with you to get J," I say. "End of discussion."

Warner glances from me to the dead body, and then back again. "Fine," he says, and sighs.

~~ELLA~~
JULIETTE

I've been standing outside the door staring at a smooth, polished stone wall for at least fifteen minutes before I check my wrist for a summons.

Still nothing.

When I'm with Anderson I don't have a lot of flexibility to look around, but standing here has given me time to freely examine my surroundings. The stretch of the hallway is eerily quiet, empty of doctors or soldiers in a way that unsettles me. There are long, vertical grates underfoot where the floor should be, and I've been standing here long enough to have become attuned to the incessant drips and mechanical roars that fill the background.

I glance at my wrist again.

Glance around the hall.

The walls aren't gray, like I originally thought. It turns out they're a dull white. Heavy shadows make them appear darker than they are—and in fact, make this entire floor appear darker. The overhead lights are unusual honeycomb clusters arranged along both the walls and ceilings. The oddly shaped lights scatter illumination, casting oblong hexagons in all directions, plunging some walls into complete darkness. I take a cautious step forward, peering more closely at a rectangle of blackness I'd previously ignored.

It's a hallway, I realize, cast entirely in shadow.

I feel a sudden compulsion to explore its depths, and I have to physically stop myself from stepping forward. My duty is here, at this door. It's not my business to explore or ask questions unless I've been explicitly asked to explore or ask questions.

My eyelids flutter.

Heat presses down on me, flames like fingers digging into my mind. Heat travels down my spine, wraps around my tailbone. And then shoots upward, fast and strong, forcing my eyes open. I'm breathing hard, spinning around.

Confused.

Suddenly, it makes perfect sense that I should explore the darkened hallway. Suddenly there seems no need at all to question my motives or any possible consequences for my actions.

But I've only taken a single step into the darkness when I'm pushed aggressively back. A girl's face peers out at me.

"Did you need something?" she says.

I throw up my hands, then I hesitate. I might not be authorized to hurt this person.

She steps forward. She's wearing civilian clothes, but doesn't appear to be armed. I wait for her to speak, and she doesn't.

"Who are you?" I demand. "Who gave you the authority to be down here?"

"I am Valentina Castillo. I have authority everywhere."

I drop my hands.

Valentina Castillo is the daughter of the supreme commander of South America, Santiago Castillo. I don't know what Valentina is supposed to look like, so this girl might be an impostor. Then again, if I take a risk and I'm wrong—

I could be executed.

I peer around her and see nothing but blackness. My curiosity—and unease—is growing by the minute.

I glance at my wrist. Still no summons.

"Who are you?" she says.

"I am Juliette Ferrars. I am a supreme soldier for our North American commander. Let me pass."

Valentina stares at me, her eyes scanning me from head to toe.

I hear a dull *click*, like the sound of something opening, and I spin around, looking for the source of the sound. There's no one.

"You have unlocked your message, Juliette Ferrars."

"What message?"

"Juliette? *Juliette.*"

Valentina's voice changes. She suddenly sounds like she's scared and breathless, like she's on the move. Her voice echoes. I hear the sounds of footsteps pounding the floor, but they seem far away, like she's not the only one running.

"*Viste*, there wasn't much time," she says, her Spanish accent getting thicker. "This was the best I could do. I have a plan, but *no sé si será posible. Este mensaje es en caso de emergencia.*

"They took Lena and Nicolás down in this direction," she says, pointing toward the darkness. "I'm on my way to try and find them. But if I can't—"

Her voice begins to fade. The light illuminating her face begins to glitch, almost like she's disappearing.

"Wait—" I say, reaching out. "Where are you—"

My hand moves straight through her and I gasp. She has no form. Her face is an illusion.

A hologram.

"I'm sorry," she says, her voice beginning to warp. "I'm sorry. This was the best I could do."

Once her form evaporates completely, I push into the darkness, heart pounding. I don't understand what's happening, but if the daughter of the supreme commander of South America is in trouble, I have a duty to find her and protect her.

I know that my loyalty is to Anderson, but that strange, familiar heat is still pressing against the inside of my mind, quieting the impulse telling me to turn around. I find I'm grateful for it. I realize, distantly, that my mind is a strange mess of contradictions, but I don't have more than a moment to dwell on it.

This hall is far too dark for easy access, but I'd observed earlier that what I once thought were decorative grooves in the walls were actually inset doors, so here, instead of relying on my eyes, I use my hands.

I run my fingers along the wall as I walk, waiting for a disruption in the pattern. It's a long hallway—I expect there to be multiple doors to sort through—but there appears to be little in this direction. Nothing visible by touch or sight, at least. When I finally feel the familiar pattern of a door, I hesitate.

I press both my hands against the wall, prepared to destroy it if I have to, when it suddenly fissures open beneath my hands, as if it was waiting for me.

Expecting me.

I move into the room, my senses heightened. Dim blue light pulses out along the floors, but other than that, the space is almost completely dark. I keep moving, and even though I don't need to use a gun, I reach for the rifle strapped across my back. I walk slowly, my soft boots soundless, and follow the distant, pulsing lights. As I move deeper into the room, lights begin to flicker on.

Overhead lights in that familiar honeycomb pattern flare to life, shattering the floor in unusual slants of light. The vast dimensions of the room begin to take shape. I stare up at the massive dome-shaped room, at the empty tank of water taking up an entire wall. There are abandoned desks, their respective chairs askew. Touchpads are stacked precariously on floors and desks, papers and binders piling everywhere. This place looks haunted. Deserted.

But it's clear it was once in full use.

Safety goggles hang from a nearby rack. Lab coats from another. There are large, empty glass cases standing upright in seemingly random and intermittent locations, and as I move even farther into the room, I notice a steady purple glow emanating from somewhere nearby.

I round the corner, and there's the source:

Eight glass cylinders, each as tall as the room and as wide as a desk, are arranged in a perfect line, straight across the laboratory. Five of them contain human figures. Three on the end remain empty. The purple light originates from within the individual cylinders, and as I approach, I realize the bodies are suspended in the air, bound entirely by light.

There are three boys I don't recognize. One girl I don't recognize. The other—

I step closer to the tank and gasp.

Valentina.

"What are you doing here?"

I spin around, rifle up and aimed in the direction of the voice. I drop my gun when I see Anderson's face. In an instant, the pervasive heat retreats from my head.

My mind is returned to me.

My mind, my name, my station, my place—my shameful, disloyal, reckless behavior. Horror and fear flood through me, coloring my features. How do I explain what I do not understand?

Anderson's face remains stony.

"Sir," I say quickly. "This young woman is the daughter of the supreme commander of South America. As a servant of The Reestablishment, I felt compelled to help her."

Anderson only stares at me.

Finally, he says: "How do you know that this girl is the daughter of the supreme commander of South America?"

I shake my head. "Sir, there was . . . some kind of vision. Standing in the hallway. She told me that she was Valentina Castillo, and that she needed help. She knew my name. She told me where to go."

Anderson exhales, his shoulders releasing their tension. "This is not the daughter of a supreme commander of The Reestablishment," he says quietly. "You were misled by a practice exercise."

Renewed mortification sends a fresh heat to my face.

Anderson sighs.

"I'm so sorry, sir. I thought— I thought it was my duty to help her, sir."

Anderson meets my eyes again. "Of course you did."

I hold my head steady, but shame sears me from within.

"And?" he says. "What did you think?"

Anderson gestures at the line of glass cylinders, at the figures displayed within.

"I think it's a beautiful display, sir."

Anderson almost smiles. He takes a step closer, studying me. "A beautiful display, indeed."

I swallow.

His voice changes, becomes soft. Gentle. "You would never betray me, would you, Juliette?"

"No, sir," I say quickly. "Never."

"Tell me something," he says, lifting his hand to my face. The backs of his knuckles graze my cheek, trail down my jawline. "Would you die for me?"

My heart is thundering in my chest. "Yes, sir."

He takes my face in his hand now, his thumb brushing, gently, across my chin. "Would you do anything for me?"

"Yes, sir."

"And yet, you deliberately disobeyed me." He drops his hand. My face feels suddenly cold. "I asked you to wait outside," he says quietly. "I did not ask you to wander. I did not ask you to speak. I did not ask you to think for yourself or to save anyone who claimed to need saving. Did I?"

"No, sir."

"Did you forget," he says, "that I am your master?"

"No, sir."

"*Liar*," he cries.

My heart is in my throat. I swallow hard. Say nothing.

"I will ask you one more time," he says, locking eyes with me. "Did you forget that I am your master?"

"Y-yes, sir."

His eyes flash. "Should I remind you, Juliette? Should I remind you to whom you owe your life and your loyalty?"

"Yes, sir," I say, but I sound breathless. I feel sick with fear. Feverish. Heat prickles my skin.

He retrieves a blade from inside his jacket pocket. Carefully, he unfolds it, the metal glinting in the neon light.

He presses the hilt into my right hand.

He takes my left hand and explores it with both of his own, tracing the lines of my palm and the shapes of my fingers, the seams of my knuckles. Sensations spiral through me, wonderful and horrible.

He presses down lightly on my index finger. He meets

my eyes.

"This one," he says. "Give it to me."

My heart is in my throat. In my gut. Beating behind my eyes.

"Cut it off. Place it in my hand. And all will be forgiven."

"Yes, sir," I whisper.

With shaking hands, I press the blade to the tender skin at the base of my finger. The blade is so sharp it pierces the flesh instantly, and with a stifled, agonized cry I press it deeper, hesitating only when I feel resistance. Knife against bone. The pain explodes through me, blinding me.

I fall on one knee.

There's blood everywhere.

I'm breathing so hard I'm heaving, trying desperately not to vomit from either the pain or the horror. I clench my teeth so hard it sends shocks of fresh pain upward, straight to my brain, and the distraction is helpful. I have to press my bloodied hand against the dirty floor to keep it steady, but with one final, desperate cry, I cut through the bone.

The knife falls from my trembling hand, clattering to the floor. My index finger is still hanging on to my hand by a single scrap of flesh, and I rip it off in a quick, violent motion. My body is shaking so excessively I can hardly stand, but somehow I manage to deposit the finger in Anderson's outstretched palm before collapsing to the ground.

"Good girl," he says softly. "Good girl."

It's all I hear him say before I black out.

KENJI

We both stare at the bloody scene a moment longer before Warner suddenly straightens and heads out the door. I tuck my gun into the waistband of my pants and chase after him, remembering to close the door behind us. I don't want those scorpions getting loose.

"Hey," I say, catching up to him. "Where are you going?"

"To find Castle."

"Cool. Okay. But do you think that maybe next time, instead of just, you know, leaving without a word, you could tell me what the hell is going on? I don't like chasing after you like this. It's demeaning."

"That sounds like a personal problem."

"Yeah but I thought personal problems were your area of expertise," I say. "You've got what, at least a few thousand personal problems, right? Or was it a few million?"

Warner shoots me a dark look. "You'd do well to address your own mental turbulence before criticizing mine."

"Uh, what's that supposed to mean?"

"It means that a rabid dog could sniff out your desperate, broken state. You're in no position to judge me."

"Excuse me?"

"You lie to yourself, Kishimoto. You hide your true

feelings behind a thin veneer, playing the clown, when all the while you're amassing emotional detritus you refuse to examine. At least I do not hide from myself. I know where my faults lie and I accept them. But you," he says. "Perhaps you should seek help."

My eyes widen to the point of pain, my head whipping back and forth between him and the path in front of me. "You have got to be kidding me right now. *You're* telling *me* to get help with my issues? What is happening?" I look up at the sky. "Am I dead? Is this hell?"

"I want to know what's happening with you and Castle."

I'm so surprised I briefly stop in place.

"What?" I blink at him. Still confused. "What are you talking about? There's nothing wrong with me and Castle."

"You've been more profane in the last several weeks than in the entire time I've known you. Something is wrong."

"I'm stressed," I say, feeling myself bristle. "Sometimes I swear when I'm stressed."

He shakes his head. "This is different. You're experiencing an unusual amount of stress, even for you."

"Wow." My eyebrows fly up. "I really hope you didn't bother using your"—I make air quotes—*"supernatural ability to sense emotions"*—I drop the air quotes—"to figure that one out. Obviously I'm extra stressed out right now. The world is on fucking fire. The list of things stressing me out is so long I can't even keep track. We're up to our necks in shit. J is gone. Adam defected. Nazeera's been shot. You've had your head so far up your own ass I thought you'd never emerge—"

He tries to cut me off but I keep talking.

"—and literally five minutes ago," I say, "someone from the Sanctuary—ha, hilarious, horrible name—just tried to kill you, and I killed her for it. *Five minutes ago.* So yeah, I think I'm experiencing an unusual amount of stress right now, genius."

Warner dismisses my speech with a single shake of his head. "Your use of profanity increases exponentially when you're irritated with Castle. Your language appears to be directly connected to your relationship with him. Why?"

I try not to roll my eyes. "Not that this information is actually relevant, but Castle and I struck a deal a few years ago. He thought that my"—I make more air quotes—"*overreliance on profanity was inhibiting my ability to express my emotions in a constructive manner*."

"So you promised him you'd tone down your language."

"Yeah."

"I see. It seems you've reneged on the terms of that arrangement."

"Why do you care?" I ask. "Why are we even talking about this? Why are we losing sight of the fact that we were just attacked by someone from *inside* of the Sanctuary? We need to find Sam and Nouria and find out who this girl was, because she was clearly from this camp, and they should know th—"

"You can tell Sam and Nouria whatever you want," Warner says. "But I need to talk to Castle."

Something in his tone frightens me. "Why?" I demand.

"What is going on? Why are you so obsessed with Castle right now?"

Finally, Warner stops moving. "Because," he says. "Castle had something to do with this."

"What?" I feel the blood drain from my body. "No way. Not possible."

Warner says nothing.

"Come on, man, don't be crazy— Castle's not perfect, but he would never—"

"Hey— What the hell just happened?" Winston, breathless and panicked, comes running up to us. "I heard a gunshot coming from the direction of your tent, but when I went to check on you, I saw— I saw—"

"Yeah."

"What happened?" Winston's voice is shrill. Terrified.

At that exact moment, more people come running. Winston starts offering people explanations I don't bother to edit, because my head is still full of steam. I have no idea what the hell Warner is getting at, but I'm also worried that I know him too well to deny his mind. My heart says Castle would never betray us, but my brain says that Warner is usually right when it comes to sussing out this kind of shit. So I'm freaking out.

I spot Nouria in the distance, her dark skin gleaming in the bright sun, and relief floods through me.

Finally.

Nouria will know more about the girl with the scorpions. She has to. And whatever she knows will almost certainly help absolve Castle of any affiliation with this mess. And as soon as we can resolve this freak accident, Warner and I can get the hell out of here and start searching for J.

That's it.

That's the plan.

It makes me feel good to have a plan. But when we're close enough, Nouria narrows her eyes at both me and Warner, and the look on her face sends a brand-new wave of fear through my body.

"Follow me," she says.

We do.

Warner looks *livid*.

Castle looks freaked out.

Nouria and Sam look like they're sick and tired of all of us.

I might be imagining things, but I'm pretty sure Sam just shot Nouria a look—the subtext of which was probably *Why the hell did you have to let your dad come stay with us?*—that was so withering Nouria didn't even get upset, she just shook her head, resigned.

And the problem is, I don't even know whose side I'm on.

In the end, Warner was right about Castle, but he was also wrong. Castle wasn't plotting anything nefarious; he didn't send that girl—her name was Amelia—after Warner. Castle's mistake was thinking that all rebel groups shared the same worldview.

At first it didn't occur to me, either, that the vibe might

be different around here. Different from our group at Point, at least. At Point we were led by Castle, who was more of a nurturer than a warrior. In his days before The Reestablishment he was a social worker. He saw tons of kids coming in and out of the system, and with Omega Point he sought to build a home and refuge for the marginalized. We were all about love and community at Point. And even though we knew that we were gearing up for a fight against The Reestablishment, we didn't always resort to violence; Castle didn't like using his powers in authoritative ways. He was more like a father figure to most of us.

But here—

It didn't take long to realize that Nouria was different from her dad. She's nice enough, but she's also all business. She doesn't like to spend much time on small talk, and she and Sam mostly keep to themselves. They don't always take their meals with everyone else. They don't always participate in group things. And when it comes right down to it, Sam and Nouria are ready and willing to set shit on fire. Hell, they seem to be looking forward to it.

Castle was never really that guy.

I think he was a little blindsided when we showed up here. He was suddenly out of a job when he realized that Nouria and Sam weren't going to take orders from him. And then, when he tried to get to know people—

He was disappointed.

"Amelia was a bit of a zealot," Sam says, sighing. "She'd never exhibited dangerous, violent tendencies, of course, which is why we let her stay—but we all felt that her views were a little intense. She was one of the rare members who felt like the lines between The Reestablishment and the rebel groups should be clear and finite. She never felt safe with the children of the supreme commanders in our midst, and I know that because she took me aside to tell me so. I had a long talk with her about the situation, but I see now that she wasn't convinced."

"Obviously," I mutter.

Nouria shoots me a look. I clear my throat.

Sam goes on: "When everyone but Warner was basically kidnapped—and Nazeera was shot—Amelia probably figured she could finish the job and get rid of Warner, too." She shakes her head. "What a horrible situation."

"Did you have to shoot her?" Nouria says to me. "Was she really that dangerous?"

"She had *three* scorpions!" I cry. "She pulled a gun on Warner!"

"What else was he supposed to think?" Castle says gently. He's staring at the ground, his long dreads freed from their usual tie at the base of his neck. I wish I could see the expression on his face. "If I hadn't known Amelia personally, even I would've thought she was working for someone."

"Tell me, again," Warner says to Castle, "exactly what you said to her about me."

Castle looks up. Sighs.

"She and I got into a bit of a heated discussion," he

says. "Amelia was determined that members of The Reestablishment could never change, that they were evil and would remain evil. I told her I didn't believe that. I told her that I believed that all people were capable of change."

I raise an eyebrow. "Wait, like, you mean you think even someone like Anderson is capable of change?"

Castle hesitates. And I know, just by looking at his eyes, what he's about to say. My heart jumps in my chest. In fear.

"I think if Anderson were truly remorseful," Castle says, "that he, too, could make a change. Yes. I do believe that."

Nouria rolls her eyes.

Sam drops her head in her hands.

"Wait. Wait." I hold up a finger. "So, like, in a hypothetical situation— If Anderson came to Point asking for amnesty, claiming to be a changed man, you'd . . . ?"

Castle just looks at me.

I throw myself back in my chair with a groan.

"Kenji," Castle says softly. "You know better than anyone else how we did things at Omega Point. I dedicated my life to giving second—and third—chances to those who'd been cast out by the world. You'd be stunned if you knew how many people's lives were derailed by a simple mistake that snowballed, escalating beyond their control because no one was ever there to offer a hand or even an hour of assistance—"

"Castle. Sir." I hold up my hands. "I love you. I really do. But Anderson isn't a regular person. He—"

"Of course he's a regular person, son. That's exactly the

point. We're all just regular people, when you strip us down. There's nothing to be afraid of when you look at Anderson; he's just as human as you or me. Just as terrified. And I'm sure if he could go back and do his life over again, he'd make very different decisions."

Nouria shakes her head. "You don't know that, Dad."

"Maybe not," he says quietly. "But it's what I believe."

"Is that what you believe about me, too?" Warner asks. "Is that what you told her? That I was just a nice boy, a defenseless child who'd never lift a finger to hurt her? That if I could do it all over again I'd choose to live my life as a monk, dedicating my days to giving charity and spreading goodwill?"

"No," Castle says sharply. It's clear he's starting to get irritated. "I told her that your anger was a defense mechanism, and that you couldn't help that you were born to an abusive father. I told her that in your heart, you're a good person, and that you don't *want* to hurt anyone. Not really."

Warner's eyes flash. "I want to hurt people all the time," he says. "Sometimes I can't sleep at night because I'm thinking about all the people I'd like to murder."

"Great." I nod, leaning back in my chair. "This is super great. All of this information we're collecting is super helpful and useful." I count off on my fingers: "Amelia was a psycho, Castle wants to be BFFs with Anderson, Warner has midnight fantasies about killing people, and Castle made Amelia think that Warner is a lost little bunny trying to find his way home."

When everyone stares at me, confused, I clarify:

"Castle basically gave Amelia the idea that she could walk into a room and murder Warner! He pretty much told her that Warner was about as harmful as a dumpling."

"*Oh*," Sam and Nouria say at the same time.

"I don't think she wanted to murder him," Castle says quickly. "I'm sure she just—"

"Dad, please." Nouria's voice is sharp and final. "Enough." She shares a glance with Sam, and takes a deep breath.

"Listen," she says, trying for a calmer tone. "We knew, when you got here, that we'd have to deal with this situation eventually, but I think it's time we had a talk about our roles and responsibilities around here."

"Oh. I see." Castle clasps his hands. Stares at the wall. He looks so sad and small and ancient. Even his dreads seem more silver than black these days. Sometimes I forget he's almost fifty. Most people think he's, like, fifteen years younger than he actually is, but that's just because he's always looked really, really good for his age. But for the first time in years, I feel like I'm beginning to see the number on his face. He looks tired. Worn out.

But that doesn't mean he's done here.

Castle's still got so much more to do. So much more to give. And I can't just sit here and let him be shoved aside. Ignored. I want to shout at someone. I want to tell Nouria and Sam that they can't just kick Castle to the curb like this.

Not after everything. Not like this.

And I'm about to say something exactly like that, when Nouria speaks.

"Sam and I," she says, "would like to offer you an official position as our senior adviser here at the Sanctuary."

Castle's head perks up. "Senior adviser?" He stares at Nouria. Stares at Sam. "You're not asking me to leave?"

Nouria looks suddenly confused.

"Leave? Dad, you just got here. Sam and I want you to stay for as long as you like. We just think it's important that we all know what we're doing here, so that we can manage things in as efficient and organized a manner as possible. It's hard for Sam and me to be effective at our jobs if we're worried about tiptoeing around your feelings, and even though it's hard to have conversations like this, we figured it would be best to jus—"

Castle pulls Nouria into a hug so fierce, so full of love, I feel my eyes sting with emotion. I actually have to look away for a moment.

When I turn back, Castle is beaming.

"I'd be honored to advise in any way that I can," Castle says. "And if I haven't said it enough, let me say it again: I'm so proud of you, Nouria. So proud of both of you," he says, looking at Sam. "The boys would've been so proud."

Nouria's eyes go glassy with emotion. Even Sam seems moved.

One more minute of this, and I'm going to need a tissue.

"Right, well." Warner is on his feet. "I'm glad the attempt

on my life was able to bring your family together. I'm leaving now."

"Wait—" I grab Warner's arm and he shoves me off.

"If you keep touching me without my permission, I will remove your hands from your body."

I ignore that. "Shouldn't we tell them that we're leaving?"

Sam frowns. *"Leaving?"*

Nouria's eyebrows fly up. *"We?"*

"We're going to get J," I explain. "She's back in Oceania. James told us everything. Speaking of which— You should probably talk to him. He's got some news about Adam you won't like, news that I don't care to repeat."

"Kent betrayed all of you to save himself."

"To save *James*," I clarify, shooting Warner a dirty look. "And that was not cool, man. I just said I didn't want to talk about it."

"I'm trying to be efficient."

Castle looks stunned. He says nothing. He just looks stunned.

"Talk to James," I say. "He'll tell you what's happening. But Warner and I are going to catch a plane—"

"Steal a plane."

"Right, steal a plane, before the end of the day. And, uh, you know—we'll just go get J and be back real quick, *bim bam boom.*"

Nouria and Sam are staring at me like I'm an idiot.

"Bim bam boom?" Warner says.

"Yeah, you know, like"—I clap my hands together—"*boom*.

Done. Easy."

Warner turns away from me with a sigh.

"Wait— So, just the two of you are doing this?" Sam asks. She's frowning.

"Honestly, the fewer, the better," Nouria answers for me. "That way, there are fewer bodies to hide, fewer actions to coordinate. Regardless, I'd offer to come with you, but we have so many still wounded that we need to care for—and now that Amelia is dead, there's sure to be more emotional upheaval to manage."

Castle's eyes light up. "While they're going after Ella," he says to Nouria and Sam, "and the two of you are running things here, I was thinking I'd reach out to the friends in my network. Let them know what's happening, and that change is afoot. I can help coordinate our moves around the globe."

"That's a great idea," Sam says. "Maybe we c—"

"I don't care," Warner says loudly, and turns for the door. "And I'm leaving now. Kishimoto, if you're coming, keep up."

"Right," I say, trying to sound important. "Yup. Bye." I shoot a quick two-finger salute at everyone and run straight for the door only to slam hard into Nazeera.

Nazeera.

Holy shit. She's awake. She's perfect.

She's *pissed*.

"You two aren't going anywhere without me," she says.

~~ELLA~~
JULIETTE

I am a thief.

I stole this notebook and this pen from one of the doctors, from one of his lab coats when he wasn't looking, and I shoved them both down my pants. This was just before he ordered those men to come and get me. The ones in the strange suits with the thick gloves and the gas masks with the foggy plastic windows hiding their eyes. They were aliens, I remember thinking. I remember thinking they must've been aliens because they couldn't have been human, the ones who handcuffed my hands behind my back, the ones who strapped me to my seat. They stuck Tasers to my skin over and over for no reason other than to hear me scream but I wouldn't. I whimpered but I never said a word. I felt the tears streak down my cheeks but I wasn't crying.

I think it made them angry.

They slapped me awake even though my eyes were open when we arrived. Someone unstrapped me without removing my handcuffs and kicked me in both kneecaps before ordering me to rise. And I tried. I tried but I couldn't and finally 6 hands shoved me out the door and my face was bleeding on the concrete for a while. I can't really remember the part where they dragged me inside.

I feel cold all the time.

I feel empty, like there is nothing inside of me but this broken heart, the only organ left in this hell. I feel the bleats echo within me, I feel the thumping reverberate around my skeleton. I have a heart, says science, but I am a monster, says society. And I know it, of course I know it. I know what I've done. I'm not asking for sympathy.

But sometimes I think—sometimes I wonder—if I were a monster—surely, I would feel it by now?

I would feel angry and vicious and vengeful.

I'd know blind rage and bloodlust and a need for vindication.

Instead I feel an abyss within me that's so deep, so dark I can't see within it; I can't see what it holds. I do not know what I am or what might happen to me.

I do not know what I might do again.

—*An excerpt from Juliette's journals in the asylum*

KENJI

I stand stock-still for a moment, letting the shock of everything settle around me, and when it finally hits me that Nazeera is really here, really awake, really okay, I pull her into my arms. Her defensive posture melts away, and suddenly she's just a girl—*my girl*—and happiness rockets through me. She's not even close to being short, but in my arms, she feels small. Pocket-sized. Like she was always meant to fit here, against my chest.

It's like heaven.

When we finally pull apart, I'm beaming like an idiot. I don't even care that everyone is staring at us. I just want to live in this moment.

"Hey," I say to her. "I'm so happy you're okay."

She takes a deep, unsteady breath, and then—smiles. It changes her whole face. It makes her look a lot less like a mercenary and a lot more like an eighteen-year-old girl. Though I think I like both versions, if I'm being honest.

"I'm so happy you're okay, too," she says quietly.

We stare at each other a moment longer before I hear someone clear their throat in a dramatic fashion.

Reluctantly, I turn around.

I know, in an instant, that the throat-clearing came

from Nouria. I can tell by the way her arms are crossed, the way her eyes are narrowed. Sam, on the other hand, looks amused.

But Castle looks happy. Surprised, but happy.

I grin at him.

Nouria's frown deepens. "You two know Warner left, right?"

That wipes the smile off my face. I spin around, but there's no sign of him. I turn back, swearing quietly under my breath.

Nazeera shoots me a look.

"I know," I say, shaking my head. "He's going to try and leave without us."

She almost laughs. "Definitely."

I'm about to say my good-byes again when Nouria jumps to her feet. "Wait," she says.

"No time," I say, already backing out the door. "Warner is going to bail on us, and I c—"

"He's about to take a shower," Sam says, cutting me off.

I freeze so fast I nearly fall over. I turn around, eyebrows high. "He's what now?"

"He's about to take a shower," she says again.

I blink at her slowly, like I'm stupid, which, honestly, is kind of how I'm feeling at the moment. "You mean you're, like, watching him get ready to take a shower?"

"It's not weird," Nouria says flatly. "Stop making it weird."

I squint at Sam. "What's Warner doing right now?" I ask

her. "Is he in the shower yet?"

"Yes."

Nazeera raises a single eyebrow. "So you're just, like, watching a naked Warner in the shower right now?"

"I'm not looking at his body," Sam says, sounding very close to irritated.

"But you *could*," I say, stunned. "That's what's so weird about this. You *could* just watch any of us take extremely naked showers."

"You know what?" Nouria says sharply. "I was going to do something to make things easier for you guys on your way out, but I think I've changed my mind."

"Wait—" Nazeera says. "Make things easier how?"

"I was going to help you steal a jet."

"Okay, all right, I take it back," I say, holding up my hands in apology. "I retract all my previous comments about nakedness. I would also like to formally apologize to Sam, who we all know is way too nice and way too cool to ever spy on anyone in the shower."

Sam rolls her eyes. Cracks a smile.

Nouria sighs. "I don't understand how you deal with him," she says to Castle. "I can't stand all the jokes. It would drive me insane to have to listen to this all day."

I'm about to protest when Castle responds.

"That's only because you don't know him well enough," Castle says, smiling at me. "Besides, we don't love him for his jokes, do we, Nazeera?" The two of them lock eyes for a moment. "We love him for his heart."

At that, the smile slips from my face. I'm still processing the weight of that statement—the generosity of such a statement—when I realize I've already missed a beat.

Nouria is talking.

"The air base isn't far from here," she's saying, "and I guess this is as good a time as any to let you all know that Sam and I are about to take a page out of Ella's playbook and take over Sector 241. Stealing a plane will be the least of the damage—and, in fact, I think it's a great way to launch our offensive strategy." She glances over her shoulder. "What do you think, Sam?"

"Brilliant," she says, "as usual."

Nouria smiles.

"I didn't realize that was your strategy," Castle says, the smile fading from his face. "Don't you think, based on how things turned out the last time, that m—"

"Why don't we discuss this after we've sent the kids off on their mission? Right now it's more important that we get them situated and give them a proper send-off before it's officially too late."

"Hey, speaking of which," I say quickly, "what makes you think we're not already too late?"

Nouria meets my eyes. "If they'd done the transfer," she says, "we would've felt it."

"Felt it how?"

It's Sam who responds: "In order for their plan to work, Emmaline has to die. They won't let that happen naturally, of course, because a natural death could occur in any number of ways, which leaves too many factors up in the air. They need to be able to control the experiment at all times—which is why they were so desperate to get their hands on Ella *before* Emmaline died. They're almost certainly going to kill Emmaline in a controlled environment, and they'll set it up in a way that leaves no room for error. Even so, we're bound to feel something change.

"That infinitesimal shift—after Emmaline's powers recede, but before they're funneled into a new host body—will dramatically glitch our visual of the world. And that moment hasn't happened yet, which makes us think that Ella is probably still safe." Sam shrugs. "But it could be happening any minute now. Time really is of the essence."

"How do you know so much about this?" Nazeera asks, her brows furrowed. "For years I tried to get my hands on this information, and I came up with nothing, despite being so close to the source. But you seem to know all of this on some kind of personal level. It's incredible."

"It's not that incredible," Nouria says, shaking her head. "We've just been focused in our search. All rebel groups have a different strength or core principle. For some, it's safety. For others, it's war. For us, it's been research. The things we've seen have been out there for everyone to see—there are glitches all the time—but when you're not looking for them, you don't notice them. But I noticed. Sam noticed. It was one of the things that brought us together."

The two women share a glance.

"We felt really sure that part of our oppression was in

an illusion," Sam says. "And we've been chasing down the truth with every resource we've got. Unfortunately, we still don't know everything."

"But we're closer than most," Nouria says. She takes a sharp breath, refocusing. "We'll be holding down our end of things while you're gone. Hopefully, when you return, we'll have flipped more than one sector to our side."

"You really think you'll be able to accomplish that much in such a short period of time?" I ask, eyes wide. "I was hoping we wouldn't be gone for more than a couple days."

Nouria smiles at me then, but it's a strange smile, a searching smile. "Don't you understand?" she says. "This is it. This is the end. This is the defining moment we've all been fighting for. The end of an era. The end of a revolution. We currently—finally—have every advantage. We have people on the inside. If we do this right, we could collapse The Reestablishment in a matter of days."

"But all of that hinges on us getting to J on time," I say. "What if we're too late?"

"You'll have to kill her."

"*Nouria*," Castle gasps.

"You're joking," I say. "Tell me you're joking."

"Not joking in the slightest," she says. "If you get there and Emmaline is dead and Ella has taken her place, you must kill Ella. You have to kill her and as many of the supreme commanders as you can."

My jaw has come unhinged.

"What about all that shit you said to J the night we got

here? What about all that talk about how inspiring she is and how so many people were moved by her actions—how she's basically a hero? What happened to all that nonsense?"

"It wasn't nonsense," Nouria says. "I meant every word. But we're at war, Kishimoto. We don't have time to be sentimental."

"Sentimental? Are you out of your—"

Nazeera places a calming hand on my arm. "We'll find another way. There has to be another way."

"It's impossible to reverse the process once it's in effect," Sam says calmly. "Operation Synthesis will remove every trace of your old friend. She will be unrecognizable. A super soldier in every sense of the word. Beyond salvation."

"I'm not listening to this," I say angrily. "I'm not listening to this."

Nouria puts up her hands. "This conversation might turn out to be unnecessary. As long as you can get to her in time, it won't matter. But remember: if you get there and Ella is still alive, you need to make sure that she kills Emmaline above all else. Removing Emmaline is key. Once she's gone, the supreme commanders become easy targets. Vulnerable."

"Wait." I frown, still angry. "Why does it have to be J who kills Emmaline? Couldn't one of us do it?"

Nouria shakes her head. "If it were that simple," she says, "don't you think it would've been done by now?"

I raise my eyebrows. "Not if no one knew she existed."

"We knew she existed," Sam says quietly. "We've known

about Emmaline for a while now."

Nouria goes on: "Why do you think we reached out to your team? Why do you think we risked the life of one of our own to get a message to Ella? Why do you think we opened our doors to you, even when we knew we'd be exposing ourselves to a possible attack? We made a series of increasingly difficult decisions, putting the lives of all those who depended on us at risk." She sighs. "But even now, after suffering a disastrous loss, Sam and I think that, ultimately, we did the right thing. Can you imagine why?"

"Because you're . . . Good Samaritans?"

"Because we realized, months ago, that Ella was the only one strong enough to kill her own sister. We need her just as much as you do. Not just us"—Nouria gestures to herself and Sam—"but the whole world. If Ella is able to kill Emmaline before any powers can be transferred, then she's killed The Reestablishment's greatest weapon. If she doesn't kill Emmaline now, while power still runs through Emmaline's veins, The Reestablishment can continue to harness and transfer that power to a new host."

"We once thought that Ella would have to fight her sister," Sam says. "But based on the information Ella shared with us while she was here, it seems like Emmaline is ready and willing to die." Sam shakes her head. "Even so, killing her is not as simple as pulling a plug. Ella will be going to war with the ghost of her mother's genius. Evie undoubtedly put in place numerous fail-safes to keep Emmaline invulnerable to attacks from others and from herself. I have no idea what

Ella will be up against, but I can guarantee it won't be easy."

"Jesus." I drop my head into my hands. I thought I was already living with peak levels of stress, but I was wrong. This stress I'm experiencing now is on a whole new level.

I feel Nazeera's hand on my back and I look up. Her face looks as uncertain as mine feels, and somehow, it makes me feel better.

"Pack your bags," Nouria says. "Catch up with Warner. I'll meet the three of you at the entrance in twenty minutes."

~~ELLA~~ JULIETTE

In the darkness, I imagine light.

I dream of suns, moons, mothers. I see children laughing, crying, I see blood, I smell sugar. Light shatters across the blackness pressing against my eyes, fracturing nothing into something. Nameless shapes expand and spin, crash into each other, dissolving on contact. I see dust. I see dark walls, a small window, I see water, I see words on a page—

I am not insane I am not insane I am not insane I am not insane
I am not insane I am not insane I am not insane I am not insane
I am not insane I am not insane I am not insane I am not insane
I am not insane I am not insane I am not insane I am not insane
I am not insane I am not insane I am not insane I am not insane
I am not insane I am not insane I am not insane I am not insane
I am not insane I am not insane I am not insane I am not insane
I am not insane I am not insane I am not insane I am not insane
I am not insane I am not insane I am not insane I am not insane
I am not insane I am not insane I am not insane I am not insane
I am not insane I am not insane I am not insane I am not insane
I am not insane I am not insane I am not insane I am not insane
I am not insane I am not insane I am not insane I am not insane

I am not insane I am not insane I am not insane I am not insane
I am not insane I am not insane I am not insane I am not insane
I am not insane I am not insane I am not insane I am not insane
I am not insane I am not insane I am not insane I am not insane
I am not insane I am not insane I am not insane I am not insane
I am not insane I am not insane I am not insane I am not insane
I am not insane I am not insane I am not insane I am not insane
I am not insane I am not insane I am not insane I am not insane
I am not insane I am not insane I am not insane I am not insane
I am not insane I am not insane I am not insane I am not insane
I am not insane I am not insane I am not insane

In the pain, I imagine bliss.

My thoughts are like wind, rushing, curling into the depths of myself, expelling, dispelling darkness

I imagine love, I imagine wind, I imagine gold hair and green eyes and whispers, laughter

I imagine

        Me

extraordinary, unbroken

the girl who shocked herself by surviving, the girl who loved herself through learning, the girl who respected her skin, understood her worth, found her strength

s t r o n g

   s t r o n g e r

              strongest

Imagine me

master of my own universe

I am everything I ever dreamed of

KENJI

We're in the air.

We've been in the air for hours now. I spent the first four hours sleeping—I can usually fall asleep anywhere, in any position—and I spent the last two hours eating all the snacks on the plane. We've got about an hour left in our flight and I'm so bored I've begun poking myself in the eye just to pass the time.

We got off to a good start—Nouria helped us steal a plane, as promised, by shielding our actions with a sheet of light—but now that we're up here, we're basically on our own. Nazeera had to fend off a few questions over the radio, but because most of the military has no idea what level of shit has already gone down, she still has the necessary clout to bypass inquiries from nosy sector leaders and soldiers. We realize it's only a matter of time, though, before someone realizes we don't have the authority to be up here.

Until then—

I glance around. I'm sitting close enough to the cockpit to be within earshot of Nazeera, but she and I both decided that I should hang back to keep an eye on Warner, who's sitting just far enough away to keep me safe from his scowl. Honestly, the look on his face is so intense I'm surprised he hasn't started aging prematurely.

Suffice it to say that he didn't like Nouria's game plan.

I mean, I don't like it, either—and I have no intentions of following through with it—but Warner looked like he might shoot Nouria for even *thinking* that we might have to kill J. He's been sitting stiffly in the back of the plane ever since we boarded, and I've been wary of approaching him, despite our recent reconciliation. Semi-reconciliation? I'm calling it a reconciliation.

But right now I think he needs space.

Or maybe it's me, maybe I'm the one who needs space. He's exhausting to deal with. Without J around, Warner has no soft edges. He never smiles. He rarely looks at people. He's always irritated.

Right now, I honestly can't remember why J likes him so much.

In fact, in the last couple of months I'd forgotten what he was like without her around. But this reminder has been more than enough. Too much, in fact. I don't want any more reminders. I can guarantee that I will never again forget that Warner is not a fun guy to spend time with. That dude carries so much tension in his body it's practically contagious. So yeah, I'm giving him space.

So far, I've given him seven hours' worth of space.

I steal another glance at him, wondering how he holds himself so still—so stiff—for seven hours straight. How does he not pull a muscle? Why does he never have to use the bathroom? Where does it all go?

The only concession we got from Warner was that he showed up looking more like his normal self. Sam was right: Warner took a shower. You'd think he was going on a date, not a murder/rescue mission. It's obvious he wants to make a good impression.

He's wearing more Haider castoffs: a pale green blazer, matching pants. Black boots. But because these pieces were selected by Haider, the blazer is not a normal blazer. Of course it isn't. This blazer has no lapels, no buttons. The silhouette is cut in sharp lines that force the jacket to hang open, exposing Warner's shirt underneath—a simple white V-neck that shows more of his chest than I feel comfortable staring at. Still, he looks okay. A little nervous, but—

"Your thoughts are very loud," Warner says, still staring out the window.

"Oh my God, I'm so sorry," I say, feigning shock. "I'd turn the volume down, but I'd have to *die* in order for my brain to stop working."

"A problem easily rectified," he mutters.

"I heard that."

"I meant for you to hear that."

"Hey," I say, realizing something. "Doesn't this feel like some kind of weird déjà vu?"

"No."

"No, no, I'm being serious. What are the odds that the three of us would be on a trip like this again? Though the last time we were all on a trip like this, we ended up being shot out of the sky, so—yeah, I don't want to relive that.

Also, J isn't here. So. Huh." I hesitate. "Okay, I think I'm realizing that maybe I don't actually understand what déjà vu means."

"It's French," Warner says, bored. "It literally means *already seen.*"

"Wait, so then I do know what it means."

"That you know what anything means is astonishing to me."

Before I have a chance to defend myself, Nazeera's voice carries over from the cockpit.

"Hey," she calls. "Are you guys being friends again?"

I hear the familiar click and slide of metal—a sound that means Nazeera is unbuckling herself from pilot mode. Every once in a while she puts the plane on cruise control (or whatever) and makes her way over to me. But it's been at least half an hour since her last break, and I've missed her.

She folds herself into the chair next to me.

I beam at her.

"I'm so glad you two are finally talking," she says, sighing as she sinks into the seat. "The silence has been depressing."

My smile dies.

Warner's expression darkens.

"Listen," she says, looking at Warner. "I know this whole thing is horrible—that the very reason we're on this plane is horrible—but you have to stop being like this. We have, like, thirty minutes left on this flight, which means we're about to go out there, together, to do something huge. Which means we all have to get on the same page. We have to be able to trust each other and work together. If we don't, or if you don't let us, we could end up losing everything."

When Warner says nothing, Nazeera sighs again.

"I don't care what Nouria thinks," she says, trying for a gentle tone. "We're not going to lose Ella."

"You don't understand," Warner says quietly. He's still not looking at us. "I've already lost her."

"You don't know that," Nazeera says forcefully. "Ella might still be alive. We can still turn this around."

Warner shakes his head. "She was different even before she was taken," he says. "Something had changed inside of her, and I don't know what it was, but I could feel it. I've always been able to feel her—I've always been able to sense her energy—and she wasn't the same. Emmaline did something to her, changed something inside of her. I have no idea what she's going to be like when I see her again. If I see her again." He stares out the window. "But I'm here because I can do nothing else. Because this is the only way forward."

And then, even though I know it's going to piss him off, I say to Nazeera:

"Warner and J were engaged."

"What?" Nazeera stills. Her eyes go wide. Super wide. Wider than the plane. Her eyes go so wide they basically fill the sky. "When? How? Why did no one tell me?"

"I told you that in confidence," Warner says sharply, shooting me a glare.

"I know." I shrug. "But Nazeera's right. We're a team now, whether you like it or not, and we should get all of this out in the open. Air it out."

"Out in the open? What about the fact that you and Nazeera are in a relationship that you never bothered mentioning?"

"Hey," I say, "I was going t—"

"Wait. *Wait*." Nazeera cuts me off. She holds up her hands. "Why are we changing the subject? Warner, engaged! Oh my God, this is— This is so good. This is a big deal, it could give us a per—"

"It's not *that* big of a deal." I turn, frown at her. "We all knew this kind of thing was coming. The two of them are basically destined to be together, even I can admit that." I tilt my head, considering. "I mean, true, I think they're a little young, but—"

Nazeera is shaking her head. "No. No. That's not what I'm talking about. I don't care about the actual engagement." She stops, glances up at Warner. "I mean—um, congratulations and everything."

Warner looks beyond annoyed.

"I just mean that this reminded me of something. Something so good. I don't know why I didn't think of this sooner. God, it would give us the perfect edge."

"What would?"

But Nazeera is out of her chair, stalking over to Warner and, cautiously, I follow. "Do you remember," she says to him, "when you and Lena were together?"

Warner shoots Nazeera a venomous look and says, with dramatic iciness, "I'd really rather not."

Nazeera waves away his statement with her hand. "Well, I remember. I remember a lot more than I should, probably, because Lena used to complain to me about your relationship all the time. And I remember, specifically, how much your dad and her mom wanted you guys to, like, I don't know—promise yourselves to each other for the foreseeable future, for the protection of the movement—"

"Promise themselves?" I frown.

"Yes, like—" She hesitates, her arms pinwheeling as she gathers her thoughts, but Warner suddenly sits up straighter in his seat, seeming to understand.

"Yes," he says calmly. The irritation is gone from his eyes. "I remember my father saying something to me about the importance of uniting our families. Unfortunately, my recollection of the interaction is vague, at best."

"Right, well, I'm sure your parents were both chasing after the idea for political gain, but Lena was—and probably still is—like, genuinely in love with you, and was always sort of obsessed with the idea of being your wife. She was always talking to me about marrying you, about her dreams for the future, about what your children would look like—"

I glance at Warner to catch his reaction to that statement, and the revolted look on his face is surprisingly satisfying.

"—but I remember her saying something even then, about how detached you were, and how closed off, and how one day, when the two of you got married, she'd finally be able to link your family profiles in the database, which would grant her the necessary security clearance to track your—"

The plane gives a sudden, violent jolt.

Nazeera goes still, words dying in her throat. Warner jumps to his feet. We all make a dash for the cockpit.

The lights are flashing, screaming alerts I don't understand. Nazeera scans the monitor at the same time as Warner, and the two of them share a look.

The plane gives another violent jolt, and I slam, hard, into the something sharp and metal. I let out a long string of curses and for some reason, when Nazeera reaches out to help me up—

I freak out.

"Will someone tell me what the hell is going on? What's happening? Are we being shot out of the sky right now?" I spin around, taking in the flashing lights, the steady beep echoing through the cabin. "Fucking déjà vu! I knew it!"

Nazeera takes a deep breath. Closes her eyes. "We're not being shot out of the sky."

"Then—"

"When we entered Oceania's airspace," Warner explains, "their base was alerted to the presence of our unauthorized aircraft." He glances at the monitor. "They know we're here, and they're not happy about it."

"Right, I get that, but—"

Another violent jolt and I hit the floor. Warner doesn't even seem to startle. Nazeera stumbles, but gracefully, and collapses into the cockpit seat. She looks strangely deflated.

"So, um, okay— What's happening?" I'm breathing hard. My heart is racing. "Are you sure we're not being shot out of the sky again? Why is no one freaking out? Am I having a heart attack?"

"You're not having a heart attack, and they're not shooting us out of the sky," Nazeera says again, her fingers flying over the dials, swiping across screens. "But they've activated remote control of the aircraft. They've taken over the plane."

"And you can't override it?"

She shakes her head. "I don't have the authority to override a supreme commander's missive."

After a beat of silence, she straightens. Turns to face us.

"Maybe this isn't so bad," she says. "I mean, I wasn't exactly sure how we'd land here or how it would all go down, but it's got to be a good sign that they want us to walk in there alive, right?"

"Not necessarily," Warner says quietly.

"Right." Nazeera frowns. "Yeah, I realized that was wrong only after I said it out loud."

"So we're just supposed to wait here?" I'm feeling my intense panic begin to fade, but only a little. "We just wait here until they land our plane and then when they land our plane they surround us with armed soldiers and then when we walk off the plane they murder us and then—you know, we're dead? That's the plan?"

"That," Nazeera says, "or they could tell our plane to crash itself into the ocean or something."

"Oh my God, Nazeera, this isn't funny."

Warner looks out the window. "She wasn't joking."

"Okay, I'm only going to ask this one more time: Why am I the only one who's freaking out?"

"Because I have a plan," Nazeera says. She glances at the dashboard once more. "We have exactly fourteen minutes before the plane lands, but that gives me more than enough time to tell you both exactly what we're going to do."

~~ELLA~~
JULIETTE

First, I see light.

Bright, orange, flaring behind my eyelids. Sounds begin to emerge shortly thereafter but the reveal is slow, muddy. I hear my own breath, then faint beeping. A metal *shhh*, a rush of air, the sound of laughter. Footsteps, footsteps, a voice that says—

Ella

Just as I'm about to open my eyes a flood of heat flushes through my body, burns through bone. It's violent, pervasive. It presses hard against my throat, choking me.

Suddenly, I'm numb.

Ella, the voice says.

Ella

Listen

"Any minute now."
Anderson's familiar voice breaks through the haze of

my mind. My fingers twitch against cotton sheets. I feel the insubstantial weight of a thin blanket covering the lower half of my body. The pinch and sting of needles. A roar of pain. I realize, then, that I cannot move my left hand.

Someone clears their throat.

"This is twice now that the sedative hasn't worked the way it should," someone says. The voice is unfamiliar. Angry. "With Evie gone this whole place is going to hell."

"Evie made substantial changes to Ella's body," Anderson says, and I wonder who he's talking about. "It's possible that something in her new physical makeup prevents the sedative from clearing as quickly as it should."

A humorless laugh. "Your friendship with Max has gotten you many things over the last couple of decades, but a medical degree is not one of them."

"It's only a theory. I think it might be po—"

"I don't care to know your theories," the man says, cutting him off. "What I want to know is why on earth you thought it would be a good idea to injure our key subject, when maintaining her physical and mental stability is *crucial* to—"

"Ibrahim, be reasonable," Anderson interjects. "After what happened last time, I just wanted to be sure that everything was working as it should. I was only testing her lo—"

"We all know about your fetish for torture, Paris, but the novelty of your singularly sick mind has worn off. We're out of time."

"We are not out of time," Anderson says, sounding remarkably calm. "This is only a minor setback; Max was able to fix it right away."

"*A minor setback?*" Ibrahim thunders. "The girl lost consciousness. We're still at high risk for regression. The subject is supposed to be in stasis. I allowed you free rein of the girl, once again, because I honestly didn't think you would be this stupid. Because I don't have time to babysit you. Because Tatiana, Santiago, and Azi and I all have our hands full trying to do both your job *and* Evie's in addition to our own. In addition to everything else."

"I was doing my own job just fine," Anderson says, his voice like acid. "No one asked you to step in."

"You're forgetting that you lost your job and your continent the moment Evie's daughter shot you in the head and claimed your leavings for herself. You let a teenage girl take your life, your livelihood, your children, and your soldiers from right under your nose."

"You know as well as I do that she's not an ordinary teenage girl," Anderson says. "She's Evie's daughter. You know what she's capable of—"

"But *she* didn't!" Ibrahim cries. "Half the reason the girl was meant to live a life of isolation was so that she'd never know the full extent of her powers. She was meant only to metamorphose quietly, undetected, while we waited for the right moment to establish ourselves as a movement. She was only entrusted to your care because of your decades-long friendship with Max—and because you were a scheming, conniving upstart who was willing to take whatever job you could get in order to move up."

"That's funny," Anderson says, unamused. "You used to like me for being a scheming, conniving upstart who was willing to take whatever job I could get."

"I liked you," Ibrahim says, seething, "when you got the job done. But in the last year, you've been nothing but deadweight. We've given you ample opportunity to correct your mistakes, but you can't seem to get things right. You're lucky Max was able to fix her hand so quickly, but we still know nothing of her mental state. And I swear to you, Paris, if there are unanticipated, irreversible consequences for your actions I will challenge you before the committee."

"You wouldn't dare."

"You might've gotten away with this nonsense while Evie was still alive, but the rest of us know that the only reason you even made it this far was because of Evie's indulgence of Max, who continues to vouch for you for reasons unfathomable to the rest of us."

"For reasons unfathomable to the rest of us?" Anderson laughs. "You mean you can't remember why you've kept me around all these years? Let me help refresh your memory. As I recall, you liked me best when I was the only one willing to do the abject, immoral, and unsavory jobs that helped get this movement off the ground." A pause. "You've kept me around all these years, Ibrahim, because in exchange, I've kept the blood off your hands. Or have you forgotten? You once called me your savior."

"I don't care if I once called you a prophet." Something shatters. Metal and glass slamming hard into something else. "We can't continue to pay for your careless mistakes. We are at *war* right now, and at the moment we're barely holding on to our lead. If you can't understand the possible ramifications of even a minor setback at this critical hour, you don't deserve to stand among us."

A sudden crash. A door, slamming shut.

Anderson sighs, long and slow. Somehow I can tell, even from the sound of his exhalation, that he's not angry.

I'm surprised.

He just seems tired.

By degrees, the fingers of heat uncurl from around my throat. After a few more seconds of silence, my eyes flutter open.

I stare up at the ceiling, my eyes adjusting to the intense burst of white light. I feel slightly immobilized, but I seem to be okay.

"Juliette?"

Anderson's voice is soft. Far more gentle than I'd expected. I blink at the ceiling and then, with some effort, manage to move my neck. I lock eyes with him.

He looks unlike himself. Unshaven. Uncertain.

"Yes, sir," I say, but my voice is rough. Unused.

"How are you feeling?"

"I feel stiff, sir."

He hits a button and my bed moves, readjusting me so that I'm sitting relatively upright. Blood rushes from my head to my extremities and I'm left slightly dizzy. I blink, slowly, trying to recalibrate. Anderson turns off the machines attached to my body, and I watch, fascinated.

And then he straightens.

He turns his back to me, faces a small, high window. It's too far up for me to see the view. He raises his arms and runs his hands through his hair with a sigh.

"I need a drink," he says to the wall.

Anderson nods to himself and walks out the adjoining door. At first, I'm surprised to be left alone, but when I hear muffled sounds of movement and the familiar trill of glasses, clinking, I'm no longer surprised.

I'm confused.

I realize then that I have no idea where I am. Now that the needles have been removed from my body, I can more easily move, and as I swivel around to take in the space, it dawns on me that I am not in a medical wing, as I first suspected. This looks more like someone's bedroom.

Or maybe even a hotel room.

Everything is extremely white. Sterile. I'm in a big white bed with white sheets and a white comforter. Even the bed frame is made of a white, blond wood. Next to the various carts and now-dead monitors, there's a single nightstand decorated with a single, simple lamp. There's a slim door standing ajar, and through a slant of light I think I spy what serves as a closet, though it appears to be empty. Adjacent to the door is a suitcase, closed but unzipped. There's a screen mounted on the wall directly opposite me, and underneath it, a bureau. One of the drawers isn't completely closed, and it piques my interest.

It occurs to me then that I am not wearing any clothes. I'm wearing a hospital gown, but no real clothes. My eyes scan the room for my military uniform and I come up short.

There's nothing here.

I remember then, in a moment of clarity, that I must've bled all over my clothes. I remember kneeling on the floor. I remember the growing puddle of my own blood in which I collapsed.

I glance down at my injured hand. I only injured my index finger, but my entire left hand is bound in gauze. The pain has reduced to a dull throb. I take that as a good sign.

Gingerly, I begin to remove the bandages.

Just then, Anderson reappears. His suit jacket is gone. His tie, gone. The top two buttons of his shirt are undone, the black curl of ink more clearly visible, and his hair is disheveled. He seems more relaxed.

He remains in the doorway and takes a long drink from a glass half-full of amber liquid.

When he makes eye contact with me, I say:

"Sir, I was wondering where I am. I was also wondering where my clothes are."

Anderson takes another sip. He closes his eyes as he swallows, leans back against the doorframe. Sighs.

"You're in my room," he says, his eyes still closed. "This compound is vast, and the medical wings—of which there are many—are, for the most part, situated on the opposite end of the facility, about a mile away. After Max attended to your needs, I had him deposit you here so that I'd be able to keep a close eye on you through the night. As to your clothes, I have no idea." He takes another sip. "I think Max had them incinerated. I'm sure someone will bring you replacements soon."

"Thank you, sir."

Anderson says nothing.

I say nothing more.

With his eyes closed, I feel safer to stare at him. I take advantage of the rare opportunity to peer closer at his tattoo, but I still can't make sense of it. Mostly, I stare at his face, which I've never seen like this: Soft. Relaxed. Almost smiling. Even so, I can tell that something is troubling him.

"What?" he says without looking at me. "What is it now?"

"I was wondering, sir, if you're okay."

His eyes open. He tilts his head to look at me, but his gaze is inscrutable. Slowly, he turns.

He throws back the last of his drink, rests the glass on the nightstand, and sits down in a nearby armchair. "I had you cut off your own finger last night, do you remember?"

"Yes, sir."

"And today you're asking me if I'm okay."

"Yes, sir. You seem upset, sir."

He leans back in the chair, looking thoughtful. Suddenly, he shakes his head. "You know, I realize now that I've been too hard on you. I've put you through too much. Tested your loyalty perhaps too much. But you and I have a long history,

Juliette. And it's not easy for me to forgive. I certainly don't forget."

I say nothing.

"You have no idea how much I hated you," he says, speaking more to the wall than to me. "How much I still hate you, sometimes. But now, finally—"

He sits up, looks me in the eye.

"Now you're perfect." He laughs, but there's no heart in it. "Now you're absolutely perfect and I have to just give you away. Toss your body to science." He turns toward the wall again. "What a shame."

Fear creeps up, through my chest. I ignore it.

Anderson stands, grabs the empty glass off the nightstand, and disappears for a minute to refill it. When he returns, he stares at me from the doorway. I stare back. We remain like that for a while before he says, suddenly—

"You know, when I was very young, I wanted to be a baker."

Surprise shoots through me, widens my eyes.

"I know," he says, taking another swallow of the amber liquid. He almost laughs. "Not what you'd expect. But I've always had a fondness for cake. Few people realize this, but baking requires infinite precision and patience. It is an exacting, cruel science. I would've been an excellent baker." And then: "I'm not really sure why I'm telling you this. I suppose it's been a long time since I've felt I could speak openly with anyone."

"You can tell me anything, sir."

"Yes," he says quietly. "I'm beginning to believe that."

We're both silent then, but I can't stop staring at him, my mind suddenly overrun with unanswerable questions.

Another twenty seconds of this and he finally breaks the silence.

"All right, what is it?" His voice is dry. Self-mocking. "What is it you're *dying* to know?"

"I'm sorry, sir," I say. "I was just wondering— Why didn't you try? To be a baker?"

Anderson shrugs, spins the glass around in his hands. "When I got a bit older, my mother used to force bleach down my throat. Ammonia. Whatever she could find under the sink. It was never enough to kill me," he says, meeting my eyes. "Just enough to torture me for all of eternity." He throws back the rest of the drink. "You might say that I lost my appetite."

I can't mask my horror quickly enough. Anderson laughs at me, laughs at the look on my face.

"She never even had a good reason for doing it," he says, turning away. "She just hated me."

"Sir," I say, "Sir, I—"

Max barges into the room. I flinch.

"What the hell did you do?"

"There are so many possible answers to that question," Anderson says, glancing back. "Please be more specific. By the way, what did you do with her clothes?"

"I'm talking about Kent," Max says angrily. "What did you do?"

Anderson looks suddenly uncertain. He glances from Max to me then back again. "Perhaps we should discuss this elsewhere."

But Max looks beyond reason. His eyes are so wild I can't tell if he's angry or terrified. "Please tell me the tapes were tampered with. Tell me I'm wrong. Tell me you didn't perform the procedure on yourself."

Anderson looks at once relieved and irritated. "Calm yourself," he says. "I watched Evie do this kind of thing countless times—and the last time, on me. The boy had already been drained. The vial was ready, just sitting there on the counter, and you were so busy with"—he glances at me—"anyway, I had a while to wait, and I figured I'd make myself useful while I stood around."

"I can't believe— Of course you don't see the problem," Max says, grabbing a fistful of his own hair. He's shaking his head. "You never see the problem."

"That seems an unfair accusation."

"Paris, there's a reason why most Unnaturals only have one ability." He's beginning to pace now. "The occurrence of two supernatural gifts in the same person is exceedingly rare."

"What about Ibrahim's girl?" he says. "Wasn't that your work? Evie's?"

"No," Max says forcefully. "That was a random, natural error. We were just as surprised by the discovery as anyone else."

Anderson goes suddenly solid with tension. "What,

exactly, is the problem?"

"It's not—"

A sudden blare of sirens and the words die in Max's throat. "Not again," he whispers. "God, not again."

Anderson spares me a single glance before he disappears into his room, and this time, he reappears fully assembled. Not a hair out of place. He checks the cartridge of a handgun before he tucks it away, in a hidden holster.

"Juliette," he says sharply.

"Yes, sir?"

"I am ordering you to remain here. No matter what you see, no matter what you hear, you are not to leave this room. You are to do nothing unless I command you otherwise. Do you understand? "

"Yes, sir."

"Max, get her something to wear," Anderson barks. "And then keep her hidden. Guard her with your life."

KENJI

This was the plan:

We were all supposed to go invisible—Warner borrowing his power from me and Nazeera—and jump out of the plane just before it landed. Nazeera would then activate her flying powers, and with Warner bolstering her power, the three of us would bypass the welcoming committee intent on murdering us. We'd then make our way directly into the heart of the vast compound, where we'd begin our search for Juliette.

This is what actually happens:

All three of us go invisible and jump out of the plane as it lands. That part worked. The thing we weren't expecting, of course, was for the welcoming/murdering committee to so thoroughly anticipate our moves.

We're up in the air, flying over the heads of at least two dozen highly armed soldiers and one dude who looks like he might be Nazeera's dad, when someone flashes some kind of long-barreled gun up, into the sky. He seems to be searching for something.

Us.

"He's scanning for heat signatures," Warner says.

"I realize that," Nazeera says, sounding frustrated. She

picks up speed, but it doesn't matter.

Seconds later, the guy with the heat gun shouts something to someone else, who aims a different weapon at us, one that immediately disables our powers.

It's just as horrifying as it sounds.

I don't even have a chance to scream. I don't have time to think about the fact that my heart is racing a mile a minute, or that my hands are shaking, or that Nazeera—fearless, invulnerable Nazeera—looks suddenly terrified as the sky falls out from under her. Even Warner seems stunned.

I was already super freaked out about the idea of being shot out of the sky again, but I can honestly say that I wasn't mentally prepared for this. This is a whole new level of terror. The three of us are suddenly visible and spiraling to our deaths and the soldiers below are just staring at us, waiting.

For what? I think.

Why are they just staring at us as we die? Why go to all the trouble to take over our plane and land us here, safely, just to watch us fall out of the sky?

Do they find this entertaining?

Time feels strange. Infinite and nonexistent. Wind is rushing up against my feet, and all I can see is the ground, coming at us too fast, but I can't stop thinking about how, in all my nightmares, I never thought I'd die like this. I never thought I'd die because of gravity. I didn't think that *this* was the way I was destined to exit the world, and it seems wrong, and it seems unfair, and I'm thinking about how quickly we failed, how we never stood a chance—when I hear a sudden explosion.

A flash of fire, discordant cries, the faraway sounds of Warner shouting, and then I'm no longer falling, no longer visible.

It all happens so fast I feel dizzy.

Nazeera's arm is wrapped around me and she's hauling me upward, struggling a bit, and then Warner materializes beside me, helping to prop me up. His sharp voice and familiar presence are my only proof of his existence.

"Nice shot," Nazeera says, her breathless words loud in my ear. "How long do you think we have?"

"Ten seconds before it occurs to them to start shooting blindly at us," Warner calls out. "We have to move out of range. Now."

"On it," Nazeera shouts back.

We narrowly avoid gunfire as the three of us plummet, at a sharp diagonal, to the ground. We were already so close to the ground that it doesn't take us long to land in the middle of a field, far enough away from danger to be able to breathe a momentary sigh of relief, but too far from the compound for the relief to last long.

I'm bent over, hands on my knees, gasping for breath, trying to calm down. "What did you do you? What the hell just happened?"

"Warner threw a grenade," Nazeera explains. Then, to Warner: "You found that in Haider's bag, didn't you?"

"That, and a few other useful things. We need to move."

I hear the sound of his retreating footsteps—boots crushing grass—and I hurry to follow.

"They'll regroup quickly," Warner is saying, "so we have only moments to come up with a new plan. I think we should split up."

"No," Nazeera and I say at the same time.

"There's no time," Warner says. "They know we're here, and they've obviously had ample opportunity to prepare for our arrival. Unfortunately, our parents aren't idiots; they know we're here to save Ella. Our presence has almost certainly inspired them to begin the transfer if they haven't done so already. The three of us together are inefficient. Easy targets."

"But one of us has to stay with you," Nazeera says. "You need us within close proximity if you're going to use stealth to get around."

"I'll take my chances."

"No way," Nazeera says flatly. "Listen, I know this compound, so I'll be okay on my own. But Kenji doesn't know this place well enough. The entire footprint measures out to about a hundred and twenty acres of land—which means you can easily get lost if you don't know where to look. You two stick together. Kenji will lend you his stealth, and you can be his guide. I'll go alone."

"What?" I say, panicked. "No, no way—"

"Warner's not wrong," Nazeera says, cutting me off. "The three of us, as a group, really do make for an easier target. There are too many variables. Besides, I have something

I need to do, and the sooner I can get to a computer, the smoother things will go for you both. It's probably best if I tackle that on my own."

"Wait, what?"

"What are you planning?" Warner asks.

"I'm going to trick the systems into thinking that your family and Ella's are linked," she says to Warner. "There's protocol for this sort of thing already in place within The Reestablishment, so if I can create the necessary profiles and authorizations, the database will recognize you as a member of the Sommers family. You'll be granted easy access to most of the high-security rooms throughout the compound. But it's not foolproof. The system does a self-scan for anomalies every hour. If it's able to see through my bullshit, you'll be locked out and reported. But until then—you'll be able to more easily search the buildings for Ella."

"Nazeera," Warner says, sounding unusually impressed. "That's . . . great."

"Better than great," I add. "That's amazing."

"Thanks," she says. "But I should get going. The sooner I start flying, the sooner I can get started, which hopefully means that by the time you reach base, I'll have made something happen."

"But what if you get caught?" I ask. "What if you can't do it? How will we find you?"

"You won't."

"But— Nazeera—"

"We're at war, Kishimoto," she says, a slight smile in her voice. "We don't have time to be sentimental."

"That's not funny. I hate that joke. I hate it so much."

"Nazeera is going to be fine," Warner says. "You obviously don't know her well if you think she's easily captured."

"She literally just woke up! After being shot! In the chest! She nearly died!"

"That was a fluke," Warner and Nazeera say at the same time.

"But—"

"Hey," Nazeera says, her voice suddenly close. "I have a feeling I'm about four months away from falling madly in love with you, so please don't get yourself killed, okay?"

I'm about to respond when I feel a sudden rush of air. I hear her launching up, into the sky, and even though I know I won't see her, I crane my neck as if to watch her go.

And just like that—

She's gone.

My heart is pounding in my chest, blood rushing to my head. I feel confused: terrified, excited, hopeful, horrified. All the best and worst things always seem to happen to me at the same time.

It's not fair.

"Fucking hell," I say out loud.

"Come on," Warner says. "Let's move out."

~~ELLA~~ JULIETTE

Max is staring at me like I'm an alien.

He hasn't moved since Anderson left; he just stands there, stiff and strange, rooted to the floor. I remember the look he gave me the first time we met—the unguarded hostility in his eyes—and I blink at him from my bed, wondering why he hates me so much.

After an uncomfortable stretch of silence, I clear my throat. It's obvious that Anderson respects Max—likes him, even—so I decide I should address him with a similar level of respect.

"Sir," I say. "I'd really like to get dressed."

Max startles at the sound of my voice. His body language is entirely different now that Anderson isn't here, and I'm still struggling to figure him out. He seems skittish. I wonder if I should feel threatened by him. His affection for Anderson is no indication that he might treat me as anything but a nameless soldier.

A subordinate.

Max sighs. It's a loud, rough sound that seems to shake him from his stupor. He shoots me a last look before he disappears into the adjoining room, from where I hear indiscernible, shuffling sounds. When he reappears, his arms are empty.

He stares blankly at me, looking more rattled than he did a moment ago. He shoves a hand through his hair. It sticks up in places.

"Anderson doesn't have anything that would fit you," he says.

"No, sir," I say carefully. Still confused. "I was hoping I might be given a replacement uniform."

Max turns away, stares at nothing. "A replacement uniform," he says to himself. "Right." But when he takes in a long, shuddering breath, it becomes clear to me that he's trying to stay calm.

Trying to stay calm.

I realize, suddenly, that Max might be afraid of me. Maybe he saw what I did to Darius. Maybe he's the doctor who patched him up.

Still—

I don't see what reason he'd have to think I'd hurt him. After all, my orders come from Anderson, and as far as I'm aware, Max is an ally. I watch him closely as he lifts his wrist to his mouth, quietly requesting that someone deliver a fresh set of clothes for me.

And then he backs away from me until he's flush with the wall. There's a single, sharp thud as the heels of his boots hit the baseboards, and then, silence.

Silence.

It erupts, settling completely into the room, the quiet reaching even the farthest corners. I feel physically trapped by it. The lack of sound feels oppressive.

Paralyzing.

I pass the time by counting the bruises on my body. I don't think I've spent this much time looking at myself in the last few days; I hadn't realized how many wounds I had. There seem to be several fresh cuts on my arms and legs, and I feel a vague stinging along my lower abdomen. I pull back the collar of the hospital gown, peering through the overly large neck hole at my naked body underneath.

Pale. Bruised.

There's a small, fresh scar running vertically down the side of my torso, and I don't know what I did to acquire it. In fact, my body seems to have amassed an entire constellation of fresh incisions and faded bruises. For some reason, I can't remember where they came from.

I glance up, suddenly, when I feel the heat of Max's gaze.

He's staring at me as I study myself, and the sharp look in his eyes makes me wary. I sit up. Sit back.

I don't feel comfortable asking him any of the questions piling in my mouth.

So I look at my hands.

I've already removed the rest of my bandages; my left hand is mostly healed. There's no visible scar where my finger was detached, but my skin is mottled up to my forearm, mostly purple and dark blue, a few spots of yellow. I curl my fingers into a fist, let it go. It hurts only a little. The pain is fading by the hour.

The next words leave my lips before I can stop them:

"Thank you, sir, for fixing my hand."

Max stares at me, uncertain, when his wrist lights up. He glances down at the message, and then at the door, and as he darts to the entrance, he tosses strange, wild looks at me over his shoulder, as if he's afraid to turn his back on me.

Max grows more bizarre by the moment.

When the door opens, the room is flooded with sound. Flashing lights pulse through the slice of open doorway, shouts and footsteps thundering down the hall. I hear metal crashing into metal, the distant blare of an alarm.

My heart picks up.

I'm on my feet before I can even stop myself, my sharpened senses oblivious to the fact that my hospital gown does little to cover my body. All I know is a sudden, urgent need to join the commotion, to do what I can to assist, and to find my commander and protect him. It's what I was built to do.

I can't just stand here.

But then I remember that my commander gave me explicit orders to remain here, and the fight leaves my body.

Max shuts the door, silencing the chaos with that single motion. I open my mouth to say something, but the look in his eyes warns me not to speak. He places a stack of clothes on the bed—refusing to even come near me—and steps out of the room.

I change into the clothes quickly, shedding the loose gown for the starched, stiff fabric of a freshly washed military uniform. Max brought me no undergarments, but

I don't bother pointing this out; I'm just relieved to have something to wear. I'm still buttoning the front placket, my fingers working as quickly as possible, when my gaze falls once more to the bureau directly opposite the bed. There's a single drawer left slightly open, as if it was closed in a hurry.

I'd noticed it earlier.

I can't stop staring at it now.

Something pulls me forward, some need I can't explain. It's becoming familiar now—almost normal—to feel the strange heat filling my head, so I don't question my compulsion to move closer. Something somewhere inside of me is screaming at me to stand down, but I'm only dimly aware of it. I hear Max's muffled, low voice in the other room; he's speaking with someone in harried, aggressive tones. He seems fully distracted.

Encouraged, I step forward.

My hand curls around the drawer pull, and it takes only a little effort to tug it open. It's a smooth, soft system. The wood makes almost no sound as it moves. And I'm just about to peer inside when—

"What are you doing?"

Max's voice sends a sharp note of clarity through my brain, clearing the haze. I take a step back, blinking. Trying to understand what I was doing.

"The drawer was open, sir. I was going to close it." The lie comes automatically. Easily.

I marvel at it.

Max slams the drawer closed and stares, suspiciously, at

my face. I blink at him, blithely meeting his gaze.

I notice then that he's holding my boots.

He shoves them at me; I take them. I want to ask him if he has a hair tie—my hair is unusually long; I have a vague memory of it being much shorter—but I decide against it.

He watches me closely as I pull on my boots, and once I'm upright again, he barks at me to follow him.

I don't move.

"Sir, my commander gave me direct orders to remain in this room. I will stay here until otherwise instructed."

"You're currently being instructed. I'm instructing you."

"With all due respect, sir, you are not my commanding officer."

Max sighs, irritation darkening his features, and he lifts his wrist to his mouth. "Did you hear that? I told you she wouldn't listen to me." A pause. "Yes. You'll have to come get her yourself."

Another pause.

Max is listening on an invisible earpiece not unlike the one I've seen Anderson use—an earpiece I'm now realizing must be implanted in their brains.

"Absolutely not," Max says, his anger so sudden it startles me. He shakes his head. "I'm not touching her."

Another beat of silence, and—

"I realize that," he says sharply. "But it's different when her eyes are open. There's something about her face. I don't like the way she looks at me."

My heart slows.

Blackness fills my vision, flickers back to light. I hear my heart beating, hear myself breathe in, breathe out, hear my own voice, loud—so loud—

There was something about my face

The words slur, slow down

there wassomething about my facesssomething about my facesssomething about my eyes, the way I looked at her

My eyes fly open with a start. I'm breathing hard, confused, and I have hardly a moment to reflect on what just happened in my head before the door flies open again. A roar of noise fills my ears—more sirens, more shouts, more sounds of urgent, chaotic movement—

"Juliette Ferrars."

There's a man in front of me. Tall. Forbidding. Black hair, brown skin, green eyes. I can tell, just by looking at him, that he wields a great deal of power.

"I am Supreme Commander Ibrahim."

My eyes widen.

Musa Ibrahim is the supreme commander of Asia. By all accounts, the supreme commanders of The Reestablishment have equal levels of authority—but Supreme Commander Ibrahim is widely known to be one of the founders of the movement, and one of the only supreme commanders to have held the position from the beginning. He's extremely well respected.

So when he says, "Come with me," I say—

"Yes, sir."

I follow him out the door and into the chaos, but I don't have long to take in the pandemonium before we make a sharp turn into a dark hallway. I follow Ibrahim down a slim, narrow path, the lights dimming as we go. I glance back a few times to see if Max is still with us, but he seems to have gone in another direction.

"This way," Ibrahim says sharply.

We make one more turn and, suddenly, the narrow path opens onto a large, brightly lit landing area. There's an industrial stairwell to the left and a large, gleaming steel elevator to the right. Ibrahim heads for the elevator, and places his hand flat against the seamless door. After a moment, the metal emits a quiet beep, hissing as it slides open.

Once we're both inside, Ibrahim gives me a wide berth. I wait for him to direct the elevator—I scan the interior for buttons or a monitor of some kind—but he does nothing. A second later, without prompting, the elevator moves.

The ride is so smooth it takes me a minute to realize we're moving sideways, rather than up or down. I glance around, taking the opportunity to more closely examine the interior, and only then do I notice the rounded corners. I thought this unit was rectangular; it appears to be circular. I wonder, then, if we're moving as a bullet would, boring through the earth.

Surreptitiously, I glance at Ibrahim.

He says nothing. Indicates nothing. He seems neither interested nor perturbed by my presence, which is new. He holds himself with a certainty that reminds me a great deal of Anderson, but there's something else about Ibrahim— something more—that feels unique. Even from a passing glance it's obvious that he feels absolutely sure about himself. I'm not sure even Anderson feels absolutely sure of himself. He's always testing and prodding—examining and questioning. Ibrahim, on the other hand, seems comfortable. Unbothered. Effortlessly confident.

I wonder what that must feel like.

And then I shock myself for wondering.

Once the elevator stops, it makes three brief, harsh, buzzing sounds. A moment later, the doors open. I wait for Ibrahim to exit first, and then I follow.

When I cross the threshold, I'm first stunned by the smell. The air quality is so poor that I can't even open my eyes properly. There's an acrid smell in the air, something reminiscent of sulfur, and I step through a cloud of smoke so thick it immediately makes my eyes burn. It's not long before I'm coughing, covering my face with my arm as I force my way through the room.

I don't know how Ibrahim can stand this.

Only after I've pushed through the cloud does the stinging smell begin to dissipate, but by then, I've lost track of Ibrahim. I spin around, trying to take in my surroundings, but there are no visual cues to root me. This laboratory doesn't seem much different from the others I've seen. A great deal of glass and steel. Dozens of long, metal tables stretched across the room, all of them covered in beakers and test tubes and what look like massive microscopes. The one big difference here is that there are huge glass domes drilled into the walls, the smooth, transparent semicircles appearing more like portholes than anything else. As I get closer I realize that they're planters of some kind, each one containing unusual vegetation I've never seen. Lights flicker on as I move through the vast space, but much of it is still shrouded in darkness, and I gasp, suddenly, when I walk straight into a glass wall.

I take a step back, my eyes adjusting to the light.

It's not a wall.

It's an aquarium.

An aquarium larger than I am. An aquarium the size of a wall. It's not the first water tank I've seen in a laboratory here in Oceania, and I'm beginning to wonder why there are so many of them. I take another step back, still trying to make sense of what I'm seeing. Dissatisfied, I step closer again. There's a dim blue light in the tank, but it doesn't do much to illuminate the large dimensions. I crane my neck to see the top of it, but I lose my balance, catching myself against the glass at the last second. This is a futile effort.

I need to find Ibrahim.

Just as I'm about to step back, I notice a flash of movement in the tank. The water trembles within, begins to thrash.

A hand slams hard against the glass.

I gasp.

Slowly, the hand retreats.

I stand there, frozen in fear and fascination, when someone clamps down on my arm.

This time, I almost scream.

"Where have you been?" Ibrahim says angrily.

"I'm sorry, sir," I say quickly. "I got lost. The smoke was so thick that I—"

"What are you talking about? What smoke?"

The words die in my throat. I thought I saw smoke. Was there no smoke? Is this another test?

Ibrahim sighs. "Come with me."

"Yes, sir."

This time, I keep my eyes on Ibrahim at all times.

And this time, when we walk through the darkened laboratory into a blindingly bright, circular room, I know I'm in the right place. Because something is wrong.

Someone is dead.

KENJI

When we finally make it to the compound, I'm exhausted, thirsty, and really have to use the bathroom. Warner is none of those things, apparently, because Warner is made of uranium or plutonium or some shit, so I have to beg him to let me take a quick break. And by begging him I mean I grab him by the back of the shirt and force him to slow down—and then I basically collapse behind a wall. Warner shoves away from me, and the sound of his irritated exhalation is all I need to know that my "break" is half a second from over.

"We don't take breaks," he says sharply. "If you can't keep up, stay here."

"Bro, I'm not asking to stop. I'm not even asking for a real break. I just need a second to catch my breath. Two seconds. Maybe five seconds. That's not crazy. And just because I have to catch my breath doesn't mean I don't love J. It means we just ran like a thousand miles. It means my lungs aren't made of steel."

"Two miles," he says. "We ran two miles."

"In the sun. Uphill. You're in a fucking suit. Do you even sweat? How are you not tired?"

"If by now you don't understand, I certainly can't teach you."

I haul myself to my feet. We start moving again.

"I'm not sure I even want to know what you're talking about," I say, lowering my voice as I reach for my gun. We're rounding the corner to the entrance, where our big, fancy plan to break into the building involves waiting for someone to open the door, and catching that door before it closes.

No luck yet.

"Hey," I whisper.

"What?" Warner sounds annoyed.

"How'd you end up proposing?"

Silence.

"Come on, bro. I'm curious. Also, I, uh, really have to pee, so if you don't distract me right now all I'm going to think about is how much I have to pee."

"You know, sometimes I wish I could remove the part of my brain that stores the things you say to me."

I ignore that.

"So? How'd you do it?" Someone comes through the door and I tense, ready to jump forward, but there's not enough time. My body relaxes back against the wall. "Did you get the ring like I told you to?"

"No."

"What? What do you mean, *no*?" I hesitate. "Did you at least, like, light a candle? Make her dinner?"

"No."

"Buy her chocolates? Get down on one knee?"

"No."

"No? No, you didn't do even one of those things? None

of them?" My whispers are turning into whisper-yells. "You didn't do a single thing I told you to do?"

"No."

"Son of a bitch."

"Why does it matter?" he asks. "She said yes."

I groan. "You're the worst, you know that? The *worst*. You don't deserve her."

Warner sighs. "I thought that was already obvious."

"Hey— Don't you dare make me feel sorry for y—"

I cut myself off when the door suddenly opens. A small group of doctors (scientists? I don't know) exits the building, and Warner and I jump to our feet and get into position. This group has just enough people—and they take just long enough exiting—that when I grab the door and hold it open for a few seconds longer, it doesn't seem to register.

We're in.

And we've only been inside for less than a second before Warner slams me into the wall, knocking the air from my lungs.

"Don't move," he whispers. "Not an inch."

"Why not?" I wheeze.

"Look up," he says, "but only with your eyes. Don't move your head. Do you see the cameras?"

"No."

"They anticipated us," he says. "They anticipated our moves. Look up again, but do it carefully. Those small black dots are cameras. Sensors. Infrared scanners. Thermal imagers. They're searching for inconsistencies in the security footage."

"*Shit.*"

"Yes."

"So what do we do?"

"I'm not sure," Warner says.

"You're not sure?" I say, trying not to freak out. "How can you not be sure?"

"I'm thinking," he whispers, irritated. "And I don't hear you contributing any ideas."

"Listen, bro, all I know is that I really, really need to p—"

I'm interrupted by the distant sound of a toilet flushing. A moment later, a door swings open. I turn my head a millimeter and realize we're right next to the men's bathroom.

Warner and I seize the moment, catching the door before it falls closed. Once inside the bathroom we press up against the wall, our backs to the cold tile. I'm trying hard not to think about all the pee residue touching my body, when Warner exhales.

It's a brief, quiet sound—but he sounds relieved.

I'm guessing that means there are no scanners or cameras in this bathroom, but I can't be sure, because Warner doesn't say a word, and it doesn't take a genius to figure out why.

We're not sure if we're alone in here.

I can't see him do it, but I'm pretty sure Warner is checking the stalls right now. It's what I'm doing, anyway. This isn't a huge bathroom—as I'm sure it's one of many—and it's right by the entrance/exit of the building, so right now it doesn't seem to be getting a lot of traffic.

When we're both certain the room is clear, Warner says—

"We're going to go up, through the vent. If you truly need to use the bathroom, do it now."

"Okay, but why do you have to sound so disgusted about it? Do you really expect me to believe that you never have to use the bathroom? Are basic human needs below you?"

Warner ignores me.

I see the stall door open, and I hear his careful sounds as he climbs the metal cubicles. There's a large vent in the ceiling just above one of the stalls, and I watch as his invisible hands make short work of the grate.

Quickly, I use the bathroom. And then I wash my hands as loudly as possible, just in case Warner feels the need to make a juvenile comment about my hygiene.

Surprisingly, he doesn't.

Instead, he says, "Are you ready?" And I can tell by the echoing sound of his voice that he's already halfway up the vent.

"I'm ready. Just let me know when you're in."

More careful movement, the metal drumming as he goes. "I'm in," he says. "Make sure you reattach the grate after you climb up."

"Got it."

"On a related note, I hope you're not claustrophobic. Though if you are . . . Good luck."

I take a deep breath.

Let it go.

And we begin our journey into hell.

ELLA JULIETTE

Max, Anderson, a blond woman, and a tall black man are all standing in the center of the room, staring at a dead body, and they look up only when Ibrahim approaches.

Anderson's eyes home in on me immediately.

I feel my heart jump. I don't know how Max got here before we did, and I don't know if I'm about to be punished for obeying Supreme Commander Ibrahim.

My mind spirals.

"What's she doing here?" Anderson asks, his expression wild. "I told her to stay in the r—"

"I overruled your orders," Ibrahim says sharply, "and told her to come with me."

"My bedroom is one of the most secure locations on this wing," Anderson says, barely holding on to his anger. "You've put us all at risk by moving her."

"We are currently under attack," Ibrahim says. "You left her alone, completely unattended—"

"I left her with Max!"

"Max, who's too terrified of his own creation to spend even a few minutes alone with the girl. You forget, there's a reason he was never granted a military position."

Anderson shoots Max a strange, confused look.

Somehow, the confusion on Anderson's face makes me feel better about my own. I have no idea what's happening. No idea to whom I should answer. No idea what Ibrahim meant by *creation*.

Max just shakes his head.

"The children are here," Ibrahim says, changing the subject. "They're here, in our midst, completely undetected. They're going room by room searching for her, and already they've killed four of our key scientists in the process." He nods at the dead body—a graying, middle-aged man, blood pooling beneath him. "How did this happen? Why haven't they been spotted yet?"

"Nothing has registered on the cameras," Anderson says. "Not yet, anyway."

"So you're telling me that this—and the three other dead bodies we've found so far—was the work of ghosts?"

"They must've found a way to trick the system," the woman says. "It's the only possible answer."

"Yes, Tatiana, I realize that—but the question is *how*." Ibrahim pinches his nose between his thumb and index finger. And it's clear he's talking to Anderson when he says: "All the preparations you claimed to have made in anticipation of a possible assault—they were all for nothing?"

"What did you expect?" Anderson is no longer trying to control his anger. "They're our children. We bred them for this. I'd be disappointed if they were stupid enough to fall into our traps right away."

Our children?

"Enough," Ibrahim cries. "Enough of this. We need to initiate the transfer now."

"I already told you why we can't," Max says urgently. "Not yet. We need more time. Emmaline still needs to fall below ten percent viability in order for the procedure to operate smoothly, and right now, she's at twelve percent. Another few days—maybe a couple of weeks—and we should be able to move forward. But anything above ten percent viability means there's a chance she'll still be strong enough to resis—"

"I don't care," Ibrahim says. "We've waited long enough. And we've wasted enough time and money trying to keep both her alive and her sister in our custody. We can't risk another failure."

"But initiating the transfer at twelve percent viability has a thirty-eight percent chance of failure," Max says, speaking quickly. "We could be risking a great deal—"

"Then find more ways to reduce viability," Ibrahim snaps.

"We're already at the top end of what we can do right now," Max says. "She's still too strong—she's fighting our efforts—"

"That's only more reason to get rid of her sooner," Ibrahim says, cutting him off again. "We're expending an egregious amount of resources just to keep the other kids isolated from her advances—when God only knows what damage she's already done. She's been meddling everywhere, causing needless disaster. We need a new host. A healthy one. And we need it now."

"Ibrahim, don't be rash," Anderson says, trying to sound calm. "This could be a huge mistake. Juliette is a perfect soldier—she's more than proven herself—and right now she could be a huge help. Instead of locking her away, we should be sending her out. Giving her a mission."

"Absolutely not."

"Ibrahim, he makes a good point," the tall black man says. "The kids won't be expecting her. She'd be the perfect lure."

"See? Azi agrees with me."

"I don't." Tatiana shakes her head. "It's too dangerous," she says. "Too many things could go wrong."

"What could possibly go wrong?" Anderson asks. "She's more powerful than any of them, and completely obedient to me. To us. To the movement. You all know as well as I do that she's proven her loyalty again and again. She'd be able to capture them in a matter of minutes. This could all be over in an hour, and we'd be able to move on with our lives." Anderson locks eyes with me. "You wouldn't mind rounding up a few rebels, would you, Juliette?"

"I would be happy to, sir."

"See?" Anderson gestures to me.

A sudden alarm blares, the sound so loud it's painful. I'm still rooted in place, so overwhelmed and confused by this sudden flood of dizzying information that I don't even know what to do with myself. But the supreme commanders look suddenly terrified.

"Azi, where is Santiago?" Tatiana cries. "You were last with him, weren't you? Someone check in with Santiago—"

"He's down," Azi says, tapping against his temple. "He's not responding."

"*Max*," Anderson says sharply, but Max is already rushing out the door, Azi and Tatiana on his heels.

"Go collect your son," Ibrahim barks at Anderson.

"Why don't you go collect your daughter?" Anderson shoots back.

Ibrahim's eyes narrow. "I'm taking the girl," he says quietly. "I'm finishing this job, and I'll do it alone if I have to."

Anderson glances from me to Ibrahim. "You're making a mistake," he says. "She's finally become our asset. Don't let your pride keep you from seeing the answer in front of us. Juliette should be the one tracking down the kids right now. The fact that they won't be anticipating her as an assailant makes them easier targets. It's the most obvious solution."

"You are out of your mind," Ibrahim shouts, "if you think I'm foolish enough to take such a risk. I will not just hand her over to her friends like some common idiot."

Friends?

I have friends?

"*Hey, princess,*" someone whispers in my ear.

KENJI

Warner just about slaps me upside the head.

He yanks me back, grabbing me roughly by the shoulder, and drags us both across the overly bright, extremely creepy laboratory.

Once we're far enough away from Anderson, Ibrahim, and Robot J, I expect Warner to say something—anything—

He doesn't.

The two of us watch the distant conversation grow more heated by the moment, but we can't really hear what they're saying from here. Though I think even if we could hear what they were saying, Warner wouldn't be paying attention. The fight seems to have left his body. I can't even see him right now, but I can feel it. Something about his movements, his quiet sighs.

His mind is on Juliette.

Juliette, who looks the same. Better, in fact. She looks healthy, her eyes bright, her skin glowing. Her hair is down—long, heavy, dark—the way it was the first time I ever saw her.

But she's not the same. Even I can see that.

And it's devastating.

I guess this is somehow better than if she'd replaced

Emmaline altogether, but this weird, robotic, super-soldier version of J is also deeply concerning.

I think.

I keep waiting for Warner to finally break the silence, to give me some indication of his feelings and/or theories on the matter—and maybe, while he's at it, offer me his professional opinion on what the hell we should be doing next—but the seconds continue to pass in perfect silence.

Finally, I give up.

"All right, get it out," I whisper. "Tell me what you're thinking."

Warner lets out a long breath. "This doesn't make sense."

I nod, even though he can't see me. "I get that. Nothing makes sense in situations like these. I always feel like it's unfair, you know, like the worl—"

"I'm not being philosophical," Warner says, cutting me off. "I mean it literally doesn't make sense. Nouria and Sam said that Operation Synthesis would turn Ella into a super soldier—and that once the program went into effect, the result would be irreversible.

"But this is not Operation Synthesis," he says. "Operation Synthesis is literally about synthesizing Ella's and Emmaline's powers, and right now, there's no—"

"Synthesis," I say. "I get it."

"This doesn't feel right. They did things out of order."

"Maybe they freaked out after Evie's attempt to wipe J's mind didn't work. Maybe they needed to find a way to fix that fail, and quick. I mean, it's much easier to keep her around if she's docile, right? Loyal to their interests. It's much easier than keeping her in a holding cell, anyway. Babysitting her constantly. Monitoring her every movement. Always worried she's going to magic the toilet paper into a shiv and break out.

"Honestly"—I shrug—"it feels to me like they're just getting lazy. I think they're sick and tired of J always breaking out and fighting back. This is literally the path of least resistance."

"Yes," Warner says slowly. "Exactly."

"Wait— Exactly what?"

"Whatever they did to her—prematurely initiating this phase—was done hastily. It was a patch job."

A lightbulb flickers to life in my head. "Which means their work was sloppy."

"And if their work was sloppy—"

"—there are definitely holes in it."

"Stop finishing my sentences," he says, irritated.

"Stop being so predictable."

"Stop acting like a child."

"*You* stop acting like a child."

"You are being ridicu—"

Warner goes suddenly silent as Ibrahim's shaking, angry voice booms across the laboratory.

"I said, *get out of the way*."

"I can't let you do this," Anderson says, his voice growing louder. "Did you not just hear that alarm? Santiago is out. They took out yet another supreme commander. How much longer are we going to let this go on?"

"*Juliette*," Ibrahim says sharply. "You're coming with me."

"Yes, sir."

"Juliette, stop," Anderson demands.

"Yes, sir."

What the hell is happening?

Warner and I dart forward to get a better look, but it doesn't matter how close we get; I still can't believe my eyes.

The scene is surreal.

Anderson is guarding Juliette. The same Anderson who's spent so much of his energy trying to murder her—is now standing in front of her with his arms out, guarding her with his life.

What the hell happened while she was here? Did Anderson get a new brain? A new heart? A parasite?

And I know I'm not alone in my confusion when I hear Warner mutter, "*What on earth?*" under his breath.

"Stop being foolish," Anderson says. "You're taking advantage of a tragedy to make an unauthorized decision, when you know as well as I do that we all need to agree on something this important before moving forward. I'm just asking you to wait, Ibrahim. Wait for the others to return, and we'll put it to a vote. Let the council decide."

Ibrahim pulls a gun on Anderson.

Ibrahim pulls a gun on Anderson.

I nearly lose my shit. I gasp so loud I almost blow our

cover.

"Step aside, Paris," he says. "You've already ruined this mission. I've given you dozens of chances to get this right. You gave me your word that we'd intercept the children before they even stepped foot in the building, and look how that turned out. You've promised me—all of us—time and time again that you would make this right, and instead all you do is cost us our time, our money, our power, our lives. *Everything*.

"It's now up to me to make this right," Ibrahim says, anger making his voice unsteady. He shakes his head. "You don't even understand, do you? You don't understand how much Evie's death has cost us. You don't understand how much of our success was built with her genius, her technological advances. You don't understand that Max will never be what Evie was—that he could never replace her. And you don't seem to understand that she's no longer here to forgive your constant mistakes.

"No," he says. "It's up to me now. It's up to me to fix things, because I'm the only one with his head on straight. I'm the only one who seems to grasp the enormity of what's ahead of us. I'm the only one who sees how close we are to complete and utter ruination. I am determined to make this right, Paris, even if it means taking you out in the process. So step aside."

"Be reasonable," Anderson says, his eyes wary. "I can't just step aside. I want our movement—everything we've worked so hard to build—I want it to be a success, too.

Surely you must realize that. You must realize that I haven't given up my life for nothing; you must know that my loyalty is to you, to the council, to The Reestablishment. But you must also know that she's worth too much. I can't let this go so easily. We've come too far. We've all made too many sacrifices to screw this up now."

"Don't force my hand, Paris. Don't make me do this."

J steps forward, about to say something, and Anderson pushes her body behind him. "I ordered you to remain silent," he says, glancing back at her. "And I am now ordering you to remain safe, at all costs. Do you hear me, Juliette? Do y—"

When the shot rings out, I don't believe it.

I think my mind is playing tricks on me. I think this is some kind of weird interlude—a strange dream, a moment of confusion—I keep waiting for the scene to change. Clear. Reset.

It doesn't.

No one thought it would happen like this. No one thought the supreme commanders would destroy themselves. No one thought we'd see Anderson felled by one his own, no one thought he'd clutch his bleeding chest and use his last gasp of breath to say:

"Run, Juliette. *Run*—"

Ibrahim shoots again, and this time, Anderson goes silent.

"Juliette," Ibrahim says, "you're coming with me."

J doesn't move.

She's frozen in place, staring at Anderson's still figure. It's so weird. I keep waiting for him to wake up. I keep waiting for his healing powers to kick in. I keep waiting for that annoying moment when he comes back to life, clutching a pocket square to his wound—

But he doesn't move.

"Juliette," Ibrahim says sharply. "You will answer to me now. And I am ordering you to follow me."

J looks up at him. Her face is blank. Her eyes are blank. "Yes, sir," she says.

And that's when I know.

That's when I know exactly what's going to happen next. I can feel it, can feel some strange electricity in the air before he makes his move. Before he blows our cover.

Warner pulls back his invisibility.

He stands there motionless for only a moment, for just long enough for Ibrahim to register his presence, to cry out, to reach for his gun. But he's not fast enough.

Warner is standing ten feet away when Ibrahim goes suddenly slack, when he chokes and the gun slips from his hand, when his eyes bulge. A thin red line appears in the middle of Ibrahim's forehead, a terrifying trickle of blood that precipitates the sudden, soft sound of his skull breaking open. It's the sound of tearing flesh, an innocuous sound that reminds me of ripping open an orange. And it doesn't take long before Ibrahim's knees hit the floor. He falls without grace, his body collapsing into itself.

I know he's dead because I can see directly into his

skull. Clumps of his fleshy brain matter leak out onto the floor.

This, I think, is the kind of horrifying shit J is capable of.

This is what she's always been capable of. She's just always been too good a person to use it.

Warner, on the other hand—

He doesn't even seem bothered by the fact that he just ripped open a man's skull. He seems totally calm about the brain matter dripping on the floor. No, he's only got eyes for J, who's staring back at him, confused. She glances from Ibrahim's limp body to Anderson's limp body and she throws her arms forward with a sudden, desperate cry—

And nothing happens.

Robo J has no idea that Warner can absorb her powers.

Warner takes a step toward her and she narrows her eyes before slamming her fist into the floor. The room begins to shake. The floor begins to fissure. My teeth are rattling so hard I lose my balance, slam against the wall, and accidentally pull back my invisibility. When Juliette spots me, she screams.

I fly out of the way, throwing myself forward, diving over a table. Glass crashes to the floor, shatters everywhere.

I hear someone groan.

I peek through the legs of a table just in time to see Anderson begin to move. This time, I actually gasp.

The whole world seems to pause.

Anderson struggles up, to his feet. He doesn't look okay. He looks sick, pale—an imitation of his former self.

Something is wrong with his healing power, because he looks only half-alive, blood oozing from two places on his torso. He sways as he gets to his feet, coughing up blood. His skin goes gray. He uses his sleeve to wipe blood from his mouth.

J goes rushing toward him, but Anderson lifts a hand in her direction, and she halts. His bleak face registers a moment of surprise as he gazes at Ibrahim's dead body.

He laughs. Coughs. Wipes away more blood.

"Did you do this?" he says, his eyes locked on his own kid. "You did me a favor."

"What have you done to her?" Warner demands.

Anderson smiles. "Why don't I show you?" He glances at J. "Juliette?"

"Yes, sir."

"Kill them."

"Yes, sir."

J moves forward just as Anderson pulls something from his pocket, aiming its sharp, blue light in Warner's direction. This time, when J throws her arm out, Warner goes flying, his body slamming hard against the stone wall.

He falls to the floor with a gasp, the wind knocked from his lungs, and I take advantage of the moment to rush forward, pulling my invisibility around us both.

He shoves me away.

"Come on, bro, we have to get out of here— This isn't a fair fight—"

"You go," he says, clutching his side. "Go find Nazeera,

and then find the other kids. I'll be fine."

"You're not going to be fine," I hiss. "She's going to kill you."

"That's fine, too."

"Don't be stupid—"

The metal tables providing us our only bit of cover go flying, crashing hard against the opposite wall. I take one last glance at Warner and make a split-second decision.

I throw myself into the fight.

I know I only have a second before my brain matter joins Ibrahim's on the floor, so I make it count. I pull my gun from its holster and shoot three, four times.

Five.

Six.

I bury lead in Anderson's body until he's knocked back by the force of it, sagging to the floor with a hacking, bloody cough. J rushes forward but I disappear, darting behind a table, and once the weapon in Anderson's hand clatters to the floor, I shoot that, too. It pops and cracks, briefly catching fire as the tech explodes.

J cries out, falling to her knees beside him.

"Kill them," Anderson gasps, blood staining the edges of his lips. "Kill them all. Kill anyone who stands in your way."

"Yes, sir," Juliette says.

Anderson coughs. Fresh blood seeps from his wounds.

J gets to her feet and turns around, scanning the room for us, but I'm already rushing over to Warner, throwing my invisibility over us both. Warner seems a little stunned, but he's miraculously uninjured.

I try to help him to his feet, and for the first time, he doesn't push away my arm. I hear him inhale. Exhale.

Never mind, he's a little injured.

I wait for him to do something, say something, but he just stands there, staring at J. And then—

He pulls back his invisibility.

I nearly scream.

J pivots when she spots him, and immediately runs forward. She picks up a table, throws it at us.

We dive out of the way so hard I nearly break my nose against the ground. I can still hear things shattering around us when I say,

"What the hell were you thinking? You just blew our chance to get out of here!"

Warner shifts, glass crunching beneath him. He's breathing hard.

"I was serious about what I said, Kishimoto. You should go. Find Nazeera. But this is where I need to be."

"You mean you need to be getting killed right now? That's where you need to be? Do you even hear yourself?"

"Something is wrong," Warner says, dragging himself to his feet. "Her mind is trapped, trapped inside of something. A program. A virus. Whatever it is, she needs help."

J screams, sending another earthquake through the room. I slam into a table and stumble backward. A sharp pain shoots through my gut and I suck in my breath. Swear.

Warner has one arm out against the wall, steadying

himself. I can tell he's about to step forward, directly into the fight, and I grab his arm, pull him back.

"I'm not saying we give up on her, okay? I'm saying that there has to be another way. We need to get out of here, regroup. Come up with a better plan."

"No."

"Bro, I don't think you understand." I glance at J, who's stalking forward, eyes burning, the ground fissuring before her. "She's really going to kill you."

"Then I will die."

That's it.

Warner's last words before he leaves.

He meets J in the middle of the room and she doesn't hesitate before taking a violent swing at his face.

He blocks.

She swings again. He blocks. She kicks. He ducks.

He's not fighting her.

He only matches her, move for move, meeting her blows, anticipating her mind. It reminds me of his fight with Anderson back at the Sanctuary—how he never struck his father, only defended himself. It was obvious then that he was just trying to enrage his father.

But this—

This is different. It's clear that he's not enjoying this. He's not trying to enrage her, and he's not trying to defend himself. He's fighting her for *her*. To protect her.

To save her, somehow.

And I have no idea if this is going to work.

J clenches her fists and screams. The walls shake, the floor continues to crack open. I stumble, catch myself against a table.

And I'm just standing here like an idiot, racking my brain for a clue, trying to figure out what to do, how to help—

"Holy shit," Nazeera says. "What the hell is going on?"

Relief floods through me fast and hot. I have to resist the impulse to pull her invisible body into my arms. To tuck her close to my chest and keep her from leaving again.

Instead, I pretend to be cool.

"How'd you get here?" I ask. "How'd you find us?"

"I was hacking the systems, remember? I saw you on the cameras. You guys aren't exactly being quiet up here."

"Right. Good point."

"Hey, I have news, by the way, I foun—" She cuts herself off abruptly, her words fading to nothing. And then, after a beat, she says quietly:

"Who killed my dad?"

My stomach turns to stone.

I take a sharp breath before I say, "Warner did that."

"Oh."

"You okay?"

I hear her exhale. "I don't know."

J screams again and I look up.

She's furious.

I can tell, even from here, that she's frustrated. She can't use her powers on Warner directly, and he's too good a fighter to be beat without an edge. She's resorted to throwing very large, very heavy objects at him. Whatever she can find. Random medical equipment. Pieces of the wall.

This is not good.

"He wouldn't leave," I tell Nazeera. "He wanted to stay. He thinks he can help her."

She sighs. "We should let him try. In the interim, I could use your help."

I turn, reflexively, to face her, forgetting for a moment that she's invisible. "Help with what?" I ask.

"I found the other kids," she says. "That's why I was gone for so long. Getting that security clearance for you guys was way easier than I thought it'd be. So I stuck around to do some deep-level hacking into the cameras—and I found out where they're hiding the other supreme kids. But it's not pretty. And I could use a hand."

I look up to catch one last glimpse of Warner.

Of J.

But they're gone.

~~ELLA~~
JULIETTE

Run, Juliette

run

faster, run until your bones break and your shins split and your muscles atrophy

Run run run

until you can't hear their feet behind you

Run until you drop dead.

Make sure your heart stops before they ever reach you. Before they ever touch you.

Run, I said.

The words appear, unbidden, in my mind. I don't know where they come from and I don't know why I know them, but I say them to myself as I go, my boots pounding the ground, my head a strangled mess of chaos. I don't understand what just happened. I don't understand what's happening to me. I don't understand anything anymore.

The boy is close.

He moves more swiftly than I anticipated, and I'm surprised. I didn't expect him to be able to meet my blows. I didn't expect him to face me so easily. Mostly, I'm stunned he's somehow immune to my power. I didn't even know that was possible.

I don't understand.

I'm racking my brain, trying desperately to comprehend how such a thing might've happened—and whether I might've been responsible for the anomaly—but nothing makes sense. Not his presence. Not his attitude. Not even the way he fights.

Which is to say: he doesn't.

He doesn't even want to fight. He seems to have no interest in beating me, despite the ample evidence that we are well matched. He only fends me off, making only the most basic effort to protect himself, and still I haven't killed him.

There's something strange about him. Something about him that's getting under my skin. Unsettling me.

But he dashed out of sight when I threw another table at him, and he's been running ever since.

It feels like a trap.

I know it, and yet, I feel compelled to find him. Face him. Destroy him.

I spot him, suddenly, at the far end of the laboratory, and he meets my eyes with an insouciance that enrages me. I charge forward but he moves swiftly, disappearing through an adjoining door.

This is a trap, I remind myself.

Then again, I'm not sure it matters whether this is a trap. I am under orders to find him. Kill him. I just have to be better. Smarter.

So I follow.

From the time I met this boy—from the first moment we began exchanging blows—I've ignored the dizzying sensations coursing through my body. I've tried to deny my sudden, feverish skin, my trembling hands. But when a fresh wave of nausea nearly sends me reeling, I can no longer deny my fear:

There's something wrong with me.

I catch another glimpse of his golden hair and my vision blurs, clears, my heart slows. For a moment, my muscles seem to spasm. There is a creeping, tremulous terror clenching its fist around my lungs and I don't understand it. I keep hoping the feeling will change. Clear. Disappear. But as the minutes pass and the symptoms show no signs of abating, I begin to panic.

I'm not tired, no. My body is too strong. I can feel it—can feel my muscles, their strength, their steadiness—and I can tell that I could keep fighting like this for hours. Days. I'm not worried about giving up, I'm not worried about breaking down.

I'm worried about my head. My confusion. The uncertainty seeping through me, spreading like a poison.

Ibrahim is dead.

Anderson, nearly so.

Will he recover? Will he die? Who would I be without him? What was it Ibrahim wanted to do to me? From what was Anderson trying to protect me? Who are these children I'm meant to kill? Why did Ibrahim call them my friends?

My questions are endless.

I kill them.

I shove aside a series of steel desks and catch a glimpse of the boy before he darts around a corner. Anger punches through me, shooting a jolt of adrenaline to my brain, and I start running again, renewed determination focusing my mind. I charge through the dimly lit room, shoving my way through an endless sea of medical paraphernalia. When I stop moving, silence descends.

Silence so pure it's deafening.

I spin around, searching. The boy is gone. I blink, confused, scanning the room as my pulse races with renewed fear. Seconds pass, gather into moments that feel like minutes, hours.

This is a trap.

The laboratory is perfectly still—the lights so perfectly dim—that as the silence drags on I begin to wonder if I'm caught in a dream. I feel suddenly paranoid, uncertain. Like maybe that boy was a figment of my imagination. Like maybe all of this is some strange nightmare, and maybe I'll wake up soon and Anderson will be back in his office, and Ibrahim will be a man I've never met, and tomorrow I'll wake up in my pod by the water.

Maybe, I think, this is all just another test.

A simulation.

Maybe Anderson is challenging my loyalty one last time. Maybe it's my job to stay put, to keep myself safe like he asked me to, and to destroy anyone who tries to stand in my way. Or maybe—

Stop.

I sense movement.

Movement so fine it's nearly imperceptible. Movement so gentle it could've been a breeze, except for one thing:

I hear a heart beating.

Someone is here, someone motionless, someone sly. I straighten, my senses heightened, my heart racing in my chest.

Someone is here someone is here someone is here—

Where?

There.

He appears, as if out of a dream, standing before me like a statue, still as cooling steel. He stares at me, green eyes the color of sea glass, the color of celadon.

I never really had a chance to see his face.

Not like this.

My heart races as I assess him, his white shirt, green jacket, gold hair. Skin like porcelain. He does not slouch or fidget and, for a moment, I'm certain I was right, that perhaps he's nothing more than a mirage. A program.

Another hologram.

I reach out, uncertain, the tips of my fingers grazing the exposed skin at his throat and he takes a sharp, shaky breath.

Real, then.

I flatten my hand against his chest, just to be sure, and I feel his heart racing under my palm. Fast, lightning fast.

I glance up, surprised.

He's nervous.

Another unsteady breath escapes him and this time, takes with it a measure of control. He steps back, shakes his head, stares up at the ceiling.

Not nervous.

He is distraught.

I should kill him now, I think. *Kill him now.*

A wave of nausea hits me so hard it nearly knocks me off my feet. I take a few unsteady steps backward, catching myself against a steel table. My fingers grip the cold metal edge and I hang on, teeth clenched, willing my mind to clear.

Heat floods my body.

Heat, torturous heat, presses against my lungs, fills my blood. My lips part. I feel parched. I look up and he's right in front of me and I do nothing. I do nothing as I watch his throat move.

I do nothing as my eyes devour him.

I feel faint.

I study the sharp line of his jaw, the gentle slope where his neck meets shoulder. His lips look soft. His cheekbones high, his nose sharp, his brows heavy, gold. He is finely made. Beautiful, strong hands. Short, clean nails. I notice he wears a jade ring on his left pinkie finger.

He sighs.

He shakes off his jacket, carefully folding it over the back of a nearby chair. Underneath he wears only a simple white T-shirt, the sculpted contours of his bare arms catching the attention of the dim lights. He moves slowly, his motions unhurried. When he begins to pace I watch him, study the shape of him. I am not surprised to discover that he moves beautifully. I am fascinated by him, by his form, his measured strides, the muscles honed under skin. He seems like he might be my age, maybe a little older, but there's something about the way he looks at me that makes him seem older than our years combined.

Whatever it is, I like it.

I wonder what I'm supposed to do with this, all of this. Is it truly a test? If so, why send someone like him? Why a face so refined? Why a body so perfectly honed?

Was I meant to enjoy this?

A strange, delirious feeling stirs inside of me at the thought. Something ancient. Something wonderful. It is almost too bad, I think, that I will have to kill him. And it is the heat, the dullness, the inexplicable numbness in my mind that compels me to say—

"Where did they make you?"

He startles. I didn't think he would startle. But when he turns to look at me, he seems confused.

I explain: "You are unusually beautiful."

His eyes widen.

His lips part, press together, tremble into a curve that surprises me. Surprises him.

He smiles.

He smiles and I stare—two dimples, straight teeth, shining eyes. A sudden, incomprehensible heat rushes across my skin, sets me aflame. I feel violently hot. Sick with fever.

Finally, he says: "So you *are* in there."

"Who?"

"Ella," he says, but he's speaking softly now. "Juliette. They said you'd be gone."

"I'm not gone," I say, my hands shaking as I pull myself together. "I am Juliette Ferrars, supreme soldier to our North American commander. Who are you?"

He moves closer. His eyes darken as he stares at me, but there's no true darkness there. I try to stand taller, straighter. I remind myself that I have a task, that this is my moment to attack, to fulfill my orders. Perhaps I sh—

"Love," he whispers.

Heat flashes across my skin. Pain presses against my mind, a vague realization that I've left something overlooked. Dusty emotion trembles inside of me, and I kill it.

He steps forward, takes my face in his hands. I think about breaking his fingers. Snapping his wrists. My heart is racing.

I cannot move.

"You shouldn't touch me," I say, gasping the words.

"Why not?"

"Because I will kill you."

Gently, he tilts my head back, his hands possessive, persuasive. An ache seizes my muscles, holds me in place. My eyes close reflexively. I breathe him in and my mouth fills with flavor—fresh air, fragrant flowers, heat, happiness—and I'm struck by the strangest idea that we've been here before, that I've lived this before, that I've known him before and then I feel, I feel his breath on my skin and the sensation, the sensation is—

heady,

disorienting.

I'm losing track of my mind, trying desperately to locate my purpose, to focus my thoughts, when

he moves

the earth tilts, his lips graze my jaw and I make a sound, a desperate, unconscious sound that stuns me. My skin is frenzied, burning. That familiar warmth contaminates my blood, my temperature spiking, my face flushing.

"Do I—"

I try to speak but he kisses my neck and I gasp, his hands still caught around my face. I'm breathless, heart pounding, pulse pounding, head pounding. He touches me like he knows me, knows what I want, knows what I need. I feel insane. I don't even recognize the sound of my own voice when I finally manage to say,

"Do I know you?"

"Yes."

My heart leaps. The simplicity of his answer strangles my mind, digs for truth. It feels true. Feels true that I've known these hands, this mouth, those eyes.

Feels real.

"Yes," he says again, his own voice rough with feeling. His hands leave my face and I'm lost in the loss, searching for warmth. I press closer to him without even meaning to, asking him for something I don't understand. But then his hands slide under my shirt, his palms pressing against my back, and the magnitude of the sudden, skin-to-skin contact sets my body on fire.

I feel explosive.

I feel dangerously close to something that might kill me, and still I lean into him, blinded by instinct, deaf to everything but the ferocious beat of my own heart.

He pulls back, just an inch.

His hands are still caught under my shirt, his bare arms wrapped around my bare skin and his mouth lingers above mine, the heat between us threatening to ignite. He pulls me closer and I bite back a moan, losing my head as the hard lines of his body sink into me. He is everywhere, his scent, his skin, his breath. I see nothing but him, sense nothing but him, his hands spreading across my torso, my lungs compressing under his careful, searing exploration. I lean into the sensations, his fingers grazing my stomach, the small of my back. He touches his forehead to mine and I press up, onto my toes, asking for something, begging for something—

"What," I gasp, "what is happening—"

He kisses me.

Soft lips, waves of sensation. Feeling overflows the vacancies in my mind. My hands begin to shake. My heart beats so hard I can hardly keep still when he nudges my mouth open, takes me in. He tastes like heat and peppermint, like summer, like the sun.

I want more.

I take his face in my hands and pull him closer and he makes a soft, desperate sound in the back of his throat that sends a spike of pleasure directly to my brain. Pure, electric heat lifts me up, outside of myself. I seem to be floating here, surrendered to this strange moment, held in place by an ancient mold that fits my body perfectly. I feel frantic, seized by a need to know more, a need I don't even understand.

When we break apart his chest his heaving and his face is flushed and he says—

"Come back to me, love. Come back."

I'm still struggling to breathe, desperately searching his eyes for answers. Explanations. "Where?"

"Here," he whispers, pressing my hands to his heart. "Home."

"But I don't—"

Flashes of light streak across my vision. I stumble backward, half-blind, like I'm dreaming, reliving the caress of a forgotten memory, and it's like an ache looking to be soothed, it's a steaming pan thrown in ice water, it's a flushed cheek pressed to a cool pillow on a hot hot night and heat gathers, collects behind my eyes, distorting sights, dimming sounds.

Here.

This.

My bones against his bones. This is my home.

I return to my skin with a sudden, violent shudder and feel wild, unstable. I stare at him, my heart seizing, my lungs fighting for air. He stares back, his eyes such a pale green in the light that, for a moment, he doesn't even seem human.

Something is happening to my head.

Pain is collecting in my blood, calcifying around my heart. I feel at war with myself, lost and wounded, my mind spinning with uncertainty. "What is your name?" I ask.

He steps forward, so close our lips touch. Part. His breath whispers across my skin and my nerves hum, spark.

"You know my name," he says quietly.

I try to shake my head. He catches my chin.

This time, he's not careful.

This time, he's desperate. This time, when he kisses me he breaks me open, heat coming off him in waves. He tastes like springwater and something sweet, something searing.

I feel dazed. Delirious.

When he breaks away I'm shaking, my lungs shaking, my breaths shaking, my heart shaking. I watch, as if in a dream, as he pulls off his shirt, tosses it to the ground. And then he's here again, he's back again, he's caught me in his arms and he's kissing me so deeply my knees give out.

He picks me up, bracing my body as he sets me down on the long, steel table. The cool metal seeps through the fabric of my pants, sending goose bumps along my heated skin and I gasp, my eyes closing as he straddles my legs, claims my mouth. He presses my hands to his chest, drags my fingers down his naked torso and I make a desperate, broken sound, pleasure and pain stunning me, paralyzing me.

He unbuttons my shirt, his deft hands moving quickly even as he kisses my neck, my cheeks, my mouth, my throat. I cry out when he moves, his kisses shifting down my body, searching, exploring. He pushes aside the two halves of my shirt, his mouth still hot against my skin, and then he closes the gap between us, pressing his bare chest to mine, and my heart explodes.

Something snaps inside of me.

Severs.

A sudden, fractured sob escapes my throat. Unbidden tears sting my eyes, startling me as they fall down my face. Unknown emotion soars through me, expanding my heart, confusing my head. He pulls me impossibly closer, our bodies soldered together. And then he presses his forehead to my collarbone, his body trembling with emotion when he says—

"Come back."

My head is full of sand, sound, sensations spinning in my mind. I don't understand what's happening to me, I don't understand this pain, this unbelievable pleasure. I'm staining his skin with my tears and he only pulls me tighter, pressing our hearts together until the feeling sinks its teeth into my bones, splits open my lungs. I want to bury myself in this moment, I want to pull him into me, I want to drag myself out of myself but there's something wrong, something blocked, something stopped—

Something broken.

Realization arrives in gentle waves, theories lapping and overlapping at the shores of my consciousness until I'm drenched in confusion. Awareness.

Terror.

"You know my name," he says softly. "You've always known me, love. I've always known you. And I'm so—I'm so desperately in love with you—"

The pain begins in my ears.

It collects, expanding, pressure building to a peak so acute it transforms, sharpening into a torture that stops my heart.

First I go deaf, stiff. Second I go blind, slack.

Third, my heart restarts.

I come back to life with a sudden, terrifying inhalation that nearly chokes me, blood rushing to my ears, my eyes, leaking from my nose. I taste it, taste my own blood in my mouth as I begin to understand: there is something inside of me. A poison. A violence. Something wrong something wrong something *wrong*

And then, as if from miles away, I hear myself scream.

There's cold tile under my knees, rough grout pressing into my knuckles. I scream into the silence, power building power, electricity charging my blood. My mind is separating from itself, trying to identify the poison, this parasite residing inside of me.

I have to kill it.

I scream, forcing my own energy inward, screaming until the explosive energy building inside of me ruptures my eardrums. I scream until I feel the blood drip from my ears and down my neck, I scream until the lights in the laboratory begin to pop and break. I scream until my teeth bleed, until the floor fissures beneath my feet, until the skin at my knees begins to crack. I scream until the monster inside of me begins to die.

And only then—

Only when I'm certain I've killed some small part of my own self do I finally collapse.

I'm choking, coughing up blood, my chest heaving from the effort expended. The room swims. Swings around.

I press my forehead to the cold floor and fight back a wave of nausea. And then I feel a familiar, heavy hand against my back. With excruciating slowness, I manage to lift my head.

A blur of gold appears, disappears before me.

I blink once, twice, and try to push up with my arms but a sharp, searing pain in my wrist nearly blinds me. I look down, examining the strange, hazy sight. I blink again. Ten times more.

Finally, my eyes focus.

The skin inside my right arm has split open. Blood is smeared across my skin, dripping on the floor. From within the fresh wound, a single blue light pulses from a steel, circular body, the edges of which push up against my torn flesh.

With one final effort, I rip the flashing mechanism from my arm, the last vestige of this monster. It drops from my shaking fingers, clatters to the floor.

And this time, when I look up, I see his face.

"Aaron," I gasp.

He drops to his knees.

He pulls my bleeding body into his arms and I break, I break apart, sobs cracking open my chest. I cry until the pain spirals and peaks, I cry until my head throbs and my eyes swell. I cry, pressing my face against his neck, my fingers digging into his back, desperate for purchase. Proof.

He holds me, silent and steady, gathering my blood and bones against his body even as the tears recede, even when I begin to tremble. He holds me tight as my body shakes, holds me close when the tears start anew, holds me in his arms and strokes my hair and tells me that everything, everything is going to be okay.

KENJI

I was assigned to keep watch outside this door, which, initially, was supposed to be a good thing—assisting in the rescue mission, et cetera—but the longer I wait out here, guarding Nazeera while she hacks the computers keeping the supreme kids in some freaky state of hypersleep, the more things go wrong.

This place is falling apart.

Literally.

The lights in the ceiling are beginning to spark and sputter, the massive staircases are beginning to groan. The huge windows lining either side of this fifty-story building are beginning to crack.

Doctors are running, screaming. Alarms are flashing like crazy, sirens blaring. Some robotic voice is announcing a crisis over the speakers like it's the most casual thing in the world.

I have no idea what's happening right now, though if I had to guess, I'd say it had something to do with Emmaline. But I just have to stand here, bracing myself against the door so as not to be accidentally trampled, and wait for whatever is happening to come to an end. The problem is, I don't know if it's going to be a happy ending or a sad one—

For anyone.

I haven't heard anything from Warner since we split up, and I'm trying really, really hard not to think about it. I'm choosing to focus, instead, on the positive things that happened today, like the fact that we managed to kill three supreme commanders—four if you count Evie—and that Nazeera's genius hacking work was a success, because without her, there's no way we'd have made much headway at all.

After our sojourn through the vents, Warner and I managed to drop down into the heart of the compound, undetected. It was easier to avoid the cameras once we were in the center of things; the rooms were closer together, and though the higher security areas have more security *access* points—some of them have fewer cameras. So as long as we avoided certain angles, the cameras didn't notice us, and with the fake clearance Nazeera built for us, we got through easily. It was because of her that we were in the right place—after having unintentionally killed a super-important scientist—when all the supreme commanders began to swarm.

It was because of her that we were able to take out Ibrahim and Anderson. And it was because of her that Warner is locked up with Robo J somewhere. Honestly, I don't even know how to feel about it all. I haven't really allowed myself to think about the fact that J might never come back, that I might never see my best friend again. If I think about it too much, I start feeling like I can't breathe, and I can't afford to stop breathing right now. Not yet.

So I try not to think about it.

But Warner—

Warner is either going to come out of this alive and happy, or dead doing something he believed in.

And there's nothing I can do about it.

The problem is, I haven't seen him in over an hour, and I have no idea what that means. It could either be really good news or really, really bad. He never shared his plan with me—surprise surprise—so I don't even know exactly what he'd planned to do to once he got her alone. And even though I know better than to doubt him, I have to admit that there's a tiny part of me that wonders if he's even alive right now.

An ancient, earsplitting groan interrupts my thoughts.

I look up, toward the source of the sound, and realize that the ceiling is caving in. The roof is coming apart. The walls are beginning to crumble. The long, circuitous hallways all ring around an interior courtyard within which lives a massive, prehistoric-looking tree. For no reason I can understand, the steel railings around the hallways are beginning to melt apart. I watch in real time as the tree catches fire, flames roaring higher at an astonishing rate. Smoke builds, curling in my direction, already beginning to suffocate the halls, and my heart is racing as I look around, my panic spiking. I start banging on the door, not caring who hears me now.

It's the end of the fucking world out here.

I'm screaming for Nazeera, begging her to come out, to get out here before it's too late, and I'm coughing now, smoke catching in my lungs, still hoping desperately that she'll hear my voice when suddenly, violently—

The door swings open.

I'm knocked backward by the force of it, and when I look up, eyes burning, Nazeera is there. Nazeera, Lena, Stephan, Haider, Valentina, Nicolás, and Adam.

Adam.

I can't explain exactly what happens next. There's so much shouting. So much running. Stephan punches a clean hole through a crumbling wall, and Nazeera helps fly us all out to safety. It happens in a blur. I see things unfold in flashes, in screams.

It feels like a dream. My eyes stinging, tearing.

I'm crying because of the fire, I think. It's the heat, the sky, the roaring flames devouring everything.

I watch the capital of Oceania—all 120 acres of it—go up in flames.

And Warner and Juliette go with it.

ELLA (JULIETTE)

The first thing we do is find Emmaline.

I reach out to her in my mind and she answers right away. Heat, fingers of heat, curling around my bones. Sparking to life in my heart. She was always here, always with me.

I understand now.

I understand that the moments that saved me were gifts from my sister, gifts she was able to give only by destroying herself in return. She's so much weaker now than she was two weeks ago because she expended so much of herself to keep me alive. To keep their machinations from reaching my heart. My soul.

I remember everything now. My mind is sharpened to a new point, honed to a clarity I've never before experienced. I see everything. Understand everything.

It doesn't take long to find her.

I don't apologize for the people I scatter, the walls I shatter along the way. I don't apologize for my anger or my pain. I don't stop moving when I see Tatiana and Azi; I don't have to. I snap their necks from where I'm standing. I tear their bodies in half with a single gesture.

When I reach my sister, the agony inside of me reaches its peak. She is limp inside her tank, a desiccated fish, a dying spider. She's curled into herself in its darkest corner, her long dark hair wrapping around her wrinkled, sagging figure. A low keening emanates from her tank.

She is crying.

She is small. Scared. She reminds me of another version of myself, a person I can hardly remember, a young girl thrown in prison, too broken by the world to realize that she'd always had the power to break herself free. To conquer the earth.

I had that luxury.

Emmaline didn't.

The sight of her makes me want to fall to pieces. My heart rages with anger, devastation. When I think about what they did to her—what they've done to her—

Don't

I don't.

I take a deep, shuddering breath. Try to collect myself. I feel Aaron take my hand and I squeeze his fingers in gratitude. It steadies me to have him here. To know he's beside me. With me.

My partner in everything.

Tell me what you want, I say to Emmaline. *Anything at all. Whatever it is, I'll do it.*

Silence.

Emmaline?

A sharp, desperate fear jumps through me.

Her fear, not mine.

Distorted sensations flash behind my eyes—flares of color, the sounds of grinding metal—and her panic intensifies. Tightens. I feel it hum down my spine.

"What's wrong?" I say out loud. "What happened?"

Here

Here

Her milky form disappears into the tank, sinking deep underwater. Goose bumps rise along my arms.

"You seem to have forgotten about me."

My father steps into the room, his tall rubber boots thudding softly against the floor.

I throw my arms out immediately, hoping to rip out his spleen, but he's too fast—his movements too fast. He presses a single button on a small, handheld remote, and I hardly have time to take a breath before my body begins to convulse. I cry out, my eyes blinded by violent, violet light, and manage to turn my head only in small, excruciating movements.

Aaron.

He and I are both frozen here, bathed in a toxic light

emanating from the ceiling. Gasping for breath. Shaking uncontrollably. My mind spins, working desperately to think of a plan, a loophole, a way out.

"I am astonished by your arrogance," my father says. "Astonished that you thought you could just walk in here and assist in your sister's suicide. You thought it would be simple? You thought there wouldn't be consequences?"

He turns a dial and my body seizes more violently, lifting off the floor. The pain is blinding. Light flashes in and out of my eyes, stunning my mind, numbing my ability to think. I hang in the air, no longer able to turn my head. Gravity pushes and pulls at my body, threatens to tear apart my limbs.

If I could scream, I would.

"Anyway, it's good you're here. Best to get this over with now. We've waited long enough." He nods, absently, at Emmaline's tank. "Obviously you've seen how desperate we are for a new host."

NO

The word is like a scream inside my head.

Max stiffens.

He looks up, staring at precisely nothing, the anger in his eyes barely held in check. I only realize then that he can hear her, too.

Of course he can.

Emmaline pounds against her tank, the sounds dull,

the effort alone seeming to exhaust her. Still, she presses forward, her sunken cheek flattening against the glass.

Max hesitates, vacillating.

He's no good at hiding his emotions—and his present uncertainty is easily discernible. It's clear, even from my disoriented perspective, that he's trying to decide which of us he needs to deal with first. Emmaline pounds her fist again, weaker this time.

NO

Another scream inside my head.

With a stifled sigh, Max decides on Emmaline.

I watch him pivot, stalk toward her tank. He presses his hand flat against the glass and it brightens to a neon blue. The blue light expands, then scatters around the chamber, slowly revealing an intricate series of electrical circuits. The neon veins are thicker in some places, occasionally braided, mostly fine. It resembles a cardiovascular system not unlike the one inside my own body.

My own body.

Something gasps to life inside of me. Reason. Rational thought. I'm trapped here, tricked by the pain into thinking I have no control over my powers, but that's not true. When I force myself to remember, I can feel it. My energy still thrums through me. It's a faint, desperate whisper—but it's there.

Bit by agonizing bit, I gather my mind.

I grit my teeth, focusing my thoughts, clenching my body

to its breaking point. Slowly, I braid together the disparate strands of my power, holding on to the threads for dear life.

And even more slowly, I claw my hand through the light.

The effort splits open my knuckles, the tips of my fingers. Fresh blood streaks across my hand and spills down my wrist as I lift my arm in a sluggish, excruciating arc above my head.

As if from light-years away, I hear beeping.

Max.

He's inputting new codes into Emmaline's tank. I have no idea what that means for her, but I can't imagine it's good.

Hurry.

Hurry, I tell myself.

Violently, I force my arm through the light, biting back a scream as I do. One by one, my fingers uncurl above my head, blood dripping from each digit down my bleeding wrist and into my eyes. My hand opens, palm up toward the ceiling. Fresh blood snakes down the planes of my face as I drive my energy into the light.

The ceiling shatters.

Aaron and I fall to the floor, hard, and I hear something snap in my leg, the pain screaming through me.

I fight it back.

The lights pop and shriek, the polished concrete ceiling beginning to crack. Max spins around, horror seizing his face as I throw my hand forward.

Close my fist.

Emmaline's tank fissures with a sudden, violent crack.

"NO!" he cries. Feverishly, he pulls the remote free from his lab coat, hitting its now useless buttons. "No! No, *no*—"

The glass groans open with an angry yawn, giving way with one final, shattering roar. Max goes comically still.

Stunned.

He dies, then, with exactly that expression on his face. And it's not me who kills him. It's Emmaline.

Emmaline, who pulls her webbed hands free of the broken glass and presses her fingers to her father's head. She kills him with nothing more than the force of her own mind.

The mind he gave her.

When she is done, his skull has split open. Blood leaks from his dead eyes. His teeth have fallen out of his face, onto his shirt. His intestines spill out from a severe rupture in his torso.

I look away.

Emmaline collapses to the floor. She's gasping through the regulator fused to her face. Her already weak limbs begin to tremble, violently, and she's making sounds I can only assume are meant to be words she's no longer able to speak.

She is more amphibian than human.

I realize this only now, only when faced with the proof of her incompatibility with our air, with the outside world. I crawl toward her, dragging my broken, bloodied leg behind me.

Aaron tries to help, but when we lock eyes, he falls back.

He understands that I need to do this myself.

I gather my sister's small, withered body against my own, pulling her wet limbs into my lap, pressing her head against my chest. And I say to her, for the second time:

"Tell me what you want. Anything at all. Whatever it is, I'll do it."

Her slick fingers clutch at my neck, clinging for dear life. A vision fills my head, a vision of everything going up in flames. A vision of this compound, her prison, disintegrating. She wants it razed, returned to dust.

"Consider it done," I say to her.

She has another request. Just one more.

And I say nothing for too long.

Please

Her voice is in my heart, begging. Desperate. Her agony is acute. Her terror palpable.

Tears spring to my eyes.

I press my cheek against her wet hair. I tell her how much I love her. How much she means to me. How much more I wish we could've had. I tell her that I will never forget her.

That I will miss her, every single day.

And then I ask her to let me take her body home with me when I am done.

A gentle warmth floods my mind, a heady feeling.

Happiness.

Yes, she says.

When it's done, when I've ripped the tubes from her body, when I've gathered her wet, trembling bones against my own, when I've pressed my poisonous cheek to hers, when I've leeched out what little life was left in her body.

When it is done, I curl myself around her cold corpse and cry.

I clutch her hollow body against my heart and feel the injustice of it all roar through me. I feel it fracture me apart. I feel her take part of me with her as she goes.

And then I scream.

I scream until I feel the earth move beneath my feet, until I feel the wind change directions. I scream until the walls collapse, until I feel the electricity spark, until I feel the lights catch fire. I scream until the ground fissures, until all falls down.

And then we carry my sister home.

EPILOGUE

WARNER

one.

The wall is unusually white.

More white than is usual. Most people think white walls are true white, but the truth is, they only seem white, and are not actually white. Most shades of white are mixed in with a bit of yellow, which helps soften the harsh edges of a pure white, making it more of an ecru, or ivory. Various shades of cream. Egg white, even. True white is practically intolerable as a color, so white it's nearly blue.

This wall, in particular, is not so white as to be offensive, but a sharp enough shade of white to pique my curiosity, which is nothing short of a miracle, really, because I've been staring at it for the greater part of an hour. Thirty-seven minutes, to be exact.

I am being held hostage by custom. Formality.

"Five more minutes," she says. "I promise."

I hear the rustle of fabric. Zippers. A shudder of—

"Is that tulle?"

"You're not supposed to be listening!"

"You know, love, it occurs to me now that I've lived through actual hostage situations far less torturous than this."

"Okay, okay, it's off. Packed away. I just need a second to

put on my cl—"

"That won't be necessary," I say, turning around. "Surely this part, I should be allowed to watch."

I lean against the unusually white wall, studying her as she frowns at me, her lips still parted around the shape of a word she seems to have forgotten.

"Please continue," I say, gesturing with a nod. "Whatever you were doing before."

She holds on to her frown for a moment longer than is honest, her eyes narrowing in a show of frustration that is pure fraud. She compounds this farce by clutching an article of clothing to her chest, feigning modesty.

I do not mind, not one single bit.

I drink her in, her soft curves, her smooth skin. Her hair is beautiful at any length, but it's been longer lately. Long and rich, silky against her skin, and when I'm lucky—against mine.

Slowly, she drops the shirt.

I suddenly stand up straighter.

"I'm supposed to wear this under the dress," she says, her fake anger already forgotten. She fidgets with the boning of a cream-colored corset, her fingers lingering absently along the garter belt, the lace-trimmed stockings. She can't meet my eyes. She's gone suddenly shy, and this time, it's real.

Do you like it?

The unspoken question.

I assumed, when she invited me into this dressing room, that it was for reasons beyond me staring at the color variations in an unusually white wall. I assumed she wanted me here to see something.

To see her.

I see now that I was correct.

"You are so beautiful," I say, unable to shed the awe in my voice. I hear it, the childish wonder in my tone, and it embarrasses me more than it should. I know I shouldn't be ashamed to feel deeply. To be moved.

Still, I feel awkward.

Young.

Quietly, she says, "I feel like I just spoiled the surprise. You're not supposed to see any of this until the wedding night."

My heart actually stops for a moment.

The wedding night.

She closes the distance between us and twines her arms around me, freeing me from my momentary paralysis. My heart beats faster with her here, so close. And though I don't know how she knew that I suddenly required the reassurance of her touch, I'm grateful. I exhale, pulling her fully against me, our bodies relaxing, remembering each other.

I press my face into her hair, breathe in the sweet scent of her shampoo, her skin. It's only been two weeks. Two weeks since the end of an old world. The beginning of a new one.

She still feels like a dream to me.

"Is this really happening?" I whisper.

A sharp knock at the door startles my spine straight.

Ella frowns at the sound. "Yes?"

"So sorry to bother you right now, miss, but there's a gentleman here wishing to speak with Mr. Warner."

Ella and I lock eyes.

"Okay," she says quickly. "Don't be mad."

My eyes narrow. "Why would I be mad?"

Ella pulls away to better look me in the eye. Her own eyes are bright, beautiful. Full of concern. "It's Kenji."

I force down a spike of anger so violent I think I give myself a stroke. It leaves me light-headed. "What is he doing here?" I manage to get out. "How on earth did he know how to find us?

She bites her lip. "We took Amir and Olivier with us."

"I see." We took extra guards along, which means our outing was posted to the public security bulletin. Of course.

Ella nods. "He found me just before we left. He was worried—he wanted to know why we were heading back into the old regulated lands."

I try to say something then, to marvel aloud at Kenji's inability to make a simple deduction despite the abundance of contextual clues right before his eyes—but she holds up a finger.

"I told him," she says, "that we were looking for replacement outfits, and reminded him that, for now, the supply centers are still the only places to shop for food or clothing or"—she waves a hand, frowns—"anything, at the moment. Anyway, he said he'd try to meet us here. He said he wanted to help."

My eyes widen slightly. I feel another stroke incoming. "He said he wanted to *help*."

She nods.

"Astonishing." A muscle ticks in my jaw. "And funny, too, because he's already helped so much—just last night he helped us both a great deal by destroying my suit and your dress, forcing us to now purchase clothing from a"—I look around, gesture at nothing—"a *store* on the very day we're supposed to get married."

"Aaron," she whispers. She steps closer again. Places a hand on my chest. "He feels terrible about it."

"And you?" I say, studying her face, her feelings. "Don't *you* feel terrible about it? Alia and Winston worked so hard to make you something beautiful, something designed precisely for you—"

"I don't mind." She shrugs. "It's just a dress."

"But it was your wedding dress," I say, my voice failing me now, practically breaking on the word.

She sighs, and in the sound I hear her heart break, more for me than for herself. She turns around and unzips the massive garment bag hanging on a hook above her head.

"You're not supposed to see this," she says, tugging yards of tulle out of the bag, "but I think it might mean more to you than it does to me, so"—she turns back, smiles—"I'll let you help me decide what to wear tonight."

I nearly groan aloud at the reminder.

A nighttime wedding. Who on earth is married at night?

Only the hapless. The unfortunate. Though I suppose we now count among their ranks.

Rather than reschedule the entire thing, we pushed it forward by a few hours so that we'd have time to purchase new clothes. Well, I have clothes. My clothes don't matter as much.

But her dress. He destroyed her dress the night before our wedding. Like a monster.

I'm going to murder him.

"You can't murder him," she says, still pulling handfuls of fabric out of the bag.

"I'm certain I said no such thing out loud."

"No," she says, "but you were thinking it, weren't you?"

"Wholeheartedly."

"You can't murder him," she says simply. "Not now. Not ever."

I sigh.

She's still struggling to unearth the gown. "Forgive me, love, but if all this"—I nod at the garment bag, the explosion of tulle—"is for a single dress, I'm afraid I already know how I feel about it."

She stops tugging. Turns around, eyes wide. "You don't like it? You haven't even seen it yet."

"I've seen enough to know that whatever this is, it's not a gown. This is a haphazard layering of polyester." I lean around her, pinching the fabric between my fingers. "Do they not carry silk tulle in this store? Perhaps we can speak to the seamstress."

"They don't have a seamstress here."

"This is a clothing store," I say. I turn the bodice inside out, frowning at the stitches. "Surely there must be a seamstress. Not a very good one, clearly, but—"

"These dresses are made in a factory," she says to me. "Mostly by machine."

I straighten.

"You know, most people didn't grow up with private tailors at their disposal," she says, a smile playing at her lips. "The rest of us had to buy clothes off the rack. Premade. Ill-fitting."

"Yes," I say stiffly. I feel suddenly stupid. "Of course. Forgive me. The dress is very nice. Perhaps I should wait for you to try it on. I gave my opinion too hastily."

For some reason, my response only makes things worse.

She groans, shooting me a single, defeated look before folding herself into the little dressing room chair.

My heart plummets.

She drops her face in her hands. "It really is a disaster, isn't it?"

Another swift knock at the door. "Sir? The gentleman seems very eager t—"

"He's certainly not a gentleman," I say sharply. "Tell him to wait."

A moment of hesitation. Then, quietly: "Yes, sir."

"Aaron."

I don't need to look up to know that she's unhappy with my rudeness. The owners of this particular supply center shut down their entire store for us, and they've been excruciatingly kind. I know I'm being cruel. At present, I can't seem to help it.

"*Aaron.*"

"Today is your wedding day," I say, unable to meet her eyes. "He has ruined your wedding day. Our wedding day."

She gets to her feet. I feel her frustration fade. Transform. Shuffle through sadness, happiness, hope, fear, and finally—

Resignation.

One of the worst possible feelings on what should be a joyous day. Resignation is worse than frustration. Far worse.

My anger calcifies.

"He hasn't ruined it," she says finally. "We can still make this work."

"You're right," I say, pulling her into my arms. "Of course you're right. It doesn't matter, really. None of it does."

"But it's my wedding day," she says. "And I have nothing to wear."

"You're right." I kiss the top of her head. "I'm going to kill him."

A sudden pounding at the door.

I stiffen. Spin around.

"Hey, guys?" More pounding. "I know you're super pissed at me, but I have good news, I swear. I'm going to fix this. I'm going to make it up to you."

I'm just about to respond when Ella tugs at my hand, silencing my scathing retort with a single motion. She shoots me a look that plainly says—

Give him a chance.

I sigh as the anger settles inside my body, my shoulders dropping with the weight of it. Reluctantly, I step aside to allow her to deal with this idiot in the manner she prefers.

It is her wedding day, after all.

Ella steps closer to the door. Points at it, jabbing her finger at the unusually white paint as she speaks. "This better be good, Kenji, or Warner is going to kill you, and I'm going to help him do it."

And then, just like that—

I'm smiling again.

two.

We're driven back to the Sanctuary the same way we're driven everywhere these days—in a black, all-terrain, bulletproof SUV—but the car and its heavily tinted windows only make us more conspicuous, which I find worrisome. But then, as Castle likes to point out, I have no ready solution for the problem, so we remain at an impasse.

I try to hide my reaction as we drive up through the wooded area just outside the Sanctuary, but I can't help my grimace or the way my body locks down, preparing for a fight. After the fall of The Reestablishment, most rebel groups emerged from hiding to rejoin the world—

But not us.

Just last week we cleared this dirt path for the SUV, enabling it to now get as close as possible to the unmarked entrance, but I'm not sure it's doing much to help. A mob of people has already crowded in so tightly around us that we're moving no more than an inch at a time. Most of them are well-meaning, but they scream and pound at the car with the enthusiasm of a belligerent crowd, and every time we endure this circus I have to physically force myself to remain calm. To sit quietly in my seat and ignore the urge to remove the gun from its holster beneath my jacket.

Difficult.

I know Ella can protect herself—she's proven this fact a thousand times over—but still, I worry. She's become notorious to a near-terrifying degree. To some extent, we all have. But Juliette Ferrars, as she's known around the world, can go nowhere and do nothing without drawing a crowd.

They say they love her.

Even so, we remain cautious. There are still many around the globe who would love to bring back to life the emaciated remains of The Reestablishment, and assassinating a beloved hero would be the most effective start to such a scheme. Though we have unprecedented levels of privacy in the Sanctuary, where Nouria's sight and sound protections around the grounds grant us freedoms we enjoy nowhere else, we've been unable to hide our precise location. People know, generally, where to find us, and that small bit of information has been feeding them for weeks. The civilians wait here—thousands and thousands of them—every single day.

For no more than a glimpse.

We've had to put barricades in place. We've had to hire extra security, recruiting armed soldiers from the local sectors. This area is unrecognizable from what it was a month ago. It's a different world already. And I feel my body go solid as we approach the entrance. Nearly there now.

I look up, ready to say something—

"Don't worry." Kenji locks eyes with me. "Nouria upped the security. There should be a team of people waiting for us."

"I don't know why all this is necessary," Ella says, still staring out the window. "Why can't I just stop for a minute and talk to them?"

"Because the last time you did that you were nearly trampled," Kenji says, exasperated.

"Just the one time."

Kenji's eyes go wide with outrage, and on this point, he and I are in full agreement. I sit back and watch as he counts off on his fingers. "The same day you were nearly trampled, someone tried to cut off your hair. Another day a bunch of people tried to kiss you. People literally throw their newborn babies at you. Plus, I've already counted six people who've peed their pants in your presence, which, I have to add, is not only upsetting, but unsanitary, especially when they try to hug you while they're still wetting themselves." He shakes his head. "The mobs are too big, princess. Too strong. Too passionate. Everyone screams in your face, fights to put their hands on you. And half the time we can't protect you."

"But—"

"I know that most of these people are well-intentioned," I say, taking her hand. She turns in her seat, meets my eyes. "They are, for the most part, kind. Curious. Overwhelmed with gratitude and desperate to put a face to their freedom.

"I know this," I say, "because I always check the crowds, searching their energy for anger or violence. And though the vast majority of them are good"—I sigh, shake my head—"sweetheart, you've just made a lot of enemies. These massive, unfiltered crowds are not safe. Not yet. Maybe not ever."

She takes a deep breath, lets it out slowly. "I know you're right," she says quietly. "But somehow it feels wrong not to be able to talk to the people we've been fighting for. I want them to know how I feel. I want them to know how much we care—and how much we're still planning on doing to rebuild, to get things right."

"You will," I say. "I'll make sure you have the chance to say all those things. But it's only been two weeks, love. And right now we don't have the necessary infrastructure to make that happen."

"But we're working on it, right?"

"We're working on it," Kenji says. "Which, actually—not that I'm making excuses or anything—but if you hadn't asked me to prioritize the reconstruction committee, I probably wouldn't have issued orders to knock down a series of unsafe buildings, one of which included Winston and Alia's studio, which"—he holds up his hands—"for the record, I didn't know was their studio. And again, not that I'm making excuses for my reprehensible behavior or anything—but how the hell was I supposed to know it was an art studio? It was officially listed in the books as unsafe, marked for demolition—"

"They didn't know it was marked for demolition," Ella says, a hint of impatience in her voice. "They made it into their studio precisely because no one was using it."

"Yes," Kenji says, pointing at her. "Right. But, see, I didn't know that."

"Winston and Alia are your friends," I point out unkindly.

"Isn't it your business to know things like that?"

"Listen, man, it's been a really hectic two weeks since the world fell apart, okay? I've been busy."

"We've all been busy."

"Okay, enough," Ella says, holding up a hand. She's looking out the window, frowning. "Someone is coming."

Kent.

"What's Adam doing here?" Ella asks. She turns back to look at Kenji. "Did you know he was coming?"

If Kenji responds, I don't hear him. I'm peering out of the very-tinted windows at the scene outside, watching Adam push his way through the crowd toward the car. He appears to be unarmed. He shouts something into the sea of people, but they won't be quieted right away. A few more tries—and they settle down. Thousands of faces turn to stare at him.

I struggle to make out his words.

And then, slowly, he stands back as ten heavily armed men and women approach our car. Their bodies form a barricade between the vehicle and the entrance into the Sanctuary, and Kenji jumps out first, invisible and leading the way. He projects his power to protect Ella, and I steal his stealth for myself. The three of us—our bodies invisible—move cautiously toward the entrance.

Only once we're on the other side, safely within the boundaries of the Sanctuary, do I finally relax.

A little.

I glance back, the way I always do, at the crowd gathered just beyond the invisible barrier that protects our camp.

Some days I just stand here and study their faces, searching for something. Anything. A threat still unknown, unnamed.

"Hey—awesome," Winston says, his unexpected voice shaking me out of my reverie.

I turn back to look at him, discovering him sweaty and out of breath as he pulls up to us.

"So glad you guys are back," he says, still panting. "Do any of you happen to know anything about fixing pipes? We've got kind of a sewage problem in one of the tents, and it's all hands on deck."

Our return to reality is swift.

And humbling.

But Ella steps forward, already reaching for the—dear God, is it wet?—wrench in Winston's hand, and I almost can't believe it. I wrap an arm around her waist, tugging her back.

"Please, love. Not today. Any other day, maybe. But not today."

"What?" She glances back. "Why not? I'm really good with a wrench. Hey, by the way," she says, turning to the others, "did you know that Ian is secretly really good at woodworking?"

Winston laughs.

"It's only been a secret to you, princess," Kenji says.

She frowns. "Well, we were fixing one of the more savable buildings the other day, and he taught me how to use everything in his toolbox. I helped him repair the roof," she says, beaming.

"That's a strange justification for spending the hours before your wedding digging feces out of a toilet." Kent saunters up to us. He's laughing.

My brother.

So strange.

He's a happier, healthier version of himself than I've ever seen before. He took a week to recover after we got him back here, but when he regained consciousness and we told him what happened—and assured him that James was safe—he fainted.

And didn't wake up for another two days.

He's become an entirely different person in the days since. Practically jubilant. Happy for everyone. A darkness still clings to all of us—will probably cling to all of us forever—

But Adam seems undeniably changed.

"I just wanted to give you guys a heads-up," he says, "that we're doing a new thing now. Nouria wants me to go out there and do a general deactivation before anyone enters or exits the grounds. Just as a precaution." He looks at Ella. "Juliette, is that okay with you?"

Juliette.

So many things changed when we came home, and this was one of them. She took back her name. Reclaimed it. She said that by erasing Juliette from her life she feared she was giving the ghost of my father too much power over her. She realized she didn't want to forget her years as Juliette—or to diminish the young woman she was, fighting against all odds to survive. Juliette Ferrars is who she was when she was made known to the world, and she wants it to remain that way.

I'm the only one allowed to call her Ella now.

It's just for us. A tether to our shared history, a nod to our past, to the love I've always felt for her, no matter her name.

I watch her as she laughs with her friends, as she pulls a hammer free from Winston's tool belt and pretends to hit Kenji with it—no doubt for something he deserves. Lily and Nazeera come out of nowhere, Lily carrying a small bundle of a dog she and Ian saved from an abandoned building nearby. Ella drops the hammer with a sudden cry and Adam jumps back in alarm. She takes the dirty, filthy creature into her arms, smothering it with kisses even as it barks at her with a wild ferocity. And then she turns to look at me, the animal still yipping in her ear, and I realize there are tears in her eyes. She is crying over a dog.

Juliette Ferrars, one of the most feared, most lauded heroes of our known world, is crying over a dog. Perhaps no one else would understand, but I know that this is the first time she's ever held one. Without hesitation, without fear, without danger of causing an innocent creature any harm. For her, this is true joy.

To the world, she is formidable.

To me?

She is the world.

So when she dumps the creature into my reluctant arms, I hold it steady, uncomplaining when the beast licks my face with the same tongue it used, no doubt, to clean its hindquarters. I remain steady, betraying nothing even when warm drool drips down my neck. I hold still as its grimy feet dig into my coat, nails catching at the wool. I am so still, in fact, that eventually the creature quiets, his anxious limbs settling against my chest. He whines as he stares at me, whines until I finally lift a hand, drag it over his head.

When I hear her laugh, I am happy.

The brand new YA fantasy romance series from the author of *TikTok* sensation, **Shatter Me**

DEFY ME

DEAN

First published in the USA 2019 by HarperCollins Children's Books
First published in Great Britain 2019 by Electric Monkey, part of Farshore
This edition published 2021 by Dean, part of Farshore
An imprint of HarperCollins*Publishers*
1 London Bridge Street, London SE1 9GF
www.farshore.co.uk

HarperCollins*Publishers*
Macken House, 39/40 Mayor Street Upper,
Dublin 1, D01 C9W8, Ireland

Published by arrangement with HarperCollins Children's Books,
a division of HarperCollins Publishers, New York, New York, USA

Text copyright © 2019 Tahereh Mafi

ISBN 978 0 603 58069 7
Printed and Bound in the UK using 100% Renewable Electricity
at CPI Group (UK) Ltd
015

A CIP catalogue record for this title is available from the British Library.

All rights reserved. No part of this publication may be reproduced,
stored in a retrieval system, or transmitted, in any form or by any means,
electronic, mechanical, photocopying, recording or otherwise, without
the prior permission of the publisher and copyright owner.

Stay safe online. Farshore is not responsible for content hosted by third parties.

This book is produced from independently certified FSC™ paper
to ensure responsible forest management.

For more information visit: www.harpercollins.co.uk/green

DEFY ME

TAHEREH MAFI

DEAN

KENJI

She's screaming.

She's just screaming words, I think. They're just *words*. But she's screaming, screaming at the top of her lungs, with an agony that seems almost an exaggeration, and it's causing devastation I never knew possible. It's like she just—imploded.

It doesn't seem real.

I mean, I knew Juliette was strong—and I knew we hadn't discovered the depth of her powers—but I never imagined she'd be capable of this.

Of this:

The ceiling is splitting open. Seismic currents are thundering up the walls, across the floors, chattering my teeth. The ground is rumbling under my feet. People are frozen in place even as they shake, the room vibrating around them. The chandeliers swing too fast and the lights flicker ominously. And then, with one last vibration, three of the massive chandeliers rip free from the ceiling and shatter as they hit the floor.

Crystal flies everywhere. The room loses half its light, bathing the cavernous space in a freakish glow, and it's suddenly hard to see what's happening. I look at Juliette and see her staring, slack-jawed, frozen at the sight of the devastation, and I realize she must've stopped screaming a minute ago. She can't stop this. She already put the energy into the world and now—

It has to go somewhere.

The shudders ripple with renewed fervor across the floorboards, ripping through walls and seats and *people*.

I don't actually believe it until I see the blood. It seems fake, for a second, all the limp bodies in seats with their chests butterflied open. It seems staged—like a bad joke, like a bad theater production. But when I see the blood, thick and heavy, seeping through clothes and upholstery, dripping down frozen hands, I know we'll never recover from this.

Juliette just murdered six hundred people at once.

There's no recovering from this.

I shove my way through the quiet, stunned, still-breathing bodies of my friends. I hear Winston's soft, insistent whimpers and Brendan's steady, reassuring response that the wound isn't as bad as it looks, that he's going to be okay, that he's been through worse than this and survived it—

And I know my priority right now needs to be Juliette.

When I reach her I pull her into my arms, and her cold, unresponsive body reminds me of the time I found her standing over Anderson, a gun aimed at his chest. She was so terrified—*so surprised*—by what she'd done that she could hardly speak. She looked like she'd disappeared into herself somewhere—like she'd found a small room in her brain and had locked herself inside. It took a minute to coax her back out again.

She hadn't even killed anyone that time.

I try to warm some sense into her, begging her now to return to herself, to hurry back to her mind, to the present moment.

"I know everything is crazy right now, but I need you to snap out of this, J. Wake up. Get out of your head. We have to get out of here."

She doesn't blink.

"Princess, please," I say, shaking her a little. "We have to go—*now*—"

And when she still doesn't move, I figure I have no choice but to move her myself. I start hauling her backward. Her limp body is heavier than I expect, and she makes a small, wheezing sound that's almost like a sob. Fear sparks in my nerves. I nod at Castle and the others to go, to move on without me, but when I glance around, looking for Warner, I realize I can't find him anywhere.

What happens next knocks the wind from my lungs.

The room tilts. My vision blackens, clears, and then darkens only at the edges in a dizzying moment that lasts hardly a second. I feel off-center. I stumble.

And then, all at once—

Juliette is gone.

Not figuratively. She's literally gone. Disappeared. One

second she's in my arms, and the next, I'm grasping at air. I blink and spin around, convinced I'm losing my mind, but when I scan the room I see the audience members begin to stir. Their shirts are torn and their faces are scratched, but no one appears to be dead. Instead, they begin to stand, confused, and as soon as they start shuffling around, someone shoves me, hard. I look up to see Ian swearing at me, telling me to get moving while we still have a chance, and I try to push back, try to tell him that we lost Juliette—that I haven't seen Warner—and he doesn't hear me, he just forces me forward, offstage, and when the murmur of the crowd grows into a roar, I know I have no choice.

I have to go.

WARNER

"I'm going to kill him," she says, her small hands forming fists. "I'm going to kill him—"

"Ella, don't be silly," I say, and walk away.

"One day," she says, chasing after me, her eyes bright with tears. "If he doesn't stop hurting you, I swear I'll do it. You'll see."

I laugh.

"It's not funny!" she cries.

I turn to face her. "No one can kill my dad. He's unkillable."

"No one is unkillable," she says.

I ignore her.

"Why doesn't your mum do anything?" she says, and she grabs my arm.

When I meet her eyes she looks different. Scared.

"Why doesn't anyone stop him?"

The wounds on my back are no longer fresh, but, somehow, they still hurt. Ella is the only person who knows about these scars, knows what my dad started doing to me on my birthday two years ago. Last year, when all the families came to visit us in California, Ella had barged into my room, wanting to know where Emmaline and Nazeera had gone off to, and she'd caught me staring at my back in the mirror.

I begged her not to say anything, not to tell anyone what she saw, and she started crying and said that we had to tell someone, that she was going to tell her mom and I said, "If you tell your mom I'll only get into more trouble. Please don't say anything, okay? He won't do it again."

But he did do it again.

And this time he was angrier. He told me I was seven years old now, and that I was too old to cry.

"We have to do something," she says, and her voice shakes a little. Another tear steals down the side of her face and, quickly, she wipes it away. "We have to tell someone."

"Stop," I say. "I don't want to talk about it anymore."

"But—"

"Ella. Please."

"No, we have t—"

"Ella," I say, cutting her off. "I think there's something wrong with my mom."

Her face falls. Her anger fades. "What?"

I'd been terrified, for weeks, to say the words out loud, to make my fears real. Even now, I feel my heart pick up.

"What do you mean?" she says. "What's wrong with her?"

"She's . . . sick."

Ella blinks at me. Confused. "If she's sick we can fix her. My mum and dad can fix her. They're so smart; they can fix anything. I'm sure they can fix your mum, too."

I'm shaking my head, my heart racing now, pounding in my ears. "No, Ella, you don't understand—I think—"

"What?" She takes my hand. Squeezes. "What is it?"

"I think my dad is killing her."

KENJI

We're all running.

Base isn't far from here, and our best option is to go on foot. But the minute we hit the open air, the group of us—myself, Castle, Winston, injured Brendan, Ian, and Alia—go invisible. Someone shouts a breathless *thanks* in my direction, but I'm not the one doing this.

My fists clench.

Nazeera.

These last couple of days with her have been making my head spin. I never should've trusted her. First she hates me, then she hates me even more, and then, suddenly, she decides I'm not an asshole and wants to be my friend? I can't believe I fell for it. I can't believe I'm such an idiot. She's been playing me this whole time. This girl just shows up out of nowhere, magically mimics my exact supernatural ability, and then—right when she pretends to be best friends with Juliette—we're ambushed at the symposium and Juliette sort of murders six hundred people?

No way. I call bullshit.

No way this was all some big coincidence.

Juliette attended that symposium because *Nazeera* encouraged her to go. Nazeera convinced Juliette it was the right thing to do. And then five seconds before Brendan gets shot, Nazeera tells me to run? Tells me we have the same powers?

Bullshit.

I can't believe I let myself be distracted by a pretty face. I should've trusted Warner when he told me she was hiding something.

Warner.

God. I don't even know what happened to him.

The minute we get back to base our invisibility is lifted. I can't know for sure if that means Nazeera went her own way, but we can't slow down long enough to find out. Quickly, I project a new layer of invisibility over our team; I'll have to keep it up just long enough to get us all to a safe space, and just being back on base isn't assurance enough. The soldiers are going to ask questions, and right now I don't have the answers they need.

They're going to be pissed.

We make our way, as a group, to the fifteenth floor, to our home on base in Sector 45. Warner only just finished having this thing built for us. He cleared out the entire top floor for our new headquarters—we'd hardly even settled in—and things have already gone to shit. I can't even allow myself to think about it now, not yet.

It makes me feel sick to my stomach.

Once we're gathered in our largest common room, I do a head count. All original, remaining Omega Point members are present. Adam and James show up to find out what happened, and Sonya and Sara stick around just long enough to gather intel before carting Brendan over to the medical wing. Winston disappears down the hall behind them.

Juliette and Warner never show.

Quickly, we share our own versions of what we saw. It doesn't take long to confirm we all witnessed basically the same thing: blood, mayhem, murdered bodies, and then—a slightly less-bloody version of the same thing. No one seems as surprised by the twisted turn of events as I was, because, according to Ian, "Weird supernatural shit happens around here all the time, it's not that weird," but, more important:

No one saw what happened to Warner and Juliette.

No one but me.

For a few seconds, we all stare at each other. My heart pounds hard and heavy in my chest. I feel like I might be on fire, burning with indignation.

Denial.

Alia is the first to speak. "You don't think they're dead, do you?"

Ian says, "Probably."

And I jump to my feet. "STOP. They're not dead."

"How can you be sure?" Adam says.

"I would know if they were dead."

"What? How w—"

"I would just know, okay?" I cut him off. "I would know. And they're not dead." I take a deep, steadying breath. "We're not going to freak out," I say as calmly as possible.

"There has to be a logical explanation. People don't just *disappear*, right?"

Everyone stares at me.

"You know what I mean," I snap, irritated. "We all know that Juliette and Warner wouldn't, like, run away together. They weren't even on speaking terms before the symposium. So it makes the most sense that they would be kidnapped." I pause. Look around again. "Right?"

"Or dead," Ian says.

"If you keep talking like that, Sanchez, I can guarantee that at least one person *will* be dead tonight."

Ian sighs, hard. "Listen, I'm not trying to be an asshole. I know you were close with them. But let's be real: they weren't close with the rest of us. And maybe that makes me less invested in all this, but it also makes me more levelheaded."

He waits, gives me a chance to respond.

I don't.

Ian sighs again. "I'm just saying that maybe you're letting emotion cloud your better judgment right now. I know you don't *want* them to be dead, but the possibility that they *are* dead is, like, really high. Warner was a traitor to The Reestablishment. I'm surprised they didn't try to kill him sooner. And Juliette—I mean, that's obvious, right? She murdered Anderson and declared herself ruler of North America." He raises his eyebrows in a knowing gesture. "Those two have had targets on their backs for months."

My jaw clenches. Unclenches. Clenches again.

"So," Ian says quietly. "We have to be smart about this. If they're dead, we need to be thinking about our next moves. Where do we go?"

"Wait—what do you mean?" Adam says, sitting forward. "What next moves? You think we have to leave?"

"Without Warner and Juliette, I don't think we're safe here." Lily takes Ian's hand in a show of emotional support that makes me feel violent. "The soldiers paid their allegiance to the two of them—to Juliette in particular. Without her, I'm not sure they'd follow the rest of us anywhere."

"And if The Reestablishment had Juliette murdered," Ian adds, "they're obviously just getting started. They'll be coming to reclaim Sector 45 any second now. Our best chance of survival is to first consider what's best for our team. Since we're the obvious next targets, I think we should bail. Soon." A pause. "Maybe even tonight."

"Bro, are you insane?" I drop down into my chair too hard, feeling like I might scream. "We can't just bail. We need to look for them. We need to be planning a rescue mission right now!"

Everyone just stares at me. Like *I'm* the one who's lost his mind.

"Castle, sir?" I say, trying and failing to keep the sharp edge out of my voice. "Do you want to chime in here?"

But Castle has sunk down in his chair. He's staring up, at the ceiling, at nothing. He looks dazed.

I don't have the chance to dwell on it.

"Kenji," Alia says quietly. "I'm sorry, but Ian's right. I

don't think we're safe here anymore."

"We're not leaving," Adam and I say at exactly the same time.

I spin around, surprised. Hope shoots through me fast and strong. Maybe Adam feels more for Juliette than he lets on. Maybe Adam will surprise us all. Maybe he'll finally stop hiding, stop cowering in the background. *Maybe*, I think, Adam is back.

"Thank you," I say, and point at him in a gesture that says to everyone:

See? This is loyalty.

"James and I aren't running anymore," Adam says, his eyes going cold as he speaks. "I understand if the rest of you have to leave, but James and I will stay here. I was a Sector 45 soldier. I lived on this base. Maybe they'll give me immunity."

I frown. "But—"

"James and I aren't leaving," Adam says. Loudly. Definitively. "You can make your plans without us. We have to take off for the night, anyway." Adam stands, turns to his brother. "It's time to get ready for bed."

James stares at the floor.

"James," Adam says, a gentle warning in his voice.

"I want to stay and listen," James says, crossing his arms. "You can go to bed without me."

"James—"

"But I have a theory," the ten-year-old says. He says the word *theory* like it's brand-new to him, like it's an interesting sound in his mouth. "And I want to share it with Kenji."

Adam looks so tense that the strain in his shoulders is stressing *me* out. I think I haven't been paying close enough attention to him, because I didn't realize until right now that Adam looks worse than tired. He looks ragged. Like he could collapse, crack in half, at any moment.

James catches my eye from across the room, his own eyes round and eager.

I sigh.

"What's your theory, little man?"

James's face lights up. "I was just thinking: maybe all the fake-killing thing was, like, a distraction."

I raise an eyebrow.

"Like, if someone wanted to kidnap Warner and Juliette," James says. "You know? Like you said earlier. Causing a scene like that would be the perfect distraction, right?"

"Well. Yeah," I say, and frown. "I guess. But why would The Reestablishment need a distraction? When have they ever been secretive about what they want? If a supreme commander wanted to take Juliette or Warner, for example, wouldn't they just show up with a shit ton of soldiers and take what they wanted?"

"*Language,*" Adam says, outraged.

"My bad. Strike the word *shit* from the record."

Adam shakes his head. He looks like he might throttle me. But James is smiling, which is really all that matters.

"No. I don't think they'd rush in like that, not with so many soldiers," James says, his blue eyes bright. "Not if they had something to hide."

"You think they'd have something to hide?" Lily pipes up. "From *us*?"

"I don't know," James says. "Sometimes people hide things." He steals a split-second glance at Adam as he says it, a glance that sets my pulse racing with fear, and I'm about to respond when Lily beats me to it.

"I mean, it's possible," she says. "But The Reestablishment doesn't have a long history of caring about pretenses. They stopped pretending to care about the opinion of the public a long time ago. They mow people down in the street just because they feel like it. I don't think they're worried about hiding things from us."

Castle laughs, out loud, and we all spin around to stare at him. I'm relieved to finally see him react, but he still seems lost in his head somewhere. He looks angry. I've never really seen Castle get angry.

"They hide a great deal from us," he says sharply. "And from each other." After a long, deep breath, he finally gets to his feet. Smiles, warily, at the ten-year-old in the room. "James, you are wise indeed."

"Thank you," James says, blinking up at him.

"Castle, sir?" I say, my voice coming out harder than I'd intended. "Will you please tell us what the hell is going on? Do you know something?"

Castle sighs. Rubs the stubble on his chin with the flat of his palm. "All right, Nazeera," he says, turning toward nothing, like he's speaking to a ghost. "Go ahead."

When Nazeera appears, as if out of thin air, I'm not the only one who's pissed. Okay, maybe I'm the only one who's pissed.

But everyone else looks surprised, at least.

They're staring at her, at each other, and then all of them—*all of them*—turn to look at me.

"Bro, did you know about this?" Ian asks.

I scowl.

Invisibility is *my* thing. My thing, goddammit.

No one ever said I had to share that with anyone. Especially not with someone like Nazeera, a lying, manipulative—

Gorgeous. Gorgeous human being.

Shit.

I turn, stare at the wall. I can't be distracted by her anymore. She knows I'm into her—my infatuation is apparently obvious to everyone within a ten-mile radius, according to Castle—and she's clearly been using my idiocy to her best advantage.

Smart. I respect the tactic.

But that also means I have to keep my guard up when she's around. No more staring. No more daydreaming about her. No more thinking about how she looked at me when she smiled. Or the way she laughed, like she meant it, the same night she yelled at me for asking reasonable questions. Which, by the way—

I don't think I was crazy for wondering out loud how the daughter of a supreme commander could get away with wearing an illegal headscarf. She told me later that she wears the scarf symbolically, every once in a while, that she can't get away with wearing it all the time because it's illegal. But when I pointed this out to her, she gave me hell. And then she gave me shit for being confused.

I'm *still* confused.

She's not covering her hair now, either, but no one else seems to have registered this fact. Maybe they'd already seen her like this. Maybe everyone but me already had that conversation with her, already heard her story about wearing it symbolically, occasionally.

Illegally, when her dad wasn't watching.

"Kenji," she says, and her voice is so sharp I look up, stare at her despite my own very explicit orders to keep my eyes on the wall. All it takes is two seconds of eye contact and my heart hits itself.

That mouth. Those eyes.

"Yeah?" I cross my arms.

She looks surprised, like she wasn't expecting me to be upset, and I don't care. She should know that I'm pissed. I want her to know that invisibility is my thing. That I know I'm petty and I don't care. Plus, I don't trust her. Also, what is up with these kids of the supreme commanders all being super-good-looking? It's almost like they did it on purpose, like they made these kids in test tubes or some shit.

I shake my head to clear it.

Carefully, Nazeera says, "I really think you should sit down for this."

"I'm good."

She frowns. For a second she looks almost hurt, but before I have a chance to feel bad about it, she shrugs. Turns away.

And what she says next nearly splits me in half.

JULIETTE

I'm sitting on an orange chair in the hallway of a dimly lit building. The chair is made of cheap plastic, its edges coarse and unfinished. The floor is a shiny linoleum that occasionally sticks to the soles of my shoes. I know I've been breathing too loudly but I can't help it. I sit on my hands and swing my legs under my seat.

Just then, a boy comes into view. His movements are so quiet I only notice him when he stops directly in front of me. He leans against the wall opposite me, his eyes focused on a point in the distance.

I study him for a moment.

He seems about my age, but he's wearing a suit. There's something strange about him; he's so pale and stiff he seems close to dead.

"Hi," I say, and try to smile. "Do you want to sit down?"

He doesn't return my smile. He won't even look at me. "I'd prefer to stand," he says quietly.

"Okay."

We're both silent awhile.

Finally, he says, "You're nervous."

I nod. My eyes must be a little red from crying, but I'd been hoping no one would notice. "Are you here to get a new family, too?"

"No."

"Oh." *I look away. Stop swinging my feet. I feel my bottom lip tremble and I bite it, hard.* "Then why are you here?"

He shrugs. I see him glance, briefly, at the three empty chairs next to me, but he makes no effort to sit down. "My father made me come."

"He made you come *here*?"

"Yes."

"Why?"

He stares at his shoes and frowns. "I don't know."

"Shouldn't you be in school?"

And then, instead of answering me, he says, "Where are you from?"

"What do you mean?"

He looks up then, meets my eyes for the first time. He has such unusual eyes. They're a light, clear green.

"You have an accent," *he says.*

"Oh," *I say.* "Yeah." *I look at the floor.* "I was born in New Zealand. That's where I lived until my mum and dad died."

"I'm sorry to hear that."

I nod. Swing my legs again. I'm about to ask him another question when the door down the hall finally opens. A tall man in a navy suit walks out. He's carrying a briefcase.

It's Mr. Anderson, my social worker.

He beams at me. "You're all set. Your new family is dying to meet you. We have a couple more things to do before you can go, but it won't take too lon—"

I can't hold it in anymore.

I start sobbing right there, all over the new dress he bought me. Sobs rack my body, tears hitting the orange chair, the sticky floor.

Mr. Anderson sets down his briefcase and laughs. "Sweetheart, there's nothing to cry about. This is a great day! You should be happy!"

But I can't speak.

I feel stuck, stuck to the seat. Like my lungs have been stuck together. I manage to calm the sobs but I'm suddenly hiccuping, tears spilling quietly down my cheeks. "I want—I want to go h-home—"

"You are going home," he says, still smiling. "That's the whole point."

And then—

"Dad."

I look up at the sound of his voice. So quiet and serious. It's the boy with the green eyes. Mr. Anderson, I realize, is his father.

"She's scared," the boy says. And even though he's talking to his dad, he's looking at me. "She's really scared."

"Scared?" Mr. Anderson looks from me to his son, then back again. "What's there to be scared of?"

I scrub at my face. Try and fail to stop the tears.

"What's her name?" the boy asks. He's still staring at me, and this time, I stare back. There's something in his eyes, something that makes me feel safe.

"This is Juliette," Mr. Anderson says, and looks me over. "Tragic"—he sighs—"just like her namesake."

KENJI

Nazeera was right. I should've sat down.

I'm looking at my hands, watching a tremor work its way across my fingers. I nearly lose my grip on the stack of photos I'm clutching. The photos. The photos Nazeera passed around after telling us that Juliette is not who we think she is.

I can't stop staring at the pictures.

A little brown girl and a little white girl running in a field, both of them smiling tiny-toothed smiles, long hair flying in the wind, small baskets full of strawberries swinging from their elbows.

Nazeera and Emmaline at the strawberry patch, it read on the back.

Little Nazeera being hugged, on either side, by two little white girls, all three of them laughing so hard they look like they're about to fall over.

Ella and Emmaline and Nazeera, it read.

A close-up of a little girl smiling right into the camera, her eyes huge and blue-green, lengths of soft brown hair framing her face.

Ella on Christmas morning, it read.

"Ella Sommers," Nazeera says.

She says her real name is Ella Sommers, sister to Emmaline Sommers, daughter of Maximillian and Evie Sommers.

"Something is wrong," Nazeera says.

"Something is happening," she says. She says she woke up six weeks ago remembering Juliette—sorry, Ella—

"Remembering her. I was *remembering* her, which means I'd forgotten her. And when I remembered Ella," she says, "I remembered Emmaline, too. I remembered how we'd all grown up together, how our parents used to be friends. I remembered but I didn't understand, not right away. I thought maybe I was confusing dreams with memory. Actually, the memories came back to me so slowly I thought, for a while, that I might've been hallucinating."

She says the hallucinations, as she called them, were impossible to shake, so she started digging, started looking for information.

"I learned the same thing you did. That two girls named Ella and Emmaline were donated to The Reestablishment, and that only Ella was taken out of their custody, so Ella was given an alias. Relocated. Adopted. But what you didn't know was that the parents who gave up their daughters were also members of The Reestablishment. They were doctors and scientists. You didn't know that Ella—the girl you know to be Juliette—is the daughter of Evie Sommers, the current supreme commander of Oceania. She and I grew up together. She, like the rest of us kids, was built to serve The Reestablishment."

Ian swears, loudly, and Adam is so stunned he doesn't complain.

"That can't be possible," Adam says. "Juliette—The girl I went to school with? She was"—he shakes his head—"I knew Juliette for years. She wasn't made like you or Warner. She was this quiet, timid, sweet girl. She was always so *nice*. She never wanted to hurt anyone. All she ever wanted was to, like, connect with people. She was trying to *help* that little boy in the grocery store. But then it just—everything ended so badly and she got sucked into this whole mess and I tried," he says, looking suddenly distraught, "I tried to help her, I tried to keep her safe. I wanted to protect her from this. I wanted t—"

He cuts himself off. Pulls himself together.

"She wasn't like this," he says, and he's staring at the ground now. "Not until she started spending all that time with Warner. After she met him she just—I don't know what happened. She lost herself, little by little. Eventually she became someone else." He looks up. "But she wasn't made to be this way, not like you. Not like Warner. There's no way she's the daughter of a supreme commander—she's not a born murderer. Besides," he says, taking a sharp breath, "if she were from Oceania she would have an *accent*."

Nazeera tilts her head at Adam.

"The girl you knew had undergone severe physical and emotional trauma," she says. "She'd had her native memories forcibly removed. She was shipped across the globe as a specimen and convinced to live with abusive adoptive parents who beat the life out of her." Nazeera shakes her head slowly. "The Reestablishment—and Anderson, in particular—made sure that Ella could never remember why she was suffering, but just because she couldn't remember what happened to her didn't change the fact that it happened. Her body was repeatedly used and abused by a rotating cast of monsters. And that shit leaves its mark."

Nazeera looks Adam straight in the eye.

"Maybe you don't understand," she says. "I read all the reports. I hacked into all my father's files. I found *everything*. What they did to Ella over the course of twelve years is *unspeakable*. So yes, I'm sure you remember a very different person. But I don't think she became someone she wasn't. My guess is she finally gathered the strength to remember who she'd always been. And if you don't get that, I'm glad things didn't work out between the two of you."

In an instant, the tension in the room is nearly suffocating.

Adam looks like he might be on fire. Like fire might literally come out of his eyeballs. Like it might be his new superpower.

I clear my throat. I force myself to say something—anything—to break the silence. "So you guys, uh, you all knew about Adam and Juliette, too, huh? I didn't realize you knew about that. Huh. Interesting."

Nazeera takes her time turning in her seat to look me in

the eye. "Are you kidding?" she says, staring at me like I'm worse than an idiot.

I figure it's best not to press the issue.

"Where did you get these photos?" Alia asks, changing the subject more deftly than I did. "How can we trust that they're real?"

At first, Nazeera only looks at her. And she seems resigned when she says, "I don't know how to convince you that the photos are real. I can only tell you that they are."

The room goes silent.

"Why do you even care?" Lily says. "Why are we supposed to believe you care about this? About Juliette—about *Ella*? What do you have to gain from helping us? Why would you betray your parents?"

Nazeera sits back in her seat. "I know you all think the children of the supreme commanders are a bunch of carefree, amoral psychopaths, happy to be the military robots our parents wanted us to be, but nothing is ever that straightforward. Our parents are homicidal maniacs intent on ruling the world; that part is true. But the thing no one seems to understand is that our parents *chose* to be homicidal maniacs. We, on the other hand, were forced to be. And just because we've been trained to be mercenaries doesn't mean we like it. None of us got to choose this life. None of us enjoyed being taught to torture before we could even drive. And it's not insane to imagine that sometimes even horrible people are searching for a way out of their own darkness."

Nazeera's eyes flash with feeling as she speaks, and her words puncture the life vest around my heart. Emotion drowns me again.

Shit.

"Is it really so crazy to think I might care about the girls I once loved as my own sisters?" she's saying. "Or about the lies my parents forced me to swallow, or the innocent people I watched them murder? Or maybe even something simpler than that—that I might've opened my eyes one day and realized that I was part and parcel of a system that was not only ravaging the world but also slaughtering everyone in it?"

Shit.

I can feel it, can feel my heart filling out, filling up. My chest feels tight, like it's swollen, like my lungs don't fit anymore. I don't want to care about Nazeera. Don't want to feel her pain or feel connected to her or feel *anything*. I just want to keep a level head. Be cool.

I force myself to think about a joke James told me the other day, a stupid pun—something to do with muffins—a joke that was so lame I nearly cried. I focus on the memory, the way James laughed at his own lameness, snorting so hard a little food fell out of his mouth. I smile and glance at James, who looks like he might be falling asleep in his seat.

Soon, the tightness in my chest begins to abate.

Now I'm really smiling, wondering if it's weird that I love bad jokes even more than good ones, when I hear Ian say—

"It's not that you seem heartless. It's just that these

photos seem so convenient. You had them ready to share." He stares down at the single photo he's holding. "These kids could be anyone."

"Look closely," Nazeera says, standing up to get a better look at the picture in his hands. "Who do you think that is?"

I lean over—Ian isn't far from me—and peer over his shoulder. There's really no point denying it anymore; the resemblance is insane.

Juliette. *Ella*.

She's just a kid, maybe four or five years old, standing in front of the camera, smiling. She's holding a bouquet of dandelions up to the cameraman, as if to offer him one. And then, just off to the side, there's another figure. A little blond boy. So blond his hair is white. He's staring, intensely, at a single dandelion in his hands.

I nearly fall out of my chair. Juliette is one thing, but this—

"Is that *Warner*?" I say.

Adam looks up sharply. He glances from me to Nazeera, then stalks over to look at the photo. His eyebrows fly up his head.

"No way," he says.

Nazeera shrugs.

"No way," Adam says again. "*No way*. That's impossible. There's no way they knew each other this long. Warner had no idea who Juliette was before she came here." When Nazeera seems unmoved, Adam says, "I'm serious. I know you think I'm full of shit, but I'm not wrong about this. I was *there*. Warner literally interviewed me for the job of being her cellmate in the asylum. He didn't know who she was. He'd never met her. Never seen her face, not up close, anyway. Half the reason he chose me to be her roommate was because she and I had history, because he found that useful. He'd grill me for hours about her."

Nazeera sighs slowly, like she's surrounded by idiots.

"When I found these photos," she says to Adam, "I couldn't understand how I came across them so easily. I didn't understand why anyone would keep evidence like this right under my nose or make it so easy to find. But I know now that my parents never expected me to look. They got lazy. They figured that, even if I found these photos, I'd never know what I was looking at. Two months ago I could've seen these pictures and assumed that this girl"—she plucks a photo of herself, what appears to be a young Haider, and a thin brown-haired girl with bright blue eyes, out of a pile—"was a neighbor kid, someone I used to know but couldn't be bothered to remember.

"But I do remember," she says. "I remember all of it. I remember the day our parents told us that Ella and Emmaline had drowned. I remember crying myself to sleep every night. I remember the day they took us to a place I thought was a hospital. I remember my mother telling me I'd feel better soon. And then, I remember *remembering* nothing. Like time, in my brain, just folded in on itself." She raises her eyebrows. "Do you get what I'm trying to say to you, Kent?"

He glares at her. "I get that you think I'm an idiot."

She smiles.

"Yes, I get what you're saying," he says, obviously irritated. "You're saying you all had your memories wiped. You're saying Warner doesn't even know that they knew each other."

She holds up a finger. "*Didn't* know," she says. "He didn't know until just before the symposium. I tried to warn him—and Castle," she says, glancing at Castle, who's looking at the wall. "I tried to warn them both that something was wrong, that something big was happening and I didn't really understand what or why. Warner didn't believe me, of course. I'm not sure Castle did, either. But I didn't have time to give them proof."

"Wait, what?" I say, my eyebrows furrowing. "You told Warner and Castle? *Before* the symposium? You told them all of this?"

"I tried," she says.

"Why wouldn't you just tell Juliette?" Lily asks.

"You mean Ella."

Lily rolls her eyes. "Sure. Ella. Whatever. Why not warn her directly? Why tell everyone else?"

"I didn't know how she'd take the news," Nazeera says. "I'd been trying to take her temperature from the moment I got here, and I could never figure out how she felt about me. I didn't think she really trusted me. And then after everything that happened"—she hesitates—"it never seemed like the right time. She got shot, she was in recovery, and then she and Warner broke up, and she just . . . I don't know. Spiraled. She wasn't in a healthy headspace. She'd already had to stomach a bunch of revelations and she didn't seem to be handling them well. I wasn't sure she could take much more, to be honest, and I was worried what she might do."

"Murder six hundred people, maybe," Ian mutters under his breath.

"Hey," I snap. "She didn't murder anyone, okay? That was some kind of magic trick."

"It was a distraction," Nazeera says firmly. "James was the only one who saw this for what it was." She sighs. "I think this whole thing was staged to make Ella appear volatile and unhinged. That scene at the symposium will no doubt undermine her position here, at Sector 45, by instilling fear in the soldiers who pledged their allegiance to her. She'll be described as unstable. Irrational. Weak. And then—easily captured. I knew The Reestablishment wanted Ella gone, but I thought they'd just burn the whole sector to the ground. I was wrong. This was a far more efficient tactic. They didn't need to kill off a regiment of perfectly good soldiers and a population of obedient workers," Nazeera says. "All they needed to do was to discredit Ella as their leader."

"So what happens now?" Lily says.

Nazeera hesitates. And then, carefully, she says, "Once they've punished the citizens and thoroughly quashed any hope for rebellion, The Reestablishment will turn everyone against you. Put bounties on your heads, or, worse, threaten to murder loved ones if civilians and soldiers don't turn you in. You were right," she says to Lily. "The soldiers and citizens paid allegiance to Ella, and with both her *and* Warner gone, they'll feel abandoned. They have no reason to trust the rest of you." A pause. "I'd say you have about twenty-four hours before they come for your heads."

Silence falls over the room. For a moment, I think everyone actually stops breathing.

"*Fuck*," Ian says, dropping his head in his hands.

"Immediate relocation is your best course of action," Nazeera says briskly, "but I don't know that I can be much help in that department. Where you go will be up to your discretion."

"Then what are you even doing here?" I say, irritated. I understand her a little better now—I know that she's been trying to help—but that doesn't change the fact that I still feel like shit. Or that I still don't know how to feel about her. "You showed up just to tell us we're all going to die and that's it?" I shake my head. "So helpful, thanks."

"Kenji," Castle says, finally breaking his silence. "There's no need to attack our guest." His voice is a calm, steadying sound. I've missed it. "She really did try to talk to me—to warn me—while she was here. As for a contingency plan," he says, speaking to the room, "give me a little time. I have friends. We're not alone, as you well know, in our resistance. There's no need to panic, not yet."

"Not yet?" Ian says, incredulous.

"Not yet," Castle says. Then: "Nazeera, what of your brother? Were you able to convince him?"

Nazeera takes a steadying breath, losing some of the tension in her shoulders. "Haider knows," she explains to the rest of us. "He's been remembering things about Ella, too, but his memories of her aren't as strong as mine, and he didn't understand what was happening to him until last night when I decided to tell him what I'd discovered."

"Whoa—Wait," Ian says. "You trust him?"

"I trust him enough," she says. "Besides, I figured he had a right to know; he knew Ella and Emmaline, too. But he wasn't entirely convinced. I don't know what he'll decide to do, not yet, but he definitely seemed shaken up about it, which I think is a good sign. I asked him to do some digging, to find out if any of the other kids were beginning to remember things, too, and he said he would. Right now, that's all I've got."

"Where *are* the other kids?" Winston asks, frowning. "Do they know you're still here?"

Nazeera's expression grows grim. "All the kids were supposed to report back as soon as the symposium was over. Haider should be on his way back to Asia by now. I tried to convince my parents I was staying behind to do more reconnaissance, but I don't think they bought it. I'm sure I'll hear from them soon. I'll handle it as it comes."

"So—Wait—" I glance from her to Castle. "You're staying with us?"

"That wasn't really my plan."

"Oh," I say. "Good. That's good."

She raises an eyebrow at me.

"You know what I mean."

"I don't think I do," she says, and she looks suddenly irritated. "Anyway, even though it *wasn't* my plan to stay, I think I might have to."

My eyes widen. "What? Why?"

"Because," she says, "my parents have been lying to me since I was a kid—stealing my memories and rewriting my history—and I want to know why. Besides"—she takes a deep breath—"I think I know where Ella and Warner are, and I want to help."

WARNER

"Goddammit."

I hear the barely restrained anger in my father's voice just before something slams, hard, into something else. He swears again.

I hesitate outside his door.

And then, impatiently—

"What do you want?"

His voice is practically a growl. I fight the impulse to be intimidated. I make my face a mask. Neutralize my emotions. And then, carefully, I step into his office.

My father is sitting at his desk, but I see only the back of his chair and the unfinished glass of Scotch clutched in his left hand. His papers are in disarray. I notice the paperweight on the floor; the damage to the wall.

Something has gone wrong.

"You wanted to see me," I say.

"What?" My father turns in his chair to face me. "See you for what?"

I say nothing. I've learned by now never to remind him when he's forgotten something.

Finally, he sighs. Says, "Right. Yes." And then: "We'll have to discuss it later."

"Later?" This time, I struggle to hide my feelings. "You said you'd give me an answer today—"

"Something's come up."

Anger wells in my chest. I forget myself. "Something more important than your dying wife?"

My father won't be baited. Instead, he picks up a stack of papers on his desk and says, "Go away."

I don't move.

"I need to know what's going to happen," I say. "I don't want to go to the capital with you—I want to stay here, with Mom—"

"Jesus," he says, slamming his glass down on the desk. "Do you hear yourself?" He looks at me, disgusted. "This behavior is unhealthy. It's disturbing. I've never known a sixteen-year-old boy to be so obsessed with his mother."

Heat creeps up my neck, and I hate myself for it. Hate him for making me hate myself when I say, quietly, "I'm not obsessed with her."

Anderson shakes his head. "You're pathetic."

I take the emotional hit and bury it. With some effort, I manage to sound indifferent when I say, "I just want to know what's going to happen."

Anderson stands up, shoves his hands in his pockets. He looks out the massive window in his office, at the city just beyond.

The view is bleak.

Freeways have become open-air museums for the skeletons of forgotten vehicles. Mountains of trash form ranges along the terrain. Dead birds litter the streets, carcasses still occasionally falling out of the sky. Untamed fires rage in the distance, heavy winds stoking their flames. A thick layer of smog has permanently settled over the city, and the remaining clouds are gray, heavy with rain. We've already begun the process of regulating what passes for livable and unlivable turf, and entire sections of the city have since been shut down. Most of the coastal areas, for example, have been evacuated, the streets and homes flooded, roofs slowly collapsing.

By comparison, the inside of my father's office is a veritable paradise. Everything is still new in here; the wood still smells like wood, every surface shines. The Reestablishment was voted into power just four months ago, and my father is currently the commander and regent of one of our brand-new sectors.

Number 45.

A sudden gust of wind hits the window, and I feel the shudder reverberate through the room. The lights flicker. He doesn't flinch. The world may be falling apart, but The Reestablishment has been doing better than ever. Their plans fell into place more swiftly than they'd expected. And even though my father is already being considered for a huge promotion—to supreme commander of North America—no amount of success seems to soothe him. Lately, he's been more volatile than usual.

Finally, he says, "I have no idea what's going to happen. I don't even know if they'll be considering me for the promotion anymore."

I'm unable to mask my surprise. "Why not?"

Anderson smiles, unhappily, at the window. "A babysitting job gone awry."

"I don't understand."

"I don't expect you to."

"So—we're not moving anymore? We won't be going to the capital?"

Anderson turns back around. "Don't sound so excited. I said I don't know yet. First, I have to figure out how to deal with the problem."

Quietly, I say, "What's the problem?"

Anderson laughs; his eyes crinkle and he looks, for a moment, human. "Suffice it to say that your girlfriend is ruining my goddamn day. As usual."

"My what?" I frown. "Dad, Lena isn't my girlfriend. I don't care what she's telling any—"

"Different girlfriend," Anderson says, and sighs. He won't meet my eyes now. He snatches a file folder from his desk, flips it open, and scans the contents.

I don't have a chance to ask another question.

There's a sudden, sharp knock at the door. At my dad's signal, Delalieu steps inside. He seems more than a little surprised to see me, and, for a moment, says nothing.

"Well?" My dad seems impatient. "Is she here?"

"Y-yes, sir." Delalieu clears his throat. His eyes flit to me again. "Should I bring her up, or would you prefer to meet elsewhere?"

"Bring her up."

Delalieu hesitates. "Are you quite certain, sir?"

I look from my dad to Delalieu. Something is wrong.

My father meets my eyes when he says, "I said, bring her up."

Delalieu nods, and disappears.

My head is a stone, heavy and useless, my eyes cemented to my skull. I maintain consciousness for only seconds at a time. I smell metal, taste metal. An ancient, roaring noise grows loud, then soft, then loud again.

Boots, heavy, near my head.

Voices, but the sounds are muffled, light-years away. I can't move. I feel as though I've been buried, left to rot. A weak orange light flickers behind my eyes and for just a second—just a second—

No.

Nothing.

Days seem to pass. Centuries. I'm only aware enough to know I've been heavily sedated. Constantly sedated. I'm parched, dehydrated to the point of pain. I'd kill for water. Kill for it.

When they move me I feel heavy, foreign to myself. I land hard on a cold floor, the pain ricocheting up my body as if from a distance. I know that, too soon, this pain will catch up to me. Too soon, the sedative will wear off and I'll be alone with my bones and this dust in my mouth.

A swift, hard kick to the gut and my eyes fly open, blackness devouring my open, gasping mouth, seeping into the sockets of my eyes. I feel blind and suffocated at once, and when the shock finally subsides, my limbs give out. Limp.

The spark dies.

KENJI

"Do you want to tell me what the hell is going on?"

I stop, frozen in place, at the sound of Nazeera's voice. I was heading back to my room to close my eyes for a minute. To try to do something about the massive headache ringing through my skull.

We finally, finally, took a break.

A brief recess after hours of exhausting, stressful conversations about next steps and blueprints and something about stealing a plane. It's too much. Even Nazeera, with all her intel, couldn't give me any real assurance that Juliette—sorry, Ella—and Warner were still alive, and just the *chance* that someone out there might be torturing them to death is, like, more than my mind can handle right now. Today has been a shitstorm of shit. A tornado of shit. I can't take it anymore. I don't know whether to sit down and cry or set something on fire.

Castle said he'd brave his way down to the kitchens to see about scrounging up some food for us, and that was the best news I'd heard all day. He also said he'd do his best to placate the soldiers for just a little longer—just long enough for us to figure out exactly what we're going to do next—but I'm not sure how much he can do. It was bad enough when

J got shot. The hours she spent in the medical wing were stressful for the rest of us, too. I really thought the soldiers would revolt right then. They kept stopping me in the halls, yelling about how they thought she was supposed to be *invincible*, that this wasn't the plan, that they didn't decide to risk their lives for a *regular* teenage girl who couldn't take a bullet and goddammit she was supposed to be some supernatural phenomenon, something more than human—

It took forever to calm them down.

But now?

I can only imagine how they'll react when they hear what happened at the symposium. It'll be mutiny, most likely.

I sigh, hard.

"So you're just going to ignore me?"

Nazeera is standing inches away from me. I can feel her, hovering. Waiting. I still haven't said anything. Still haven't turned around. It's not that I don't want to talk—I think I might, sort of, want to talk. Maybe some other day. But right now I'm out of gas. I'm out of James's jokes. I'm fresh out of fake smiles. Right now I'm nothing but pain and exhaustion and raw emotion, and I don't have the bandwidth for another serious conversation. I really don't want to do this right now.

I'd nearly made my escape, too. I'm right here, right in front of my door. My hand is on the handle.

I could just walk away, I think.

I could be that kind of guy, a Warner kind of guy. A jackass kind of guy. Just walk away without a word. Too tired, no thank you, don't want to talk.

Leave me alone.

Instead, I slump forward, rest my hands and forehead against the closed bedroom door. "I'm tired, Nazeera."

"I can't believe you're upset with me."

My eyes close. My nose bumps against the wood. "I'm not upset with you. I'm half asleep."

"You were *mad*. You were mad at me for having the same ability as you. Weren't you?"

I groan.

"Weren't you?" she says again, this time angrily.

I say nothing.

"*Unbelievable.* That is the most petty, ridiculous, *immature*—"

"Yeah, well."

"Do you know how hard it was for me to tell you that? Do you have any idea—" I hear her sharp, angry huff. "Will you at least look at me when I'm talking to you?"

"Can't."

"What?" She sounds startled. "What do you mean you can't?"

"Can't look at you."

She hesitates. "Why not?"

"Too pretty."

She laughs, but angrily, like she might punch me in the face. "Kenji, I'm trying to be serious with you. This is important to me. This is the first time in my whole life I've ever shown other people what I can do. It's the first time I've ever interacted with other people like me. Besides," she says, "I thought we decided we were going to be friends. Maybe that's not a big deal to you, but it's a big deal to me, because I don't make friends easily. And right now you're making me doubt my own judgment."

I sigh so hard I nearly hurt myself.

I push off the door, stare at the wall. "Listen," I say, swallowing hard. "I'm sorry I hurt your feelings. I just— There was a minute back there, before you really started talking, when I thought you'd just, like, lied about things. I didn't understand what was happening. I thought maybe you'd set us up. A bunch of stuff seemed too crazy to be a coincidence. But we've been talking for hours now, and I don't feel that way anymore. I'm not mad anymore. I'm sorry. Can I go now?"

"Of course," she says. "I just . . ." She trails off, like she's confused, and then she touches my arm. No, she doesn't just touch my arm. She takes my arm. She wraps her hand around my bare forearm and tugs, gently.

The contact is hot and immediate. Her skin is soft. My brain feels dim. Dizzy.

"Stop," I say.

She drops her hand.

"Why won't you look at me?" she says.

"I already told you why I won't look at you, and you laughed at me."

She's quiet for so long I wonder if she's walked away. Finally, she says, "I thought you were joking."

"Well, I wasn't."

More silence.

Then: "Do you always say exactly what you're thinking?"

"Most of the time, yeah." Gently, I bang my head against the door. I don't understand why this girl won't let me wallow in peace.

"What are you thinking right now?" she asks.

Jesus Christ.

I look up, at the ceiling, hoping for a wormhole or a bolt of lightning or maybe even an alien abduction—anything to get me out of here, this moment, this relentless, exhausting conversation.

In the absence of miracles, my frustration spikes.

"I'm thinking I want to go to sleep," I say angrily. "I'm thinking I want to be left alone. I'm thinking I've already told you this, a thousand times, and you won't let me go even though I apologized for hurting your feelings. So I guess what I'm really thinking is *I don't understand what you're doing here.* Why do you care so much about what I think?"

"What?" she says, startled. "I don't—"

Finally, I turn around. I feel a little unhinged, like my brain is flooded. There's too much happening. Too much to feel. Grief, fear, exhaustion. Desire.

Nazeera takes a step back when she sees my face.

She's perfect. Perfect everything. Long legs and curves. Her face is insane. Faces shouldn't look like that. Bright, honey-colored eyes and skin like dusk. Her hair is so brown it's nearly black. Thick, heavy, straight. She reminds me of something, of a feeling I don't even know how to describe. And there's something about her that's made me stupid. Drunk, like I could just stare at her and be happy, float forever in this feeling. And then I realize, with a start, that I'm staring at her mouth again.

I never mean to. It just happens.

She's always touching her mouth, tapping that damn diamond piercing under her lip, and I'm just dumb, my eyes following her every move. She's standing in front of me with her arms crossed, running her thumb absently against the edge of her bottom lip, and I can't stop staring. She startles, suddenly, when she realizes I'm looking. Drops her hands to her sides and blinks at me. I have no idea what she's thinking.

"I asked you a question," I say, but this time my voice comes out a little rough, a little too intense. I knew I should've kept my eyes on the wall.

Still, she only stares at me.

"All right. Forget it," I say. "You keep begging me to talk, but the minute I ask *you* a question, you say nothing. That's just great."

I turn away again, reach for the door handle.

And then, still facing the door, I say:

"You know—I'm aware that I haven't done a good job being smooth about this, and maybe I'll never be that kind of guy. But I don't think you should treat me like this, like I'm some idiot nothing, just because I don't know how to be a douchebag."

"What? Kenji, I don't—"

"*Stop*," I say, jerking away from her. She keeps touching my arm, touching me like she doesn't even know she's doing it. It's driving me crazy. "Don't do that."

"Don't do what?"

Finally, angrily, I spin around. I'm breathing hard, my chest rising and falling too fast. "Stop messing with me," I say. "You don't know me. You don't know anything about me. You say you want to be my friend, but you talk to me like I'm an idiot. You touch me, constantly, like I'm a child, like you're trying to comfort me, like you have no idea that I'm a grown-ass man who might *feel* something when you put your hands on me like that." She tries to speak and I cut her off. "I don't care what you think you know about me—or how stupid you think I am—but right now I'm exhausted, okay? I'm done. So if you want nice Kenji maybe you should check back in the morning, because right now all I've got is jack shit in the way of pleasantries."

Nazeera looks frozen. Stunned. She stares at me, her lips slightly parted, and I'm thinking this is it, this is how I die, she's going to pull out a knife and cut me open, rearrange my organs, put on a puppet show with my intestines. What a way to go.

But when she finally speaks, she doesn't sound angry. She sounds a little out of breath.

Nervous.

"I don't think you're a child," she says.

I have no idea what to say to that.

She takes a step forward, presses her hands flat against my torso, and I turn into a statue. Her hands seem to sear into my body, heat pressing between us, even through my shirt.

I feel like I might be dreaming.

She runs her hands up my chest and that simple motion feels so good I'm suddenly terrified. I feel magnetized to her, frozen in place. Afraid to wake up.

"What are you doing?" I whisper.

She's still staring at my chest when she says, again, "I don't think you're a child."

"Nazeera."

She lifts her head to meet my eyes, and a flash of feeling, hot and painful, shoots down my spine.

"And I don't think you're stupid," she says.

Wrong.

I'm definitely stupid.

So stupid. I can't even think right now.

"Okay," I say stupidly. I don't know what to do with my hands. I mean, I *know* what to do with my hands, I'm just worried that if I touch her she might laugh and then, probably, kill me.

She smiles then, smiles so big I feel my heart explode, make a mess inside my chest. "So you're not going to make a move?" she says, still smiling. "I thought you liked me. I thought that's what this whole thing was all about."

"*Like* you?" I blink at her. "I don't even know you."

"Oh," she says, and her smile disappears. She begins to

pull away and she can't meet my eyes and then, I don't know what comes over me—

I grab her hand, open my bedroom door, and lock us both inside.

She kisses me first.

I have an out-of-body moment, like I can't believe this is actually happening to me. I can't understand what I did to make this possible, because according to my calculations I messed this up on a hundred different levels and, in fact, I was pretty sure she was pissed at me up until, like, five minutes ago.

And then I tell myself to shut up.

Her kiss is soft, her hands tentative against my chest, but I wrap my arms around her waist and kiss her, really kiss her, and then somehow we're against the wall and her hands are around my neck and she parts her lips for me, sighs in my mouth, and that small sound of pleasure drives me crazy, floods my body with heat and desire so intense I can hardly stand.

We break apart, breathing hard, and I stare at her like an idiot, my brain still too numb to figure out exactly how I got here. Then again, who cares how I got here. I kiss her again and it nearly kills me. She feels so good, so soft. Perfect. She's perfect, fits perfectly in my arms, like we were made for this, like we've done this a thousand times before, and she smells like shampoo, like something sweet. Perfume, maybe. I don't know. Whatever it is, it's in my head now.

Killing brain cells.

When we break apart she looks different, her eyes darker, deeper. She turns away and when she turns back again she's smiling at me and for a second I think we might both be thinking the same thing. But I'm wrong, of course, so wrong, because I was thinking about how I'm, like, the luckiest guy on the planet and *she*—

She puts her hand on my chest and says, softly:

"You're really not my type."

That knocks the wind out of me. I drop my arms from around her waist and take a sudden, uncertain step backward.

She cringes, covers her face with both hands. "I don't—wow—I don't mean you're not my *type*." She shakes her head, hard. "I just mean I don't normally—I don't usually do this."

"Do what?" I say, still wounded.

"This," she says, and gestures between us. "I don't—I don't, like, just go around kissing guys I barely know."

"Okay." I frown. "Do you want to leave?"

"No." Her eyes widen.

"Then what do you want?"

"I don't know," she says, and her eyes go soft again. "I kind of just want to look at you for a minute. I meant what I said about your face," she says, and smiles. "You have a great face."

I go suddenly weak in the knees. I literally have to sit down. I walk over to my bed and collapse backward, my head hitting the pillow. It feels too good to be horizontal. If there weren't a gorgeous woman in my room right now, I'd be asleep already.

"Just so you know, this is not a move," I say, mostly to the ceiling. "I'm not trying to get you to sleep with me. I just literally had to lie down. Thank you for appreciating my face. I've always thought I had an underappreciated face."

She laughs, hard, and sits next to me, teetering on the edge of the bed, near my arm. "You're really not what I was expecting," she says.

I peer at her. "What were you expecting?"

"I don't know." She shakes her head. Smiles at me. "I guess I wasn't expecting to like you so much."

My chest goes tight. Too tight. I force myself to sit up, to meet her eyes.

"Come here," I say. "You're too far away."

She kicks off her boots and shifts closer, folding her legs up underneath her. She doesn't say a word. Just stares at me. And then, carefully, she touches my face, the line of my jaw. My eyes close, my mind swimming with nonsense. I lean back, rest my head against the wall behind us. I know it doesn't say much for my self-confidence that I'm so surprised this is happening, but I can't help it.

I never thought I'd get this lucky.

"Kenji," she says softly.

I open my eyes.

"I can't be your girlfriend."

I blink. Sit up a little. "Oh," I say.

It hadn't occurred to me until exactly this moment that I might even want something like that, but now that I'm thinking about it, I know that I do. A girlfriend is exactly what I want. I want a relationship. I want something real.

"It would never work, you know?" She tilts her head, looks at me like it's obvious, like I know as well as she does why things would never work out between us. "We're not—" She motions between our bodies to indicate something I don't understand. "We're so different, right? Plus, I don't even live here."

"Right," I say, but my mouth feels suddenly numb. My whole face feels numb. "You don't even live here."

And then, just as I'm trying to figure out how to pick up the pieces of my obliterated hopes and dreams, she climbs into my lap. Zero to sixty. My body malfunctions. Overheats.

She presses her face into my cheek and kisses me, softly, just underneath my jaw, and I feel myself melt into the wall, into the air.

I don't understand what's happening anymore. She likes me but she doesn't want to be with me. She's not going to be with me but she's going to sit on my lap and kiss me into oblivion.

Sure. Okay.

I let her touch me the way she wants to, let her put her hands on my body and kiss me wherever, however she wants. She touches me in a proprietary way, like I already belong to her, and I don't mind. I kind of love it. And I let her take the lead for as long as I can bear it. She's pulling up my shirt, running her hands across my bare skin and telling me how much she likes my body, and I really feel like—like I can't breathe. I feel too hot. Delirious but sharp, aware of this moment in an almost primal way.

She helps me pull off my shirt and then she just looks at me, first at my face and then at my chest, and she runs her hands across my shoulders, down my arms. "Wow," she says softly. "You're so gorgeous."

That's it for me.

I pick her up off my lap and lay her down, on her back, and she gasps, stares at me like she's surprised. And then, *deep*, her eyes go deep and dark, and she's looking at my mouth but I decide to kiss her neck, the curve of her shoulder.

"Nazeera," I whisper, hardly recognizing the sound of my own voice. "I want you so badly it might kill me."

Suddenly, someone is banging on my door.

"Bro, where the hell did you go?" Ian shouts. "Castle brought dinner up like ten minutes ago."

I sit up too fast. I nearly pull a muscle. Nazeera laughs out loud, and even though she claps a hand over her mouth to muffle the sound, she's not quick enough.

"Uh—Hello?" Ian again. "Kenji?"

"I'll be right there," I shout back.

I hear him hesitate—his footsteps uncertain—and then he's gone. I drop my head into my hands. Suddenly, everything comes rushing back to me. For a few minutes this moment with Nazeera felt like the whole world, a welcome reprieve from all the war and death and struggle. But now, with a little oxygen in my brain, I feel stupid. I don't know what I was thinking.

Juliette might be *dead*.

I get to my feet. I pull my shirt on quickly, careful not to meet her eyes. For some reason, I can't bring myself to look at Nazeera. I have no regrets about kissing her—it's just that I also feel suddenly guilty, like I was doing something wrong. Something selfish and inappropriate.

"I'm sorry," I say. "I don't know what got into me."

Nazeera is tugging on her boots. She looks up, surprised. "What do you mean?"

"What we just"—I sigh, hard—"I don't know. I forgot, for a moment, everything we have to do. The fact that Juliette might be out there, somewhere, being tortured to death. Warner might be dead. We'll have to pack up and run, leave this place behind. God, there's so much happening and I just—My head was in the wrong place. I'm sorry."

Nazeera is standing up now. She looks upset. "Why do you keep apologizing to me? Stop apologizing to me."

"You're right. I'm sorry." I wince. "I mean—You know what I mean. Anyway, we should go."

"Kenji—"

"Listen, you said you didn't want a relationship, right? You didn't want to be my girlfriend? You don't think that this"—I mimic what she did earlier, motioning between us—"could ever work? Well, then—" I take a breath. Run a hand through my hair. "This is what not being my girlfriend looks like. Okay? There are only a few people in my life who actually care about me, and right now my best friend is probably being murdered by a bunch of psychopaths, and I should be out there, doing something."

"I didn't realize you and Warner were so close," she says quietly.

"What?" I frown. "No, I'm talking about Juliette," I say. "Ella. Whatever."

Nazeera's eyebrows go high.

"Anyway, I'm sorry. We should probably just keep this professional, right? You're not looking for anything serious, and I don't know how to have casual relationships anyway. I always end up caring too much, to be honest, so this probably wasn't a good idea."

"Oh."

"Right?" I look at her, hoping, suddenly, that there was something I missed, something more than the cool distance in her eyes. "Didn't you just tell me that we're too different? That you don't even live here?"

She turns away. "Yes."

"And have you changed your mind in the last thirty seconds? About being my girlfriend?"

She's still staring at the wall when she says, "No."

Pain shoots up my spine, gathers in my chest. "Okay then," I say, and nod. "Thanks for your honesty. I have to go."

She cuts past me, walks out the door. "I'm coming, too."

JULIETTE

I've been sitting in the back of a police car for over an hour. I haven't been able to cry, not yet. And I don't know what I'm waiting for, but I know what I did, and I'm pretty sure I know what happens next.

I killed a little boy.

I don't know how I did it. I don't know why it happened. I just know that it was me, my hands, me. I did that. Me.

I wonder if my parents will show up.

Instead, three men in military uniforms march up to my window. One of them flings open the door and aims a machine gun at my chest.

"Get out," he barks. "Out with your hands up."

My heart is racing, terror propelling me out of the car so fast I stumble, slamming my knee into the ground. I don't need to check to know that I'm bleeding; the pain of the fresh wound is already searing. I bite my lip to keep from crying out, force the tears back.

No one helps me up.

I want to tell them that I'm only fourteen, that I don't know a lot about a lot of things, but that I know enough. I've watched TV shows about this sort of thing. I know they can't charge me as an adult. I know that they shouldn't be treating me like this.

But then I remember that the world is different now. We have a new government now, one that doesn't care how we used to do things. Maybe none of that matters anymore.

My heart beats faster.

I'm shoved into the backseat of a black car, and before I know it, I'm deposited somewhere new: somewhere that looks like an ordinary office building. It's tall. Steel gray. It seems old and decrepit—some of its windows are cracked—and the whole thing looks sad.

But when I walk inside I'm stunned to discover a blinding, gleaming interior. I look around, taking in the marble floors, the rich carpets and furnishings. The ceilings are high, the architecture modern but elegant. It's all glass and marble and stainless steel.

I've never been anywhere so beautiful.

And I haven't even had a moment to take it all in before I'm greeted by a thin, older man with even thinner brown hair.

The soldiers flanking me step back as he steps forward.

"Ms. Ferrars?" he says.

"Yes?"

"You are to come with me."

I hesitate. "Who are you?"

He studies me a moment and then seems to make a decision. "You may call me Delalieu."

"Okay," I say, the word disappearing into a whisper.

I follow Delalieu into a glass elevator and watch him use a key card to authorize the lift. Once we're in motion, I find the courage to speak.

"Where am I?" I ask. "What's happening?"

His answer comes automatically. "You are in Sector 45

headquarters. You're here to have a meeting with the chief commander and regent of Sector 45." He doesn't look at me when he speaks, but there's nothing in his tone that feels threatening. So I ask another question.

"Why?"

The elevator doors ping as they open. Delalieu finally turns to look at me. "You'll find out in just a moment."

I follow Delalieu down a hall and wait, quietly, outside a door while he knocks. He peeks his head inside when the door opens, announces his presence, and then motions for me to follow him in.

When I do, I'm surprised.

There's a beautiful man in military uniform—I'm assuming he's the commander—standing in front of a large, wooden desk, his arms crossed against his chest. He's staring me straight in the eye, and I'm suddenly so overwhelmed I feel myself blush.

I've never seen anyone so handsome before.

I look down, embarrassed, and study the laces of my tennis shoes. I'm grateful for my long hair. It serves as a dark, heavy curtain, shielding my face from view.

"Look at me."

The command is sharp and clear. I look up, nervously, to meet his eyes. He has thick, dark brown hair. Eyes like a storm. He looks at me for so long I feel goose bumps rise along my skin. He won't look away, and I feel more terrified by the moment. This man's eyes are full of anger. Darkness. There's something genuinely frightening about him, and my heart begins to hammer.

"You're growing up quickly," he says.

I stare at him, confused, but he's still studying my face.

"Fourteen years old," he says quietly. "Such a complicated age for a young girl." Finally, he sighs. Looks away. "It always breaks my heart to break beautiful things."

"I don't—I don't understand," I say, feeling suddenly ill.

He looks up again. "You're aware of what you did today?"

I freeze. Words pile up in my throat, die in my mouth.

"Yes or no?" he demands.

"Y-yes," I say quickly. "Yes."

"And do you know why you did it? Do you know how you did it?"

I shake my head, my eyes filling fast with tears. "It was an accident," I whisper. "I didn't know—I didn't know that this—"

"Does anyone else know about your sickness?"

"No." I stare at him, my eyes wide even as tears blur my vision. "I mean, n-not, not really—just my parents—but no one really understands what's wrong with me. I don't even understand—"

"You mean you didn't plan this? It wasn't your intention to murder the little boy?"

"No!" I cry out, and then clap both hands over my mouth. "No," I say, quietly now. "I was trying to help him. He'd fallen to the floor and I—I didn't know. I swear I didn't know."

"Liar."

I'm still shaking my head, wiping away tears with shaking hands. "It was an accident. I swear, I didn't mean to—I d-didn't—"

"Sir." It's Delalieu. His voice.

I didn't realize he was still in the room.

I sniff, hard, wiping quickly at my face, but my hands are still *shaking. I try, again, to swallow back the tears. To pull myself together.*

"Sir," Delalieu says more firmly, "perhaps we should conduct this interview elsewhere."

"I don't see why that's necessary."

"I don't mean to seem impertinent, sir, but I really feel that you might be better served conducting this interview privately."

I dare to turn, to look up at him. And that's when I notice the third person in the room.

A boy.

My breath catches in my throat with an almost audible gasp. A single tear escapes down my cheek and I brush it away, even as I stare at him. I can't help it—I can't look away. He has the kind of face I've never seen in real life. He's more handsome than the commander. More beautiful. Still, there's something unnerving about him, something cold and alien about his face that makes him difficult to look at. He's almost too perfect. He has a sharp jawline and sharp cheekbones and a sharp, straight nose. Everything about him reminds me of a blade. His face is pale. His eyes are a stunning, clear green, and he has rich, golden hair. And he's staring at me, his eyes wide with an emotion I can't decipher.

A throat clears.

The spell is broken.

Heat floods my face and I avert my eyes, mortified I didn't look away sooner.

I hear the commander mutter angrily under his breath. "Unbelievable," *he says.* "Always the same."

I look up.

"Aaron," he says sharply. "Get out."

The boy—his name must be Aaron—startles. He stares at the commander for a second, and then glances at the door. But he doesn't move.

"Delalieu, please escort my son from the room, as he seems presently unable to remember how to move his legs."

His son.

Wow. That explains the face.

"Yes, sir, of course, sir."

Aaron's expression is impossible to read. I catch him looking at me, just once more, and when he finds me staring, he frowns. It's not an unkind look.

Still, I turn away.

He and Delalieu move past me as they exit, and I pretend not to notice when I hear him whisper—

"Who is she?"

—as they walk away.

"Ella? Are you all right?"

I blink, slowly clearing the webbing of blackness obscuring my vision. Stars explode and fade behind my eyes and I try to stand, the carpet pressing popcorn impressions into my palms, metal digging into my flesh. I'm wearing manacles, glowing cuffs that emit a soft, blue light that leaches the life from my skin, makes my own hands seem sinister.

The woman at my door is staring at me. She smiles.

"Your father and I thought you might be hungry," she

says. "We made you dinner."

I can't move. My feet seem bolted in place, the pinks and purples of the walls and floors assaulting me from every corner. I'm standing in the middle of the bizarre museum of what was likely my childhood bedroom—staring at what might be my biological mother—and I feel like I might throw up. The lights are suddenly too bright, the voices too loud. Someone walks toward me and the movement feels exaggerated, the footsteps thudding hard and fast in my ears. My vision goes in and out and the walls seem to shake. The floor shifts, tilts backward.

I fall, hard, onto the floor.

For a minute, I hear nothing but my heartbeat. Loud, so loud, pressing in on me, assaulting me with a cacophony of sound so disturbing I double over, press my face into the carpet and scream.

I'm hysterical, my bones shaking in my skin, and the woman picks me up, reels me in, and I tear away, still screaming—

"Where is everyone?" I scream. "What's happening to me?" I scream. "Where am I? Where's Warner and Kenji and oh my God—*oh my God*—all those people—all those people I k-killed—"

Vomit inches up my throat, choking me, and I try and fail to suppress the images, the horrible, terrifying images of bodies cleaved open, blood snaking down ridges of poorly torn flesh and something pierces my mind, something sharp and blinding and suddenly I'm on my knees, heaving the meager contents of my stomach into a pink basket.

I can hardly breathe.

My lungs are overworked, my stomach still threatening to betray me, and I'm gasping, my hands shaking hard as I try to stand. I spin around, the room moving more quickly than I do, and I see only flashes of pink, flashes of purple.

I sway.

Someone catches me again, this time new arms, and the man who calls me his daughter holds me like I'm his child and he says, "Honey, you don't have to think about them anymore. You're safe now."

"Safe?" I rear back, eyes wild. "Who *are* you—?"

The woman takes my hand. Squeezes my fingers even as I wrench free from her grip. "I'm your mother," she says. "And I've decided it's time for you to come home."

"What"—I grab two fistfuls of her shirt—"have you done *with my friends*?" I scream. And then I shake her, shake her so hard she actually looks scared for a second, and then I try to pick her up and throw her into the wall but remember, with a start, that my powers have been cut off, that I have to rely on mere anger and adrenaline and I turn around, suddenly furious, feeling more certain by the second that I've begun to hallucinate, hallucinate, when

unexpectedly

she slaps me in the face.

Hard.

I blink, stunned, but manage to stay upright.

"Ella Sommers," she says sharply, "you will pull yourself

together." Her eyes flash as she appraises me. "What is this ridiculous, dramatic behavior? Worried about your *friends*? Those people are not your friends."

My cheek burns and half my mouth feels numb but I say, "Yes, yes they're my fr—"

She slaps me again.

My eyes close. Reopen. I feel suddenly dizzy.

"We are your parents," she says in a harsh whisper. "Your father and I have brought you home. You should be grateful."

I taste blood. I reach up, touch my lip. My fingers come away red. "Where's Emmaline?" Blood is pooling in my mouth and I spit it out, onto the floor. "Have you kidnapped her, too? Does she know what you've done? That you donated us to The Reestablishment? Sold our bodies to the world?"

A third, swift slap.

I feel it ring in my skull.

"*How dare you.*" My mother's face flushes crimson. "How *dare* you—You have no idea what we've built, all these years—The sacrifices we made for our *future*—"

"Now, Evie," my dad says, and places a calming hand on her shoulder. "Everything is going to be okay. Ella just needs a little time to settle in, that's all." He glances at me. "Isn't that right, Ella?"

It hits me then, in that moment. Everything. It hits me, all at once, with a frightening, destabilizing force—

I've been kidnapped by a pair of crazy people and I might

never see my friends again. In fact, my friends might be dead. My *parents* might've killed them. All of them.

The realization is like suffocation.

Tears fill my throat, my mouth, my eyes—

"Where," I say, my chest heaving, "is Warner? What did you do to him?"

Evie's expression goes suddenly murderous. "You and that damn boy. If I have to hear his name one more time—"

"Where's Warner?" I'm screaming again. "Where is he? Where's Kenji? What did you do with them?"

Evie looks suddenly exhausted. She pinches the bridge of her nose between her thumb and index finger.

"Darling," she says, but she isn't looking at me, she's looking at my father. "Will you handle this, please? I have a terrible headache and several urgent phone calls to return."

"Of course, my love." And he pulls a syringe from his pocket and stabs it, swiftly, into my neck.

KENJI

The common room is really growing on me.

I used to walk by, all the time, and wonder why Warner ever thought we'd need a common room this big. There's tons of seating and a lot of room to spread out, but I always thought it was a waste of space. I secretly wished Warner had used the square footage for our bedrooms.

Now I get it.

When Nazeera and I walk in, ten minutes late to the impromptu pizza party, everyone is here. *Brendan* is here. He's sitting in a corner being fussed over by Castle and Alia, and I nearly tackle him. I don't, of course, because it's obvious he's still in recovery, but I'm relieved to find that he looks okay. Mostly he looks wrung-out, but he's not wearing a sling or anything, so I'm guessing the girls didn't run into any problems when they were patching him up. That's a great sign.

I spot Winston walking across the room and I catch up to him, clap him on the back. "Hey," I say, when he turns around. "You okay?"

He's balancing a couple of paper plates, both of which are already sagging under the weight of too much pizza, and he smiles with his whole face when he says, "I hate today.

Today is a garbage fire. I hate everything about today except for the fact that Brendan is okay and we have pizza. Other than that, today can go straight to hell."

"Yeah. I feel that so much." And then, after a pause, I say quietly: "So I'm guessing you never had that conversation with Brendan, huh?"

Winston goes suddenly pink. "I said I was waiting for the right time. Does this seem like the right time to you?"

"Good point." I sigh. "I guess I was just hoping you had some good news. We could all use some good news right now."

Winston shoots me a sympathetic look. "No word on Juliette?"

I shake my head. Feel suddenly sick. "Has anyone told you her real name is Ella?"

"I heard," Winston says, raising his eyebrows. "That whole story is batshit."

"Yeah," I say. "Today is the worst."

"Fuck today," Winston says.

"Don't forget about tomorrow," I say. "Tomorrow's going to suck, too."

"What? Why?" The paper plates in Winston's hands are going translucent from pizza grease. "What's happening tomorrow?"

"Last I heard we were jumping ship," I say. "Running for our lives. I'm assuming it's going to suck."

"*Shit*." Winston nearly drops his plates. "Seriously? Brendan needs more time to rest." Then, after a beat:

"Where are we going to go?"

"The other side of the continent, apparently," Ian says as he walks over.

He hands me a plate of pizza. I murmur a quick thanks and stare at the pizza, wondering whether I'd be able to shove the whole thing in my mouth at once. Probably not.

"Do you know something we don't?" Winston says to Ian, his glasses slipping down the bridge of his nose. Winston tries, unsuccessfully, to shove them back up with his forearm, and Ian steps up to do it for him.

"I know a lot of things you don't know," Ian says. "The first of which is that Kenji was definitely hooking up with Nazeera, like, five seconds ago."

My mouth nearly falls open before I remember there's food in it. I swallow, too quickly, and choke. I'm still coughing as I look around, panicking that Nazeera might be within earshot. Only when I spot her across the room speaking with Sonya and Sara do I finally relax.

I glare at Ian. "What the hell is wrong with you?"

Winston, at least, has the decency to whisper-yell when he says, "You were hooking up with Nazeera? We were only gone a few hours!"

"I did not hook up with Nazeera," I lie.

Ian takes a bite of pizza. "Whatever, bro. No judgment. The world's on fire. Have some fun."

"We didn't"—I sigh, look away—"it wasn't like that. It's not even anything. We were just, like—" I make some random gesture with my hand that means exactly nothing.

Ian raises his eyebrows.

"Okay," Winston says, shooting me a look. "We'll talk about the Nazeera thing later." He turns to Ian. "What's happening tomorrow?"

"We bail," Ian says. "Be ready to go at dawn."

"Right, I heard that part," Winston says, "but where are we going?"

Ian shrugs. "Castle has the news," he says. "That's all I heard. He was waiting for Kenji and Nazeera to put their clothes back on before he told everyone the details."

I tilt my head at Ian, threatening him with a single look. "Nothing is going on with me and Nazeera," I say. "Drop it."

"All right," he says, picking at his pizza. "Makes sense. I mean she's not even that pretty."

My plate falls out of my hand. Pizza hits the floor. I feel a sudden, unwelcome need to punch Ian in the face. "Are you—Are you out of your mind? Not even—She's, like, the most beautiful woman I've ever seen in my *life*, and you're out here saying she's *not even that pretty*? Have y—"

"See what I'm saying?" Ian cuts me off. He's looking at Winston.

"Wow," Winston says, staring solemnly at the pizza on the ground. "Yeah, Kenji is definitely full of shit."

I drag a hand across my face. "I hate you guys."

"Anyway," Ian says, "I heard Castle's news has something to do with Nouria."

My head snaps back up.

Nouria.

I nearly forgot. This morning, just before the symposium, the twins told me they'd uncovered something—something to do with the poison in the bullets Juliette had been shot with—that led them back to Nouria.

But so much happened today that I never had the chance to follow up. Find out what happened.

"Did you hear about that?" Ian asks me, raising an eyebrow. "She sent a message, apparently. That's what the girls are saying."

"Yeah," I say, and frown. "I heard."

I honestly have no idea how this might shake out.

It's been at least ten years since the last time Castle saw his daughter, Nouria. Darrence and Jabari, his two boys, were murdered by police officers when they refused to let the men into their house without a warrant. This was before The Reestablishment took over.

Castle wasn't home that day, but Nouria was.

She watched it happen. Castle said he felt like he'd lost three children that day. Nouria never recovered. Instead, she grew detached. Listless. She stopped coming home at normal hours and then—one day—she disappeared. The Reestablishment was always picking kids up off the street and shipping them wherever they felt there was a need to fill. Nouria was collected against her will; picked up and packaged for another sector. Castle knew for certain that it happened, because The Reestablishment sent him a receipt for his child. A fucking receipt.

Everyone from Point knew Castle's story. He always

made an effort to be honest, to share the hardest, most painful memories from his life so that the rest of us didn't feel like we were suffering alone.

Castle thought he'd never see Nouria again.

So if she's reaching out now—

Just then, Castle catches my eye. He glances at me, then at Nazeera. A hint of a smile touches his lips and then it's gone, his spine straight as he addresses the room. He looks good, I realize. He looks bright, alive like I haven't seen him in years. His locs are pulled back, tied neatly at the base of his neck. His faded blue blazer still fits him perfectly, even after all these years.

"I have news," he says.

But I'm pretty sure I know what's coming next.

Nouria lives in Sector 241, thousands of miles away, and cross-sector communication is nearly unheard of. Only rebel groups are brave enough to risk sending coded messages across the continent. Ian and Winston know this. I know this.

Everyone knows this.

Which means Castle is probably here to tell us that Nouria has gone rogue.

Ha.

Like father, like daughter.

WARNER

"Hi," I say.

She turns at the sound of my voice and startles when she sees my face. Her eyes widen. And I feel it, right away, when her emotions change.

She's attracted to me.

She's attracted to me, and the revelation makes me happy. I don't know why. It's not new. I learned, long ago, that lots of people find me attractive. Men. Women. Especially older women, a phenomenon I still don't understand. But this—

It makes me happy.

"Hi," she says, but she won't look at me.

I realize she's blushing. I'm surprised. There's something sweet about her, something gentle and sweet I wasn't really expecting.

"Are you doing all right?" I ask.

It's a stupid question. The girl is clearly in an awful position. Right now she's only in our custody for as long as it takes my father to decide what to do with her. She's currently in a fairly comfortable holding facility here on base, but she'll likely end up in a juvenile detention center. I'm not sure. I've heard my father talk about running more tests on her first. Her parents are apparently hysterical, desperate for us to take her in and deal with her. Offer a diagnosis. They think she killed the little boy on purpose. They *think their daughter is insane.*

I think she seems just fine.

I can't stop looking at her. My eyes travel her face more than once, studying her features carefully. She seems so familiar to me, like I might've seen her before. Maybe in a dream.

I'm aware, even as I think it, that my thoughts are ridiculous.

But I was drawn down here, magnetized to her by something beyond my control. I know I shouldn't have come. I have no business talking to her, and if my father found me in here he'd likely murder me. But I've tried, for days, to forget her face, and I couldn't. I try to sleep at night and her likeness materializes in the blackness. I needed to see her again.

I don't know how to defend it.

Finally, she speaks, and I shake free from my reverie. I remind myself that I've asked her a question.

"Yes, thank you," she says, her eyes on the floor. "I'm doing fine."

She's lying.

I want her to look up, to meet my eyes. She doesn't, and I find it frustrating.

"Will you look at me?" I say.

That works well enough.

But when she looks me directly in the eye I feel my heart go suddenly, terrifyingly still. A skipped beat. A moment of death.

And then—

Fast. My heart is racing too fast.

I've never understood my ability to be so aware of others, but it's often served me well. In most cases, it offers me an advantage.

In this case, it's nothing short of overwhelming.

Right now, everything is hitting me twice as hard. I feel two sets of emotions—hers and mine, the both of them intertwined. We seem to be feeling the same things at the same time. It's disorienting, so heady I can hardly catch my breath.

"Why?" she says.

I blink. "What?"

"Why do you want me to look at you?"

I take a breath. Clear my head, consider my options. I could tell the truth. I could tell a lie. I could be evasive, change the subject.

Finally, I say, "Do I know you?"

She laughs and looks away. "No," she says. "Definitely not."

She bites her lip and I feel her sudden nervousness, hear the spike in her breathing. I draw closer to her almost without realizing it.

She looks up at me then, and I realize, with a thrill, how close we are. Her eyes are big and beautiful, blue green. Like the globe, I think. Like the whole world.

She's looking at me and I feel suddenly off-balance.

"What's wrong?" she says.

I have to step away from her. "I don't—" I look at her again. "Are you sure I don't know you?"

And she smiles. Smiles at me and my heart shatters.

"Trust me," she says. "I'd remember you."

KENJI

Delalieu.

I can't believe we forgot about Delalieu.

I thought Castle's news would be about Nouria. I thought he was going to tell us that she reached out to say that she was some fancy resistance leader now, that we'd be welcome to crash at her place for a while. Instead, Castle's news was—

Delalieu.

Homeboy came through.

Castle steps aside and allows the lieutenant to enter the room, and even though he seems stiff and out of place, Delalieu looks genuinely upset. I feel it, like a punch to the gut, the moment I see his face. *Grief.*

He clears his throat two or three times.

When he finally speaks, his voice is steadier than I've ever heard it. "I've come to reassure you," he says, "in person, that I'll make sure your group remains safe here, for as long as I can manage." A pause. "I don't know yet exactly what's happening right now, but I know it can't be good. I'm worried it won't end well if you stay, and I'm committed to helping you while you plan your escape."

Everyone is quiet.

"Um, thank you," I say, breaking the silence. I look around the room when I say, "We really appreciate that. But, uh, how much time do we have?"

Delalieu shakes his head. "I'm afraid I can't guarantee your safety for more than a week. But I'm hoping a few days' reprieve will give you the necessary time to figure out your next steps. Find a safe place to go. In the meantime, I'll provide whatever assistance I can."

"Okay," Ian says, but he looks skeptical. "That's really . . . generous."

Delalieu clears his throat again. "It must be hard to know whether you should trust me. I understand your concerns. But I fear I've stayed silent for t-too long," he says, his voice losing its steadiness. "And now—with—With what's happened to Warner and to Ms. Ferrars—" He stops, his voice breaking on the last word. He looks up, looks me in the eye. "I'm sure Warner told none of you that I am his grandfather."

My jaw drops open. Actually drops open.

Castle is the only person in the room who doesn't look shocked.

"You're Warner's grandfather?" Adam says, getting to his feet. The terrified look in his eyes breaks my heart.

"Yes," Delalieu says quietly. "On his mother's side." He meets Adam's eyes, acknowledging, silently, that he knows. Knows that Adam is Anderson's illegitimate son. That he knows everything.

Adam sits back down, relief apparent on his face.

"I can only imagine what an unhappy life yours must've been," Brendan says. I turn to look at him, surprised to hear his voice. He's been so quiet all this time. But then, of course Brendan would be compassionate. Even to someone like Delalieu, who stepped aside and said nothing while Anderson set the world on fire. "But I'm grateful—we're all grateful," Brendan says, "for your help today."

Delalieu manages a smile. "It's the least I can do," he says, and turns to go.

"Did you know her?" Lily says, her voice sharp. "As Ella?"

Delalieu freezes in place, still half turned toward the exit.

"Because if you're Warner's grandfather," Lily says, "and you've been working under Anderson for this long—you must've known her."

Slowly, very slowly, Delalieu turns to face us. He seems tense, nervous like I've never seen him. He says nothing, but the answer is written all over his face. The twitch in his hands.

Jesus.

"How long?" I say, anger building inside of me. "How long did you know her and say nothing?"

"I don't—I d-don't—"

"*How long?*" I say, my hand already reaching for the gun tucked in the waistband of my pants.

Delalieu takes a jerky step backward. "Please don't," he says, his eyes wild. "Please don't ask this of me. I can give you aid. I can provide you with weapons and transportation—anything you need—but I can't—You don't underst—"

"*Coward,*" Nazeera says, standing up. She looks stunning,

tall and strong and steady. I love watching that girl move. Talk. Breathe. Whatever. "You watched and said nothing as Anderson tortured his own children. Didn't you?"

"No," Delalieu says desperately, his face flushing with emotion I've never seen in him before. "No, that's not—"

Castle picks up a chair with single flick of his hand and drops it, unceremoniously, in front of Delalieu.

"Sit down," he says, a violent, unguarded rage flashing in his eyes.

Delalieu obeys.

"How long?" I say again. "How long have you known her as Ella?"

"I—I've"—Delalieu hesitates, looks around—"I've known Ella s-since she was a child," he says finally.

I feel the blood leave my body.

His clear, explicit confession is too much. It means too much. I sag under the weight of it—the lies, the conspiracies. I sink back into my chair and my heart splinters for Juliette, for all she's suffered at the hands of the people meant to protect her. I can't form the words I need to tell Delalieu he's a spineless piece of shit. It's Nazeera who still has the presence of mind to spear him.

Her voice is soft—lethal—when she speaks.

"You've known Ella since she was a child," Nazeera says. "You've been here, working here, helping Anderson since Ella was a *child*. That means you helped Anderson put her in the custody of abusive, adoptive parents and you stood by as they tortured her, as Anderson tortured her, over and over—"

"No," Delalieu cries out. "I d-didn't condone any of that. Ella was supposed to grow up in a normal home environment. She was supposed to be given nurturing parents and a stable upbringing. Those were the terms everyone agreed t—"

"Bullshit," Nazeera says, her eyes flashing. "You know as well as I do that her adoptive parents were monsters—"

"Paris changed the terms of the agreement," Delalieu shouts angrily.

Nazeera raises an eyebrow, unmoved.

But something seems to have loosened Delalieu's tongue, something like fear or guilt or pent-up rage, because suddenly the words rush out of him.

"Paris went back on his word as soon as Ella was in his custody," he says. "He thought no one would find out. Back then he and I were about the same, as far as rank went, in The Reestablishment. We often worked closely together because of our family ties, and I was, as a result, privy to the choices he made."

Delalieu shakes his head.

"But I discovered too late that he purposely chose adoptive parents who exhibited abusive, dangerous behavior. When I confronted him about it he argued that any abuse Ella suffered at the hands of her surrogate parents would only encourage her powers to manifest, and he had the statistics to support his claim. I tried to voice my concerns—I reported him; I told the council of commanders that he was hurting her, *breaking* her—but he made my concerns sound like the desperate histrionics of someone unwilling to do what was necessary for the cause."

I can see the color creeping up Delalieu's neck, his anger only barely contained.

"I was repeatedly overruled. Demoted. I was punished for questioning his tactics.

"But I knew Paris was wrong," he says quietly. "Ella withered. When I first met her she was a strong girl with a joyful spirit. She was unfailingly kind and upbeat." He hesitates. "It wasn't long before she grew cold and closed-off. Withdrawn. Paris moved up in rank quickly, and I was soon relegated to little more than his right hand. I was the one he sent to check on her at home, at school. I was ordered to monitor her behavior, write the reports outlining her progress.

"But there were no results. Her spirit had been broken. I begged Paris to put her elsewhere—to, at the very least, return her to a regular facility, one that I might oversee personally—and still he insisted, over and over again, that the abuse she suffered would spur results." Delalieu is on his feet now, pacing. "He was hoping to impress the council, hoping his efforts would be rewarded with yet another promotion. It soon became his single task to wait, to have me watch Ella closely for developments, for any sign that she'd changed. Evolved." He stops in place. Swallows, hard. "But Paris was careless."

Delalieu drops his head into his hands.

The room around us has gone so quiet I can almost

hear the seconds pass. We're all waiting for him to keep going, but he doesn't lift his head. I'm studying him—his shaking hands, the tremble in his legs, his general loss of composure—and my heart hammers in my chest. I feel like he's about to break. Like he's close to telling us something important.

"What do you mean?" I say quietly. "Careless how?"

Delalieu looks up, his eyes red-rimmed and wild.

"I mean *it was his one job*," he says, slamming his fist against the wall. He hits it, hard, his knuckles breaking through the plaster, and for a moment, I'm genuinely stunned. I didn't think Delalieu had it in him.

"You don't understand," he says, losing the fire. He stumbles back, sags against the wall. "My greatest regret in life has been watching those kids suffer and doing nothing about it."

"Wait," Winston says. "Which kids? Who are you talking about?"

But Delalieu doesn't seem to hear him. He only shakes his head. "Paris never took Ella's assignment seriously. It was his fault she lost control. It was his fault she didn't know better, it was his fault she hadn't been prepared or trained or properly guarded. It was his fault she killed that little boy," he says, now so broken his voice is shaking. "What she did that day nearly destroyed her. Nearly ruined the entire operation. Nearly exposed us to the world."

He closes his eyes, presses his fingers to his temples. And then he sinks back down into his chair. He looks unmoored.

Castle and I share a knowing glance from across the room. Something is happening. Something is about to happen.

Delalieu is a resource we never realized we had. And for all his protests, he actually seems like he wants to talk. Maybe Delalieu is the key. Maybe he can tell us what we need to know about—about everything. About Juliette, about Anderson, about The Reestablishment. It's obvious a dam broke open in Delalieu. I'm just hoping we can keep him talking.

It's Adam who says, "If you hated Anderson so much, why didn't you stop him when you had the chance?"

"Don't you understand?" Delalieu says, his eyes big and round and sad. "I *never* had the chance. I didn't have the authority, and we'd only just been voted into power. Leila— my daughter—was sicker every day and I was—I wasn't myself. I was unraveling. I suspected foul play in her illness but had no proof. I spent my work hours overseeing the crumbling mental and physical health of an innocent young woman, and I spent my free hours watching my daughter die."

"Those are excuses," Nazeera says coldly. "You were a coward."

He looks up. "Yes," he says. "That's true. I was a coward." He shakes his head, turns away. "I said nothing, even when Paris spun Ella's tragedy into a victory. He told everyone that what Ella did to that boy was a blessing in disguise. That, in fact, it was exactly what he'd been working toward.

He argued that what she did that day, regardless of the consequences, was the exact manifestation of her powers he'd been hoping for all along." Delalieu looks suddenly sick. "He got away with everything. Everything he ever wanted, he was given. And he was always reckless. He did lazy work, all the while using Ella as a pawn to fulfill his own sadistic desires."

"Please be more specific," Castle says coolly. "Anderson had a great deal of sadistic desires. Which are you referring to?"

Delalieu goes pale. His voice is lower, weaker, when he says, "Paris has always been perversely fond of destroying his own son. I never understood it. I never understood his need to break that boy. He tortured him a thousand different ways, but when Paris discovered the depth of Aaron's emotional connection to Ella, he used it to drive that boy near to madness."

"That's why he shot her," I say, remembering what Juliette—Ella—told me after Omega Point was bombed. "Anderson wanted to kill her to teach Warner a lesson. Right?"

But something changes in Delalieu's face. Transforms him, sags him down. And then he laughs—a sad, broken laugh. "You don't understand, you don't understand, *you don't understand*," he cries, shaking his head. "You think these recent events are everything. You think Aaron fell in love with your friend of several months, a rebel girl named Juliette. You don't know. You don't know. You don't know that Aaron has been in love with Ella for the better part of his entire life. They've known each other since childhood."

Adam makes a sound. A stunned sound of disbelief.

"Okay, I have to be honest—I don't get it," Ian says. He steals a wary glance at Nazeera before he says, "Nazeera said Anderson has been wiping their memories. If that's true, then how could Warner be in love with her for so long? Why would Anderson wipe their memories, tell them all about how they know each other, and then wipe their memories again?"

Delalieu is shaking his head. A strange smile begins to form on his face, the kind of shaky, terrified smile that isn't a smile at all. "No. *No*. You don't—" He sighs, looks away. "Paris has never told either of them about their shared history. The reason he had to keep wiping their memories was because it didn't matter how many times he reset the story or remade the introductions—Aaron always fell in love with her. Every time.

"In the beginning Paris thought it was a fluke. He found it almost funny. Entertaining. But the more it happened, the more it began to drive Paris insane. He thought there was something wrong with Aaron—that there was something wrong with him on a genetic level, that he'd been plagued by a sickness. He wanted to crush what he saw as a weakness."

"Wait," Adam says, holding up his hands. "What do you mean, *the more it happened*? How many times did it happen?"

"At least several times."

Adam looks shell-shocked. "They met and fell in love

several times?"

Delalieu takes a shaky breath. "I don't know that they always fell in love, exactly. Paris seldom let them spend that much time alone. But they were always drawn together. It was obvious, every time he put them in the same room, they were like"—Delalieu claps his hands—"magnets."

Delalieu shakes his head at Adam.

"I'm sorry to be the one to tell you all this. I'm sure it's painful to hear, especially considering your history with Ella. It's not fair that you were pulled into Paris's games. He never should've p—"

"Whoa, whoa—Wait. What games?" Adam says, stunned. "What are you talking about?"

Delalieu runs a hand across his sweaty forehead. He looks like he's melting, crumbling under pressure. Maybe someone should get him some water.

"There's too much," he says wearily. "Too much to tell. Too much to explain." He shakes his head. "I'm sorry, I—"

"I need you to try," Adam says, his eyes flashing. "Are you saying our relationship was fake? That everything she said—everything she felt was fake?"

"No," Delalieu says quickly, even as he uses his shirtsleeve to wipe the sweat from his face. "No. As far as I'm aware, her feelings for you were as real as anything else. You came into her life at a particularly difficult time, and your kindness and affection no doubt meant a great deal to her." He sighs. "I only mean that it wasn't coincidence that both of Paris's boys fell in love with the same girl. Paris liked toying with things. He liked cutting things open to study them. He liked experiments. And Paris pit you and Warner against each other on *purpose*.

"He planted the soldier at your lunch table who let slip that Warner was monitoring a girl with a lethal touch. He sent another to speak with you, to ask you about your history with her, to appeal to your protective nature by discussing Aaron's plans for her—Do you remember? You were persuaded, from every angle, to apply for the position. When you did, Paris pulled your application from the pile and encouraged Aaron to interview you. He then made it clear that you should be chosen as her cellmate. He let Aaron think he was making all his own decisions as CCR of Sector 45—but Paris was always there, manipulating everything. I watched it happen."

Adam looks so stunned it takes him a moment to speak. "So . . . he knew? My dad always knew about me? Knew where I was—what I was doing?"

"Knew?" Delalieu frowns. "Paris *orchestrated* your lives. That was the plan, from the beginning." He looks at Nazeera. "All the children of the supreme commanders were to become case studies. You were engineered to be soldiers. You and James," he says to Adam, "were unexpected, but he made plans for you, too."

"What?" Adam goes white. "What's his plan for me and James?"

"This, I honestly don't know."

Adam sits back in his chair, looking suddenly ill.

"Where is Ella now?" Winston says sharply. "Do you know where they're keeping her?"

Delalieu shakes his head. "All I know is that she can't be dead."

"What do you mean she *can't* be dead?" I ask. "Why not?"

"Ella's and Emmaline's powers are critical to the regime," he says. "Critical to the continuation of everything we've been working toward. The Reestablishment was built with the promise of Ella and Emmaline. Without them, Operation Synthesis means nothing."

Castle bolts upright. His eyes are wide. "Operation Synthesis," he says breathlessly, "has to do with *Ella*?"

"The Architect and the Executioner," Delalieu says. "It—"

Delalieu falls back with a small, surprised gasp, his head hitting the back of his chair. Everything, suddenly, seems to slow down.

I feel my heart rate slow. I feel the world slow. I feel formed from water, watching the scene unfold in slow motion, frame by frame.

A bullet between his eyes.

Blood trickling down his forehead.

A short, sharp scream.

"You traitorous son of a bitch," someone says.

I'm seeing it, but I don't believe it.

Anderson is here.

JULIETTE

I'm given no explanations.

My father doesn't invite me to dinner, like Evie promised. He doesn't sit me down to offer me long histories about my presence or his; he doesn't reveal groundbreaking information about my life or the other supreme commanders or even the nearly six hundred people I just murdered. He and Evie are acting like the horrors of the last seventeen years never happened. Like *nothing* strange has ever happened, like I never stopped being their daughter—not in the ways that matter, anyway.

I don't know what was in that needle, but the effects are unlike anything I've experienced. I feel both awake and asleep, like I'm spinning in place, like there's too much grease turning the wheels in my brain and I try to speak and realize my lips no longer move on command. My father carries my limp body into a blindingly silver room, props me up in a chair, straps me down, and panic pours into me, hot and terrifying, flooding my mind. I try to scream. Fail. My brain is slowly disconnecting from my body, like I'm being removed from myself. Only basic, instinctual functions seem to work. Swallowing. Breathing.

Crying.

Tears fall quietly down my face and my father whistles a tune, his movements light and easy even as he sets up an IV drip. He moves with such startling efficiency I don't even realize he's removed my manacles until I see the scalpel.

A flash of silver.

The blade is so sharp he meets no resistance as he slices clean lines into my forearms and blood, blood, heavy and warm, spills down my wrists and into my open palms and it doesn't seem real, not even when he stabs several electrical wires into my exposed flesh.

The pain arrives just seconds later.

Pain.

It begins at my feet, blooms up my legs, unfurls in my stomach and works its way up my throat only to explode behind my eyes, *inside my brain*, and I cry out, but only in my mind, my useless hands still limp on the armrests, and I'm so certain he's going to kill me—

but then he smiles.

And then he's gone.

I lie in agony for what feels like hours.

I watch, through a delirious fog, as blood drips off my fingertips, each drop feeding the crimson pools growing in the folds of my pants. Visions assault me, memories of a girl I might've been, scenes with people I might've known. I want to believe they're hallucinations, but I can't be certain of anything anymore. I don't know if Max and Evie are planting things in my mind. I don't know that I can trust anything I might've once believed about myself.

I can't stop thinking about Emmaline.

I'm adrift, suspended in a pool of senselessness, but something about her keeps tugging, sparking my nerves, errant currents pushing me to the surface of something—an emotional revelation—that trembles into existence only to evaporate, seconds later, as if it might be terrified to exist.

This goes on and on and on and on and on

Lightyears.

Eons.

over

and

over

    whispers of clarity

        g a s p s o f o x y g e n

and I'm tossed back out to sea.

Bright, white lights flicker above my head, buzzing in unison with the low, steady hum of engines and cooling units. Everything smells sharp, like antiseptic. Nausea makes my head swim. I squeeze my eyes shut, the only command my body will obey.

Me and Emmaline at the zoo

Me and Emmaline, first trip on a plane
Me and Emmaline, learning to swim
Me and Emmaline, getting our hair cut

Images of Emmaline fill my mind, moments from the first years of our lives, details of her face I never knew I could conjure. I don't understand it. I don't know where they're coming from. I can only imagine that Evie put these images here, but why Evie would want me to see *this*, I don't understand. Scenes play through my head like I might be flipping through a photo album, and they make me miss my sister. They make me remember Evie as my mother. Make me remember I had a family.

Maybe Evie wants me to reminisce.

My blood has hit the floor. I hear it, the familiar drip, the sound like a broken faucet, the slow

tap

tap

of tepid fluid on tile.

Emmaline and I held hands everywhere we went, often wearing matching outfits. We had the same long brown hair, but her eyes were pure blue, and she was a few inches taller than me. We were only a year apart, but she looked so much older. Even then, there was something in her eyes that looked hard. Serious. She held my hand like she was trying to protect me. Like maybe she knew more than I did.

Where are you? I wonder. *What did they do to you?*

I have no idea where I am. No idea what they've done

to me. No idea of the hour or the day, and pain blisters everywhere. I feel like a live wire, like my nerves have been stapled to the outside of my body, sensitive to every minute change in environment. I exhale and it hurts. Twitch and it takes my breath away.

And then, in a flash of movement, my mother returns.

The door opens and the motion forces a gentle rush of air into the room, a whisper of a breeze, gentle even as it grazes my skin, and somehow the sensation is so unbearable I'm certain I'll scream.

I don't.

"Feeling better?" she says.

Evie is holding a silver box. I try to look more closely but the pain is in my eyes now. Searing.

"You must be wondering why you're here," she says softly. I hear her working on something, glass and metal touching together, coming apart, touching together, coming apart. "But you must be patient, little bird. You might not even get to stay."

I close my eyes.

I feel her cold, slender fingers on my face just seconds before she yanks my eyelids back. Swiftly, she replaces her fingers with sharp, steel clamps, and I muster only a low, guttural sound of agony.

"Keep your eyes open, Ella. Now's not the time to fall asleep."

Even then, in that painful, terrifying moment, the words sound familiar. Strange and familiar. I can't figure out why.

"Before we make any concrete plans to keep you here, I need to make sure"—she tugs on a pair of latex gloves—"that you're still viable. See how you've held up after all these years."

Her words send waves of dread coursing through me.

Nothing has changed.

Nothing has changed.

I'm still no more than a receptacle. My body exchanges hands exchanges hands in exchange for what

My mother has no love for me.

What has she done to my sister.

"Where is Emmaline?" I try to scream, but the words don't leave my mouth. They expand in my head, explosive and angry, pressing against the ridges of my mind even as my lips refuse to obey me.

Dying.

The word occurs to me suddenly, as if it were something I've just remembered, the answer to a question I forgot existed.

I don't comprehend it.

Evie is standing in front of me again.

She touches my hair, sifts through the short, coarse strands like she might be panning for gold. The physical contact is excruciating.

"Unacceptable," she says. "This is unacceptable."

She turns away, makes notes in a tablet she pulls out of

her lab coat. Roughly, she takes my chin in her hand, lifts my face toward hers.

Evie counts my teeth. Runs the tip of one finger along my gums. She examines the insides of my cheeks, the underside of my tongue. Satisfied, she rips off the gloves, the latex making harsh snapping sounds that collide and echo, shattering the air around me.

A mechanical purr fills my ears and I realize Evie is adjusting my chair. I was previously in a reclining position, now I'm flat on my back. She takes a pair of shears to my clothes, cutting straight through my pants, my shirt, my sleeves.

Fear threatens to rip my chest open, but I only lie there, a perfect vegetable, as she strips me down.

Finally, Evie steps back.

I can't see what's happening. The hum of an engine builds into a roar. Sounds like scissors, slicing the air. And then: Sheets of glass materialize at the edges of my vision, move toward me from all sides. They lock into place easily, seams sealing shut with a cool *click* sound.

I'm being burned alive.

Heat like I've never known it, fire I can't see or stop. I don't know how it's happening but I feel it. I *smell* it. The scent of charred flesh fills my nose, threatens to upend the contents of my stomach. The top layer of skin is being slowly singed off my body. Blood beads along my body like morning dew, and a fine mist follows the heat, cleansing and cooling. Steam fogs up the glass around me and then, just when I think I might die from the pain, the glass fissures open with a sudden gasp.

I wish she would just kill me.

Instead, Evie is meticulous. She catalogs my every physical detail, making notes, constantly, in her pocket tablet. For the most part, she seems frustrated with her assessment. My arms and legs are too weak, she says. My shoulders too tense, my hair too short, my hands too scarred, my nails too chipped, my lips too chapped, my torso too long.

"We made you too beautiful," she says, shaking her head at my naked body. She prods at my hips, the balls of my feet. "Beauty can be a terrifying weapon, if you know how to wield it. But all this seems deeply unnecessary now." She makes another note.

When she looks at me again, she looks thoughtful.

"I gave this to you," she says. "Do you understand? This container you live in. I grew it, shaped it. You belong to me. Your life belongs to me. It's very important that you understand that."

Rage, sharp and hot, sears through my chest.

Carefully, Evie cracks open the silver box. Inside are dozens of slim glass cylinders. "Do you know what these are?" she says, lifting a few vials of shimmering, white liquid. "Of course you don't."

Evie studies me awhile.

"We did it wrong the first time," she finally says. "We didn't expect emotional health to supersede the physical in such dramatic fashion. We expected stronger minds, from both of you. Of course—" Evie hesitates. "She was the superior specimen, your sister. Infinitely superior. You were always a bit doe-eyed as a child. A little moonier than I'd have liked. Emmaline, on the other hand, was pure fire. We never dreamed she'd deteriorate so quickly. Her failures have been a great personal disappointment."

I inhale sharply and choke on something hot and wet in my throat. Blood. So much blood.

"But then," Evie says with a sigh, "such is the situation. We must be adaptable to the unexpected. Amenable to change when necessary."

Evie hits a switch and something seizes inside of me. I feel my spine straighten, my jaw go slack. Blood is now bubbling up my throat in earnest, and I don't know whether to let it up or swallow it down. I cough, violently, and blood spatters across my face. My arms. Drips down my chest, my fresh pink skin.

My mother drops into a crouch. She takes my chin in her hand and forces me to look at her. "You are far too full of emotion," she says softly. "You feel too much for this world. You call people your friends. You imagine yourself in love." She shakes her head slowly. "That was never the plan for you, little bird. You were meant for a solitary existence. We put you in isolation on purpose." She blinks. "Do you understand?"

I'm hardly breathing. My tongue feels rough and heavy, foreign in my mouth. I swallow my own blood and it's revolting, thick and lukewarm, gelatinous with saliva.

"If Aaron were anyone else's son," she says, "I would've had him executed. I'd have him executed right now, if I could. Unfortunately, I alone do not have the authority."

A force of feeling seizes my body.

I'm half horror, half joy. I didn't know I had any hope left that Warner was alive until just this moment.

The feeling is explosive.

It takes root inside of me. Hope catches fire in my blood, a feeling more powerful than these drugs, more powerful than myself. I cling to it with my whole heart, and, suddenly, I'm able to feel my hands. I don't know why or how but I feel a quiet strength surge up my spine.

Evie doesn't notice.

"I regret our mistakes," she's saying. "I regret the oversights that seem so obvious now. We couldn't have known so many years ago that things would turn out like this. We didn't expect to be blindsided by something so flimsy as your emotions. We couldn't have known, at the onset, that things would escalate in this way.

"Paris," she says, "had convinced everyone that bringing you on base in Sector 45 would be beneficial to us all, that he'd be able to monitor you in a new environment rife with experiences that would motivate your powers to evolve. Your father and I thought it was a stupid plan, stupider still for placing you under the direct supervision of a nineteen-year-old boy with whom your history was . . . complicated." She looks away. Shakes her head. "But Anderson delivered results. With Aaron you made progress at a rate we'd only dreamed of, and we were forced to let it be. Still," she says. "It backfired."

Her eyes linger, for a moment, on my shaved head.

"There are few people, even in our inner circle, who really understand what we're doing here. Your father understands. Ibrahim understands. But Paris, for security reasons, was never told everything about you. He wasn't yet a supreme commander when we gave him the job, and we decided to keep him informed on a need-to-know basis. Another mistake," Evie says, her voice both sad and terrifying.

She presses the back of her hand to her forehead.

"Six months and everything falls apart. You run away. You join some ridiculous gang. You drag Aaron into all of this and Paris, the oblivious fool, tries to *kill* you. Twice. I nearly slit his throat for his idiocy, but my mercy may as well have been for nothing, what with your attempt to murder him. Oh, Ella," she says, and sighs. "You've caused me a great deal of trouble this year. The paperwork alone." She closes her eyes. "I've had the same splitting headache for six months."

She opens her eyes. Looks at me for a long time.

"And now," she says, gesturing at me with the tablet in her hand, "there's this. Emmaline needs to be replaced, and we're not even sure you're a suitable substitute. Your body is operating at *maybe* sixty-five percent efficiency, and your mind is a complete disaster." She stops. A vein jumps in her forehead. "Perhaps it's impossible for you to understand how I'm feeling right now. Perhaps you don't care to know the depth of my disappointments. But you and Emmaline are my life's work. I was the one who found a way to isolate the gene that was causing widespread transformations in the population. I was the one who managed to re-create the transformation. I was the one who rewrote your genetic code." She frowns at me, looking, for the first time, like a real person. Her voice softens. "I *remade* you, Ella. You and your sister were the greatest accomplishments of my career. Your failures," she whispers, touching the tips of her fingers to my face, "are my failures."

I make a harsh, involuntary sound.

She stands up. "This is going to be uncomfortable for you. I won't pretend otherwise. But I'm afraid we have no choice. If this is going to work, I'll need you to have a healthy, unpolluted headspace. We have to start fresh. When we're done, you won't remember anything but what I tell you to remember. Do you understand?"

My heart picks up and I hear its wild, erratic beats amplified on a nearby monitor. The sounds echo around the room like a siren.

"Your temperature is spiking," Evie says sharply. "There's no need to panic. This is the merciful option. Paris is still clamoring to have you killed, after all. But Paris"—she hesitates—"Paris can be melodramatic. We've all known how much he's hated you for your effect on Aaron. He blames you, you know." Evie tilts her head at me. "He thinks you're part of the reason Aaron is so weak. Honestly, sometimes I wonder if he's right."

My heart is beating too fast now. My lungs feel fit to burst. The bright lights above my head bleed into my eyes, into my brain—

"Now. I'm going to download this information"—I hear her tap the silver box—"directly into your mind. It's a lot of data to process, and your body will need some time to accept it all." A long pause. "Your mind might try to reject this, but it's up to you to let things take their course, do you understand? We don't want to risk splicing the past and present. It's only painful in the first few hours, but if you can survive those first hours, your pain receptors will begin to fail, and the rest of the data should upload without incident."

I want to scream.

Instead, I make a weak, choking sound. Tears spill fast down my cheeks and my mother stands there, her fingers small and foreign on my face, and I see, but cannot feel, the enormous needle going into the soft flesh at my temple. She empties and refills the syringe what feels like a thousand times, and each time it's like being submerged underwater, like I'm slowly drowning, suffocating over and over again and never allowed to die. I lie there, helpless and mute, caught in an agony so excruciating I no longer breathe, but rasp, as she leans over me to watch.

"You're right," she says softly. "Maybe this is cruel. Maybe it would've been kinder to simply let you die. But this isn't about you, Ella. This is about me. And right now," she says, stroking my hair, "this is what I need."

KENJI

The whole thing happens so quickly it takes me a second to register exactly what went down.

Delalieu is dead.

Delalieu is dead and Anderson is alive.

Anderson is back from the dead.

I mean, right now he's flat on the ground, buried under the weight of every single piece of furniture in this room. Castle stares, intently, from across the space, and when I hear Anderson wheezing, I realize Castle isn't trying to kill him; he's only using the furniture to contain him.

I inch closer to the crowd forming around Anderson's gasping figure. And then I notice, with a start, that Adam is pressed up against the wall like a statue, his face frozen in horror.

My heart breaks for him.

I'm so glad Adam dragged James off to bed hours ago. So glad that kid doesn't have to see any of this right now.

Castle finally makes his way across the room. He's standing a few feet away from Anderson's prone figure when he asks the question we're all thinking:

"How are you still alive?"

Anderson attempts a smile. It comes out crooked. Crazy.

"You know what's always been so great about you, Castle?" He says Castle's name like it's funny, like he's saying it out loud for the first time. He takes a tight, uneven breath. "You're so predictable. You like to collect strays. You love a good sob story."

Anderson cries out with a sudden, rough exhalation, and I realize Castle probably turned up the pressure. When Anderson catches his breath, he says, "You're an idiot. You're an idiot for trusting so easily."

Another harsh, painful gasp.

"Who do you think called me here?" he says, struggling to speak now. "Who do you think has been keeping me apprised"—another strained breath—"of every single thing you've been discussing?"

I freeze. A horrible, sick feeling gathers in my chest.

We all turn, as a group, to face Nazeera. She's standing apart from everyone else, the personification of calm, collected intensity. She has no expression on her face. She looks at me like I might be a wall.

For a split second I feel so dizzy I think I might actually pass out.

Wishful thinking.

That's it—that's the thing that does it. A room full of extremely powerful people and yet, it's this moment, this brief, barely there moment of shock that ruins us all. I feel the needle in my neck before I even register what's happening, and I have only a few seconds to scan the room—glimpsing the horror on my friends' faces—before I fall.

WARNER

I'm sitting in my office listening to an old record when I get the call. I worry, at first, that it might be Lena, begging me to come back to her, but my feeling of revulsion quickly transforms to hate when I hear the voice on the line. My father. He wants me downstairs.

The mere sound of his voice fills me with a feeling so violent it takes me a minute to control myself.

Two years away.

Two years becoming the monster my father always wanted me to be. I glance in the mirror, loathing myself with a new, profound intensity I'd never before experienced. Every morning I wake up hoping only to die. To be done with this life, with these days.

He knew, when he made that deal, what he was asking me to do. I didn't. I was sixteen, still young enough to believe in hope, and he took advantage of my naiveté. He knew what it would do to me. He knew it would break me. And it was all he'd ever wanted.

My soul.

I sold my soul for a few years with my mother, and now, after everything, I don't even know if it'll be worth it. I don't know if I'll be able to save her. I've been away too long. I've missed too much. My mother is doing so much worse now, and no doctor has been able to help her. Nothing has helped. My efforts have been worse than futile.

I gave up everything—for nothing.

I wish I'd known how those two years would change me. I wish I'd known how hard it would be to live with myself, to look in the mirror. No one warned me about the nightmares, the panic attacks, or the dark, destructive thoughts that would follow. No one explained to me how darkness works, how it feasts on itself or how it festers. I hardly recognize myself these days. Becoming an instrument of torture destroyed what was left of my mind.

And now, this: I feel empty, all the time. Hollowed out.

Beyond redemption.

I didn't want to come back here. I wanted to walk directly into the ocean. I wanted to fade into the horizon. I wanted to disappear.

Of course, he'd never let that happen.

He dragged me back here and gave me a title. I was rewarded for being an animal. Celebrated for my efforts as a monster. Never mind the fact that I wake up in the middle of every night strangled by irrational fears and a sudden, violent urge to upend the contents of my stomach.

Never mind that I can't get these images out of my head.

I glance at the expensive bottle of bourbon my father left for me in my room and feel suddenly disgusted. I don't want to be like him. I don't want his opiate, his preferred form of oblivion.

At least, soon, my father will be gone. Any day now, he'll be gone, and this sector will become my domain. I'll finally be on my own.

Or something close to it.

Reluctantly, I pull on my blazer and take the elevator down.

When I finally arrive in his quarters as he requested, he spares me only the briefest look.

"Good," he says. "You've come."

I say nothing.

He smiles. "Where are your manners? You're not going to greet our guest?"

Confused, I follow his line of sight. There's a young woman sitting on a chair in the far corner of the room, and, at first, I don't recognize her.

When I do, the blood drains from my face.

My father laughs. "You kids remember each other, right?"

She was sitting so quietly, so still and small that I almost hadn't noticed her at all. My dead heart jumps at the sight of her slight frame, a spark of life trying, desperately, to ignite.

"Juliette," I whisper.

My last memory of her was from two years ago, just before I left home for my father's sick, sadistic assignment. He ripped her away from me. Literally ripped her out of my arms. I'd never seen that kind of rage in his eyes, not like that, not over something so innocent.

But he was wild.

Out of his mind.

She and I hadn't done anything more than talk to each other. I'd started stealing down to her room whenever I could get away, and I'd trick the cameras' feeds to give us privacy. We'd talk, sometimes for hours. She'd become my friend.

I never touched her.

She said that after what happened with the little boy, she was afraid to touch anyone. She said she didn't understand what was happening to her and didn't trust herself anymore. I asked her if she wanted to touch me, to test it out and see if anything would happen, and she looked scared and I told her not to worry. I promised it'd be okay. And when I took her hand, tentatively, waiting for disaster—

Nothing happened.

Nothing happened except that she burst into tears. She threw herself into my arms and wept and told me she'd been terrified that there was something wrong with her, that she'd turned into a monster—

We only had a month, altogether.

But there was something about her that felt right to me, from the very beginning. I trusted her. She felt familiar, like I'd always known her. But I also knew it seemed a dramatic sort of thought, so I kept it to myself.

She told me about her life. Her horrible parents. She'd shared her fears with me, so I shared mine. I told her about my mom, how I didn't know what was happening to her, how worried I was that she was going to die.

Juliette cared about me. Listened to me the way no one else did.

It was the most innocent relationship I'd ever had, but it meant more to me than anything. For the first time in years, I felt less alone.

The day I found out she was finally being transferred, I pulled her close. I pressed my face into her hair and breathed her in and she cried. She told me she was scared and I promised I'd try to do something—I promised to talk to my dad even though I knew he wouldn't care—

And then, suddenly, he was there.

He ripped her out of my arms, and I noticed then that he was wearing gloves. "What the hell are you doing?" he cried. "Have you lost your mind? Have you lost yourself entirely?"

"Dad," I said, panicking. "Nothing happened. I was just saying good-bye to her."

His eyes widened, round with shock. And when he spoke, his words were whispers. "You were just—You were saying good-bye to her?"

"She's leaving," I said stupidly.

"You think I don't know that?"

I swallowed, hard.

"Jesus," he said, running a hand across his mouth. "How long have you been doing this? How long have you been coming down here?"

My heart was racing. Fear pulsed through me. I was shaking my head, unable to speak.

"What did you do?" my dad demanded, his eyes flashing. "Did you touch her?"

"No." Anger surged through me, giving me back my voice even as my face flushed with embarrassment. "No, of course not."

"Are you sure?"

"Dad, why are you"—I shook my head, confused—"I don't understand why you're so upset. You've been pushing me and Lena

together for months, even though I've told you a hundred times that I don't like her, but now, when I actually—" I hesitated, looking at Juliette, her face half hidden behind my dad. *"I was just getting to know her. That's all."*

"You were just getting to know her?" He stared at me, disgusted. "Of all the girls in the world, you fall for this one? The child-murderer bound for prison? The likely insane test tube experiment? What is wrong with you?"

"Dad, please—Nothing happened. We're just friends. We just talk sometimes."

"Just friends," he said, and laughed. The sound was demented. "You know what? I'll let you take this with you. I'll let you keep this one while you're gone. Let it sit with you. Let it teach you a lesson."

"What? Take what with me?"

"A warning." He leveled me with a lethal look. "Try something like this again," he said, "and I'll kill her. And I'll make sure you get to watch."

I stared at him, my heart beating out of my chest. This was insane. We hadn't even done anything. I'd known that my dad would probably be angry, but I never thought he'd threaten to kill her. If I'd known, I never would've risked it. And now—

My head was spinning. I didn't understand. He was dragging her down the hall and I didn't understand.

Suddenly, she screamed.

She screamed and I stood there, helpless as he dragged her away. She called my name—cried out for me—and he shook her, told her to shut up, and I felt something inside of me die. I felt it as it happened. Felt something break apart inside of me as I watched her go.

I'd never hated myself so much. I'd never been more of a coward.

And now, here we are.

That day feels like a lifetime ago. I never thought I'd see her again.

Juliette looks up at me now, and she looks different. Her eyes are glassy with tears. Her skin has lost its pallor; her hair has lost its sheen. She looks thinner. She reminds me of myself.

Hollow.

"Hi," I whisper.

Tears spill, silently, down her cheeks.

I have to force myself to remain calm. I have to force myself not to lose my head. My mother warned me, years ago, to hide my heart from my father, and every time I slipped—every time I let myself hope he might not be a monster—he punished me, mercilessly.

I wasn't going to let him do that to me again. I didn't want him to know how much it hurt to see her like this. How painful it was to sit beside her and say nothing. Do nothing.

"What is she doing here?" I ask, hardly recognizing my own voice.

"She's here," he says, "because I had her collected for us."

"Collected for what? You said—"

"I know what I said." He shrugs. "But I wanted to see this moment. Your reunion. I'm always interested in your reunions. I *find the dynamics of your relationship fascinating."*

I look at him, feel my chest explode with rage and somehow, fight it back. "You brought her back here just to torture me?"

"You flatter yourself, son."

"Then what?"

"I have your first task for you," he says, pushing a stack of files across his desk. "Your first real mission as chief commander and regent of this sector."

My lips part, surprised. "What does that have to do with her?"

My father's eyes light up. "Everything."

I say nothing.

"I have a plan," he says. "One that will require your assistance. In these files"—he nods at the stack in front of me—"is everything you need to know about her illness. Every medical report, every paper trail. I want you to reform the girl. Rehabilitate her. And then I want you to weaponize her abilities for our own use."

I meet his eyes, failing to conceal my horror at the suggestion. "Why? Why would you come to me with this? Why would you ask me to do something like this, when you know our history?"

"You are uniquely suited to the job. It seems silly to waste my time explaining this to you now, as you won't remember most of this conversation tomorrow—"

"What?" I frown. "Why wouldn't I—"

"—but the two of you seem to have some kind of immutable connection, one that might, I hope, inspire her abilities to develop more fully. More quickly."

"That doesn't make any sense."

He ignores me. Glances at Juliette. Her eyes are closed, her head resting against the wall behind her. She seems almost asleep, except for the tears still streaking softly down her face.

It kills me just to look at her.

"As you can see," my father says, "she's a bit out of her mind right now. Heavily sedated. She's been through a great deal these last two years. We had no choice but to turn her into a sort of guinea pig. I'm sure you can imagine how that goes."

He stares at me with a slight smile on his face. I know he's waiting for something. A reaction. My anger.

I refuse to give it to him.

His smile widens.

"Anyhow," he says happily, "I'm going to put her back in isolation for the next six months—maybe a year, depending on how things develop. You can use that opportunity to prepare. To observe her."

But I'm still fighting back my anger. I can't bring myself to speak.

"Is there a problem?" he says.

"No."

"You remember, of course, the warning I gave you the last time she was here."

"Of course," *I say, my voice flat. Dead.*

And then, as if out of nowhere: "How is Lena, by the way? I hope she's well."

"I wouldn't know."

It's barely there, but I catch the sudden shift in his voice. The anger when he says, "And why is that?"

"I broke things off with her last week."

"And you didn't think to tell me?"

Finally, I meet his eyes. "I never understood why you wanted us to be together. She's not right for me. She never was."

"You don't love her, you mean."

"I can't imagine how anyone would."

"That," he says, "is exactly why she's perfect for you."

I blink at him, caught off guard. For a moment, it almost sounded like my father cared about me. Like he was trying to protect me in some perverse, idiotic way.

Eventually, he sighs.

He picks up a pen and a pad of paper and begins writing something down. "I'll see what I can do about repairing the damage you've done. Lena's mother must be hysterical. Until then, get to work." He nods at the stack of files he's set before me.

Reluctantly, I pick a folder off the top.

I glance through the documents, scanning the general outline of the mission, and then I look up at him, stunned. "Why does the paperwork make it sound like this was my idea?"

He hesitates. Puts down his pen. "Because you don't trust me."

I stare at him, struggling to understand.

He tilts his head. "If you knew this was my idea, you'd never trust it, would you? You'd look too closely for holes. Conspiracies. You'd never follow through the way I'd want you to. Besides," he says, picking up his pen again. "Two birds. One stone. It's time to finally break the cycle."

I replace the folder on the pile. I'm careful to temper the tone of my voice when I say, "I have no idea what you're talking about."

"I'm talking about your new experiment," he says coolly. "Your little tragedy. This," he says, gesturing between me and Juliette. "This needs to end. And she is unlikely to return your affections when she wakes up to discover you are not her friend but her oppressor. Isn't she?"

And I can no longer keep the fury or the hysteria out of my voice when I say, "Why are you doing this to me? Why are you purposely torturing me?"

"Is it so crazy to imagine that I might be trying to do you a favor?" My father smiles. "Look more closely at those files, son. If you've ever wanted a chance at saving your mother—this might be it."

I've become obsessed with time.

Still, I can only guess at how long I've been here, staring at these walls without reprieve. No voices, only the occasional warped sounds of faraway speech. No faces, not a single person to tell me where I am or what awaits me. I've watched the shadows chase the light in and out of my cell for weeks, their motions through the small window my only hope for marking the days.

A slim, rectangular slot in my door opens with sudden, startling force, the aperture shot through with what appears to be artificial light on the other side.

I make a mental note.

A single, steaming bun—no tray, no foil, no utensils—is shoved through the slot and my reflexes are still fast enough to catch the bread before it touches the filthy floor. I have enough sense to understand that the little food I'm given every day is poisoned. Not enough to kill me. Just enough to slow me down. Slight tremors rock my body, but I force my eyes to stay open as I turn the soft bun around in my hand, searching its flaky skin for information. It's unmarked. Unextraordinary. It could mean nothing.

There's no way to be sure.

This ritual happens exactly twice a day. I am fed an insignificant, tasteless portion of food twice a day. For hours at a time my thoughts slur; my mind swims and hallucinates. I am slow. Sluggish.

Most days, I fast.

To clear my head, to cleanse my body of the poison, and to collect information. I have to find my way out of here before it's too late.

Some nights, when I'm at my weakest, my imagination runs wild; my mind is plagued by horrible visions of what might've happened to her. It's torture not knowing what they've done with her. Not knowing where she is, not knowing how she is, not knowing if someone is hurting her.

But the nightmares are perhaps the most disconcerting.

At least, I think they're nightmares. It's hard to separate fact from fiction, dreams from reality; I spend too much time with poison running through my veins. But Nazeera's words to me before the symposium—her warning that Juliette was someone else, that Max and Evie are her true, biological parents . . .

I didn't want to believe it then.

It seemed a possibility too perverse to be real. Even my father had lines he wouldn't cross, I told myself. Even The Reestablishment had some sense of invented morality, I told myself.

But I saw them as I was carried away—I saw the familiar faces of Evie and Maximillian Sommers—the supreme commander of Oceania and her husband. And I've been thinking of them ever since.

They were the key scientists of our group, the quiet brains of The Reestablishment. They were military, yes, but they were medical. The pair often kept to themselves. I had few memories of them until very recently.

Until *Ella* appeared in my mind.

But I don't know how to be sure that what I'm seeing is real. I have no way of knowing that this isn't simply another part of the torture. It's impossible to know. It's agony, boring a hole through me. I feel like I'm being assaulted on both sides—mental and physical—and I don't know where or how to begin fighting back. I've begun clenching my teeth so hard it's causing me migraines. Exhaustion feasts, slowly, on my mind. I'm fairly certain I've got at least two fractured ribs, and my only hours of rest are achieved standing up, the single position that eases the pain in my torso. It'd be easy to give up. Give in. But I can't lose myself to these mind games.

I won't.

So I compile data.

I spent my whole life preparing for moments like these by people like this and they will take full advantage of that knowledge. I know they'll expect me to prove that I deserve to survive, and—unexpectedly—knowing this brings me a much-needed sense of calm. I feel none of my usual anxiety here, being carefully poisoned to death.

Instead, I feel at home. Familiar.

Fortified by adrenaline.

Under any other circumstances I'd assume my meals were offered once in the morning and once at night—but I know better than to assume anything anymore. I've been charting the shadows long enough to know that I'm never fed at regular hours, and that the erratic schedule is intentional. There must be a message here: a sequence of numbers, a pattern of information, something I'm not grasping—because I know that this, like everything else, is a test.

I am in the custody of a supreme commander.

There can be no accidents.

I force myself to eat the warm, flavorless bun, hating the way the gummy, overly processed bread sticks to the roof of my mouth. It makes me wish for a toothbrush. They've given me my own sink and toilet, but I have little else to keep my standards of hygiene intact, which is possibly the greatest indignity here. I fight a wave of nausea as I swallow the last bite of bread and a sudden, prickling heat floods my body. Beads of sweat roll down my back and I clench my fists to keep from succumbing too quickly to the drugs.

I need a little more time.

There's a message here, somewhere, but I haven't yet decided where. Maybe it's in the movements of the shadows. Or in the number of times the slot opens and closes. It might be in the names of the foods I'm forced to eat, or in the exact number of footsteps I hear every day—or perhaps it's in the occasional, jarring knock at my door that accompanies silence.

There's something here, something they're trying to tell me, something I'm supposed to decipher—I gasp, reach out blindly as a shock of pain shoots through my gut—

I can figure this out, I think, even as the drug drags me down. I fall backward, onto my elbows. My eyes flutter open and closed and my mind drowns even as I count the sounds outside my door—

one hard step
two dragging steps
one hard step

—and there's something there, something deliberate in the movement that speaks to me. I know this. I know this language, I know its name, it's right there at the tip of my tongue but I can't seem to grasp it.

I've already forgotten what I was trying to do.

My arms give out. My head hits the floor with a dull thud. My thoughts melt into darkness.

The nightmares take me by the throat.

KENJI

I thought I'd spent time in some pretty rough places in my life, but this shit is like nothing else. Perfect darkness. No sounds but the distant, tortured screams of other prisoners. Food is disgusting slop shoved through a slot in the door. No bathrooms except that they open the doors once a day, just long enough for you to kill yourself trying to find the disgusting showers and toilets. I know what this is. I remember when Juliette—

Ella. *Ella*. Ella used to tell me about this place.

Some nights we'd stay up for hours talking about it. I wanted to know. I wanted to know everything. And those conversations are the only reason I knew what the open door means.

I don't really know how long I've been here—a week? Maybe two? I don't understand why they won't just kill me. I try to tell myself, every minute of every damn day, that they're just doing this to mess with our heads, that the tortured mind is a worse fate than a bullet in the brain, but I can't lie. This place is starting to get to me.

I feel myself starting to go weird.

I'm starting to hear things. See things. I'm beginning to freak myself out about what might've happened to my friends or whether I'll ever get out of here.

I try not to think about Nazeera.

When I think about Nazeera I want to punch myself in the face. I want to shoot myself in the throat.

When I think about Nazeera I feel a rage so acute I'm actually convinced, for a minute, that I might be able to break out of these neon handcuffs with nothing but brute force. But it never happens. These things are unbreakable, even as they strip me of my powers. And they emit a soft, pulsing blue glow, the only light I ever see.

J told me her cell had a window. Mine doesn't.

A harsh buzzing sound fills my cell. I hear a smooth click in the heavy metal door. I jump to my feet.

The door swings open.

I feel my way down the dripping corridor, the dim, pulsing light of my cuffs doing little to guide my way.

The shower is quick and cold. Awful in every way. There are no towels in this shithole, so I'm always freezing until I can get back to my room and wrap myself in the threadbare blanket. I'm thinking about that blanket now, trying to keep my thoughts focused and my teeth from chattering as I wend my way down the dark tunnels.

I don't see what happens next.

Someone comes up on me from behind and puts me in a choke hold, suffocating me with a technique so perfect I don't even know if it's worth a struggle. I'm definitely about to die.

Super weird way to go, but this is it. I'm done.

Shit.

~~JULIETTE~~

ELLA

Mr. Anderson says I can have lunch at his house before I meet my new family. It wasn't his idea, but when Aaron, his son—that was the boy's name—suggested it, Mr. Anderson seemed okay with it.

I'm grateful.

I'm not ready to go live with a bunch of strangers yet. I'm scared and nervous and worried about so many things, I don't even know where to start. Mostly, I feel angry. I'm angry with my parents for dying. Angry with them for leaving me behind.

I'm an orphan now.

But maybe I have a new friend. Aaron said that he was eight years old—about two years older than me—so there isn't any chance we'd be in the same grade, but when I said that we'd probably be going to the same school anyway, he said no, we wouldn't. He said he didn't go to public school. He said his father was very particular about these kinds of things and that he'd been homeschooled by private tutors his whole life.

We're sitting next to each other in the car ride back to his house when he says, quietly, "My dad never lets me invite people over to our house. He must like you."

I smile, secretly relieved. I really hope that this means I'll have a new friend. I'd been so scared to move here, so scared to be somewhere new and to be all alone, but now, sitting next to this strange blond boy with the light green eyes, I'm beginning to feel like things might be okay.

At least now, even if I don't like my new parents, I'll know I'm not completely alone. The thought makes me both happy and sad.

I look over at Aaron and smile. He smiles back.

When we get to his house, I take a moment to admire it from the outside. It's a big, beautiful old house painted the prettiest blue. It has big white shutters on the windows and a white fence around the front yard. Pink roses are growing around the edges, peeking through the wooden slats of the fence, and the whole thing looks so peaceful and lovely that I feel immediately at home.

My worries vanish.

I'm so grateful for Mr. Anderson's help. So grateful to have met his son. I realize, then, that Mr. Anderson might've brought his son to my meeting today just to introduce me to someone my own age. Maybe he was trying to make me feel at home.

A beautiful blond lady answers the front door. She smiles at me, bright and kind, and doesn't even say hello to me before she pulls me into her arms. She hugs me like she's known me forever, and there's something so comfortable about her arms around me that I embarrass everyone by bursting into tears.

I can't even look at anyone after I pull away from her—she told me her name was Mrs. Anderson, but that I could call her Leila, if I wanted—and I wipe at my tears, ashamed of my overreaction.

Mrs. Anderson tells Aaron to take me upstairs to his room while she makes us some snacks before lunch.

Still sniffling, I follow him up the stairs.

His room is nice. I sit on his bed and look at his things. Mostly it's pretty clean except that there's a baseball mitt on his nightstand and there are two dirty baseballs on the floor. Aaron catches me staring and scoops them up right away. He seems embarrassed as he tucks them in his closet, and I don't understand why. I was never very tidy. My room was always—

I hesitate.

I try to remember what my old bedroom looked like but, for some reason, I can't. I frown. Try again.

Nothing.

And then I realize I can't remember my parents' faces.

Terror barrels through me.

"What's wrong?"

Aaron's voice is so sharp—so intense—that I look up, startled. He's staring at me from across the room, the fear on his face reflected in the mirrors on his closet doors.

"What's wrong?" he says again. "Are you okay?"

"I—I don't—" I falter, feeling my eyes refill with tears. I hate that I keep crying. Hate that I can't stop crying. "I can't remember my parents," I say. "Is that normal?"

Aaron walks over, sits next to me on his bed. "I don't know," he says.

We're both quiet for a while. Somehow, it helps. Somehow, just sitting next to him makes me feel less alone. Less terrified.

Eventually, my heart stops racing.

After I've wiped away my tears, I say, "Don't you get lonely, being homeschooled all the time?"

He nods.

"Why won't your dad let you go to a normal school?"

"I don't know."

"What about birthday parties?" I ask. "Who do you invite to your birthday parties?"

Aaron shrugs. He's staring into his hands when he says, "I've never had a birthday party."

"What? Really?" I turn to face him more fully. "But birthday parties are so fun. I used to—" I blink, cutting myself off.

I can't remember what I was about to say.

I frown, trying to remember something, something about my old life, but when the memories don't materialize, I shake my head to clear it. Maybe I'll remember later.

"Anyway," I say, taking a quick breath, "you have to have a birthday party. Everyone has birthday parties. When is your birthday?"

Slowly, Aaron looks up at me. His face is blank even as he says, "April twenty-fourth."

"April twenty-fourth," I say, smiling. "That's great. We can have cake."

The days pass in a stifled panic, an excruciating crescendo toward madness. The hands of the clock seem to close around my throat and still, I say nothing, do nothing.

I wait.

Pretend.

I've been paralyzed here for two weeks, stuck in the prison of this ruse, this compound. Evie doesn't know that her plot to bleach my mind failed. She treats me like a foreign object, distant but not unkind. She instructed me to call her *Evie*, told me she was my doctor, and then proceeded to lie, in great detail, about how I'd been in a terrible accident, that I'm suffering from amnesia, that I need to stay in bed in order to recover.

She doesn't know that my body won't stop shaking, that my skin is slick with sweat every morning, that my throat burns from the constant return of bile. She doesn't know what's happening to me. She could never understand the sickness plaguing my heart. She couldn't possibly understand this agony.

Remembering.

The attacks are relentless.

Memories assault me while I sleep, jolting me upright, my chest seizing in panic over and over and over until, finally, I meet dawn on the bathroom floor, the smell of vomit clinging to my hair, the inside of my mouth. I can only drag myself back to bed every morning and force my face to smile when Evie checks on me at sunrise.

Everything feels wrong.

The world feels strange. Smells confuse me. Words don't feel right in my mouth anymore. The sound of my own name feels at once familiar and foreign. My memories of people and places seem warped, fraying threads coming together to form a ragged tapestry.

But Evie. *My mother.*

I remember her.

"Evie?"

I pop my head out of the bathroom, clutching a robe to my wet body. I search my room for her face. "Evie, are you there?"

"Yes?" I hear her voice just seconds before she's suddenly standing before me, holding a set of fresh sheets in her hands. She's stripping my bed again. "Did you need something?"

"We're out of towels."

"Oh—easily rectified," she says, and hurries out the door. Not seconds later she's back, pressing a warm, fresh towel into my hands. She smiles faintly.

"Thanks," I say, forcing my own smile to stretch, to spark life in my eyes. And then I disappear into the bathroom.

The room is steaming; the mirrors fogged, perspiring. I grip the towel with one hand, watching as beads of water race down my bare skin. Condensation wears me like a suit; I wipe at the damp metal cuffs locked around my wrists and ankles, their glowing blue light my constant reminder that I am in hell.

I collapse, with a heavy breath, onto the floor.

I'm too hot to put on clothes, but I'm not ready to leave the privacy of the bathroom yet, so I sit here, wearing nothing but these manacles, and drop my head into my hands.

My hair is long again.

I discovered it like this—long, heavy, dark—one morning, and when I asked her about it, I nearly ruined everything.

"What do you mean?" Evie said, narrowing her eyes at me. "Your hair has always been long."

I blinked at her, remembering to play dumb. "I know."

She stared at me awhile longer before she finally let it go, but I'm still worried I'll pay for that slip. Sometimes it's hard to remember how to act. My mind is being attacked, assaulted every day by emotion I never knew existed. My memories were supposed to be erased. Instead, they're being replenished.

I'm remembering everything:

My mother's laugh, her slender wrists, the smell of her shampoo, and the familiarity of her arms around me.

The more I remember, the less this place feels foreign to me. The less these sounds and smells—these mountains in the distance—feel unknown. It's as if the disparate parts of my most desperate self are stitching back together, as if the gaping holes in my heart and head are healing, filling slowly with sensation.

This compound was my home. These people, my family. I woke up this morning remembering my mother's favorite shade of lipstick.

Bloodred.

I remember watching her paint her lips some evenings. I remember the day I snuck into her room and stole the glossy metal tube; I remember when she found me, my hands and mouth smeared in red, my face a grotesque reimagining of herself.

The more I remember my parents, the more I begin to finally make sense of myself—my many fears and insecurities, the myriad ways in which I've often felt lost, searching for something I could not name.

It's devastating.

And yet—

In this new, turbulent reality, the one person I recognize anymore is *him*. My memories of him—memories of us—have done something to me. I've changed somewhere deep inside. I feel different. Heavier, like my feet have been more firmly planted, liberated by certainty, free to grow roots here in my own self, free to trust unequivocally in the strength and steadiness of my own heart. It's an empowering discovery, to find that I can trust myself—even when I'm not myself—to make the right choices. To know for certain now that there was at least one mistake I never made.

Aaron Warner Anderson is the only emotional through line in my life that ever made sense. He's the only constant. The only steady, reliable heartbeat I've ever had.

Aaron, Aaron, Aaron, Aaron

I had no idea how much we'd lost, no idea how much of him I'd longed for. I had no idea how desperately we'd been fighting. How many years we'd fought for moments—minutes—to be together.

It fills me with a painful kind of joy.

But when I remember how I left things between us, I want to *scream*.

I have no idea if I'll ever see him again.

Still, I'm holding on to the hope that he's alive, out there, somewhere. Evie said she couldn't kill him. She said that she alone didn't have the authority to have him executed.

And if Aaron is still alive, I will find a way to get to him. But I have to be careful. Breaking out of this new prison won't be easy—As it is, Evie almost never lets me out of my room. Worse, she sedates me during the day, allowing me only a couple of lucid hours. There's never enough time to *think*, much less to plan an escape, to assess my surroundings, or to wander the halls outside my door.

Only once did she let me go outside.

Sort of.

She let me onto a balcony overlooking the backyard. It wasn't much, but even that small step helped me understand a bit about where we were and what the layout of the building might look like.

The assessment was chilling.

We appeared to be in the center of a settlement—a small city—in the middle of nowhere. I leaned over the edge of the balcony, craning my neck to take in the breadth of it, but the view was so vast I couldn't see all the way around. From where I stood I saw at least twenty different buildings, all connected by roads and navigated by people in miniature, electric cars. There were loading and unloading docks, massive trucks filing in and out, and there was a landing strip in the distance, a row of jets parked neatly in a concrete lot. I understood then that I was living in the middle of a massive operation—something so much more terrifying than Sector 45.

This is an international base.

This has to be one of the capitals. Whatever this

is—whatever they do here—it makes Sector 45 look like a joke.

Here, where the hills are somehow still green and beautiful, where the air is fresh and cool and everything seems alive. My accounting is probably off, but I think we're nearing the end of April—and the sights outside my window are unlike anything I've ever seen in Sector 45: vast, snowcapped mountain ranges; rolling hills thick with vegetation; trees heavy with bright, changing leaves; and a massive, glittering lake that looks close enough to run to. This land looks healthy. Vibrant.

I thought we'd lost a world like this a long time ago.

Evie's begun to sedate me less these days, but some days my vision seems to fray at the edges, like a satellite image glitching, waiting for data to load.

I wonder, sometimes, if she's poisoning me.

I'm wondering this now, remembering the bowl of soup she sent to my room for breakfast. I can still feel the gluey residue as it coated my tongue, the roof of my mouth.

Unease churns my stomach.

I haul myself up off the bathroom floor, my limbs slow and heavy. It takes me a moment to stabilize. The effects of this experiment have left me hollow.

Angry.

As if out of nowhere, my mind conjures an image of Evie's face. I remember her eyes. Deep, dark brown. Bottomless. The same color as her hair. She has a short, sharp bob, a heavy curtain constantly whipping against her chin. She's a beautiful woman, more beautiful at fifty than she was at twenty.

Coming.

The word occurs to me suddenly, and a bolt of panic shoots up my spine. Not a second later there's a sharp knock at my bathroom door.

"Yes?"

"Ella, you've been in the bathroom for almost half an hour, and you know how I feel about wasting ti—"

"*Evie.*" I force myself to laugh. "I'm almost done," I say. "I'll be right out."

A pause.

The silence stretches the seconds into a lifetime. My heart jumps up, into my throat. Beats in my mouth.

"All right," she says slowly. "Five more minutes."

I close my eyes as I exhale, pressing the towel to the racing pulse at my neck. I dry off quickly before wringing the remaining water from my hair and slipping back into my robe.

Finally, I open the bathroom door and welcome the cool morning temperature against my feverish skin. But I hardly have a chance to take a breath before she's in my face again.

"Wear this," she says, forcing a dress into my arms. She's smiling but it doesn't suit her. She looks deranged. "You love wearing yellow."

I blink as I take the dress from her, feeling a sudden,

disorienting wave of déjà vu. "Of course," I say. "I love wearing yellow."

Her smile grows thinner, threatens to turn her face inside out.

"Could I just—?" I make an abstract gesture toward my body.

"Oh," she says, startled. "Right." She shoots me another smile and says, "I'll be outside."

My own smile is brittle.

She watches me. She always watches me. Studies my reactions, the timing of my responses. She's scanning me, constantly, for information. She wants confirmation that I've been properly hollowed out. *Remade.*

I smile wider.

Finally, she takes a step back. "Good girl," she says softly.

I stand in the middle of my room and watch her leave, the yellow dress still pressed against my chest.

There was another time when I'd felt trapped, just like this. I was held against my will and given beautiful clothes and three square meals and demanded to be something I wasn't and I fought it—fought it with everything I had.

It didn't do me any good.

I swore that if I could do it again I'd do it differently. I said if I could do it over I'd wear the clothes and eat the food and play along until I could figure out where I was and how to break free.

So here's my chance.

This time, I've decided to play along.

KENJI

I wake up, bound and gagged, a roaring sound in my ears. I blink to clear my vision. I'm bound so tightly I can't move, so it takes me a second to realize I can't see my legs.

No legs. No arms, either.

The revelation that I'm invisible hits me with full, horrifying force.

I'm not doing this.

I didn't bring myself here, bind and gag myself, and make myself invisible.

There's only one other person who would.

I look around desperately, trying to gauge where I am and what my chances might be for escape, but when I finally manage to heave my body to one side—just long enough to crane my neck—I realize, with a terrifying jolt, that I'm on a plane.

And then—voices.

It's Anderson and Nazeera.

I hear them discussing something about how we'll be landing soon, and then, minutes later, I feel it when we touch ground.

The plane taxis for a while and it seems to take forever before the engines finally turn off.

I hear Anderson leave. Nazeera hangs back, saying something about needing to clean up. She shuts down the plane and its cameras, doesn't acknowledge me.

Finally, I hear her footsteps getting closer to my head. She uses one foot to roll me onto my back, and then, just like that, my invisibility is gone. She stares at me for a little while longer, says nothing.

Finally, she smiles.

"Hi," she says, removing the gag from my mouth. "How are you holding up?"

And I decide right then that I'm going to have to kill her.

"Okay," she says, "I know you're probably upset—"

"UPSET? YOU THINK I'M UPSET?" I jerk violently against the ties. "Jesus Christ, woman, get me out of these goddamn restraints—"

"I'll get you out of the restraints when you calm down—"

"HOW CAN YOU EXPECT ME TO BE CALM?"

"I'm trying to save your life right now, so, actually, I expect a lot of things from you."

I'm breathing hard. "Wait. What?"

She crosses her arms, stares down at me. "I've been trying to explain to you that there was really no other way to do this. And don't worry," she says. "Your friends are okay. We should be able to get them out of the asylum before any permanent damage is done."

"What? What do you mean *permanent damage*?"

Nazeera sighs. "Anyway, this was the only way I could think of stealing a plane without attracting notice. I needed to track Anderson."

"So you knew he was alive, that whole time, and you said nothing about it."

She raises her eyebrows. "Honestly, I thought you knew."

"How the hell was I supposed to know?" I shout. "How was I supposed to know *anything*?"

"Stop shouting," she says. "I went to all this trouble to save your life but I swear to God I will kill you if you don't stop shouting right now."

"Where," I say, "THE HELL," I say, "ARE WE?"

And instead of killing me, she laughs. "Where do you think we are?" She shakes her head. "We're in Oceania. We're here to find Ella."

WARNER

"We can live in the lake," she says simply.

"What?" I almost laugh. "What are you talking about?"

"I'm serious," she says. "I heard my mum talking about how to make it so people can live underwater, and I'm going to ask her to tell me, and then we can live in the lake."

I sigh. "We can't live in the lake, Ella."

"Why not?" She turns and looks at me, her eyes wide, startlingly bright. Blue green. Like the globe, I think. Like the whole world. "Why can't we live in the lake? My mum says th—"

"Stop it, Ella. Stop—"

I wake suddenly, jerking upward as my eyes fly open, my lungs desperate for air. I breathe in too fast and cough, choking on the overcorrection of oxygen. My body bows forward, chest heaving, my hands braced against the cold, concrete floor.

Ella.

Ella.

Pain spears me through the chest. I stopped eating the poisoned food two days ago, but the visions linger even when I'm lucid. There's something hyperreal about this one in particular, the memory barreling into me over and over, shooting swift, sharp pains through my gut. It's breathtaking, this disorienting rush of emotion.

For the first time, I'm beginning to believe.

I thought nightmares. Hallucinations, even. But now I know.

Now it seems impossible to deny.

I heard my mum talking about how to make it so people can live underwater

I didn't understand right away why Max and Evie were keeping me captive here, but they must blame me for something—maybe something my father is responsible for. Something I unknowingly took part in.

Maybe something like torturing their daughter Emmaline.

When I was sent away for two years, I was never told where I was going. The details of my location were never disclosed, and during that time period I lived in a veritable prison of my own, never allowed to step outside, never allowed to know more than was absolutely necessary about the task at hand. The breaks I was given were closely guarded, and I was required to wear a blindfold as I was ushered on and off the jet, which always made me think I must've been working somewhere easily identifiable. But those two years also comprised some of the darkest, saddest days of my life; all I knew was my desperate need for oblivion. I was so buried in self-loathing that it seemed only right to find solace in the arms of someone who meant nothing to me. I hated myself every day. Being with Lena was both relief and torture.

Even so, I felt numb, all the time.

After two weeks here, I'm beginning to wonder if this prison isn't one I've known before. If this isn't the same place I spent those two horrible years of my life. It's hard to explain the intangible, irrational reasons why the view outside my window is beginning to feel familiar to me, but two years is a long time to grow familiar with the rhythms of a land, even one you don't understand.

I wonder if Emmaline is here, somewhere.

It makes sense that she'd be here, close to home—close to her parents, whose medical and scientific advances are the only reason she's even alive. Or something close to alive, anyway.

It makes sense that they'd bring Juliette—*Ella*, I remind myself—back here, to her home. The question is—

Why bring her here? What are they hoping to do with her?

But then, if her mother is anything like my father, I think I can imagine what they might have in mind.

I push myself off the floor and take a steadying breath. My body is running on mere adrenaline, so starved for sleep and sustenance that I have to—

Pain.

It's swift and sudden and I gasp even as I recognize the familiar sting. I have no idea how long it'll take for my ribs to fully heal. Until then, I clench my teeth as I stand, feeling blindly for purchase against the rough stone. My hands shake as I steady myself and I'm breathing too hard again, eyes darting around the familiar cell.

I turn on the sink and splash ice-cold water on my face.

The effect is immediate. Focusing.

Carefully, I strip down to nothing. I soak my undershirt under the running water and use it to scrub my face, my neck, the rest of my body. I wash my hair. Rinse my mouth. Clean my teeth. And then I do what little I can for the rest of my clothes, washing them by hand and wringing them dry. I slip back into my underwear even though the cotton is still slightly damp, and I fight back a shiver in the darkness. Hungry and cold is at least better than drugged and delirious.

This is the end of my second week in confinement, and my third day this week without food. It feels good to have a clear head, even as my body slowly starves. I'd already been leaner than usual, but now the lines of my body feel unusually sharp, even to myself, all necessary softness gone from my limbs. It's only a matter of time before my muscles atrophy and I do irreparable damage to my organs, but right now I have no choice. I need access to my mind.

To *think*.

And something about my sentencing feels off.

The more I think about it, the less sense it makes that Max and Evie would want me to suffer for what I did to Emmaline. They were the ones who donated their daughters to The Reestablishment in the first place. My work overseeing Emmaline was assigned to me—in fact, it was likely a job they'd approved. It would make more sense that I were here for treason. Max and Evie, like any other commanders, would want me to suffer for turning my back on The Reestablishment.

But even this theory feels wrong. Incongruous.

The punishment for treason has always been public execution. Quick. Efficient. I should be murdered, with only a little fanfare, in front of my own soldiers. But this—locking people up like this—slowly starving them while stripping them of their sanity and dignity—this is uncivilized. It's what The Reestablishment does to others, not to its own.

It's what they did to Ella. They tortured her. Ran tests on her. She wasn't locked up to inspire penitence. She was in isolation because she was part of an ongoing experiment.

And I am in the unique position to know that such a prisoner requires constant maintenance.

I figured I'd be kept here for a few days—maybe a week—but locking me up for what seems to be an indeterminate amount of time—

This must be difficult for them.

For two weeks they've managed to remain just slightly ahead of me, a feat they accomplished by poisoning my food. In training I'd never needed more than a week to break my way out of high-security prisons, and they must've known this. By forcing me to choose between sustenance and clarity every day, they've given themselves an advantage.

Still, I'm unconcerned.

The longer I'm here, the more leverage I gain. If they know what I'm capable of, they must also know that this is unsustainable. They can't use shock and poison to destabilize me indefinitely. I've now been here long enough to have taken stock of my surroundings, and I've been filing away information for nearly two weeks—the movements of the sun, the phases of the moon, the manufacturer of the locks, the sink, the unusual hinges on the door. I suspected, but now know for certain, that I'm in the southern hemisphere, not only because I know Max and Evie hail from Oceania, but because the northern constellations outside my window are upside down.

I must be on their base.

Logically, I know I must've been here a few times in my life, but the memories are dim. The night skies are clearer here than they were in Sector 45. The stars, brighter. The lack of light pollution means we are far from civilization, and the view out the window proves that we are surrounded, on all sides, by the wild landscape of this territory. There's a massive, glittering lake not far in the distance, which—

Something jolts to life in my mind.

The memory from earlier, expanded:

She shrugs and throws a rock in the lake. It lands with a dull splash. "Well, we'll just run away," she says.

"We can't run away," I say. "Stop saying that."

"We can, too."

"There's nowhere to go."

"There are plenty of places to go."

I shake my head. "You know what I mean. They'd find us wherever we went. They watch us all the time."

"We can live in the lake," she says simply.

"What?" I almost laugh. "What are you talking about?"

"I'm serious," she says. "I heard my mum talking about how to make it so people can live underwater, and I'm going to ask her to tell me, and then we can live in the lake."

I sigh. "We can't live in the lake, Ella."

"Why not?" She turns and looks at me, her eyes wide, startlingly bright. Blue green. Like the globe, I think. Like the whole world. "Why can't we live in the lake? My mum says th—"

"Stop it, Ella. Stop—"

A cold sweat breaks out on my forehead. Goose bumps rise along my skin. *Ella.*

Ella Ella Ella

Over and over again.

Everything about the name is beginning to sound familiar. The movement of my tongue as I form the word, familiar. It's as if the memory is in my muscle, as if my mouth has made this shape a thousand times.

I force myself to take a steadying breath.

I need to find her. *I have to find her.*

Here is what I know:

It takes just under thirty seconds for the footsteps to disappear down the hall, and they're always the same—same stride, same cadence—which means there's only one person attending to me. The paces are long and heavy, which means my attendant is tall, possibly male. Maybe Max himself, if they've deemed me a high-priority prisoner. Still, they've left me unshackled and unharmed—*why?*—and though I've been given neither bed nor blanket, I have access to water from the sink.

There's no electricity in here; no outlets, no wires. But there must be cameras hidden somewhere, watching my every move. There are two drains: one in the sink, and one underneath the toilet. There's one square foot of window—likely bulletproof glass, maybe eight to ten centimeters thick—and a single, small air vent in the floor. The vent has no visible screws, which means it must be bolted from inside, and the slats are too narrow for my fingers, the steel blades visibly welded in place. Still, it's only an average level of security for a prison vent. A little more time and clarity, and I'll find a way to remove the screen and repurpose the parts. Eventually, I'll find a way to dismantle everything in this room. I'll take apart the metal toilet, the flimsy metal sink. I'll make my own tools and weapons and find a way to slowly, carefully disassemble the locks and hinges. Or perhaps I'll damage the pipes and flood the room and its adjoining hallway, forcing someone to come to the door.

The sooner they send someone to my room, the better. If they've left me alone in my cell this long, it's been for their own protection, not my suffering. I excel at hand-to-hand combat.

I know myself. I know my capacity to withstand

complicated physical and mental torture. If I wanted to, I could give myself two—maybe three—weeks to forgo the poisoned meals and survive on water alone before I lost my mind or mobility. I know how resourceful I can be, given the opportunity, and this—this effort to contain me—must be exhausting. Great care went into selecting these sounds and meals and rituals and even this vigilant lack of communication.

It doesn't make sense that they'd go to all this trouble for treason. No. I must be in purgatory for something else.

I rack my brain for a motive, but my memories are surprisingly thin when it comes to Max and Evie. Still forming.

With some difficulty, I'm able to conjure up flickers of images.

A brief handshake with my father.

A burst of laughter.

A cheerful swell of holiday music.

A laboratory and my mother.

I stiffen.

A laboratory and my mother.

I focus my thoughts, homing in on the memory—*bright lights, muffled footsteps, the sound of my own voice asking my father a question* and then, painfully—

My mind goes blank.

I frown. Stare into my hands.

Nothing.

I know a great deal about the other commanders and

their families. It's been my business to know. But there's an unusual dearth of information where Oceania is concerned, and for the first time, it sends a shock of fear through me. There are two timelines merging in my mind—a life with Ella, and a life without her—and I'm still learning to sift through the information for something real.

Still, thinking about Max and Evie now seems to strain something in my brain. It's as if there's something there, something just out of reach, and the more I force my mind to recall them—their faces, their voices—the more it hurts.

Why all this trouble to imprison me?

Why not simply have me killed?

I have so many questions it's making my head spin.

Just then, the door rattles. The sound of metal on metal is sharp and abrasive, the sounds like sandpaper against my nerves.

I hear the bolt unlock and feel unusually calm. I was built to handle this life, its blows, its sick, sadistic ways. Death has never scared me.

But when the door swings open, I realize my mistake.

I imagined a thousand different scenarios. I prepared for a myriad of opponents. But I had not prepared for this.

"Hi birthday boy," he says, laughing as he steps into the light. "Did you miss me?"

And I'm suddenly unable to move.

~~JULIETTE~~

ELLA

"Stop—stop it, oh my God, that's disgusting," Emmaline cries. "Stop it. Stop touching each other! You guys are so gross."

Dad pinches Mum's butt, right in front of us.

Emmaline screams. "Oh my God, I said stop!"

It's Saturday morning, and Saturday morning is when we make pancakes, but Mum and Dad don't really get around to cooking anything because they won't stop kissing each other. Emmaline hates it.

I think it's nice.

I sit at the counter and prop my face in my hands, watching. I prefer watching. Emmaline keeps trying to make me work, but I don't want to. I like sitting better than working.

"No one is making pancakes," Emmaline cries, and she spins around so angrily she knocks a bowl of batter to the ground. "Why am I doing all the work?"

Dad laughs. "Sweetheart, we're all together," he says, scooping up the fallen bowl. He grabs a bunch of paper towels and says, "Isn't that more important than pancakes?"

"No," Emmaline says angrily. "We're supposed to make pancakes. It's Saturday, which means we're supposed to make pancakes, and you and Mum are just kissing, and Ella is being lazy—"

"Hey—" I say, and stand up.

"—and no one is doing what they're supposed to be doing and instead I'm doing it all by myself—"

Mum and Dad are both laughing now.

"It's not funny!" Emmaline cries, and now she's shouting, tears streaking down her face. "It's not funny, and I don't like it when no one listens to me, and I don't—"

Two weeks ago, I was lying on an operating table, limp, naked, and leaking blood through an aperture in my temple the size of a gunshot wound. My vision was blurred. I couldn't hear much more than the sound of my own breathing, hot and heavy and everywhere, building in and around me. Suddenly, Evie came into view. She was staring at me; she seemed frustrated. She'd been trying to complete the process of *physical recalibration*, as she called it.

For some reason, she couldn't finish the job.

She'd already emptied the contents of sixteen syringes into my brain, and she'd made several small incisions in my abdomen, my arms, and my thighs. I couldn't see exactly what she did next, but she spoke, occasionally, as she worked, and she claimed that the simple surgical procedures she was performing would strengthen my joints and reinforce my muscles. She wanted me to be stronger, to be more resilient on a cellular level. It was a preventative measure, she said. She was worried my build was too slight; that my muscles might degenerate prematurely in the face of intense physical challenges. She didn't say it, but I felt it: she wanted me to be stronger than my sister.

"Emmaline," I whispered.

It was lucky that I was too exhausted, too broken, too sedated to speak clearly. It was lucky that I only lay there, eyes fluttering open and closed, my chapped lips making it impossible to do more than mutter the name. It was lucky that I couldn't understand, right away, that I was still *me*. That I still remembered everything despite Evie's promises to dissolve what was left of my mind.

Still, I'd said the wrong thing.

Evie stopped what she was doing. She leaned over my face and studied me, nose to nose.

I blinked.

Don't

The words appeared in my head as if they'd been planted there long ago, like I was remembering, remembering

Evie jerked backward and immediately started speaking into a device clenched in her fist. Her voice was low and rough and I couldn't make out what she was saying.

I blinked again. Confused. I parted my lips to say something, when—

Don't

The thought came through more sharply this time.

A moment later Evie was in my face again, this time

drilling me with questions.

who are you
where are you
what is your name
where were you born
how old are you
who are your parents
where do you live

I was suddenly aware enough to understand that Evie was checking her work. She wanted to make sure my brain had been wiped clean. I wasn't sure what I was supposed to say or do, so I said nothing.

Instead, I blinked.

Blinked a lot.

Evie finally—reluctantly—stepped away, but she didn't seem entirely convinced of my stupidity. And then, when I thought she might murder me just to be safe, she stopped. Stared at the wall.

And then she left.

I was trembling on the operating table for twenty minutes before the room was swarmed by a team of people. They unstrapped my body, washed and wrapped my open wounds.

I think I was screaming.

Eventually the combination of pain, exhaustion, and the slow drip of opiates caught up with me, and I passed out.

I never understood what happened that day.

I couldn't ask, Evie never explained, and the strange, sharp voice in my head never returned. But then, Evie sedated me so much in my first weeks on this compound that it's possible there was never even a chance.

Today, for the first time since that day, I hear it again.

I'm standing in the middle of my room, this gauzy yellow dress still bunched in my arms, when the voice assaults me.

It knocks the wind out of me.

Ella

I spin around, my breaths coming in fast. The voice is louder than it's ever been, frightening in its intensity. Maybe I was wrong about Evie's experiment, maybe this is part of it, maybe hallucinating and hearing voices is a precursor to oblivion—

No

"Who are you?" I say, the dress dropping to the floor. It occurs to me, as if from a distance, that I'm standing in my underwear, screaming at an empty room, and a violent shudder goes through my body.

Roughly, I yank the yellow dress over my head, its light, breezy layers like silk against my skin. In a different lifetime, I would've loved this dress. It's both beautiful and comfortable, the perfect sartorial combination. But there's no time for that kind of frivolity anymore.

Today, this dress is just a part of the role I must play.

The voice in my head has gone quiet, but my heart is still racing. I feel propelled into motion by instinct alone, and, quickly, I slip into a pair of simple white tennis shoes, tying the laces tightly. I don't know why, but today, *right now*, for some reason—I feel like I might need to run.

Yes

My spine straightens.

Adrenaline courses through my veins and my muscles feel tight, burning with an intensity that feels brand-new to me; it's the first time I've felt any positive effects of Evie's procedures. This strength feels like it's been grafted to my bones, like I could launch myself into the air, like I could scale a wall with one hand.

I've known superstrength before, but that strength always felt like it was coming from elsewhere, like it was something I had to harness and release. Without my supernatural abilities—when I turned off my powers—I was left with an unimpressive, flimsy body. I'd been undernourished for years, forced to endure extreme physical and mental conditions, and my body suffered for it. I'd only begun to learn proper forms of exercise and conditioning in the last couple of months, and while the progress I made was helpful, it was only the first step in the right direction.

But this—

Whatever Evie did to me? This is different.

Two weeks ago I was in so much pain I could hardly move. The next morning, when I could finally stand on my own, I saw no discernible difference in my body except that I was seven shades of purple from top to bottom. Everything was bruised. I was walking agony.

Evie told me, as my doctor, that she kept me sedated so that I'd be forced to remain still in order to heal more quickly, but I had no reason to believe her. I still don't. But this is the first time in two weeks that I feel almost normal. The bruises have nearly faded. Only the incision sites, the most painful entry points, still look a little yellow.

Not bad.

I flex my fists and feel powerful, truly powerful, even with the glowing manacles clamped around my wrists and ankles. I've desperately missed my powers, missed them more than I ever thought I could miss something I'd spent so many years hating about myself. But for the first time in weeks, I feel strong. I know Evie did this to me—did this to my muscles—and I know I should distrust it, but it feels so good to feel good that I almost can't help but revel in it.

And right now, I feel like I could—

Run

I go still.

RUN

"What?" I whisper, turning to scan the walls, the ceiling. "Run where?"

Out

The word thunders through me, reverberates along my rib cage. *Out.* As if it were that simple, as if I could turn the doorknob and be rid of this nightmare. If it were that easy to leave this room, I would've done it already. But Evie reinforces the locks on my door with multiple layers of security. I only saw the mechanics of it once, when she returned me to my room after allowing me to look outside for a few minutes. In addition to the discreet cameras and retina displays, there's a biometric scanner that reads Evie's fingerprints to allow her access to the room. I've spent hours trying to get my bedroom door open, to no avail.

Out

Again, that word, loud and harsh inside my head. There's something terrifying about the hope that snakes through me at the thought of escape. It clings and tugs and tempts me to be crazy enough to listen to the absurd hallucinations attacking my mind.

This could be a trap, I think.

This could all be Evie's doing. I could be playing directly

into her hand.

Still.

I can't help myself.

I cross the room in a few quick strides. I hesitate, my hand hovering over the handle, and, with a final exhalation, I give in.

The door swings opens easily.

I stand in the open doorway, my heart racing harder. A heady rush of feeling surges through me and I look around desperately, studying the many hallways stretching out before me.

This seems impossible.

I have no idea where to go. No idea if I'm crazy for listening to a manipulative voice in my head after my psychotic mother spent hours injecting things into my mind.

It's only when I remember that I first heard this voice the night I arrived—just moments before Evie began torturing me—that I begin to doubt my doubt.

Dying

That was what the voice said to me that first night. *Dying*.

I was lying on an operating table, unable to move or speak. I could only shout inside my head and I wanted to know where Emmaline was. I tried to scream it.

Dying, the voice had said.

A cold, paralyzing fear fills my blood.
"Emmaline?" I whisper. "Is that you?"

Help

I take a certain step forward.

WARNER

"I'm a little early," he says. "I know your birthday is tomorrow, but I just couldn't wait any longer."

I stare at my father as though he might be a ghost. Worse, a poltergeist. I can't bring myself to speak, and for some reason he doesn't seem to mind my silence.

Then—

He smiles.

It's a true smile, one that softens his features and brightens his eyes. We're in something that looks like a sitting room, a bright, open space with plush couches, chairs, a round table, and a small writing desk in the corner. There's a thick carpet underfoot. The walls are a pleasant, pale yellow, sun pouring in through large windows. My father's figure is backlit. He looks ethereal. Glowing, like he might be an angel.

This world has a sick sense of humor.

He tossed me a robe when he walked into my cell, but hasn't offered me anything else. I haven't been given a chance to change. I haven't been offered food or water. I feel underdressed—vulnerable—sitting across from him in nothing but cold underwear and a thin robe. I don't even have socks. Slippers. *Something.*

And I can only imagine what I must look like right now, considering it's been a couple of weeks since I've had a shave or a haircut. I managed to keep myself clean in prison, but my hair is a bit longer now. Not like it used to be, but it's getting there. And my face—

I touch my face almost without thinking.

Touching my face has become a bit of a habit these last couple of weeks. I have a beard. It's not much of a beard, but it's enough to surprise me, every time. I have no idea how I must look right now.

Untamed, perhaps.

Finally, I say, "You're supposed to be dead."

"Surprise," he says, and smiles.

I only stare at him.

My father leans against the table and stuffs his hands into his pants' pockets in a way that makes him look boyish. Charming.

It makes me feel ill.

I look away, scanning the room for help. Details. Something to root me, something to explain *him*, something to arm me against what might be coming.

I come up short.

He laughs. "You know, you could stand to show a bit more emotion. I actually thought you might be happy to see me."

That gets my attention. "You thought wrong," I say. "I was happy to hear you were dead."

"Are you sure?" He tilts his head. "You're sure you didn't

shed a single tear for me? Didn't miss me even the tiniest bit?"

All it takes is a moment of hesitation. The half-second delay during which I remember the weeks I spent caught in a prison of half grief, hating myself for mourning him, and hating that I ever cared at all.

I open my mouth to speak and he cuts me off, his smile triumphant. "I know this must be a bit unsettling. And I know you're going to pretend you don't care. But we both know that your bleeding heart has always been the source of all our problems, and there's no point trying to deny that now. So I'll be generous and offer to overlook your treasonous behavior."

My spine stiffens.

"You didn't think I'd just forget, did you?" My father is no longer smiling. "You try to overthrow *me*—my government, my continent—and then you stand aside like a perfect, pathetic piece of garbage as your girlfriend attempts to *murder* me—and you thought I'd never mention it?"

I can't look at him anymore. I can't stand the sight of his face, so like my own. His skin is still perfect, unscarred. As if he'd never been injured. Never taken a bullet to the forehead.

I don't understand it.

"No? You still won't be inspired to respond?" he says. "In that case, you might be smarter than I gave you credit for."

There. That feels more like him.

"But the fact remains that we're at an important crossroads right now. I had to call in a number of favors to have you transported here unharmed. The council was going to vote to have you executed for treason, and I was able to convince them otherwise."

"Why would you even bother?"

His eyes narrow as he appraises me. "I save your life," he says, "and this is your reaction? Insolence? Ingratitude?"

"This," I say sharply, "is your idea of saving my life? Throwing me in prison and having me poisoned to death?"

"That should've been a picnic." His gaze grows cold. "You really would be better off dead if those circumstances were enough to break you."

I say nothing.

"Besides, we had to punish you somehow. Your actions couldn't go unchecked." My father looks away. "We've had a lot of messes to clean up," he says finally. "Where do you think I've been all this time?"

"As I said, I thought you were dead."

"Close, but not quite. Actually," he says, taking a breath, "I spent a great deal of time convalescing. *Here*. I was airlifted back here, where the Sommerses have been reviving me." He pulls up the hem of his pants and I glimpse the silver gleam of metal where his ankle should be. "I've got new feet," he says, and laughs. "Can you believe it?"

I can't. I can't believe it.

I'm stunned.

He smiles, obviously satisfied with my reaction. "We let

you and your friends think you'd had a victory just long enough to give me time to recover. We sent the rest of the kids down to distract you, to make it seem like The Reestablishment might actually accept its new, self-appointed commander." He shakes his head. "A seventeen-year-old child declaring herself the ruler of North America," he says, almost to himself. And then, looking up: "That girl really was a piece of work, wasn't she?"

Panic gathers in my chest. "What did you do to her? Where is she?"

"No." My father's smile disappears. "Absolutely not."

"What does that mean?"

"It means *absolutely not*. That girl is done. She's gone. No more afternoon specials with your buddies from Omega Point. No more running around naked with your little girlfriend. No more sex in the afternoon when you should be working."

I feel both ill and enraged. "Don't you dare—Don't *ever* talk about her like that. You have no right—"

He sighs, long and loud. Mutters something foul. "When are you going stop this? When will you grow out of this?"

It takes everything I've got to bite back my anger. To sit here, calmly, and say nothing. Somehow, my silence makes things worse.

"Dammit, Aaron," he says, getting to his feet. "I keep waiting for you to move on. To get over her. To *evolve*," he says, practically shouting at me now. "It's been over a decade of the same bullshit."

Over a decade.

A slip.

"What do you mean," I say, studying him carefully. "'Over a decade'?"

"I'm exaggerating," he says, biting off the words. "Exaggerating to make a point."

"*Liar.*"

For the first time, something uncertain flashes through my father's eyes.

"Will you admit it?" I say quietly. "Will you admit to me what I already know?"

He sets his jaw. Says nothing.

"*Admit it,*" I say. "Juliette was an alias. Juliette Ferrars is actually Ella Sommers, the daughter of Evie and Maximillian Som—"

"How—" My father catches himself. He looks away and then, too soon, he looks back. He seems to be deciding something.

Finally, slowly, he nods.

"You know what? It's better this way. Better for you to know," he says quietly. "Better for you to understand exactly why you're never going to see her again."

"That's not up to you."

"Not up to me?" Rage flashes in and out of his eyes, his cool mask quickly crumbling. "That girl has been the bane of my existence for *twelve years,*" he says. "She's caused me more problems than you can even begin to understand, not the least of which has been to distract my idiot son for the better part of the last decade. Despite my every effort to break you apart—to remove this cancer from our lives—you've insisted, over and over again, on falling in love with her." He looks me in the eye, his own eyes wild with fury. "She was never meant for you. She was never meant for any of this. That girl was sentenced to death," he says viciously, "the moment I named her Juliette."

My heart is beating so hard it feels as though I'm dreaming. This must be a nightmare. I have to force myself to speak. To say:

"What are you talking about?"

My father's mouth twists into an imitation of a smile.

"Ella," he says, "was designed to become a tool for war. She and her sister both, right from the beginning. Decades before we took over, sicknesses were beginning to ravage the population. The government was trying to bury the information, but we knew. I saw the classified files. I tracked down one of the secret bunkers. People were malfunctioning, metamorphosing—so much so that it felt almost like the next phase of evolution. Only Evie had the presence of mind to see the sickness as a tool. She was the one who first began studying the Unnaturals. She was the reason we created the asylums—she wanted access to more varieties of the illness—and she was the one who learned how to isolate and reproduce the alien DNA. It was her idea to use the findings to help our cause. Ella and Emmaline," he says angrily, "were only ever meant to be Evie's science experiments. Ella was never meant for you. Never meant for *anyone*," he shouts. "Get her out of your head."

I feel frozen as the words settle around me. Within me. The revelation isn't entirely new and yet—the pain is fresh. Time seems to slow down, speed up, spin backward. My eyes fall closed. My memories collect and expand, exploding with renewed meaning as they assault me, all at once—

Ella through the ages.

My childhood friend.

Ella, ripped away from me when I was seven years old. Ella and Emmaline, who they'd said had drowned in the lake. They told me to forget, to forget the girls ever existed and, finally, tired of answering my questions, they told me they'd make things easier for me. I followed my father into a room where he promised he'd explain everything.

And then—

I'm strapped to a chair, my head held in place with heavy metal clamps. Bright lights flash and buzz above me.

I hear the monitors chirping, the muffled sounds of voices around me. The room feels large and cavernous, gleaming. I hear the loud, disconcerting sounds of my own breathing and the hard, heavy beats of my heart. I jump, a little, at the unwelcome feel of my father's hand on my arm, telling me I'll feel better soon.

I look up at him as if emerging from a dream.

"What is it?" he says. "What just happened?"

I part my lips to speak, wonder if it's safe to tell him the truth.

I decide I'm tired of the lies.

"I've been remembering her," I say.

My father's face goes unexpectedly blank, and it's the only reaction I need to understand the final, missing piece.

"You've been stealing my memories," I say to him, my voice unnaturally calm. "All these years. You've been tampering with my mind. It was you."

He says nothing, but I see the tension in his jaw, the sudden jump of a vein under skin. "What are you remembering?"

I shake my head, stunned as I stare at him. "I should've known. After everything you've done to me—" I stop, my vision shifts, unfocused for a moment. "Of course you wouldn't let me be master of my own mind."

"What, exactly, are you remembering?" he says, hardly able to control the anger in his voice now. "What else do you know?"

At first, I feel nothing.

I've trained myself too well. Years of practice have taught me to bury my emotions as a reflex—especially in his presence—and it takes a few seconds for the feelings to emerge. They form slowly, infinite hands reaching up from infinite graves to fan the flames of an ancient rage I've never really allowed myself to touch.

"You stole my memories of her," I say quietly. "Why?"

"Always so focused on the girl." He glares at me. "She's not the center of everything, Aaron. I stole your memories of lots of things."

I'm shaking my head. I get to my feet slowly, at once out of my mind and perfectly calm, and I worry, for a moment, that I might actually expire from the full force of everything I feel for him. Hatred so deep it might boil me alive.

"Why would you do something like this except to torture me? You knew how I felt about her. You did it on purpose. Pushing us together and pulling us apart—" I stop suddenly. Realization dawns, bright and piercing and I look at him, unable to fathom the depth of his cruelty.

"You put Kent under my command on purpose," I say.

My father meets my eyes with a vacant expression. He says nothing.

"I find it hard to believe you didn't know the whereabouts of your illegitimate children," I say to him. "I don't believe for a second that you weren't having Kent's every move monitored. You must've known what he was doing with his life. You must've been notified the moment he enlisted.

"You could've sent him anywhere," I say. "You had the power to do that. Instead, you let him remain in Sector 45— under *my* jurisdiction—on purpose. Didn't you? And when you had Delalieu show me those files—when he came to me, convinced me that Kent would be the perfect cellmate for Juliette because here was proof that he'd known her, that they'd gone to school together—"

Suddenly, my father smiles.

"I've always tried to tell you," he says softly. "I've tried to tell you to stop letting your emotions rule your mind. Over and over, I tried to teach you, and you never listened. You never learned." He shakes his head. "If you suffer now, it's because you brought it upon yourself. You made yourself an easy target."

I'm stunned.

Somehow, even after everything, he manages to shock me. "I don't understand how you can stand there, defending your actions, after you spent twenty years torturing me."

"I've only ever been trying to teach you a lesson, Aaron. I didn't want you to end up like your mother. She was weak, just like you."

I need to kill him.

I picture it: what it would be like to pin him to the ground, to stab him repeatedly through the heart, to watch the light go out of his eyes, to feel his body go cold under my hands.

I wait for fear.

Revulsion.

Regret.

They don't come.

I have no idea how he survived the last attempt on his life, but I no longer care to know the answer. I want him dead. I want to watch his blood pool in my hands. I want to rip his throat out.

I spy a letter opener on the writing desk nearby, and in the single second I take to swipe it, my father laughs.

Laughs.

Out loud. Doubled over, one hand holding his side. When he looks up, there are actual tears in his eyes.

"Have you lost your mind?" he says. "Aaron, don't be ridiculous."

I step forward, the letter opener clutched loosely in my fist, and I watch, carefully, for the moment he understands that I'm going to kill him. I want him to know that it's going to be me. I want him to know that he finally got what he wanted.

That he finally broke me.

"You made a mistake sparing my life," I say quietly. "You made a mistake showing your face. You made a mistake thinking you could ask me to come back, after all you've done—"

"You misunderstand me." He's standing straight again, the laughter gone from his face. "I'm not asking you to come back. You don't have a choice."

"Good. That makes this easier."

"Aaron." He shakes his head. "I'm not unarmed. I'm entirely willing to kill you if you step out of line. And though I can't claim that murdering my son is my favorite way to spend a morning, that doesn't mean I won't do it. So you need to stop and think, for just a moment, before you step forward and commit suicide."

I study him. My fingers flex around the weapon in my hand. "Tell me where she is," I say, "and I'll consider sparing your life."

"You fool. Have you not been listening to me? *She's gone.*"

I stiffen. Whatever he means by that, he's not lying. "Gone where?"

"*Gone,*" he says angrily. "Disappeared. The girl you knew no longer exists."

He pulls a remote out of his jacket pocket and points it at the wall. An image appears instantly, projected from elsewhere, and the sound that fills the room is so sudden—so jarring and unexpected—it nearly brings me to my knees.

It's Ella.

She's screaming.

Blood drips down her open, screaming mouth, the agonizing sounds punctured only by the heaving sobs that pull ragged, aching breaths from her body. Her eyes are half open, delirious, and I watch as she's unstrapped from a chair and dragged onto a stretcher. Her body spasms, her arms and legs jerking uncontrollably. She's in a white hospital gown, the insubstantial ties coming undone, the thin fabric damp with her own blood.

My hands shake uncontrollably as I watch, her head whipping back and forth, her body straining against her restraints. She screams again and a bolt of pain shoots through me, so excruciating it nearly bends me in half. And then, quickly, as if out of nowhere, someone steps forward and stabs a needle in her neck.

Ella goes still.

Her body is frozen, her face captured in a single moment of agony before the drug kicks in, collapsing her. Her screams dissolve into smaller, steadier whimpers. She cries, even as her eyes close.

I feel violently ill.

My hands are shaking so hard I can no longer form a fist, and I watch, as if from afar, as the letter opener falls to the floor. I hold still, forcing back the urge to vomit, but the action provokes a shudder so disorienting I almost lose my balance. Slowly, I turn to face my father, whose eyes are inscrutable.

It takes two tries before I'm able to form a single, whispered word:

"What?"

He shakes his head, the picture of false sympathy. "I'm trying to get you to understand. This," he says, nodding at the screen, "this is what she's destined for. Forever. Stop imagining your life with her. Stop thinking of her as a *person*—"

"This can't be real," I say, cutting him off. I feel wild. Unhinged. "This—Tell me this isn't real. What are you doing to me? Is this—"

"Of course it's real," he says. "Juliette is gone. Ella is gone. She's as good as dead. She had her mind wiped *weeks* ago. But you," he says, "you still have a life to live. Are you listening to me? You have to pull yourself together."

But I can't hear him over the sound of Ella sobbing.

She's still weeping—the sounds softer, sadder, more desperate. She looks terrified. Small and helpless as foreign hands bandage the open wounds on her arms, the backs of her legs. I watch as glowing metal cuffs are shackled to her wrists and ankles. She whimpers once more.

And I feel insane.

I must be. Listening to her scream—watching her fight for her life, watching her choke on her own blood while I stand here, powerless to help her—

I'll never be able to forget the sound.

No matter what happens, no matter where I run, these screams—her screams—will haunt me forever.

"You wanted me to watch this?" I'm whispering now; I can hardly speak. "Why would you want me to watch this?"

He says something to me. Shouts something at me. But I feel suddenly deaf.

The sounds of the world seem warped, faraway, like my head has been submerged underwater. The fire in my brain has been snuffed out, replaced by a sudden, absolute calm. A sense of certainty. I know what I need to do now. And I know that there's nothing—nothing I won't do to get to her.

I feel it, feel my thin morals dissolving. I feel my flimsy, moth-eaten skin of humanity begin to come apart, and with it, the veil keeping me from complete darkness. There are no lines I won't cross. No illusions of mercy.

I wanted to be better for her. For her happiness. For her future.

But if she's gone, what good is goodness?

I take a deep, steadying breath. I feel oddly liberated, no longer shackled by an obligation to decency. And in one simple move, I pick up the letter opener I dropped on the floor.

"Aaron," he says, a warning in his voice.

"I don't want to hear you speak," I say. "I don't want you

to talk to me ever again."

I throw the knife even before the words have left my mouth. It flies hard and fast, and I enjoy the second it soars through the air. I enjoy the way the second expands, exploding in the strangeness of time. It all feels like slow motion. My father's eyes widen in a rare display of unmasked shock, and I smile at the sound of his gasp when the weapon finds its mark. I was aiming for his jugular, and it looks like my aim was true. He chokes, his eyes bulging as his hands move, shakily, to yank the letter opener from its home in his neck.

He coughs, suddenly, blood spattering everywhere, and with some effort, he's able to pull the thing free. Fresh blood gushes down his shirt, seeps from his mouth. He can't speak; the blade has penetrated his larynx. Instead, he gasps, still choking, his mouth opening and closing like a dying fish.

He falls to his knees.

His hands grasp at air, his veins jumping under his skin, and I step toward him. I watch him as he begs, silently, for something, and then I pat him down, pocketing the two guns I find concealed on his person.

"Enjoy hell," I whisper, before walking away.

Nothing matters anymore.

I have to find her.

~~JULIETTE~~

ELLA

Left.
Right.
Straight.
Left.

The commands keep my feet moving safely down the hall. This compound is vast. Enormous. My bedroom was so ordinary that the truth of this facility is jarring. An open framework reveals many dozens of floors, hallways and staircases intertwining like overpasses and freeways. The ceiling seems miles away, high and arched and intricate. Exposed steel beams meet clean white walkways centered around an open, interior courtyard. I had no idea I was so high up. And, somehow, for such a huge building, I haven't yet been spotted.

Things are growing more eerie by the minute.

I encounter no one as I go; I'm ordered to run, detour, or hide just in time to avoid passersby. It's uncanny. Still, I've been walking for at least twenty minutes, and I don't seem to be getting closer to anything. I have no idea where I am in the scheme of things, and there are no windows nearby. The whole facility feels like a gilded prison.

A long stretch of silence between myself and my imaginary friend starts making me nervous. I think this voice might be Emmaline's, but she still hasn't confirmed it. And though I want to say something, I feel silly speaking out loud. So I speak only inside my mind when I say:

Emmaline? Are you there?

No response.
My nervousness reaches its peak and I stop walking.

Where are you taking me?

This time, the answer comes quickly:

Escape

Are we getting closer? I ask.

Yes

I take a deep breath and forge ahead, but I feel a creeping dread infiltrate my senses. The longer I walk—down hallways and infinite staircases—the closer I seem to be getting to *something*—something that fills me with fear. I can't explain it.

It's clear I'm going underground.

The lights are growing dimmer as I go. The halls are

beginning to narrow. The windows and staircases are beginning to disappear. And I know I'm only getting closer to the bowels of the building when the walls change. Gone are the smooth, finished white walls of the upper floors. Here, everything is unfinished cement. It smells cold and wet. Earthy. The lights buzz and hum, occasionally snapping.

Fear continues to pulse up my spine.

I shuffle down a slight slope, my shoes slipping a little as I go. My lungs squeeze. My heartbeat feels loud, too loud, and a strange sensation begins to fill my arms and legs. Feeling. Too much feeling. It makes my skin crawl, makes my bones itch. I feel suddenly restless and anxious. And just as I'm about to lose hope in this crazy, meandering escape route—

Here

I stop.

I'm standing in front of a massive stone door. My heart is racing in my throat. I hesitate, fear beginning to fissure my certainty.

Open

"Who are you?" I ask again, this time speaking out loud. "This doesn't look like an escape route."

Open

I squeeze my eyes shut; fill my lungs with air.

I came all this way, I tell myself. I have no other options at the moment. I may as well see it through.

But when I open the door I realize it's only the first of several. Wherever I'm headed is protected by multiple layers of security. The mechanisms required to open each door are baffling—there are no knobs or handles, no traditional hinges—but all I have to do is touch the door for it to swing open.

It's too easy.

Finally, I'm standing in front of a steel wall. There's nothing here to indicate there might be a room beyond.

Touch

Tentatively, I touch my fingers to the metal.

More

I press my whole hand firmly against the door, and within seconds, the wall melts away. I look around nervously and step forward.

Immediately, I know I've been led astray.

I feel sick as I look around, sick and terrified. This place is so far from an escape I almost can't believe I fell for it. I'm in a laboratory.

Another laboratory.

Panic collapses something inside me, bones and organs

knocking together, blood rushing to my head. I run for the door and it seals shut, the steel wall forming easily, as if from air.

I pull in a few sharp breaths, begging myself to stay calm.

"Show yourself," I shout. "Who are you? What do you want with me?"

Help

My heart shudders to a stop. I feel my fear expand and contract.

Dying

Goosebumps rise along my skin. My breath catches; my fists clench. I take a step farther into the room, and then a few more. I'm still wary, worried this is all yet another part of the trick—

Then I see it.

A glass cylinder as tall and wide as the wall, filled to the hilt with water. There's a creature floating inside of it. Something greater than fear is driving me forward, greater than curiosity, greater than wonder.

Feeling washes over me.

Memories crash into me.

A spindly arm reaches through the murky water, shaky fingers forming a loose fist that pounds, weakly, against the glass.

At first, all I see is her hand.

But the closer I get, the more clearly I'm able to see what they've done to her. And I can't hide my horror.

She inches closer to the glass and I catch sight of her face. She no longer has a face, not really. Her mouth has been permanently sealed around a regulator, skin spiderwebbing over silicone. Her hair is a couple feet long, dark and wild and floating around her head like wispy tentacles. Her nose has melted backward into her skull and her eyes are permanently closed, long dark lashes the only indication they ever used to open. Her hands and feet are webbed. She has no fingernails. Her arms and legs are mostly bone and sagging, wrinkled skin.

"Emmaline," I whisper.

Dying

The tears come hot and fast, hitting me without warning, breaking me from within.

"What did they do to you?" I say, my voice ragged. "How could they do this to you?"

A dull, metallic sound. Twice.

Emmaline is floating closer. She presses her webbed fingers against the barrier between us and I reach up, hastily wiping my eyes before I meet her there. I press my palm to the glass and somehow, impossibly, I feel her take my hand. Soft. Warm. Strong.

And then, with a gasp—

Feeling pulses through me, wave after wave of *feeling*, emotions as infinite as time. Memories, desires, long-extinguished hopes and dreams. The force of everything sends my head spinning; I slump forward and grit my teeth, steadying myself by pressing my forehead against the barrier between us. Images fill my mind like stilted frames from an old movie.

Emmaline's life.

She wants me to know. I feel like I'm being pulled into her, like she's reeling me into her own body, immersing me in her mind. Her memories.

I see her younger, much younger, eight or nine years old. She was spirited, furious. Difficult to control. Her mind was stronger than she could handle and she didn't know how to feel about her powers. She felt cursed, strangled by them. But unlike me, she was kept at home, here, in this exact laboratory, forced to undergo test after test administered by her own parents. I feel her rage pierce through me.

For the first time, I realize I had the luxury of forgetting. She didn't.

Max and Evie—and even Anderson—tried to wipe Emmaline's memory multiple times, but each time, Emmaline's body prevailed. Her mind was so strong that she was able to convince her brain to reverse the chemistry meant to dissolve her memories. No matter what Max and Evie tried, Emmaline could never forget them.

Instead, she watched as her own parents turned on her.

Turned her inside out.

Emmaline is telling me everything without saying a word. She can't speak. She's lost four of her five senses.

She went blind first.

She lost her sense of smell and sensation a year later, both at the same time. Finally, she lost the ability to speak. Her tongue and teeth disintegrated. Her vocal cords eroded. Her mouth sealed permanently shut.

She can only hear now. But poorly.

I see the scenes change, see her grow a little older, a little more broken. I see the fire go out of her eyes. And then, when she realizes what they have planned for her—The entire reason they wanted her, so desperately—

Violent horror takes my breath away.

I fall, kneecaps knocking the floor. The force of her feelings rips me open. Sobs break my back, shudder through my bones. I feel everything. Her pain, her endless pain.

Her inability to end her own suffering.

She wants this to end.

End, she says, the word sharp and explosive.

With some effort, I manage to lift my head to look at her. "Was it you this whole time?" I whisper. "Did you give me back my memories?"

Yes

"How? Why?"

She shows me.

I feel my spine straighten as the vision moves through me. I see Evie and Max, hear their warped conversations from inside the glass prison. They've been trying to make Emmaline stronger over the years, trying to find ways to enhance Emmaline's telekinetic abilities. They wanted her skills to evolve. They wanted her to be able to perform mind control.

Mind control of the masses.

It backfired.

The more they experimented on her—the further they pushed her—the stronger and weaker she became. Her mind was able to handle the physical manipulations, but her heart couldn't take it. Even as they built her up, they were breaking her down.

She'd lost the will to live. To fight.

She no longer had complete control over her own body; even her powers were now regulated through Max and Evie. She'd become a puppet. And the more listless she became, the more they misunderstood. Max and Evie thought Emmaline was growing compliant.

Instead, she was deteriorating.

And then—

Another scene. Emmaline hears an argument. Max and Evie are discussing *me*. Emmaline hasn't heard them mention me in years; she had no idea I was still alive. She hears that I've been fighting back. That I've been resisting, that I tried to kill a supreme commander.

Emmaline feels hope for the first time in years.

I clap my hands over my mouth. Take a step back.

Emmaline has no eyes, but I feel her staring at me. Watching me for a reaction. I feel unsteady, alert but overcome.

I finally understand.

Emmaline has been using her last gasp of strength to contact me—and not just me, but all the other children of the supreme commanders.

She shows me, inside my own mind, how she's taken advantage of Max and Evie's latest effort to expand her capabilities. She'd never been able to reach out to people individually before, but Max and Evie got greedy. In Emmaline they laid the foundation for their own demise.

Emmaline thinks we're the last hope for the world. She wants us to stand up, fight, save humanity. She's been slowly returning our minds to us, giving back what our parents once stole. She wants us to see the truth.

Help, she says.

"I will," I whisper. "I promise I will. But first I'm going to get you out of here."

Rage, hot and violent, sends me reeling. Emmaline's anger is sharp and terrifying, and a resounding

NO

fills my brain.

I go still. Confused.

"What do you mean?" I say. "I have to help you get out of here. We'll escape together. I have friends—healers—who can restore y—"

NO

And then, in a flash—

She fills my mind with an image so dark I think I might be sick.

"No," I say, my voice shaking. "I won't do it. I'm not going to kill you."

Anger, hot, ferocious anger, attacks my mind. Image after image assaults me, her failed suicide attempts, her inability to turn her own powers against herself, the infinite fail-safes Max and Evie put in place to make sure Emmaline couldn't take her own life, and that she couldn't harm theirs—

"Emmaline, please—"

HELP

"There has to be another way," I say desperately. "This can't be it. You don't have to die. We can get through this together."

She bangs her open palm against the glass. Tremors rock her emaciated body.

Already

dying

I step forward, press my hands to her prison. "It wasn't supposed to end like this," I say, the words broken. "There has to be another way. Please. I want my sister back. I want you to live."

More anger, hot and wild, begins to bloom in my mind and then—
a spike of fear.
Emmaline goes rigid in her tank.

Coming

I look around, steeling myself. Adrenaline spikes in my veins.

Wait

Emmaline has wrapped her arms around her body, her face pinched in concentration. I can still feel her with an immediacy so intimate it feels almost like her thoughts are my own.

And then, unexpectedly—

My shackles pop open.

I spin around as they fall to the floor with a rich clatter. I rub at my aching wrists, my ankles. "How did you—?"

Coming

I nod.

"Whatever happens today," I whisper, "I'm coming back for you. This isn't over. Do you hear me? Emmaline, I won't let you die here."

For the first time, Emmaline seems to relax.

Something warm and sweet fills my head, affection so unexpected it pricks my eyes.

I fight back the emotion.

Footsteps.

Fear has fled my body. I feel unusually calm. I'm stronger than I've ever been. There's strength in my bones, strength in my mind. And now that the cuffs are off, my powers are back on and a familiar feeling is surging through me; it's like being joined by an old friend.

I meet Evie's eyes as she walks through the door.

She's already pointing a gun at me. Not a gun—something that looks like a gun. I don't know what's in it.

"What are you doing here?" she says, her voice only slightly hysterical. "What have you done?"

I shake my head.

I can't look at her face anymore without feeling blind

rage. I can't even think her name without feeling a violent, potent, animalistic need to murder her with my bare hands. Evie Sommers is the worst kind of human being. A traitor to humanity. An unadulterated sociopath.

"What have you done?" she says again, this time betraying her fear. Her panic. The gun trembles in her fist. Her eyes are wide, crazed, darting from me to Emmaline, still trapped in the tank behind me.

And then—

I see it. I see the moment she realizes I'm not wearing my manacles.

Evie goes pale.

"I haven't done anything," I say softly. "Not yet."

Her gun falls, with a clatter, to the floor.

Unlike Paris, my mother isn't stupid. She knows there's no point trying to shoot me. She *created* me. She knows what I'm capable of. And she knows—I can see it in her eyes—she knows I'm about to kill her, and she knows there's nothing she can do to stop it.

Still, she tries.

"Ella," she says, her voice unsteady. "Everything we did—everything we've ever done—was to try to help you. We were trying to save the world. You have to understand."

I take a step forward. "I do understand."

"I just wanted to make the world a better place," she says. "Don't you want to make the world a better place?"

"Yes," I say. "I do."

She almost smiles. A small, broken breath escapes her body.

Relief.

I take two swift, running steps and punch her through the chest, ribs breaking under my knuckles. Her eyes widen and she chokes, staring at me in stunned, paralyzed silence. She coughs and blood spatters, hot and thick, across my face. I turn away, spitting her blood out of my mouth, and by the time I look back, she's dead.

With one last tug, I rip her heart out of her body.

Evie falls to the floor with a heavy thud, her eyes cold and glassy. I'm still holding my mother's heart, watching it die in my hands, when a familiar voice calls out to me.

Thank you

Thank you

Thank you

WARNER

I realize, upon quitting the crime scene, that I have no idea where I am. I stand in the middle of the hallway outside the room within which I just murdered my father, and try to figure out my next moves. I'm nearly naked. No socks. Completely barefoot. Far from ideal.

Still, I need to keep moving.

If only.

I don't make it five feet before I feel the familiar pinch of a needle. I feel it—even as I try to fight it—I feel it as a foreign chemical enters my body. It's only a matter of time before it pulls me under.

My vision blurs.

I try to beat it, try to remain standing, but my body is weak. After two weeks of near starvation, constant poisoning, and violent exhaustion, I've run out of reserves. The last dregs of my adrenaline have left me.

This is it.

I fall to the floor, and the memories consume me.

I gasp as I'm returned to consciousness, taking in great lungfuls of air as I sit up too fast, my head spinning.

There are wires taped to my temples, my limbs, the

plastic ends pinching the soft hinges of my arms and legs, pulling at the skin on my bare chest. I rip them off, causing great distress to the monitors nearby. I yank the needle out of my arm and toss it to the floor, applying pressure to the wound for a few seconds before deciding to let it bleed. I get to my feet, spinning around to assess my surroundings, but still feel off-balance.

I can only guess at who must've shot me with a tranquilizer; even so, I feel no urgency to panic. Killing my father has instilled in me an extraordinary serenity. It's a perverse, horrible thing to celebrate, but to murder my father was to vanquish my greatest fear. With him dead, anything seems possible.

I feel free.

Still, I need to focus on where I am, on what's happening. I need to be forming a plan of attack, a plan of escape, a plan to rescue Ella. But my mind is being pulled in what feels like a hundred different directions.

The memories are growing more intense by the minute.

I don't know how much more of this I can take. I don't know how long this barrage will last or how much more will be uncovered, but the emotional revelations are beginning to take their toll on me.

A few months ago, I knew I loved Ella. I knew I felt for her what I'd never felt before for anyone. It felt new and precious and tender.

Important.

But every day—every minute—of the last couple of

weeks I've been bombarded by memories of her I never even knew I had. Moments with her from years ago. The sound of her laughter, the smell of her hair, the look in her eyes when she smiled at me for the first time. The way it felt to hold her hand when everything was new and unknown—

Three years ago.

How could it be possible that I touched her like that three years ago? How could we have known then, without actually knowing *why*, that we could be together? That she could touch me without hurting me? How could any of these moments have been ripped from my mind?

I had no idea I'd lost so much of her. But then, I had no idea there'd been so much to lose.

A profound, painful ache has rooted inside of me, carrying with it the weight of years. Being apart from Juliette—*Ella*—has always been hard, but now it seems unsurvivable.

I'm being slowly decimated by emotion.

I need to see her. To hold her. To bind her to me, somehow. I won't believe a word my father said until I see her and speak with her in person.

I can't give up. Not yet.

To hell with what happened between us back on base. Those events feel like they happened lifetimes ago. Like they happened to different people. Once I find her and get her to safety I will find a way to make things right between us. It feels like something long dead inside of me is being slowly returned to life—like my hopes and dreams are being resuscitated, like the holes in my heart are being slowly, carefully mended. I will find her. And when I do, I will find a way to move forward with her, by my side, forever.

I take a deep breath.

And then I get to my feet.

I brace myself, expecting the familiar sting of my broken ribs, but the pain in my side is gone. Gingerly, I touch my torso; the bruising has disappeared. I touch my face and I'm surprised to discover that my skin is smooth, clean-shaven. I touch my hair and find it's been returned to its original length—exactly as it was before I had to cut it all off.

Strange.

Still, I feel more like myself than I have in a long time, and I'm quietly grateful. The only thing bothering me is that I'm wearing nothing but a dressing grown, under which I'm completely naked.

I'm sick of being naked.

I want my clothes. I want a proper pair of pants. I want—

And then, as if someone has read my mind, I notice a fresh set of clothes on a nearby table. Clothes that look exactly my size.

I pick up the sweater. Examine it.

These are my actual clothes. I know these pieces. Recognize them. And if that wasn't enough, my initials—AWA—are monogrammed on the cuff of the sweater. This was no accident. Someone brought my clothes here. From my own closet.

They were expecting me.

I dress quickly, grateful for the clean outfit regardless of the circumstances, and I'm nearly done with the straps on my boots when someone walks in.

"Max," I say, without lifting my head. Carefully, I step on the needle I'd tossed earlier to the floor. "How are you?"

He laughs out loud. "How did you know it was me?"

"I recognized the rhythm of your footfalls."

He goes quiet.

"Don't bother trying to deny it," I say, hiding the syringe in my hand as I sit up. I meet his eyes and smile. "I've been listening to your heavy, uneven gait for the last two weeks."

Max's eyes widen. "I'm impressed."

"And I appreciate the clean shave," I say, touching my face.

He laughs again, more softly this time. "You were pretty close to dead when I brought you in here. Imagine my surprise to find you nearly naked, severely dehydrated, half-starved, vitamin-deficient. You had three broken ribs. Your father's blood all over your hands."

"Three broken ribs? I thought it was two."

"Three broken ribs," Max says, and nods. "And still, you managed to sever Paris's carotid artery. Nicely done."

I meet his eyes. Max thinks this is funny.

And then I understand.

"He's still alive, isn't he?" I say.

Max smiles wider. "Quite alive, yes. Despite your best efforts to murder him."

"That seems impossible."

"You sound irritated," Max says.

"I am irritated. That he survived is an insult to my skill set."

Max fights back another laugh. "I don't remember you being so funny."

"I'm not trying to be funny."

But Max can't wipe the smile off his face.

"So you're not going to tell me how he survived?" I say. "You're just going to bait me?"

"I'm waiting for my wife," he says.

"I understand. Does she help you sound out the big words?"

Max's eyebrows jump up his forehead. "Watch yourself, Aaron."

"Apologies. Please step out of my way."

"As I said, I'm waiting for my wife. She has something she wants to say to you."

I study him, looking closely at his face in a way I can't remember ever having done. He has dark brown hair, light brown skin, and bright blue-green eyes. He's aged well. On a different day, I might've even described his face as warm, friendly. But knowing now that he's Ella's father—I almost can't believe I didn't notice sooner. She has his eyes.

I hear a second set of footsteps drawing nearer to the door. I expect to see Evie, Supreme Sommers, and instead—

"Max, how long do you think it'll take bef—"

My father. His voice.

I can hardly believe it.

He stops, just inside the doorway, when he sees my face.

He's holding a bloodied towel to his throat. "You *idiot*," he says to me.

I don't have a chance to respond.

A sharp alarm sounds, and Max goes suddenly rigid. He glances at a monitor on the wall before looking back at my father.

"Go," Anderson says. "I can handle him."

Max glances at me just once before he disappears.

"So," I say, nodding at my father's face, his healing wound. "Are you going to explain?"

He merely stares at me.

I watch, quietly, as he uses his free hand to pull a handkerchief from his pocket. He wipes the remaining blood from his lips, refolds the handkerchief, and tucks it back inside his pocket.

Something between us has changed.

I can feel it. Can feel the shift in his attitude toward me. It takes a minute to piece together the various emotional cues long enough to understand, but when it finally hits me, it hits me hard.

Respect.

For the first time in my life, my father is staring at me with something like respect. I tried to kill him, and instead of being angry with me, he seems pleased. Maybe even impressed.

"You did good work back there," he says quietly. "It was a strong throw. Solid."

It feels strange to accept his compliment, so I don't.

My father sighs.

"Part of the reason I wanted custody of those healer twins," he says finally, "was because I wanted Evie to study them. I wanted her to replicate their DNA and braid it into my own. Healing powers, I realized, were extremely useful."

A sharp chill goes up my spine.

"But I didn't have them under my control for as long as I wanted," he says. "I was only able to extract a few blood samples. Evie did the best she could with the time we had."

I blink. Try to control the expression on my face. "So you have healing powers now?"

"We're still working on it," he says, his jaw tight. "It's not yet perfect. But it was enough that I was able to survive the wounds to the head just long enough to be shipped to safety." He smiles a bitter smile. "My feet, on the other hand, didn't make it."

"How unfortunate," I lie.

I test the weight of the syringe in my hand. I wonder how much damage it could do. It's not substantial enough to do much more than stun, but a carefully angled attack could result in temporary nerve pain that would buy me a sizable amount of time. But then, so might a single, precise stab in the eye.

"Operation Synthesis," my father says sharply.

I look up. Surprised.

"You're ready, Aaron." His gaze is steady. "You're ready for a real challenge. You've got the necessary fire. The drive. I'm seeing it in your eyes for the first time."

I'm too afraid to speak.

Finally, after all these years, my father is giving me praise. He's telling me I'm capable. As a child, it was everything I'd ever wanted.

But I'm not a child anymore.

"You've seen Emmaline," my father says. "But you haven't seen her recently. You don't know what state she's in."

I wait.

"She's dying," he says. "Her body isn't strong enough to survive her mind or her environment, and despite Max and Evie's every effort, they don't know if there's anything else they can do to help her. They've been working for years to prolong her life as much as possible, but they've reached the end of the line. There's nothing left to do. She's deteriorating at a rate they can no longer control."

Still, I say nothing.

"Do you understand?" my father says to me. "Do you understand the importance of what I'm saying to you? Emmaline is not only a psychokinetic, but a telepath," he says. "As her body deteriorates, her mind grows wilder. She's too strong. Too explosive. And lately, without a strong enough body to contain her, she's become volatile. If she's not given a n—"

"Don't you dare," a voice barks, loudly, into the room. "Don't you dare say another word. You thickheaded *fool*."

I spin around, surprise catching in my throat.

Supreme Commander Ibrahim. He seems taller than I

remember him. Dark skin, dark hair. *Angry.*

"It's okay," my father says, unbothered. "Evie has taken care of—"

"Evie is *dead*," Ibrahim says angrily. "We need to initiate the transfer immediately."

"What?" My father goes pale. I've never seen him pale. I've never seen him terrified. "What do you mean she's dead?"

Ibrahim's eyes flash. "I mean we have a serious problem." He glances at me. "This boy needs to be put back in isolation. We can't trust any of them right now. We don't know what she might've done."

And just as I'm trying to decide my next move, I hear a whisper at my ear.

"Don't scream," she says.

Nazeera.

~~JULIETTE~~

ELLA

I'm running for my life, bolting down hallways and up staircases. A low, insistent alarm has gone off, its high, piercing sound sending shocks of fear through me even as my feet pound the floor. I feel strong, steady, but I'm increasingly aware of my inability to navigate these snaking paths. I could see—could feel—Emmaline growing weaker as I left, and now, the farther I get from her, the dimmer our connection becomes. She showed me, in her memories, how Max and Evie slowly stripped her of control; Emmaline is more powerful than anyone, but now she can only use her powers on command. It took all her strength to push past the fail-safes long enough to use her strength at will, and now that her voice has retreated from my mind, I know she won't be back. Not anytime soon. I have to figure out my own way out of here.

I will.

My power is back on. I can get through anything from here. I have to. And when I hear someone shout I spin around, ready to fight—

But the face in the distance is so familiar I stop, stunned, in my tracks.

Kenji barrels into me.

Kenji.

Kenji is hugging me. Kenji is hugging me, and he's uninjured. He's perfect.

And just as I begin to return his embrace he swears, violently, and launches himself backward. "Jesus, woman— Are you trying to kill me? You can't turn that shit off for a second? You have to go and ruin our dramatic reunion by nearly murdering me even after I've gone to all the trouble of f—"

I launch myself into his arms again and he stiffens, relaxing only when he realizes I've pulled my power back. I forgot, for a second, how much of my skin was exposed in this dress.

"Kenji," I breathe. "You're alive. You're okay. Oh my God."

"Hey," he says. "*Hey.*" He pulls back, looks me in the eye. "I'm okay. You okay?"

I don't really know how to answer the question. Finally, I say, "I'm not sure."

He studies my face for a second. He looks concerned.

And then, the knot of fear growing only more painful in my throat, I ask the question killing me most:

"Where's Warner?"

Kenji shakes his head.

I feel myself begin to unravel.

"I don't know yet," Kenji says quietly. "But we're going to find him, okay? Don't worry."

I nod. My bottom lip trembles and I bite it down but the

tremble won't be killed. It grows, multiplies, evolves into a tremor that shakes me from stem to sternum.

"Hey," Kenji says.

I look up.

"You want to tell me where all the blood came from?"

I blink. "What blood?"

He raises his eyebrows at me. "The *blood*," he says, gesturing, generally, at my body. "On your face. Your dress. All over your hands."

"Oh," I say, startled. I look at my hands as if seeing them for the first time. "The blood."

Kenji sighs, squints at something over my shoulder. He pulls a pair of gloves out of his back pocket and tugs them on. "All right, princess, turn your power back on. We have to move."

We break apart. Kenji pulls his invisibility over us both.

"Follow me," he says, taking my hand.

"Where are we going?" I say.

"What do you mean, *where are we going*? We're getting the hell out of here."

"But—What about Warner?"

"Nazeera is looking for him as we speak."

I stop so suddenly I nearly stumble. "Nazeera is here?"

"Uh, yeah—So—It's a really long story? But the short answer is yes."

"So that's how you got in here," I say, beginning to understand. "Nazeera."

Kenji makes a sound of disbelief. "Wow, right off the

bat you give me no credit, huh? C'mon, J, you know I love a good rescue mission. I know some things. I can figure things out, too."

For the first time in weeks I feel a smile tug at my lips. A laugh builds and breaks inside my body. I've missed this so much. I've missed my friends so much. Emotion wells in my throat, surprising me.

"I missed you, Kenji," I say. "I'm so happy you're here."

"*Hey*," Kenji says sharply. "Don't you dare start crying. If you start crying I'll start crying and we do not have time to cry right now. We have too much shit to do, okay? We can cry later, at a more convenient time. Okay?"

When I say nothing, he squeezes my hand.

"Okay?" he says again.

"Okay," I say.

I hear him sigh. "Damn," he says. "They really messed you up in here, didn't they?"

"Yeah."

"I'm so sorry," he says.

"Can we cry about it later? I'll tell you everything."

"Hell yeah we can cry about it later." Kenji tugs gently on my hand to get us moving again. "I have so much shit to cry about, J. So much. We should make, like, a list."

"Good idea," I say, but my heart is in my throat again.

"Hey, don't worry," Kenji says, reading my thoughts. "Seriously. We'll find Warner. Nazeera knows what she's doing."

"But I don't think I can just wait while Nazeera goes

searching for him. I can't just stand around—I need to do something. I need to look for him myself—"

"Uh-uh. No way. Nazeera and I split up on purpose. *My* mission is to get you on the plane. *Her* mission is to get Warner on the plane. That's how math works."

"Wait—You have a plane?"

"How else did you think we got here?"

"I have no idea."

"Well, that's another long story, and I'll fill you in later, but the highlights are that Nazeera is very confusing but helpful, and according to her calculations, we need to be getting the hell out of here yesterday. We're running out of time."

"But wait, Kenji—What happened to everyone? Last time I saw you, you were bleeding. Brendan had been shot. Castle was down. I thought everyone was dead."

Kenji doesn't answer me at first. "You really have no idea what happened, huh?" he says finally.

"I only know that I didn't actually kill all those people at the symposium."

"Oh yeah?" He sounds surprised. "Who told you?"

"Emmaline."

"Your *sister*?"

"Yeah," I say, sighing heavily. "There's so much I have to tell you. But first—Please tell me everyone is still alive."

Kenji hesitates. "I mean, I think so? Honestly, I don't know. Nazeera says they're alive. She's promising to come through on getting them to safety, so I'm still holding my breath. But get this." He stops walking, puts an invisible hand on my shoulder. "You're never going to believe this."

"Let me guess," I say. "Anderson is alive."

I hear Kenji's sharp intake of breath. "How did you know?"

"Evie told me."

"So you know about how he came back to Sector 45?"

"What?" I say. "No."

"Well, what I was about to tell you, right now, was that Anderson came back to base. He's resumed his position as supreme commander of North America. He was there right before we left. Nazeera told me he made up this whole story about how he'd been ill and how our team had spread false rumors while he was recovering—and that you'd been executed for your deception."

"What?" I say, stunned. "That's insane."

"This is what I'm saying."

"So what are we going to do when we get back to Sector 45?" I say. "Where do we go? Where do we stay?"

"Shit if I know," Kenji says. "Right now, I'm just hoping we can get out of here alive."

Finally, we reach the exit. Kenji has a security card that grants him access to the door, and it opens easily.

From there, it's almost too simple. Our invisibility keeps us undetected. And once we're on the plane, Kenji checks his watch.

"We've only got thirty minutes, just so you know. That was the rule. Thirty minutes and if Nazeera doesn't show up with Warner, we have to go."

My heart drops into my stomach.

WARNER

I have no time to register my shock, or to ask Nazeera when on earth she was going to tell me she had the power to turn herself invisible, so I do the only thing I can, in the moment.

I nod, the movement almost imperceptible.

"Kenji is getting Ella onto a plane. I'm going to wait for you just outside this door," she says. "Do you think you can make it? If you go invisible in front of everyone, they'll be on to us, and it'd be better if they think you're just trying to run."

Again, I nod.

"All right then. I'll see you out there."

I wait a second or two, and then I head for the door.

"Hey—" Ibrahim bellows.

I hesitate, turning back slightly, on my heel.

"Yes?"

"Where do you think you're going?" he says. He pulls a gun from the inside of his jacket and points it at me.

"I have to use the bathroom."

Ibrahim doesn't laugh. "You're going to wait here until Max gets back. And then we decide what we're going to do with you."

I tilt my head at him. The gun he's pointing at me looks

suspiciously like one of the guns I stole from my father earlier.

Not that it matters.

I take a quick breath. "I'm afraid that's not how this is going to work," I say, attempting a smile. "Though I'm sure we'll all be seeing each other soon, so I wouldn't worry about missing me too much."

And then, before anyone has a chance to protest, I run for the door, but not before Ibrahim fires his weapon.

Three times.

In close range.

I fight back the urge to cry out as one of the bullets shoots clean through my calf, even as the pain nearly takes my breath away.

Once I'm on the other side of the door, Nazeera pulls her invisibility over me. I don't make it far before I take a sharp breath, slumping against the wall.

"*Shit*," she says. "Did you get shot?"

"Obviously," I bite out, trying to keep my breathing even.

"Dammit, Warner, what the hell is wrong with you? We have to get back to the plane in the next fifteen minutes, or they're going to leave without us."

"What? Why would—"

"Because I told them to. We have to get Ella out of here no matter what. I can't have them waiting around for us and risk getting killed in the process."

"Your sympathy is truly heartwarming. Thank you."

She sighs. "Where did you get shot?"

"In my leg."

"Can you walk?"

"I should be able to in just a minute."

I hear her hesitate. "What does that mean?"

"If I manage to live long enough, maybe I'll tell you."

She's unamused. "Can you really start running in just a minute?"

"Oh, now it's running? A moment ago you were asking if I could walk."

"Running would be better."

I offer her a bitter laugh. It's hard from this distance, but I've been drawing on my father's new ability, harnessing it as best I can from where I am. I feel the wound healing, slowly regenerating nerves and veins and even a bit of bone, but it's taking longer than I'd like.

"How long is the flight back?" I say. "I can't remember."

"We've got the jet, so it should only take about eight hours."

I nod, even though she can't see me. "I don't think I can survive eight hours with an open wound."

"Well, it's a good thing I don't give a shit. I'm giving you two more minutes before I carry you out of here myself."

I grunt in response, focusing all of my energy on drawing up the healing powers into my body. I've never tried to do something like this while wounded, and I didn't realize how demanding it was, both emotionally and physically. I feel drained. My head is throbbing, my jaw aching from the intense pressure I've used to bite back the pain, and my leg feels like it's on *fire*. There's nothing pleasant about the healing process. I have to imagine that my father is on the move—probably searching for me with Ibrahim—because harnessing his power is harder than any of the others I've tried to take.

"We're leaving in thirty seconds," Nazeera says, a warning in her voice.

I grit my teeth.

"Fifteen."

"*Shit*."

"Did you just swear?" Nazeera says, stunned.

"I'm in an extraordinary amount of pain."

"All right, that's it, we're out of time."

And before I manage to get a word in, she picks me up, off the ground.

And we're in the air.

~~JULIETTE~~

ELLA

Kenji and I have been staring at each other in nervous silence for the last minute. I spent the first ten minutes telling him a little about Emmaline, which was its own stressful distraction, and then Kenji helped me wash the blood off my hands and face with the few supplies we have on board. Now we're both staring into the silence, our combined terror filling the plane.

It's a nice plane, I think. I'm not sure. I haven't actually had the presence of mind to look around. Or to ask him who, exactly, among us even knows how to fly a plane. But none of that will matter, of course, if Nazeera and Warner don't get back here soon.

It won't matter because I won't be leaving without him.

And my thoughts must be easy to read, because suddenly Kenji frowns. "Listen," he says, "I'm just as worried about them as you are. I don't want to leave Nazeera behind and I sure as hell don't want to imagine anything bad happening to her while she's out there, but we have to get you out of here."

"Kenji—"

"We don't have a choice, J," he says, cutting me off. "We have to get you out of here whether you like it or not. The

Reestablishment is up to some shady shit, and you're right in the center of it. We have to keep you safe. Right now, keeping you safe is my entire mission."

I drop my face in my hands, and then, just as quickly, look up again. "This is all my fault, you know? I could've prevented this."

"What are you talking about?"

I look him straight in the eye. "I should've done more research on The Reestablishment. I should've read up on its history—and my history within it. I should've learned more about the supreme commanders. I should've been better prepared. Hell, I should've demanded we search the water for Anderson's dead body instead of just *assuming* he'd sunk with the ship." I shake my head, hard. "I wasn't ready to be supreme commander, Kenji. You knew it; Castle knew it. I put everyone's lives in danger."

"Hey," he says sharply, "I never said you weren't—"

"Only Warner ever tried to convince me I was good enough, but I don't think I ever really believed it."

"J, listen to me. I never said you weren't—"

"And now he's gone. Warner is gone. Everyone from Omega Point might be dead. Everything we built . . . everything we worked toward—" I feel myself break, snap open from the inside. "I can't lose him, Kenji." My voice is shaking. My hands are shaking. "I can't—You don't know— You don't—"

Kenji looks at me with actual pain in his eyes. "Stop it, J. You're breaking my heart. I can't hear this."

And I realize, as I swallow back the lump in my throat, how much I'd needed to have this conversation. These feelings had been building inside of me for weeks, and I'd desperately needed someone to talk to.

I needed my friend.

"I thought I'd been through some hard things," I say, my eyes now filling with tears. "I thought I'd lived through my share of awful experiences. But this—I honestly think these have been the worst days of my life."

Kenji's eyes are deep. Serious. "You want to tell me about it?"

I shake my head, wiping furiously at my cheeks. "I don't think I'll be able to talk about any of it until I know Warner is okay."

"I'm so sorry, J. I really am."

I sniff, hard. "You know my name is Ella, right?"

"Right," he says, his eyebrows pulling together. "Yeah. Ella. That's wild."

"I like it," I say. "I like it better than Juliette."

"I don't know. I think both names are nice."

"Yeah," I say, turning away. "But *Juliette* was the name Anderson picked out for me."

"And *Ella* is the name you were born with," Kenji says, shooting me a look. "I get it."

"Yeah."

"Listen," he says with a sigh. "I know this has been a rough couple of weeks for you. I heard about the memory thing. I heard about lots of things. And I can't pretend to imagine I have any idea what you must be going through right now. But you can't blame yourself for any of this. It's not your fault. None of it is your fault. You've been a pawn at the center of this conspiracy your entire life. The last month wasn't going to change that, okay? You have to be kinder to yourself. You've already been through so much."

I offer Kenji a weak smile. "I'll try," I say quietly.

"Feeling any better now?"

"No. And thinking about leaving here without Warner—not knowing if he'll even make it onto this plane—It's killing me, Kenji. It's boring a hole through my body."

Kenji sighs, looks away. "I get it," he says. "I do. You're worried you won't have a chance to make things right with him."

I nod.

"Shit."

"I won't do it. I can't do it, Kenji."

"I understand where you're coming from, kid, I swear. But we can't afford to do this. If they're not back here in five minutes, we have to go."

"Then you'll have to leave without me."

"No way, not an option," he says, getting to his feet. "I don't want to do this any more than you do, but I know Nazeera well enough to know that she can handle herself out there, and if she's not back yet, it's probably because she's waiting for a safer moment. She'll find her way. And you have to trust that she'll bring Warner back with her. Okay?"

"No."

"C'mon—"

"Kenji, stop." I get to my feet, too, anger and heartbreak colliding.

"Don't do this," he says, shaking his head. "Don't force me to do something I don't want to do. Because if I have to, I will tackle you to the floor, J, I swear—"

"You wouldn't do that," I say quietly. The fight leaves my body. I feel suddenly exhausted, hollowed out by heartache. "I know you wouldn't. You wouldn't make me leave him behind."

"Ella?"

I turn around, a bolt of feeling leaving me breathless. Just the sound of his voice has my heart racing in a way that feels dangerous. The jarring shift from fear to joy has my head pounding, delirious with feeling. I'd been so worried, all this time, and to know now—

He's unharmed.

His face, unmarked. His body, intact. He's perfect and beautiful and he's *here*. I don't know how, but he's here.

I clap my hands over my mouth.

I'm shaking my head and searching desperately for the right words but find I can't speak. I can only stare at him as he steps forward, his eyes bright and burning.

He pulls me into his arms.

Sobs break my body, the culmination of a thousand fears and worries I hadn't allowed myself to process. I press my face into his neck and try, but fail, to pull myself together.

"I'm sorry," I say, gasping the words, tears streaming fast down my face. "Aaron, I'm so sorry. I'm so, so sorry."

I feel him stiffen.

He pulls away, staring at me with strange, scared eyes. "Why would you say that?" He looks around wildly, glances at Kenji, who only shakes his head. "What happened, love?" He pushes the hair out of my eyes, takes my face in his hands. "What are you sorry for?"

Nazeera pushes past us.

She nods at me, just once, before heading to the cockpit. Moments later I hear the roar of the engine, the electric sounds of equipment coming online.

I hear her voice in the speakers overhead, her crisp, certain commands filling the plane. She tells us to take our seats and get strapped in and I stare at Warner just once more, promising myself that we'll have a chance to talk. Promising myself that I'll make this right.

When we take off, he's holding my hand.

We've been climbing higher for several minutes now, and Kenji and Nazeera were generous enough to give us some illusion of privacy. They both shot me separate but similar looks of encouragement just before they slipped off into the cockpit. It finally feels safe to keep talking.

But emotion is like a fist in my chest, hard and heavy.

There's too much to say. Too much to discuss. I almost don't even know where to start. I don't know what happened to him, what he learned or what he remembers. I don't know if he's feeling the same things I'm feeling anymore. And all the unknowns are starting to scare me.

"What's wrong?" he says.

He's turned in his seat to face me. He reaches up, touches my face, and the feeling of his skin against mine is overwhelming—so powerful it leaves me breathless. Feeling shoots up my spine, sparks in my nerves.

"You're afraid, love. Why are you afraid?"

"Do you remember me?" I whisper. I have to force myself to remain steady, to fight back the tears that refuse to die. "Do you remember me the way I remember you?"

Something changes in his expression. His eyes change, pull together in pain.

He nods.

"Because I remember you," I say, my voice breaking on the last word. "I remember you, Aaron. I remember everything. And you have to know—You have to know how sorry I am. For the way I left things between us." I'm crying again. "I'm sorry for everything I said. For everything I put you thr—"

"Sweetheart," he says gently, the question in his eyes resolving to a measure of understanding. "None of that matters anymore. That fight feels like it happened in another lifetime. To different people."

I wipe away my tears. "I know," I say. "But being here—All of this—I thought I might never see you again. And it *killed* me to remember how I left things between us."

When I look up again Warner is staring at me, his own

eyes bright, shining. I watch the movement in his throat as he swallows, hard.

"Forgive me," I whisper. "I know it all seems stupid now, but I don't want to take anything for granted anymore. Forgive me for hurting you. Forgive me for not trusting you. I took my pain out on you and I'm so sorry. I was selfish, and I hurt you, and I'm so sorry."

He's silent for so long I almost can't bear it.

When he finally speaks, his voice is rough with emotion. "Love," he says, "there's nothing to forgive."

WARNER

Ella is asleep in my arms.

Ella.

I can't really think of her as *Juliette* anymore.

We've been in the air for an hour now, and Ella cried until her tears ran dry, cried for so long I thought it might kill me. I didn't know what to say. I was so stunned I didn't know how to soothe her. And only when the exhaustion overcame the tears did she finally go still, collapsing fully and completely into my arms. I've been holding her against my chest for at least half an hour, marveling at what it does to me to just be this close to her. Every once in a while, it feels like a dream. Her face is pressed against my neck. She's clinging to me like she might never let go and it does something to me, something heady, to know that she could possibly want me—or need me—like this. It makes me want to protect her even if she doesn't need protecting. It makes me want to carry her away. Lose track of time.

Gently, I stroke her hair. Press my lips to her forehead.

She stirs, but only slightly.

I had not been expecting this.

Of all the things I thought might happen when I finally saw her, I could never have dreamed a scenario such as this.

No one has ever apologized to me before. Not like this.

I've had men fall to their knees before me, begging me to spare their lives—but I can't remember a single time in my life when someone apologized to me for hurting my feelings. No one has ever cared about my feelings long enough to apologize for hurting them. In my experience, I'm usually the monster. I'm the one expected to make amends.

And now—

I'm stunned. Stunned by the experience, by how strange it feels. All this time, I'd been preparing to win her back. To try to convince her, somehow, to see past my demons. And up until just this moment, I don't think I was ever truly convinced anyone would see me as human enough to forgive my sins. To give me a second chance.

But now, she knows everything.

Every dark corner of my life. Every awful thing I ever tried to hide. She knows and she still loves me.

God. I run a tired hand across my face. She asked me to forgive *her*. I almost don't know what to do with myself. I feel joy and terror. My heart is heavy with something I don't even know how to describe.

Gratitude, perhaps.

The ache in my chest has grown stronger, more painful. Being near her is somehow both a relief and a new kind of agony. There's so much ahead of us, so much we still need to face, together, but right now I don't want to think about any of it. Right now I just want to enjoy her proximity. I want to watch the gentle motions of her breathing. I want to inhale the soft scent of her hair and lean into the steadying warmth of her body.

Carefully, I touch my fingers to her cheek.

Her face is smooth, free from pain and tension. She looks peaceful. She looks *beautiful*.

My love.

My beautiful love.

Her eyes flutter open and I worry, for a moment, that I might've spoken out loud. But then she looks up at me, her eyes still soft with sleep, and I bring my hand to her face, this time trailing my fingers lightly along her jaw. She closes her eyes again. Smiles.

"I love you," she whispers.

A shock of feeling swells inside of me, makes it hard for me to breathe. I can only look at her, studying her face, the lines and angles I've somehow always known.

Slowly, she sits up.

She leans back, stretching out her sore, stiff muscles. When she catches me watching her, she offers me a shy smile.

She leans in, takes my face in her hands.

"Hi," she says, her words soft, her hands gentle as she tilts my chin down, toward her mouth. She kisses me, once, her lips full and sweet. It's a tender kiss, but feeling strikes through me with a sharp, desperate need. "I missed you so much," she says. "I still can't believe you're here." She kisses me again, this time deeper, hungrier, and my heart beats so fast it roars in my ears. I can hardly hear anything else. I can't bring myself to speak.

I feel stunned.

When we break apart, her eyes are worried. "Aaron," she says. "Is everything okay?"

And I realize then, in a moment that terrifies me, that I want this, forever. I want to spend the rest of my life with her. I want to build a future with her. I want to grow old with her.

I want to marry her.

~~JULIETTE~~

ELLA

"Aaron?" I say again, this time softly. "Are you all right?"

He blinks, startled. "Yes," he says, drawing in a sharp breath. "Yes. Yes, I'm perfect."

I manage a small smile. "I'm glad you finally agree with me."

He frowns, confused, and then, as realization hits—

He *blushes*.

And for the first time in weeks, a full, genuine grin spreads across my face. It feels good. Human.

But Aaron shakes his head, clearly mortified. He can't meet my eyes. His voice is careful, quiet when he says, "That's not at all what I meant."

"Hey," I say, my smile fading. I take his hands in mine, squeeze. "Look at me."

He does.

And I forget what I was going to say.

He has that kind of face. The kind of face that makes you forget where you are, who you are, what you might've been about to do or say. I've missed him so much. Missed his eyes. It's only been a couple of weeks, but it feels like forever since the last time I saw him, a lifetime full of horrible revelations that threatened to break us both. I can't believe he's here, that we found each other and made things right.

It's no small thing.

Even with everything else—with all the other horrors we've yet to contend with—being here with him feels like a huge victory. Everything feels new. My mind feels new, my memories, new. Even Aaron's face is new, in its own way. He looks a little different to me now.

Familiar.

Like he's always been here. Always lived in my heart.

His hair, thick and golden and beautiful, is how I remember it best—Evie must've done something to his hair, too, somehow. And even though he looks more exhausted than I'd like, his face is still striking. Beautiful, sharp lines. Piercing green eyes so light and bright they're almost painful to look at. Everything about him is finely crafted. His nose. His chin. His ears and eyebrows. He has a beautiful mouth.

I linger too long there, my eyes betraying my mind, and Aaron smiles. *Aaron.* Calling him Warner doesn't feel right anymore.

"What are you doing, love?"

"Just enjoying the view," I say, still staring at his mouth. I reach up, touch two fingers to his bottom lip. Memories flood through me in a sudden, breathless rush. Long nights. Early mornings. His mouth, on me. Everywhere. Over and over again.

I hear him exhale, suddenly, and I glance up at him.

His eyes are darker, heavy with feeling. "What are you thinking?"

I shake my head, feeling suddenly shy. It's strange, considering how close we've been, that I'd feel shy around him now. But he feels at once old and new to me—like we're still learning about each other. Still discovering what our relationship means and what we mean to each other. Things feel deeper, desperate.

More important.

I take his hands again. "How are you?" I whisper.

He's staring at our hands, entwined, when he says: "My father is still alive."

"I heard. I'm so sorry."

He nods. Looks away.

"Did you see him?"

Another nod. "I tried to kill him."

I go still.

I know how hard it's been for Aaron to face his father. Anderson has always been his most formidable opponent; Aaron has never been able to fight him head on. He's never been able to bring himself to actually follow through with his threats to kill his father.

It's astonishing he even came close.

And then Aaron tells me how his father has semifunctional healing powers, how Evie tried to re-create the twins' DNA for him.

"So your dad is basically invincible?"

Aaron laughs quietly. Shakes his head. "I don't think so. It makes him harder to kill, but I definitely think there's a chink to be found in his armor." He sighs. "Believe it or not, the strangest part of the whole thing was that, afterward, my father was proud of me. Proud of me for trying to kill him." Aaron looks up, looks me in the eye. "Can you imagine?"

"Yes," I whisper. "I can."

Aaron's eyes go deep with emotion. He pulls me close. "I'm so sorry, love. I'm so sorry for everything they did to you. For everything they've put you through. It kills me to know that you were suffering. That I couldn't be there for you."

"I don't want to think about it right now." I shake my head. "Right now all I want is *this*. I just want to be here. With you. Whatever comes next, we'll face it together."

"Ella," he says softly.

A wave of feeling washes over me. Hearing him say my name—my real name—makes everything feel real. Makes *us* feel real.

I meet his eyes.

He smiles. "You know—I feel everything when you touch me, love. I can feel your excitement. Your nervousness. Your pleasure. And I love it," he says quietly. "I love the way you respond to me. I love the way you *want* me. I feel it, when you lose yourself, the way you trust me when we're together. And I feel your love for me," he whispers. "I feel it in my bones."

He turns away.

"I have loved you my entire life." He looks up, looks at me with so much feeling it nearly breaks my heart. "And after everything we've been through—after all the lies and the secrets and the misunderstandings—I feel like we've been given a chance to start fresh. I want to start over," he says. "I never want to lie to you again. I want us to trust each other and be true partners in everything. No more misunderstandings," he says. "No more secrets. I want us to begin again, here, in this moment."

I nod, pulling back so I can see his face more clearly. Emotions well in my throat, threaten to overcome me. "I want that, too. I want that so much."

"Ella," he says, his voice rough with feeling. "I want to spend the rest of my life with you."

My heart stops.

I stare at him, uncertain, thoughts pinwheeling in my head. I touch his cheek and he looks away, takes a sudden, shaky breath.

"What are you saying?" I whisper.

"I love you, Ella. I love you more th—"

"*Wow*. You two seriously couldn't wait until we got back to base, huh? You couldn't spare my eyes?"

The sound of Kenji's voice pulls me suddenly, abruptly out of my head. I turn too quickly, awkwardly disengaging from Aaron's body.

Aaron, on the other hand, goes suddenly white.

Kenji throws a thin airplane pillow at him. "You're welcome," he says.

Aaron chucks the pillow back without a word, his eyes burning in Kenji's direction. He seems both shocked and angry, and he leans forward in his seat, his elbows balanced on his knees, the heels of his hands pressed against his eyes.

"You are a plague upon my life, Kishimoto."

"I said *you're welcome*."

Aaron sighs, heavily. "What I would give to snap your neck right now, you have no idea."

"Hey—*you* have no idea what I just did for you," Kenji says. "So I'm going to repeat myself one more time: You are *welcome*."

"I never asked for your help."

Kenji crosses his arms. When he speaks, he overenunciates each word, like he might be talking to an idiot. "I don't think you're thinking clearly."

"I'm thinking clearer than I ever have."

"You really thought that would be a good idea?" Kenji says, shaking his head. "Here? Now?"

Aaron's jaw clenches. He looks mutinous.

"Bro, this is not the moment."

"And when, exactly, did you become an expert on this sort of thing?"

I look between the two of them. "What is going on?" I say. "What are you guys talking about?"

"Nothing," they say at the same time.

"Um, okay." I stare at them, still confused, and I'm about to ask another question when Kenji says, suddenly:

"Who wants lunch?"

My eyebrows shoot up my forehead. "We have lunch?"

"It's pretty awful," Kenji says, "but Nazeera and I have a picnic basket we brought with us, yeah."

"I guess I'm up for trying the contents of the mystery basket." I smile at Aaron. "Are you hungry?"

But Aaron says nothing. He's still staring at the floor. I touch his hand and, finally, he sighs. "I'm not hungry," he says.

"Not an option," Kenji says sharply. "I'm pretty sure you haven't eaten a damn thing since you got out of fake prison."

Aaron frowns. And when he looks up, he says, "It wasn't *fake* prison. It was a very real prison. They poisoned me for weeks."

"What?" My eyes widen. "You never t—"

Kenji cuts me off with the wave of his hand. "They gave you food, water, and let you keep the clothes on your back, didn't they?"

"Yes, but—"

He shrugs. "Sounds like you had a little vacation."

Aaron sighs. He looks both annoyed and exhausted as he runs a hand down the length of his face.

I don't like it.

"Hey—Why are you giving him such a hard time?" I say, frowning at Kenji. "Just before he and Nazeera showed up you were going on and on about how wonderful he is, and n—"

Kenji swears, suddenly, under his breath. "Jesus, J." He shoots me a dark look. "What did I say to you about repeating that conversation out loud?"

Aaron sits up, the frustration in his eyes slowly giving way to surprise. "You think I'm wonderful?" he says, one hand pressed against his chest in mock affection. "That's so sweet."

"I *never* said you were wonderful."

Aaron tilts his head. "Then what, exactly, did you say?"

Kenji turns away. Says nothing.

I'm grinning at Kenji's back when I say, "He said you looked good in everything and that you were good at everything."

Aaron's smile deepens.

Aaron almost never smiles widely enough for me to see his dimples, but when he does, they transform his face. His eyes light up. His cheeks go pink with feeling. He looks suddenly sweet. *Adorable*.

It takes my breath away.

But he's not looking at me, he's looking at Kenji, his eyes full of laughter when he says, "Please tell me she's not serious."

Kenji gives us both the finger.

Aaron laughs. And then, leaning in—

"You really think I look good in everything?"

"Shut up, asshole."

Aaron laughs again.

"Stop having fun without me," Nazeera shouts from the cockpit. "No more making jokes until I put this thing on cruise control."

I stiffen. "Do planes have cruise control?"

"Um"—Kenji scratches his head—"I don't actually know?"

But then Nazeera saunters over to us, tall and beautiful and unbothered. She's not covering her hair today, which I suppose makes sense, considering it's generally illegal, but I feel a faint panic spread through my body when I realize she's in no hurry to return to the cockpit.

"Wait—No one is flying the plane," I say. "Shouldn't someone be flying the plane?"

She waves me down. "It's fine. These things are practically automatic now, anyway. I don't have to do more than input coordinates and make sure everything is operating smoothly."

"But—"

"Everything is fine," she says, shooting me a sharp look. "We're fine. But someone needs to tell me what's going on."

"Are you sure we're fine?" I ask once more, quietly.

She levels me with a dark look.

I sigh. "Well, in that case," I say. "You should know that Kenji was just admiring Aaron's sense of style."

Nazeera turns to Kenji. Raises a single eyebrow.

Kenji shakes his head, visibly irritated. "I wasn't—Dammit, J, you have no loyalty."

"I have plenty of loyalty," I say, slightly wounded. "But when you guys fight like this it stresses me out. I just want Aaron to know that, secretly, you care about him. I love you both and I want the two of you to be frien—"

"Wait"—Aaron frowns—"What do you mean you love us both?"

I glance between him and Kenji, surprised. "I mean I

care about both of you. I love you both."

"Right," Aaron says, hesitating, "but you don't *actually* love us both. That's just a figure of speech, isn't it?"

It's my turn to frown. "Kenji is my best friend," I say. "I love him like a brother."

"But—"

"I love you, too, princess," Kenji says, a little too loudly. "And I appreciate you saying that."

Aaron mutters something under his breath that sounds suspiciously like, *"Unwashed idiot."*

"What did you just say to me?" Kenji's eyes widen. "I'll have you know I wash *all the time*—"

Nazeera places a calming hand on Kenji's arm, and he startles at her touch. He looks up at her, blinking.

"We have another five hours ahead of us on this flight," she says, and her voice is firm but kind. "So I recommend we put this conversation to bed. I think it's clear to everyone that you and Warner secretly enjoy each other's friendship, and it's not doing anyone any good to pretend otherwise."

Kenji blanches.

"Does that sound like a reasonable plan?" She looks around at all of us. "Can we all agree that we're on the same team?"

"Yes," I say enthusiastically. "I do. I agree."

Aaron says, "Fine."

"Great," Nazeera says. "Kenji, you okay?"

He nods and mumbles something under his breath.

"Perfect. Now here's the plan," she says briskly. "We're

going to eat and then take turns trying to get some sleep. We'll have a ton of things to deal with when land, and it's best if we hit the ground running when we do." She tosses a few vacuum-sealed bags at each of us. "That's your lunch. There are water bottles in the fridge up front. Kenji and I will take the first shift—"

"No way," Kenji says, crossing his arms. "You've been up for twenty-four hours straight. I'll take the first shift."

"But—"

"Warner and I will take the first shift together, actually." Kenji shoots Warner a look. "Isn't that right?"

"Yes, of course," Aaron says. He's already on his feet. "I'd be happy to."

"Great," Kenji says.

Nazeera is already stifling a yawn, pulling a bunch of thin blankets and pillows from a storage closet. "All right, then. Just wake us up in a couple of hours, okay?"

Kenji raises an eyebrow at her. "Sure."

"I'm serious."

"Yup. Got it." Kenji offers her a mock salute, Aaron offers me a quick smile, and the two of them disappear into the cockpit.

Kenji closes the door behind them.

I'm staring at the closed door, wondering what on earth is going on between the two of them, when Nazeera says—

"I had no idea you two were so intense."

I look up, surprised. "Who? Me and Aaron?"

"No," she says, smiling. "You and Kenji."

"Oh." I frown. "I don't think we're intense."

She shoots me a funny look.

"I'm serious," I say. "I think we have a pretty normal friendship."

Instead of answering me, she says, "Did you two ever"—she waves a hand at nothing—"date?"

"What?" My eyes widen. A traitorous heat floods my body. "*No.*"

"Never?" she says, her smile slow.

"Never. I swear. Not even close."

"Okay."

"Not that there's anything wrong with him," I hurry to add. "Kenji is wonderful. The right person would be lucky to be with him."

Nazeera laughs, softly.

She carries the stack of pillows and blankets over to the row of airplane seats and begins reclining the backs. I watch her as she works. There's something so smooth and refined about her movements—something intelligent in her eyes at all times. It makes me wonder what she's thinking, what she's planning. Why she's here at all.

Suddenly, she sighs. She's not looking at me when she says, "Do you remember me yet?"

I raise my eyebrows, surprised. "Of course," I say quietly.

She nods. She says, "I've been waiting awhile for you to catch up," and sits down, inviting me to join her by patting the seat next to her.

I do.

Wordlessly, she hands me a couple of blankets and pillows. And then, when we're both settled in and I'm staring, suspiciously, at the vacuum-sealed package of "food" she threw at me, I say—

"So you remember me, too?"

Nazeera tears open her vacuum-sealed package. Peers inside to study the contents. "Emmaline guided me to you," she says quietly. "The memories. The messages. It was her."

"I know," I say. "She's trying to unify us. She wants us to band together."

Nazeera shakes out the contents of the bag into her hand, picks through the bits of freeze-dried fruit. She glances at me. "You were five when you disappeared," she says. "Emmaline was six. I'm six months older than you, and six months younger than Emmaline."

I nod. "The three of us used to be best friends."

Nazeera looks away, looks sad. "I really loved Emmaline," she says. "We were inseparable. We did everything together." She shrugs, even as a flash of pain crosses her face. "That was all we got. Whatever we might've been was stolen from us."

She picks out two pieces of fruit and pops them into her mouth. I watch as she chews, thoughtfully, and wait for more.

But the seconds pass and she says nothing, and I figure I should fill the silence. "So," I say. "We're not actually getting any sleep, are we?"

That gets her to smile. Still, she doesn't look at me.

Finally, she says, "I know you and Warner got the absolute worst of it, I do. But if it makes you feel any better, they wiped all of our memories, in the beginning."

"I know. Emmaline told me."

"They didn't want us to remember you," she says. "They didn't want us to remember a lot of things. Did Emmaline tell you she's reached out to all of us? You, me, Warner, my brother—all the kids."

"She told me a little bit, yeah. Have you talked to any of the others about it?"

Nazeera nods. Pops another piece of fruit in her mouth.

"And?"

She tilts her head. "We'll see."

My eyes widen. "What does that mean?"

"I'll know more when we land, that's all."

"So—How did you even know?" I say, frowning a little. "If you'd only ever had memories of me and Emmaline as children—how did you tie it all back to the present? How did you know that I was the Ella from our childhood?"

"You know—I wasn't a hundred percent positive I was right about everything until I saw you at dinner that first night on base."

"You recognized me?" I say. "From when I was five?"

"No," she says, and nods at my right hand. "From the scar on the back of your wrist."

"This?" I say, lifting my hand. And then I frown, remembering that Evie repaired my skin. I used to have faded scars all over my body; the ones on my hands were the worst. My adoptive mom put my hands in the fire, once. And I hurt myself a lot while I was locked up; lots of burns, lots of poorly healed wounds. I shake my head at Nazeera when I say, "I used to have scars on my hand from my time in the asylum. Evie got rid of them."

Nazeera takes my hand, flips it over so my palm is up, open. Carefully, she traces a line from my wrist to my forearm. "Do you remember the one that was here?"

"Yes." I raise my eyebrows.

"My dad has a really extensive sword collection," she says, dropping my hand. "Really gorgeous blades—gilded, handmade, ancient, ornate stuff. Anyway," she says, tapping the invisible scar on my wrist. "I did that to you. I broke into my dad's sword room and thought it'd be fun for us to practice a little hand-to-hand combat. But I sliced you up pretty bad, and my mom just about beat the crap out of me." She laughs. "I will never forget that."

I frown at her, at where my scar used to be. "Didn't you say that we were friends when we were *five*?"

She nods.

"We were five and we thought it would be fun to play with real swords?"

She laughs. Looks confused. "I never said we had a *normal* childhood. Our lives were so messed up," she says, and laughs again. "I never trusted my parents. I always knew they were knee-deep in some dark shit; I always tried to learn more. I'd been trying, for years, to hack into Baba's electronic files," she says. "And for a long time, I only ever accessed basic information. I learned about the asylums. The Unnaturals."

"That's why you hid your abilities from them," I say, finally understanding.

She nods. "But I wanted to know more. I knew I was only scratching the surface of something big. But the levels of security built into my dad's account are unlike anything I'd ever seen before. I was able to get through the first few levels of security, which is how I learned of yours and Emmaline's existence, a few years back. Baba had tons of records, reports on your daily habits and activities, a log with the time and date of every memory they stole from you—and they were all from recent years and months."

I gasp.

Nazeera shoots me a sympathetic look. "There were brief mentions of a sister in your files," she says, "but nothing substantial; mostly just a note that you were both powerful, and had been donated to the cause by your parents. But I couldn't find anything on the unknown sister, which made me think that her files were more protected. I spent the last couple of years trying to break into the deeper levels of Baba's account and never had any success. So I let it go for a while."

She pops another piece of dried fruit in her mouth.

"It wasn't until my dad started losing his *mind* after you almost killed Anderson that I started getting suspicious. That was when I began to wonder if the *Juliette Ferrars* he kept screaming about wasn't someone important." She studies me out of the corner of her eye. "I knew you couldn't have been some random *Unnatural*. I just knew it. Baba went *ballistic*. So I started hacking again."

"Wow," I say.

"Yeah," she says, nodding. "Right? Anyway, all I'm trying to say is that I've been trying to sniff out the bullshit in this situation for a few years, and now, with Emmaline in my head, I'm finally getting close to figuring it all out."

I glance up at her.

"The only thing I still don't know is *why* Emmaline is locked up. I don't know what they're doing with her. And I don't understand why it's such a secret."

"I do," I say.

Her head snaps up. She looks at me, wide-eyed. "Way to get to the point, Ella."

I laugh, but the sound is sad.

WARNER

As soon as we take our seats, Kenji turns on me. "You want to tell me what the hell is going on?" he says.

"No."

Kenji rolls his eyes. He rips open his little snack bag and doesn't even inspect the contents before he tips the bag directly into his mouth. He closes his eyes as he chews. Makes little satisfied noises.

I manage to fight the impulse to cringe, but I can't stop myself from saying—

"You eat like a caveman."

"No, I don't," he says angrily. And then, a moment later: "Do I?"

I hesitate, feeling his sudden wave of embarrassment. Of all the emotions I hate experiencing, secondhand embarrassment might be the worst. It hits me right in the gut. Makes me want to turn my skin inside out.

And it's by far the easiest way to make me capitulate.

"No," I say heavily. "You don't eat like a caveman. That was unfair."

Kenji glances at me. There's too much hope in his eyes.

"I've just never seen anyone eat food with as much enthusiasm as you do."

Kenji raises an eyebrow. "I'm not enthusiastic. I'm hungry."

Carefully, I tear open my own package. Shake out a few bits of the fruit into my open hand.

They look like desiccated worms.

I return the fruit to the bag, dust off my hands, and offer my portion to Kenji.

"You sure?" he says, even as he takes it from me.

I nod.

He thanks me.

We both say nothing for a while.

"So," Kenji says finally, still chewing. "You were going to propose to her. Wow."

I exhale a long, heavy breath. "How you could have even known something like that?"

"Because I'm not deaf."

I raise my eyebrows.

"It echoes in here."

"It certainly does not echo in here."

"Stop changing the subject," he says, shaking more fruit into his mouth. "The point is, you were going to propose. Do you deny it?"

I look away, run a hand along the side of my neck, massaging the sore muscles. "I do not deny it," I say.

"Then congratulations. And yes, I'd be happy to be your best man at the wedding."

I look up, surprised. "I've no interest in addressing the latter part of what you just said, but—Why offer congratulations? I thought you were vehemently opposed to the idea."

Kenji frowns. "What? I'm not opposed to the idea."

"Then why were you so angry?"

"I thought you were stupid for doing it *here*," he says. "Right now. I didn't want you to do something you would regret. That you'd both regret."

"Why would I regret proposing right now? This seems as good a time as any."

Kenji laughs, but somehow manages to keep his mouth closed. He swallows another bite of food and says, "Don't you want, to, like, I don't know—buy her some roses? Light a candle? Maybe hand her a box of chocolates or some shit? Or, hell, uh, I don't know—maybe you'd want to get her a *ring* first?"

"I don't understand."

"C'mon, bro—Have you never seen, like, a movie?"

"No."

Kenji stares at me, dumbfounded. "You're shitting me," he says. "Please tell me you're shitting me."

I bristle. "I was never allowed to watch movies growing up, so I never picked up the habit, and after The Reestablishment took over, that sort of thing was outlawed anyway. Besides, I don't enjoy sitting still in the dark for that long. And I don't enjoy the emotional manipulations of cinema."

Kenji brings his hands to his face, his eyes wide with something like horror. "You have got to be kidding me."

"Why would—I don't understand why that's strange. I was homeschooled. My father was very—"

"There are so many things about you that never made sense to me," Kenji says, staring, flabbergasted, at the wall behind me. "Like, everything about you is weird, you know?"

"No," I say sharply. "I don't think I'm weird."

"But now it all makes sense." He shakes his head. "It all makes so much sense. Wow. Who knew."

"*What* makes sense?"

Kenji doesn't seem to hear me. Instead, he says, "Hey, is there anything else you've never done? Like—I don't know, have you ever gone swimming? Or, like, blown out candles on a birthday cake?"

"Of course I've been swimming," I say, irritated. "Swimming was an important part of my tactical training. But I've never—" I clear my throat. "No, I never had my own birthday cake."

"Jesus."

"What is wrong with you?"

"Hey," Kenji says suddenly. "Do you even know who Bruce Lee is?"

I hesitate.

There's a challenge in his voice, but Kenji isn't generating much more in the way of emotional cues, so I don't understand the importance of the question. Finally, I say, "Bruce Lee was an actor. Though he's also considered to be one of the greatest martial artists of our time. He founded a system of martial arts called jeet kune do, a type of Chinese kung fu that eschews patterns and form. His Chinese name is Lee Jun-fan."

"Well shit," Kenji says. He sits back in his chair, staring at me like I might be an alien. "Okay. I wasn't expecting that."

"What does Bruce Lee have to do with anything?"

"First of all," he says, holding up a finger, "Bruce Lee has everything to do with everything. And second of all, can you just, like, do that?" He snaps his fingers in the direction of my head. "Can you just, like, remember shit like that? Random facts?"

"They're not random facts. It's information. Information about our world, its fears, histories, fascinations, and pleasures. It's my job to know this sort of thing."

"But you've never seen a single movie?"

"I didn't have to. I know enough about pop culture to know which films mattered or made a difference."

Kenji shakes his head, looks at me with something like awe. "But you don't know anything about the *best* films. You never saw the really good stuff. Hell, you've probably never even heard of the good stuff."

"Try me."

"Have you ever heard of *Blue Streak*?"

I blink at him. "That's the name of a movie?"

"*Romeo Must Die*? *Bad Boys*? *Rush Hour*? *Rush Hour 2*? *Rush Hour 3*? Actually, *Rush Hour 3* wasn't that great. *Tangled*?"

"That last one, I believe, is a cartoon about a girl with very long hair, inspired by the German fairy tale 'Rapunzel.'"

Kenji looks like he might be choking. "A *cartoon*?" he says, outraged. "*Tangled* is not a *cartoon*. *Tangled* is one of the greatest movies of all time. It's about fighting for freedom and true love."

"Please," I say, running a tired hand across my face. "I really don't care what kinds of cartoons you like to watch in your free time. I only want to know why you're so certain I was making a mistake today."

Kenji sighs so deeply his shoulders sag. He slumps down in his chair. "I can't believe you've never seen *Men in Black*. Or *Independence Day*." He looks up at me, his eyes bright. "Shit, you'd love *Independence Day*. Will Smith punches an alien in the face, for God's sake. It's so good."

I stare blankly at him.

"My dad and I used to watch movies all the time," he says quietly. "My dad loved movies." Kenji only allows himself to feel his grief for a moment, but when he does, it hits me in a wild, desperate wave.

"I'm so sorry for your loss," I say quietly.

"Yeah, well." Kenji runs a hand over his face. Rubs at his eyes and sighs. "Anyway, do whatever you want. I just think you should buy her a ring or something before you get down on one knee."

"I wasn't planning on getting down on one knee."

"What?" He frowns. "Why not?"

"That seems illogical."

Kenji laughs. Rolls his eyes. "Listen, just trust me and at least pick out a ring first. Let her know you actually thought about it. Think it through for a beat, you know?"

"I did think it through."

"For, what, five seconds? Or did you mean that you were planning this proposal while you were being poisoned in prison?" Kenji laughs. "Bro, you literally saw her—for the first time—*today*, like, two hours ago, after two weeks of being apart, and you think proposing to her is a rational, clearheaded move?" Kenji shakes his head. "Just take some time. Think about it. Make some plans."

And then, suddenly, his reaction makes sense to me.

"You don't think she's going to say yes." I sit back, stunned. Look at the wall. "You think she'll refuse me."

"What? I never said that."

"But it's what you think, isn't it?"

"Listen," he says, and sighs. "I have no idea what she'll say. I really don't. I mean I think it's more than obvious that she loves you, and I think if she's ready to call herself the supreme commander of North America she's probably ready to handle something as big as this, but"—he rubs his chin, looks away—"I mean, yeah, I think maybe you should, like, think about it for a minute."

I stare at him. Consider his words.

Finally, I say, "You think I should get her a ring."

Kenji smiles at the floor. He seems to be fighting back a laugh. "Uh. Yeah, I do."

"I don't know anything about jewelry."

He looks up, his eyes bright with humor. "Don't worry. I'm sure the files in that thick head of yours have tons of information on this sort of thing."

"But—"

The plane gives a sudden, unexpected jolt, and I'm thrown backward in my seat. Kenji and I stare at each other for a protracted second, caution giving way to fear, fear building slowly into panic.

The plane jolts again. This time harder.

And then, once more.

"That's not turbulence," I say.

Kenji swears, loudly, and jumps to his feet. He scans the dashboard for a second before turning back, his head in a viselike grip between his hands. "I can't read these dials," he says, "I have no idea how to read these goddamn dials—"

I shove the cockpit door open just as Nazeera runs forward. She pushes her way past me to scan the dashboard and when she pulls away she looks suddenly terrified. "We've lost one of our engines," she says, her words barely a whisper. "Someone is shooting us out of the sky."

"What? How is that—"

But there's no time to discuss it. And Nazeera and I hardly have a chance to try to figure out a way to fix it before the plane jolts, once more, and this time the emergency oxygen masks fall out of their overhead compartments. Sirens are wailing. Lights overhead blink rapidly, insistent, sharp beeps warning us that the system is crashing.

"We have to try to land the plane," Nazeera is saying. "We have to figure out—Shit," she says. She covers her mouth with one hand. "We just lost another engine."

"So we're just going to fall out of the goddamn sky?" This, from Kenji.

"We can't land the plane," I say, my heart beating furiously even as I try to keep a level head. "Not like this, not when we're missing two engines. Not while they're still shooting at us."

"So what do we do?" she says.

It's Ella, at the door, who says quietly, "We have to jump."

~~JULIETTE~~

ELLA

"*What?*"

The three of them turn to face me.

"What are you talking about?" Kenji says.

"Love, that's really not a good idea—We don't have any parachutes on this plane, and without them—"

"No, she's right," Nazeera says carefully. She's looking me in the eye. She seems to understand what I'm thinking.

"It'll work," I say. "Don't you think?"

"Honestly, I have no idea," she says. "But it's definitely worth a shot. It might be our only shot."

Kenji is beginning to pace. "Okay, someone needs to tell me what the hell is going on."

Aaron has gone pale. "Love," he says again, "what—"

"Nazeera can fly," I explain. "If we all find a way to secure ourselves to one another, she can use her powers to bolster us, you can use your power to bolster *her* power, and because there's little chance either of you could use that much of your strength while still carrying our combined weight, we'll eventually, slowly, be dragged down to the ground."

Nazeera glances at the dash again. "We're eight thousand feet in the air and losing altitude quickly. If we're going to do this, we should jump now, while the plane is still relatively stable."

"Wait—where are we?" Kenji says. "Where are we going to land?"

"I'm not sure," she says. "But it looks like we're somewhere over the general vicinity of sectors 200 through 300." She looks at Aaron. "Do you have any friends in this region?"

Aaron shoots her a dark look. "I have friends nowhere."

"Zero people skills," Kenji mutters.

"We're out of time," I say. "Are we going to do this?"

"I guess so. It's the only plan we've got," Kenji says.

"I think it's a solid plan," Aaron says, and shoots me a hesitant, but encouraging look. "But I think we should find a way to strap ourselves together. Some kind of harness or something—so we don't lose each other in the air."

"We don't have time for that." Nazeera's calm is quickly giving way to panic. "We'll just have to hold on tight."

Kenji nods, and with a sudden heave, shoves open the airplane door. Air rushes in fast and hard, nearly knocking us off our feet.

Quickly, we all link arms, Nazeera and Aaron holding up the outer edges, and with a few reassuring shouts through the howling wind—

We jump.

It's a terrifying sensation.

The wind pushes up fast and hard and then, all at once, stills. We seem to be frozen in time, whirring in place even as we watch the jet fall, steadily, into the distance. Nazeera and Aaron appear to be doing their jobs almost too well. We're not falling fast enough, and not only is it freezing up here, oxygen is scarce.

"I'm going to drop my hold on your power," Aaron calls out to Nazeera, and she shouts back her agreement.

Slowly, we begin to descend.

I watch as the world blurs around us. We drift downward, unhurried, the wind pushing hard against our feet. And then, suddenly, the bottom seems to drop out from under us, and we go shooting down, hard, into the terrain below.

I give out a single, terrified scream—

Or was that Kenji?

—before we pull to a sudden stop, a foot above the ground. Aaron squeezes my arm and I look at him, grateful for the catch.

And then we fall to the ground.

I land badly on my ankle and wince, but I can put weight on my foot, so I know it's all right. I look around to assess the state of my friends, but realize, too late, that we're not alone.

We're in a vast, wide-open field. This was, once upon a time, almost certainly farmland, but it's now been reduced to little more than ash. In the distance appears a thin band of people, quickly closing in on us.

I harness my powers, ready to fight. Ready to face whatever comes our way. Energy is thrumming inside me, sparking in my blood.

I am not afraid.

Aaron puts his arm around me, pulls me close. "Together," he whispers. "No matter what."

Finally, after what feels like immeasurable minutes, two bodies separate from their group. Slowly, they walk up to us.

My whole body is tense in preparation for an attack, but as they get closer, I'm able to discern their faces.

They're two adults:

One, a slender, stunning woman with closely cropped hair and skin so dark it gleams. She's luminous as she walks, her smile widening with every step. Beside her is another smiling face, but the familiar sight of his brown skin and long dreadlocks sends shock and panic and hope rushing through me. I feel dazed.

Castle.

His presence here could be either good or bad. A thousand questions run through my mind, among them: What is he doing here? How did he get here? The last time I saw him, I didn't think he was on my side at all—has he turned against us completely?

The woman is the first to speak.

"I'm glad to see you're all right," she says. "I'm afraid we had no choice but to shoot your plane out of the sky."

"What? What are y—"

"Castle?" Kenji's quiet, tentative voice reaches out from behind me.

Castle steps forward just as Kenji moves toward him,

and the two embrace, Castle pulling him in so tightly I can practically feel the tension from where I'm standing. They're both visibly emotional, and the moment is so touching it puts my fears at ease.

"You're okay," Kenji says. "I thought—"

Haider and Stephan, the son of the supreme commander of Africa, step out of the crowd. Shock seizes my body at the sight of them. They nod at Nazeera and the three of them separate to form a new group, off to the side. They speak in low, hurried whispers.

Castle takes a deep breath. "We have a lot to talk about." And then, to me, he says, "Ella, I'd like you to meet my daughter, Nouria."

My eyebrows fly up my forehead. I glance at Aaron, who seems as stunned as I am, but Kenji lets out a sudden *whoop*, and tackles Castle all over again. The two of them laugh. Kenji is saying, *No way, no way*

Nouria pointedly ignores them and smiles at me. "We call our home the Sanctuary," she says. "My wife and I are the leaders of the resistance here. Welcome."

Another woman separates from the crowd and steps forward. She's petite, with long blond hair. She shakes my hand. "It's an honor to meet you," she says. "My name is Samantha."

I study both of them, Nouria and Samantha standing side by side. Castle's happiness. The smile on Kenji's face. The cluster of Nazeera, Haider, and Stephan off to the side. The larger group crowded in the distance.

"The honor is ours," I say, and smile. Then: "But are we safe out here? Out in the open like this?"

Nouria nods. "My powers allow me to manipulate light in unusual ways," she says. "I've cast a protective shield around us right now, so that if someone were to look in our direction, they'd see only a painful brightness that would force them to look away."

"Whoa." Kenji's eyes widen. "That's cool."

"Thank you," Nouria says. She's practically emanating light, her dark brown skin shimmering even as she stands still. There's something breathtaking about just being near her.

"Are those your people?" I hear Aaron say, speaking for the first time. He's peering over her head, at the small crowd in the distance.

She nods.

"And are they here to make sure we don't hurt you?"

Nouria smiles. "They're here to make sure no one hurts *you*," she says. "Your group is welcome here. You've more than proven yourselves worthy." And then, "We've heard all the stories about Sector 45."

"You have?" I say, surprised. "I thought The Reestablishment buried everything."

Nouria shakes her head. "Whispers travel faster than anyone can control. The continent is buzzing with the news of all you've been doing these past couple of months. It's truly a privilege to meet you," she says to me, and holds out her hand. "I've been so inspired by your work."

I take her hand, feeling at once proud and embarrassed. "Thank you," I say quietly. "That's very kind of you."

But then Nouria's eyes grow somber. "I *am* sorry we had to shoot you out of the sky," she says. "That must've been terrifying. But Castle assured me that there were two among you who would be able to fly."

"Wait, what?" Kenji hazards a look at Castle. "You planned this?"

"It was the only way," he says. "Once we were able to get free of the asylum"—he nods gratefully at Nazeera—"I knew the only place left for us was here, with Nouria. But we couldn't have radioed to tell you to land here; our communication would've been intercepted. And we couldn't have you land at the air base, for obvious reasons. So we've been tracking your plane, waiting for the right moment. Shooting you out of the sky punts the problem straight back to the military. They'll think it was action from another unit, and by the time they begin to figure it out, we'll have destroyed all evidence of our being here."

"So—Wait—" I say. "How did you and Nouria coordinate this? How'd you find each other?" And then: "Castle, if you've abandoned the citizens—Won't Anderson just murder them all? Shouldn't you have stayed to protect them? Tried to fight back?"

He shakes his head. "We had no choice but to evacuate Omega Point members from Sector 45. After the two of you"—he nods at me and Aaron—"were taken, things fell into complete chaos. We were all taken hostage and thrown in prison. It was only because of Nazeera—who connected us with Haider and Stephan—that we were able to make our way here. Sector 45 has since been returned to its original state as a prison." Castle takes a tight breath. "There's a great deal we need to share with each other. So much has happened in the last two weeks it'll be impossible to discuss it all quickly. But it *is* important that you know, right now, a little bit about Nouria's role in all this."

He turns to Nouria and gives her a small nod.

Nouria looks me in the eye and says, "That day you were shot on the beach," she says quietly. "Do you remember?"

I hesitate. "Of course."

"I was the one who issued that order against you."

I'm so stunned I visibly flinch.

"*What?*" Aaron steps forward, outraged. "Castle, are you *insane*? You ask us to take refuge in the home of a person who nearly murdered Ella?" He turns back, stares at me with a wild look in his eyes. "How could y—"

"Castle?" There's a warning in Kenji's voice. "What is going on?"

But Nouria and Castle are staring at each other, and a heavy look passes between them.

Finally, Castle sighs.

"Let's get settled before we keep talking," he says. "This is a long conversation, and it's an important one."

"Let's have it now," Aaron says.

"Yes," Kenji says angrily. "Now."

"She tried to murder me," I say, finally finding my voice.

"Why would you bring me here? What are you trying to do?"

"You've had a long, difficult journey," Castle says. "I want you to have a chance to get settled. Take a shower and eat some food. And then, I promise—we'll give you all the answers you want."

"But how can we trust that we'll be safe?" I say. "How can we know Nouria isn't trying to hurt us?"

"Because," she says steadily, "I did what I did to help you."

"And how is that plausible?" Aaron says sharply.

"It was the only way I knew how to get a message to you," Nouria says, still staring at me. "I was never trying to kill you—and I knew that your own defenses would help protect you from certain death."

"That was a dangerous bet to make."

"Believe me," she says quietly, "it was a difficult decision to make. It came at great cost to us—we lost one of our own in the process."

I feel myself tense, but otherwise betray no emotion. I remember the day Nazeera saved me—the day she killed my assailant.

"But I had to reach you," Nouria says, her dark brown eyes deep with feeling. "It was the only way I could do it without rousing suspicion."

My curiosity beats out my skepticism. For the moment.

"So—Why? Why did you do it?" I ask. "Why poison me?"

Unexpectedly, Nouria smiles. "I needed you to see what I saw. And according to Castle, it worked."

"What worked?"

"Ella—" She hesitates. "May I call you by your real name?"

I blink. Stare at Castle. "You told her about me?"

"He didn't have to. Things don't stay secret for very long around here," Nouria says. "No matter what The Reestablishment has you believe, we're all finding ways to pass messages to each other. All the resistance groups across the globe know the truth about you by now. And they love you more for it."

I don't know what to say.

"Ella," she says softly, "I was able to figure out why your parents have kept your sister a secret for so long. And I just wanted t—"

"I already know," I say, the words coming out quietly.

I haven't talked to anyone about this yet; haven't told a soul. There's been no time to discuss something this big. No time to have a long conversation. But I guess we're going to have it now.

Nouria is staring at me, stunned. "You know?"

"Emmaline told me everything."

A hush falls over the crowd. Everyone turns to look at me. Even Haider, Stephan, and Nazeera finally stop talking amongst themselves long enough to stare.

"She's kept in captivity," I say. "She lives in a holding tank, where she exists almost permanently underwater. Her brain waves are connected to tidal turbines that convert the kinetic energy of her mind into electricity. Evie, my mother, found a way to harness that electricity—and project it outward. All over the world." I take a deep breath. "Emmaline is stronger than I've ever been or ever will be. She has the power to bend the minds of the people—she can warp and distort realities—Here. Everywhere."

Kenji's face is a perfect encapsulation of horror, and his expression is reflected on dozens of other faces around me. Nazeera, on the other hand, looks stricken.

"What you see here?" I say. "Around us? The decay of society, the broken atmosphere, the birds gone from the sky—It's all an illusion. It's true that our climate has changed, yes—we've done serious damage to the atmosphere, to the animals, to the planet as a whole—but that damage is not irreparable. Scientists were hopeful that, with a careful, concerted effort, we could fix our Earth. Save the future. But The Reestablishment didn't like that angle," he says. "They didn't want the people to hope. They wanted people to think that our Earth was beyond salvation. And with Emmaline they were able to do just that."

"Why?" Kenji says, stunned. "Why would they do that? What do they gain?"

"Desperate, terrified people," Nouria says solemnly, "are much easier to control. They used Ella's sister to create the illusion of irreversible devastation, and then they preyed upon the weak and the hopeless, and convinced them to turn to The Reestablishment for support."

"Emmaline and I were designed for something called Operation Synthesis. She was meant to be the architect of the world, and I was to be the executioner. But Emmaline is dying. They need another powerful weapon with which to control the people. A contingency. A backup plan."

Aaron takes my hand.

"The Reestablishment wanted me to replace my sister," I say.

For the first time, Nouria has gone still. No one knew this part. No one but me. "How?" she says. "You have such different abilities."

It's Castle who says, "It's easy to imagine, actually." But he looks terrified. "If they were to magnify Ella's powers the way they did her sister's, she would become the equivalent of a human atom bomb. She could cause mass destruction. Excruciating pain. Death when they please. Across tremendous distances."

"We have no choice." Nazeera's voice rings out, sharp and clear. "We have to kill Evie."

And I'm looking out, far into the distance, when I say, quietly, "I already did."

A collective gasp goes through the crowd. Aaron goes still beside me.

"And now," I say, "I have to kill my sister. It's what she wants. It's the only way."

WARNER

Nouria's headquarters are both strange and beautiful. They have no need to hide underground, because she's found a way to imbue objects with her power—an evolution of our abilities even Castle hadn't foreseen. The Sanctuary's campsite is protected by a series of twenty-foot-tall pole lights that border the edges of the clearing. Fused with Nouria's power, the lights work together as a barrier that makes it impossible to look in the direction of their campsite. She says her abilities not only have the power to blind, but that she can also use light to warp sounds. So they live here, out in the open, their words and actions protected in plain sight. Only those who know the location can find their way here.

Nouria says that the illusion has kept them safe for years.

The sun begins its descent as we make our way toward the campsite—the vast, unusually green field dotted with cream-colored tents—and the scene is so breathtaking I can't help but stop to appreciate the view. Fire streaks across the sky, golden light flooding the air and earth. It feels both beautiful and bleak, and I shiver as a gust of wind wraps around my body.

Ella takes my hand.

I look at her, surprised, and she smiles at me, the fading

sun glinting in her eyes. I feel her fear, her hope, her love for me. But there's something else, too—something like pride. It's faint, but it's there, and it makes me so happy to see her like this. She *should* be proud. I can speak for myself, at least, when I say that I've never been so proud of her. But then, I always knew she would go on to greatness. It doesn't surprise me at all that, even after everything she's been through—after all the horrors she's had to face— she's still managed to inspire the world. She's one of the strongest people I've ever known. My father might be back from the dead, and Sector 45 might be out of our hands, but Ella's impact can't be ignored. Nouria says that no one really believed that she was actually dead, but now that it's official—now that word has spread that Ella is still alive— she's become more notorious than ever. Nouria says that the rumbles underground are already getting stronger. People are more desperate to act, to get involved, and to stand up to The Reestablishment. Resistance groups are growing. The civilians are finding ways to get smarter—to get stronger, together. And Ella has given them a figure to rally around. Everyone is talking about her.

She's become a symbol of hope for so many.

I squeeze Ella's hand, returning her smile, and when her cheeks flush with color I have to fight back the urge to pull her into my arms.

She amazes me more every day.

My conversation with Kenji is still, despite everything, at the forefront of my mind. Things always feel so desperate these days that I feel a new, nagging insistence that this window of calm might be my only chance at happiness. We're almost constantly at war, either fighting for our lives or on the run—and there's no guarantee of a future. No guarantee that I'll live to see another year. No promise to grow old. It makes me feel li—

I stop, suddenly, and Ella nearly stumbles.

"Are you okay?" she says, squeezing my hand.

I nod. I offer her a distracted smile and vague apology as we begin walking again, but—

I run the numbers once more.

Finally, I say, without looking up, "Does anyone happen to know what day it is?"

And someone responds, a voice from the group I can't be bothered to identify, confirming what I already thought might be true. My father wasn't lying.

Tomorrow is my birthday.

I'll be twenty years old.

Tomorrow.

The revelation thunders through me. This birthday feels like more of a milestone than usual, because my life, exactly one year ago, was nearly unrecognizable. Almost everything in my life is different now. One year ago I was a different person. I was in an awful, self-destructive relationship with a different person. One year ago my anxiety was so crippling that five minutes alone with my own mind would leave me spiraling for days. I relied entirely upon my routines and schedules to keep me tethered to the endless horrors of my job and its demands. I was inflexible beyond reason. I was hanging on to humanity by a thread. I felt both wild and nearly out of my mind, all the time. My private thoughts and fears were so dark that I spent nearly all my free hours either exercising, in my shooting range, or in the bowels of Sector 45, running training simulations that, I'm not proud to admit, I designed specifically to experience killing myself, over and over again.

That was one year ago. Less than a year ago. Somehow, it feels like a lifetime ago. And when I think back on who I was and what that version of myself thought my life would be like today—

I'm left deeply and profoundly humbled.

Today is not forever. Happiness does not *happen*. Happiness must be uncovered, separated from the skin of pain. It must be claimed. Kept close.

Protected.

"Would you prefer a chance to shower and change before reuniting with the others?" Nouria is saying.

Her voice is sharp and clear and it shakes me from my reverie. "Yes," I say quickly. "I'd really appreciate the time to rest."

"No problem. We meet for dinner in the main tent in two hours. I'll show you to your new residences." She hesitates. "I hope you'll forgive me for being presumptuous, but I assumed the two of you"—she looks at me and Ella—"would like to share a space. But of course if that's not—"

"Yes, thank you," Ella says quickly. Her cheeks are

already pink. "We're grateful for your thoughtfulness."

Nouria nods. She seems pleased. And then she turns to Kenji and Nazeera and says, "If you'd like, I can arrange to join your separate rooms so that y—"

Kenji and Nazeera respond at the same time.

"What? No."

"Absolutely not."

"*Oh*, I'm so sorry," Nouria says quickly. "My apologies. I shouldn't have assumed."

For the first time ever, Nazeera looks flustered. She can hardly get out the words when she says, "Why would you think we'd want to share a room?"

Nouria shakes her head. She shares a quick, confused glance with Castle, but seems suddenly mortified. "I don't know. I'm sorry. You seemed—"

"Separate rooms are perfect," Kenji says sharply.

"Great," Nouria says a little too brightly. "I'll lead the way."

And I watch, amused, as Castle tries and fails to hide a smile.

Our residence, as Nouria called it, is more than I could've hoped for. I thought we'd be camping; instead, inside of each tent is a miniature, self-contained home. There's a bed, a small living area, a tiny kitchen, and a full bathroom. The furnishings are spare but bright, well made and clean.

And when Ella walks in, slips off her shoes, and throws herself backward onto the bed, I can almost imagine us together like this—maybe, someday—in our own home. The thought sends a wave of disorienting euphoria through my body.

And then—fear.

It seems like tempting fate to even hope for a happiness like that. But there's another part of me, a small, but insistent part of me, that clings to that hope nonetheless. Ella and I overcame what I once thought impossible. I never dreamed she'd still love me once she knew everything about me. I never dreamed that the heartbreak and horrors of recent events would only bring us closer, or that my love for her could somehow increase tenfold in two weeks. I grew up thinking that the joys of this world were for other people to enjoy. I was certain that I was fated to a bleak, solitary life, forever barred from the contentment offered by human connection.

But now—

Ella yawns soundlessly, hugging a pillow to her chest as she curls up on her side. Her eyes close.

A smile tugs at my mouth as I watch her.

I'm still amazed at how just the sight of her could bring me so much peace. She shifts, again, burrowing more deeply into the pillows, and I realize she must be exhausted. And as much as I'd love to pull her into my arms, I decide to give her space. I back away quietly, and instead use the time to explore the rest of our new, temporary home.

I'm still surprised by how much I like it.

We have more privacy here, in these new headquarters,

than we ever did before. More freedom. Here, I'm a visitor, welcome to take my time showering and resting before dinner. No one expects me to run their world. I have no correspondence to attend to. No awful tasks to attend to. No civilians to oversee. No innocents to torture. I feel so much freer now that someone else has taken the reins.

It's both alien and wonderful.

It feels so good to have space with Ella—literal and figurative space—to be ourselves, to be together, to simply be and breathe. Ella and I shared my bedroom back on base, but it never felt like home there. Everything was cold, sterile. I hated that building. Hated that room. Hated every minute of my life. Those walls—my own personal rooms—were suffocating, infused with awful memories. But here, even though the room is small, the tight quarters manage to be cozy. This place feels fresh and new and serene. The future doesn't seem improbable here. Hope doesn't feel ridiculous.

It feels like a chance to begin again.

And it doesn't feel dangerous to dream that one day, Ella might be mine in every way. My wife. My family. My future.

I've never, ever dared to think of it.

But my hope is snuffed out just as quickly as it appeared. Kenji's warnings flash through my mind, and I feel suddenly agitated. Apparently proposing to Ella is more complicated than I'd originally thought it might be. Apparently I need some kind of plan. A ring. A moment on one knee. It all sounds ridiculous to me. I don't even know why it sounds ridiculous, exactly, just that it doesn't feel like *me*. I don't know how to put on a performance. I don't want to make a scene. I'd find it excruciating to be so vulnerable in front of other people or in an unfamiliar setting. I wouldn't know what to do with myself.

Still, these problems seem surmountable in the pursuit of forever with her. I would get on one knee if Ella wanted me to. I'd propose in a room filled with her closest friends if that was what she needed.

No, my fear is something much greater than that.

The thing Kenji said to me today that rattled me to my core was the possibility that Ella might say no. It's *unconscionable* that it never occurred to me that she might say no.

Of course she might say no.

She could be uninterested for any number of reasons. She might not be ready, for example. Or she might not be interested in the institution of marriage as a whole. *Or*, I think, she simply might not want to tether herself to me in such a permanent way.

The thought sends a chill through my body.

I suppose I assumed she and I were on the same page, emotionally. But my assumptions in this department have landed me in trouble more times than I'd like to admit, and the stakes are too high now not to take Kenji's concerns seriously. I'm not prepared to acknowledge the damage it would do to my heart if she rejected my proposal.

I take a deep, sharp breath.

Kenji said I need to get her a ring. So far he's been right

about most of the things I've done wrong in our relationship, so I'm inclined to believe he might have a point. But I have no idea where I'd be able to conjure up a ring in a place like this. Maybe if we were back home, where I was familiar with the area and its artisans—

But here?

It's almost too much to think about right now.

There's so much to think about, in fact, that I can't quite believe I'm even considering something like this—at a time like this. I haven't even had a moment to reconcile the apparent regeneration of my father, or literally any of the other new, outrageous revelations our families have thrown at us. We're in the middle of a fight for our lives; we're fighting for the future of the *world*.

I squeeze my eyes shut. Maybe I really am an idiot.

Five minutes ago, the end of the world seemed like the right reason to propose: to take everything I can in this transitory world—and grieve nothing. But suddenly, it feels like this really might be an impulsive decision. Maybe this isn't the right time, after all.

Maybe Kenji was right. Maybe I'm not thinking clearly. Maybe losing Ella and regaining all these memories—

Maybe it's made me irrational.

I push off the wall, trying to clear my head. I wander the rest of the small space, taking stock of everything in our tent, and peer into the bathroom. I'm relieved to discover that there's real plumbing. In fact, the more I look around, the more I realize that this isn't a tent at all. There are actual floors and walls and a single vaulted ceiling in this room, as if each unit is actually a small, freestanding building. The tents seem to be draped over the entire structure—and I wonder if they serve a more practical purpose that's not immediately obvious.

Several years, Nouria said.

Several years they've lived here and made this their home. They really found a way to make something out of nothing.

The bathroom is a nice size—spacious enough for two people to share, but not big enough for a bathtub. Still, when we first approached the clearing I wasn't even sure they'd have proper facilities or running water, so this is more than I could've hoped for. And the more I stare at the shower, the more I'm suddenly desperate to rinse these weeks from my skin. I always took pains to stay clean, even in prison, but it's been too long since I've had a hot shower with steady, running water, and I can hardly resist the temptation now. And I've already stripped off most of my clothes when I hear Ella call my name, her still-sleepy voice carrying over from what serves as our bedroom. Or bed space. It's not really a room as much as it is an area designated for a bed.

"Yes?" I call back.

"Where'd you go?" she says.

"I thought I might take a shower," I try to say without shouting. I've just stepped out of my underwear and into the standing shower, but I turn the dials in the wrong direction and cold water sprays from the showerhead. I jump backward even as I hurry to undo my mistake, and nearly collide with Ella in the process.

Ella, who's suddenly standing behind me.

I don't know whether its habit, instinct, or self-preservation, but I grab a towel from a nearby shelf and quickly press it against my exposed body. I don't even understand why I'm suddenly self-conscious. I never feel uncomfortable in my own skin. I like the way I look naked.

But this moment wasn't one I'd anticipated, and I feel defenseless.

"Hi, love," I say, taking a quick breath. I remember to smile. "I didn't see you standing there."

Ella crosses her arms, pretending to look mad, but I can see the effort she's making to fight back a smile. "Aaron," she says sternly. "You were going to take a shower without me?"

My eyebrows fly up, surprised.

For a moment, I don't know what to say. And then, carefully, "Would you like to join me?"

She steps forward, wraps her arms around my waist, and stares up at me with a sweet, secret smile. The look in her eyes is enough to make me think about dropping the towel.

I whisper her name, my heart heavy with emotion.

She pulls me closer, gently touching her lips to my chest, and I go uncomfortably still. Her kisses grow more intent, her lips leaving a trail of fire across my chest, down my torso, and feeling rushes through my veins, sets me on fire. Suddenly I forget why I was ever holding a towel.

I don't even know when it falls to the floor.

I slip my arms around her, reel her in. She feels incredible, her body fitting against me perfectly, and I tilt her face up, my hand caught somewhere behind her neck and the base of her jaw and I kiss her, soft and slow, heat filling my blood with dangerous speed. I pull her tighter and she gasps, stumbles and takes an accidental step back and I catch her, pressing her against the wall behind her. I bunch up the hem of her dress and in one smooth motion yank it upward, my hand slipping under the material to skim the smooth skin of her waist, to grip her hip, hard. I part her legs with my thigh and she makes a soft, desperate sound deep in her throat and it does something to me, to feel her like this, to hear her like this—to be assaulted by endless waves of her pleasure and desire—

It drives me *insane*.

I bury my face in her neck, my hands moving up, under her dress to feel her skin, hot and soft and sensitive to my touch. I've missed her so much. I've missed her body under my hands, missed the scent of her skin and the soft, feather-light whisper of her hair against my body. I kiss her neck, trying to ignore the tension in my muscles or the hard, desperate pressure driving me toward her, toward madness. There's an ache expanding inside of me and demanding more, demanding I flip her over and lose myself in her here, right now, and she whispers—

"How—How do you always feel so good?" She's clinging to me, her eyes half-lidded but bright with desire. Her face is flushed. Her words are heavy with feeling when she says, "How do you always do this to me?"

I break away from her.

I take two steps backward and I'm breathing hard, trying to regain control of myself even as her eyes widen, her arms going suddenly still.

"Aaron?" she says. "What's—"

"Take off your dress," I say quietly.

Understanding awakens in her eyes.

She says nothing, she only looks at me, carefully, as I watch, imprisoned in place by an acute form of agony. Her hands are trembling but her eyes are willing and wanting and nervous. She shoves the material down, past her shoulders and lets it fall to the floor. I drink her in as she steps out of the dress, my mind racing.

Gorgeous, I think. *So gorgeous.*

My pulse is wild.

When I ask her to, she unhooks her bra. Moments later, her underwear joins her bra on the floor and I can't look away from her, my mind unable to process the perfection of this happiness. She's so stunning I can hardly breathe. I can hardly fathom that she's mine, that she wants me, that she would ever love me. I can't even hear myself *think* over the rush of blood in my ears, my heart beating so fast and hard it seems to thud against my skull. The sight of her standing in front of me, vulnerable and flushed with desire, is doing wild, desperate things to my mind. God, the fantasies I've had about her. The places my mind has gone.

I step forward and pick her up and she gasps, surprised, clinging desperately to my neck as I hitch her legs around my waist, my arms settling under her thighs. I love feeling the weight of her soft curves. I love having her this close to me. I love her arms around my neck and the squeeze of her legs around my hips. I love how ready she is, her thighs already parted, every inch of her pressed against me. But then she runs her hands up my naked back and I have to resist the urge to flinch. I don't want to be self-conscious about the scars on my body. I don't want any part of me to be off-limits to her. I want her to know me exactly as I am, and, as hard as it is, I allow myself to ease into her touch, closing my eyes as she trails her hands up, across my shoulders, down my arms.

"You're so gorgeous," she says softly. "I'm always surprised. It doesn't matter how many times I see you without your clothes on, I'm always surprised. It doesn't seem fair that anyone should be this gorgeous."

She looks at me, stares at me as if expecting an answer, but I can't speak. I fear I might unravel if I do. I want her with a desperate need I've never known before—a desperate, painful need so overwhelming it's threatening to consume me. I need her. Need this. Now. I take a deep, unsteady breath, and carry her into the shower.

She screams.

Hot water hits us fast and hard and I press her against the shower wall, losing myself in her in a way I never have before. The kisses are deeper, more desperate. The heat, more explosive. Everything between us feels wild and raw and vulnerable.

I lose track of time.

I don't know how long we've been here. I don't know how long I've lost myself in her when she cries out, clutching my arms so tightly her fingernails dig into my skin, her screams muffled against my chest. I feel weak, unsteady as she collapses in my arms; I'm intoxicated by the pure, stunning power of her emotions: endless waves of love and desire, love and kindness, love and joy, love and tenderness. So much tenderness.

It's almost too much.

I step backward, bracing myself against the wall as she presses her cheek against my chest and holds me, our bodies wet and heavy with feeling, our hearts pounding with something more powerful than I ever thought possible. I kiss the curve of her shoulder, the nape of her neck. I forget where we are and all we have left to do and I just hold on, hot water rushing down my arms, my limbs still slightly shaking, too terrified to let her go.

~~Juliette~~

Ella

I wake up with a start.

After we got out of the shower, Aaron and I dried off, climbed into bed without a word, and promptly fell asleep.

I have no idea what time it is.

Aaron's body is curled around mine, one of his arms under my head, the other wrapped around my waist. His arms are heavy, and the weight of him feels so good—makes me feel so safe—that, on the one hand, I don't ever want to move. On the other hand—

I know we should probably get out of bed.

I sigh, hating to wake him up—he seems so tired—and I turn around, slowly, in his arms.

He only pulls me tighter.

He shifts so that his chin rests on my head; my face is now pressed gently against his throat, and I breathe him in, running my hands along the strong, deep lines of muscle in his arms. Everything about him feels raw. Powerful. There's something both wild and terrified about his heart, and somehow, knowing this only makes me love him more. I trace the lines of his shoulder blades, the curve of his spine. He stirs, but only a little, and buries his face in my hair, breathing me in.

"Don't go," he says quietly.

I tilt my head, gently kiss the column of his throat. "Aaron," I whisper, "I'm not going anywhere."

He sighs. Says, "Good."

I smile. "But we should probably get out of bed. We have to go to dinner. Everyone will be waiting for us."

He shakes his head, barely. Makes a disapproving sound in his throat.

"But—"

"No." And then, deftly, he helps me turn around. He hugs me close again, my back pressed against his chest. His voice is soft, husky with desire when he says. "Let me enjoy you, love. You feel so good."

And I give in. Melt back into his arms.

The truth is, I love these moments most. The quiet contentment. The peace. I love the weight of him, the feel of him, his naked body wrapped around mine. I never feel closer to him than I do like this, when there's nothing between us.

Gently, he kisses my temple. Pulls me, somehow, even tighter. And his lips are at my ear when he says,

"Kenji said I was supposed to get you a ring."

I stiffen, confused. Try to turn around when I say, "What do you mean?"

But Aaron eases my body back down. He rests his chin on my shoulder. His hands move down my arms, trace the curve of my hips. He kisses my neck once, twice, so softly. "I know I'm doing this wrong," he says. "I know I'm not good at this sort of thing, love, and I hope you'll forgive me for it, but I don't know how else to do it." A pause. "And I'm starting to think it might kill me if I don't."

My body is frozen, even as my heart pounds furiously in my chest. "Aaron," I say, hardly daring to breathe. "What are you talking about?"

He says nothing.

I turn around again, and this time, he doesn't stop me. His eyes flare with emotion, and I watch the gentle movement in his throat as he swallows. A muscle jumps in his jaw.

"Marry me," he whispers.

I stare at him, disbelief and joy colliding. And it's the look in his eyes—the hopeful, terrified look in his eyes—that nearly kills me.

I'm suddenly crying.

I clap my hands over my face. A sob escapes my mouth. Gently, he pries my hands away from my face.

"Ella?" he says, his words hardly a whisper.

I'm still crying when I throw my arms around his neck, still crying when he says, a little nervously—

"Sweetheart, I really need to know if this means yes or no—"

"Yes," I cry, slightly hysterical. "Yes. Yes to everything with you. Yes to forever with you. *Yes.*"

WARNER

Is this joy?

I think it might kill me.

"Aaron?"

"Yes, love?"

She takes my face in her hands and kisses me, kisses me with a love so deep it releases my brain from its prison. My heart starts beating violently.

"Ella," I say. "You're going to be my wife."

She kisses me again, crying again, and suddenly I don't recognize myself. I don't recognize my hands, my bones, my heart. I feel new. Different.

"I love you," she whispers. "I love you so much."

"That you could love me at all seems like some kind of miracle."

She smiles, even as she shakes her head. "That's ridiculous," she says. "It's very, very easy to love you."

And I don't know what to say. I don't know how to respond.

She doesn't seem to mind.

I reel her in, kiss her, again, and lose myself in the taste and feel of her, in the fantasy of what we might have. What we might be. And then I pull her gently onto my lap and she straddles my body, settling over me until we're pressed together, her cheek against my chest. I wrap my arms around her, spread my hands along her back. I feel her gentle breaths on my skin, her eyelashes tickling my chest as she blinks, and I decide I'm never, ever leaving this bed.

A happy, wonderful silence settles between us.

"You asked me to marry you," she says softly.

"Yes."

"Wow."

I smile, my heart filled suddenly with inexpressible joy. I hardly recognize myself. I can't remember the last time I ever smiled this much. I can't recall ever feeling this kind of pure, unburdened bliss.

Like my body might float away without me.

I touch her hair, gently. Run my fingers through the soft, silky strands. When I finally sit up, she sits up, too, and she blushes as I stare at her, mesmerized by the sight of her. Her eyes are wide and bright. Her lips full and pink. She's perfect, perfect here, bare and beautiful in my arms.

I press my forehead to the curve of her shoulder, my lips brushing against her skin. "I love you, Ella," I whisper. "I will love you for the rest of my life. My heart is yours. Please don't ever give it back to me."

She says nothing for what feels like an eternity.

Finally, I feel her move. Her hand touches my face.

"Aaron," she whispers. "Look at me."

I shake my head.

"Aaron."

I look up, slowly, to meet her eyes, and her expression is at once sad and sweet and full of love. I feel something thaw inside of me as I stare at her, and just as she's about to say something, a complicated chime echoes through the room.

I freeze.

Ella frowns. Looks around. "That sounds like a doorbell," she says.

I wish I could deny the possibility.

I sit back, even though she's still sitting on my lap. I want this interruption to end. I want to go back to our conversation. I want to stick to my original plan to spend the rest of the night here, in bed, with my perfect, naked fiancée.

The chime sounds again, and this time, I say something decidedly ungentlemanly under my breath.

Ella laughs, surprised. "Did you just swear?"

"No."

A third chime. This time, I stare up at the ceiling and try to clear my head. Try to convince myself to move, to get dressed. This must be some kind of emergency, or else—

Suddenly, a voice:

"Listen—I didn't want to come, okay? I really didn't. I hate being this guy. But Castle sent me to come get you guys because you missed dinner. It's getting super late and everyone is a little worried, and now you're not even answering the door, and—Jesus Christ, open the goddamn door—"

I can't believe it. I can't believe he's here. He's always

here, ruining my life.

I'm going to *kill* him.

I nearly trip trying to pull on my pants and get to the door at the same time, but when I do, I rip the door open, practically tearing it off its hinges.

"Unless someone is dead, dying, or we are under attack, I want you gone before I've even finished this sentence."

Kenji narrows his eyes at me, and then pushes past me into the room. And I'm so stunned by his gall that it takes me a moment to realize I'm going to have to murder him.

"J—?" he says, looking around as he walks in. "You in here?"

Ella is holding the bedsheet up to her neck. "Uh, hi," she says. She smiles nervously. "What are you doing here?"

"Hey, is it cool if I still call you J?" he says. "I know your name is Ella and everything, but I got so used to calling you J that it just feels right, you know?"

"You can still call me J," she says. And then she frowns. "Kenji, what's wrong?"

I groan.

"Get out," I snap at him. "I don't know why you're here, and I don't care. We don't wish to be disturbed. *Ever*."

Ella shoots me a sharp look. She ignores me when she says, to Kenji, "It's okay. I care. Tell me what's wrong."

"Nothing is wrong," Kenji says. "But I know your boyfriend won't listen to me, so I wanted to let *you* know that it's almost midnight and we really need you guys to get down to the dining tent ASAP, okay?" He shoots Ella a loaded look, and her eyes widen. She nods. I feel a sudden rush of excitement move through her, and it leaves me confused.

"What's going on?" I say.

But Kenji is already walking away.

"Bro, you really need to, like, eat a pizza or something," he says, slapping me on the shoulder as he leaves. "You have too many abs."

"What?" My eyebrows pull together. "That's not—"

"I'm *joking*," Kenji says, pausing in the doorway just before he leaves. "Joking," he says again. "It was a joke. Jesus."

And then he slams the door behind him. I turn around.

"What's going on?" I say again.

But she only smiles. "We should get dressed."

"Ella—"

"I promise I'll explain as soon as we get there."

I shake my head. "Did something happen?"

"No—I'm just—I'm really excited to see everyone from Omega Point again, and they're all waiting for us in the dining tent." She gets out of bed still holding the bedsheet to her body, and I have to clench my fists to keep from pulling it away from her. From pinning her against the wall.

And before I even have a chance to respond, she disappears into the bathroom, the sheet dragging on the floor as she goes.

I follow her.

She's looking for her clothes, oblivious to my presence,

but her dress is on the floor in a corner she hasn't glimpsed yet, and I doubt she'd want to put that bloodied dress back on anyway. I should tell her that I found a drawer full of simple, standard clothes we're probably allowed to borrow.

Maybe later.

For now, I step behind her, slip my hands around her waist. She startles and the sheet falls to the floor. "Ella," I say softly, tugging her body against mine. "Sweetheart, you have to tell me what's going on."

I turn her around, slowly. She looks down at herself, surprised—always surprised—by the sight of her naked body. "I don't have any clothes on," she whispers.

"I know," I say, smiling as I run my hands down her back, appreciating her softness, her perfect curves. I wish I could store these moments. I wish I could revisit them. Relive them. She shivers in my arms and I pull her closer.

"It's not fair," she says, wrapping her arms around me. "It's not fair that you can sense emotions. That it's impossible to keep secrets from you."

"What's not fair," I say, "is that you're about to put your clothes on and force me to leave this bedroom and I don't know why."

She stares at me, her eyes wide and nervous even as she smiles. I can sense that she's torn, her heart in two places at once. "Aaron," she says softly. "Don't you like surprises?"

"I hate surprises."

She laughs. Shakes her head. "I guess I should've known that."

I stare at her, my eyebrows raised, still waiting for an explanation.

"They're going to kill me for telling you," she says. And then at the look in my eyes, "Not—I mean, not literally. But just—" Finally, she sighs. And she won't look at me when she says—

"We're throwing you a birthday party."

I'm certain I've heard her wrong.

~~Juliette~~

ELLA

It took more work than I imagined to get him to believe me. He wanted to know how anyone even knew that tomorrow was his birthday and how we could've possibly planned a party when we had no idea we were going to crash the plane here and why would anyone throw him a party and he wasn't even sure he liked parties and on and on and on

And it wasn't until we literally walked through the doors of the dining tent and everyone screamed happy birthday at him that he finally believed me. It wasn't much, of course. We hadn't really had time to prepare. I knew his birthday was coming up because I'd been keeping track of it ever since the day he told me what his father used to do to him, every year, on his birthday. I swore to myself I would do whatever I could to replace those memories with better ones. That forever and ever I would try to drown out the darkness that had inhaled his entire young life.

I told Kenji, when he found me, that tomorrow was Aaron's birthday, and I made him promise me that, no matter what happened, when we found him we would find a way to celebrate, in some small way.

But this—

This was more than I could've hoped for. I thought

maybe, given our time constraints, we'd just get a group to sing him "Happy Birthday," or maybe eat dessert in his honor, but this—

There's an actual cake.

A cake with candles in it, waiting to be lit.

Everyone from Omega Point is here—the whole crew of familiar faces: Brendan and Winston, Sonya and Sara, Alia and Lily, and Ian and Castle. Only Adam and James are missing, but we have new friends, too—

Haider is here. So is Stephan. Nazeera.

And then there's the new resistance. The members of the Sanctuary that we've yet to meet, all come forward, gathered around a single, modest sheet cake. It reads—

HAPPY BIRTHDAY WARNER

in red icing.

The piping is a little sloppy. The icing is imperfect. But when someone dims the lamps and lights the candles, Aaron goes suddenly still beside me. I squeeze his hand as he looks at me, his eyes round with a new emotion.

There's tragedy and beauty in his eyes: something stoic that refuses to be moved, and something childlike that can't help but feel joy. He looks, in short, like he's in pain.

"Aaron," I whisper. "Is this okay?"

He takes a few seconds to respond, but when he finally does, he nods. Just once—but it's enough.

"Yes," he says softly. "This is okay."

And I feel myself relax.

Tomorrow, there will be pain and devastation to contend

with. Tomorrow we'll dive into a whole new chapter of hardship. There's a world war brewing. A battle for our lives—for the whole world. Right now, little is certain. But tonight, I'm choosing to celebrate. We're going to celebrate the small and large joys. Birthdays and engagements. We're going to find time for happiness. Because how can we stand against tyranny if we ourselves are filled with hate? Or worse—

Nothing?

I want to remember to celebrate more. I want to remember to experience more joy. I want to allow myself to be happy more frequently. I want to remember, forever, this look on Aaron's face, as he's bullied into blowing out his birthday candles for the very first time.

This is, after all, what we're fighting for, isn't it?

A second chance at joy.

The brand new YA fantasy romance series from the author of *TikTok* sensation, **Shatter Me**

RESTORE ME

ALSO BY TAHEREH MAFI

SHATTER ME SERIES:

Shatter Me

Unravel Me

Ignite Me

Restore Me

Defy Me

Imagine Me

NOVELLA COLLECTIONS:

Unite Me (Destroy Me & Fracture Me)

Find Me (Shadow Me & Reveal Me)

Believe Me

A Very Large Expanse of Sea

An Emotion of Great Delight

This Woven Kingdom

These Infinite Threads

RESTORE ME

TAHEREH MAFI

DEAN

DEAN

First published in the USA 2018 by HarperCollins Children's Books
First published in Great Britain 2018 by Electric Monkey, part of Farshore
This edition published 2021 by Dean, part of Farshore
An imprint of HarperCollins*Publishers*
1 London Bridge Street, London SE1 9GF
www.farshore.co.uk

HarperCollins*Publishers*
Macken House, 39/40 Mayor Street Upper,
Dublin 1, D01 C9W8, Ireland

Published by arrangement with HarperCollins Children's Books,
a division of HarperCollins Publishers, New York, New York, USA

Text copyright © 2018 Tahereh Mafi

ISBN 978 0 603 58068 0
Printed and Bound in the UK using 100% Renewable Electricity
at CPI Group (UK) Ltd
015

A CIP catalogue record for this title is available from the British Library.

All rights reserved. No part of this publication may be reproduced,
stored in a retrieval system, or transmitted, in any form or by any means,
electronic, mechanical, photocopying, recording or otherwise, without
the prior permission of the publisher and copyright owner.

Stay safe online. Farshore is not responsible for content hosted by third parties.

This book is produced from independently certified FSC™ paper
to ensure responsible forest management.

For more information visit: www.harpercollins.co.uk/green

For Jodi Reamer, who always believed

JULIETTE

I don't wake up screaming anymore. I do not feel ill at the sight of blood. I do not flinch before firing a gun.

I will never again apologize for surviving.

And yet—

I'm startled at once by the sound of a door slamming open. I silence a gasp, spin around, and, by force of habit, rest my hand on the hilt of a semiautomatic hung from a holster at my side.

"J, we've got a serious problem."

Kenji is staring at me—eyes narrowed—his hands on his hips, T-shirt taut across his chest. This is angry Kenji. Worried Kenji. It's been sixteen days since we took over Sector 45—since I crowned myself the supreme commander of The Reestablishment—and it's been quiet. Unnervingly so. Every day I wake up, filled with half terror, half exhilaration, anxiously awaiting the inevitable missives from enemy nations who would challenge my authority and wage war against us—and now, finally, it seems that moment has arrived. So I take a deep breath, crack my neck, and look Kenji in the eye.

"Tell me."

He presses his lips together. Looks up at the ceiling. "So,

okay—the first thing you need to know is that this isn't my fault, okay? I was just trying to help."

I falter. Frown. "What?"

"I mean, I knew his punkass was a major drama queen, but this is just beyond ridiculous—"

"I'm sorry—what?" I take my hand off my gun; feel my body unclench. "Kenji, what are you talking about? This isn't about the war?"

"The war? What? J, are you not paying attention? Your boyfriend is having a freaking conniption right now and you need to go handle his ass before I do."

I exhale, irritated. "Are you serious? *Again* with this nonsense? Jesus, Kenji." I unlatch the holster from my back and toss it on the bed behind me. "What did you do this time?"

"See?" Kenji points at me. "See—why are you so quick to judge, huh, princess? Why assume that *I* was the one who did something wrong? Why me?" He crosses his arms against his chest, lowers his voice. "And you know, I've been meaning to talk to you about this for a while, actually, because I really feel that, as supreme commander, you can't be showing preferential treatment like this, but clearly—"

Kenji goes suddenly still.

At the creak of the door Kenji's eyebrows shoot up; a soft click and his eyes widen; a muted rustle of movement and suddenly the barrel of a gun is pressed against the back of his head. Kenji stares at me, his lips making no sound as he mouths the word *psychopath* over and over again.

The psychopath in question winks at me from where

he's standing, smiling like he couldn't possibly be holding a gun to the head of our mutual friend. I manage to suppress a laugh.

"Go on," Warner says, still smiling. "Please tell me exactly how she's failed you as a leader."

"*Hey*—" Kenji's arms fly up in mock surrender. "I never said she failed at anything, okay? And you are clearly overreact—"

Warner knocks Kenji on the side of the head with the weapon. "Idiot."

Kenji spins around. Yanks the gun out of Warner's hand. "What the hell is wrong with you, man? I thought we were cool."

"We were," Warner says icily. "Until you touched my *hair*."

"You asked me to give you a haircut—"

"I said nothing of the sort! I asked you to trim the edges!"

"And that's what I did."

"*This*," Warner says, spinning around so I might inspect the damage, "is not trimming the edges, you incompetent moron—"

I gasp. The back of Warner's head is a jagged mess of uneven hair; entire chunks have been buzzed off.

Kenji cringes as he looks over his handiwork. Clears his throat. "Well," he says, shoving his hands in his pockets. "I mean—whatever, man, beauty is subjective—"

Warner aims another gun at him.

"Hey!" Kenji shouts. "I am not here for this abusive

relationship, okay?" He points at Warner. "I did not sign up for this shit!"

Warner glares at him and Kenji retreats, backing out of the room before Warner has another chance to react; and then, just as I let out a sigh of relief, Kenji pops his head back into the doorway and says

"I think the cut looks cute, actually"

and Warner slams the door in his face.

Welcome to my brand-new life as supreme commander of The Reestablishment.

Warner is still facing the closed door as he exhales, his shoulders losing their tension as he does, and I'm able to see even more clearly the mess Kenji has made. Warner's thick, gorgeous, golden hair—a defining feature of his beauty—chopped up by careless hands.

A disaster.

"Aaron," I say softly.

He hangs his head.

"Come here."

He turns around, looking at me out of the corner of his eye like he's done something to be ashamed of. I clear the guns off the bed and make room for him beside me. He sinks into the mattress with a sad sigh.

"I look hideous," he says quietly.

I shake my head, smiling, and touch his cheek. "Why did you let him cut your hair?"

Warner looks up at me then; his eyes round and green and perplexed. "You told me to spend time with him."

I laugh out loud. "So you let Kenji cut your hair?"

"I didn't let him *cut* my hair," he says, scowling. "It was"—he hesitates—"it was a gesture of camaraderie. It was an act of trust I'd seen practiced among my soldiers. In any case," he says, turning away, "it's not as though I have any experience building friendships."

"Well," I say. "We're friends, aren't we?"

At this, he smiles.

"And?" I nudge him. "That's been good, hasn't it? You're learning to be nicer to people."

"Yes, well, I don't want to be nicer to people. It doesn't suit me."

"I think it suits you beautifully," I say, beaming. "I love it when you're nice."

"You would say that." He almost laughs. "But being kind does not come naturally to me, love. You'll have to be patient with my progress."

I take his hand in mine. "I have no idea what you're talking about. You're perfectly kind to me."

Warner shakes his head. "I know I promised I would make an effort to be nicer to your friends—and I will continue to make that effort—but I hope I've not led you to believe I'm capable of an impossibility."

"What do you mean?"

"Only that I hope I won't disappoint you. I might, if pressed, be able to generate some degree of warmth, but you must know that I have no interest in treating anyone the way I treat you. *This*," he says, touching the air between us, "is an exception to a very hard rule." His eyes are on my lips now; his hand has moved to my neck. "*This*," he says softly, "is very, very unusual."

I stop

stop breathing, talking, thinking—

He's hardly touched me and my heart is racing; memories crash over me, scalding me in waves: the weight of his body against mine; the taste of his skin; the heat of his touch and his sharp gasps for air and the things he's said to me only in the dark.

Butterflies invade my veins, and I force them out.

This is still so new, his touch, his skin, the scent of him, so new, so new and so incredible—

He smiles, tilts his head; I mimic the movement and with one soft intake of air his lips part and I hold still, my lungs flung to the floor, fingers feeling for his shirt and for what comes next when he says

"I'll have to shave my head, you know"

and pulls away.

I blink and he's still not kissing me.

"And it is my very sincere hope," he says, "that you will still love me when I return."

And then he's up up and away and I'm counting on one hand the number of men I've killed and marveling at how little it's done to help me hold it together in Warner's presence.

I nod once as he waves good-bye, collect my good sense from where I left it, and fall backward onto the bed, head spinning, the complications of war and peace heavy on my mind.

I did not think it would be *easy* to be a leader, exactly, but I do think I thought it would be easier than this:

I am racked with doubt in every moment about the decisions I have made. I am infuriatingly surprised every time a soldier follows my lead. And I am growing more terrified that we—that *I*—will have to kill many, many more before this world is settled. Though I think it's the silence, more than anything else, that's left me shaken.

It's been sixteen days.

I've given speeches about what's to come, about our plans for the future; we've held memorials for the lives lost in battle and we're making good on promises to implement change. Castle, true to his word, is already hard at work, trying to address issues with farming, irrigation, and, most urgent, how best to transition the civilians out of the compounds. But this will be work done in stages; it will be a slow and careful build—a fight for the earth that may take a century. I think we all understand that. And if it were only the civilians I had to worry about, I would not worry so much. But I worry because I know too well that nothing can be done to fix this world if we spend the next several decades at war within it.

Even so, I'm prepared to fight.

It's not what I want, but I'll gladly go to war if it's what we need to do to make a change. I just wish it were that simple. Right now, my biggest problem is also the most confusing:

Wars require enemies, and I can't seem to find any.

In the sixteen days since I shot Anderson in the forehead I have faced zero opposition. No one has tried to arrest me. No other supreme commanders have challenged me. Of the 554 remaining sectors on this continent alone, not a single one has defected, declared war, or spoken ill of me. No one has protested; the people have not rioted. For some reason, The Reestablishment is playing along.

Playing pretend.

And it deeply, deeply unnerves me.

We're in a strange stalemate, stuck in neutral when I desperately want to be doing more. More for the people of Sector 45, for North America, and for the world as a whole. But this strange quiet has thrown all of us off-balance. We were so sure that, with Anderson dead, the other supreme commanders would rise up—that they'd command their armies to destroy us—to destroy *me*. Instead, the leaders of the world have made our insignificance clear: they're ignoring us as they would an annoying fly, trapping us under glass where we're free to buzz around, banging broken wings against the walls for only as long as the oxygen lasts. Sector 45 has been left to do as it pleases; we've been allowed autonomy and the authority to revise the infrastructure of our sector with no interference. Everywhere else—and everyone else—is pretending as though nothing in the world has changed. Our revolution occurred in a vacuum. Our subsequent victory has been reduced to something so small it might not even exist.

Mind games.

Castle is always visiting, advising. It was his suggestion that I be proactive—that I take the upper hand. Instead of waiting around, anxious and defensive, I should reach out, he said. I should make my presence known. Stake a claim, he said. Take a seat at the table. And attempt to form alliances before launching assaults. Connect with the five other supreme commanders around the world.

Because I may speak for North America—but what of the rest of the world? What of South America? Europe? Asia? Africa? Oceania?

Host an international conference of leaders, he said.

Talk.

Aim for peace first, he said.

"They must be dying of curiosity," Castle said to me. "A seventeen-year-old girl taking over North America? A teenage girl killing Anderson and declaring herself ruler of this continent? Ms. Ferrars—you must know that you have great leverage at the moment! Use it to your advantage!"

"Me?" I said, stunned. "How do I have leverage?"

Castle sighed. "You certainly are brave for your age, Ms. Ferrars, but I'm sorry to see your youth so inextricably tied to inexperience. I will try to put it plainly: you have superhuman strength, nearly invincible skin, a lethal touch, only seventeen years to your name, and you have single-handedly felled the despot of this nation. And yet you doubt that you might be capable of intimidating the world?"

I cringed.

"Old habits, Castle," I said quietly. "Bad habits. You're right, of course. Of course you're right."

He leveled me with a straight stare. "You must understand that unanimous, collective silence from your enemies is no act of coincidence. They've certainly been in touch with one another—they've certainly agreed to this approach—because they're waiting to see what you do next." He shook his head. "They are awaiting your next move, Ms. Ferrars. I implore you to make it a good one."

So I'm learning.

I did as he suggested and three days ago I sent word through Delalieu and contacted the five other supreme commanders of The Reestablishment. I invited them to join me here, in Sector 45, for a conference of international leaders next month.

Just fifteen minutes before Kenji barged into my room, I'd received my first RSVP.

Oceania said yes.

And I'm not sure what that means.

WARNER

I've not been myself lately.

The truth is I've not been myself for what feels like a long time, so much so that I've begun to wonder whether I ever really knew. I stare, unblinking, into the mirror, the din of buzzing hair clippers echoing through the room. My face is only dimly reflected in my direction, but it's enough for me to see that I've lost weight. My cheeks are hollow; my eyes, wider; my cheekbones more pronounced. My movements are both mournful and mechanical as I shear off my own hair, the remnants of my vanity falling at my feet.

My father is dead.

I close my eyes, steeling myself against the unwelcome strain in my chest, the clippers still humming in my clenched fist.

My father is dead.

It's been just over two weeks since he was killed, shot twice in the forehead by someone I love. She was doing me a kindness by killing him. She was braver than I'd ever been, pulling the trigger when I never could. He was a monster. He deserved worse.

And still—

This pain.

I take in a tight breath and blink open my eyes, grateful for the time to be alone; grateful, somehow, for the opportunity to tear asunder something, anything from my flesh. There's a strange catharsis in this.

My mother is dead, I think, as I drag the electric blade across my skull. *My father is dead*, I think, as the hair falls to the floor. Everything I was, everything I did, everything I am, was forged from the twins of their action and inaction.

Who am I, I wonder, in their absence?

Shorn head, blade switched off, I rest my palms against the edge of the sink and lean in, still trying to catch a glimpse of the man I've become. I feel old and unsettled, my heart and mind at war. The last words I ever spoke to my father—

"Hey."

My heart speeds up as I spin around; I'm affecting nonchalance in an instant. "Hi," I say, forcing my limbs to slow, to be steady as I dust errant strands of hair from my shoulders.

She's looking at me with big eyes, beautiful and worried.

I remember to smile. "How do I look? Not too horrible, I hope."

"Aaron," she says quietly. "Are you okay?"

"I'm fine," I say, and glance again in the mirror. I run a hand over the soft/spiky half inch of hair I have left and wonder at how the cut manages to makes me look harsher— and colder—than before. "Though I confess I don't really recognize myself," I add aloud, attempting a laugh. I'm standing in the middle of the bathroom wearing nothing but boxer briefs. My body has never been leaner, the sharp lines of muscle never more defined; and the rawness of my body is now paired with the rough cut of my hair in a way that feels almost uncivilized—and so unlike me that I have to look away.

Juliette is now right in front of me.

Her hands settle on my hips and pull me forward; I trip a little as I follow her lead. "What are you doing?" I begin to say, but when I meet her eyes I find tenderness and concern. Something thaws inside of me. My shoulders relax and I reel her in, drawing in a deep breath as I do.

"When will we talk about it?" she says against my chest. "All of it? Everything that's happened—"

I flinch.

"Aaron."

"I'm okay," I lie to her. "It's just hair."

"You know that's not what I'm talking about."

I look away. Stare at nothing. We're both quiet a moment.

It's Juliette who finally breaks the silence.

"Are you upset with me?" she whispers. "For shooting him?"

My body stills.

Her eyes widen.

"No—*no*." I say the words too quickly, but I mean them. "No, of course not. It's not that."

Juliette sighs.

"I'm not sure you're aware of this," she says finally, "but

it's okay to mourn the loss of your father, even if he was a terrible person. You know?" She peers up at me. "You're not a robot."

I swallow back the lump growing in my throat and gently extricate myself from her arms. I kiss her on the cheek and linger there, against her skin, for only a second. "I need to take a shower."

She looks heartbroken and confused, but I don't know what else to do. It's not that I don't love her company, it's just that right now I'm desperate for solitude and I don't know how else to find it.

So I shower. I take baths. I go for long walks.

I tend to do this a lot.

When I finally come to bed she's already asleep.

I want to reach for her, to pull her soft, warm body against my own, but I feel paralyzed. This horrible half-grief has made me feel complicit in darkness. I worry that my sadness will be interpreted as an endorsement of his choices—of his very existence—and in this matter I don't want to be misunderstood, so I cannot admit that I grieve him, that I care at all for the loss of this monstrous man who raised me. And in the absence of healthy action I remain frozen, a sentient stone in the wake of my father's death.

Are you upset with me? For shooting him?

I hated him.

I hated him with a violent intensity I've never since

experienced. But the fire of true hatred, I realize, cannot exist without the oxygen of affection. I would not hurt so much, or hate so much, if I did not care.

And it is this, my unrequited affection for my father, that has always been my greatest weakness. So I lie here, marinating in a sorrow I can never speak of, while regret consumes my heart.

I am an orphan.

"Aaron?" she whispers, and I'm pulled back to the present.

"Yes, love?"

She moves in a sleepy, sideways motion, and nudges my arm with her head. I can't help but smile as I open up to make room for her against me. She fills the void quickly, pressing her face into my neck as she wraps an arm around my waist. My eyes close as if in prayer. My heart restarts.

"I miss you," she says. It's a whisper I almost don't catch.

"I'm right here," I say, gently touching her cheek. "I'm right here, love."

But she shakes her head. Even as I pull her closer, even as she falls back asleep, she shakes her head.

And I wonder if she's not wrong.

JULIETTE

I'm having breakfast by myself this morning—alone, but not lonely.

The breakfast room is full of familiar faces, all of us catching up on something: sleep; work; half-finished conversations. Energy levels in here are always dependent on the amount of caffeine we've had, and right now, things are still pretty quiet.

Brendan, who's been nursing the same cup of coffee all morning, catches my eye and waves. I wave back. He's the only one among us who doesn't actually need caffeine; his gift for creating electricity also works as a backup generator for his whole body. He's exuberance, personified. In fact, his stark-white hair and ice-blue eyes seem to emanate their own kind of energy, even from across the room. I'm starting to think Brendan keeps up appearances with the coffee cup mostly out of solidarity with Winston, who can't seem to survive without it. The two of them are inseparable these days—even if Winston occasionally resents Brendan's natural buoyancy.

They've been through a lot together. We all have.

Brendan and Winston are sitting with Alia, who's got her sketchbook open beside her, no doubt designing something new and amazing to help us in battle. I'm too tired to move, otherwise I'd get up to join their group; instead, I drop my chin in one hand and study the faces of my friends, feeling grateful. But the scars on Brendan's and Winston's faces take me back to a time I'd rather not remember—back to a time when we thought we'd lost them. When we'd lost two others. And suddenly my thoughts are too heavy for breakfast. So I look away. Drum my fingers against the table.

I'm supposed to be meeting Kenji for breakfast—it's how we begin our workdays—which is the only reason I haven't grabbed my own plate of food. Unfortunately, his lateness is beginning to make my stomach grumble. Everyone in the room is cutting into fresh stacks of fluffy pancakes, and they look delicious. All of it is tempting: the mini pitchers of maple syrup; the steaming heaps of breakfast potatoes; the little bowls of freshly cut fruit. If nothing else, killing Anderson and taking over Sector 45 got us much better breakfast options. But I think we might be the only ones who appreciate the upgrades.

Warner never has breakfast with the rest of us. He pretty much never stops working, not even to eat. Breakfast is another meeting for him, and he takes it with Delalieu, just the two of them, and even then I'm not sure he actually eats anything. Warner never appears to take pleasure in food. For him, food is fuel—necessary and, most of the time, annoying—in that his body requires it to function. Once, while he was deeply immersed in some important paperwork at dinner, I put a cookie on a plate in front of him just to see what would happen. He glanced up at me, glanced back at his work, whispered a quiet *thank you*, and ate the cookie with a knife and fork. He didn't even seem to enjoy it. This, needless to say, makes him the polar opposite of Kenji, who loves to eat everything, all the time, and who later told me that watching Warner eat a cookie made him want to cry.

Speaking of Kenji, him flaking on me this morning is more than a little weird, and I'm beginning to worry. I'm just about to glance at the clock for the third time when, suddenly, Adam is standing next to my table, looking uncomfortable.

"Hi," I say, just a little too loudly. "What's, uh, what's up?"

Adam and I have interacted a couple of times in the last two weeks, but it's always been by accident. Suffice it to say that it's unusual for Adam to be standing in front of me on purpose, and I'm so surprised that for a moment I almost miss the obvious:

He looks bad.

Rough. Ragged. More than a little exhausted. In fact, if I didn't know any better, I would've sworn Adam had been crying. Not over our failed relationship, I hope.

Still, old instinct gnaws at me, tugs at ancient heartstrings.

We speak at the same time:

"You okay . . . ?" I ask.

"Castle wants to talk to you," he says.

"Castle sent *you* to come get me?" I say, feelings forgotten.

Adam shrugs. "I was walking past his room at the right time, I guess."

"Um. Okay." I try to smile. Castle is always trying to make nice between me and Adam; he doesn't like the tension. "Did he say he wants to see me right now?"

"Yep." Adam shoves his hands in his pockets. "Right away."

"All right," I say, and the whole thing feels awkward. Adam just stands there as I gather my things, and I want to tell him to go away, to stop staring at me, that this is weird, that we broke up forever ago and it was *weird*, you made it *so weird*, but then I realize he isn't staring at me. He's looking at the floor like he's stuck, lost in his head somewhere.

"Hey—are you okay?" I say again, this time gently.

Adam looks up, startled. "What?" he says. "What, oh—yeah, I'm fine. Hey do you know, uh"—he clears his throat, looks around—"do you, uh—"

"Do I what?"

Adam rocks on his heels, eyes darting around the room. "Warner is never here for breakfast, huh?"

My eyebrows shoot up my forehead. "You're looking for Warner?"

"What? No. I'm just, uh, wondering. He's never here. You know? It's weird."

I stare at him.

He says nothing.

"It's not that weird," I say slowly, studying Adam's face. "Warner doesn't have time for breakfast with us. He's always working."

"Oh," Adam says, and the word seems to deflate him. "That's too bad."

"Is it?" I frown.

But Adam doesn't seem to hear me. He calls for James, who's putting away his breakfast tray, and the two of them meet in the middle of the room and then disappear.

I have no idea what they do all day. I've never asked.

The mystery of Kenji's absence at breakfast is solved the moment I walk up to Castle's door: the two of them are here, heads together.

I knock on the open door as a courtesy. "Hey," I say. "You wanted to see me?"

"Yes, yes, Ms. Ferrars," Castle says eagerly. He gets to his feet and waves me inside. "Please, have a seat. And if you would"—he gestures behind me—"close the door."

I'm nervous in an instant.

I take a tentative step into Castle's makeshift office and glance at Kenji, whose blank face does nothing to allay my fears. "What's going on?" I say. And then, only to Kenji: "Why weren't you at breakfast?"

Castle motions for me to take a seat.

I do.

"Ms. Ferrars," he says urgently. "You have news of Oceania?"

"Excuse me?"

"The RSVP. You received your first RSVP, did you not?"

"Yeah, I did," I say slowly. "But no one is supposed to know about that yet—I was going to tell Kenji about it over breakfast this morning—"

"Nonsense." Castle cuts me off. "Everyone knows. Mr. Warner knows, certainly. And Lieutenant Delalieu knows."

"What?" I glance at Kenji, who shrugs. "How is that possible?"

"Don't be so easily shocked, Ms. Ferrars. Obviously all of your correspondence is monitored."

My eyes widen. "What?"

Castle makes a frustrated motion with his hand. "Time is of the essence, so if you would, I'd really—"

"Time is of *what* essence?" I say, irritated. "How am I supposed to help you when I don't even know what you're talking about?"

Castle pinches the bridge of his nose. "Kenji," he says suddenly. "Will you leave us, please?"

"Yep." Kenji jumps to his feet with a mock salute. He heads toward the door.

"Wait," I say, grabbing his arm. "What's going on?"

"I have no idea, kid." Kenji laughs, shakes his arm free. "This conversation doesn't concern me. Castle called me in here earlier to talk about cows."

"*Cows?*"

"Yeah, you know." He arches an eyebrow. "Livestock. He's been having me do reconnaissance on several hundreds of acres of farmland that The Reestablishment has been keeping off the radar. Lots and lots of cows."

"Exciting."

"It is, actually." His eyes light up. "The methane makes

it all pretty easy to track. Makes you wonder why they wouldn't do something to preve—"

"*Methane?*" I say, confused. "Isn't that a kind of gas?"

"I take it you don't know much about cow shit."

I ignore that. Instead, I say, "So that's why you weren't at breakfast this morning? Because you were looking at cow poop?"

"Basically."

"Well," I say. "At least that explains the smell."

It takes Kenji a second to catch on, but when he does, he narrows his eyes. Taps me on the forehead with one finger. "You're going straight to hell, you know that?"

I smile, big. "See you later? I still want to go on our morning walk."

He makes a noncommittal grunt.

"C'mon," I say, "it'll be fun this time, I promise."

"Oh yeah, big fun." Kenji rolls his eyes as he turns away, and shoots Castle another two-finger salute. "See you later, sir."

Castle nods his good-bye, a bright smile on his face.

It takes a minute for Kenji to finally walk out the door and shut it behind him, but in that minute Castle's face transforms. His easy smile, his eager eyes: gone. Now that he and I are fully alone, Castle looks a little shaken, a little more serious. Maybe even . . . scared?

And he gets right down to business.

"When the RSVP came through, what did it say? Was there anything memorable about the note?"

"No." I frown. "I don't know. If all my correspondence is being monitored, wouldn't you already know the answer to this question?"

"Of course not. I'm not the one monitoring your mail."

"So who's monitoring my mail? Warner?"

Castle only looks at me. "Ms. Ferrars, there is something deeply unusual about this response." He hesitates. "Especially as it's your first, and thus far, only RSVP."

"Okay," I say, confused. "What's unusual about it?"

Castle looks into his hands. At the wall. "How much do you know about Oceania?"

"Very little."

"How little?"

I shrug. "I can point it out on a map."

"And you've never been there?"

"Are you serious?" I shoot him an incredulous look. "Of course not. I've never been anywhere, remember? My parents pulled me out of school. Passed me through the system. Eventually threw me in an insane asylum."

Castle takes a deep breath. Closes his eyes as he says, very carefully, "Was there anything at all memorable about the note you received from the supreme commander of Oceania?"

"No," I say. "Not really."

"Not really?"

"I guess it was little informal? But I don't thi—"

"Informal, how?"

I look away, remembering. "The message was really

brief," I explain. "It said *Can't wait to see you*, with no sign-off or anything."

"'Can't wait to see you'?" Castle looks suddenly puzzled.

I nod.

"Not can't wait to *meet* you," he says, "but can't wait to *see* you."

I nod again. "Like I said, a little informal. But it was polite, at least. Which I think is a pretty positive sign, all things considered."

Castle sighs heavily as he turns in his chair. He's facing the wall now, his fingers steepled under his chin. I'm studying the sharp angles of his profile as he says quietly,

"Ms. Ferrars, how much has Mr. Warner told you about The Reestablishment?"

WARNER

I'm sitting alone in the conference room, running an absent hand over my new haircut, when Delalieu arrives. He's pulling a small coffee cart in behind him, wearing the tepid, shaky smile I've come to rely upon. Our workdays have been busier than ever lately; thankfully, we've never made time to discuss the uncomfortable details of recent events, and I doubt we ever will.

For this I am forever grateful.

It's a safe space for me here, with Delalieu, where I can pretend that things in my life have changed very little.

I am still chief commander and regent to the soldiers of Sector 45; it's still my duty to organize and lead those who will help us stand against the rest of The Reestablishment. And with that role comes responsibility. We've had a lot of restructuring to do while we coordinate our next moves, and Delalieu has been critical to these efforts.

"Good morning, sir."

I nod a greeting as he pours us both a cup of coffee. A lieutenant such as himself need not pour his own coffee in the morning, but we've come to prefer the privacy.

I take a sip of the black liquid—I've recently learned to enjoy its bitter tang—and lean back in my chair. "Updates?"

Delalieu clears his throat.

"Yes, sir," he says, hastily returning his coffee cup to its saucer, spilling a little as he does. "Quite a few this morning, sir."

I tilt my head at him.

"Construction of the new command station is going well. We're expecting to be done with all the details in the next two weeks, but the private rooms will be move-in ready by tomorrow."

"Good." Our new team, under Juliette's supervision, comprises many people now, with many departments to manage and, with the exception of Castle, who's carved out a small office for himself upstairs, thus far they've all been using my personal training facilities as their central headquarters. And though this had seemed like a practical idea at its inception, my training facilities are accessible only through my personal quarters; and now that the group of them are living freely on base, they're often barging in and out of my rooms, unannounced.

Needless to say, it's driving me insane.

"What else?"

Delalieu checks his list and says, "We've finally managed to secure your father's files, sir. It's taken all this time to locate and retrieve the bulk of it, but I've left the boxes in your room, sir, for you to open at your leisure. I thought"—he clears his throat—"I thought you might like to look through his remaining personal effects before they are inherited by our new supreme commander."

A heavy, cold dread fills my body.

"There's quite a lot of it, I'm afraid," Delalieu is still saying. "All his daily logs. Every report he'd ever filed. We even managed to locate a few of his personal journals." Delalieu hesitates. And then, in a tone only I know how to decipher: "I do hope his notes will be useful to you, somehow."

I look up, meet Delalieu's eyes. There's concern there. Worry.

"Thank you," I say quietly. "I'd nearly forgotten."

An uncomfortable silence settles between us and, for a moment, neither of us knows exactly what to say. We still haven't discussed this, the death of my father. The death of Delalieu's son-in-law. The horrible husband of his late daughter, my mother. We never talk about the fact that Delalieu is my grandfather. That he is the only kind of father I have left in the world.

It's not what we do.

So it's with a halting, unnatural voice that Delalieu attempts to pick up the thread of conversation.

"Oceania, as, as I'm sure you've heard, sir, has said that, that they would attend a meeting organized by our new madam, madam supreme—"

I nod.

"But the others," he says, the words rushing out of him now, "will not respond until they've spoken with you, sir."

At this, my eyes widen perceptibly.

"They're"—Delalieu clears his throat again—"well, sir,

as you know, they're all old friends of the family, and they—well, they—"

"Yes," I whisper. "Of course."

I look away, at the wall. My jaw feels suddenly wired shut with frustration. Secretly, I'd been expecting this. But after two weeks of silence I'd actually begun to hope that maybe they'd continue to play dumb. There's been no communication from these old friends of my father, no offers of condolences, no white roses, no sympathy cards. No correspondence, as was our daily ritual, from the families I'd known as a child, the families responsible for the hellscape we live in now. I thought I'd been happily, mercifully, cut off.

Apparently not.

Apparently treason is not enough of a crime to be left alone. Apparently my father's many daily missives expounding my "grotesque obsession with an experiment" were not reason enough to oust me from the group. He loved complaining aloud, my father, loved sharing his many disgusts and disapprovals with his old friends, the only people alive who knew him face-to-face. And every day he humiliated me in front of the people we knew. He made my world, my thoughts, and my feelings seem small. Pathetic. And every day I'd count the letters piling up in my in-box, screeds from his old friends begging me to see *reason*, as they called it. To remember myself. To stop embarrassing my family. To listen to my father. To grow up, be a man, and stop crying over my sick mother.

No, these ties run too deep.

I squeeze my eyes shut to quell the rush of faces, memories of my childhood, as I say, "Tell them I'll be in touch."

"That won't be necessary, sir," says Delalieu.

"Excuse me?"

"Ibrahim's children are already *en route*."

It happens swiftly: a sudden, brief paralysis of my limbs.

"What do you mean?" I say, only barely managing to stay calm. "*En route* where? Here?"

Delalieu nods.

A wave of heat floods my body so quickly I don't even realize I'm on my feet until I have to grab the table for support. "How *dare* they," I say, somehow still clinging to the edge of composure. "Their complete disregard— To be so unbearably entitled—"

"Yes, sir, I understand, sir," Delalieu says, looking newly terrified, "it's just—as you know—it's the way of the supreme families, sir. A time-honored tradition. A refusal on my part would've been interpreted as an open act of hostility—and Madam Supreme has instructed me to be diplomatic for as long as possible so I thought, I—I thought—Oh, I'm very sorry, sir—"

"She doesn't know who she's dealing with," I say sharply. "There is no diplomacy with these people. Our new supreme commander might have no way of knowing this, but you," I say, more upset than angry now, "you should've known better. War would've been worth avoiding this."

I don't look up to see his face when he says, his voice trembling, "I'm deeply, deeply sorry, sir."

A time-honored tradition, indeed.

The right to come and go was a practice long ago agreed upon. The supreme families were always welcome in each other's lands at any time, no invitations necessary. While the movement was young and the children were young, our families held fast. And now those families—and their children—rule the world.

This was my life for a very long time. On Tuesday, a playdate in Europe; on Friday, a dinner party in South America. Our parents insane, all of them.

The only *friends* I ever knew had families even crazier than mine. I have no wish to see any of them ever again.

And yet—

Good God, I have to warn Juliette.

"As to the, as to the matter of the, of the civilians"—Delalieu is prattling on—"I've been communicating with Castle, per, per your request, sir, on how best to proceed with their transition out of the, out of the compounds—"

But the rest of our morning meeting passes by in a blur.

When I finally manage to loose myself from Delalieu's shadow, I head straight back to my own quarters. Juliette is usually here this time of day, and I'm hoping to catch her, to warn her before it's too late.

Too soon, I'm intercepted.

"Oh, um, hey—"

I look up, distracted, and quickly stop in place. My eyes widen, just a little.

"Kent," I say quietly.

One swift appraisal is all I need to know that he's not okay. In fact, he looks terrible. Thinner than ever; dark circles under his eyes. Thoroughly worn-out.

I wonder whether I look just the same to him.

"I was wondering," he says, and looks away, his face pinched. He clears his throat. "I was, uh"—he clears his throat again—"I was wondering if we could talk."

I feel my chest tighten. I stare at him a moment, cataloging his tense shoulders, his unkempt hair, his deeply bitten fingernails. He sees me staring and quickly shoves his hands into his pockets. He can hardly meet my eyes.

"Talk," I manage to say.

He nods.

I exhale quietly, slowly. We haven't spoken a word to each other since I first found out we were brothers, nearly three weeks ago. I thought the emotional implosion of the evening had ended as well anyone could've hoped, but so much has happened since that night. We haven't had a chance to rip open that wound again. "Talk," I say again. "Of course."

He swallows hard. Stares at the ground. "Cool."

And I'm suddenly compelled to ask a question that unsettles both of us: "Are you all right?"

He looks up, stunned. His blue eyes are round and red-rimmed, bloodshot. His Adam's apple bobs in his throat. "I don't know who else to talk to about this," he whispers. "I don't know anyone else who would even understand—"

And I do. All at once.

I understand.

When his eyes go abruptly glassy with emotion; when his shoulders tremble even as he tries to hold himself still—

I feel my own bones rattle.

"Of course," I say, surprising myself. "Come with me."

JULIETTE

It's another cold day today, all silver ruins and snow-covered decay. I wake up every morning hoping for even a slant of sunlight, but the bite in the air remains unforgiving as it sinks hungry teeth into our flesh. We've finally left the worst of winter behind, but even these early weeks of March feel inhumanly frosty. I pull my coat up around my neck and huddle into it.

Kenji and I are on what has become our daily walk around the forgotten stretches of Sector 45. It's been both strange and liberating to be able to walk so freely in the fresh air. Strange, because I can't leave the base without a small troop for protection, and liberating because it's the first time I've been able to acquaint myself with the land. I'd never had a chance to walk calmly through these compounds; I had no way of seeing, firsthand, exactly what'd happened to this world. And now, to be able to roam freely, unquestioned—

Well, sort of.

I glance over my shoulder at the six soldiers shadowing our every move, machine guns held tightly against their chests as they march. No one really knows what to do about me yet; Anderson had a very different system in place as supreme commander—he never showed his face to anyone except those he was about to kill, and never traveled anywhere without his Supreme Guard. But I don't have rules about either and, until I decide exactly how I want to rule, this is my new situation:

I'm to be babysat from the moment I step outside.

I tried to explain that I don't need protection—I tried to remind everyone of my very literal, lethal touch; my superhuman strength; my functional invincibility—

"But it would be very helpful to the soldiers," Warner had explained, "if you would at least go through the motions. We rely on rules, regulation, and constant discipline in the military, and soldiers need a system upon which they might depend, at all times. Do this for them," he said. "Maintain the pretense. We can't change everything all at once, love. It'd be too disorienting."

So here I am.

Being followed.

Warner has been my constant guide these last couple of weeks. He's been teaching me every day about all the many things his dad did and all the things he, himself, is responsible for. There are an infinite number of things Warner needs to do every day just to run this sector—never mind the bizarre (and seemingly endless) list of things I need to do to lead an entire continent.

I'd be lying if I didn't say that, sometimes, it all feels impossible.

I had one day, just one day to exhale and enjoy the relief of overthrowing Anderson and reclaiming Sector 45. One day to sleep, one day to smile, one day to indulge in the luxury of imagining a better world.

It was at the end of Day 2 that I discovered a nervous-looking Delalieu standing behind my door.

He seemed frantic.

"Madam Supreme," he'd said, a crazy smile half hung on his face. "I imagine you must be very overwhelmed lately. So much to do." He looked down. Wrung his hands. "But I fear—that is—I think—"

"What is it?" I'd said to him. "Is something wrong?"

"Well, madam—I haven't wanted to bother you—you've been through so much and you've needed time to adjust—"

He looked at the wall.

I waited.

"Forgive me," he said. "It's just that it's been nearly thirty-six hours since you've taken control of the continent and you haven't been to visit your quarters once," he said in a rush. "And you've already received so much mail that I don't know where to put it anymo—"

"*What?*"

He froze. Finally met my eyes.

"What do you mean, *my quarters*? I have *quarters*?"

Delalieu blinked, dumbfounded. "Of course you do, madam. The supreme commander has his or her own quarters in every sector on the continent. We have an entire wing here dedicated to your offices. It's where the late supreme commander Anderson used to stay whenever he visited us on base. And as everyone around the world knows that you've made Sector 45 your permanent residence, this is where they've sent all your mail, both physical and digital. It's where your intelligence briefings will be delivered every morning. It's where other sector leaders have been sending their daily reports—"

"You're not serious," I said, stunned.

"Very serious, madam." He looked desperate. "And I worry about the message you might be sending by ignoring all correspondence at this early stage." He looked away. "Forgive me. I don't mean to overstep. I just—I know you'd like to make an effort to strengthen your international relationships—but I worry about the consequences you might face for breaking your many continental accords—"

"No, no, of course. Thank you, Delalieu," I said, head spinning. "Thank you for letting me know. I'm—I'm very grateful to you for intervening. I had no idea"—I clapped a hand to my forehead—"but maybe tomorrow morning?" I said. "Tomorrow morning you could meet me after my morning walk? Show me where these quarters are located?"

"Of course," he said with a slight bow. "It would be my pleasure, Madam Supreme."

"Thank you, Lieutenant."

"Certainly, madam." He looked so relieved. "Have a pleasant evening."

I stumbled then as I said good-bye to him, tripping over my feet in a daze.

Not much has changed.

My shoes scuff on the concrete, my feet knocking into

each other as I startle myself back into the present. I take a more certain step forward, this time bracing myself against another sudden, biting gust. Kenji shoots me a look of concern. I look, but don't really see him. I'm looking beyond him now, eyes narrowed at nothing in particular. My mind continues on its course, whirring in time with the wind.

"You okay, kid?"

I look up, squinting sideways at Kenji. "I'm okay, yeah."

"Convincing."

I manage to smile and frown at the same time.

"So," Kenji says, exhaling the word. "What'd Castle want to talk to you about?"

I turn away, irritated in an instant. "I don't know. Castle is being weird."

That gets Kenji's attention. Castle is like a father to him—and I'm pretty sure if he had to choose, Kenji would choose Castle over me—so it's clear where his loyalties lie when he says, "What do you mean? How is Castle being weird? He seemed fine this morning."

I shrug. "He just seems really paranoid all of a sudden. And he said some things about Warner that just—" I cut myself off. Shake my head. "I don't know."

Kenji stops walking. "Wait, what things did he say about Warner?"

I shrug again, still irritated. "He thinks Warner is hiding stuff from me. Like, not hiding stuff from me, exactly—but that there's a lot I don't know about him? So I was like, 'If you know so much about Warner, why don't *you* tell me what I need to know about him?' and Castle was like, 'No, blah blah, Mr. Warner should tell you himself, blah blah.'" I roll my eyes. "Basically he was telling me it's weird that I don't know that much about Warner's past. But that's not even true," I say, looking at Kenji now. "I know a bunch about Warner's past."

"Like?"

"Like, I don't know—I know all that stuff about his mom."

Kenji laughs. "You don't know shit about his mom."

"Sure I do."

"Whatever, J. You don't even know that lady's name."

At this, I falter. I search my mind for the information, certain he must've mentioned it—

and come up short.

I glance at Kenji, feeling small.

"Her name was Leila," he says. "Leila Warner. And I only know this because Castle does his research. We had files on all persons of interest back at Omega Point. Never knew she had powers that made her sick, though," he says, looking thoughtful. "Anderson did a good job keeping that quiet."

"Oh," is all I manage to say.

"So that's why you thought Castle was being weird?" Kenji says to me. "Because he very correctly pointed out that you know nothing about your boyfriend's life?"

"Don't be mean," I say quietly. "I know some things."

But the truth is, I don't know much.

What Castle said to me this morning hit a nerve. I'd be lying if I said I didn't wonder, all the time, what Warner's life was like before I met him. In fact, I think often of that day—that awful, awful day—in the pretty blue house on Sycamore, the house where Anderson shot me in the chest.

We were all alone, me and Anderson.

I never told Warner what his father said to me that day, but I've never forgotten. Instead, I've tried to ignore it, to convince myself that Anderson was playing games with my mind to confuse and immobilize me. But no matter how many times I've played back the conversation in my head—trying desperately to break it down and dismiss it—I've never been able to shake the feeling that, maybe, just maybe, it wasn't all for show. Maybe Anderson was telling me the truth.

I can still see the smile on his face as he said it. I can still hear the musical lilt in his voice. He was enjoying himself. Tormenting me.

Did he tell you how many other soldiers wanted to be in charge of Sector 45? How many fine candidates we had to choose from? He was only eighteen years old!

Did he ever tell you what he had to do to prove he was worthy?

My heart pounds in my chest as I remember, and I close my eyes, my lungs knotting together—

Did he ever tell you what I made him do to earn it?

No.

I suspect he didn't want to mention that part, did he? I bet he didn't want to include that part of his past, did he?

No.

He never did. And I've never asked.

I think I never want to know.

"Don't worry," Anderson said to me then. *"I won't spoil it for you. Best to let him share those details with you himself."*

And now, this morning—I get the same line from Castle:

"No, Ms. Ferrars," Castle had said, refusing to look me in the eye. "No, no, it's not my place to tell. Mr. Warner needs to be the one to tell you the stories about his life. Not I."

"I don't understand," I said, frustrated. "How is this even relevant? Why do you suddenly care about Warner's past? And what does any of that have to do with Oceania's RSVP?"

"Warner knows these other commanders," Castle said. "He knows the other supreme families. He knows how The Reestablishment operates from within. And there's still a great deal he needs to tell you." He shook his head. "Oceania's response is deeply unusual, Ms. Ferrars, for the simple reason that it is the only response you've received. I feel very certain that the moves made by these commanders are not only coordinated but also intentional, and I'm beginning to feel more worried by the moment that there is an entirely *other* message here—one that I'm still trying to translate."

I could feel it then, could feel my temperature rising, my jaw tensing as anger surged through me. "But you're the one who told me to reach out to all the supreme commanders! This was your idea! And now you're terrified that someone actually reached out? What do y—"

And then, all at once, I understood.

My words were soft and stunned when I said, "Oh my God, you didn't think I'd get any responses, did you?"

Castle swallowed hard. Said nothing.

"*You didn't think anyone would respond?*" I said, my voice rising in pitch.

"Ms. Ferrars, you must understand—"

"Why are you playing games with me, Castle?" My fists clenched. "What are you doing?"

"I'm not playing games with you," he said, the words coming out in a rush. "I just—I thought—" he said, gesticulating wildly. "It was an exercise. An experiment—"

I felt flashes of heat spark behind my eyes. Anger welled in my throat, vibrated along my spine. I could feel the rage building inside me and it took everything I had to clamp it down. "I am no longer anyone's experiment," I said. "And I need to know what the hell is going on."

"You must speak with Mr. Warner," he said. "He will explain everything. There's still so much you need to know about this world—and The Reestablishment—and time is of the essence," he said. He met my eyes. "You must be prepared for whatever comes next. You need to know more, and you need to know now. Before things escalate."

I looked away, my hands shaking from the surge of unspent energy. I wanted to—needed to—break something. Anything. Instead, I said, "This is bullshit, Castle. Complete bullshit."

And he looked like the saddest man in the world when he said—

"I know."

I've been walking around with a splitting headache ever since.

So it doesn't make me feel any better when Kenji pokes me in the shoulder, startling me back to life, and says,

"I've said it before and I'll say it again: You guys have a weird relationship."

"No, we don't," I say, and the words are reflexive, petulant.

"Yes," Kenji says. "You do." And he saunters off, leaving me alone in the abandoned streets, tipping an imaginary hat as he walks away.

I throw my shoe at him.

The effort, however, is fruitless; Kenji catches my shoe midair. He's now waiting for me, ten steps ahead, holding my tennis shoe in his hand as I hop awkwardly in his direction. I don't have to turn around to see the smirks on the soldiers' faces some distance behind us. I'm pretty sure everyone thinks I'm a joke of a supreme commander. And why wouldn't they?

It's been over two weeks and I still feel lost.

Half paralyzed.

I'm not proud of my inability to get it together, not proud of the revelation that, as it turns out, I'm not smart enough, fast enough, or shrewd enough to rule the world. I'm not proud that, at my lowest moments, I look around at all that I have to do in a single day and wonder, in awe, at how organized Anderson was. How accomplished. How very, very talented.

I'm not proud that I've thought that.

Or that, in the quietest, loneliest hours of the morning I lie awake next to the son Anderson tortured nearly to death and wish that Anderson would return from the dead and take back the burden I stole from his shoulders.

And then there's this thought, all the time, all the time:

That maybe I made a mistake.

"Uh, hello? Earth to princess?"

I look up, confused. Lost in my mind today. "Did you say something?"

Kenji shakes his head as he hands me my shoe. I'm struggling to put it on when he says, "So you forced me to take a stroll through this nasty, frozen shitland just to ignore me?"

I raise a single eyebrow at him.

He raises both, waiting, expectant. "What's the deal, J? *This*," he says, gesturing at my face, "is more than whatever weirdness you got from Castle this morning." He tilts his head at me, and I read genuine concern in his eyes when he says, "So what's going on?"

I sigh; the exhalation withers my body.

You must speak with Mr. Warner. He will explain everything.

But Warner isn't known for his communication skills. He doesn't make small talk. He doesn't share details about himself. He doesn't do *personal*. I know he loves me—I can feel, in our every interaction, how deeply he cares for me—but even so, he's only ever offered me the vaguest information about his life. He is a vault to which I'm only occasionally granted access, and I often wonder how much I have left to learn about him. Sometimes it scares me.

"I'm just—I don't know," I finally say. "I'm really tired. I've got a lot on my mind."

"Rough night?"

I peer up at Kenji, shading my eyes against the cold sunlight. "You know, I don't really sleep anymore," I say to him. "I'm up at four in the morning every day, and I still haven't gotten through *last week's* mail. Isn't that crazy?"

Kenji shoots me a sideways glance, surprised.

"And I have to, like, approve a million things every day? Approve this, approve that. Not even, like, big things," I say to him. "It's stupid stuff, like, like"—I pull a crumpled sheet of paper out of my pocket and shake it at the sky—"like this nonsense: Sector 418 wants to extend their soldiers' lunch hour by an additional three minutes, and they need my approval. Three minutes? *Who cares?*"

Kenji fights back a smile; shoves his hands in his pockets.

"Every day. All day. I can't get anything *real* done. I thought I'd be doing something big, you know? I thought I'd be able to, like, unify the sectors and broker peace or something, and instead I spend all day trying to avoid Delalieu, who's in my face every five minutes because he needs me to sign something. *And that's just the mail.*"

I can't seem to stop talking now, finally confessing to Kenji all the things I feel I can never say to Warner, for fear of disappointing him. It's liberating, but then, suddenly, it also feels dangerous. Like maybe I shouldn't be telling *anyone* that I feel this way, not even Kenji.

So I hesitate, wait for a sign.

Kenji isn't looking at me anymore, but he still appears to be listening. His head is cocked to the side, his mouth playing at a smile when he says, after a moment, "Is that all?"

And I shake my head, hard, relieved and grateful to keep complaining. "I have to log everything, all the time. I have to fill out reports, read reports, file reports. There are five hundred and fifty-four other sectors in North America, Kenji. *Five hundred and fifty-four.*" I stare at him. "That means I have to read five hundred and fifty-four reports, every single day."

Kenji stares back, unmoved.

"Five hundred and fifty-four!"

He crosses his arms.

"The reports are ten pages long!"

"Uh-huh."

"Can I tell you a secret?" I say.

"Hit me."

"This job blows."

Now Kenji laughs, out loud. Still, he says nothing.

"What?" I say. "What are you thinking?"

He musses my hair and says, "Aww, J."

I jerk my head away from his hand. "That's all I get? Just an '*Aww, J,*' and that's it?"

Kenji shrugs.

"*What?*" I demand.

"I mean, I don't know," he says, cringing a little as he says it. "Did you think this was going to be . . . easy?"

"No," I say quietly. "I just thought it would be better than this."

"Better, how?"

"I guess, I mean, I thought it would be . . . cooler?"

"Like, you thought you'd be killing a bunch of bad dudes by now? High-kicking your way through politics? Like you could just kill Anderson and all of a sudden, *bam*, world peace?"

And now I can't bring myself to look at him, because I'm lying, lying through my teeth when I say,

"No, of course not. I didn't think it would be like that."

Kenji sighs. "This is why Castle was always so apprehensive, you know? With Omega Point it was always about being slow and steady. Waiting for the right moment. Knowing our strengths—and our weaknesses. We had a lot going for us, but we always knew—Castle always said—that we could never take out Anderson until we were ready to lead. It's why I didn't kill him when I had the chance. Not even when he was half dead already and standing right in front of me." A pause. "It just wasn't the right moment."

"So—you think I made a mistake?"

Kenji frowns, almost. Looks away. Looks back, smiles a little, but only with one side of his mouth. "I mean, I think you're great."

"But you think I made a mistake."

He shrugs in a slow, exaggerated way. "Nah, I didn't say that. I just think you need a little more training, you know? I'm guessing the insane asylum didn't prep you for this gig."

I narrow my eyes at him.

He laughs.

"Listen, you're good with the people. You talk pretty. But this job comes with a lot of paperwork, and it comes with a lot of bullshit, too. Lots of playing nice. Lots of ass-kissing. I mean, what are we trying to do right now? We're trying to be cool. Right? We're trying to, like, take over but, like, not cause absolute anarchy. We're trying *not* to go to war right now, right?"

I don't respond quickly enough and he pokes me in the shoulder.

"Right?" he says. "Isn't that the goal? Maintain the peace for now? Attempt diplomacy before we start blowing shit up?"

"Yes, right," I say quickly. "Yeah. Prevent war. Avoid casualties. Play nice."

"Okay then," he says, and looks away. "So you have to keep it together, kid. Because if you start losing it now? The Reestablishment is going to eat you alive. It's what they want. In fact, it's probably what they're expecting—they're waiting for you to self-destruct all this shit for them. So you can't let them see this. You can't let these cracks show."

I stare at him, feeling suddenly scared.

He wraps one arm around my shoulder. "You can't be

getting stressed out like this. Over some paperwork?" He shakes his head. "Everyone is watching you now. Everyone is waiting to see what happens next. We either go to war with the other sectors—hell, with the rest of the world—or we manage to be cool and negotiate. And you have to be *chill*, J. Just be chill."

And I don't know what to say.

Because the truth is, he's right. I'm so far in over my head I don't even know where to start. I didn't even graduate from high school. And now I'm supposed to have a lifetime's worth of knowledge about international relations?

Warner was designed for this life. Everything he does, is, breathes—

He was built to lead.

But me?

What on earth, I think, *have I gotten myself into?*

Why did I think I'd be capable of running an entire continent? How did I allow myself to imagine that a supernatural ability to kill things with my skin would suddenly grant me a comprehensive understanding of political science?

I clench my fists too hard and—

pain, fresh pain

—as my fingernails pierce the flesh.

How did I think people ruled the world? Did I really imagine it would be so simple? That I might control the fabric of society from the comfort of my boyfriend's bedroom?

I'm only now beginning to understand the breadth of

this delicate, intricately developed spiderweb of people, positions, and power already in place. I said I was up for the task. Me, a seventeen-year-old nobody with very little life experience; I volunteered for this position. And now—basically overnight—I have to keep up. And I have no *idea* what I'm doing.

But if I don't learn how to manage these many relationships? If I don't at least pretend to have even the slightest idea of how I'm going to rule?

The rest of the world could so easily destroy me.

And sometimes I'm not sure I'll make it out of this alive.

WARNER

"How's James?"

I'm the first to break the silence. It's a strange feeling. New for me.

Kent nods his head in response, his eyes focused on the hands he's clasped in front of him. We're on the roof, surrounded by cold and concrete, sitting next to each other in a quiet corner to which I sometimes retreat. I can see the whole sector from here. The ocean far off in the distance. The sun making its sluggish, midday approach. Civilians like toy soldiers marching to and fro.

"He's good," Kent finally says. His voice is tight. He's wearing nothing but a T-shirt and doesn't seem to be bothered by the blistering cold. He takes in a deep breath. "I mean—he's great, you know? He's so great. Doing great."

I nod.

Kent looks up, laughs a short, nervous sort of laugh and looks away. "Is this crazy?" he says. "Are we crazy?"

We're both silent a minute, the wind whistling harder than before.

"I don't know," I finally say.

Kent pounds a fist against his leg. Exhales through his nose. "You know, I never said this to you. Before." He looks up, but doesn't look at me. "That night. I never said it, but I wanted you to know that it meant a lot to me. What you said."

I squint into the distance.

It's an impossible thing to do, really, to apologize for attempting to kill someone. Even so, I tried. I told him I understood him then. His pain. His anger. His actions. I told him that he'd survived the upbringing of our father to become a much better person than I'd ever be.

"I meant it," I say to him.

Kent now taps his closed fist against his mouth. Clears his throat. "I'm sorry, too, you know." His voice is hoarse. "Things got so screwed up. Everything. It's such a mess."

"Yes," I say. "It is."

"So what do we do now?" He finally turns to look at me, but I'm still not ready to meet his eyes. "How—how do we fix this? Can we even fix this? Is it too far gone?"

I run a hand over my newly shorn hair. "I don't know," I say, too quietly. "But I'd like to fix it."

"Yeah?"

I nod.

Kent nods several times beside me. "I'm not ready to tell James yet."

I falter, surprised. "Oh."

"Not because of you," he says quickly. "It's not you I'm worried about. I just—explaining *you* means explaining something so much bigger. And I don't know how to tell him his dad was a monster. Not yet. I really thought he'd never have to know."

At this, I look up. "James doesn't know? Anything?"

Kent shakes his head. "He was so little when our mom died, and I always managed to keep him out of sight when our dad came around. He thinks our parents died in a plane crash."

"Impressive," I hear myself say. "That was very generous of you."

I hear Kent's voice crack when he next speaks. "God, why am I so messed up over him? Why do I *care*?"

"I don't know," I say, shaking my head. "I'm having the same problem."

"Yeah?"

I nod.

Kent drops his head in his hands. "He really screwed us up, man."

"Yes. He did."

I hear Kent sniff twice, two sharp attempts at keeping his emotions in check, and even so, I envy him his ability to be this open with his feelings. I pull a handkerchief from the inside pocket of my jacket and hand it to him.

"Thanks," he says tightly.

Another nod.

"So, um—what's up with your hair?"

I'm so caught off guard by the question I almost flinch. I actually consider telling Kent the whole story, but I'm worried he'll ask me why I'd ever let Kenji touch my hair, and then I'd have to explain Juliette's many, many requests that I befriend the idiot. And I don't think she's a safe topic for us yet. So instead I say, "A little mishap."

Kent raises his eyebrows. Laughs. "Uh-huh."

I glance in his direction, surprised.

He says, "It's okay, you know."

"What is?"

Kent is sitting up straighter now, staring into the sunlight. I'm beginning to see shades of my father in his face. Shades of myself. "You and Juliette," he says.

I freeze.

He glances at me. "Really. It's okay."

I can't help it when I say, stunned, "I'm not sure it would've been okay with me, had our roles been reversed."

Kent smiles, but it looks sad. "I was a real dick to her at the end," he says. "So I guess I got what I deserved. But it wasn't actually about her, you know? All of that. It wasn't about her." He looks up at me out of the corner of his eye. "I'd been drowning for a while, actually. I was just really unhappy, and really stressed, and then"—he shrugs, turns away—"honestly, finding out you were my brother nearly killed me."

I blink. Surprised once more.

"Yeah." He laughs, shaking his head. "I know it seems weird now, but at the time I just—I don't know, man, I thought you were a sociopath. I was so worried you'd figure out we were related and then, I mean—I don't know, I thought you'd try to murder me or something."

He hesitates. Looks at me.

Waits.

It's only then that I realize—surprised, yet again—that he wants me to deny this. To say it wasn't so.

But I can understand his concern. So I say, "Well. I did try to kill you once, didn't I?"

Kent's eyes go wide. "It's too soon for that, man. That shit is still not funny."

I look away as I say, "I wasn't making a joke."

I can feel Kent looking at me, studying me, trying, I assume, to make some sense of me or my words. Perhaps both. But it's hard to know what he's thinking. It's frustrating to have a supernatural ability that allows me to know everyone's emotions, except for his. It makes me feel off-kilter around him. Like I've lost my eyesight.

Finally, Kent sighs.

I seem to have passed a test.

"Anyway," he says, but he sounds a bit uncertain now, "I was pretty sure you would come after me. And all I could think was that if I died, James would die. I'm his whole world, you know? You kill me, you kill him." He looks into his hands. "I stopped sleeping at night. Stopped eating. I was losing my mind. I couldn't handle it, any of it—and you were, like, living with us? And then everything with Juliette—I just—I don't know." He sighs, long and loud. Shaky. "I was an asshole. I took everything out on her. Blamed her for everything. For walking away from what I thought was one of the few sure things in my life. It's my own fault, really. My own baggage. I've still got a lot of shit to work out," he says finally. "I've got issues with people leaving me behind."

For a moment, I'm rendered speechless.

I'd never thought of Kent as capable of complex thought. My ability to sense emotions and his ability to extinguish preternatural gifts has made for a strange pairing—I'd always been forced to conclude that he was devoid of all thought and feeling. It turns out he's quite a bit more emotionally adept than I'd expected. Vocal, too.

But it's strange to see someone with my shared DNA speak so freely. To admit aloud his fears and shortcomings. It's too raw, like looking directly at the sun. I have to look away.

Ultimately, I say only, "I understand."

Kent clears his throat.

"So. Yeah," he says. "I guess I just wanted to say that Juliette was right. In the end, she and I grew apart. All of this"—he makes a gesture between us—"made me realize a lot of things. And she was right. I've always been so desperate for something, some kind of love, or affection, or *something*. I don't know," he says, shaking his head. "I guess I wanted to believe she and I had something we didn't. I was in a different place then. Hell, I was a different person. But I know my priorities now."

I look at him then, a question in my eyes.

"My family," he says, meeting my gaze. "That's all I care about now."

JULIETTE

We're making our way slowly back to base.

I'm in no hurry to find Warner only to have what will probably be a difficult, stressful conversation, so I take my time. I pick my way through the detritus of war, winding through the gray wreckage of the compounds as we leave behind unregulated territory and the smudged remnants of what used to be. I'm always sorry when our walk is nearly at an end; I feel great nostalgia for the cookie-cutter homes, the picket fences, the small, boarded-up shops and old, abandoned banks and buildings that make up the streets of unregulated turf. I'd like to find a way to bring it all back again.

I take a deep breath and enjoy the rush of crisp, icy air as it burns through my lungs. Wind wraps around me, pulling and pushing and dancing, whipping my hair into a frenzy, and I lean into it, get lost in it, open my mouth to inhale it. I'm about to smile when Kenji shoots me a dark look and I cringe, apologizing with my eyes.

My halfhearted apology does little to placate him.

I forced Kenji to take another detour down to the ocean, which is often my favorite part of our walk. Kenji, on the other hand, really hates it—and so do his boots, one of which got stuck in the muck that now clings to what used to be clean sand.

"I still can't believe you like staring at that nasty, piss-infested—"

"It's not infested, exactly," I point out. "Castle says it's definitely more water than pee."

Kenji only glares at me.

He's still muttering under his breath, complaining about his shoes being soaked in "piss water," as he likes to call it, as we make our way up the main road. I'm happy to ignore him, determined to enjoy the last of this peaceful hour, as it's one of the only hours I have for myself these days. I linger and look back at the cracked sidewalks and caving roofs of our old world, trying—and occasionally succeeding—to remember a time when things weren't so bleak.

"Do you ever miss it?" I ask Kenji. "The way things used to be?"

Kenji is standing on one foot, shaking some kind of sludge from one leather boot, when he looks up and frowns. "I don't know what you think you remember, J, but the way things used to be wasn't much better than the way they are now."

"What do you mean?" I ask, leaning against the pole of an old street sign.

"What do *you* mean?" he counters. "How can you miss anything about your old life? I thought you hated your life with your parents. I thought you said they were horrible and abusive."

"They were," I say, turning away. "And we didn't have much. But there were some things I like to remember—some nice moments—back before The Reestablishment was in power. I guess I just miss the small things that used to make me happy." I look back at him and smile. "You know?"

He raises an eyebrow.

"Like—the sound of the ice cream truck in the afternoons," I say to him. "Or the mailman making his rounds. I used to sit by the window and watch people come home from work in the evenings." I look away, remembering. "It was nice."

"Hm."

"You don't think so?"

Kenji's lips quirk up into an unhappy smile as he inspects his boot, now free of sludge. "I don't know, kid. Those ice cream trucks never came into my neighborhood. The world I remember was tired and racist and volatile as hell, ripe for a hostile takeover by a shit regime. We were already divided. The conquering was easy." He takes a deep breath. Blows it out as he says, "Anyway, I ran away from an orphanage when I was eight, so I don't remember much of that cutesy shit, regardless."

I freeze, stunned. It takes me a second to find my voice. "You lived in an orphanage?"

Kenji nods before offering me a short, humorless laugh. "Yep. I'd been living on the streets for a year, hitchhiking my way across the state—you know, before we had sectors—until Castle found me."

"What?" My body goes rigid. "Why have you never told me this story? All this time—and you never said—"

He shrugs.

"Did you ever know your parents?"

He nods but doesn't look at me.

I feel my blood run cold. "What happened to them?"

"It doesn't matter."

"Of course it matters," I say, and touch his elbow. *"Kenji—"*

"It's not important," he says, breaking away. "We've all got problems. We've all got baggage. No need to dwell on it."

"This isn't about dwelling on the past," I say. "I just want to know. Your life—your past—it matters to me." And for a moment I'm reminded again of Castle—his eyes, his urgency—and his insistence that there's more I need to know about Warner's past, too.

There's so much left to learn about the people I care about.

Kenji finally smiles, but it makes him look tired. Eventually, he sighs. He jogs up a few cracked steps leading to the entrance of an old library and sits down on the cold concrete. Our armed guards are waiting for us, just out of sight.

Kenji pats the place next to him.

I scramble up the steps to join him.

We're staring out at an ancient intersection, old stoplights and electric lines smashed and tangled on the pavement, when he says,

"So, you know I'm Japanese, right?"

I nod.

"Well. Where I grew up, people weren't used to seeing faces like mine. My parents weren't born here; they spoke Japanese and broken English. Some people didn't like that. Anyway, we lived in a rough area," he explains, "with a lot of ignorant people. And just before The Reestablishment started campaigning, promising to solve all our people problems by obliterating cultures and languages and religions and whatever, race relations were at their worst. There was a lot of violence, all across the continent. Communities clashing. Killing each other. If you were the wrong color at the wrong time"—he makes a finger gun, shoots it into the air—"people would make you disappear. We avoided it, mostly. The Asian communities never had it as bad as the black communities, for example. The black communities had it the worst—Castle can tell you all about that," he says. "Castle's got the craziest stories. But the worst that ever happened to my family, usually, was people would talk shit when we were out together. I remember my mom never wanted to leave the house."

I feel my body tense.

"Anyhow." He shrugs. "My dad just—you know—he couldn't just stand there and let people say stupid, foul shit about his family, right? So he'd get mad. It wasn't like this was always happening or whatever—but when it *did* happen, sometimes the altercation would end in an argument, and sometimes nothing. It didn't seem like the end of the world. But my mom was always begging my dad to let it go, and he couldn't." His face darkens. "And I don't blame him.

"One day," Kenji says, "it ended really badly. Everyone had guns in those days, remember? *Civilians* had guns. Crazy to imagine now, under The Reestablishment, but back then, everyone was armed, out for themselves." A short pause. "My dad bought a gun, too. He said we needed it, just in case. For our own protection." Kenji isn't looking at me when he says, "And the next time some stupid shit went down, my dad got a little too brave. They used his own gun against him. Dad got shot. Mom got shot trying to make it stop. I was seven."

"You were there?" I gasp.

He nods. "Saw the whole thing go down."

I cover my mouth with both hands. My eyes sting with unshed tears.

"I've never told anyone that story," he says, his forehead creasing. "Not even Castle."

"What?" I drop my hands. My eyes widen. "Why not?"

He shakes his head. "I don't know," he says quietly, and stares off into the distance. "When I met Castle everything was still so fresh, you know? Still too real. When he wanted to know my story, I told him I didn't want to talk about it. Ever." Kenji glances over at me. "Eventually, he just stopped asking."

I can only stare at him, stunned. Speechless.

Kenji looks away. He's almost talking to himself when he says, "It feels so weird to have said all of that out loud." He takes a sudden, sharp breath, jumps to his feet, and turns his head so I can't see his face. I hear him sniff hard, twice. And then he stuffs his hands in his pockets and says, "You know, I think I might be the only one of us who doesn't have daddy issues. I loved the *shit* out of my dad."

I'm still thinking about Kenji's story—and how much more there is to know about him, about Warner, about everyone I've come to call a friend—when Winston's voice startles me back to the present.

"We're still figuring out exactly how to divvy up the rooms," he's saying, "but it's coming together nicely. In fact, we're a little ahead of schedule on the bedrooms," he says. "Warner fast-tracked the work on the east wing, so we can actually start moving in tomorrow."

There's a brief round of applause. Someone cheers.

We're taking a brief tour of our new headquarters.

The majority of the space is still under construction, so, for the most part, what we're staring at is a loud, dusty mess, but I'm excited to see the progress. Our group has desperately needed more bedrooms, more bathrooms, desks and studios. And we need to set up a real command center from which we can get work done. This will, hopefully, be the beginning of that new world. The world wherein I'm the supreme commander.

Crazy.

For now, the details of what I do and control are still unfolding. We won't be challenging other sectors or their leaders until we have a better idea of who our allies might be, and that means we'll need a little more time. "The destruction of the world didn't happen overnight, and neither will saving it," Castle likes to say, and I think he's right. We need to make thoughtful decisions as we move forward—and making an effort to be diplomatic might be the difference between life and death. It would be far easier to make global progress, for example, if we weren't the only ones with the vision for change.

We need to forge alliances.

But Castle's conversation with me this morning has left me a little rattled. I'm not sure how to feel anymore—or what to hope for. I only know that, despite the brave face I put on for the civilians, I don't *want* to jump from one war to another; I don't *want* to have to slaughter everyone who stands in my way. The people of Sector 45 are trusting me with their loved ones—with their children and spouses who've become my soldiers—and I don't want to risk any more of their lives unless absolutely necessary. I'm hoping to ease into this. I'm hoping that there's a chance—even the smallest chance—that the semicooperation of my fellow sectors and the five other supreme commanders could mean good things for the future. I'm wondering if we might be able to come together without more bloodshed.

"That's ridiculous. And *naive*," Kenji says.

I look up at the sound of his voice, look around. He's talking to Ian. Ian Sanchez—tall, lanky guy with a bit of an attitude but a good heart. The only one of us with no superpowers, though. Not that it matters.

Ian is standing tall, arms crossed against his chest, head turned to the side, eyes up at the ceiling. "I don't care what you think—"

"Well, I do." I hear Castle cut in. "I care what Kenji thinks," he's saying.

"But—"

"I care what you think, too, Ian," Castle says, "But you have to see that Kenji is right in this instance. We have to approach everything with a great deal of caution. We can't know for certain what will happen next."

Ian sighs, exasperated. "That's not what I'm saying. What I'm saying is I don't understand why we need all this space. It's unnecessary."

"Wait—what's the issue here?" I ask, looking around. And then, to Ian: "Why don't you like the new space?"

Lily puts an arm around Ian's shoulders. "Ian is just sad," she says, smiling. "He doesn't want to break up the slumber party."

"What?" I frown.

Kenji laughs.

Ian scowls. "I just think we're fine where we are," he says. "I don't know why we need to move up into all *this*," he says, his arms wide as he scans the cavernous space. "It feels like tempting fate. Doesn't anyone remember what happened the last time we built a huge hideout?"

I watch Castle flinch.

I think we all do.

Omega Point, destroyed. Bombed into nothingness.

Decades of hard work obliterated in a moment.

"That's not going to happen again," I say firmly. "Besides, we're more protected here than we ever were before. We have an entire army behind us now. We're safer in this building than we would be anywhere else."

My words are met with an immediate chorus of support, but still I bristle, because I know that what I've said is only partly true.

I have no way of knowing what's going to happen to us or how long we'll last here. What I *do* know is that we need the new space—and we need to set up shop while we still have the funds. No one has tried to cut us off or shut us down yet; no sanctions have been imposed by fellow continents or commanders. Not yet, anyway. Which means we need to rebuild while we still have the means to do so.

But this—

This enormous space dedicated only to our efforts?

This was all Warner's doing.

He was able to empty out an entire floor for us—the top floor, the fifteenth story—of Sector 45 headquarters. It took an enormous amount of effort to transfer and distribute a whole floor's worth of people, work, and furnishings to other departments, but somehow, he managed it. Now the level is being refitted specifically for our needs.

Once it's all done we'll have state-of-the-art technology that will allow us not only the access to the research and surveillance we'll need, but the necessary tools for Winston and Alia to continue building any devices, gadgets, and uniforms we might require. And even though Sector 45 already has its own medical wing, we'll need a secure area for Sonya and Sara to work, from where they'll be able to continue developing antidotes and serums that might one day save our lives.

I'm just about to point this out when Delalieu walks into the room.

"Supreme," he says, with a nod in my direction.

At the sound of his voice, we all spin around.

"Yes, Lieutenant?"

There's a slight quiver in his words when he says, "You have a visitor, madam. He's requesting ten minutes of your time."

"A visitor?" I turn instinctively, finding Kenji with my eyes. He looks just as confused as I am.

"Yes, madam," says Delalieu. "He's waiting downstairs in the main reception room."

"But who is this person?" I ask, concerned. "Where did he come from?"

"His name is Haider Ibrahim. He's the son of the supreme commander of Asia."

I feel my body lock in sudden apprehension. I'm not sure I'm any good at hiding the panic that jolts through me as I say, *"The son of the supreme commander of Asia?* Did he say why he was here?"

Delalieu shakes his head. "I'm sorry to say that he refused to answer any of my more detailed questions, madam."

I'm breathing hard, head spinning. Suddenly all I can

think about is Castle's concern over Oceania this morning. The fear in his eyes. The many questions he refused to answer.

"What shall I tell him, madam?" Delalieu again.

I feel my heart pick up. I close my eyes. *You are a supreme commander*, I say to myself. *Act like it.*

"Madam?"

"Yes, of course, tell him I'll be right th—"

"Ms. Ferrars." Castle's sharp voice pierces the fog of my mind.

I look in his direction.

"Ms. Ferrars," he says again, a warning in his eyes. "Perhaps you should wait."

"Wait?" I say. "Wait for what?"

"Wait to meet with him until Mr. Warner can be there, too."

My confusion bleeds into anger. "I appreciate your concern, Castle, but I can do this on my own, thank you."

"Ms. Ferrars, I would beg you to reconsider. Please," he says, more urgently now, "you must understand—this is no small thing. The son of a supreme commander—it could mean so much—"

"As I said, thank you for your concern." I cut him off, my cheeks inflamed. Lately, I've been feeling like Castle has no faith in me—like he isn't rooting for me at all—and it makes me think back to this morning's conversation. It makes me wonder if I can trust anything he says. What kind of ally would stand here and point out my ineptitude in front of everyone? It's all I can do not to shout at him when I say, "I can assure you, I'll be fine."

And then, to Delalieu:

"Lieutenant, please tell our visitor that I'll be down in a moment."

"Yes, madam." Another nod, and Delalieu's gone.

Unfortunately, my bravado walks out the door with him.

I ignore Castle as I search the room for Kenji's face; for all my big talk, I don't actually want to do this alone. And Kenji knows me well.

"Hey—I'm right here." He's crossed the room in just a few strides, by my side in seconds.

"You're coming with me, right?" I whisper, tugging at his sleeve like a child.

Kenji laughs. "I'll be wherever you need me to be, kid."

WARNER

I have a great fear of drowning in the ocean of my own silence.

In the steady thrum that accompanies quiet, my mind is unkind to me. I think too much. I feel, perhaps, far more than I should. It would be only a slight exaggeration to say that my goal in life is to outrun my mind, my memories.

So I have to keep moving.

I used to retreat belowground when I wanted a distraction. I used to find comfort in our simulation chambers, in the programs designed to prepare soldiers for combat. But as we've recently moved a team of soldiers underground in all the chaos of the new construction, I'm without reprieve. I've no choice now but to go up.

I enter the hangar at a brisk pace, my footsteps echoing in the vast space as I move, almost instinctively, toward the army choppers parked in the far right wing. Soldiers see me and jump quickly out of my way, their eyes betraying their confusion even as they salute me. I nod only once in their direction, offering no explanation as I climb up and into the aircraft. I place the headphones over my head and speak quietly into the radio, alerting our air-traffic controllers of my intent to take flight, and strap myself into the front seat.

The retinal scanner takes my identification automatically. Preflight checks are clear. I turn on the engine and the roar is deafening, even through the noise-canceling headphones. I feel my body begin to unclench.

Soon, I'm in the air.

My father taught me to shoot a gun when I was nine years old. When I was ten he sliced open the back of my leg and showed me how to suture my own wounds. At eleven he broke my arm and abandoned me in the wild for two weeks. At age twelve I was taught to build and defuse my own bombs. He began teaching me how to fly planes when I was thirteen.

He never did teach me how to ride a bike. I figured that out on my own.

From thousands of feet above the ground, Sector 45 looks like a half-assembled board game. Distance makes the world feel small and surmountable, a pill easily swallowed. But I know the deceit too well, and it is here, above the clouds, that I finally understand Icarus. I, too, am tempted to fly too close to the sun. It is only my inability to be impractical that keeps me tethered to the earth. So I take a steadying breath, and get back to work.

I'm making my aerial rounds a bit earlier than usual, so the sights below are different from the ones I've begun to expect every day. On an average day I'm up here in the late afternoon, checking in on civilians as they leave work to exchange their REST dollars at local Supply Centers. They usually scurry back to their compounds shortly thereafter, weighted down with newly purchased necessities and the disheartening realization that they'll have to do it all again the following day. Right now, everyone is still at work, leaving the land empty of its worker ants. The landscape is bizarre and beautiful from afar, the ocean vast, blue, and breathtaking. But I know only too well our world's pockmarked surface.

This strange, sad reality my father helped create.

I squeeze my eyes shut, my hand clutching the throttle. There's simply too much to contend with today.

First, the disarming realization that I have a brother whose heart is as complicated and flawed as my own.

Second, and perhaps most offensive: the impending, anxiety-inducing arrival of my past.

I still haven't talked to Juliette about the imminent arrival of our guests, and, if I'm being honest, I'm no longer sure I want to. I've never discussed much of my life with her. I've never told her stories of my childhood friends, their parents, the history of The Reestablishment and my role within it. There's never been time. Never the right moment. If Juliette has been supreme commander for seventeen days now, she and I have only been in a relationship for two days longer than that.

We've both been busy.

And we've only just overcome so much—all the complications between us, all the distance and confusion, the misunderstandings. She's mistrusted me for so long.

I know I have only myself to blame for what's transpired between us, but I worry that the past ugliness has inspired in her an instinct to doubt me; it's likely a well-developed muscle now. And I feel certain that telling her more about my ignoble life will only make things worse at the onset of a relationship I want desperately to preserve. To protect.

So how do I begin? Where do I start?

The year I turned sixteen, our parents, the supreme commanders, decided we should all take turns shooting each other. Not to kill, merely to disable. They wanted us to know what a bullet wound felt like. They wanted us to be able to understand the recovery process. Most of all, they wanted us to know that even our friends might one day turn on us.

I feel my mouth twist into an unhappy smile.

I suppose it was a worthwhile lesson. After all, my father is now six feet under the ground and his old friends don't seem to care. But the problem that day was that I'd been taught by my father, a master marksman. Worse, I'd already been practicing every day for five years—two years earlier than the others—and, as a result, I was faster, sharper, and crueler than my peers. I didn't hesitate. I'd shot all my friends before they'd even picked up their weapons.

That was the first day I felt, with certainty, that my father was proud of me. I'd spent so long desperately seeking his approval and that day, I finally had it. He looked at me the way I'd always hoped he would: like he cared for me. Like a father who saw a bit of himself in his son. The realization sent me into the forest, where I promptly threw up in the bushes.

I've only been struck by a bullet once.

The memory still mortifies me, but I don't regret it. I deserved it. For misunderstanding her, for mistreating her, for being lost and confused. But I've been trying so hard to be a different man; to be, if not kinder, then at the very least, *better*. I don't want to lose the love I've come to cherish.

And I don't want Juliette to know my past.

I don't want to share stories from my life that only disgust and revolt me, stories that would color her impression of me. I don't want her to know how I spent my time as a child. She doesn't need to know how many times my father forced me to watch him skin dead animals, how I can still feel the vibrations of his screams in my ear as he kicked me, over and over again, when I dared to look away. I'd rather not remember the hours I spent shackled in a dark room, compelled to listen to the manufactured sounds of women and children screaming for help. It was all supposed to make me strong, he'd said. It was supposed to help me survive.

Instead, life with my father only made me wish for death.

I don't want to tell Juliette how I'd always known my father was unfaithful, that he'd abandoned my mother long, long ago, that I'd always wanted to murder him, that I'd dreamt of it, planned for it, hoped to one day break his neck using the very skills he'd given me.

How I failed. Every time.

Because I am weak.

I don't miss him. I don't miss his life. I don't want his friends or his footprint on my soul. But for some reason, his old comrades won't let me go.

They're coming to collect their pound of flesh, and I fear that this time—as I have every time—I will end up paying with my heart.

JULIETTE

Kenji and I are in Warner's room—what's become my room—and we're standing in the middle of the closet while I fling clothes at him, trying to figure out what to wear.

"What about this?" I say to him, throwing something glittery in his direction. "Or this?" I toss another ball of fabric at him.

"You don't know shit about clothes, do you?"

I turn around, tilt my head. "I'm sorry, when was I supposed to learn about fashion, Kenji? When I was growing up alone and tortured by my horrible parents? Or maybe when I was festering in an insane asylum?"

That shuts him up.

"*So?*" I say, nodding with my chin. "Which one?"

He picks up the two pieces I threw at him and frowns. "You're making me choose between a short, shiny dress and a pair of pajama bottoms? I mean—I guess I choose the dress? But I don't think it'll go well with those ratty tennis shoes you're always wearing."

"Oh." I glance down at my shoes. "Well, I don't know. Warner picked this stuff out for me a long time ago—before he even met me. It's all I have," I say, looking up. "These clothes are left over from when I first got to Sector 45."

"Why don't you just wear your suit?" Kenji says, leaning against the wall. "The new one Alia and Winston made for you?"

I shake my head. "They haven't finished fixing it yet. And it's still got bloodstains from when I shot Warner's dad. Besides," I say, taking a deep breath, "that was a different me. I wore those head-to-toe suits when I thought I had to protect people from my skin. But I'm different now. I can turn my power off. I can be . . . normal." I try to smile. "So I want to dress like a normal person."

"But you're not a normal person."

"I know that." A frustrating flush of heat warms my cheeks. "I just . . . I think I'd like to dress like one. Maybe for a little while? I've never been able to act my age and I just want to feel a little bit—"

"I get it," Kenji says, cutting me off with one hand. He looks me up and down. Says, "Well, I mean, if that's the look you're going for, I think you look like a normal person right now. This'll work." He waves in the general direction of my body.

I'm wearing jeans and a pink sweater. My hair is pulled up into a high ponytail. I feel comfortable and normal—but I also feel like an unaccomplished seventeen-year-old playing pretend.

"But I'm supposed to be the supreme commander of North America," I say. "Do you think it's okay if I'm dressed like this? Warner is always wearing fancy suits, you know? Or just, like, really nice clothes. He always looks so poised—so intimidating—"

"Where is he, by the way?" Kenji cuts me off. "I mean, I know you don't want to hear this, but I agree with Castle. Warner should be here for this meeting."

I take a deep breath. Try to be calm. "I know that Warner knows everything, okay? I know he's the best at basically everything, that he was born for this life. His father was grooming him to lead the world. In another life, another reality? This was supposed to be his role. I know that. I do."

"But?"

"But it's *not* Warner's job, is it?" I say angrily. "It's mine. And I'm trying not to rely on him all the time. I want to try to do some things on my own now. To take charge."

Kenji doesn't seem convinced. "I don't know, J. I think maybe this is one of those times when you should still be relying on him. He knows this world way better than we do—and, bonus, he'd be able to tell you what you should be wearing." Kenji shrugs. "Fashion really isn't my area of expertise."

I pick up the short, shiny dress and examine it.

Just over two weeks ago I single-handedly fought off hundreds of soldiers. I crushed a man's throat in my fist. I put two bullets through Anderson's forehead with no hesitation or regret. But here, staring at an armoire full of clothes, I'm intimidated.

"Maybe I *should* call Warner," I say, peeking over my shoulder at Kenji.

"Yep." He points at me. "Good idea."

But then,

"No—never mind," I say. "It's okay. I'll be okay, right? I mean what's the big deal? He's just a kid, right? Just the *son* of a supreme commander. Not an actual supreme commander. Right?"

"Uhhh—all of it is a big deal, J. The kids of the commanders are all, like, other Warners. They're basically mercenaries. And they've all been prepped to take their parents' places—"

"Yeah, no, I should definitely do this on my own." I'm looking in a mirror now, pulling my ponytail tight. "Right?"

Kenji is shaking his head.

"Yes. Exactly." I nod.

"Uh-uh. No. I think this is a bad idea."

"I'm capable of doing *some* things on my own, Kenji," I snap. "I'm not totally clueless."

Kenji sighs. "Whatever you say, princess."

WARNER

"Mr. Warner—please, Mr. Warner, slow down, son—"

I stop too suddenly, pivoting sharply on my heel. Castle is chasing me down the hall, waving a frantic hand in my direction. I meet his eyes with a mild expression.

"Can I help you?"

"Where have you been?" he says, obviously out of breath. "I've been looking for you everywhere."

I raise an eyebrow, fighting back the urge to tell him that my whereabouts are none of his business. "I had a few aerial rounds to make."

Castle frowns. "Don't you usually do that later in the afternoon?"

At this, I almost smile. "You've been watching me."

"Let's not play games. You've been watching me, too."

Now I actually smile. "Have I?"

"You think so little of my intelligence."

"I don't know what to think of you, Castle."

He laughs out loud. "Goodness, you're an excellent liar."

I look away. "What do you need?"

"He's here. He's here right now and she's with him and I tried to stop her but she wouldn't listen to me—"

I turn back, alarmed. "Who's here?"

For the first time, I see actual anger flicker in Castle's eyes. "Now is not the time to play dumb with me, son. Haider Ibrahim is here. Right now. And Juliette is meeting with him alone, completely unprepared."

Shock renders me, for a moment, speechless.

"Did you hear what I said?" Castle is nearly shouting. "She's meeting with him *now*."

"How?" I say, coming back to myself. "How is he here already? Did he arrive alone?"

"Mr. Warner, please listen to me. You have to talk to her. You have to explain and you have to do it now," he says, grabbing my shoulders. "They're coming back for h—"

Castle is thrown backward, hard.

He cries out as he catches himself, his arms and legs splayed out in front of him as if caught in a gust of wind. He remains in that impossible position, hovering several inches off the ground, and stares at me, chest heaving. Slowly, he steadies. His feet finally touch the floor.

"You would use my own powers against me?" he says, breathing hard. "I am your *ally*—"

"Never," I say sharply, "ever put your hands on me, Castle. Or next time I might accidentally kill you."

Castle blinks. And then I feel it—I can sense it, close my fingers around it: his pity. It's everywhere. Awful. Suffocating.

"Don't you dare feel sorry for me," I say.

"My apologies," he says quietly. "I didn't mean to invade your personal space. But you must understand the urgency here. First, the RSVP—and now, Haider's arrival? This is just the beginning," he says, lowering his voice. "They are mobilizing."

"You are overthinking this," I say, my voice clipped. "Haider's arrival today is about *me*. Sector 45's inevitable infestation by a swarm of supreme commanders is about *me*. I've committed treason, remember?" I shake my head, begin walking away. "They're just a little . . . angry."

"Stop," he says. "Listen to me—"

"You don't need to concern yourself with this, Castle. I'll handle it."

"Why aren't you listening to me?" He's chasing after me now. "They're coming to take her back, son! We can't let that happen!"

I freeze.

I turn to face him. My movements are slow, deliberate. "What are you talking about? Take her back where?"

Castle doesn't respond. Instead, his face goes slack. He stares, confused, in my direction.

"I have a thousand things to do," I say, impatient now, "so if you would please make this quick and tell me what on earth you're talking about—"

"He never told you, did he?"

"Who? Told me what?"

"Your father," he says. "He never told you." Castle runs a hand down the length of his face. He looks abruptly ancient, about to expire. "My God. He never told you."

"What do you mean? What did he never tell me?"

"The truth," he says. "About Ms. Ferrars."

I stare at him, my chest constricting in fear.

Castle shakes his head as he says, "He never told you where she really came from, did he? He never told you the truth about her parents."

JULIETTE

"Stop squirming, J."

We're in the glass elevator, making our way down to one of the main reception areas, and I can't stop fidgeting.

My eyes are squeezed shut. I keep saying, "Oh my God, I *am* totally clueless, aren't I? What am I doing? I don't look professional at all—"

"You know what? Who cares what you're wearing?" Kenji says. "It's all in the attitude, anyway. It's about how you carry yourself."

I look up at him, feeling the height difference between us more acutely than ever. "But I'm so short."

"Napoleon was short, too."

"Napoleon was horrible," I point out.

"Napoleon got shit done, didn't he?"

I frown.

Kenji nudges me with his elbow. "You might want to spit the gum out, though."

"Kenji," I say, only half hearing him, "I've just realized I've never met any foreign officials before."

"I know, right? Me neither," he says, mussing my hair. "But it'll be okay. You just need to calm down. Anyway, you look cute. You'll do great."

I slap his hand away. "I may not know much about being a supreme commander yet, but I do know that I'm not supposed to be *cute*."

Just then, the elevator dings open.

"Who says you can't be cute and kick ass at the same time?" Kenji winks at me. "I do it every day."

"Oh, man—you know what? Never mind," is the first thing Kenji says to me.

He's cringing, shooting me a sidelong glance as he says, "Maybe you really *should* work on your wardrobe?"

I might die of embarrassment.

Whoever this guy is, whatever his intentions are, Haider Ibrahim is dressed unlike anyone I've ever seen before. He *looks* like no one I've ever seen before.

He stands up as we enter the room—tall, very tall—and I'm instantly struck by the sight of him. He's wearing a dark gray leather jacket over what I can only assume is meant to be a shirt, but is actually a series of tightly woven chains strung across his body. His skin is heavily tanned and half exposed, his upper body only barely concealed by his chain-link shirt. His closely tapered black pants disappear into shin-high combat boots, and his light brown eyes—a startling contrast to his brown skin—are rimmed in a flutter of thick black lashes.

I tug at my pink sweater and nervously swallow my gum.

"Hi," I say, and begin to wave, but Kenji is kind enough to push down my hand. I clear my throat. "I'm Juliette."

Haider steps forward cautiously, his eyes drawn together in what looks like confusion as he appraises my appearance. I feel uncomfortably self-conscious. Wildly underprepared. And I suddenly really need to use the bathroom.

"Hello," he finally says, but it sounds more like a question.

"Can we help you?" I say.

"Tehcheen Arabi?"

"Oh." I glance at Kenji, then at Haider. "Um, you don't speak English?"

Haider raises a single eyebrow. "Do you only speak English?"

"Yes?" I say, feeling now more nervous than ever.

"That's too bad." He sighs. Looks around. "I'm here to see the supreme commander." He has a rich, deep voice but speaks with a slight accent.

"Yep, hi, that's me," I say, and smile.

His eyes widen with ill-concealed confusion. "You are"—he frowns—"the supreme?"

"Mm-hm." I paste on a brighter smile. Diplomacy, I tell myself. *Diplomacy.*

"But we were told that the new supreme was wild, lethal—terrifying—"

I nod. Feel my face warm. "Yes. That's me. I'm Juliette Ferrars."

Haider tilts his head, his eyes scanning my body. "But you're so small." And I'm still trying to figure out how to respond to that when he shakes his head and says, "I apologize, I meant to say—that you are so young. But then, also, very small."

My smile is beginning to hurt.

"So it was you," he says, still confused, "who killed Supreme Anderson?"

I nod. Shrug.

"But—"

"I'm sorry," Kenji interjects. "Did you have a reason for being here?"

Haider looks taken aback by the question. He glances at Kenji. "Who is this?"

"He's my second-in-command," I say. "And you should feel free to respond to him when he speaks to you."

"Oh, I see," Haider says, understanding in his eyes. He nods at Kenji. "A member of your Supreme Guard."

"I don't have a Supr—"

"That's right," Kenji says, throwing a swift *shut up* elbow in my ribs. "You'll have to forgive me for being a little overprotective." He smiles. "I'm sure you know how it is."

"Yes, of course," Haider says, looking sympathetic.

"Should we all sit down?" I say, gesturing to the couches across the room. We're still standing in the entryway and it's starting to get awkward.

"Certainly." Haider offers me his arm in anticipation of the fifteen-foot journey to the couches, and I shoot Kenji a quick look of confusion.

He shrugs.

The three of us settle into our seats; Kenji and I sit across from Haider. There's a long, wooden coffee table between us, and Kenji presses the slim button underneath to call for a tea and coffee service.

Haider won't stop staring at me. His gaze is neither flattering nor threatening—he looks genuinely confused—and I'm surprised to find that it's *this* reaction I find most unsettling. If his eyes were angry or objectifying, I might better know how to react. Instead, he seems mild and pleasant, but—surprised. And I'm not sure what to do with it. Kenji was right—I wish more than ever that Warner were here; his ability to sense emotions would give me a clearer idea of how to respond.

I finally break the silence between us.

"It's really very nice to meet you," I say, hoping I sound kinder than I feel, "but I'd love to know what brings you here. You've come such a long way."

Haider smiles then. The action adds a necessary warmth to his face that makes him look younger than he first appeared. "Curiosity," he says simply.

I do my best to mask my anxiety.

It's becoming more obvious by the moment that he was sent here to do some kind of reconnaissance for his father. Castle's theory was right—the supreme commanders must be dying to know who I am. And I'm beginning to wonder if this is only the first of several visits I'll soon receive from prying eyes.

Just then, the tea and coffee service arrives.

The ladies and gentlemen who work in Sector 45—here,

and in the compounds—are peppier than ever these days. There's an infusion of hope in our sector that doesn't exist anywhere else on the continent, and the two older ladies who hurry into our room with the food cart are no exception to the effects of recent events. They flash big, bright smiles in my direction, and arrange the china with an exuberance that does not go unnoticed. I see Haider watching our interaction closely, examining the ladies' faces and the comfortable way in which they move in my presence. I thank them for their work and Haider is visibly stunned. Eyebrows raised, he sits back in his seat, hands clasped in his lap like the perfect gentleman, silent as salt until the moment they leave.

"I will impose upon your kindness for a few weeks," Haider says suddenly. "That is—if that's all right."

I frown, begin to protest, and Kenji cuts me off.

"Of course," he says, smiling wide. "Stay as long as you like. The son of a supreme commander is always welcome here."

"You are very kind," he says with a simple bow of his head. And then he hesitates, touches something at his wrist, and our room is swarmed in an instant by what appear to be members of his personal staff.

Haider stands up so swiftly I almost miss it.

Kenji and I hurry to our feet.

"It was a pleasure meeting you, Supreme Commander Ferrars," Haider says, stepping forward to reach for my hand, and I'm surprised by his boldness. Despite the many rumors

I know he's heard about me, he doesn't seem to mind being near my skin. Not that it really matters, of course—I've now learned how to turn my powers on and off at will—but not everyone knows that yet.

Either way, he presses a brief kiss to the back of my hand, smiles, and bows his head very slightly.

I manage an awkward smile and a small nod.

"If you tell me how many people are in your party," Kenji says, "I can begin to arrange accommodations for y—"

Haider laughs out loud, surprised. "Oh, that won't be necessary," he says. "I've brought my own residence."

"You've brought"—Kenji frowns—"you brought your own *residence*?"

Haider nods without looking at Kenji. When he next speaks he speaks only to me. "I look forward to seeing you and the rest of your guard at dinner tonight."

"Dinner," I say, blinking fast. "Tonight?"

"Of course," Kenji says swiftly. "We look forward to it."

Haider nods. "Please send my warmest regards to your Regent Warner. It's been several months since our last visit, but I look forward to catching up with him. He has mentioned me, of course?" A bright smile. "We've known each other since our infancy."

Stunned, I nod slowly, realization overcoming my confusion. "Yes. Right. Of course. I'm sure he'll be thrilled to see you again."

Another nod, and Haider's gone.

Kenji and I are alone.

"What the f—"

"Oh"—Haider pops his head back in the room—"and please tell your chef that I do not eat meat."

"For sure," Kenji says, nodding and smiling. "Yep. You got it."

WARNER

I'm sitting in the dark with my back to the bedroom door when I hear it open. It's only midafternoon, but I've been sitting here, staring at these unopened boxes for so long that even the sun, it seems, has grown tired of staring.

Castle's revelation left me in a daze.

I still don't trust Castle—don't trust that he has any idea what he's talking about—but at the end of our conversation I couldn't shake a terrible, frightening feeling in my gut begging for verification. I needed time to process the possibilities. To be alone with my thoughts. And when I expressed as much to Castle, he said, "Process all you like, son, but don't let this distract you. Juliette should not be meeting with Haider on her own. Something doesn't feel right here, Mr. Warner, and you have to go to them. Now. Show her how to navigate your world."

But I couldn't bring myself to do it.

Despite my every instinct to protect her, I won't undermine her like that. She didn't ask for my help today. She made a choice to not tell me what was happening. My abrupt and unwelcome interruption would only make her think that I agreed with Castle—that I didn't trust her to do the job on her own. And I *don't* agree with Castle; I think he's an idiot for underestimating her. So I returned here, instead, to these rooms, to think. To stare at my father's unopened secrets. To await her arrival.

And now—

The first thing Juliette does is turn on the light.

"Hey," she says carefully. "What's going on?"

I take a deep breath and turn around. "These are my father's old files," I say, gesturing with one hand. "Delalieu had them collected for me. I thought I should take a look, see if there's anything here that might be useful."

"Oh, wow," she says, her eyes alight with recognition. "I was wondering what those were for." She crosses the room to crouch beside the stacks, carefully running her fingers along the unmarked boxes. "Do you need help moving these into your office?"

I shake my head.

"Would you like me to help you sort through them?" she says, glancing at me over her shoulder. "I'd be happy t—"

"No," I say too quickly. I get to my feet, make an effort to appear calm. "No, that won't be necessary."

She raises her eyebrows.

I try to smile. "I think I'd like the time alone with them."

At this, she nods, misunderstanding all at once, and her sympathetic smile makes my chest tighten. I feel an indistinct, icy feeling stab at somewhere inside of me. She thinks I want space to deal with my grief. That going through my father's things will be difficult for me.

She doesn't know. I wish I didn't.

"So," she says, walking toward the bed, the boxes forgotten. "It's been an . . . interesting day."

The pressure in my chest intensifies. "Has it?"

"I just met an old friend of yours," she says, and flops backward onto the mattress. She reaches behind her head to pull her hair free of its ponytail, and sighs.

"An old friend of mine?" I say. But I can only stare at her as she speaks, study the shape of her face. I can't, at the present moment, know with perfect certainty whether or not what Castle told me is true; but I do know that I'll find the answers I seek in my father's files—in the boxes stacked inside this room.

Even so, I haven't yet gathered the courage to look.

"Hey," she says, waving a hand at me from the bed. "You in there?"

"Yes," I say reflexively. I take in a sharp breath. "Yes, love."

"So . . . do you remember him?" she says. "Haider Ibrahim?"

"Haider." I nod. "Yes, of course. He's the eldest son of the supreme commander of Asia. He has a sister," I say, but I say it robotically.

"Well, I don't know about his sister," she says. "But Haider is here. And he's staying for a few weeks. We're all having dinner with him tonight."

"At his behest, I'm sure."

"Yeah." She laughs. "How'd you know?"

I smile. Vaguely. "I remember Haider very well."

She's silent a moment. Then: "He said you'd known each other since your infancy."

And I feel, but do not acknowledge, the sudden tension in the room. I merely nod.

"That's a long time," she says.

"Yes. A very long time."

She sits up. Drops her chin in one hand and stares at me. "I thought you said you never had any friends."

At this, I laugh, but the sound is hollow. "I don't know that I would call us friends, exactly."

"No?"

"No."

"And you don't care to expand on that?"

"There's little to say."

"Well—if you're not friends, exactly, then why is he here?"

"I have my suspicions."

She sighs. Says, "Me too," and bites the inside of her cheek. "I guess this is where it starts, huh? Everyone wants to take a look at the freak show. At what we've done—at who I am. And we have to play along."

But I'm only half listening.

Instead, I'm staring at the many boxes looming behind her, Castle's words still settling in my mind. I remember I should say something, anything, to appear engaged in the conversation. So I try to smile as I say, "You didn't tell me he'd arrived earlier. I wish I could've been there to assist somehow."

Her cheeks, suddenly pink with embarrassment, tell one story; her lips tell another. "I didn't think I needed to tell you everything, all the time. I can handle some things on my own."

Her sharp tone is so surprising it forces my mind to focus. I meet her eyes to find she's staring straight through me now, bright with both hurt and anger.

"That's not at all what I meant," I say. "You know I think you can do anything, love. But I could've been a help to you. I know these people."

Her face is now pinker, somehow. She can't meet my eyes.

"I know," she says quietly. "I know. I've just been feeling a little overwhelmed lately. And I had a talk with Castle this morning that kind of messed with my head." She sighs. "I'm in a weird place today."

My heart starts beating too fast. "You had a talk with Castle?"

She nods.

I forget to breathe.

"He said I need to talk to you about something?" She looks up at me. "Like, there's more about The Reestablishment that you haven't told me?"

"More about The Reestablishment?"

"Yeah, like, there's something you need to tell me?"

"Something I need to tell you."

"Um, are you just going to keep repeating what I'm saying to you?" she says, and laughs.

I feel my chest unclench. A little.

"No, no, of course not," I say. "I just—I'm sorry, love. I confess I'm also a bit distracted today." I nod at the boxes laid out across the room. "It seems there's a lot left to discover about my father."

She shakes her head, her eyes big and sad. "I'm so sorry. It must be awful to have to go through all his stuff like this."

I exhale, and say, mostly to myself, "You have no idea," before looking away. I'm still staring at the floor, my head heavy with the day and its demands, when she reaches out, tentatively, with a single word.

"Aaron?"

And I can feel it then, can feel the change, the fear, the pain in her voice. My heart still beats too hard, but now it's for an entirely different reason.

"What's wrong?" I say, looking up at once. I take a seat next to her on the bed, study her eyes. "What's happened?"

She shakes her head. Stares into her open hands. Whispers the words when she says, "I think I made a mistake."

My eyes widen as I watch her. Her face pulls together. Her feelings pinwheel out of control, assaulting me with their wildness. She's afraid. She's angry. She's angry with herself for being afraid.

"You and I are so different," she says. "Meeting Haider today, I just"—she sighs—"I remembered how different we are. How differently we grew up."

I'm frozen. Confused. I can feel her fear and apprehension, but I don't know where she's going with this. What she's trying to say.

"So you think you've made a mistake?" I say. "About—*us*?"

Panic, suddenly, as she understands. "No, oh my God, no, not about us," she says quickly. "No, I just—"

Relief floods through me.

"—I still have so much to learn," she says. "I don't know anything about ruling . . . anything." She makes an impatient, angry sound. She can hardly get the words out. "I had no idea what I was signing up for. And every day I feel so incompetent," she says. "Sometimes I'm just not sure I can keep up with you. With any of this." She hesitates. And then, quietly, "This job should've been yours, you know. Not mine."

"No."

"Yes," she says, nodding. She can no longer look at me. "Everyone's thinking it, even if they don't say it. Castle. Kenji. I bet even the soldiers think so."

"Everyone can go to hell."

She smiles, only a little. "I think they might be right."

"People are idiots, love. Their opinions are worthless."

"Aaron," she says, frowning. "I appreciate you being angry on my behalf, I really do, but not *all* people are idio—"

"If they think you incapable it is because they are idiots. Idiots who've already forgotten that you were able to accomplish in a matter of *months* what they had been trying to do for decades. They are forgetting where you started, what you've overcome, how quickly you found the courage to fight when they could hardly stand."

She looks up, looks defeated. "But I don't know anything about politics."

"You are inexperienced," I say to her, "that is true. But you can learn these things. There's still time. And I will help you." I take her hand. "Sweetheart, you inspired the people of this sector to follow you into *battle*. They put their lives on the line—they sacrificed their loved ones—because they believed in you. In your strength. And you didn't let them down. You can never forget the enormity of what you've done," I say. "Don't allow anyone to take that away from you."

She stares at me, her eyes wide, shining. She blinks as she looks away, wiping quickly at a tear escaping down the side of her face.

"The world tried to crush you," I say, gently now, "and you refused to be shattered. You've recovered from every setback a stronger person, rising from the ashes only to astonish everyone around you. And you will continue to surprise and confuse those who underestimate you. It is an inevitability," I say. "A foregone conclusion.

"But you should know now that being a leader is a thankless occupation. Few will ever be grateful for what you do or for the changes you implement. Their memories will be short, convenient. Your every success will be scrutinized. Your accomplishments will be brushed aside, breeding only greater expectations from those around you. Your power will push you further away from your friends." I look away, shake my head. "You will be made to feel lonely. Lost. You will long for validation from those you once admired, agonizing between pleasing old friends and doing what is right." I look up. I feel my heart swell with pride as I stare at her. "But you must never, ever let the idiots into your head. They will only lead you astray."

Her eyes are bright with unshed tears. "But how?" she says, her voice breaking on the word. "How do I get them out of my head?"

"Set them on fire."

Her eyes go wide.

"In your mind," I say, attempting a smile. "Let them fuel the fire that keeps you striving." I reach out, touch my fingers to her cheek. "Idiots are highly flammable, love. Let them all burn in hell."

She closes her eyes. Turns her face into my hand.

And I pull her in, press my forehead to hers. "Those who do not understand you," I say softly, "will always doubt you."

She leans back, just an inch. Looks up.

"And I," I say, "I have never doubted you."

"Never?"

I shake my head. "Not once."

She looks away. Wipes her eyes. I press a kiss against her cheek, taste the salt of her tears.

She turns toward me.

I can feel it, as she looks at me; I can feel her fears disappearing, can feel her emotions becoming something else. Her cheeks flush. Her skin is suddenly hot, electric, under my hands. My heart beats faster, harder, and she doesn't have to say a word. I can feel the temperature change between us.

"Hey," she says. But she's staring at my mouth.

"Hi."

She touches her nose to mine and something inside me jolts to life. I hear my breath catch. My eyes close, unbidden.

"I love you," she says.

The words do something to me every time I hear them. They change me. Build something new inside of me. I swallow, hard. Fire consumes my mind.

"You know," I whisper, "I never get tired of hearing you say that."

She smiles. Her nose brushes the line of my jaw as she turns, presses her lips against my throat. I'm holding my breath, terrified to move, to leave this moment.

"I love you," she says again.

Heat fills my veins. I can feel her in my blood, her whispers overwhelming my senses. And for a sudden, desperate second I think I might be dreaming.

"Aaron," she says.

I'm losing a battle. We have so much to do, so much to take care of. I know I should move, should snap out of this, but I can't. I can't think.

And then she climbs into my lap and I take a quick, desperate breath, fighting against a sudden rush of pleasure and pain. There's no pretending anything when she's this close to me; I know she can feel me, can feel how badly I want her.

I can feel her, too.

Her heat. Her desire. She makes no secret of what she wants from me. What she wants me to do to her. And knowing this makes my torment only more acute.

She kisses me once, softly, her hands slipping under my sweater, and wraps her arms around me. I pull her in and she shifts forward, adjusting herself in my lap, and I take another painful, anguished breath. My every muscle tightens. I try not to move.

"I know it's late," she says. "I know we have a bunch of things to do. But I miss you." She reaches down, her fingers trailing along the zipper of my pants, and the movement sears through me. My vision goes white. For a moment I hear nothing but my heart, pounding in my head.

"You are trying to kill me," I say.

"Aaron." I can feel her smile as she whispers the word in my ear. She's unbuttoning my pants. "Please."

And I, I am gone.

My hand is suddenly behind her neck, the other wrapped around her waist, and I kiss her, melting into her, falling backward onto the bed and pulling her down with me. I used to dream about this—times like this—what it would be like to unzip her jeans, to run my fingers along her bare skin, to feel her, hot and soft against my body.

I stop, suddenly. Break away. I want to see her, to study her. To remind myself that she's really here, really mine. That she wants me just as much I want her. And when I meet her eyes the feeling overwhelms me, threatens to drown me. And then she's kissing me, even as I fight to catch my breath, and every thing, every thought and worry is wicked away, replaced by the feel of her mouth against my skin. Her hands, claiming my body.

God, it's an impossible drug.

She's kissing me like she knew. Like she knows—knows how desperately I need this, need her, need this comfort and release.

Like she needs it, too.

I wrap my arms around her, flip her over so quickly she actually squeaks in surprise. I kiss her nose, her cheeks, her lips. The lines of our bodies are welded together. I feel myself dissolving, becoming pure emotion as she parts her lips, tastes me, moans into my mouth.

"I love you," I say, gasping the words. *"I love you."*

It's interesting, really, how quickly I've become the kind of person who takes late-afternoon naps. The person I used to be would never have wasted so much time sleeping. Then again, that person never knew how to relax. Sleep was brutal, elusive. But this—

I close my eyes, press my face to the back of her neck and breathe.

She stirs almost imperceptibly against me.

Her naked body is flush against the length of mine, my arms wrapped entirely around her. It's six o'clock, I have a thousand things to do, and I never, ever want to move.

I kiss the top of her shoulder and she arches her back, exhales, and turns to face me. I pull her closer.

She smiles. Kisses me.

I shut my eyes, my skin still hot with the memory of her. My hands search the shape of her body, her warmth. I'm always stunned by how soft she is. Her curves are gentle and smooth. I feel my muscles tighten with longing and I surprise myself with how much I want her.

Again.

So soon.

"We'd better get dressed," she says softly. "I still need to meet with Kenji to talk about tonight."

All at once I recoil.

"Wow," I whisper, turning away. "That was not at all what I was hoping you'd say."

She laughs. Out loud. "Hmm. Kenji is a big turnoff for you. Got it."

I frown, feeling petty.

She kisses my nose. "I really wish you two could be friends."

"He's a walking disaster," I say. "Look what he did to my hair."

"But he's my best friend," she says, still smiling. "And I don't want to have to choose between the two of you all the time."

I look at her out of the corner of my eye. She's sitting up now, wearing nothing but the bedsheet. Her brown hair is long and tousled, her cheeks pinked, her eyes big and round and still a little sleepy.

I'm not sure I could ever say no to her.

"Please be nice to him," she says, and crawls over to me, the bedsheet catching under her knee and undoing her composure. I yank the rest of the sheet away from her and she gasps, surprised by the sight of her own naked body, and I can't help but take advantage of the moment, tucking her underneath me all over again.

"Why," I say, kissing her neck, "are you always so attached to that bedsheet?"

She looks away and blushes, and I'm lost again, kissing her.

"Aaron," she gasps, breathless, "I really—I have to go."

"Don't," I whisper, leaving light kisses along her collarbone. "Don't go." Her face is flushed, her lips bright red. Her eyes are closed in pleasure.

"I don't want to," she says, her breath hitching as I catch her bottom lip between my teeth, "I really don't, but Kenji—"

I groan and fall backward, pulling a pillow over my head.

JULIETTE

"Where the hell have you been?"

"What? Nothing," I say, heat flashing through my body. "I just—"

"What do you mean, nothing?" Kenji says, nearly stepping on my heels as I attempt to outpace him. "I've been waiting down here for almost two hours."

"I know—I'm sorry—"

He grabs my shoulder. Spins me around. Takes one look at my face and—

"Oh, gross, J, what the *hell*—"

"What?" I widen my eyes, all innocence, even as my face inflames.

Kenji glares at me.

I clear my throat.

"I told you to ask him a *question*."

"I did!"

"Jesus Christ." Kenji rubs an agitated hand across his forehead. "Do time and place mean nothing to you?"

"Hmm?"

He narrows his eyes at me.

I smile.

"You guys are terrible."

"Kenji," I say, reaching out.

"Ew, don't touch me—"

"Fine." I frown, crossing my arms.

He shakes his head, looks away. Makes a face and says, "You know what? Whatever," and sighs. "Did he at least tell you anything useful before you—uh, changed the subject?"

We've just walked back into the reception area where we first met with Haider.

"Yes he did," I say, determined. "He knew exactly who I was talking about."

"And?"

We sit down on the couches—Kenji choosing to sit across from me this time—and I clear my throat. I wonder aloud if we should order more tea.

"No tea." Kenji leans back, legs crossed, right ankle propped up on his left knee. "What did Warner say about Haider?"

Kenji's gaze is so focused and unforgiving I'm not sure what to do with myself. I still feel weirdly embarrassed; I wish I'd remembered to tie my hair back again. I have to keep pushing it out of my face.

I sit up straighter. Pull myself together. "He said they were never really friends."

Kenji snorts. "No surprise there."

"But he remembered him," I say, pointing at nothing in particular.

"And? What does he remember?"

"Oh. Um." I scratch an imaginary itch behind my ear. "I don't know."

"You didn't ask?"

"I . . . forgot?"

Kenji rolls his eyes. "Shit, man, I knew I should've gone myself."

I sit on my hands and try to smile. "Do you want to order some tea?"

"*No tea.*" Kenji shoots me a look. He taps the side of his leg, thinking.

"Do you want t—"

"Where is Warner now?" Kenji cuts me off.

"I don't know," I say. "I think he's still in his room. He had a bunch of boxes he wanted to sort through—"

Kenji is on his feet in an instant. He holds up one finger. "I'll be right back."

"Wait! Kenji—I don't think that's a good idea—"

But he's already gone.

I slump into the couch and sigh.

As I suspected. Not a good idea.

Warner is standing stiffly beside my couch, hardly looking at Kenji. I think he still hasn't forgiven him for the terrible haircut, and I can't say I blame him. Warner looks different without his golden hair—not bad, no—but different. His hair is barely half an inch long, one uniform length throughout, a shade of blond that registers only dimly as a color now. But the most interesting change in his face is that he's got a soft, subtle shadow of stubble—as though he's forgotten to shave lately—and I'm surprised to find that it doesn't bother me. He's too naturally good-looking to have his genetics undone by a simple haircut and, the truth is, I kind of like it. I'd hesitate to say this to Warner, as I don't know whether he'd appreciate the unorthodox compliment, but there's something nice about the change. He looks a little coarser now; a little rougher around the edges. He's less beautiful but somehow, impossibly—

Sexier.

Short, uncomplicated hair; a five o'clock shadow; a deeply, deeply serious face.

It works for him.

He's wearing a soft, navy-blue sweater—the sleeves, as always, pushed up his forearms—and slim black pants tucked into shiny black ankle boots. It's an effortless look. And right now he's leaning against a column, his arms crossed against his chest, feet crossed at the ankles, looking more sullen than usual, and I'm really kind of enjoying the view.

Kenji, however, is not.

The two of them look more irritated than ever, and I realize I'm to blame for the tension. I keep trying to force them to spend time together. I keep hoping that, with enough experience, Kenji will come to see what I love about Warner, and that Warner will learn to admire Kenji the way that I do—but it doesn't seem to be working. Forcing them to spend time together is beginning to backfire.

"*So*," I say, clapping my hands together. "Should we talk?"

"Sure," Kenji says, but he's staring at the wall. "Let's talk."

No one talks.

I tap Warner's knee. When he looks at me, I gesture for him to sit down.

He does.

"Please," I whisper.

Warner frowns.

Finally, reluctantly, he sighs. "You said you had questions for me."

"Yeah, first question: Why are you such a dick?"

Warner stands up. "Sweetheart," he says quietly, "I hope you will forgive me for what I'm about to do to his face."

"Hey, asshole, I can still hear you."

"Okay, seriously, this has to stop." I'm tugging on Warner's arm, trying to get him to sit down, and he won't budge. My superhuman strength is totally useless on Warner; he just absorbs my power. "Please, sit down. Everyone. And you," I say, pointing at Kenji, "you need to stop instigating fights."

Kenji throws a hand in the air, makes a sound of disbelief. "Oh, so it's always my fault, huh? Whatever."

"No," I say heavily. "It's not your fault. This is my fault."

Kenji and Warner turn to look at me at the same time, surprised.

"This?" I say, gesturing between them. "I caused this. I'm sorry I ever asked you guys to be friends. You don't have to be friends. You don't even have to like each other. Forget I said anything."

Warner drops his crossed arms.

Kenji raises his eyebrows.

"I promise," I say. "No more forced hangout sessions. No more spending time alone without me. Okay?"

"You swear?" Kenji says.

"I swear."

"Thank God," Warner says.

"*Same*, bro. Same."

And I roll my eyes, irritated. This is the first thing they've managed to agree on in over a week: their mutual hatred of my hopes for their friendship.

But at least Kenji is finally smiling. He sits down on the couch and seems to relax. Warner takes the seat next to me—still composed, but far less tense.

And that's it. That's all it takes. The tension is gone. Now that they're free to hate each other, they seem perfectly friendly. I don't understand them at all.

"So—you have questions for me, Kishimoto?" Warner says.

Kenji nods, leans forward. "Yeah—yeah, I want to know everything you remember about the Ibrahim family. We've got to be prepared for whatever Haider throws at us at dinner tonight, which"—Kenji looks at his watch, frowns—"is in, like, twenty minutes, no thanks to you guys, but anyway I'm wondering if you can tell us anything about his possible motivations. I'd like to be one step ahead of this dude."

Warner nods. "Haider's family will take more time to unpack. As a whole, they're intimidating. But Haider himself is far less complex. In fact, he's a strange choice for this situation. I'm surprised Ibrahim didn't send his daughter instead."

"Why?"

Warner shrugs. "Haider is less competent. He's self-righteous. Spoiled. Arrogant."

"Wait—are we describing you or Haider?"

Warner doesn't seem to mind the gibe. "You are misunderstanding a key difference between us," he says. "It's true that I am confident. But Haider is arrogant. We are not the same."

"Sounds like the same thing to me."

Warner clasps his hands and sighs, looking for all the world like he's trying to be patient with a difficult child. "Arrogance is false confidence," he says. "It is born from insecurity. Haider pretends to be unafraid. He pretends to be crueler than he is. He lies easily. That makes him unpredictable and, in some ways, a more dangerous opponent. But the majority of the time his actions are inspired by fear." Warner looks up, looks Kenji in the eye. "And that makes him weak."

"Huh. Okay." Kenji sinks further into the couch, processing. "Anything particularly interesting about him? Anything we should be aware of?"

"Not really. Haider is mediocre at most things. He excels only occasionally. He's obsessed mainly with his physique, and most talented with a sniper rifle."

Kenji's head pops up. "Obsessed with his physique, huh? You sure you two aren't related?"

At this, Warner's face sours. "I am *not* obsessed with m—"

"Okay, okay, calm down." Kenji waves his hands around. "No need to worry your pretty little face about it."

"I detest you."

"I love that we feel the same way about each other."

"All right, guys," I say loudly. "Focus. We're having dinner with Haider in like five minutes, and I seem to be the only one worried about this revelation that he's a super-talented sniper."

"Yeah, maybe he's here for some, you know"—Kenji makes a finger gun motion at Warner, and then at himself—"target practice."

Warner shakes his head, still a little annoyed. "Haider is all show. I wouldn't worry about him. As I said, I would only worry if his sister were here—which means we should probably plan to worry very soon." He exhales. "She will almost certainly be arriving next."

At this, I raise my eyebrows. "Is she really scary?"

Warner tilts his head. "Not scary, exactly," he says to me. "She's very cerebral."

"So she's . . . what?" says Kenji. "Psycho?"

"Not at all. But I've always been able to get a sense of people and their emotions, and I could never get a good read on her. I think her mind moves too quickly. There's something kind of . . . flighty about the way she thinks. Like a hummingbird." He sighs. Looks up. "Anyhow, I haven't seen her in several months, at least, but I doubt much about her has changed."

"Like a *hummingbird*?" says Kenji. "So, is she, like, a fast talker?"

"No," says Warner. "She's usually very quiet."

"Hmm. Okay, well, I'm glad she's not here," Kenji says. "Sounds boring."

Warner almost smiles. "She would disembowel you."

Kenji rolls his eyes.

And I'm just about to ask another question when a sudden, harsh ring interrupts the conversation.

Delalieu has come to collect us for dinner.

WARNER

I genuinely dislike being hugged.

There are very few exceptions to this rule, and Haider is not one of them. Even so, every time I see him, he insists on hugging me. He kisses the air on either side of my face, clamps his hands around my shoulders, and smiles at me like I am actually his friend.

"Hela habibi shlonak? It's so good to see you."

I attempt a smile. *"Ani zeyn, shukran."* I nod at the table. "Please, have a seat."

"Sure, sure," he says, and looks around. *"Wenha Nazeera . . . ?"*

"Oh," I say, surprised. "I thought you came alone."

"La, habibi," he says as he sits down. *"Heeya shwaya mitakhira.* But she should be here any minute now. She was very excited to see you."

"I highly doubt that."

"Um, I'm sorry, but am I the only one here who didn't know you speak Arabic?" Kenji is staring at me, wide-eyed.

Haider laughs, eyes bright as he analyzes my face. "Your new friends know so little about you." And then, to Kenji, "Your Regent Warner speaks seven languages."

"You speak *seven* languages?" Juliette says, touching my arm.

"Sometimes," I say quietly.

It's a small group of us for dinner tonight; Juliette is sitting at the head of the table. I'm seated to her right; Kenji sits to the right of me.

Across from me now sits Haider Ibrahim.

Across from Kenji is an empty chair.

"So," says Haider, clapping his hands together. "This is your new life? So much has changed since I saw you last."

I pick up my fork. "What are you doing here, Haider?"

"*Wallah*," he says, clutching his chest, "I thought you'd be happy to see me. I wanted to meet all your new friends. And of course, I had to meet your new supreme commander." He appraises Juliette out of the corner of his eye; the movement is so quick I almost miss it. And then he picks up his napkin, drapes it carefully across his lap, and says, very softly, "*Heeya jidan helwa*."

My chest tightens.

"And is that enough for you?" He leans forward suddenly, speaking so quietly only I can hear him. "A pretty face? And you so easily betray your friends?"

"If you've come here to fight," I say, "please, let's not bother eating dinner."

Haider laughs out loud. Picks up his water glass. "Not yet, *habibi*." He takes a drink. Sits back. "There's always time for dinner."

"Where is your sister?" I say, turning away. "Why didn't you arrive together?"

"Why don't you ask her yourself?"

I look up, surprised to find Nazeera standing at the door. She studies the room, her eyes lingering on Juliette's face just a second longer than everyone else's, and takes her seat without a word.

"Everyone, this is Nazeera," Haider says, jumping to his feet with a wide smile. He wraps an arm around his sister's shoulder even as she ignores him. "She'll be here for the duration of my stay. I hope you will welcome her as warmly as you've welcomed me."

Nazeera does not say hello.

Haider's face is open, an exaggeration of happiness. Nazeera, however, wears no expression at all. Her eyes are blank, her jaw solemn. The only similarities in these siblings are physical: she bears a remarkable resemblance to her brother. She has his warm brown skin, his light brown eyes, and the same long, dark eyelashes that shutter shut her expression from the rest of us. But she's grown up quite a bit since I last saw her. Her eyes are bigger, deeper than Haider's, and she has a small, diamond piercing centered just underneath her bottom lip. Two more diamonds above her right eyebrow. The only other marked distinction between them is that I cannot see her hair.

She wears a silk shawl around her head.

And I can't help but be quietly shocked. This is new. The Nazeera I remember did not cover her hair—and why would she? Her head scarf is a relic; a part of our past life. It's an artifact of a religion and culture that no longer exists under The Reestablishment. Our movement long ago expunged all symbols and practices of faith or culture in an effort at resetting identities and allegiances; so much so that places of worship were among the first institutions around the world to be destroyed. Civilians, it was said, were to bow before The Reestablishment and nothing else. Crosses, crescents, Stars of David—turbans and yarmulkes, head scarves and nun's habits—

They're all illegal.

And Nazeera Ibrahim—the daughter of a supreme commander—has a staggering amount of nerve. Because this simple scarf, an otherwise insubstantial detail, is nothing less than an open act of rebellion. And I'm so stunned I almost can't help what I say next.

"You cover your hair now?"

At this, she looks up, meets my eyes. She takes a long sip of her tea and studies me. And then, finally—

Says nothing.

I feel my face about to register surprise and I have to force myself to be still. Clearly, she has no interest in discussing the subject. I decide to move on. I'm about to say something to Haider, when,

"So you don't think anyone will notice? That you cover your hair?" It's Kenji, speaking and chewing at the same time. I touch my fingers to my lips and look away, fighting to hide my revulsion.

Nazeera stabs at a piece of lettuce on her plate. Eats it.

"I mean you have to know," Kenji says to her, still chewing, "that what you're wearing is an offense punishable by imprisonment."

She seems surprised to find Kenji still pursuing the subject, her eyes appraising him like he might be an idiot. "I'm sorry," she says softly, putting down her fork, "but who are you, exactly?"

"*Nazeera*," Haider says, trying to smile as he shoots her a careful, sidelong glance. "Please remember that we are guests—"

"I didn't realize there was a dress code here."

"Oh—well, I guess we don't have a dress code *here*," Kenji says between bites, oblivious to the tension. "But that's only because we have a new supreme commander who's not a psychopath. But it's illegal to dress like that," he says, gesturing at her face with his spoon, "like, literally everywhere else. Right?" He looks around, but no one responds. "Isn't it?" he says to me, eager for confirmation.

I nod. Slowly.

Nazeera takes another long drink of her tea, careful to replace the cup in its saucer before she leans back, looks us both in the eye and says, "What makes you think I care?"

"I mean"—Kenji frowns—"don't you have to care? Your dad is a supreme commander. Does he even know that you wear that thing"—another abstract gesture at her head—"in public? Won't he be pissed?"

This is not going well.

Nazeera, who'd just picked up her fork again to spear some bit of food on her plate, puts down her fork and sighs. Unlike her brother, she speaks perfectly unaccented English.

She's looking only at Kenji when she says, "This *thing*?"

"Sorry," he says sheepishly, "I don't know what it's called."

She smiles at him, but there's no warmth in it. Only a warning. "Men," she says, "are always so baffled by women's clothing. So many opinions about a body that does not belong to them. Cover up, don't cover up"—she waves a hand—"no one can seem to decide."

"But—that's not what I—" Kenji tries to say.

"You know what I think," she says, still smiling, "about someone telling me what's legal and illegal about the way I dress?"

She holds up two middle fingers.

Kenji chokes.

"Go ahead," she says, her eyes flashing angrily as she picks up her fork again. "Tell my dad. Alert the armies. I don't give a shit."

"*Nazeera*—"

"Shut up, Haider."

"Whoa—hey—I'm sorry," Kenji says suddenly, looking panicked. "I didn't mean—"

"Whatever," she says, rolling her eyes. "I'm not hungry." She stands up suddenly. Elegantly. There's something interesting about her anger. Her unsubtle protest. And she's more impressive standing up.

She has the same long legs and lean frame as her brother, and she carries herself with great pride, like someone who was born into position and privilege. She wears a gray tunic cut from fine, heavy fabric; skintight leather pants; heavy boots; and a set of glittering gold knuckles on both hands.

And I'm not the only one staring.

Juliette, who's been watching quietly this whole time, is looking up, amazed. I can practically see her thought process as she suddenly stiffens, glances down at her own outfit, and crosses her arms over her chest as if to hide her pink sweater from view. She's tugging at her sleeves as though she might tear them off.

It's so adorable I almost kiss her right then.

A heavy, uncomfortable silence settles between us after Nazeera's gone.

We'd all been expecting an in-depth interrogation from Haider tonight; instead, he pokes quietly at his food, looking tired and embarrassed. No amount of money or prestige can save any of us from the agony of awkward family dinners.

"Why'd you have to say anything?" Kenji elbows me, and I flinch, surprised.

"Excuse me?"

"This is your fault," he hisses, low and anxious. "You shouldn't have said anything about her scarf."

"I asked *one* question," I say stiffly. "*You're* the one who kept pushing—"

"Yeah, but you started it! Why'd you even have to say anything?"

"She's the daughter of a supreme commander," I say, fighting to keep my voice down. "She knows better than anyone else that what she's wearing is illegal under the laws of The Reestablishment—"

"Oh my God," Kenji says, shaking his head. "Just—just stop, okay?"

"How dare you—"

"What are you two whispering about?" Juliette says, leaning in.

"Just that your boyfriend doesn't know when to shut his mouth," Kenji says, scooping up another spoonful of food.

"*You're* the one who can't keep his mouth shut." I turn away. "You can't even manage it while you're eating a bite of food. Of all the disgusting things—"

"Shut up, man. I'm hungry."

"I think I'll retire for the evening also," Haider says suddenly. He stands.

We all look up.

"Of course," I say. I get to my feet to bid him a proper good night.

"*Ani aasef*," Haider says, looking down at his half-eaten dinner. "I was hoping to have a more productive conversation with all of you this evening, but I'm afraid my sister is unhappy to be here; she didn't want to leave home." He sighs. "But you know Baba," he says to me. "He gave her no choice." Haider shrugs. Attempts a smile. "She doesn't understand yet that what we do—the way we live now"—he hesitates—"it's the life we are given. None of us has a choice."

And for the first time tonight he surprises me; I see something in his eyes I recognize. A flicker of pain. The weight of responsibility. Expectation.

I know too well what it is to be the son of a supreme commander of the Reestablishment—and dare to disagree.

"Of course," I say to him. "I understand."

I really do.

JULIETTE

Warner escorts Haider back to his residence, and soon after they're gone, the rest of our party breaks apart. It was a weird, too-short dinner with a lot of surprises, and my head hurts. I'm ready for bed. Kenji and I are making our way to Warner's rooms in silence, both of us lost in thought.

It's Kenji who speaks first.

"So—you were pretty quiet tonight," he says.

"Yeah." I laugh, but there's no life in it. "I'm exhausted, Kenji. It was a weird day. An even weirder night."

"Weird how?"

"Um, I don't know, how about we start with the fact that Warner speaks *seven languages*?" I look up, meet his eyes. "I mean, what the hell? Sometimes I think I know him so well, and then something like this happens and it just"—I shake my head—"blows my mind. You were right," I say. "I still know nothing about him. Plus, what am I even doing anymore? I didn't say anything at dinner because I have no idea what to say."

Kenji blows out a breath. "Yeah. Well. Seven languages is pretty crazy. But, I mean, you have to remember that he was born into this, you know? Warner's had schooling you've never had."

"That's exactly my point."

"Hey, you'll be okay," Kenji says, squeezing my shoulder. "It's going to be okay."

"I was just starting to feel like maybe I could do this," I say to him. "I just had this whole talk with Warner today that actually made me feel better. And now I can't even remember why." I sigh. Close my eyes. "I feel so stupid, Kenji. Every day I feel stupider."

"Maybe you're just getting old. Senile." He taps his head. "You know."

"Shut up."

"So, uh"—he laughs—"I know it was a weird night and everything, but—what'd you think? Overall?"

"Of what?" I glance at him.

"Of Haider and Nazeera," he says. "Thoughts? Feelings? Sociopaths, yes or no?"

"Oh." I frown. "I mean, they're so different from each other. Haider is so loud. And Nazeera is . . . I don't know. I've never met anyone like her before. I guess I respect that she's standing up to her dad and The Reestablishment, but I have no idea what her real motivations are, so I'm not sure I should give her too much credit." I sigh. "Anyway, she seems really . . . angry."

And really beautiful. And really intimidating.

The painful truth is that I'd never felt so intimidated by another girl before, and I don't know how to admit that out loud. All day—and for the last couple of weeks—I've felt like an imposter. A child. I hate how easily I fade in and out of confidence, how I waver between who I was and who I could be. My past still clings to me, skeleton hands holding me back even as I push forward into the light. And I can't help but wonder how different I'd be today if I'd ever had someone to encourage me when I was growing up. I never had strong female role models. Meeting Nazeera tonight—seeing how tall and brave she was—made me wonder where she learned to be that way.

It made me wish I'd had a sister. Or a mother. Someone to learn from and lean on. A woman to teach me how to be brave in this body, among these men.

I've never had that.

Instead, I was raised on a steady diet of taunts and jeers, jabs at my heart, slaps in the face. Told repeatedly I was worthless. A monster.

Never loved. Never protected from the world.

Nazeera doesn't seem to care at all what other people think, and I wish so much that I had her confidence. I know I've changed a lot—that I've come a long way from who I used to be—but I want more than anything to just *be* confident and unapologetic about who I am and how I feel, and not have to try so hard all the time. I'm still working on that part of myself.

"Right," Kenji is saying. "Yeah. Pretty angry. But—"

"Excuse me?"

At the sound of her voice we both spin around.

"Speak of the devil," Kenji says under his breath.

"I'm sorry—I think I'm lost," Nazeera says. "I thought

I knew this building pretty well, but there's a bunch of construction going on and it's . . . throwing me off. Can either of you tell me how to get outside?"

She almost smiles.

"Oh, sure," I say, and almost smile back. "Actually"—I pause—"I think you might be on the wrong side of the building. Do you remember which entrance you came in from?"

She stops to think. "I think we're staying on the south side," she says, and flashes me a full, real smile for the first time. Then falters. "Wait. I *think* it was the south side. I'm sorry," she says, frowning. "I just arrived a couple of hours ago—Haider got here before me—"

"I totally understand," I say, cutting her off with a wave. "Don't worry—it took me a while to navigate the construction, too. Actually, you know what? Kenji knows his way around even better than I do. This is Kenji, by the way—I don't think you guys were formally introduced tonight—"

"Yeah, hi," she says, her smile gone in an instant. "I remember."

Kenji is staring at her like an idiot. Eyes wide, blinking. Lips parted ever so slightly. I poke his arm and he yelps, startled, but comes back to life. "Oh, right," he says quickly. "Hi. Hi—yeah, hi, um, sorry about dinner."

She raises an eyebrow at him.

And for the first time in all the time I've known him, Kenji actually blushes. *Blushes*. "No, really," he says. "I, uh, I think your—scarf—is, um, really cool."

"Uh-huh."

"What's it made of?" he says, reaching forward to touch her head. "It looks so soft—"

She slaps his hand away, recoiling visibly even in this dim light. "What the hell? Are you serious right now?"

"What?" Kenji blinks, confused. "What'd I do?"

Nazeera laughs, her expression a mixture of confusion and vague disgust. "How are you *so* bad at this?"

Kenji freezes in place, his mouth agape. "I don't, um—I just don't know, like, what the rules are? Like, can I call you sometime or—"

I laugh suddenly, loud and awkward, and pinch Kenji in the arm.

Kenji swears out loud. Shoots me an angry look.

I plant a bright smile on my face and speak only to Nazeera. "So, yeah, um, if you want to get to the south exit," I say quickly, "your best bet is to go back down the hall and make three lefts. You'll see the double doors on your right— just ask one of the soldiers to take you from there."

"Thanks," Nazeera says, returning my smile before shooting a weird look in Kenji's direction. He's still massaging his injured shoulder as he waves her a weak good-bye.

It's only after she's gone again that I finally spin around, hiss, "What the hell is wrong with you?" and Kenji grabs my arm, goes weak in the knees, and says,

"Oh my God, J, I think I'm in love."

I ignore him.

"No, seriously," he says, "like, is this what that is?

Because I've never been in love before, so I don't know if this is love or if I just have, like, food poisoning?"

"You don't even know her," I say, rolling my eyes, "so I'm guessing it's probably food poisoning."

"You think so?"

I glance up at him, eyes narrowed, but one look is all it takes to lose my thread of anger. His expression is so weird and silly—so slap-happy—I almost feel bad for him.

I sigh, shoving him forward. He keeps stopping in place for no reason. "I don't know. I think maybe you're just, you know—attracted to her? God, Kenji, you gave me so much crap for acting like this over Adam and Warner and now here you are, being all hormonal—"

"Whatever. You owe me."

I frown at him.

He shrugs, still beaming. "I mean, I know she's probably a sociopath. And, like, would definitely murder me in my sleep. But damn she's, wow," he says. "She's, like, batshit pretty. The kind of pretty that makes a man think getting murdered in his sleep might not be a bad way to go."

"Yeah," I say, but I say it quietly.

"Right?"

"I guess."

"What do you mean, *you guess*? I wasn't asking a question. That girl is objectively beautiful."

"Sure."

Kenji stops, takes my shoulders in his hands. "What is your deal, J?"

"I don't know what you're—"

"Oh my God," he says, stunned. "Are you jealous?"

"*No*," I say, but I practically yell the word at him.

He's laughing now. "That's crazy. Why are you jealous?"

I shrug, mumble something.

"Wait, what's that?" He cups his hand over his ear. "You're worried I'm going to leave you for another woman?"

"Shut up, Kenji. I'm not jealous."

"Aw, J."

"I'm not. I swear. I'm not jealous. I'm just—I'm just . . ."

I'm having a hard time.

But I never have a chance to say the words. Kenji suddenly picks me up, spins me around and says, "Aw, you're so cute when you're jealous—"

And I kick him in the knee. Hard.

He drops me to the floor, grabs his leg, and shouts words so foul I don't even recognize half of them. I sprint away, half guilty, half pleased, his promises to kick my ass in the morning echoing after me as I go.

WARNER

I've joined Juliette on her morning walk today.

She seems deeply nervous now, more so than ever before, and I blame myself for not better preparing her for what she might face as supreme commander. She came back to our room last night in a panic, said something about wishing she spoke more languages, and then refused to talk about it.

I feel like she's hiding from me.

Or maybe I've been hiding from her.

I've been so absorbed in my own head, in my own issues, that I haven't had much of a chance to speak with her, at length, about how she's doing lately. Yesterday was the first time she'd ever brought up her worries about being a good leader, and it makes me wonder how long these fears have been wearing away at her. How long she's been bottling everything up. We have to find more time to talk this all through; but I worry we might both be drowning in revelations.

I'm certain I am.

My mind is still full of Castle's nonsense. I'm fairly certain he'll be proven misinformed, that he's misunderstood some crucial detail. Still, I'm desperate for real answers, and I haven't yet had a chance to go through my father's files.

So I remain here, in this uncertain state.

I'd been hoping to find some time today, but I don't trust Haider and Nazeera to be alone with Juliette. I gave her the space she needed when she first met Haider, but leaving her alone with them now would just be irresponsible. Our visitors are here for all the wrong reasons and likely looking for any reason to play cruel mental Olympics with her emotions. I'd be surprised if they didn't want to terrify and confuse her. To bully her into cowardice. And I'm beginning to worry.

There's so much Juliette doesn't know.

I think I've not made enough of an effort to imagine how she must be feeling. I take too much for granted in this military life, and things that seem obvious to me are still brand-new to her. I need to remember that. I need to tell her that she has her own armory. That she has a fleet of private cars; a personal chauffeur. Several private jets and pilots at her disposal. And then I wonder, suddenly, whether she's ever been on a plane.

I stop, suspended in thought.

Of course she hasn't. She has no recollection of a life lived anywhere but in Sector 45. I doubt she's ever gone for a *swim*, much less sailed on a ship in the middle of the ocean. She's never lived anywhere but in books and memories.

There's still so much she has to learn. So much to overcome. And while I sympathize deeply with her struggles, I really do not envy her in this, the enormity of the task ahead. After all, there's a simple reason I never wanted the job of supreme commander myself—

I never wanted the responsibility.

It's a tremendous amount of work with far less freedom than one might expect; worse, it's a position that requires a great deal of people skills. The kind of people skills that include both killing *and* charming a person at a moment's notice. Two things I detest.

I tried to convince Juliette that she was perfectly capable of stepping into my father's shoes, but she doesn't seem at all persuaded. And with Haider and Nazeera now here, I understand why she seems more uncertain than ever. The two of them—well, it was only Haider, really—asked to join Juliette on her morning walk to the water this morning. She and Kenji had been discussing the matter under their breaths, but Haider has sharper hearing than we suspected. So here we are, the five of us walking along the beach in an awkward silence. Haider and Juliette and I have unintentionally formed a group. Nazeera and Kenji follow some paces behind.

No one is speaking.

Still, the beach isn't a terrible place to spend a morning, despite the strange stench arising from the water. It's actually rather peaceful. The sounds of the breaking waves make for a soothing backdrop against the otherwise already-stressful day.

"So," Haider finally says to me, "will you be attending the Continental Symposium this year?"

"Of course," I answer quietly. "I will attend as I always

have." A pause. "Will you be returning home to attend your own event?"

"Unfortunately not. Nazeera and I were hoping to accompany you to the North American arm, but of course—I wasn't sure if Supreme Commander Ferrars"—he glances at Juliette—"would be making an appearance, so—"

She leans in, eyes wide. "I'm sorry, what are we talking about?"

Haider frowns only a little in response, but I can feel the depth of his surprise. "The Continental Symposium," he says. "Surely you've heard of it?"

Juliette looks at me, confused, and then—

"Oh, yes, of course," she says, remembering. "I've gotten a bunch of letters about that. I didn't realize it was such a big deal."

I have to fight the impulse to cringe.

This was another oversight on my part.

Juliette and I have talked about the symposium, of course, but only briefly. It's a biannual congress of all 555 regents from across the continent. Every sector leader gathered in one place.

It's a massive production.

Haider tilts his head, studying her. "Yes, it's a very big deal. Our father," he says, "is busy preparing for the Asia event, so it's been on my mind quite a bit lately. But as the late Supreme Anderson never attended public gatherings, I wondered whether you would be following in his footsteps."

"Oh, no, I'll be there," Juliette says quickly. "I'm not

hiding from the world the way he did. Of course I'll be there."

Haider's eyes widen slightly. He looks from me to her and back again.

"When is it, exactly?" she says, and I feel Haider's curiosity grow suddenly more intense.

"You've not looked at your invitation?" he asks, all innocence. "The event is in two days."

She suddenly turns away, but not before I see that her cheeks are flushed. I can feel her sudden embarrassment and it breaks my heart. I hate Haider for toying with her like this.

"I've been very busy," she says quietly.

"It's my fault," I cut in. "I was supposed to follow up on the matter and I forgot. But we'll be finalizing the program today. Delalieu is already hard at work arranging all the details."

"Wonderful," Haider says to me. "Nazeera and I look forward to joining you. We've never been to a symposium outside of Asia before."

"Of course," I say. "We'll be delighted to have you with us."

Haider looks Juliette up and down then, examining her outfit, her hair, her plain, worn tennis shoes; and though he says nothing, I can feel his disapproval, his skepticism and ultimately—his disappointment in her.

It makes me want to throw him in the ocean.

"What are your plans for the rest of your stay here?" I

ask, watching him closely now.

He shrugs, perfect nonchalance. "Our plans are fluid. We're only interested in spending time with all of you." He glances at me. "Do old friends really need a reason to see each other?" And for a moment, the briefest moment, I sense genuine pain behind his words. A feeling of neglect.

It surprises me.

And then it's gone.

"In any case," Haider is saying, "I believe Supreme Commander Ferrars has already received a number of letters from our other friends. Though it seems their requests to visit were met with silence. I'm afraid they felt a bit left out when I told them Nazeera and I were here."

"What?" Juliette says, glancing at me before looking back at Haider. "What other friends? Do you mean the other supreme commanders? Because I haven't—"

"Oh—no," Haider says. "No, no, not the other commanders. Not yet, anyway. Just us kids. We were hoping for a little reunion. We haven't gotten the whole group together in far too long."

"The whole group," Juliette says softly. Then she frowns. "How many more kids are there?"

Haider's fake exuberance turns suddenly strange. Cold. He looks at me with both anger and confusion when he says, "You've told her nothing about us?"

Now Juliette is staring at me. Her eyes widen perceptibly; I can feel her fear spike. And I'm still trying to figure out how to tell her not to worry when Haider clamps down on my arm, hard, and pulls me forward.

"What are you doing?" he whispers, the words urgent, violent. "You turned your back on all of us—for what? For *this*? For a *child*? *Inta kullish ghabi*," he says. "So very, very stupid. And I promise you, *habibi*, this won't end well."

There's a warning in his eyes.

I feel it then, when he suddenly lets go—when he unlocks a secret deep within his heart—and something awful settles into the pit of my stomach. A feeling of nausea. Terrible dread.

And I finally understand:

The commanders are sending their children to do the groundwork here because they don't think it's worth their time to come themselves. They want their offspring to infiltrate and examine our base—to use their youth to appeal to the new, young supreme commander of North America, to fake camaraderie—and, ultimately, to send back information. They're not interested in forging alliances.

They're only here to figure out how much work it will take to destroy us.

I turn away, anger threatening to undo my composure, and Haider clamps down harder on my arm. I meet his eyes. It's only my determination to keep things civil for Juliette's sake that prevents me from breaking his fingers off my body.

Hurting Haider would be enough to start a world war.

And he knows this.

"What's happened to you?" he says, still hissing in my ear. "I didn't believe it when I first heard that you'd fallen in love with some idiot psychotic girl. I had more faith in you. I *defended* you. But this," he says, shaking his head, "this is truly heartbreaking. I can't believe how much you've changed."

My fingers tense, itching to form fists, and I'm just about to respond when Juliette, who's been watching us closely from a distance, says, "Let go of him."

And there's something about the steadiness of her voice, something about the barely restrained fury in her words that captures Haider's attention.

He drops my arm, surprised. Spins around.

"Touch him one more time," Juliette says quietly, "and I will rip your heart out of your body."

Haider stares at her. "Excuse me?"

She steps forward. She looks suddenly terrifying. There's a fire in her eyes. A murderous stillness in her movements. "If I ever catch you putting your hands on him again, I will tear open your chest," she says, "and rip out your heart."

Haider's eyebrows fly up his forehead. He blinks. Hesitates. And then: "I didn't realize that was something you could do."

"For you," she says, "I'd do it with pleasure."

Now, Haider smiles. Laughs, out loud. And for the first time since he's arrived, he actually looks sincere. His eyes crinkle with delight. "Would you mind," he says to her, "if I borrowed your Warner for a bit? I promise I won't put my hands on him. I'd just like to speak with him."

She looks at me then, a question in her eyes.

But I can only smile at her. I want to scoop her up and carry her away. Take her somewhere quiet and lose myself in her. I love that the girl who blushes so easily in my arms is the same one who would kill a man for hurting me.

"I won't be long," I say.

And she returns my smile, her face transformed once again. It lasts only a couple of seconds, but somehow time slows down long enough for me to gather the many details of this moment and place it among my favorite memories. I'm grateful, suddenly, for this unusual, supernatural gift I have for sensing emotions. It's still my secret, known only by a few—a secret I'd managed to keep from my father, and from the other commanders and their children. I like how it makes me feel separate—different—from the people I've always known. But best of all, it makes it possible for me to know how deeply Juliette loves me. I can always feel the rush of emotion in her words, in her eyes. The certainty that she would fight for me. Protect me. And knowing this makes my heart feel so full that, sometimes, when we're together, I can hardly breathe.

I wonder if she knows that I would do anything for her.

JULIETTE

"Oh, look! A fish!" I run toward the water and Kenji catches me around the waist, hauls me back.

"That water is *disgusting*, J. You shouldn't get near it."

"What? Why?" I say, still pointing. "Can't you see the fish? I haven't seen a fish in the water in a really long time."

"Yeah, well, it's probably dead."

"What?" I look again, squinting. "No—I don't think—"

"Oh, yeah, it's definitely dead."

We both look up.

It's the first thing Nazeera has said all morning. She's been very quiet, watching and listening to everything with an eerie stillness. Actually, I've noticed she spends most of her time watching her brother. She doesn't seem interested in me the way Haider seems to be, and I find it confusing. I don't understand yet exactly why they're here. I know they're curious about who I am—which, honestly, I get— but there's got to be more to it than just that. And it's this unknowable part—the tension between brother and sister, even—that I can't comprehend.

So I wait for her to say more.

She doesn't.

She's still watching her brother, who's off in the distance

with Warner now, the two of them discussing something we can no longer hear.

It's an interesting scene, the two of them.

Warner is wearing a dark, blood-red suit today. No tie, and no overcoat—even though it's freezing outside—just a black shirt underneath the blazer, and a pair of black boots. He's clutching the handle of a briefcase and a pair of gloves in the same hand, and his cheeks are pink from the cold. Beside him, Haider's hair is a wild, untamed shock of blackness in the gray morning light. He's wearing slim black slacks and yesterday's chain-link shirt underneath a long blue velvet coat, and doesn't seem at all bothered by the wind blowing the jacket open to reveal his heavily built, very bronzed upper body. In fact, I'm pretty sure it's intentional. The two of them walking tall and alone on the deserted beach—heavy boots leaving prints in the sand—makes for a striking image, but they're definitely overdressed for the occasion.

If I were being honest, I'd be forced to admit that Haider is just as beautiful as his sister, despite his aversion to wearing shirts. But Haider seems deeply aware of how handsome he is, which somehow works against him. In any case, none of that matters. I'm only interested in the boy walking beside him. So it's Warner I'm staring at when Kenji says something that pulls me suddenly back to the present.

"I think we better get back to base, J." He checks the time on the watch he's only recently started wearing.

"Castle said he needs to talk to you ASAP."

"Again?"

Kenji nods. "Yeah, and I have to talk to the girls about their progress with James, remember? Castle wants a report. By the way, I think Winston and Alia are finally done fixing your suit, and they actually have a new design for you to look at when you have a chance. I know you still have to get through the rest of your mail from today, but whenever you're done maybe we could—"

"Hey," Nazeera says, waving at us as she walks up. "If you guys are heading back to base, could you do me a favor and grant me clearance to walk around the sector on my own today?" She smiles at me. "I haven't been back here in over a year, and I'd like to look around a little. See what's changed."

"Sure," I say, and smile back. "The soldiers at the front desk can take care of that. Just give them your name, and I'll have Kenji send them my pre-authorizati—"

"Oh—yeah, actually, you know what? Why don't I just show you around myself?" Kenji beams at her. "This place changed a lot in the last year. I'd be happy to be your tour guide."

Nazeera hesitates. "I thought I just heard you say you had a bunch of things to do."

"What? No." He laughs. "Zero things to do. I'm all yours. For whatever. You know."

"*Kenji*—"

He flicks me in the back and I flinch, scowling at him.

"Um, okay," Nazeera says. "Well, maybe later, if you have time—"

"I've got time now," he says, and he's grinning at her like an idiot. Like, an actual idiot. I don't know how to save him from himself. "Should we get going?" he says. "We can start here—I can show you around the compounds first, if you like. Or, I mean, we can start in unregulated territory, too." He shrugs. "Whatever you prefer. Just let me know."

Nazeera looks suddenly fascinated. She's staring at Kenji like she might chop him up and put him in a stew. "Aren't you a member of the Supreme Guard?" she says. "Shouldn't you stay with your commander until she's safely back to base?"

"Oh, uh, yeah—no, she'll be fine," he says in a rush. "Plus we've got these dudes"—he waves at the six soldiers shadowing us—"watching her all the time, so, she'll be safe."

I pinch him, hard, in the side of his stomach.

Kenji gasps, spins around. "We're only like five minutes from base," he says. "You'll be okay getting back by yourself, won't you?"

I glare at him. "Of course I can get back by myself," I shout-whisper. "That's not why I'm mad. I'm mad because you have a million things to do and you're acting like an idiot in front of a girl who is obviously not interested in you."

Kenji steps back, looking injured. "Why are you trying to hurt me, J? Where's your vote of confidence? Where's the love and support I require at this difficult hour? I need you to be my wingwoman."

"You do know that I can hear you, right?" Nazeera tilts her head to one side, her arms crossed loosely against her chest. "I'm standing right here."

She looks somehow even more stunning today, her hair wrapped up in silks that look like liquid gold in the light. She's wearing an intricately braided red sweater, a pair of black, textured leather leggings, and black boots with steel platforms. And she's still got those heavy gold knuckles on both her fists.

I wish I could ask her where she gets her clothes.

I only realize Kenji and I have both been staring at her for too long when she finally clears her throat. She drops her arms and steps cautiously forward, smiling—not unkindly—at Kenji, who seems suddenly unable to breathe. "Listen," she says softly. "You're cute. Really cute. You've got a great face. But this," she says, gesturing between them, "is not happening."

Kenji doesn't appear to have heard her. "You think I've got a great face?"

She laughs and frowns at the same time. Waves two fingers and says, "Bye."

And that's it. She walks away.

Kenji says nothing. His eyes are fixed on Nazeera's disappearing form in the distance.

I pat his arm, try to sound sympathetic. "It'll be okay," I say. "Rejection is har—"

"That was amazing."

"Uh. What?"

He turns to look at me. "I mean, I've always known I had a great face. But now I know, like, for sure that I've got a great face. And it's just so validating."

"You know, I don't think I like this side of you."

"Don't be like that, J." Kenji taps me on the nose. "Don't be jealous."

"I'm not je—"

"I mean, I deserve to be happy, too, don't I?" And he goes suddenly quiet. His smile slips, his laugh dies away, and Kenji looks, if only for a moment—sad. "Maybe one day."

I feel my heart seize.

"Hey," I say gently. "You deserve to be the happiest."

Kenji runs a hand through his hair and sighs. "Yeah. Well."

"Her loss," I say.

He glances at me. "I guess that was pretty decent, as far as rejections go."

"She just doesn't know you," I say. "You're a total catch."

"I know, right? I keep trying to tell people."

"People are dumb." I shrug. "I think you're wonderful."

"Wonderful, huh?"

"Yep," I say, and link my arm in his. "You're smart and funny and kind and—"

"Handsome," he says. "Don't forget handsome."

"And very handsome," I say, nodding.

"Yeah, I'm flattered, J, but I don't like you like that."

My mouth drops open.

"How many times do I have to ask you to stop falling in love with me?"

"Hey!" I say, shoving away from him. "You're terrible."

"I thought I was wonderful."

"Depends on the hour."

And he laughs, out loud. "All right, kid. You ready to head back?"

I sigh, look off into the distance. "I don't know. I think I need a little more time alone. I've still got a lot on my mind. A lot I need to sort through."

"I get it," he says, shooting me a sympathetic look. "Do your thing."

"Thanks."

"Do you mind if I get going, though? All jokes aside, I really do have a lot to take care of today."

"I'll be fine. You go."

"You sure? You'll be okay out here on your own?"

"Yes, yes," I say, and shove him forward. "I'll be more than okay. I'm never really on my own, anyway." I gesture with my head toward the soldiers. "These guys are always following me."

Kenji nods, gives me a quick squeeze on the arm, and jogs off.

Within seconds, I'm alone. I sigh and turn toward the water, kicking at the sand as I do.

I'm so confused.

I'm caught between different worries, trapped by a fear of what seems my inevitable failure as a leader and my fears of Warner's inscrutable past. And today's conversation with Haider didn't help with the latter. His unmasked shock that Warner hadn't even bothered to mention the other families—and the children—he grew up with, really blew me away. It made me wonder how much more I don't know. How much more there is to unearth.

I know exactly how I feel when I look into his eyes, but sometimes being with Warner gives me whiplash. He's so unused to communicating basic things—to anyone—that every day with him comes with new discoveries. The discoveries aren't all bad—in fact, most of the things I learn about him only make me love him more—but even the harmless revelations are occasionally confusing.

Last week I found him sitting in his office listening to old vinyl records. I'd seen his record collection before—he has a huge stack that was apportioned to him by The Reestablishment along with a selection of old books and artwork—he was supposed to be sorting through it all, deciding what to keep and what to destroy. But I'd never seen him just sit and listen to music.

He didn't notice me when I'd walked in that day.

He was sitting very still, looking only at the wall, and listening to what I later discovered was a Bob Dylan record. I know this because I peeked in his office many hours later, after he'd left. I couldn't shake my curiosity; Warner had only listened to one of the songs on the record—he'd reset the needle every time the song finished—and I wanted to know what it was. It turned out to be a song called "Like a Rolling Stone."

I still haven't told him what I saw that day; I wanted to see if he would share the story with me himself. But he never mentioned it, not even when I asked him what he did that afternoon. It wasn't a lie, exactly, but the omission made me wonder why he'd keep it from me.

There's a part of me that wants to rip his history open. I want to know the good and the bad and just get all the secrets out and be done with it. Because right now I feel certain that my imagination is much more dangerous than any of his truths.

But I'm not sure how to make that happen.

Besides, everything is moving so quickly now. We're all so busy, all the time, and it's hard enough to keep my own thoughts straight. I'm not even sure where our resistance is headed at the moment. Everything is worrying me. Castle's worries are worrying me. Warner's mysteries are worrying me. The children of the supreme commanders are worrying me.

I take in a deep breath and exhale, long and loud.

I'm staring out across the water, trying to clear my mind by focusing on the fluid motions of the ocean. It was just three weeks ago that I'd felt stronger than I ever had in my whole life. I'd finally learned how to make use of my powers; I'd learned how to moderate my strength, how to project— and, most important, how to turn my abilities on and off. And then I'd crushed Anderson's legs in my bare hands. I stood still while soldiers emptied countless rounds of lead into my body. I was invincible.

But now?

This new job is more than I bargained for.

Politics, it turns out, is a science I don't yet understand. Killing things, breaking things—destroying things? That, I understand. Getting angry and going to war, I understand. But patiently playing a confusing game of chess with a bunch of strangers from around the world?

God, I'd so much rather shoot someone.

I'm making my way back to base slowly, my shoes filling with sand as I go. I'm actively dreading whatever it is Castle wants to talk to me about, but I've been gone for too long already. There's too much to do, and there's no way out of this but through. I have to face it. Deal with it, whatever it is. I sigh as I flex and unflex my fists, feeling the power come in and out of my body. It's still a strange thrill for me, to be able to disarm myself at will. It's nice to be able to walk around most days with my powers turned off; it's nice to be able to accidentally touch Kenji's skin without worrying I'll hurt him. I scoop up two handfuls of sand. Powers on: I close my fist and the sand is pulverized to dust. Powers off: the sand leaves a vague, pockmarked impression on my skin.

I drop the sand, dusting off the remaining grains from my palms, and squint into the morning sun. I'm searching for the soldiers who've been following me this whole time, because, suddenly, I can't spot them. Which is strange, because I just saw them a minute ago.

And then I feel it—

Pain

It explodes in my back.

It's a sharp, searing, violent pain and I'm blinded by it in an instant. I spin around in a fury that immediately dulls, my senses dimming even as I attempt to harness them. I pull up my Energy, thrumming suddenly with *electricum*, and wonder at my own stupidity for forgetting to turn my powers back on, especially out in the open like this. I was too distracted. Too frustrated. I can feel the bullet in my shoulder blade incapacitating me now, but I fight through the agony to try and spot my attacker.

Still, I'm too slow.

Another bullet hits my thigh, but this time I feel it leave only a flesh wound, bouncing off before it can make much of a mark. My Energy is weak—and weakening by the minute—I think because of the blood I'm losing—and I'm frustrated, so frustrated by how quickly I've been overtaken.

Stupid stupid stupid—

I trip as I try to hurry on the sand; I'm still an open target here. My assailant could be anyone—could be anywhere—and I'm not even sure where to look when suddenly three more bullets hit me: in my stomach, my wrist, my chest. The bullets break off my body and still manage to draw blood, but the bullet buried, buried in my back, is sending blinding flashes of pain through my veins and I gasp, my mouth frozen open and I can't catch my breath and the torment is so intense I can't help but wonder if this is a special gun, if these are special bullets—

oh

The small, breathless sound leaves my body as my knees hit the sand and I'm now pretty sure, fairly certain these bullets have been laced with poison, which would mean that even these, these flesh wounds would be dangero—

I fall, head spinning, backward onto the sand, too dizzy to see straight. My lips feel numb, my bones loose and my blood, my blood all sloshing together fast and weird and I start laughing, thinking I see a bird in the sky—not just one but many of them all at once flying flying *flying*

Suddenly I can't breathe.

Someone has their arm around my neck; they're dragging me backward and I'm choking, spitting up and losing lungs and I can't feel my tongue and I'm kicking at the sand so hard I've lost my shoes and I think here it is, death again, so soon so soon I was too tired anyway and then

The pressure is gone

So swiftly

I'm gasping and coughing and there's sand in my hair and in my teeth and I'm seeing colors and birds, so many birds, and I'm spinning and—

crack

Something breaks and it sounds like bone. My eyesight sharpens for an instant and I manage to see something in front of me. Someone. I squint, feeling like my mouth might swallow itself and I think it must be the poison but it's not; it's Nazeera, so pretty, so pretty standing in front of me, her hands around a man's limp neck and then she drops him to the ground

Scoops me up

You're so strong and so pretty I mumble, so strong and I want to be like you, I say to her

And she says shhh and tells me to be still, tells me I'll be fine

and carries me away.

WARNER

Panic, terror, guilt—unbounded fears—

I can hardly feel my feet as they hit the ground, my heart beating so hard it physically hurts. I'm bolting toward our half-built medical wing on the fifteenth floor and trying not to drown in the darkness of my own thoughts. I have to fight an instinct to squeeze my eyes shut as I run, taking the emergency stairs two at a time because, of course, the nearest elevator is temporarily closed for repairs.

I've never been such a fool.

What was I thinking? What was I *thinking*? I simply walked away. I keep making mistakes. I keep making assumptions. And I've never been so desperate for Kishimoto's inelegant vocabulary. God, the things I wish I could say. The things I'd like to shout. I've never been so angry with myself. I was so sure she'd be fine, I was so sure she knew to never move out in the open unprotected—

A sudden rush of dread overwhelms me.

I will it away.

I will it away, even as my chest heaves with exhaustion and outrage. It's irrational, to be mad at agony—it's futile, I know, to be angry with this pain—and yet, here I am. I feel powerless. I want to see her. I want to hold her. I want to ask her how she could've possibly let her guard down while walking *alone*, out in the *open*—

Something in my chest feels like it might rip apart as I reach the top floor, my lungs burning from the effort. My heart is pumping furiously. Even so, I tear down the hall. Desperation and terror fuel my need to find her.

I stop abruptly in place when the panic returns.

A wave of fear bends my back and I'm doubled over, hands on my knees, trying to breathe. It's unbidden, this pain. Overwhelming. I feel a startling prick behind my eyes. I blink, hard, fight the rush of emotion.

How did this happen? I want to ask her.

Didn't you realize that someone would try to kill *you?*

I'm nearly shaking when I reach the room they're keeping her in. I almost can't make sense of her limp, blood-smeared body laid out on the metal table. I rush forward half blind and ask Sonya and Sara to do again what they've done once before: help me heal her.

It's only then that I realize the room is full.

I'm ripping off my blazer when I notice the others. Figures are pressed up against the walls—forms of people I probably know and can't be bothered to name. Still, somehow, *she* stands out to me.

Nazeera.

I could close my hands around her throat.

"Get out of here," I choke out in a voice that doesn't sound like my own.

She looks genuinely shocked.

"I don't know how you managed this," I say, "but this is your fault—you, and your brother—you did this to her—"

"If you'd like to meet the man responsible," she says, flat and cold, "you're welcome to. He has no identification, but the tattoos on his arms indicate he might be from a neighboring sector. His dead body is in a holding cell underground."

My heart stops, then starts. "What?"

"Aaron?" It's Juliette, Juliette, my Juliette—

"Don't worry, love," I say quickly, "we're going to fix this, okay? The girls are here and we're going to do this again, just like last time—"

"Nazeera," she says, eyes closed, lips half mumbling.

"Yes?" I freeze. "What about Nazeera?"

"Saved"—her mouth halts midmotion, then swallows—"my life."

I look at Nazeera, then. Study her. She seems just about carved from stone, motionless in the middle of chaos. She's staring at Juliette with a curious look on her face, and I can't read her at all. But I don't need a supernatural ability to tell me that something is off about this girl. Basic human instinct tells me there's something she knows—something she's not telling me—and it makes me distrust her.

So when she finally turns in my direction, her eyes deep and steady and frighteningly serious, I feel a bolt of panic pierce me through the chest.

Juliette is sleeping now.

I'm never more grateful for my inhuman ability to steal

and manifest other people's Energies than I am in these unfortunate moments. We've often hoped that now, in the wake of Juliette learning to turn on and off her lethal touch, that Sonya and Sara would be able to heal her—that they'd be able to place their hands on her body in case of emergency without concern for their own safety. But Castle has since pointed out that there's still a chance that, once Juliette's body has begun to heal, her half-healed trauma could instinctively trigger old defenses, even without Juliette's permission. In that state of emergency, Juliette's skin might, accidentally, become lethal once more. It is a risk—an experiment—we were hoping to never again have to face. But now?

What if I weren't around? What if I didn't have this strange gift?

I can't bring myself to think on it.

So I sit here, head in my hands. I wait quietly outside her door as she sleeps off her injuries. The healing properties are still working their way through her body.

Until then, waves of emotion continue to assault me.

It's immeasurable, this frustration. Frustration with Kenji for having left Juliette all alone. Frustration with the six soldiers who were so easily relieved of their guns and their faculties by this single, unidentified assailant. But most of all, *God*, most of all, I've never been so frustrated with myself.

I've been remiss.

I let this happen. My oversights. My stupid infatuation with my own father—the fallout with my own feelings after his death—the pathetic dramas of my past. I let myself get distracted; I was self-absorbed, consumed by my own concerns and daily dealings.

It's my fault.

It's my fault for misunderstanding.

It's my fault for thinking she was fine, that she didn't require more from me—more encouragement, more motivation, more guidance—on a daily basis. She kept showing these tremendous moments of growth and change, and they disarmed me. I'm only now realizing that these moments are misleading. She needs more time, more opportunities to solidify her new strength. She needs to practice; and she needs to be pushed to practice. To be unyielding, to always and forever fight for herself.

And she's come so far.

She is, today, almost unrecognizable from the trembling young woman I first met. She's strong. She's no longer terrified of everything. But she's still only seventeen years old. And she's only been doing this for a short while.

And I keep forgetting.

I should have advised her when she said she wanted to take over the job of supreme commander. I should've said something then. I should've made sure she understood the breadth of what she'd be getting herself into. I should've warned her that her enemies would inevitably make an attempt on her *life*—

I have to pry my hands away from my face. I've unconsciously pressed my fingers so hard into my skin that

I've given myself a brand-new headache.

I sigh and fall back against the chair, extending my legs as my head hits the cold, concrete wall behind me. I feel numb and somehow, still electric. With anger. With impotence. With this impossible need to yell at someone, anyone. My fists clench. I close my eyes. *She has to be okay.* She has to be okay for her sake and for my sake, because I need her, and because I need her to be safe—

A throat clears.

Castle sits down in the seat beside me. I do not look in his direction.

"Mr. Warner," he says.

I do not respond.

"How are you holding up, son?"

An idiotic question.

"This," he says quietly, waving a hand toward her room, "is a much bigger problem than anyone will admit. I think you know that, too."

I stiffen.

He stares at me.

I turn only an inch in his direction. I finally notice the faint lines around his eyes, his forehead. The threads of silver gleaming through the neat dreadlocks tied at his neck. I don't know how old Castle is, but I suspect he's old enough to be my father. "Do you have something to say?"

"She can't lead this resistance," he says, squinting at something in the distance. "She's too young. Too inexperienced. Too angry. You know that, don't you?"

"No."

"It should've been you," Castle says. "I always secretly hoped—from the day you showed up at Omega Point—that it would've been you. That you would join us. And lead us." He shakes his head. "You were born for this. You would've managed it all beautifully."

"I didn't want this job," I say to him, sharp and clipped. "Our nation needed change. It needed a leader with heart and passion and I am not that person. Juliette cares about these people. She cares about their hopes, their fears—and she will fight for them in a way I never would."

Castle sighs. "She can't fight for anyone if she's dead, son."

"Juliette is going to be fine," I say angrily. "She's resting now."

Castle is quiet for a time.

When he finally breaks the silence, he says, "It is my great hope that, very soon, you will stop pretending to misunderstand me. I certainly respect your intelligence too much to reciprocate the pretense." He's staring at the floor. His eyebrows pull together. "You know very well what I'm trying to get at."

"And what is your point?"

He turns to look at me. Brown eyes, brown skin, brown hair. The white flash of his teeth as he speaks. "You say you love her?"

I feel my heart pound suddenly, the sound drumming in my ears. It's so hard for me to admit this sort of thing out loud. To a veritable stranger.

"Do you really love her?" he asks again.

"Yes," I whisper. "I do."

"Then stop her. Stop her before they do. Before this experiment destroys her."

I turn away, my chest heaving.

"You still don't believe me," he says. "Even though you know I'm telling the truth."

"I only know that you *think* you're telling me the truth."

Castle shakes his head. "Her parents are coming for her," he says. "And when they do you'll know for certain that I've not led you astray. But by then," he says, "it'll be too late."

"Your theory doesn't make any sense," I say, frustrated. "I have documents stating that Juliette's biological parents died a long time ago."

He narrows his eyes. "Documents are easily falsified."

"Not in this case," I say. "It isn't possible."

"I assure you that it is."

I'm still shaking my head. "I don't think you understand," I say. "I have all of Juliette's files," I say to him, "and her biological parents' date of death has always been clearly noted. Maybe you confused these people with her *adoptive* parents—"

"The adoptive parents only ever had custody of one child—Juliette—correct?"

"Yes."

"Then how do you explain the second child?"

"What?" I stare at him. "What second child?"

"Emmaline, her older sister. You remember Emmaline, of course."

Now I'm convinced Castle is unhinged. "My God," I say. "You really have lost your mind."

"Nonsense," he says. "You've met Emmaline many times, Mr. Warner. You may not have known who she was at the time, but you've lived in her world. You've interacted with her at length. Haven't you?"

"I'm afraid you're deeply misinformed."

"Try to remember, son."

"Try to remember *what*?"

"You were sixteen. Your mother was dying. There were whispers that your father would soon be promoted from commander and regent of Sector 45 to supreme commander of North America. You knew that, in a couple of years, he was going to move you to the capital. You didn't want to go. You didn't want to leave your mother behind, so you offered to take his place. To take over Sector 45. And you were willing to do anything."

I feel the blood exit my body.

"Your father gave you a job."

"No," I whisper.

"Do you remember what he made you do?"

I look into my open, empty hands. My pulse picks up. My mind spirals.

"Do you remember, son?"

"How much do you know?" I say, but my face feels paralyzed. "About me—about *this*?"

"Not quite as much as you do. But more than most."

I sink into the chair. The room spins around me.

I can only imagine what my father would say if he were alive to see this now. *Pathetic. You're pathetic. You have no one to blame but yourself,* he'd say. *You're always ruining everything, putting your emotions before your duty—*

"How long have you known?" I look at him, anxiety sending waves of unwelcome heat up my back. "Why have you never said anything?"

Castle shifts in his chair. "I'm not sure how much I should say on this matter. I don't know how much I can trust you."

"You can't trust *me*?" I say, losing control. "You're the one who's been holding back—all this time"—I glance up suddenly, realizing—"does Kishimoto know about this?"

"No."

My features rearrange. Surprised.

Castle sighs. "He'll know soon enough. Just as everyone else will."

I shake my head in disbelief. "So you're telling me that— that girl—that was her sister?"

Castle nods.

"That's not possible."

"It is a fact."

"How can any of this be true?" I say, sitting up straighter. "I would *know* if it were true. I would have the classified data, I would have been briefed—"

"You're still only a child, Mr. Warner. You forget that

sometimes. You forget that your father didn't tell you everything."

"Then how do *you* know? How do you know any of this?"

Castle looks me over. "I know you think I'm foolish," he says, "but I'm not as simple as you might hope. I, too, once tried to lead this nation, and I did a great deal of my own research during my time underground. I spent decades building Omega Point. Do you think I did so without also understanding my enemies? I had files three feet deep on every supreme commander, their families, their personal habits, their favorite colors." He narrows his eyes. "Surely you didn't think I was that naive.

"The supreme commanders of the world have a great deal of secrets," Castle says. "And I'm privy to only a few of them. But the information I gathered on the beginnings of The Reestablishment have proven true."

I can only stare at him, uncomprehending.

"It was on the strength of what I'd uncovered that I knew a young woman with a lethal touch was being held in an asylum in Sector 45. Our team had already been planning a rescue mission when you first discovered her existence—as Juliette Ferrars, an alias—and realized how she might be useful to your own research. So we at Omega Point waited. Bided our time. In the interim, I had Kenji enlist. He was gathering information for several months before your father finally approved your request to move her out of the asylum. Kenji infiltrated the base in Sector 45 on my orders; his mission was always to retrieve Juliette.

I've been searching for Emmaline ever since."

"I still don't understand," I whisper.

"Mr. Warner," he says impatiently, "Juliette and her sister have been in the custody of The Reestablishment for twelve years. The two sisters are part of an ongoing experiment for genetic testing and manipulation, the details of which I'm still trying to unravel."

My mind might explode.

"Will you believe me now?" he says. "Have I done enough to prove I know more about your life than you think?"

I try to speak but my throat is dry; the words scrape the inside of my mouth. "My father was a sick, sadistic man," I say. "But he wouldn't have done this. He couldn't have done this to me."

"And yet," Castle says. "He did. He allowed you to bring Juliette on base knowing very well who she was. Your father had a disturbing obsession with torture and experimentation."

I feel disconnected from my mind, my body, even as I force myself to breathe. "Who are her real parents?"

Castle shakes his head. "I don't know yet. Whoever they were, their loyalties to The Reestablishment ran deep. These girls were not stolen from their parents," he says. "They were offered willingly."

My eyes widen. I feel suddenly sick.

Castle's voice changes. He sits forward, his eyes sharp. "Mr. Warner," he says. "I'm not sharing this information with you because I'm trying to hurt you. You must know that this isn't fun for me, either."

I look up.

"I need your help," he says, studying me. "I need to know what you did for those two years. I need to know the details of your assignment to Emmaline. What were you tasked to do? Why was she being held? How were they using her?"

I shake my head. "I don't know."

"You do know," he says. "You must know. *Think*, son. Try to remember—"

"I don't know!" I shout.

Castle sits back, surprised.

"He never told me," I say, breathing hard. "That was the job. To follow orders without questioning them. To do whatever was asked of me by The Reestablishment. To prove my loyalty."

Castle falls back into his seat, crestfallen. He looks shattered. "You were my one remaining hope," he says. "I thought I might finally be able to crack this."

I glance at him, heart pounding. "And I still have no idea what you're talking about."

"There's a reason why no one knows the truth about these sisters, Mr. Warner. There's a reason why Emmaline is kept under such high security. She is critical, somehow, to the structure of The Reestablishment, and I still don't know how or why. I don't know what she's doing for them." He looks me straight in the eye, then, his gaze piercing through me. "Please," he says. "Try to remember. What did he make you do to her? Anything you can remember—anything at all—"

"No," I whisper. I want to scream the word. "I don't want to remember."

"Mr. Warner," he says. "I understand that this is hard for you—"

"*Hard for me?*" I stand up suddenly. My body is shaking with rage. The walls, the chairs, the tables around us begin to rattle. The light fixtures swing dangerously overhead, the bulbs flickering. "You think this is *hard* for me?"

Castle says nothing.

"What you are telling me right now is that Juliette was planted here, in my life, as part of a larger experiment—an experiment my father had always been privy to. You're telling me that Juliette is not who I think she is. That Juliette Ferrars isn't even her real name. You're telling me that not only is she a girl with a set of living parents, but that I also spent two years unwittingly torturing her sister." My chest heaves as I stare at him. "Is that about right?"

"There's more."

I laugh, out loud. The sound is insane.

"Ms. Ferrars will find out about all this very soon," Castle says to me. "So I would advise you to get ahead of these revelations. Tell her everything as soon as possible. You must confess. Do it now."

"What?" I say, stunned. "Why me?"

"Because if you don't tell her soon," he says, "I assure you, Mr. Warner, that someone else will—"

"I don't care," I say. "You tell her."

"You're not hearing me. It is imperative that she hear this from *you*. She trusts you. She loves you. If she finds out on her own, from a less worthy source, we might lose her."

"I'll never let that happen. I'll never let anyone hurt her again, even if that means I'll have to guard her myself—"

"No, son." Castle cuts me off. "You misunderstand me. I did not mean we would lose her physically." He smiles, but the result is strange. Scared. "I meant we would *lose* her. Up here"—he taps his head—"and here"—he taps his heart.

"What do you mean?"

"Simply that you must not live in denial. Juliette Ferrars is not who you think she is, and she is not to be trifled with. She seems, at times, entirely defenseless. Naive. Even innocent. But you cannot allow yourself to forget the fist of anger that still lives in her heart."

My lips part, surprised.

"You've read about it, haven't you? In her journal," he says. "You've read where her mind has gone—how dark it's been—"

"How did you—"

"And I," he says, "I have seen it. I've seen her lose control of that quietly contained rage with my own eyes. She nearly destroyed all of us at Omega Point long before your father did. She broke the ground in a fit of madness inspired by a simple *misunderstanding*," he says. "Because she was upset about the tests we were running on Mr. Kent. Because she was confused and a little scared. She wouldn't listen to reason—and she nearly killed us all."

"That was different," I say, shaking my head. "That was a long time ago. She's different now." I look away, failing to control my frustration at his thinly veiled accusations. "She's *happy*—"

"How can she be truly happy when she's never dealt with her past? She's never addressed it—merely set it aside. She's never had the time, or the tools, to examine it. And that anger—that kind of rage," Castle says, shaking his head, "does not simply disappear. She is volatile and unpredictable. And heed my words, son: Her anger will make an appearance again."

"No."

He looks at me. Picks me apart with his eyes. "You don't really believe that."

I do not respond.

"Mr. Warner—"

"Not like that," I say. "If it comes back, it won't be like that. Anger, maybe—*yes*—but not rage. Not uncontrolled, uninhibited rage—"

Castle smiles. It's so sudden, so unexpected, I stop midsentence.

"Mr. Warner," he says. "What do you think is going to happen when the truth of her past is finally revealed to her? Do you think she will accept it quietly? Calmly? If my sources are correct—and they usually are—the whispers underground affirm that her time here is up. The experiment has come to an end. Juliette murdered a supreme commander. The system won't let her go on like this, her powers unleashed, unchecked. And I have heard that the plan is to obliterate Sector 45." He hesitates. "As for Juliette herself," he says, "it is likely they will either kill her, or place her in another facility."

My mind spins, explodes. "How do you know this?"

Castle laughs briefly. "You can't possibly believe that Omega Point was the only resistance group in North America, Mr. Warner. I'm very well connected underground. And my point still stands." A pause. "Juliette will soon have access to the information necessary to piece together her past. And she will find out, one way or another, your part in all of it."

I look away and back again, eyes wide, my voice fraying. "You don't understand," I whisper. "She would never forgive me."

Castle shakes his head. "If she learns from someone else that you've always known she was adopted? If she hears from someone else that you tortured her sister?" He nods. "Yes, it's true, she will likely never forgive you."

For a sudden, terrible moment, I lose feeling in my knees. I'm forced to sit down, my bones shaking inside me.

"But I didn't know," I say, hating how it sounds, hating that I feel like a child. "I didn't know who that girl was, I didn't know Juliette had a sister— I didn't know—"

"It doesn't matter. Without you, without context, without an explanation or an apology, all of this will be much harder to forgive. But if you tell her yourself and tell her *now*? Your relationship might still stand a chance." He shakes his head.

"Either way, you must tell her, Mr. Warner. Because we have to warn her. She needs to know what's coming, and we have to start planning. Your silence on the subject will end only in devastation."

JULIETTE

I am a thief.

I stole this notebook and this pen from one of the doctors, from one of his lab coats when he wasn't looking, and I shoved them both down my trousers. This was just before he ordered those men to come and get me. The ones in the strange suits with the thick gloves and the gas masks with the foggy plastic windows hiding their eyes. They were aliens, I remember thinking. I remember thinking they must've been aliens because they couldn't have been human, the ones who handcuffed my hands behind my back, the ones who strapped me to my seat. They stuck Tasers to my skin over and over for no reason other than to hear me scream but I wouldn't. I whimpered but I never said a word. I felt the tears streak down my cheeks but I wasn't crying.

I think it made them angry.

They slapped me awake even though my eyes were open when we arrived. Someone unstrapped me without removing my handcuffs and kicked me in both kneecaps before ordering me to rise. And I tried. I tried but I couldn't and finally six hands shoved me out the door and my face was bleeding on the concrete for a while. I can't really remember the part where they dragged me inside.

I feel cold all the time.

I feel empty, like there is nothing inside of me but this broken heart, the only organ left in this shell. I feel the bleats echo within me, I feel the thumping reverberate around my skeleton. I have a heart, says science, but I am a monster, says society. And I know it, of course I know it. I know what I've done. I'm not asking for sympathy. But sometimes I think—sometimes I wonder—if I were a monster—surely, I would feel it by now?

I would feel angry and vicious and vengeful. I'd know blind rage and bloodlust and a need for vindication.

Instead, I feel an abyss within me that's so deep, so dark I can't see within it; I can't see what it holds. I do not know what I am or what might happen to me.

I do not know what I might do again.

—AN EXCERPT FROM JULIETTE'S JOURNALS IN THE ASYLUM

I'm dreaming about birds again.

I wish they would go away already. I'm tired of thinking about them, hoping for them. Birds, birds, birds—why won't they go away? I shake my head as if to clear it, but feel my mistake at once. My mind is still dense and foggy, swimming in confusion. I blink open my eyes slowly, tentatively, but no matter how far I force them open, I can't seem to take in any light. It takes me too long to understand that I've awoken in the middle of the night.

A sharp gasp.

That's me, my voice, my breath, my quickly beating heart. Where is my head? Why is it so heavy? My eyes close fast, sand stuck in the lashes, sticking them together. I try to clear the haze—try to remember—but parts of me still feel numb, like my teeth and toes and the spaces between my ribs and I laugh, suddenly, and I don't know why—

I was shot.

My eyes fly open, my skin breaking into a sudden, cold sweat.

Oh my God I was shot, I was shot I was shot

I try to sit up and can't. I feel so heavy, so heavy with blood and bone and suddenly I'm freezing, my skin is cold rubber and clammy against the metal table I'm sticking to and all at once

I want to cry

all at once I'm back in the asylum, the cold and the metal and the pain and the delirium all confusing me and then I'm weeping, silently, hot tears warming my cheeks and I can't speak but I'm scared and I hear them, I hear them

the others

screaming

Flesh and bone breaking in the night, hushed, muffled voices—suppressed shouts—cellmates I'd never see—

Who were they? I wonder.

I haven't thought about them in so long. What happened to them. Where they came from. Who did I leave behind?

My eyes are sealed shut, my lips parted in quiet terror. I haven't been haunted like this in so long so long so long

It's the drugs, I think. **There was poison in those bullets.**

Is that why I can see the birds?

I smile. Giggle. Count them. Not just the white ones, white with streaks of gold like crowns atop their heads, but blue ones and black ones and yellow birds, too. I see them when I close my eyes but I saw them today, too, on the beach and they looked so real, so real

Why?

Why would someone try to kill me?

Another sudden jolt to my senses and I'm more alert,

more myself, panic clearing the poison for a single moment of clarity and I'm able to push myself up, onto my elbows, head spinning, eyes wild as they scan the darkness and I'm just about to lie back down, exhausted, when I see something—

"Are you awake?"

I inhale sharply, confused, trying to make sense of the sounds. The words are warped like I'm hearing them underwater and I swim toward them, trying, trying, my chin falling against my chest as I lose the battle.

"Did you see anything today?" the voice says to me. "Anything . . . strange?"

"Who—where, where are you—" I say, reaching blindly into the dark, eyes only half open now. I feel resistance and wrap my fingers around it. A hand? A strange hand. It's a mix of metal and flesh, a fist with a sharp edge of steel.

I don't like it.

I let go.

"Did you see anything today?" it says again.

I mumble.

"What did you see?" it says.

And I laugh, remembering. I could hear them—hear their *caw caws* as they flew far above the water, could hear their little feet walking along the sand. There were so many of them. Wings and feathers, sharp beaks and talons.

So much motion.

"What did you *see*—?" the voice demands again, and it makes me feel strange.

"I'm cold," I say, and lie down again. "Why is it so cold?"

A brief silence. A rustle of movement. I feel a heavy blanket drape over the simple sheet already covering my body.

"You should know," the voice says to me, "that I'm not here to hurt you."

"I know," I say, though I don't understand why I've said it.

"But the people you trust are lying to you," the voice is saying. "And the other supreme commanders only want to kill you."

I smile wide, remembering the birds. "Hello," I say.

Someone sighs.

"I'll see you in the morning. We'll talk another time," the voice says. "When you're feeling better."

I'm so warm now, warm and tired and drowning again in strange dreams and distorted memories. I feel like I'm swimming in quicksand and the harder I pull away, the more quickly I am devoured and all I can think is

here

in the dark, dusty corners of my mind

I feel a strange relief.

I am always welcome here

in my loneliness, in my sadness

in this abyss, there is a rhythm I remember. The steady drop of tears, the temptation to retreat, the shadow of my past

the life I choose to forget has not
will never
ever
forget *me*

WARNER

I've been awake all night.

Infinite boxes lie open before me, their innards splayed across the room. Papers are stacked on desks and tables, spread open on my floor. I'm surrounded by files. Many thousands of pages of paperwork. My father's old reports, his work, the documents that ruled his life—

I have read them all.

Obsessively. Desperately.

And what I've found within these pages does nothing to soothe me, no—

I am distraught.

I sit here, cross-legged on the floor of my office, suffocated on all sides by the sight of a familiar typeset and my father's too-legible scrawl. My right hand is caught behind my head, desperate for a length of hair to yank out of my skull and finding none. This is so much worse than I had feared, and I don't know why I'm so surprised.

This is not the first time my father has kept secrets from me.

It was after Juliette escaped Sector 45, after she ran away with Kent and Kishimoto and my father came here to clean up the mess—that was when I learned, for the first time, that my father had knowledge of their world. Of others with abilities.

He'd kept it from me for so long.

I'd heard rumors, of course—from the soldiers, from the civilians—of various unusual sightings and stories, but I brushed them off as nonsense. A human need to find a magical portal to escape our pain.

But there it was—all true.

After my father's revelation, my thirst for information became suddenly insatiable. I needed to know more—who these people were, where they'd come from, how much we'd known—

And I unearthed truths I wish every day I could unlearn.

There are asylums, just like Juliette's, all over the world. *Unnaturals,* as The Reestablishment calls them, were rounded up in the name of science and discovery. But now, finally, I'm understanding how it all began. Here, in these stacks of papers, are all the horrible answers I sought.

Juliette and her sister were the very first Unnatural finds of The Reestablishment. The discovery of these girls' unusual abilities led to the discoveries of other people like them, all over the world. The Reestablishment went on to collect as many Unnaturals as they could find; they told the civilians they were cleansing them of their old and their ill and imprisoning them in camps for closer medical examination.

But the truth was rather more complicated.

The Reestablishment quickly weeded out the useful Unnaturals from the nonuseful for their own benefit. The ones with the best abilities were absorbed by the system—divvied up around the world by the supreme commanders for their personal use in perpetuating the wrath of The Reestablishment—and the others were disposed of. This led to the eventual rise of The Reestablishment, and, with it, the many asylums that would house the other Unnaturals around the globe. For further studies, they'd said. For testing.

Juliette had not yet manifested abilities when she was donated to The Reestablishment by her parents. No. It was her *sister* who started it all.

Emmaline.

It was Emmaline whose preternatural gifts startled everyone around them; the sister, Emmaline, was the one who unwittingly drew attention to herself and her family. The unnamed parents were frightened by their daughter's frequent and incredible displays of psychokinesis.

They were also fanatics.

There's limited information in my father's files about the mother and father who willingly gave up their children for experimentation. I've scoured every document and was able to glean only a little about their motives, ultimately piecing together from various notes and extraneous details a startling depiction of these characters. It seems these people had an unhealthy obsession with The Reestablishment. Juliette's biological parents were devoted to the cause long before it had even gained momentum as an international movement, and they thought that studying their daughter might help shed light on the current world and its many ailments. If this was happening to Emmaline, they theorized, maybe it was happening to others—and maybe, somehow, this was information that could be used to help better the world. In no time at all The Reestablishment had Emmaline in custody.

Juliette was taken as a precaution.

If the older sibling had proven herself capable of incredible feats, The Reestablishment thought the younger sister might, too. Juliette was only five years old, and she was held under close surveillance.

After a month in a facility, Juliette showed no signs of a special ability. So she was injected with a drug that would destroy critical parts of her memory, and sent to live in Sector 45, under my father's supervision. Emmaline had kept her real name, but the younger sister, unleashed into the real world, would need an alias. They renamed her Juliette, planted false memories in her head, and assigned her adoptive parents who, only too happy to bring home a child into their childless family, followed instructions to never tell the child that she'd been adopted. They also had no idea that they were being watched. All other useless Unnaturals were, generally, killed off, but The Reestablishment chose to monitor Juliette in a more neutral setting. They hoped a home life would inspire a latent ability within her. She was too valuable as a blood relation to the very talented Emmaline to be so quickly disposed of.

It is the next part of Juliette's life that I was most familiar with.

I knew of Juliette's troubles at home, her many moves.

I knew of her family's visits to the hospital. Their calls to the police. Her stays in juvenile detention centers. She lived in the general area that used to be Southern California before she settled in a city that became firmly a part of what is now Sector 45, always within my father's reach. Her upbringing among the ordinary people of the world was heavily documented by police reports, teachers' complaints, and medical files attempting to understand what she was becoming. Eventually, upon finally discovering the extremes of Juliette's lethal touch, the vile people chosen to be her adoptive parents would go on to abuse her—for the rest of her adolescent life with them—and, ultimately, return her to The Reestablishment, which was only too happy to receive her.

It was The Reestablishment—my own father—who put Juliette back in isolation. For more tests. More surveillance.

And this was when our worlds collided.

Tonight, in these files, I was finally able to make sense of something both terrible and alarming:

The supreme commanders of the world have always known Juliette Ferrars.

They've been watching her grow up. She and her sister were handed over by their psychotic parents, whose allegiance to The Reestablishment overruled all else. Exploiting these girls—understanding their powers—was what helped The Reestablishment dominate the world. It was through the exploitation of other innocent Unnaturals that The Reestablishment was able to conquer and manipulate people and places so quickly.

This, I now realize, is why they've been so patient with a seventeen-year-old who's declared herself ruler of an entire continent. This is why they've so quietly abided the truth of her having slaughtered one of their fellow commanders.

And Juliette has no idea.

She has no idea she's being played and preyed upon. She has no idea that she has no real power here. No chance at change. No opportunity to make a difference in the world. She was, and will forever be nothing more than a toy to them—a science experiment to watch carefully, to make certain the concoction doesn't boil over too soon.

But it did.

Juliette failed their tests over a month ago, and my father tried to kill her for it. He tried to kill her because he'd decided that she'd become a distraction. Gone was the opportunity for this *Unnatural* to grow into an adversary.

The monster we've bred has tried to kill my own son. She's since attacked me like a feral animal, shooting me in both my legs. I've never seen such wildness—such blind, inhuman rage. Her mind shifts without warning. She showed no signs of psychosis upon first arrival in the house, but appeared to dissociate from any structure of rational thought while attacking me. Having seen her instability with my own eyes makes me only more certain of what needs to be done. I write this now as a decree from my hospital bed, and as a precaution to my fellow commanders. In the case that I don't recover from these wounds and am unable to follow through with what needs to be done: You, who are reading this now, you must react. Finish what I could not do. The younger sister is a failed experiment. She is, as we feared, disconnected from humanity. Worse, she's become a distraction for Aaron. He's become—in a toxic turn of events—impossibly drawn to her, with no apparent regard for his own safety. I have no idea what she's done to his mind. I only know now that I should never have entertained my own curiosity by allowing him to bring her on base. It's a shame, really, that she is nothing like her elder sister. Instead, Juliette Ferrars has become an incurable cancer we must cut out of our lives for good.

—AN EXCERPT FROM ANDERSON'S DAILY LOG

Juliette threatened the balance of The Reestablishment.

She was an experiment gone wrong. And she'd become a liability. She needed to be expunged from the earth.

My father tried so hard to destroy her.

And I see now that his failure has been of great interest to the other commanders. My father's daily logs were shared; all the supreme commanders shared their logs with one another. It was the only way for the six of them to remain apprised, at all times, of each other's daily goings-on.

So. They knew his story. They've known about my feelings for her.

And they have their orders to kill Juliette.

But they're waiting. And I have to assume there's

something more—some other explanation for their hesitation. Maybe they think they can rehabilitate her. Maybe they're wondering whether Juliette cannot still be of service to them and to their cause, much like her sister has been.

Her sister.

I'm haunted at once by a memory of her.

Brown-haired and bony. Jerking uncontrollably underwater. Long brown waves suspended, like jittery eels, around her face. Electric wires threaded under her skin. Several tubes permanently attached to her neck and torso. She'd been living underwater for so long when I first saw her that she hardly resembled a person. Her flesh was milky and shriveled, her mouth stretched out in a grotesque O, wrapped around a regulator that forced air into her lungs. She's only a year older than Juliette. And she's been held in captivity for twelve years.

Still alive, but only barely.

I had no idea she was Juliette's sister. I had no idea she was anyone at all. When I first met my assignment, she had no name. I was given only instructions, and ordered to follow them. I didn't know who or what I'd been assigned to oversee. I understood only that she was a prisoner—and I knew she was being tortured—but I didn't know then that there was anything supernatural about the girl. I was an idiot. A child.

I slam the back of my head against the wall, once. Hard. My eyes squeeze shut.

Juliette has no idea she ever had a real family—a horrible, insane family—but a family nonetheless. And if Castle is to be believed, The Reestablishment is coming for her. To kill her. To exploit her. So we have to act. I have to warn her, and I have to do it as soon as possible.

But how—how do I tell her any of this? How do I tell her without explaining my part in all of this?

I've always known Juliette was adopted, but I never told her this truth simply because I thought it would make things worse. My understanding was that Juliette's biological parents were long dead. I didn't see how telling her that she had real, dead parents would make her life any better.

But that doesn't change the fact that I knew.

And now I have to confess. Not just this, but the truth about her sister—that she is still alive and being actively tortured by The Reestablishment. That I contributed to that torture.

Or this:

That I am the true monster, completely and utterly unworthy of her love.

I close my eyes, press the back of my hand to my mouth and feel my body break apart within me. I don't know how to extricate myself from the mess made by my own father. A mess in which I was unintentionally complicit. A mess that, upon its unveiling, will destroy the little bit of happiness I've managed to piece together in my life.

Juliette will never, ever forgive me.

I will lose her.
And it will kill me.

JULIETTE

I wonder what they're thinking. My parents. I wonder where they are. I wonder if they're okay now, if they're happy now, ~~if they finally got what they wanted~~ I wonder if my mother will have another child. I wonder if someone will ever be kind enough to kill me and I wonder if hell is better than here. I wonder what my face looks like now. I wonder if I'll ever breathe fresh air again.

I wonder about so many things.

Sometimes I'll stay awake for days just counting everything I can find. I count the walls, the cracks in the walls, my fingers and toes. I count the springs in the bed, the threads in the blanket, the steps it takes to cross the room and back. I count my teeth and the individual hairs on my head and the number of seconds I can hold my breath.

But sometimes I get so tired that I forget I'm not allowed to wish for things anymore and I find myself wishing for the one thing I've always wanted. The only thing I've always dreamt about.

I wish all the time for a friend.

I dream about it. I imagine what it would be like. To smile and be smiled upon. To have a person to confide in, someone who wouldn't throw things at me or stick my hands in the fire or beat me for being born. Someone who would hear that I'd been thrown away and would try to find me, who would never be afraid of me.

Someone who'd know I'd never try to hurt them.

Someone who'd know I'd never try to hurt them.

I fold myself into a corner of this room and bury my head in my knees and rock back and forth and back and forth and back and forth and I wish and I wish and I wish and I dream of impossible things until I've cried myself to sleep.

I wonder what it would be like to have a friend.

And then I wonder who else is locked in this asylum. I wonder where the other screams are coming from.

I wonder if they're coming from me.

—AN EXCERPT FROM JULIETTE'S JOURNALS IN THE ASYLUM

I feel strange this morning.

I feel slow, like I'm wading through mud, like my bones have filled with lead and my head, *oh*—

I flinch.

My head has never been heavier.

I wonder if it's the last dregs of the poison still haunting my veins, but something feels wrong with me today. My memories of my time in the asylum are suddenly too present—perched too fully at the forefront of my mind. I thought I'd managed to shove those memories out of my head but no, here they are again, dredged out of the darkness. 264 days in perfect isolation. Nearly a year without access or outlet to the outside. To another human being.

So long, so long, so very, very long without the warmth of human contact.

I shiver involuntarily. Jerk upward.

What's wrong with me?

Sonya and Sara must've heard me moving because they're now standing before me, their voices clear but somehow, vibrating. Echoing off the walls. My ears won't stop ringing. I squint to make sense of their faces but I feel dizzy suddenly, disoriented, like my body is sideways or maybe flat on the ground or maybe *I* need to be flat on the ground, or *oh*

oh I think I might be sick—

"Thank you for the bucket," I say, still nauseous. I try to sit up and for some reason I can't remember how. My skin has broken out in a cold sweat. "What's wrong with me?" I say. "I thought you healed—healed—"

I'm gone again.

Head spinning.

Eyes closed against the light. The floor-to-ceiling windows we've installed can't seem to block the sun from invading the room and I can't help but wonder when I've ever seen the sun shine so brightly. Over the last decade our world collapsed inward, the atmosphere unpredictable, the weather changing in sharp and dramatic spikes. It snows where it shouldn't; rains where it once couldn't; the clouds are always gray; the birds gone forever from the sky. The once-bright green leaves of trees and lawns are now dull and brittle with decay. It's March now, and even as we approach spring the sky shows no sign of change. The earth is still cold, still iced over, still dark and muddy.

Or at least, it was yesterday.

Someone places a cool rag on my forehead and the cold is welcome; my skin feels inflamed even as I shiver. Slowly, my muscles unclench. But I wish someone would do something about the glaring sunlight. I'm squinting, even with my eyes closed, and it's making my headache worse.

"The wound is fully healed," I hear someone saying, "but it looks like the poison hasn't worked its way out of her system—"

"I don't understand," says another voice. "How is that possible? Why aren't you able to heal her completely?"

"Sonya," I manage to say. "Sara?"

"Yes?" The twin sisters answer at the same time, and I can feel the rush of their footsteps, hard like drumbeats against my head, as they hurry to my bedside.

I try to gesture toward the windows. "Can we do something about the sun?" I say. "It's too bright."

They help me up into a seated position and I feel my head-spin begin to steady. I blink my eyes open with a great deal of effort just in time to have someone hand me a cup of water.

"Drink this," Sonya says. "Your body is severely dehydrated."

I gulp the water down quickly, surprised by my own thirst. They hand me another glass. I drink that, too. I have to drink five glasses of water before I can hold my head up without immense difficulty.

When I finally feel more normal, I look around. Eyes wide-open. I have a massive headache, but the other symptoms are beginning to fade.

I see Warner first.

He's standing in a corner of the room, eyes bloodshot, yesterday's clothes rumpled on his body, and he's staring at me with a look of unmasked fear that surprises me. It's entirely unlike him. Warner rarely shows emotion in public.

I wish I could say something, but it doesn't feel like the right time. Sonya and Sara are still watching me carefully, their hazel eyes bright against their brown skin. But something about them looks different to me. Maybe it's that I've never looked at them this closely anywhere but underground, but the brilliant light of the sun has reduced their pupils to the size of pinpricks, and it makes their eyes look different. Bigger. *New*.

"The light is so strange today," I can't help saying. "Has it ever been this bright?"

Sonya and Sara glance out the window, glance back at me, and frown at each other. "How are you feeling?" they say. "Does your head still hurt? Do you feel dizzy?"

"My head is killing me," I say, and try to laugh. "What was in those bullets?" I pinch the bridge of my nose between my thumb and index finger. "Do you know if the headache will go away soon?"

"Honestly—we're not sure what's happening right now." This, from Sara.

"Your wound is mended," says Sonya, "but it seems the poison is still affecting your mind. We can't know for sure if it was able to cause permanent damage before we got to you."

At this, I look up. Feel my spine stiffen. "Permanent damage?" I say. "To my brain? Is that really possible?"

They nod. "We'll monitor you closely for the next couple of weeks just to be sure. The illusions you're experiencing might end up being nothing."

"What?" I look around. Look at Warner, who still won't speak. "What illusions? I just have a headache." I squint again, turning away from the window. "Yikes. Sorry," I say, eyes narrowed against the light, "it's been so long since we've had days like this"—I laugh—"I think I'm more accustomed to the dark." I place my hand over my eyes like a visor. "We really need to get some shades on these windows. Someone remind me to tell Kenji about that."

Warner has gone gray. He looks frozen in his skin.

Sonya and Sara share a look of concern.

"What is it?" I say, my stomach sinking as I look at the three of them. "What's wrong? What are you not telling me?"

"There's no sun today," Sonya says quietly. "It's snowing again."

"It's dark and cloudy, just like every other day," says Sara.

"What? What are you talking about?" I say, laughing and frowning at the same time. I can *feel* the heat of the sun on my face. I see it make a direct impact in their eyes, their pupils dilating as they move into the shadows. "You're joking, right? The sun is so bright I can barely look out the window."

Sonya and Sara shake their heads.

Warner is staring at the wall, both hands locked behind his neck.

I feel my heart begin to race. "So I'm seeing things?" I say to them. "I'm hallucinating?"

They nod.

"Why?" I say, trying not to panic. "What's happening to me?"

"We don't know," Sonya says, looking into her hands. "But we're hoping these effects are just temporary."

I try to slow my breathing. Try to remain calm. "Okay. Well. I need to go. Can I go? I have a thousand things to do—"

"Maybe you should stay here a little while longer," says Sara. "Let us watch you for a few more hours."

But I'm shaking my head. "I need to get some air—I need to go outside—"

"*No*—"

It's the first thing Warner's said since I woke up, and he nearly shouts the word at me. He's holding up his hands in a silent plea.

"No, love," he says, sounding strange. "You can't go outside again. Not—not just yet. Please."

The look on his face is enough to break my heart.

I slow down, feel my racing pulse steady as I stare at him. "I'm so sorry," I say. "I'm sorry I scared everyone. It was a moment of stupidity and it was totally my fault. I let my guard down for just a *second*." I sigh. "I think someone had been watching me, waiting for the right moment. Either way, it won't happen again."

I try to smile, and he doesn't budge. Won't smile back.

"Really," I try again. "Don't worry. I should've realized there would be people out there waiting to kill me the moment I seemed vulnerable, but"—I laugh—"believe me, I'll be more careful next time. I'll even ask to have a larger guard follow me around."

He shakes his head.

I study him, his terror. I don't understand it.

I make an effort to get to my feet. I'm in socks and a hospital gown, and Sonya and Sara hurry me into a robe and slippers. I thank them for everything they've done and they squeeze my hands.

"We'll be right outside if you need anything," they say in unison.

"Thank you again," I say, and smile. "I'll let you know how it goes with the, um"—I point to my head—"weird visions."

They nod and disappear.

I take a tentative step toward Warner.

"Hey," I say gently. "I'm going to be okay. Really."

"You could've been killed."

"I know," I say. "I've been so off lately—I wasn't thinking. But this was a mistake I will never make again." A short laugh. "Really."

Finally, he sighs. He releases the tension in his shoulders. Runs a hand along the length of his face, the back of his neck.

I've never seen him like this before.

"I'm so sorry I scared you," I say.

"Please don't apologize to me, love. You don't have to worry about me," he says, shaking his head. "I've been worried about *you*. How are you feeling?"

"Other than the hallucinating, you mean?" I crack a half grin. "I feel okay. It took me a minute to come back to myself this morning, but I feel much better now. I'm sure the strange visions will be gone soon, too." I smile, wide, more for his benefit than mine. "Anyway, Delalieu wants me to meet with him ASAP to talk about my speech for the symposium, so I'm thinking maybe I should go do that. I can't believe it's happening *tomorrow*." I shake my head. "I can't afford to waste any more time. Although"—I look down at myself—"maybe I should take a shower first? Put on some real clothes?"

I try to smile at him again, to convince him that I'm feeling fine, but he seems unable to speak. He just looks at me, his eyes red-rimmed and raw. If I didn't know him any better I'd think he'd been crying.

I'm just about to ask him what's wrong, when he says "Sweetheart."

and for some reason I hold my breath.

"I have to talk to you," he says.

He whispers it, actually.

"Okay," I say, and exhale. "Talk to me."

"Not here."

I feel my stomach flip. My instincts tell me to panic. "Is everything okay?"

It takes him a long time to say, "I don't know."

I stare at him, confused.

He stares back, his eyes such a pale green in the light

that, for a moment, he doesn't even seem human. He says nothing more.

I take a deep breath. Try to be calm. "Okay," I say. "Okay. But if we're going to go back to the room, can I at least shower first? I'd really like to get all this sand and dried blood off my body."

He nods. Still no emotion.

And now I'm really beginning to panic.

WARNER

I'm pacing the length of the hall just outside of our room, impatiently waiting for Juliette to finish her shower. My mind is ravaged. Hysteria has been clawing at my insides for hours. I have no idea what she'll say to me. How she'll react to what I need to tell her. And I'm so horrified by what I'm about to do that I don't even hear someone calling my name until they've touched me.

I spin around too fast, my reflexes faster than even my mind. I've got his hand pinched up at the wrist and wound behind his back and I've slammed him chest-first into the wall before I realize it's Kent. Kent, who's not fighting back, just laughing and telling me to let go of him.

I do.

I drop his arm. Stunned. Shake my head to clear it. I don't remember to apologize.

"Are you okay?" someone else says to me.

It's James. He's still the size of a child, and for some reason this surprises me. I take a careful breath. My hands are shaking. I've never felt further from *okay*, and I'm too confused by my anxiety to remember to lie.

"No," I say to him. I step backward, hitting the wall behind me and slumping to the floor. "No," I say again, and this time I don't know who I'm speaking to.

"Oh. Do you want to talk about it?" James is still blathering. I don't understand why Kent won't make him stop.

I shake my head.

But this only seems to encourage him. He sits down beside me. "Why not? I think you should talk about it," he says.

"C'mon, buddy," Kent finally says to him. "Maybe we should give Warner some privacy."

James will not be convinced. He peers into my face. "Were you *crying*?"

"Why do you ask so many questions?" I snap, dropping my head in one hand.

"What happened to your hair?"

I look up at Kent, astounded. "Will you please retrieve him?"

"You shouldn't answer questions with other questions," James says to me, and puts a hand on my shoulder. I nearly jump out of my skin.

"Why are you touching me?"

"You look like you could use a hug," he says. "Do you want a hug? Hugs always make me feel better when I'm sad."

"No," I say, fast and sharp. "I do not want a *hug*. And I'm not sad."

Kent appears to be laughing. He stands a few feet away from us with his arms crossed, doing nothing to help the situation. I glare at him.

"Well you *seem* sad," James says.

"Right now," I say stiffly, "all I'm feeling is irritation."

"Bet you feel better though, huh?" James smiles. Pats my arm. "See—I told you it helps to talk about it."

I blink, surprised. Stare at him.

He's not exactly correct in his theory, but oddly enough, I do feel better. Getting frustrated just now, with him—it helped clear my panic and focus my thoughts. My hands have steadied. I feel a little sharper.

"Well," I say. "Thank you for being annoying."

"*Hey.*" He frowns. He gets to his feet, dusts off his pants. "I'm not annoying."

"You most certainly are annoying," I tell him. "Especially for a child your size. Why haven't you have learned to be quieter by now? When I was your age I only spoke when I was spoken to."

James crosses his arms. "Wait a second—what do you mean, *for a child my size*? What's wrong with my size?"

I squint at him. "How old are you? Nine?"

"I'm about to turn eleven!"

"You're very small for eleven."

And then he punches me. Hard. In the thigh.

"*Owwwwwww*," he cries, overzealous in his exaggeration of the simple sound. He shakes out his fingers. Scowls at me. "Why does your leg feel like *stone*?"

"Next time," I say, "you should try picking on someone your own size."

He narrows his eyes at me.

"Don't worry," I say to him. "I'm sure you'll get taller soon. I didn't hit my growth spurt until I was about twelve or thirteen, and if you're anything like me—"

Kent clears his throat, hard, and I catch myself.

"That is—if you're anything like, ah, your brother, I'm sure you'll be just fine."

James looks back at Kent and smiles, the awkward punch apparently forgotten. "I really hope I'm like my brother," James says, beaming now. "Adam is the best, isn't he? I hope I'm just like him."

I feel the smile break off my face. This little boy. He's also mine, *my brother*, and he may never know it.

"Isn't he?" James says, still smiling.

I startle. "Excuse me?"

"Adam," he says. "Isn't Adam the best? He's the best big brother in the world."

"Oh—yes," I say to him, clearing the catch in my throat. "Yes, of course. Adam is, ah, the best. Or some approximation thereof. In any case, you're very lucky to have him."

Kent shoots me a look, but says nothing.

"I know," James says, undeterred. "I got really lucky."

I nod. Feel something twist in my gut. I get to my feet. "Yes, well, if you'll excuse me—"

"Yep. Got it." Kent nods. Waves good-bye. "We'll see you around, yeah?"

"Certainly."

"Bye!" James says as Kent tugs him down the hall. "Glad you're feeling better!"

Somehow I feel worse.

I walk back into the bedroom not quite as panicked as before, but more somber, somehow. And I'm so distracted I almost don't notice Juliette stepping out of the bathroom as I enter.

She's wearing nothing but a towel.

Her cheeks are pink from the shower. Her eyes are big and bright as she smiles as me. She's so beautiful. So unbelievably beautiful.

"I just have to grab some fresh clothes," she says, still smiling. "Do you mind?"

I shake my head. I can only stare at her.

Somehow, my reaction is insufficient. She hesitates. Frowns as she looks at me. And then, finally, moves toward me.

I feel my lungs malfunction.

"Hey," she says.

But all I can think about is what I have to say to her and how she might react. There's a small, desperate hope in my heart that's still trying to be optimistic about the outcome.

Maybe she'll understand.

"Aaron?" She steps closer, closing the gap between us. "You said you wanted to talk to me, right?"

"Yes," I say, whispering the word. "Yes." I feel dazed.

"Can it wait?" she says. "Just long enough for me to change?"

I don't know what comes over me.

Desperation. Desire. Fear.

Love.

It hits me with a painful force, the reminder. Of just how much I love her. God, I love all of her. Her impossibilities, her exasperations. I love how gentle she is with me when we're alone. How soft and kind she can be in our quiet moments. How she never hesitates to defend me.

I love her.

And she's standing in front of me now, a question in her eyes, and I can't think of anything but how much I want her in my life, forever.

Still, I say nothing. I do nothing.

And she won't walk away.

I realize, with a start, that she's still waiting for an answer.

"Yes, of course," I say quickly. "Of course it can wait."

But she's trying to read my face. "What's wrong?" she says.

I shake my head as I take her hand. Gently, so gently. She steps closer, and my hands close lightly over her bare shoulders. It's a small, simple movement, but I feel it when her emotions change. She trembles suddenly as I touch her, my hands traveling down her arms, and her reaction trips my senses. It kills me, every time, it leaves me breathless every time she reacts to me, to my touch. To know that she feels something for me. That she wants me.

Maybe she'll understand, I think. We've been through so much together. We've overcome so much. Maybe this, too, will be surmountable.

Maybe she'll understand.

"Aaron?"

Blood rushes through my veins, hot and fast. Her skin is soft and smells of lavender and I pull back, just an inch. Just to look at her. I graze her bottom lip with my thumb before my hand slips behind her neck.

"Hi," I say.

And she meets me here, in this moment, in an instant.

She kisses me without restraint, without hesitation, and wraps her arms around my neck and I'm overwhelmed, lost in a rush of emotion—

And the towel falls off her body.

Onto to the floor.

I step back, surprised, taking in the sight of her. My heart is pounding furiously in my chest. I can hardly remember what I was trying to do.

Then she steps forward, stands on tiptoe and reels me in, all warmth and heat and sweetness and I pull her against me, drugged by the feel of her, lost in the smooth expanse of her bare skin. I'm still fully clothed. She's naked in my arms. And somehow that difference between us only makes this moment more surreal. She's pushing me back gently, even as she continues to kiss me, even as she searches my body through this fabric and I fall backward onto the bed, gasping.

She climbs on top of me.

And I think I've lost my goddamned mind.

JULIETTE

This, I think, is the way to die.

I could drown in this moment and I'd never regret it. I could catch fire from this kiss and happily turn to ash. I could live here, die here, right *here*, against his hips, his lips. In the emotion in his eyes as he sinks into me, his heartbeats indistinguishable from mine.

This. Forever. This.

He kisses me again, his occasional gasps for air hot against my skin, and I taste him, his mouth, his neck, the hard line of his jaw and he fights back a groan, pulls away, pain and pleasure twining together as he moves deeper, harder, his muscles taught, his body rock solid against mine. He has one hand around the back of my neck, the other around the back of my thigh and he wraps us together, impossibly closer, overwhelming me with an extraordinary pleasure that feels like nothing I've ever known. It's nameless. Unknowable, impossible to plan for. It's different every time.

And there's something wild and beautiful in him today, something I can't explain in the way he touches me—the way his fingers linger along my shoulder blades, down the curve of my back—like I might evaporate at any moment, like this might be the first and last time we'll ever touch.

I close my eyes.

Let go.

The lines of our bodies have merged. It's wave after wave of ice and heat, melting and catching fire and it's his mouth on my skin, his strong arms wrapping me up in love and warmth. I'm suspended in midair, underwater, in outer space, all at the same time and clocks are frozen, inhibitions are out the window and I've never felt so safe, so loved or so protected than I have here, in the private fusion of our bodies.

I lose track of time.

I lose track of my mind.

I only know I want this to last forever.

He's saying something to me, running his hands down my body, and his words are soft and desperate, silky against my ear, but I can hardly hear him over the sound of my own heart beating against my chest. But I see it, when the muscles in his arms strain against his skin, as he fights to stay here, with me—

He gasps, out loud, squeezing his eyes shut as he reaches out, grabs a fistful of the bedsheets and I turn my face into his chest, trail my nose up the line of his neck and breathe him in and I'm pressed against him, every inch of my skin hot and raw with want and need and

"I love you," I whisper

even as I feel my mind detach from my body

even as stars explode behind my eyes and heat floods my

veins and I'm overcome, I'm stunned and overcome every time, every time

It's a torrent of feeling, a simultaneous, ephemeral taste of death and bliss and my eyes close, white-hot heat flashes behind my eyelids and I have to fight the need to call out his name even as I feel us shatter together, destroyed and restored all at once and he gasps

He says, *"Juliette—"*

I love the sight of his naked body.

Especially in these quiet, vulnerable moments. These brackets of time stapled between dreams and reality are my favorite. There's a sweetness in this hesitant consciousness—a careful, gentle return of form to function. I've found I love these minutes most for the delicate way in which they unfold. It's tender.

Slow motion.

Time tying its shoes.

And Warner is so still, so soft. So unguarded. His face is smooth, his brow unfurrowed, his lips wondering whether to part. And the first seconds after he opens his eyes are the sweetest. Some days I'm lucky enough to look up before he does. Today I watch him stir. I watch him blink open his eyes and orient himself. But then, in the time it takes him to find me—the way his face lights up when he sees me staring—that part makes something inside of me sing. I know everything, everything that ever matters, just by the way he looks at me in that moment.

And today, something is different.

Today, when he opens his eyes he looks suddenly disoriented. He blinks and looks around, sitting up too fast like he might want to run and doesn't remember how. Today, something is wrong.

And when I climb into his lap he stills.

And when I take his chin in my hands he turns away.

When I kiss him, softly, he closes his eyes and something inside him thaws, something unclenches in his bones, and when he opens his eyes again he looks terrified and I feel suddenly sick to my stomach.

Something is terribly, terribly wrong.

"What is it?" I say, my words scarcely making a sound. "What happened? What's wrong?"

He shakes his head.

"Is it me?" My heart is pounding. "Did I do something?"

His eyes go wide. "No, no, Juliette—you're perfect. You're—God, you're perfect," he says. He grips the back of his head, looks at the ceiling.

"Then why won't you look at me?"

So he meets my eyes. And I can't help but marvel at how much I love his face, even now, even in his fear. He's so classically handsome. So remarkably beautiful, even like this: his hair shorn, short and soft; his face unshaven, a silver-blond shadow contouring the already hard lines of his face. His eyes are an impossible shade of green. Bright. Blinking. And then—

Closed.

"I have to tell you something," he says quietly. He's looking down. He lifts a hand to touch me and his fingers trail down the side of my torso. Delicate. Terrified. "Something I should've told you earlier."

"What do you mean?" I fall back. I ball up a section of the bedsheet and hold it tightly against my body, feeling suddenly vulnerable.

He hesitates for too long. Exhales. He drags his hand across his mouth, his chin, down the back of his neck—

"I have no idea where to start."

Every instinct in my body is telling me to run. To shove cotton in my ears. To tell him to stop talking. But I can't. I'm frozen.

And I'm scared.

"Start at the beginning," I say, surprised I can even bring myself to speak. I've never seen him like this before. I can't imagine what he has to say. He's now clasping his hands together so tightly I worry he might break his own fingers by accident.

And then, finally. Slowly.

He speaks.

"The Reestablishment," he says, "went public with their campaigns when you were seven years old. I was nine. But they'd been meeting and planning for many years before that."

"Okay."

"The founders of the The Reestablishment," he says, "were once military men and women turned defense contractors. And they were responsible, in part, for the rise of the military industrial complex that built the foundation of the *de facto* military states composing what is now The Reestablishment. They'd had their plans in place for a long time before this regime went live," he says. "Their jobs had made it possible for them to have had access to weapons and technology no one had even heard of. They had extensive surveillance, fully equipped facilities, acres of private property, unlimited access to information—all for years before you were even born."

My heart is pounding in my chest.

"They'd discovered *Unnaturals*—a term The Reestablishment uses to describe those with supernatural abilities—a few years later. You were about five years old," he says, "when they made their first discovery." He looks at the wall. "That's when they started collecting, testing, and using people with abilities to expedite their goals in dominating the world."

"This is all really interesting," I say, "but I'm kind of freaking out right now and I need you to skip ahead to the part where you tell me what any of this has to do with me."

"Sweetheart," he says, finally meeting my eyes. "All of this has to do with you."

"How?"

"There was one thing I knew about your life that I never told you," he says. He swallows. He's looking into his hands when he says, "You were adopted."

The revelation is like a thunderclap.

I stumble off the bed, clutch the sheet to my body and

stand there, staring at him, stunned. I try to stay calm even as my mind catches fire.

"I was adopted."

He nods.

"So you're saying that the people who raised me—*tortured me*—are not my real parents?"

He shakes his head.

"Are my biological parents still alive?"

"Yes," he whispers.

"And you never told me this?"

No, he says quickly

No, no I didn't know they were still alive, he says

I didn't know anything except that you were adopted, he says, *I just found out, just yesterday, that your parents are still alive, because Castle*, he says, *Castle told me—*

And every subsequent revelation is like a shock wave, a sudden, unforeseen detonation that implodes within me—

BOOM

Your life has been an experiment, he says

BOOM

You have a sister, he says, *she's still alive*

BOOM

Your biological parents gave you and your sister to The Reestablishment for scientific research

and it's like the world has been knocked off its axis, like I've been flung from the earth and I'm headed directly for the sun,

like I'm being burned alive and somehow, I can still

hear him, even as my skin melts inward, as my mind turns inside-out and everything I've ever known, everything I ever thought to be true about who I am and where I come from

v a n i s h e s

I inch away from him, confused and horrified and unable to form words, unable to speak

And he says he *didn't know,* and his voice breaks when he says it, when he says he didn't know until recently that my biological parents were still alive, didn't know until Castle told him, never knew how to tell me that I'd been adopted, didn't know how I would take it, didn't know if I needed that pain, but Castle told him that The Reestablishment is coming for me, that they're coming to take me back

and your sister, he says

but I'm crying now, unable to see him through the tears and still I cannot speak and

your sister, he says, her name is Emmaline, she's one year older than you, she's very, very powerful, she's been the property of The Reestablishment *for twelve years*

I can't stop shaking my head

"Stop," I say

"No," I say

Please don't do this to me—

But he won't stop. He says I have to know. He says I have to know this now—that I have to know the truth—

STOP TELLING ME THIS, I scream

I didn't know she was your sister, he's saying,

I didn't know you had a sister

I swear I didn't know

"There were nearly twenty men and women who put together the beginnings of The Reestablishment," he says, "but there were only six supreme commanders. When the man originally chosen for North America became terminally ill, my father was being considered to replace him. I was sixteen. We lived here, in Sector 45. My father was then CCR. And becoming supreme commander meant he would be moving away, and he wanted to take me with him. My mother," he says, "was to be left behind."

Please don't say any more

Please don't say anything else, I beg him

"It was the only way I could convince him to give me his job," he says, desperate now. "To allow me to stay behind, to watch her closely. He was sworn in as supreme commander when I was eighteen. And he made me spend the two years in between—

"Aaron, please," I say, feeling hysterical, "I don't want to know—I didn't ask you to tell me— I don't want to know—"

"I perpetuated your sister's torture," he says, his voice raw, broken, "her confinement. I was ordered to oversee her continued imprisonment. I gave the orders that kept her there. Every day. I was never told why she was there or what was wrong with her. I was told to maintain her. That was it. She was allowed only four twenty-minute breaks from the water tank every twenty-four hours and she used to scream—she'd beg me to release her," he says, his voice catching. "She begged for mercy and I never gave it to her."

And I stop

Head spinning

I drop the sheet from my body as I run, run away

I'm shoving clothes on as fast as I can and when I return to the room, half wild, caught in a nightmare, I catch him half dressed, too, no shirt, just pants, and he doesn't even speak as I stare at him, stunned, one hand covering my mouth as I shake my head, tears spilling fast down my face and I don't know what to say, I don't know that I can ever say anything to him, ever again—

"It's too much," I say, choking on the words. "It's too much—it's too much—"

"*Juliette*—"

And I shake my head, hands trembling as I reach for the door and

"*Please*," he says, and tears are falling silently down his face, and he's visibly shaking as he says, "You have to believe me. I was young. And stupid. I was desperate. I thought I had nothing to live for then—nothing mattered to me but saving my mother and I was willing to do anything that would keep me here, close to her—"

"You lied to me!" I explode, anger squeezing my eyes shut as I back away from him. "You lied to me all this time, you've *lied* to me—about everything—"

"No," he says, all terror and desperation. "The only thing I've kept from you was the truth about your parents, I swear to you—"

"How could you keep that from me? All this time, all

this—*everything*—all you did was *lie to me*—"

He's shaking his head when he says *No, no, I love you, my love for you has never been a lie*—

"Then why didn't you tell me this sooner? Why would you keep this from me?"

"I thought your parents had died a long time ago—I didn't think it would help you to know about them. I thought it would only hurt you more to know you'd lost them. And I didn't know," he says, shaking his head, "I didn't know anything about your real parents or your sister, please believe me—I swear I didn't know, not until yesterday—"

His chest is heaving so hard that his body bows, his hands planted on his knees as he tries to breathe and he's not looking at me when he says, whispers, "I'm so sorry. I'm so, so sorry."

"Stop it—stop talking—"

"Please—"

"How—h-how can I ever—ever trust you again?" My eyes are wide and terrified and searching him for an answer that will save us both but he doesn't answer. He can't. He leaves me with nothing to hold on to. "How can we ever go back?" I say. "How can you expect me to forget all of this? That you lied to me about my parents? That you tortured my sister? There's so much about you I don't know," I say, my voice small and broken, "so much—and I can't—I can't do this—"

And he looks up, frozen in place, staring at me like he's finally understanding that I won't pretend this never happened, that I can't continue to be with someone I can't trust and I can see it, can see the hope go out of his eyes, his hand caught behind his head. His jaw is slack; his face is stunned, suddenly pale and he takes a step toward me, lost, desperate, pleading with his eyes

but I have to go.

I'm running down the hall and I don't know where I'm going until I get there.

WARNER

So this—

This is agony.

This is what they talk about when they talk about heartbreak. I thought I knew what it was like before. I thought I knew, with perfect clarity, what it felt like to have my heart broken, but now—now I finally understand.

Before? When Juliette couldn't decide between myself and Kent? That pain? That was child's play.

But this.

This is suffering. This is full, unadulterated torture. And I have no one to blame for this pain but myself, which makes it impossible to direct my anger anywhere but inward. If I weren't better informed, I'd think I were having an actual heart attack. It feels as though a truck has run over me, broken every bone in my chest, and now it's stuck here, the weight of it crushing my lungs. I can't breathe. I can't even see straight.

My heart is pounding in my ears. Blood is rushing to my head too quickly and it's making me hot and dizzy. I'm strangled into speechlessness, numb in my bones. I feel nothing but an immense, impossible pressure breaking apart my body. I fall backward, hard. My head is against the wall. I try to calm myself, calm my breathing. I try to be rational.

This is not a heart attack, I tell myself. *Not a heart attack.*

I know better.

I'm having a panic attack.

This has happened to me just once before, and then the pain had materialized as if out of a nightmare, out of nowhere, with no warning. I'd woken up in the middle of the night seized by a violent terror I could not articulate, convinced beyond a shadow of a doubt that I was dying. Eventually, the episode passed, but the experience never left me.

And now, this—

I thought I was prepared. I thought I had steeled myself against the possible outcome of today's conversation. I was wrong.

I can feel it devouring me.

This pain.

I've struggled with occasional anxiety over the course of my life, but I've generally been able to manage it. In the past, my experiences had always been associated with this work. With my father. But the older I got, the less powerless I became, and I found ways to manage my triggers; I found the safe spaces in my mind; I educated myself in cognitive behavioral therapies; and with time, I learned to cope. The anxiety came on with far less weight and frequency. But very rarely, it morphs into something else. Sometimes it spirals entirely out of my control.

And I don't know how to save myself this time.

I don't know if I'm strong enough to fight it now, not when I no longer know what I'm fighting for. And I've just collapsed, supine on the floor, my hand pressed against the pain in my chest, when the door suddenly opens.

I feel my heart restart.

I lift my head half an inch and wait. Hoping against hope.

"Hey, man, where the hell are you?"

I drop my head with a groan. Of all the people.

"Hello?" Footsteps. "I know you're in here. And why is this room such a mess? Why are there boxes and bedsheets everywhere?"

Silence.

"Bro, where are you? I just saw Juliette and she was freaking out, but she wouldn't tell me why, and I know your punkass is probably hiding in here like a little—"

And then there he is.

His boots right next to my head.

Staring at me.

"Hi," I say. It's all I can manage at the moment.

Kenji is looking down at me, stunned.

"What in the fresh hell are you doing on the ground? Why aren't you wearing any clothes?" And then, "Wait— were you *crying*?"

I close my eyes, pray to die.

"What's going on?" His voice is suddenly closer than it was before, and I realize he must be crouching next to me. "What's wrong with you, man?"

"I can't breathe," I whisper.

"What do you mean, *you can't breathe*? Did she shoot you again?"

That reminder spears straight through me. Fresh, searing pain.

God, I hate him so much.

I swallow, hard. "Please. Leave."

"Uh, no." I hear the rustle of movement as he sits down beside me. "What is this?" he says, gesturing to my body. "What's happening to you right now?"

Finally, I give up. Open my eyes. "I'm having a panic attack, you inconsiderate ass." I try to take a breath. "And I'd really like some privacy."

His eyebrows fly up. "You're having a what-now?"

"Panic." I breathe. "Attack."

"What the hell is that?"

"I have medicine. In the bathroom. *Please*."

He shoots me a strange look, but does as I ask. He returns in a moment with the right bottle, and I'm relieved.

"This it?"

I nod. I've never actually taken this medication before, but I've kept the prescription current at my medic's request. In case of emergencies.

"You want some water with that?"

I shake my head. Snatch the bottle from him with shaking hands. I can't remember the right dosage, but as I so rarely have an attack this severe, I take a guess. I pop three of the pills in my mouth and bite down, hard, welcoming the vile, bitter taste on my tongue.

It's only several minutes later, after the medicine begins to work its magic, that the metaphorical truck is finally extricated from its position on my chest. My ribs magically restitch themselves. My lungs remember to do their job.

And I feel suddenly limp. Exhausted.

Slow.

I drag myself up, stumble to my feet.

"*Now* do you want to tell me what's going on here?" Kenji is still staring at me, arms crossed against his chest. "Or should I go ahead and assume you did something horrible and just beat the shit out of you?"

I feel so tired suddenly.

A laugh builds in my chest and I don't know where it's coming from. I manage to fight back the laugh, but fail to hide a stupid, inexplicable smile as I say, "You should probably just beat the shit out of me."

It was the wrong thing to say.

Kenji's expression changes. His eyes are suddenly, genuinely concerned and I worry I've said too much. These drugs are slowing me down, softening my senses. I touch a hand to my lips, beg them to stay closed. I hope I haven't taken too much of the medicine.

"Hey," Kenji says gently. "What happened?"

I shake my head. Close my eyes. "What happened?" Now I actually laugh. "What happened, what happened." I open my eyes long enough to say, "Juliette broke up with me."

"*What?*"

"That is, I think she did?" I stop. Frown. Tap a finger against my chin. "I imagine that's why she ran out of here screaming."

"But—why would she break up with you? Why was she crying?"

At this, I laugh again. "Because I," I say, pointing at myself, "am a monster."

Kenji looks confused. "And how is that news to anyone?"

I smile. He's funny, I think. Funny guy.

"Where did I leave my shirt?" I mumble, feeling suddenly numb in a whole new way. I cross my arms. Squint. "Hmm? Have you seen it anywhere?"

"Bro, are you drunk?"

"What?" I slap at the air. Laugh. "I don't drink. My father is an alcoholic, didn't you know? I don't touch the stuff. No, wait"—I hold up a finger—"*was* an alcoholic. My father *was* an alcoholic. He's dead now. Quite dead."

And then I hear Kenji gasp. It's loud and strange and he whispers, "*Holy shit*," and it's enough to sharpen my senses for a second.

I turn around to face him.

He looks terrified.

"What is it?" I say, annoyed.

"What happened to your back?"

"Oh." I look away, newly irritated. "That." The many, many scars that make up the disfiguration of my entire back. I take a deep breath. Exhale. "Those are just, you know, birthday gifts from dear old dad."

"Birthday gifts from your *dad*?" Kenji blinks, fast. Looks around, speaks to the air. "What the hell kind of soap opera did I just walk into here?" He runs a hand through his hair and says, "Why am I always getting involved in other people's personal shit? Why can't I just mind my own business? Why can't I just keep my mouth shut?"

"You know," I say to him, tilting my head slightly, "I've always wondered the same thing."

"Shut up."

I smile, big. Lightbulb bright.

Kenji's eyes widen, surprised, and he laughs. He nods at my face and says, "Aw, you've got dimples. I didn't know that. That's cute."

"Shut up." I frown. "Go away."

He laughs harder. "I think you took way too many of those medicine thingies," he says to me, picking up the bottle I left on the floor. He scans the label. "It says you're only supposed to take one every three hours." He laughs again. Louder this time. "Shit, man, if I didn't know you were in a world of pain right now, I'd be filming this."

"I'm very tired," I say to him. "Please go directly to hell."

"No way, freak show. I'm not missing this." He leans against the wall. "Plus, I'm not going anywhere until your drunkass tells me why you and J broke up."

I shake my head. Finally manage to find a shirt and put it on.

"Yeah, you put that on backward," Kenji says to me.

I glare at him and fall into bed. Close my eyes.

"So?" he says, sitting down next to me. "Should I get the popcorn? What's going on?"

"It's classified."

Kenji makes a sound of disbelief. "What's classified? Why you broke up is classified? Or did you break up over classified information?"

"Yes."

"Throw me a freaking bone here."

"We broke up," I say, pulling a pillow over my eyes, "because of information I shared with her that is, as I said, *classified*."

"What? Why? That doesn't make any sense." A pause. "Unless—"

"Oh good, I can practically hear the tiny gears in your tiny brain turning."

"You lied to her about something?" he says. "Something you should've told her? Something classified—about *her*?"

I wave a hand at nothing in particular. "The man's a genius."

"Oh, *shit*."

"Yes," I say. "Very much shit."

He exhales a long, hard breath. "That sounds pretty serious."

"I am an idiot."

He clears his throat. "So, uh, you really screwed up this time, huh?"

"Quite thoroughly, I'm afraid."

Silence.

"Wait—tell me again why all these sheets are on the floor?"

At that, I pull the pillow away from my face. "Why do you think they're on the floor?"

A second's hesitation and then,

"Oh, what—*c'mon*, man, what the hell." Kenji jumps off the bed looking disgusted. "Why would you let me sit here?" He stalks off to the other side of the room. "You guys are just—*Jesus*—that is just *not okay*—"

"Grow up."

"I *am* grown." He scowls at me. "But Juliette's like my sister, man, I don't want to think about that shit—"

"Well, don't worry," I say to him, "I'm sure it'll never happen again."

"All right, all right, drama queen, calm down. And tell me about this classified business."

JULIETTE

Run, I said to myself.

Run until your lungs collapse, until the wind whips and snaps at your tattered clothes, until you're a blur that blends into the background.

Run, Juliette, run faster, run until your bones break and your shins split and your muscles atrophy and your heart dies because it was always too big for your chest and it beat too fast for too long and run.

Run run run until you can't hear their feet behind you. Run until they drop their fists and their shouts dissolve in the air. Run with your eyes open and your mouth shut and dam the river rushing up behind your eyes. Run, Juliette.

Run until you drop dead.

Make sure your heart stops before they ever reach you. Before they ever touch you.

Run, I said.

—AN EXCERPT FROM JULIETTE'S JOURNALS IN THE ASYLUM

My feet pound against the hard, packed earth, each steady footfall sending shocks of electric pain up my legs. My lungs burn, my breaths coming in fast and sharp, but I push through the exhaustion, my muscles working harder than they have in a long time, and keep moving. I never used to be any good at this. I've always had trouble breathing. But I've been doing a lot of cardio and weight training since moving on base, and I've gotten much stronger.

Today, that training is paying off.

I've covered at least a couple of miles already, panic and rage propelling me most of the way through, but now I have to break through my own resistance in order to maintain momentum. I cannot stop. I will not stop.

I'm not ready to start thinking yet.

It's a disturbingly beautiful day today; the sun is shining high and bright, impossible birds chirping merrily in half-blooming trees and flapping their wings in vast, blue skies. I'm wearing a thin cotton shirt. Dark blue jeans. Another pair of tennis shoes. My hair, loose and long, waves behind me, locked in a battle with the wind. I can feel the sun warm my face; I feel beads of sweat roll down my back.

Could this possibly be real? I wonder.

Did someone shoot me with those poison bullets on purpose? To try and tell me something?

Or are my hallucinations an altogether different issue?

I close my eyes and push my legs harder, will myself to move faster. I don't want to think yet. I don't want to stop moving.

If I stop moving, my mind might kill me.

A sudden gust of wind hits me in the face. I open my eyes again, remember to breathe. I'm back in unregulated territory now, my powers turned fully on, the energy humming through me even now, in perpetual motion. The streets of the old world are paved, but pockmarked by potholes and puddles. The buildings are abandoned, tall and cold, electric lines strapped across the skyline like the staffs of unfinished songs, swaying gently in the afternoon light. I run under a crumbling overpass and down several cascading, concrete stairs manned on either side by unkempt palm trees and burned-out lampposts, their wrought-iron handrails rough and peeling paint. I turn up and down a few side streets and then I'm surrounded, on all sides, by the skeleton of an old freeway, twelve lanes wide, an enormous metal structure half collapsed in the middle of the road. I squint more closely and count three equally massive green signs, only two of which are still standing. I read the words—

405 SOUTH LONG BEACH

—and I stop.

I fall forward, elbows on my knees, hands clasped behind my head, and fight the urge to tumble to the ground.

Inhale.

Exhale.

Over and over and over

I look up, look around.

An old bus sits not far from me, its many wheels mired in a pool of still water, rotting, half rusted, like an abandoned child steeping in its own filth. Freeway signs, shattered glass, shredded rubber, and forgotten bumpers litter what's left of the broken pavement.

The sun finds me and shines in my direction, a spotlight for the fraying girl stopped in the middle of nowhere and I'm caught in its focused rays of heat, melting slowly from within, quietly collapsing as my mind catches up to my body like an asteroid barreling to earth.

And then it hits me—

The reminders like reverberations

The memories like hands around my throat

There it is

There she is

shattered again.

I'm curled into myself against the back of the filthy bus and I've got a hand clamped over my mouth to try and trap the screams but their desperate attempts to escape my lips are fighting a tide of unshed tears I cannot allow and—

breathe

My body shakes with unspent emotion.

Vomit inches up my oesophagus.

Go away, I whisper, but only in my head

go away, I say

Please *die*

I'd chained the terrified little girl of my past in some unknowable dungeon inside of me where she and her fears had been carefully stored, sealed away.

Her memories, suffocated.

Her anger, ignored.

I do not speak to her. I don't dare look in her direction. I *hate* her.

But right now I can hear her crying.

Right now I can see her, this other version of myself, I can see her dragging her dirty fingernails against the chambers of my heart, drawing blood. And if I could reach inside myself and rip her out of me with my own two hands, I would.

I would snap her little body in half.

I would toss her mangled limbs out to sea.

I would be rid of her then, fully and truly, bleached forevermore of her stains on my soul. But she refuses to die. She remains within me, an echo. She haunts the halls of my heart and mind and though I'd gladly murder her for a chance at freedom, I cannot. It's like trying to choke a ghost.

So I close my eyes and beg myself to be brave. I take deep breaths. I cannot let the broken girl inside of me inhale all that I've become. I cannot revert back to another version of myself. I will not shatter, not again, in the wake of an emotional earthquake.

But where do I even begin?

How do I deal with any of this? These past weeks had already been too much for me; too much to handle; too much to juggle. It's been hard to admit that I'm unqualified, that I'm in way over my head, but I got there. I was willing to recognize that all this—this new life, this new world—would take time and experience. I was willing to put in the hours, to trust my team, to try to be diplomatic. But now, in light of everything—

My entire life has been an experiment.

I have a sibling. A sister. And an altogether different set of parents, biological parents, who treated me no differently than my adoptive ones did, donating my body to research as if I were nothing more than a science experiment.

Anderson and the other supreme commanders have always known me. Castle has always known the truth about me. Warner knew I'd been adopted.

And now, to know that those I've trusted most have been lying to me—manipulating me—

Everyone has been *using me*—

It rips itself from my lungs, the sudden scream. It wrenches free from my chest without warning, without permission, and it's a scream so loud, so harsh and violent it brings me to my knees. My hands are pressed against the pavement, my head half bent between my legs. The sound of my agony is lost in the wind, carried off by the clouds.

But here, between my feet, the ground has fissured open.

I jump up, surprised, and look down, spin around. I suddenly can't remember if that crack was there before.

The force of my frustration and confusion sends me back to the bus, where I exhale and lean against the back doors, hoping for a place to rest my head—except that my hands and head rip through the exterior wall as though it were made of tissue, and I fall hard on the filthy floor, my hands and knees going straight through the metal underfoot.

Somehow this only makes me angrier.

My power is out of control, stoked by my reckless mind, my wild thoughts. I can't focus my energy the way Kenji taught me to, and it's everywhere, all around me, within and without me and the problem is, I don't care anymore.

I don't care, not right now.

I reach without thinking and rip one of the bus seats from its bolts, and throw it, hard, through the windshield. Glass splinters everywhere; a large shard hits me in the eye and several more fly into my open, angry mouth; I lift a hand to find slivers stuck in my sleeve, glittering like miniature icicles. I spit the spare bits from my mouth. Remove the glass shards from my shirt. And then I pull an inch-long piece of glass out of the inside of my eyelid and toss it, with a small clatter, to the ground.

My chest is heaving.

What, I think, as I rip another seat from its bolts, *do I do now?* I throw this seat straight through a window, shattering more glass and ripping open more metal innards. Instinct alone moves my arm up to protect my face from the flying debris, but I don't flinch. I'm too angry to care. I'm too powerful at the moment to feel pain. Glass ricochets off my body. Razor-thin ribbons of steel bounce off my skin. I almost wish I felt something. Anything.

What do I do?

I punch the wall and there's no relief in it; my hand goes straight through. I kick a chair and there's no comfort in it; my foot rips through the cheap upholstery. I scream again, half outrage, half heartbreak, and watch this time as a long, dangerous crack forms along the ceiling.

That's new.

And I've hardly had time to think the thought when the bus gives a sudden, lurching heave, yawns itself into a deep shudder, and splits clean in half.

The two halves collapse on either side of me, tripping me backward. I fall into a pile of shredded metal and wet, dirty glass and, stunned, I stumble up to my feet.

I don't know what just happened.

I knew I was able to project my abilities—my strength, for certain—but I didn't know that there was any projectional power in my voice. Old impulses make me wish I had someone to discuss this with. But I have no one to talk to anymore.

Warner is out of the question.

Castle is complicit.

And Kenji—*what about Kenji?* Did he know about my parents—my sister—too? Surely, Castle would've told him?

The problem is, I can't be sure of anything anymore.

There's no one left to trust.

But those words—that simple thought—suddenly inspires

in me a memory. It's something hazy I have to reach for. I wrap my hands around it and pull. A voice? A female voice, I remember now. Telling me—

I gasp.

It was Nazeera. Last night. In the medical wing. It was her. I remember her voice now—I remember reaching out and touching her hand, I remember the feel of the metal knuckles she's always wearing and she said—

"*. . . the people you trust are lying to you—and the other supreme commanders only want to kill you . . .*"

I spin around too fast, searching for something I cannot name.

Nazeera was trying to warn me. Last night—she's barely known me and she was trying to tell me the truth long before any of the others ever did—

But why?

Just then, something hard and loud lands heavily on the half-bent steel structure blocking the road. The old freeway signs shudder and sway.

I'm looking straight at it as it happens. I'm watching this in real time, frame by frame, and yet, I'm still so shocked by what I see that I forget to speak.

It's Nazeera, fifty feet in the air, sitting calmly atop a sign that says—

10 EAST LOS ANGELES

—and she's waving at me. She's wearing a loose, brown leather hood attached to a holster that fits snugly around her shoulders. The leather hood covers her hair and shades her eyes so that only the bottom half of her face is visible from where I stand. The diamond piercing under her bottom lip catches fire in the sunlight.

She looks like a vision from an unknowable time.

I still have no idea what to say.

Naturally, she does not share my problem.

"You ready to talk yet?" she says to me.

"How—how did you—"

"Yeah?"

"How did you get here?" I spin around, scanning the distance. *How did she know I was here? Was I being followed?*

"I flew."

I turn back to face her. "Where's your plane?"

She laughs and jumps off the freeway sign. It's a long, hard fall that would've injured any normal person. "I really hope you're joking," she says to me, and then grabs me around the waist and leaps up, into the sky.

WARNER

I've seen a lot of strange things in my life, but I never thought I'd have the pleasure of seeing Kishimoto shut his mouth for longer than five minutes. And yet, here we are. In any other situation, I might be relishing this moment. Sadly, I'm unable to enjoy even this small pleasure.

His silence is unnerving.

It's been fifteen minutes since I finished sharing with him the same details I shared with Juliette earlier today, and he hasn't said a word. He's sitting quietly in the corner, his head pressed against the wall, face in a frown, and he will not speak. He only stares, his eyes narrowed at some invisible point across the room.

Occasionally he sighs.

We've been here for almost two hours, just he and I. Talking. And of all the things I thought would happen today, I certainly did not think it would involve Juliette running away from me, and my befriending this idiot.

Oh, the best-laid plans.

Finally, after what feels like a tremendous amount of time, he speaks.

"I can't believe Castle didn't tell me," is the first thing he says.

"We all have our secrets."

He looks up, looks me in the eye. It's not pleasant. "You have any more secrets I should know about?"

"None you should know about, no."

He laughs, but it sounds sad. "You don't even realize what you're doing, do you?"

"Realize what?"

"You're setting yourself up for a lifetime of pain, bro. You can't keep living like this. This," he says, pointing at my face, "this old you? This messed-up dude who never talks and never smiles and never says anything nice and never allows anyone to really know him—you can't be this guy if you want to be in any kind of relationship."

I raise an eyebrow.

He shakes his head. "You just can't, man. You can't be with someone and keep that many secrets from them."

"It's never stopped me before."

Here, Kenji hesitates. His eyes widen, just a little. "What do you mean, *before*?"

"Before," I say. "In other relationships."

"So, uh, you've been in other relationships? Before Juliette?"

I tilt my head at him. "You find that hard to believe."

"I'm still trying to wrap my head around the fact that you have *feelings*, so yeah, I find that hard to believe."

I clear my throat very quietly. Look away.

"So—umm—you, uh"—he laughs, nervously—"I'm sorry but, like, does Juliette know you've been in other relationships? Because she's never mentioned anything about that, and I think that would've been, like, I don't know? Relevant?"

I turn to face him. "No."

"No, what?"

"No, she doesn't know."

"Why not?"

"She's never asked."

Kenji gapes at me. "I'm sorry—but are you—I mean, are you actually as stupid as you sound? Or are you just messing with me right now?"

"I'm nearly twenty years old," I say to him, irritated. "Do you really think it so strange that I've been with other women?"

"No," he says, "I, personally, don't give a shit how many women you've been with. What I think is strange is that you never told your *girlfriend* that you've been with other women. And to be perfectly honest it's making me wonder whether your relationship wasn't already headed to hell."

"You have no idea what you're talking about." My eyes flash. "I *love* her. I never would've done anything to hurt her."

"They why would you lie to her?"

"Why do you keep pressing this? Who cares if I've been with other women? They meant nothing to me—"

"You're messed up in the head, man."

I close my eyes, feeling suddenly exhausted. "Of all the things I've shared with you today, *this* is the issue you're most interested in discussing?"

"I just think it's important, you know, if you and J ever try to repair this damage. You have to get your shit together."

"What do you mean, *repair this damage*?" I say, my eyes flying open. "I've already lost her. The damage is done."

At this, he looks surprised. "So that's it? You're just going to walk away? All this talk of *I love her* blah blah and that's it?"

"She doesn't want to be with me. I won't try to convince her she's wrong."

Kenji laughs. "Damn," he says. "I think you might need to get your bolts tightened."

"I beg your pardon?"

He gets to his feet. "Whatever, bro. Your life. Your business. I liked you better when you were drunk on your meds."

"Tell me something, Kishimoto—"

"What?"

"Why would I take relationship advice from *you*? What do you know about relationships aside from the fact that you've never been in one?"

A muscle twitches in his jaw. "Wow." He nods, looks away. "You know what?" He gives me the finger. "Don't pretend to know shit about me, man. You don't know me."

"You don't know me, either."

"I know that you're an *idiot*."

I suddenly, inexplicably, shut down.

My face pales. I feel unsteady. I don't have any fight left in me today and I don't have any interest in defending myself. I *am* an idiot. I know who I am. The terrible things I've done. It's indefensible.

"You're right," I say, but I say it quietly. "And I'm sure you're right that there's a great deal I don't know about you, too."

Something in Kenji seems to relax.

His eyes are sympathetic when he says, "I really don't think you have to lose her. Not like this. Not over this. What you did was, like—yeah, that shit was beyond horrible. Torturing her freaking sister? I mean. Yeah. Absolutely. Like, ten out of ten you'll probably go to hell for that."

I flinch.

"But that happened before you knew her, right? Before all this"—he waves a hand—"you know, whatever it is that happened between you guys happened. And I know her—I know how she feels about you. There might be something to save. I wouldn't lose hope just yet."

I almost crack a smile. I almost laugh.

I don't do either.

Instead, I say, "I remember Juliette telling me you gave a similar speech to Kent shortly after they broke up. That you spoke expressly against her wishes. You told Kent she still loved him—that she wanted to get back together with him. You told him the exact opposite of what she felt. And she was furious."

"That was different." Kenji frowns. "That was just . . . like . . . you know—I was just trying to help? Because, like, logistically the situation was really complicated—"

"I appreciate your trying to help me," I say to him. "But I will not beg her to return to me. Not if it's not what she wants." I look away. "In any case, she's always deserved to be with someone better. Maybe this is her chance."

"Uh-huh." Kenji lifts an eyebrow. "So if, like, tomorrow she hooks up with some other dude you're just gonna shrug and be like—I don't know? Shake the guy's hand? Take the happy couple out to dinner? Seriously?"

It's just an idea.

A hypothetical scenario.

But the possibility blooms in my mind: Juliette smiling, laughing with another man—

And then worse: his hands on her body, her eyes half closed with desire—

I feel suddenly like I've been punched in the stomach.

I close my eyes. Try to be steady.

But now I can't stop picturing it: someone else knowing her the way I've known her, in the dark, in the quiet hours before dawn—her gentle kisses, her private moans of pleasure—

I can't do it. I can't do it.

I can't breathe.

"Hey—I'm sorry—it was just a question—"

"I think you should go," I say. I whisper the words. "You should leave."

"Yeah—you know what? Yeah. Excellent idea." He nods several times. "No problem." Still, he doesn't move.

"What?" I snap at him.

"I just, uh"—he rocks back and forth on his heels—"I was wondering if you, uh, wanted any more of those medicine thingies though? Before I get out of here?"

"Get. Out."

"All right, man, no problem, yeah, I'm just gonna—"

Suddenly, someone is banging on my door.

I look up. Look around.

"Should I, um"—Kenji is looking at me, a question in his eyes—"you want me to get that?"

I glare at him.

"Yeah, I'll get it," he says, and runs to answer the door.

It's Delalieu, looking panicked.

It takes more than a concerted effort, but I manage to pull myself together.

"You couldn't have called, Lieutenant? Isn't that what our phones are for?"

"I've been trying, sir, for over an hour, but no one would answer your phone, sir—"

I roll my neck and sigh, stretching the muscles even as they tense up again.

My fault.

I disconnected my phone last night. I didn't want any distractions while I was looking through my father's files, and in the insanity of the morning I forgot to reconnect the line. I was beginning to wonder why I've had so much uninterrupted time to myself today.

"That's fine," I say, cutting him off. "What's the problem?"

"Sir," he says, swallowing hard, "I've tried to contact both you and Madam Supreme, but the two of you have been unavailable all day and, and—"

"What is it, Lieutenant?"

"The supreme commander of Europe has sent her daughter, sir. She showed up unannounced a couple of hours ago, and I'm afraid she's making quite a fuss about being ignored and I wasn't sure what to d-do—"

"Well, tell her to sit her ass down and wait," Kenji says, irritated. "What do you mean she's making a *fuss*? We've got shit to do around here."

But I've gone unexpectedly solid. Like the blood in my veins has congealed.

"I mean—right?" Kenji is saying, nudging me with his arm. "What's the deal, man? Delalieu," he says, ignoring me. "Just tell her to chill. We'll be down in a bit. This guy needs to shower and put his shirt on straight. Give her some lunch or something, okay? We'll be right there."

"Yes, sir," Delalieu says quietly. He's talking to Kenji, but flashes me another look of concern. I do not respond. I'm not sure what to say.

Things are happening too quickly. Fission and fusion in all the wrong places, all at once.

It's only once Delalieu has gone and the door is closed that Kenji finally says, "What was that about? Why do you look so freaked?"

And I unfreeze. Feeling returns slowly to my limbs.

I turn around to face him.

"You really think," I say carefully, "that I need to tell Juliette about the other women I've been with?"

"Uh, yeah," he says, "but what does that have to do with—"

I stare at him.

He stares back. His mouth drops open. "You mean—with this girl—the one downstairs—?"

"The children of the supreme commanders," I try to explain, squeezing my eyes shut as I do, "we—we all basically grew up together. I've known most of these girls all my life." I look at him, attempting nonchalance. "It was inevitable, really. It shouldn't be surprising."

But Kenji's eyebrows are high. He's trying to fight a smile as he slaps me on the back, too hard. "Oh, you are in for a world of pain, bro. A world. Of. Pain."

I shake my head. "There's no need to make this dramatic. Juliette doesn't have to know. She's not even speaking to me at the moment."

Kenji laughs. Looks at me with something that resembles pity. "You don't know anything about women, do you?" When I don't respond, he says, "Trust me, man, I bet you anything that wherever J is right now—out there somewhere—she already knows. And if she doesn't, she will soon. Girls talk about everything."

"How is that possible?"

He shrugs.

I sigh. Run a hand over my hair. "Well," I say. "Does it really matter? Don't we have more important things to contend with than the staid details of my previous relationships?"

"Normally? Yes. But when the supreme commander of North America is your ex-girlfriend, and she's already feeling really stressed about the fact that you've been lying to her? And then all of a sudden your other ex-girlfriend shows up and Juliette doesn't even *know* about her? And she realizes there are, like, a thousand other things you've lied to her about—"

"I never lied to her about any of this," I interject. "She never *asked*—"

"—and then our very powerful supreme commander gets, like, super, super pissed?" Kenji shrugs. "I don't know, man, I don't see that ending well."

I drop my head in my hands. Close my eyes. "I need to shower."

"And . . . yeah, that's my cue to go."

I look up, suddenly. "Is there anything I can do?" I say. "To stop this from getting worse?"

"Oh, so *now* you're taking relationship advice from me?"

I fight the impulse to roll my eyes.

"I don't really know man," Kenji says, and sighs. "I think, this time, you just have to deal with the consequences of your own stupidity."

I look away, bite back a laugh, and nod several times as I say, "Go to hell, Kishimoto."

"I'm right behind you, bro." He winks at me. Just once.

And disappears.

JULIETTE

~~There's something simmering inside of me.~~

~~Something I've never dared to tap into, something I'm afraid to acknowledge. There's a part of me clawing to break free from the cage I've trapped it in, banging on the doors of my heart begging to be free.~~

~~Begging to let go.~~

~~Every day I feel like I'm reliving the same nightmare. I open my mouth to shout, to fight, to swing my fists but my vocal cords are cut, my arms are heavy and weighted down as if trapped in wet cement and I'm screaming but no one can hear me, no one can reach me and I'm caught. And it's killing me.~~

~~I've always had to make myself submissive, subservient, twisted into a pleading, passive mop just to make everyone else feel safe and comfortable. My existence has become a fight to prove I'm harmless, that I'm not a threat, that I'm capable of living among other human beings without hurting them.~~

~~And I'm so tired I'm so tired I'm so tired I'm so tired and sometimes I get so angry~~

I don't know what's happening to me.

—AN EXCERPT FROM JULIETTE'S JOURNALS IN THE ASYLUM

We land in a tree.

I have no idea where we are—I don't even know if I've ever been this high, or this close to nature—but Nazeera doesn't seem bothered at all.

I'm breathing hard as I turn to face her, adrenaline and disbelief colliding, but she's not looking at me. She looks calm—happy, even—as she looks out across the sky, one foot propped up on a tree branch while the other hangs, swinging gently back and forth in the cool breeze. Her left arm rests on her left knee and her hand is relaxed, almost too casual, as it clenches and unclenches around something I can't see. I tilt my head, part my lips to ask the question when she interrupts me.

"You know," she says suddenly, "I've never, ever shown anyone what I can do."

I'm caught off guard.

"No one? Ever?" I say, stunned.

She shakes her head.

"Why not?"

She's quiet for a minute before she says, "The answer to that question is one of the reasons why I wanted to talk to you." She touches an absent hand to the diamond piercing at her lip, tapping the tip of one finger against the glittering stone. "So," she says. "Do you know anything real about your past?"

And the pain is swift, like cold steel, like knives in my chest. Painful reminders of today's revelations. "I know some things," I finally say. "I learned most of it this morning, actually."

She nods. "And that's why you ran off like you did."

I turn to face her. "You were watching me?"

"I've been shadowing you, yeah."

"Why?"

She smiles, but it looks tired. "You really don't remember me, do you?"

I stare at her, confused.

She sighs. Swings both her legs under her and looks out into the distance. "Never mind."

"No, wait—what do you mean? Am I supposed to remember you?"

She shakes her head.

"I don't understand," I say.

"Forget it," she says. "It's nothing. You just look really familiar, and for a split second I thought we'd met before."

"Oh," I say. "Okay." But now she won't look at me, and I have a strange feeling she's holding something back.

Still, she says nothing.

She looks lost in thought, chewing on her lip as she looks off in the distance, and doesn't say anything for what feels like a long time.

"Um. Excuse me? You put me in a *tree*," I finally say. "What the hell am I doing here? What do you want?"

She turns to face me. That's when I realize that the object in her hand is actually a bag of little hard candies. She holds it out to me, indicating with her head that I should take one.

But I don't trust her. "No thanks," I say.

She shrugs. Unwraps one of the colorful candies and pops it in her mouth. "So," she says. "What'd Warner tell you today?"

"Why do you want to know?"

"Did he tell you that you have a sister?"

I feel a knot of anger beginning to form in my chest. I say nothing.

"I'll take that as a yes," she says. She bites down hard on the candy in her mouth. Crunches quietly beside me. "Did he tell you anything else?"

"What do you want from me?" I say. "Who are you?"

"What did he tell you about your parents?" she asks, ignoring me even as she glances at me out of the corner of her eye. "Did he tell you that you were adopted? That your biological parents are still alive?"

I only stare at her.

She tilts her head. Studies me. "Did he tell you their names?"

My eyes widen automatically.

Nazeera smiles, and the action brightens her face. "There it is," she says, with a triumphant nod. She peels another candy from its wrapper and pops it in her mouth. "Hmm."

"There *what* is?"

"The moment," she says, "where the anger ends, and the curiosity begins."

I sigh, irritated. "You know my parents' names?"

"I never said that."

I feel suddenly exhausted. Powerless. "Does everyone know more about my life than I do?"

She glances at me. Looks away. "Not everyone," she says. "Those of us with ranks high enough in The Reestablishment know a lot, yeah," she says. "It's our business to know. Especially *us*," she says, meeting my eyes for a second. "The kids, I mean. Our parents expect us to take over one day. But, no, not everyone knows everything." She smiles at something, a private joke shared only with herself, when she says, "Most people don't know shit, actually." And then, a frown. "Though I guess Warner knows more than I thought he did."

"So," I say. "You've known Warner for a long time."

Nazeera pushes her hood back a bit so I can better see her face, leans against a branch, and sighs. "Listen," she says quietly. "I only know what my dad told us about you guys, and I'm wise enough to the game now to know that most of the things I've heard are probably nonsense. But—"

She hesitates. Bites her lip and hesitates.

"Just say it," I tell her, shaking my head as I do. "I've already heard so many people tell me I'm crazy for falling for him. You wouldn't be the first."

"What? No," she says, and laughs. "I don't think you're crazy. I mean, I get why people might think he's trouble, but he's my people, you know? I knew his parents. Anderson made my own dad seem like a nice guy. We're all kind of messed up, that's true, but Warner's not a bad person. He's just trying to find a way to survive this insanity, just like the rest of us."

"Oh," I say. Surprised.

"Anyway," she says with a shrug, "no, I understand why you like him. And even if I didn't, I mean—I'm not blind." She raises a knowing eyebrow at me. "I get you, girl."

I'm still stunned. This might be the very first time I've heard anyone but myself make an argument for Warner.

"No, what I'm trying to say is that I think it might be a good time for you to focus on yourself for a little while. Take a beat. And anyway, Lena's going to be here any minute, so it's probably best for you to stay away from that situation for as long as you can." She shoots me another knowing look. "I really don't think you need any more drama in your life, and that whole"—she gestures to the air—"*thing* is bound to just—you know—get really ugly."

"What?" I frown. "What thing? What situation? Who's Lena?"

Nazeera's surprise is so swift, so genuine, I can't help but feel instantly concerned. My pulse picks up as Nazeera turns fully in my direction and says, very, very slowly, "Lena. Lena Mishkin. She's the daughter of the supreme commander of Europe."

I stare at her. Shake my head.

Nazeera's eyes widen. "Girl, what the hell?"

"What?" I say, scared now. "Who is she?"

"Who is she? Are you serious? She's Warner's *ex-girlfriend*."

I nearly fall out of the tree.

It's funny, I thought I'd feel more than this.

Old Juliette would've cried. Broken Juliette would've split open from the sudden impact of today's many heartbreaking revelations, from the depth of Warner's lies, from the pain of feeling so deeply betrayed. But this new version of me is refusing to react; instead, my body is shutting down.

I feel my arms go numb as Nazeera offers me details about Warner's old relationship—details I do and don't want to hear. She says Lena and Warner were a big deal for the world of The Reestablishment and suddenly three fingers on my right hand begin to twitch without my permission. She says that Lena's mom and Warner's dad were excited about an alliance between their families, about a bond that would only make their regime stronger, and electric currents bolt down my legs, shocking and paralyzing me all at once.

She says that Lena was in love with him—really in love with him—but that Warner broke her heart, that he never treated her with any real affection and she's hated him for it, that "Lena's been in a rage ever since she heard the stories of how he fell for you, especially because you were supposed to be, like, fresh out of a mental asylum, you know? Apparently it was a huge blow to her ego" and hearing this does nothing to soothe me. It makes me feel strange and foreign, like a specimen in a tank, like my life was never my own, like I'm an actor in a play directed by strangers and I feel an exhalation of arctic wind blow steadily into my chest, a bitter breeze circling my heart and I close my eyes as frostbite eases my pain, its icy hands closing around the wounds festering in my flesh.

Only then

Only then do I finally breathe, luxuriating in the disconnection from this pain.

I look up, feeling broken and brand-new, eyes cold and unfeeling as I blink slowly and say, "How do you know all this?"

Nazeera breaks a leaf off a nearby branch and folds it between her fingers. She shrugs. "It's a small, incestuous circle we move in. I've known Lena forever. She and I were never close, exactly, but we move in the same world." Another shrug. "She was really messed up over him. It's all she ever wanted to talk about. And she'd talk to anyone about it."

"How long were they together?"

"Two years."

Two years.

The answer is so unexpectedly painful it spears through my new defenses.

Two years? Two years with another girl and he never said a word about it. Two years with someone else. *And how many others?* A shock of pain tries to reach me, to circumvent my new, cold heart, and I manage to fight the worst of it. Even so, a brick of something hot and horrible buries itself in my chest.

Not jealousy, no.

Inferiority. Inexperience. Naïveté.

How much more will I learn about him? How much more has he kept from me? How will I ever be able to trust him again?

I close my eyes and feel the weight of loss and resignation settle deep, deep within me. My bones shift, rearranging to make room for these new hurts.

This wave of fresh anger.

"When did they break up?" I ask.

"Like . . . eight months ago?"

Now I stop asking questions.

I want to become a tree. A blade of grass. I want to become dirt or air or nothing. *Nothing.* Yes. I want to become nothing.

I feel like such a fool.

"I don't understand why he never told you," Nazeera is saying to me now, but I can hardly hear her. "That's crazy. It was pretty big news in our world."

"Why have you been following me?" I change the subject with zero finesse. My eyes are half lidded. My fists are clenched. I don't want to talk about Warner anymore. Ever again. I want to rip my heart out of my chest and throw it in our piss-filled ocean for all the good its ever done me.

I don't want to feel anything anymore.

Nazeera sits back, surprised. "There's a lot going on right now," she says. "There's so much you don't know, so much crap you're just beginning to wade into. I mean—hell, someone tried to kill you yesterday." She shakes her head. "I'm just worried about you."

"You don't even know me. Why bother worrying about me?"

This time, she doesn't respond. She just looks at me. Slowly, she unwraps another candy. Pops it in her mouth and looks away.

"My dad forced me to come here," she says quietly. "I didn't want to have any part in any of this. I never have. I hate everything The Reestablishment stands for. But I told myself that if I had to be here, I would look out for you. So that's what I'm doing now. I'm looking out for you."

"Well, don't waste your time," I say to her, feeling callous. "I don't need your pity or your protection."

Nazeera goes quiet. Finally, she sighs. "Listen—I'm really sorry," she says. "I honestly thought you knew about Lena."

"I don't care about Lena," I lie. "I have more important things to worry about."

"Right," she says. She clears her throat. "I know. Still, I'm sorry."

I say nothing.

"Hey," Nazeera says. "Really. I didn't mean to upset you.

I just want you to know that I'm not here to hurt you. I'm trying to look out for you."

"I don't need you to look out for me. I'm doing fine."

Now she rolls her eyes. "Didn't I just save your life?"

I mumble something dumb under my breath.

Nazeera shakes her head. "You have to get it together, girl, or you're not going to get through this alive," she says to me. "You have no idea what's going on behind the scenes or what the other commanders have in store for you." When I don't respond she says, "Lena won't be the last of us to arrive here, you know. And no one is coming here to play nice."

I look up at her. My eyes are dead of emotion. "Good," I say. "Let them come."

She laughs, but there's no life in it. "So you and Warner have some drama and now you just don't care about anything? That's real mature."

Fire flashes through me. My eyes sharpen. "If I'm upset right now, it's because I've just discovered that everyone closest to me has been *lying* to me. Using me. Manipulating me for their own needs. My parents," I say angrily, "are still *alive*, and apparently they're no better than the abusive monsters who adopted me. I have a sister being actively tortured by The Reestablishment—and I never even knew she existed. I'm trying to come to terms with the fact that *nothing* is going to be the same for me, not ever again, and I have no idea who to trust or how to move forward. So yeah," I say, nearly shouting the words, "right now I don't care about *anything*. Because I don't know what I'm fighting for anymore. And I don't know who my friends are. Right now," I say, "everyone is my enemy, including *you*."

Nazeera is unmoved. "You could fight for your sister," she says.

"I don't even know who she is."

Nazeera shoots me a sidelong look, heavy with disbelief. "Isn't it enough that she's an innocent girl being tortured? I thought there was some greater good you were fighting for."

I shrug. Look away.

"You know what? You don't have to care," she says. "But I do. I care about what The Reestablishment has done to innocent people. I care that our parents are all a bunch of psychopaths. I care a great deal about what The Reestablishment has done, in particular, to those of us with abilities.

"And to answer your earlier question: I never told anyone about my powers because I saw what they did to people like me. How they locked them up. Tortured and abused them." She looks me in the eye. "And I don't want to be the next experiment."

Something inside me hollows. Mellows out. I feel suddenly empty and sad. "I do care," I finally say to her. "I care too much, probably."

And Nazeera's anger subsides. She sighs.

"Warner said The Reestablishment wants to take me back," I say.

She nods. "Seems about right."

"Where do they want to take me?"

"I'm not sure," she says. Shrugs. "They might just kill you."

"Thanks for the pep talk."

"Or," she says, smiling a little, "they'll send you to another continent, maybe. New alias. New facility."

"Another continent?" I say, curious despite myself. "I've never even been on a plane before."

Somehow, I've said the wrong thing.

Nazeera looks almost stricken for a second. Pain flashes in and out of her eyes and she looks away. Clears her throat. But when she looks back her face is neutral once more. "Yeah. Well. You're not missing much."

"Do you travel a lot?" I ask.

"Yep."

"Where are you from?"

"Sector 2. Asian continent." And then, at the look at my face: "But I was born in Baghdad."

"Baghdad," I say, almost to myself. It sounds so familiar, and I'm trying to remember, trying to place it on the map, when she says

"Iraq."

"*Oh*," I say. "Wow."

"A lot to take in, huh?"

"Yeah," I say quietly. And then—hating myself even as I say the words—I can't help but ask, "Where's Lena from?"

Nazeera laughs. "I thought you said you didn't care about Lena."

I close my eyes. Shake my head, mortified.

"She was born in Peterhof, a suburb of Saint Petersburg."

"Russia," I say, relieved to finally recognize one of these cities. *"War and Peace."*

"Great book," Nazeera says with a nod. "Too bad it's still on the burn list."

"Burn list?"

"To be destroyed," she says. "The Reestablishment has big plans to reset language, literature, and culture. They want to create a new kind of, I don't know," she says, making a random gesture with one hand, "universal humanity."

I nod, quietly horrified. I already know this. I'd first heard about this from Adam right after he was assigned to become my cellmate in the asylum. And the idea of destroying art—culture—everything that makes human beings diverse and beautiful—

It makes me feel sick to my stomach.

"Anyway," she says, "it's obviously a garbage, grotesque experiment, but we have to go through the motions. We were given lists of books to sort through, and we have to read them, write reports, decide what to keep and what to get rid of." She exhales. "I finally finished reading most of the classics a couple of months ago—but early last year they forced all of us to read *War and Peace* in five languages, because they wanted us to analyze how culture plays a role in manipulating the translation of the same text." She hesitates, remembering. "It was definitely the most fun to read in French. But I think, ultimately, it's best in Russian.

All other translations—especially the English ones—are missing that necessary . . . *toska*. You know what I mean?"

My mouth drops open a little.

It's the *way* she says it—like it's no big deal, like she's just said something perfectly normal, like anyone could read Tolstoy in five different languages and polish off the books in an afternoon. It's her easy, effortless self-assuredness that makes my heart deflate. It took me a month to read *War and Peace*. In *English*.

"Right," I say, and look away. "Yeah. That's, um, interesting."

It's becoming too familiar, this feeling of inferiority. Too powerful. Every time I think I've made progress in my life I seem to be reminded of how much further I still have to go. Though I guess it's not Nazeera's fault that she and the rest of these kids were bred to be violent geniuses.

"So," she says, clapping her hands together. "Is there anything else you want to know?"

"Yeah," I say. "What's the deal with your brother?"

She looks surprised. "Haider?" She hesitates. "What do you mean?"

"I mean, like"—I frown—"is he loyal to your dad? To The Reestablishment? Is he trustworthy?"

"I don't know if I'd call him trustworthy," she says, looking thoughtful. "But I think all of us have complicated relationships with The Reestablishment. Haider doesn't want to be here any more than I do."

"Really?"

She nods. "Warner probably doesn't consider any of us his friends, but Haider does. And Haider went through a really dark time last year." She pauses. Breaks another leaf off a nearby branch. Folds and refolds it between her fingers as she says, "My dad was putting a lot of pressure on him, forcing him through some really intense training—the details of which Haider still won't share with me—and a few weeks later he just started spiraling. He was exhibiting suicidal tendencies. Self-harming. And I got really scared. I called Warner because I knew Haider would listen to him." She shakes her head. "Warner didn't say a word. He just got on a plane. And he stayed with us for a couple of weeks. I don't know what he said to Haider," she says. "I don't know what he did or how he got him through it, but"—she looks off into the distance, shrugs—"it's hard to forget something like that. Even though our parents keep trying to pit us against each other. They're trying to keep us from getting too soft." She laughs. "But it's so much bullshit."

And I'm reeling, stunned.

There's so much to unpack here I don't even know where to begin. I'm not sure if I want to. All of Nazeera's comments about Warner just seem to spear me in the heart. They make me miss him.

They make me want to forgive him.

But I can't let my emotions control me. Not now. Not ever. So I force the feelings down, out of my head, and instead, I say, "Wow. And I just thought Haider was kind of a jerk."

Nazeera smiles. Waves an absent hand. "He's working on it."

"Does he have any . . . supernatural abilities?"

"None that I know of."

"Huh."

"Yeah."

"But you can fly," I say.

She nods.

"That's interesting."

She smiles, wide, and turns to face me. Her eyes are big and beautifully lit from the dappled light breaking through the branches, and her excitement is so pure that it makes something inside of me shrivel up and die.

"It's so much more than *interesting*," she says, and it's then that I feel a pang of something new:

Jealousy.

Envy.

Resentment.

My abilities have always been a curse—a source of endless pain and conflict. Everything about me is designed to kill and destroy and it's a reality I've never been able to fully accept. "Must be nice," I say.

She turns away again, smiling into the wind. "The best part?" she says. "Is that I can also do *this*—"

Nazeera goes suddenly invisible.

I jerk back sharply.

And then she's back, beaming. "Isn't it great?" she says, eyes glittering with excitement. "I've never been able to share this with anyone before."

"Uh . . . yeah." I laugh but it sounds fake, too high. "Very cool." And then, more quietly, "Kenji is going to be pissed."

Nazeera stops smiling. "What does he have to do with anything?"

"Well—" I nod in her general direction. "I mean, what you just did? That's Kenji's thing. And he's not good at sharing the spotlight, generally."

"I didn't know there could be someone else with the same power," she says, visibly heartbroken. "How is that possible?"

"I don't know," I say, and I feel a sudden urge to laugh. She's so determined to dislike Kenji that I'm starting to wonder why. And then I'm reminded, all at once, of today's horrible revelations, and the smile is wiped off my face. "So," I say quickly, "should we get back to base? I still have a ton of things to figure out, including how I'm going to deal with this stupid symposium tomorrow. I don't know if I should bail or just—"

"Don't bail." Nazeera cuts me off. "If you bail they might think you know something. Don't show your hand," she says. "Not yet. Just go through the motions until you get your own plan together."

I stare at her. Study her. Finally, I say, "Okay."

"And once you decide what you want to do, let me know. I can always help evacuate people. Hold down the fort. Fight. Whatever. Just say the word."

"What—?" I frown. "Evacuate people? What are you

talking about?"

She smiles as she shakes her head. "Girl, you still don't get it, do you? Why do you think we're here? The Reestablishment is planning on destroying Sector 45." She stares at me. "And that includes everyone in it."

WARNER

I never make it downstairs.

I've hardly had a second to put my shirt on straight when I hear someone banging on my door.

"I'm really sorry, bro," I hear Kenji shout, "she wouldn't listen to me—"

And then,

"Open the door, Warner. I promise this will only hurt a little."

Her voice is the same as it's always been. Smooth. Deceptively soft. Always a little rough around the edges.

"Lena," I say. "How nice to hear from you again."

"Open the door, asshole."

"You never did hold back with the flattery."

"I said *open the door*—"

Very carefully, I do.

And then I close my eyes.

Lena slaps me across the face so hard I feel it ring in my ears. Kenji screams, but only briefly, and I take a steadying breath. I look up at her without lifting my head. "Are you done?"

Her eyes go wide, enraged and offended, and I realize I've already pushed her too far. She swings without thinking, and even so, it's a punch perfectly executed. On impact she'd break, at the very least, my nose, but I can no longer entertain her daydreams of causing me physical harm. My reflexes are faster than hers—they always have been—and I catch her wrist just moments before impact. Her arm vibrates from the intensity of the unspent energy and she jerks back, shrieking as she breaks free.

"You son of a bitch," she says, breathing hard.

"I can't let you punch me in the face, Lena."

"I would do worse to you."

"And yet you wonder why things didn't work out between us."

"Always so cold," she says, and something in her voice breaks as she says it. "Always so cruel."

I rub the back of my head and smile, unhappily, at the wall. "Why have you come up to my room? Why engage me privately? You know I have little left to say to you."

"You never said *anything* to me," she suddenly screams. "Two years," she says, her chest heaving, "two years and you left a message with my *mother* telling her to let me know our relationship was over—"

"You weren't home," I say, squeezing my eyes shut. "I thought it more efficient—"

"You are a *monster*—"

"Yes," I say. "Yes, I am. I wish you'd forget about me."

Her eyes go glassy in an instant, heavy with unspent tears. I feel guilty for feeling nothing. I can only stare back at her, too tired to fight. Too busy nursing my own wounds.

Her voice is both angry and sad when she says, "Where's your new girlfriend? I'm dying to meet her."

At this, I look away again, my own heart breaking in my chest. "You should go get settled," I say. "Nazeera and Haider are here, too, somewhere. I'm sure you'll all have plenty to talk about."

"Warner—"

"Please, Lena," I say, feeling truly exhausted now. "You're upset, I understand. But it's not my fault you feel this way. I don't love you. I never have. And I never led you to believe I did."

She's quiet for so long I finally face her, realizing too late that somehow, again, I've managed to make things worse. She looks paralyzed, her eyes round, her lips parted, her hands trembling slightly at her sides.

I sigh.

"I have to go," I say quietly. "Kenji will show you to your quarters." I glance at Kenji and he nods, just once. His face is unexpectedly grim.

Still, Lena says nothing.

I take a step back, ready to close the door between us, when she lunges at me with a sudden cry, her hands closing around my throat so unexpectedly she almost knocks me over. She's screaming in my face, pushing me backward as she does, and it's all I can do to keep myself calm. My instincts are too sharp sometimes—it's hard for me to keep from reacting to physical threats—and I force myself to move in an almost liquid slow motion as I remove her hands from around my neck. She's still thrashing against me, landing several kicks at my shins when I finally manage to gentle her arms and pull her close.

Suddenly, she stills.

My lips are at her ear when I say her name once, very gently.

She swallows hard as she meets my eyes, all fire and rage. Even so, I sense her hope. Her desperation. I can feel her wonder whether I've changed my mind.

"Lena," I say again, even more softly. "Really, you must know that your actions do nothing to endear you to me."

She stiffens.

"Please go away," I say, and quickly close the door between us.

I fall backward onto my bed, cringing as she kicks violently at my door, and cradle my head in my hands. I have to stifle a sudden, inexplicable impulse to break something. My brain feels like it might split free of my skull.

How did I get here?

Unmoored. Disheveled and distracted.

When did this happen to me?

I have no focus, no control. I am every disappointment, every failure, every useless thing my father ever said I was. I am weak. I am a coward. I let my emotions win too often and now, now I've lost everything. Everything is falling apart. Juliette is in danger. Now, more than ever, she and I need to stand together. I need to talk to her. I need to warn her. I need to *protect* her—but she's gone. She despises me again.

And I'm here once more.

In the abyss.

Dissolving slowly in the acid of emotion.

JULIETTE

Loneliness is a strange sort of thing.

It creeps up on you, quiet and still, sits by your side in the dark, strokes your hair as you sleep. It wraps itself around your bones, squeezing so tight you almost can't breathe, almost can't hear the pulse racing in your blood as it rushes up your skin and touches its lips to the soft hairs at the back of your neck. It leaves lies in your heart, lies next to you at night, leaches the light out from every corner. It's a constant companion, clasping your hand only to yank you down when you're struggling to stand up, catching your tears only to force them down your throat. It scares you simply by standing by your side.

You wake up in the morning and wonder who you are. You fail to fall asleep at night and tremble in your skin. You doubt you doubt you doubt

do I

don't I

should I

why won't I

And even when you're ready to let go. When you're ready to break free. When you're ready to be brand-new. Loneliness is an old friend standing beside you in the mirror, looking you in the eye, challenging you to live your life without it. You can't find the words to fight yourself, to fight the words screaming that you're not enough never enough never ever enough.

Loneliness is a bitter, wretched companion.

Sometimes it just won't let go.

—AN EXCERPT FROM JULIETTE'S JOURNALS IN THE ASYLUM

The first thing I do upon my return back to base is order Delalieu to move all my things into Anderson's old rooms. I haven't really thought about how I'll deal with seeing Warner all the time. I haven't considered yet how to act around his ex-girlfriend. I have no idea what any of that will be like and right now I almost can't be bothered to care.

I'm too angry.

If Nazeera is to be believed, then everything we tried to do here—all of our efforts to play nice, to be diplomatic, to host an international conference of leaders—was for nothing. Everything we'd been working toward is garbage. She says they're planning on wiping out all of Sector 45. Every person. Not just the ones living at our headquarters. Not just the soldiers who stood alongside us. But all the civilians, too. Women, children—everyone.

They're going to make Sector 45 disappear.

And I'm feeling suddenly out of control.

Anderson's old quarters are enormous—they make Warner's rooms seem ridiculous in comparison—and after Delalieu has left me alone I'm free to drown in the many privileges that my fake role as supreme commander of The Reestablishment has to offer. Two offices. Two meeting rooms. A full kitchen. A large master suite. Three bathrooms. Two guest rooms. Four closets, fully stocked—like father, like son, I realize—and countless other details. I've never spent much time in any of these rooms before; the dimensions are too vast. I need only one office and, generally, that's where I spend my time.

But today I take the time to look around, and the one space that piques my interest most is one I'd never noticed before. It's the one positioned closest to the bedroom: an entire room devoted to Anderson's enormous collection of alcohol.

I don't know very much about alcohol.

I've never had a traditional teenage experience of any kind; I've never had parties to attend; I've never been subjected to the kind of peer pressure I've read about in novels. No one has ever offered me drugs or a strong drink, and probably for good reason. Still, I'm mesmerized by the myriad bottles arranged perfectly on the glass shelves lining the dark, paneled walls of this room. There's no furniture but two big, brown leather chairs and the heavily lacquered coffee table stationed between them. Atop the coffee table sits a clear—jug?—filled with some kind of amber liquid; there's a lone drinking glass set beside it. Everything in here is dark, vaguely depressing, and reeks of wood and something ancient, musty—*old*.

I reach out, run my fingers along the wooden panels, and count. Three of the four walls of the room are dedicated to housing various, ancient bottles—637 in total—most of which are full of the same amber liquid; only a couple of bottles are full of clear liquid. I move closer to inspect the labels and learn that the clear bottles are full of vodka—this is a drink I've heard of—but the amber liquid is named different things in different containers. A great deal of it is called Scotch. There are seven bottles of tequila. But most of what Anderson keeps in this room is called bourbon—523 bottles in total—a substance I have no knowledge of. I've only really heard about people who drink wine and beer and margaritas—and there's none of that here. The only wall stocked with anything but alcohol is stacked with several boxes of cigars and more of the same short, intricately cut drinking glasses. I pick up one of the glasses and nearly drop it; it's so much heavier than it looks. I wonder if these things are made of real crystal.

And then I can't help but wonder about Anderson's motivations in designing this space. It's such a strange idea, to dedicate an entire room to displaying bottles of alcohol. Why not put them in a cabinet? Or in a refrigerator?

I sit down in one of the chairs and look up, distracted by the massive, glittering chandelier hanging from the ceiling.

Why I've gravitated toward this room, I can't say. But in here I feel truly alone. Walled off from all the noise and confusion of the day. I feel properly isolated here, among these bottles, in a way that soothes me. And for the first time all day, I feel myself relax. I feel myself withdraw. Retreat. Run away to some dark corner of my mind.

There's a strange kind of freedom in giving up.

There's a freedom in being angry. In living alone. And strangest of all: in here, within the walls of Anderson's old refuge I feel I finally understand him. I finally understand how he was able to live the way he did. He never allowed himself to feel, never allowed himself to hurt, never invited emotion into his life. He was under no obligation to anyone but himself—and it liberated him.

His selfishness set him free.

I reach for the jug of amber liquid, tug off the stopper, and fill the crystal glass sitting beside it. I stare at the glass for a while, and it stares back.

Finally, I pick it up.

One sip and I nearly spit it out, coughing violently as some of the liquid catches in my throat. Anderson's drink of choice is disgusting. Like death and fire and oil and smoke. I force myself to take one quick gulp of the vile drink before setting it down again, my eyes watering as the alcohol works its way through me. I'm not even sure why I've done it—why I wanted to try it or what I'm hoping it'll do for me. I have no expectations of anything.

I'm just curious.

I'm feeling careless.

And the seconds skip by, my eyes fluttering open and shut in the welcome silence and I drag a finger across the seam of my lips, I count the many bottles again, and I'm just beginning to think the terrible taste of the drink wasn't really that bad when slowly, happily, a bloom of warmth reaches up from deep within me and unfurls individual rays of heat inside my veins.

Oh, I think

oh

My mouth smiles but it feels a little crooked and I don't mind, not really, not even that my throat feels a little numb. I pick up the still-full glass and take another large gulp of fire and this time I don't dread it. It's pleasant to be lost like this, to fill my head with clouds and wind and nothing. I feel loose and a little clumsy as I stand but it feels nice, it feels nice and warm and pleasant and I find myself wandering toward the bathroom, smiling as I search its drawers for something

something

where is it

And then I find it, a set of electric hair clippers, and I decide it's time to give myself a haircut. My hair has been bothering me forever. It's too long, too long, a memento, a keepsake from all my time in the asylum, too long from all those years I was forgotten and left to rot in hell, too thick, too suffocating, too much, too this, too that, too annoying

My fingers fumble for the plug but eventually I manage to turn the thing on, the little machine buzzing in my hand and I think I should probably take off my clothes first, don't want to get hair everywhere do I, so I should probably take my clothes off first, definitely

And then I'm standing in my underwear, thinking about how much I've always secretly wanted to do this, how I always thought it would feel so nice, so liberating—

And I drag the clippers across my head in a slightly jagged motion.

Once.

Twice.

Over and over and over and I'm laughing as my hair falls to the floor, a sea of too-long brown waves lapping at my feet and I've never felt so light, so silly silly happy

I drop the still-buzzing clippers in the sink and step back, admiring my work in the mirror as I touch my newly shorn head. I have the same haircut as Warner now. The same sharp half inch of hair, except my hair is dark where his is light and I look so much older suddenly. Harsher. Serious. I have cheekbones. A jawline. I look angry and a little scary. My eyes are bright, huge in my face, the center of attention, wide and sharp and piercing and I love it.

I love it.

I'm still giggling as I teeter down the hall, wandering Anderson's rooms in my underwear, feeling freer than I have in years. I flop down onto the big leather chair and finish the rest of the glass in two swift gulps.

Years, centuries, lifetimes pass and dimly, I hear the sound of banging.

I ignore it.

I'm sideways on the chair now, my legs flung over the arm, leaning back to watch the chandelier spin—

Was it spinning before?

—and too soon my reverie is interrupted, too soon I hear

a rush of voices I vaguely recognize and I don't move, merely squint, turning only my head toward the sounds.

"Oh shit, J—"

Kenji charges into the room and freezes in place at the sight of me. I suddenly, faintly remember that I'm in my underwear, and that another version of myself would prefer not to have Kenji see me like this—but it's not enough to motivate me to move. Kenji, however, seems very concerned.

"Oh *shit shit shit*—"

It's only then that I notice he's not alone.

Kenji and Warner are standing in front of me, the two of them staring at me like they're horrified, like I've done something wrong, and it makes me angry.

"What?" I say, annoyed. "Go away."

"Juliette—love—what did you do—"

And then Warner is kneeling beside me. I try to look at him but it's suddenly hard to focus, hard to see straight at all. My vision blurs and I have to blink several times to get his face to stop moving but then I'm looking at him, really looking at him, and something inside of me is trying to remember that we are angry with Warner, that we don't like him anymore and we do not want to see him or speak to him but then he touches my face—

and I sigh

I rest my cheek against his palm and remember something beautiful, something kind, and a rush of feeling floods through me

"Hi," I say.

And he looks so sad so sad and he's about to respond but Kenji says, "Bro, I think she drank, like, I don't know, a whole glass of this stuff. Maybe half a pint? And at her weight?" He swears under his breath. "That much whisky would destroy *me*."

Warner closes his eyes. I'm fascinated by the way his Adam's apple moves up and down his throat and I reach out, trail my fingers down his neck.

"Sweetheart," he whispers, his eyes still closed. "Why—"

"Do you know how much I love you?" I say. "I love— loved you so much. So much."

When he opens his eyes again, they're bright. Shining. He says nothing.

"Kishimoto," he says quietly. "Please turn on the shower."

"On it."

And Kenji's gone.

Warner still says nothing to me.

I touch his lips. Lean forward. "You have such a nice mouth," I whisper.

He tries to smile. It looks sad.

"Do you like my hair?" I say.

He nods.

"Really?"

"You're beautiful," he says, but he can hardly get the words out. And his voice breaks when he says, "Why did you do this, love? Were you trying to hurt yourself?"

I try to answer but feel suddenly nauseous. My head spins. I close my eyes to steady the feeling but it won't abate.

"Shower's ready," I hear Kenji shout. And then, suddenly, his voice is closer. "You got this, bro? Or do you want me to take it from here?"

"No." A pause. "No, you can go. I'll make sure she's safe. Please tell the others I'm not feeling well tonight. Send my apologies."

"You got it. Anything else?"

"Coffee. Several bottles of water. Two aspirin."

"Consider it done."

"Thank you."

"Anytime, man."

And then I'm moving, everything is moving, everything is sideways and I open my eyes and quickly close them as the world blurs before me. Warner is carrying me in his arms and I bury my face in the crook of his neck. He smells so familiar.

Safe.

I want to speak but I feel slow. Like it takes forever to tell my lips to move, like it's slow motion when they do, like the words rush together as I say them, over and over again

"I miss you already," I mumble against his skin. "I miss this, miss you, miss you" and then he puts me down, steadies me on my feet, and helps me walk into the standing shower.

I nearly scream when the water hits my body.

My eyes fly open, my mind half sobered in an instant, as the cold water rushes over me. I blink fast, breathing hard as I lean against the shower wall, staring wildly at Warner through the warped glass. Water snakes down my skin, collects in my eyelashes, my open mouth. My shoulders slow their tremble as my body acclimates to the temperature and minutes pass, the two of us staring at each other and saying nothing. My mind steadies but doesn't clear, a fog still hanging over me even as I reach forward to turn the dial, heating the water by many degrees.

I can still see his face, beautiful even blurred by the glass between us, when he says, "Are you okay? Do you feel any better?"

I step forward, studying him silently, and say nothing as I unhook my bra and let it drop to the floor. There's no response from him save the slight widening of his eyes, the slight movement in his chest and I slip out of my underwear, kicking it off behind me and he blinks several times and steps backward, looks away, looks back again.

I push open the shower door.

"Come inside," I say.

But now he won't look at me.

"Aaron—"

"You're not feeling well," he says.

"I feel fine."

"Sweetheart, please, you just drank your weight in whisky—"

"I just want to touch you," I say. "Come here."

He finally turns to face me, his eyes moving slowly up my body and I see it, I see it happen when something inside of him seems to break. He looks pained and vulnerable and he swallows hard as he steps toward me, steam filling the room now, hot drops of water breaking on my bare hips and his lips part as he looks at me, as he reaches forward, and I think he might actually come inside when

    instead

    he closes the door between us and says

    "I'll be waiting for you in the living room, love."

WARNER

Juliette is asleep.

She emerged from the shower, climbed into my lap and promptly fell asleep against my neck, all the while mumbling things I know for certain she'll regret having said in the morning. It took every bit of my self-control to unhook her soft, warm figure from around me, but somehow I managed it. I tucked her into bed and left, the pain of peeling myself away from her not unlike what I imagine it'd be like to peel the skin off my own body. She begged me to stay and I pretended not to hear her. She told me she loved me and I couldn't bring myself to respond.

She cried, even with her eyes closed.

But I can't trust that she knows what she's doing or saying in this compromised state; no, I know better. She has no experience with alcohol, but I can only imagine that when her good sense is returned to her in the daylight, she will not want to see my face. She won't want to know that she made herself so vulnerable in front of me. I wonder whether she'll even remember what happened.

As for me, I am beyond despair.

It's past three in the morning and I feel as though I've not slept in days. I can hardly bear to close my eyes; I can't be left alone with my mind or the many frailties of my person. I feel shattered, held together by nothing but necessity.

I have tried in vain to articulate the mess of emotion cluttering my mind—to Kenji, who wanted to know what happened after he left; to Castle, who cornered me not three hours ago, demanding to know what I'd said to her; even to Kent, who managed to look only a little pleased upon discovering that my brand-new relationship had already imploded.

I want to sink into the earth.

I can't go back to our bedroom—my bedroom—where the proof of her is still fresh, too alive; and I can no longer escape to the simulation chambers, as the soldiers are still stationed there, relocated in all the aftermath of the new construction.

I've no reprieve from the consequences of my actions.

Nowhere to rest my head for longer than a moment before I'm discovered and duly chastened.

Lena, laughing loudly in my face as I walked past her in the hall.

Nazeera shaking her head as I bid good night to her brother.

Sonya and Sara shooting me mournful looks upon discovering me crouched in a corner of the unfinished medical wing. Brendan, Winston, Lily, Alia, and Ian popping their heads out of their brand-new bedrooms, stopping me as I tried to get away, asking so many questions—so loudly and forcefully—that even a groggy James came to find me, tugging at my sleeve and asking me over and over again whether or not Juliette was okay.

Where did this life come from?

Who are all these people to whom I'm suddenly beholden?

Everyone is so justifiably concerned about Juliette—about the well-being of our new supreme commander—that I, because I am complicit in her suffering, am safe nowhere from prying eyes, questioning looks, and pitying faces. It's alarming, having so many people privy to my private life. When things were good between us I had to answer fewer questions; I was a subject of lesser interest. Juliette was the one who maintained these relationships; they were not for me. I never wanted any of this. I didn't want this accountability. I don't care for the responsibility of friendships. I only wanted Juliette. I wanted her love, her heart, her arms around me. And this was part of the price I paid for her affection: these people. Their questions. Their unvarnished scorn for my existence.

So. I've become a wraith.

I stalk these quiet halls. I stand in the shadows and hold myself still in the darkness and wait for something. For what, I don't know.

Danger.

Oblivion.

Anything at all to inform my next steps.

I want renewed purpose, a focus, a job to do. And then all at once I'm reminded that I am the chief commander and regent of Sector 45, that I have an infinite number of things to oversee and negotiate—and somehow that's no longer enough for me. My daily tasks are not enough to distract my mind; my deeply regimented routines have been dismantled; Delalieu is struggling under the weight of my emotional erosion and I cannot help but think of my father again and again—

How right he was about me.

He's always been right.

I've been undone by emotion, over and over. It was emotion that prompted me to take any job—at any cost—to be nearer to my mother. It was emotion that led me to find Juliette, to seek her out in search of a cure for my mother. It was emotion that prompted me to fall in love, to get shot and lose my mind, to become a broken boy all over again—one who'd fall to his knees and beg his worthless, monstrous father to spare the girl he loved. It was emotion, my flimsy emotions that cost me everything.

I have no peace. No purpose.

How I wish I'd ripped this heart from my chest long ago.

Still, there is work to be done.

The symposium is now less than twelve hours away and I never had a chance to go over the details with Juliette. I didn't think things would turn out like this. I never thought that business would go on as usual after the death of my father. I thought a greater war was imminent; I thought for certain the other supreme commanders would come for us before we'd had even a chance to pretend we had true control of Sector 45. It hadn't occurred to me that they'd have more sinister plans in mind. It hadn't occurred to me to spend more time prepping her for the tedious formalities—these monotonous routines—embedded in the structure of The Reestablishment. But I should have known better. I should have expected this. *I could have prevented this.*

I thought The Reestablishment would fall.

I was wrong.

Our supreme commander has hours to prepare before having to address a room of the 554 other chief commanders and regents in North America. She will be expected to lead. To negotiate the many intricacies of domestic and international diplomacy. Haider, Nazeera, and Lena will all be waiting to send word back to their murderous parents. And I should be by her side, helping and guiding and protecting her. Instead, I have no idea what kind of Juliette will emerge from my father's rooms in the morning. I have no idea what to expect from her, how she will treat me, or where her mind will go.

I have no idea what's going to happen.

And I have no one to blame but myself.

JULIETTE

~~I am not insane. I am not insane. I am not insane. I am not insane.~~
~~I am not insane. I am not insane. I am not insane. I am not insane.~~
~~I am not insane. I am not insane. I am not insane. I am not insane.~~
~~I am not insane. I am not insane. I am not insane. I am not insane.~~
~~I am not insane. I am not insane. I am not insane. I am not insane.~~
~~I am not insane. I am not insane. I am not insane. I am not insane.~~
~~I am not insane. I am not insane. I am not insane. I am not insane.~~
~~I am not insane. I am not insane. I am not insane. I am not insane.~~
~~I am not insane. I am not insane. I am not insane. I am not insane.~~
~~I am not insane. I am not insane. I am not insane. I am not insane.~~
~~I am not insane. I am not insane. I am not insane. I am not insane.~~
~~I am not insane. I am not insane. I am not insane. I am not insane.~~
~~I am not insane. I am not insane. I am not insane. I am not insane.~~
~~I am not insane. I am not insane. I am not insane. I am not insane.~~
~~I am not insane. I am not insane. I am not insane. I am not insane.~~
~~I am not insane. I am not insane. I am not insane. I am not insane.~~
~~I am not insane. I am not insane. I am not insane. I am not insane.~~
~~I am not insane. I am not insane. I am not insane. I am not insane.~~
~~I am not insane. I am not insane. I am not insane. I am not insane.~~
~~I am not insane. I am not insane. I am not insane. I am not insane.~~
~~I am not insane. I am not insane. I am not insane. I am not insane.~~
~~I am not insane. I am not insane. I am not insane. I am not insane.~~
~~I am not insane. I am not insane. I am not insane. I am not insane.~~

~~I am not insane. I am not insane. I am not insane. I am not insane.~~
~~I am not insane. I am not insane. I am not insane. I am not insane.~~
~~I am not insane. I am not insane. I am not insane. I am not insane.~~
~~I am not insane. I am not insane. I am not insane. I am not insane.~~
~~I am not insane.~~I am not insane.

—AN EXCERPT FROM JULIETTE'S JOURNALS IN THE ASYLUM

When I open my eyes, everything comes rushing back to me.

The evidence is here, in this drumming, pounding headache, in this sour taste in my mouth and stomach—in this unbearable thirst, like every cell in my body is dehydrated. It's the strangest feeling. It's horrible.

But worse, worse than all that are the memories. Gauzy but intact, I remember everything. Drinking Anderson's bourbon. Lying in my underwear in front of Kenji. And then, with a sudden, painful gasp—

Stripping in the shower. Asking Warner to join me.

I close my eyes as a wave of nausea overtakes me, threatens to upend the meager contents of my stomach. Mortification floods through me with an almost breathtaking efficiency, manufacturing within me a feeling of absolute self-loathing I'm unable to shake. Finally, reluctantly, I squint open my eyes again and notice someone has left me three bottles of water and two small white pills.

Gratefully, I inhale everything.

It's still dark in this room, but somehow I know the day has broken. I sit up too fast and my brain swings, rocking in my skull like a weighted pendulum and I feel myself sway even as I remain motionless, planting my hands against the mattress.

Never, I think. *Never again. Anderson was an idiot. This is a terrible feeling.* And it's not until I make my way to the bathroom that I remember, with a sudden, piercing clarity, that I shaved my head.

I stand frozen in front of the mirror, remnants of my long, brown waves still littering the floor underfoot, and stare at my reflection in awe. Horror. Fascination.

I hit the light switch and flinch, the fluorescent bulbs triggering something painful in my newly stupid brain, and it takes me a minute to adjust to the light. I turn on the shower, letting the water warm while I study my new self.

Gingerly, I touch the soft buzz of what little hair I have left. Seconds pass and I get braver, stepping so close to the mirror my nose bumps the glass. So strange, so strange but soon my apprehension dulls. No matter how long I look at myself I'm unable to drum up appropriate feelings of regret. Shock, yes, but—

I don't know.

I really, really like it.

My eyes have always been big and blue-green, miniatures of the globe we inhabit, but I've never before found them particularly interesting. But now—for the first time—I find my own face interesting. Like I've stepped out of the shadows of my own self; like the curtain I used to hide behind has been, finally, pushed back.

I'm here. Right here.

Look at me, I seem to scream without speaking.

Steam fills the room in slow, careful exhalations that

cloud my reflection and eventually, I'm forced to look away. But when I do, I'm smiling.

Because for the first time in my life, I actually like the way I look.

I asked Delalieu to arrange to have my armoire moved into Anderson's quarters before I arrived yesterday—and I find myself standing before it now, examining its depths with new eyes. These are the same clothes I've seen every time I've opened these doors; but suddenly I'm seeing them differently.

But then, I *feel* differently.

Clothes used to perplex me. I could never understand how to piece together an outfit the way Warner did. I thought it was a science I'd never crack; a skill beyond my grasp. But I'm realizing now that my problem was that I never knew who I was; I didn't understand how to dress the imposter living in my skin.

What did I like?

How did I want to be perceived?

For years my goal was to minimize myself—to fold and refold myself into a polygon of nothingness, to be too insignificant to be remembered. I wanted to appear innocent; I wanted to be thought of as quiet and harmless; I was worried always about how my very existence was terrifying to others and I did everything in my power to diminish myself, my light, my soul.

I wanted so desperately to placate the ignorant. I wanted

so badly to appease the assholes who judged me without knowing me that I lost myself in the process.

But now?

Now, I laugh. Out loud.

Now, I don't give a shit.

WARNER

When Juliette joins us in the morning, she is almost unrecognizable.

I was forced, despite every inclination to bury myself in other duties, to rejoin our group today on account of what seems now to have been the inevitable arrival of our three final guests. The twin children of the South American supreme and the son of the supreme commander of Africa all arrived early this morning. The supreme commander of Oceania has no children, so I have to assume this is the last of our visitors. And all of them have arrived in time to accompany us to the symposium. Very convenient.

I should have realized.

I had just been in the middle of introducing the three of them to Castle and Kenji, who came down to greet our new visitors, when Juliette made her first appearance of the day. It's been less than thirty seconds since she walked in, and I'm still trying and failing to take her in.

She's *stunning*.

She's wearing a simple, fitted black sweater; slim, dark gray jeans; and a pair of flat, black, ankle-length boots. Her hair is both gone and not; it's like a soft, dark crown that suits her in a way I never could've expected. Without the distraction of her long hair my eyes have nowhere to focus but directly on her face. And she has the most incredible face—large, captivating eyes—and a bone structure that's never been more pronounced.

She looks shockingly different.

Raw.

Still beautiful, but sharper. Harder. She's not a girl with a ponytail in a pink sweater anymore, no. She looks a great deal more like the young woman who murdered my father and then drank four fingers of his most expensive Scotch.

She's looking from me to the stunned expressions of Kenji and Castle to the quietly confused faces of our three new guests, and all of us appear unable to speak.

"Good morning," she finally says, but she doesn't smile when she says it. There's no warmth, no kindness in her eyes as she looks around, and I falter.

"Damn, princess, is that really you?"

Juliette appraises Kenji once, swiftly, but doesn't respond.

"Who are you three?" she says, nodding at the newcomers. They stand slowly. Uncertainly.

"These are our new guests," I say, but now I can't bring myself to look at her. To face her. "I was just about to introduce them to Castle and Kishimo—"

"And you weren't going to include me?" says a new voice. "I'd like to meet the new supreme commander, too."

I turn around to find Lena standing in the doorway, not three feet from Juliette, looking around the room like she's never been so delighted in all her life. I feel my heart pick up, my mind racing. I still have no idea if Juliette knows who Lena is—or what we were together.

And Lena's eyes are bright, too bright, her smile wide and happy.

A chill runs through me.

With them standing so close together, I can't help but notice that the differences between her and Juliette are almost too obvious. Where Juliette is petite, Lena is tall. Juliette has dark hair and deep eyes, while Lena is pale in every possible way. Her hair is almost white, her eyes are the lightest blue, her skin is almost translucent, save the many freckles spanning her nose and cheeks. But what she lacks in pigment she makes up for in presence; she's always been loud, aggressive, passionate to a fault. Juliette, by comparison, is muted almost to an extreme this morning. She betrays no emotion, not a hint of anger or jealousy. She stands still and quiet, silently studying the situation. Her energy is tightly coiled. Ready to spring.

And when Lena turns to face her, I feel everyone in the room stiffen.

"Hi," Lena says loudly. False happiness disfigures her smile, morphing it into something cruel. She holds out her hand as she says, "It's nice to finally meet Warner's girlfriend." And then: "Oh, wait—I'm sorry. I meant *ex*-girlfriend."

I'm holding my breath as Juliette looks her up and down.

She takes her time, tilting her head as she devours Lena with her eyes and I can see Lena's offered hand beginning to tire, her open fingers starting to shake.

Juliette seems unimpressed.

"You can call me the supreme commander of North America," she says.

And then walks away.

I feel an almost hysterical laughter build in my chest; I have to look down, force myself to keep a straight face. And then I'm sobered, all at once, by the realization that Juliette is no longer mine. She's no longer mine to love, mine to adore. I've never been more attracted to her in all the time I've known her and there's nothing, nothing to be done about it. My heart pounds faster as she steps more completely into the room—a gaping Lena left in her wake—and I'm struck still with regret.

I can't believe I've managed to lose her. Twice.

That she loved me. Once.

"Please identify yourselves," she says to our three guests.

Stephan speaks first.

"I'm Stephan Feruzi Omondi," he says, reaching forward to shake her hand. "I'm here to represent the supreme commander of Africa."

Stephan is tall and dignified and deeply formal, and though he was born and raised in what used to be Nairobi, he studied English abroad, and speaks now with a British accent. And I can tell from the way Juliette's eyes linger on his face that she likes the look of him.

Something tightens in my chest.

"Your parents sent you to spy on me, too, Stephan?" she says, still staring.

Stephan smiles—the movement animating his whole face—and suddenly I hate him. "We're only here to say hello," he says. "Just a little friendly union."

"Uh-huh. And you two?" She turns to the twins. "Same thing?"

Nicolás, the elder twin, only smiles at her. He seems delighted. "I am Nicolás Castillo," he says, "son of Santiago and Martina Castillo, and this is my sister, Valentina—"

"*Sister?*" Lena cuts in. She's found another opportunity to be cruel and I've never hated her so much. "Are you still doing that?"

"Lena," I say, a warning in my voice.

"What?" She looks at me. "Why does everyone keep acting like this is normal? One day Santiago's son decides he wants to be a girl and we all just, what? Look the other way?"

"Eat shit, Lena," is the first thing Valentina has said all morning. "I should've cut off your ears when I had the chance."

Juliette's eyes go wide.

"Uh, I'm sorry"—Kenji pokes his head forward, waves a hand—"am I missing something?"

"Valentina likes to play pretend," Lena says.

"*Cállate la boca, cabrona,*" Nicolás snaps at her.

"No, you know what?" Valentina says, placing a hand on her brother's shoulder. "It's okay. Let her talk. Lena thinks I like to pretend, *pero* I won't be pretending *cuando cuelge su cuerpo muerto en mi cuarto.*"

Lena only rolls her eyes.

"Valentina," I say. "Please ignore her. *Ella no tiene ninguna idea de lo que está hablando. Tenemos mucho que hacer y no debemo—*"

"Damn, bro," Kenji cuts me off. "You speak Spanish, too, huh?" He runs a hand through his hair. "I'm going to have to get used to this."

"We all speak many languages," says Nicolás, a note of irritation still clinging to his voice. "We have to be able to communi—"

"Listen, guys, I don't care about your personal dramas," Juliette says suddenly, pinching the bridge of her nose. "I have a massive headache and a million things to do today, and I'd like to get started."

"*Por su puesto, señorita.*" Nicolás bows his head a little.

"What?" she says, blinking at him. "I don't know what that means."

Nicolás only smiles. "*Entonces deberías aprender como hablar español.*"

I almost laugh, even as I shake my head. Nicolás is being difficult on purpose. "*Basta ya,*" I say to him. "*Dejala sola. Sabes que ella no habla español.*"

"What are you guys saying?" Juliette demands.

Nicolás only smiles wider, his blue eyes crinkling in delight. "Nothing of consequence, Madam Supreme. Only that we are pleased to meet you."

"And I take it you'll all be attending the symposium today?" she says.

Another slight bow. "*Claro que sí.*"

"That's a yes," I say to her.

"What other languages do you speak?" Juliette says, spinning to face me, and I'm so surprised she's addressing me in public that I forget to respond.

It's Stephan who says, "We were taught many languages from a very young age. It was critical that the commanders and their families all knew how to communicate with one another."

"But I thought The Reestablishment wanted to get rid of all the languages," she says. "I thought you were working toward a single, universal language—"

"*Sí*, Madam Supreme," says Valentina with a slight nod. "That's true. But first we had to be able to speak with each other, no?"

Juliette looks fascinated. She's forgotten her anger for just long enough to be awed by the vastness of the world again; I can see it in her eyes. Her desire to escape. "Where are you from?" she asks, the question full of innocence; wonder. Something about it breaks my heart. "Before the world was remapped—what were the names of your countries?"

"We were born in Argentina," Nicolás and Valentina say at the same time.

"My family is from Kenya," says Stephan.

"And you've visited each other?" she says, turning to scan our faces. "You travel to each other's continents?"

We nod.

"Wow," she says quietly, but mostly to herself. "That must be incredible."

"You must come visit us, too, Madam Supreme," says a smiling Stephan. "We'd love to have you stay with us. After all, you are one of us now."

Juliette's smile vanishes. Gone too soon is the wistful, faraway look on her face. She says nothing, but I can sense the anger and sadness boiling over inside her.

Too suddenly, she says,

"Warner, Castle, Kenji?"

"Yeah?"

"Yes, Ms. Ferrars?"

I merely stare.

"If we're done here, I'd like to speak with the three of you alone, please."

JULIETTE

I keep thinking I need to stay calm, that it's all in my head, that everything is going to be fine and someone is going to open the door now, someone is going to let me out of here. I keep thinking it's going to happen. I keep thinking it has to happen, because things like this don't just happen. This doesn't happen. People aren't forgotten like this. Not abandoned like this.

This doesn't just happen.

My face is caked with blood from when they threw me on the ground and my hands are still shaking even as I write this. This pen is my only outlet, my only voice, because I have no one else to speak to, no mind but my own to drown in and all the lifeboats are taken and all the life preservers are broken and I don't know how to swim I can't swim I can't swim and it's getting so hard. It's getting so hard. It's like there are a million screams caught inside of my chest but I have to keep them all in because what's the point of screaming if you'll never be heard and no one will ever hear me in here. No one will ever hear me ever again.

I've learned to stare at things.

The walls. My hands. The cracks in the walls. The lines on my fingers. The shades of gray in the concrete. The shape of my fingernails. I pick one thing and stare at it for what must be hours. I keep time in my head by counting the seconds as they pass. I keep days in my head by writing them down. Today is day two. Today is the second day. Today is a day.

Today.

It's so cold. It's so cold it's so cold.

Please please please

—AN EXCERPT FROM JULIETTE'S JOURNALS IN THE ASYLUM

I'm still staring at the three of them, waiting for confirmation when, suddenly, Kenji speaks with a start.

"Uh, yeah—no, uh, no problem," he says.

"Certainly," says Castle.

And Warner says nothing at all, looking at me like he can see through me, and for a moment all I can remember is me, naked, begging him to join me in the shower; me, curled up in his arms crying, telling him how much I miss him; me, touching his lips—

I cringe, mortified. An old impulse to blush overtakes my entire body.

I close my eyes and look away, pivoting sharply as I leave the room without a word.

"Juliette, love—"

I'm already halfway down the hall when I feel his hand on my back and I stiffen, my pulse racing in an instant. The minute I spin around I see his face change, his features shifting from scared to surprised in less than a second and it makes me so angry that he has this ability, this gift of being able to sense other people's emotions, because I am always so transparent to him, so completely vulnerable and it's infuriating, *infuriating*

"What?" I say. I try to say it harshly but it comes out all wrong. Breathless. Embarrassing.

"I just—" But his hand falls. His eyes capture mine and suddenly I'm frozen in time. "I wanted to tell you—"

"What?" And now the word is quiet and nervous and terrified all at once. I take a step back to save my own life and I see Castle and Kenji walking too slowly down the hall; they're keeping their distance on purpose—giving us space to speak. "What do you want to say?"

But now Warner's eyes are moving, studying me. He looks at me with such intensity I wonder if he's even aware he's doing it. I wonder if he knows that when he looks at me like that I can feel it as acutely as if his bare skin were pressed against my own, that it does things to me when he looks at me like that and it makes me crazy, because I hate that I can't control this, that this thread between us remains unbroken and he says finally, softly,

something

something I don't hear

because I'm looking at his lips and feeling my skin ignite with memories of him and it was just yesterday, just yesterday that he was mine, that I felt his mouth on my body, that I could *feel him inside me*—

"What?" I manage to say, blinking upward.

"I said I really like what you've done with your hair."

And I hate him, hate him for doing this to my heart, hate my body for being so weak, for wanting him, missing him, despite everything and I don't know whether to cry or kiss him or kick him in the teeth, so instead I say, without meeting his eyes,

"When were you going to tell me about Lena?"

He stops then; motionless in a moment. "Oh"—he clears his throat—"I hadn't realized you'd heard about Lena."

I narrow my eyes at him, not trusting myself to speak, and I'm still deciding the best course of action when he says

"Kenji was right," but he whispers the words, and mostly to himself.

"Excuse me?"

He looks up. "Forgive me," he says softly. "I should've said something sooner. I see that now."

"Then why didn't you?"

"She and I," he says, "it was—we were nothing. It was a relationship of convenience and basic companionship. It meant nothing to me. Truly," he says, "you have to know— if I never said anything about her it was only because I never thought about her long enough to even consider mentioning it."

"But you were together for *two years*—"

He shakes his head before he says, "It wasn't like that. It wasn't two years of anything serious. It wasn't even two years of continuous communication." He sighs. "She lives in Europe, love. We saw each other briefly and infrequently. It was purely physical. It wasn't a real relationship—"

"*Purely physical*," I say, stunned. I rock backward, nearly tripping over my own feet and I feel his words tear through my flesh with a searing physical pain I wasn't expecting. "Wow. Wow."

And now I can think of nothing but his body and hers, the two of them entwined, the *two years* he spent naked in her arms—

"No—please," he says, the urgency in his words jolting me back to the present. "That's not what I meant. I'm just—I'm—I don't know how to explain this," he says, frustrated like I've never seen him before. He shakes his head, hard. "Everything in my life was different before I met you," he says. "I was lost and all alone. I never cared for anyone. I never wanted to get close to anyone. I've never—you were the first person to ever—"

"Stop," I say, shaking my head. "Just stop, okay? I'm so tired. My head is *killing* me and I don't have the energy to hear any more of this."

"Juliette—"

"How many more secrets do you have?" I ask. "How much more am I going to learn about you? About me? My family? My history? The Reestablishment and the details of my *real life*?"

"I swear I never meant to hurt you like this," he says. "And I don't want to keep things from you. But this is all so new for me, love. This kind of relationship is so new for me and I don't—I don't know how to—"

"You've already kept so much from me," I say to him, feeling my strength falter, feeling the weight of this throbbing headache unclench my armor, feeling too much, too much all at once when I say "There's so much I don't know about you. There's so much I don't know about your past. Our present. And I have no idea what to believe anymore."

"Ask me anything," he says. "I'll tell you anything you want to know—"

"Except the truth about me? My parents?"

Warner looks suddenly pale.

"You were going to keep that from me forever," I say to him. "You had no plan to tell me the truth. That I was adopted. Did you?"

His eyes are wild, bright with feeling.

"Answer the question," I say. "Just tell me this much." I step forward, so close I can feel his breath on my face; so close I can almost hear his heart racing in his chest. "Were you ever going to tell me?"

"I don't know."

"Tell me the *truth*."

"Honestly, love," he says, shaking his head. "In all likelihood, I would have." And suddenly he sighs. The action seems to exhaust him. "I don't know how to convince you that I believed I was sparing you the pain of that particular truth. I really thought your biological parents were dead. I see now that keeping this from you wasn't the right thing to do, but then, I don't always do the right thing," he says quietly. "But you have to believe that my intention was never to hurt you. I never intended to lie to you or to purposely withhold information from you. And I do think that I would have, in time, told you what I knew to be the truth. I was just searching for the right moment."

Suddenly, I'm not sure what to feel.

I stare at him, his downcast eyes, the movement in his throat as he swallows against a swell of emotion. And something breaks apart inside of me. Some measure of resistance begins to crumble.

He looks so vulnerable. So young.

I take a deep breath and let it go, slowly, and then I look up, look into his face once more and I see it, I see the moment he senses the change in my feelings. Something comes alive in his eyes. He takes a step forward and now we're standing so close I'm afraid to speak. My heart is beating too hard in my chest and I don't have to do anything at all to be reminded of everything, every moment, every touch we've ever shared. His scent is all around me. His heat. His exhalations. Gold eyelashes and green eyes. I touch his face, almost without meaning to, gently, like he might be a ghost, like this might be a dream and the tips of my fingers graze his cheek, trail the line of his jaw and I stop when his breath catches, when his body shakes almost imperceptibly

and we lean in as if by memory

eyes closing

lips just touching

"Give me another chance," he whispers, resting his forehead against mine.

My heart aches, throbs in my chest.

"Please," he says softly, and he's somehow closer now, his lips touching mine as he speaks and I feel pinned in place by emotion, unable to move as he presses the words against my mouth, his hands soft and hesitant around my face and he says, "I swear on my life," he says, "I won't disappoint you"

and he kisses me

Kisses me

right here, in the middle of everything, in front of everyone and I'm flooded, overrun with feeling, my head spinning as he presses me against the hard line of his body and I can't save myself from myself, can't stop the sound I make when he parts my lips and I'm lost, lost in the taste of him, lost in his heat, wrapped up in his arms and

I have to tear myself away

pulling back so quickly I nearly stumble. I'm breathing too hard, my face flushed, my feelings panicked

And he can only look at me, his chest rising and falling with an intensity I feel from here, from two feet away, and I can't think of anything right or reasonable to say about what just happened or what I'm feeling except

"This isn't fair," I whisper. Tears threaten, sting my eyes. "This isn't *fair*."

And I don't wait to hear his response before I tear down the hall, bolting the rest of the way back to my rooms.

WARNER

"Trouble in paradise, Mr. Warner?"

I've got him by the throat in seconds, shock disfiguring his expression as I slam his body against the wall. "You," I say angrily. "You forced me into this impossible position. *Why?*"

Castle tries to swallow but can't, his eyes wide but unafraid. When he speaks his words are raspy, suffocated. "You had to do it," he chokes out. "It had to happen. She needed to be warned, and it had to come from you."

"I don't believe you," I shout, shoving him harder against the wall. "And I don't know why I ever trusted you."

"Please, son. Put me down."

I ease up, only a little, and he takes in several lungfuls of air before saying, "I haven't lied to you, Mr. Warner. She had to hear the truth. And if she'd heard this from anyone else she'd never forgive you. But at least now"—he coughs—"with time, she might. It's your only chance at happiness."

"What?" I drop my hand. Drop him. "Since when have you cared about my happiness?"

He's quiet for too long, massaging his throat as he stares at me. Finally, he says, "You think I don't know what your father did to you? What he put you through?"

And now I take a step back.

"You think I don't know your story, son? You think I'd let you into my world—offer you sanctuary among my people—if I really thought you were going to hurt us?"

I'm breathing hard. Suddenly confused. Feeling exposed.

"You don't know anything about me," I say, feeling the lie even as I say it.

Castle smiles, but there's something wounded in it. "You're just a boy," he says quietly. "You're only nineteen years old, Mr. Warner. And I think you forget that all the time. You have no perspective, no idea that you've only barely lived. There's still so much life ahead of you." He sighs. "I try to tell Kenji the same thing, but he's like you. Stubborn," he says. "So stubborn."

"I'm *nothing* like him."

"Did you know that you're a year younger than him?"

"Age is irrelevant. Nearly all my soldiers are older than me."

Castle laughs.

"All of you kids," he says, shaking his head. "You suffer too much. You have these horrible, tragic histories. Volatile personalities. I've always wanted to help," he says. "I've always wanted to fix that. Make this world a better place for you kids."

"Well, you can go save the world somewhere else," I say. "And feel free to babysit Kishimoto all you like. But I'm not your responsibility. I don't need your pity."

Castle only tilts his head at me. "You will never escape my pity, Mr. Warner."

My jaw clenches.

"You boys," he says, his eyes distracted for a moment, "you remind me so much of my own sons."

I pause. "You have children?"

"Yes," he says. And I feel his sudden, breathtaking wave of pain wash over me as he says, "I did."

I take several unconscious steps backward, reeling from the rush of his shared emotions. I can only stare at him. Surprised. Curious.

Sorry.

"Hey."

At the sound of Nazeera's voice I spin around, startled. She's with Haider, the two of them looking grave.

"What is it?" I say.

"We need to talk." She looks at Castle. "Your name is Castle, right?"

He nods.

"Yeah, I know you're wise to this business, Castle, so I'm going to need you to get in on this, too." Nazeera whips her finger through the air to draw a circle around the four of us. "We all need to talk. *Now*."

JULIETTE

It's a strange thing, to never know peace. To know that no matter where you go, there is no sanctuary. That the threat of pain is always a whisper away. I'm not safe locked into these 4 walls, I was never safe leaving my house, and I couldn't even feel safe in the 14 years I lived at home. The asylum kills people every day, the world has already been taught to fear me, and my home is the same place where my father locked me in my room every night and my mother screamed at me for being the abomination she was forced to raise.

She always said it was my face.

There was something about my face, she said, that she couldn't stand. Something about my eyes, the way I looked at her, the fact that I even existed. She'd always tell me to stop looking at her. She'd always scream it. Like I might attack her. Stop looking at me, she'd scream. You just stop looking at me, she'd scream.

She put my hand in the fire once.

Just to see if it would burn, she said. Just to check if it was a regular hand, she said.

I was 6 years old then.

I remember because it was my birthday.

—AN EXCERPT FROM JULIETTE'S JOURNALS IN THE ASYLUM

"Never mind," is all I say when Kenji shows up at my door.

"Never mind, what?" Kenji sticks his foot out to catch the closing door. Now he's squeezing his way in. "What's going on?"

"Never mind, I don't want to talk to any of you. Please go away. Or maybe you can all go to hell. I don't actually care."

Kenji looks stunned, like I just slapped him in the face. "Are you—wait, are you serious right now?"

"Nazeera and I are leaving for the symposium in an hour. I have to get ready."

"What? What's happening, J? What's wrong with you?"

Now, I turn to face him. *"What's wrong with me?* Oh, like you don't know?"

Kenji runs a hand through his hair. "I mean, I heard about what happened with Warner, yeah, but I'm pretty sure I just saw you guys making out in the hallway so I'm, uh, really confused—"

"He *lied* to me, Kenji. He lied to me this whole time. About so many things. And so did Castle. So did *you*—"

"Wait, what?" He grabs my arm as I turn away. "Wait—I didn't lie to you about shit. Don't mix me up in this mess. I had nothing to do with any of it. Hell, I still haven't figured out what to say to Castle. I can't believe he kept all of this from me."

I go suddenly still, my fists closing as my anger builds and breaks, holding fast to a sudden hope. "You weren't in on all of this?" I say. "With Castle?"

"Uh-uh. No way. I had no clue about any of this insanity until Warner told me about it yesterday."

I hesitate.

Kenji rolls his eyes.

"Well, how am I supposed to trust you?" I say, my voice rising in pitch like a child. "Everyone's been lying to me—"

"J," he says, shaking his head. "C'mon. You know me. You know I don't bullshit. That's not my style."

I swallow, hard, feeling suddenly small. Feeling suddenly broken inside. My eyes sting and I fight back the impulse to cry. "You promise?"

"Hey," he says softly. "Come here, kid."

I take a tentative step forward and he wraps me up in his arms, warm and strong and safe and I've never been so grateful for his friendship, for his steady existence in my life.

"It's going to be okay," he whispers. "I swear."

"Liar," I sniff.

"Well, there's a fifty percent chance I'm right."

"Kenji?"

"Mm?"

"If I find out you're lying to me about any of this I swear to God I will break all the bones in your body."

A short laugh. "Yeah, okay."

"I'm serious."

"Uh-huh." He pats my head.

"I will."

"I know, princess. I know."

Several more seconds of silence.

And then

"Kenji," I say quietly.

"Mm?"

"They're going to destroy Sector 45."

"Who is?"

"Everyone."

Kenji leans back. Raises an eyebrow. "Everyone who?"

"All the other supreme commanders," I say. "Nazeera told me everything."

Unexpectedly, Kenji's face breaks into a tremendous smile. "Oh, so Nazeera is one of the good guys, huh? She's on our team? Trying to help you out?"

"Oh my God, Kenji, please focus—"

"I'm just saying," he says, holding up his hands. "The girl is fine as hell is all I'm saying."

I roll my eyes. Try not to laugh as I wipe away errant tears.

"So." He nods his head at me. "What's the deal? The details? Who's coming? When? How? Et cetera?"

"I don't know," I say. "Nazeera is still trying to figure it out. She thinks maybe in the next week or so? The kids are here to monitor me and send back information, but they're coming to the symposium, specifically, because apparently the commanders want to know how the other sector leaders will react to seeing me. Nazeera says she thinks the information will help inform their next moves. I'm guessing we have maybe a matter of *days*."

Kenji's eyes go wide, panicked. "Oh, shit."

"Yeah, but when they decide to obliterate Sector 45 their plan is to also take me prisoner. The Reestablishment wants to bring me back in, apparently. Whatever that means."

"Bring you back in?" Kenji frowns. "For what? More testing? Torture? What do they want to do with you?"

I shake my head. "I have no idea. I have no clue who these people are. My sister," I say, the words feeling strange as I say them, "is apparently still being tested and tortured somewhere. So I'm pretty sure they're not bringing me back for a big family reunion, you know?"

"Wow." Kenji rubs his forehead. "That is some next-level drama."

"Yeah."

"So—what are we going to do?"

I hesitate. "I don't know, Kenji. They're coming to kill everyone in Sector 45. I don't think I have a choice."

"What do you mean?"

I look up. "I mean I'm pretty sure I'll have to kill them first."

WARNER

My heart is pounding frantically in my chest. My hands are clammy, unsteady. But I cannot make time to deal with my mind. Nazeera's confessions might cost me my sanity. I can only pray she is mistaken. I can only hope that she will be proven desperately and woefully wrong and there's no time, no time at all to deal with any of this. I can no longer make room in my day for these flimsy, unreliable human emotions.

I must live here now.

In my own solitude.

Today I will be a soldier only, a perfect robot if need be, and stand tall, eyes betraying no emotion as our supreme commander Juliette Ferrars takes the stage.

We're all here today, a small battalion posted up behind her like her own personal guard—myself, Delalieu, Castle, Kenji, Ian, Alia, Lily, Brendan, and Winston—even Nazeera and Haider, Lena, Stephan, Valentina, and Nicolás stand beside us, pretending to be supportive as she begins her speech. The only ones missing are Sonya, Sara, Kent, and James, who stayed behind on base. Kent cares little about anything these days but keeping James out of danger, and I can't say I blame him. Sometimes I wish I could opt out of this life, too.

I squeeze my eyes shut. Steady myself.

I just want this to be over.

The location of the biannual symposium is fairly fluid, and generally rotational. But in recognition of our new supreme commander, the event was relocated to Sector 45, an effort made possible entirely by Delalieu.

I can feel our collective group pulse with different kinds and levels of energy, but it's all so meshed together I can't tell fear and apathy apart. I'm focused instead on the audience and our leader, as their reactions are the most important. And of all the many events and symposiums I've attended over the years, I've never felt such an electric charge in the crowd as I do now.

554 of my fellow chief commanders and regents are in the audience, but so are their spouses, and even several members of their closest staff. It's unprecedented: every invitation was accepted. No one wanted to miss the opportunity to meet the new seventeen-year-old leader of North America, no. They're fascinated. They're hungry. Wolves sitting in human skin, eager to tear into the flesh of the young girl they've already underestimated.

If Juliette's powers didn't offer her body a level of functional invincibility I'd be deeply concerned about her standing alone and unguarded in front of all her enemies. The civilians of this sector may be rooting for her, but the rest of the continent has no interest in the disruption she's brought to the land—or to the threat she poses to their ranks in The Reestablishment. These men and women standing before her today are paid to be loyal to another party. They have no sympathy for her cause, for her fight for the common people.

I have no idea how long they'll let her speak before they rip into her.

But I don't have to wait long.

Juliette has only just started speaking—she's only just begun talking about the many failures of The Reestablishment and the need for a new beginning when the crowd becomes suddenly restless. They stand up, raise their fists and my mind disconnects as they shout at her, the events unfolding before my eyes as if in slow motion. She doesn't react.

One, two, sixteen people are on their feet now, and she keeps talking.

Half the room roars upward, angry words hurled in her direction and now I can feel her growing angrier, her frustration peaking, but somehow, she holds her ground. The more they protest, the more she projects her voice; she's speaking so loudly now she's practically shouting. I look quickly between her and the crowd, my mind working desperately to decide what to do. Kenji catches my eye and the two of us understand each other without speaking.

We have to intervene.

Juliette is now denouncing The Reestablishment's plans to obliterate languages and literature; she's outlining her hopes to transition the civilians out of the compounds; and she's just begun addressing our issues with the climate when a shot is fired into the room.

There's a moment of perfect silence, and then—

Juliette peels the dented bullet off her forehead. Tosses it to the ground. The gentle, tinkling sound of metal on marble reverberates around the room.

Mass chaos.

Hundreds and hundreds of people are suddenly on their feet, all of them shouting at her, threatening her, pointing guns at her, and I can feel it, I can feel it spiraling out of control.

More shots ring out, and in the seconds it takes us to form a plan, we're already too late. Brendan falls to the ground with a sudden, horrifying gasp. Winston screams; catches his body.

And that's it.

Juliette goes suddenly still, and my mind slows down.

I can feel it before it happens: I can feel the change, the static in the air. Heat ripples around her, tongues of power unfurling from her body like lightning preparing for a strike and there's no time to do anything but hold my breath when, suddenly—

She *screams*.

Long. Loud. Violent.

The world seems to blur for just a second—for just a moment everything seizes, freezes in place: contorted bodies; angry, distorted faces; all frozen in time—

Floorboards peel upward and fissure apart. Cracks like thunderclaps as they shatter up the walls. Light fixtures swing precariously before smashing to the floor.

And then, everyone.

Every single person in her line of sight. 554 people and all their guests. Their faces, their bodies, the seats they sit in: sliced open like fresh fish. Their flesh feathers outward, swelling slowly as a steady gush of blood gathers in pools around their feet.

They all drop dead.

JULIETTE

I started screaming today.
—AN EXCERPT FROM JULIETTE'S JOURNALS IN THE ASYLUM

Were you happy
Were you sad
Were you scared
Were you mad
the first time you screamed?
Were you fighting for your life your decency your dignity your humanity
When someone touches you now, do you scream?
When someone smiles at you now, do you smile back?
Did he tell you not to scream did he hit you when you cried?
Did he have one nose two eyes two lips two cheeks two ears two eyebrows.
Was he one human who looked just like you.
Color your personality.
Shapes and sizes are variety.
Your heart is an anomaly.
Your actions
are
the
only
traces
you leave
behind.

—AN EXCERPT FROM JULIETTE'S JOURNALS IN THE ASYLUM

Sometimes I think the shadows are moving.

Sometimes I think someone might be watching.

Sometimes this idea scares me and sometimes the idea makes me so absurdly happy I can't stop crying. And then sometimes I think I have no idea when I started losing my mind in here. Nothing seems real anymore and I can't tell if I'm screaming out loud or only in my head.

There's no one here to hear me.

To tell me I'm not dead.

—AN EXCERPT FROM JULIETTE'S JOURNALS IN THE ASYLUM

I don't know when it started.

I don't know why it started.

I don't know anything about anything except for the screaming.

My mother screaming when she realized she could no longer touch me. My father screaming when he realized what I'd done to my mother. My parents screaming when they'd lock me in my room and tell me I should be grateful. For their food. For their humane treatment of this thing that could not possibly be their child. For the yardstick they used to measure the distance I needed to keep away.

I ruined their lives, is what they said to me.

I stole their happiness. Destroyed my mother's hope for ever having children again.

Couldn't I see what I'd done? is what they'd ask me. Couldn't I see that I'd ruined everything?

I tried so hard to fix what I'd ruined. I tried every single day to be what they wanted. I tried all the time to be better but I never really knew how.

I only know now that the scientists are wrong.

The world is flat.

I know because I was tossed right off the edge and I've been trying to hold on for seventeen years. I've been trying to climb back up for seventeen years but it's nearly impossible to beat gravity when no one is willing to give you a hand.

When no one wants to risk touching you.

—AN EXCERPT FROM JULIETTE'S JOURNALS IN THE ASYLUM

Am I insane yet?
Has it happened yet?
How will I ever know?

—AN EXCERPT FROM JULIETTE'S JOURNALS IN THE ASYLUM

There's a moment of pure, perfect silence before everything, everything explodes. At first, I don't even realize what I've done. I don't understand what just happened. I didn't mean to kill *these* people—

And then, suddenly

It hits me

The crushing realization that I've just slaughtered a room of six hundred people.

It seems impossible. It seems fake. There were no bullets. No excess force, no violence. Just one, long, angry cry.

"*Stop it*," I screamed. I squeezed my eyes shut and screamed it, anger and heartbreak and exhaustion and crushing devastation filling my lungs. It was the weight of recent weeks, the pain of all these years, the embarrassment of false hopes manufactured in my heart, the betrayal, the loss—

Adam. Warner. Castle.

My parents, real and imagined.

A sister I might never know.

The lies that make up my life. The threats against the innocent people of Sector 45. The certain death that awaits me. The frustration of having so much power, so much power and feeling so utterly, completely powerless

"*Please,*" I screamed. "*Please stop—*"

And now—

Now this.

My limbs have gone numb from disbelief. My ears feel full of wind, my mind disconnected from my body. I couldn't have killed this many people, I think, I couldn't have just killed all these people that isn't possible, I think, it's not possible not possible that I opened my mouth and then *this*

Kenji is trying to say something to me, something that sounds like *we have to get out of here, hurry, we have to go now—*

But I'm numb, I'm dim, I'm unable to move one foot in front of the other and someone is dragging me, forcing me to move and I hear explosions

And suddenly my mind sharpens.

I gasp and spin around, searching for Kenji but he's gone. His shirt is soaked in blood and he's being dragged off in the distance, his eyes half closed and

Warner is on his knees, his hands cuffed behind his back

Castle is unconscious on the floor, blood running freely from his chest

Winston is still screaming, even as someone drags him away

Brendan is dead

Lily, Ian, Alia, dead

And I'm trying to reconnect my mind, trying to work my way through the shock seizing my body and my head is spinning, *spinning*, and I see Nazeera out of the corner of my eye with her head in her hands and someone touches me and I jump

I jerk back

"What's happening?" I say to no one. "What's going on?"

"You've done beautiful work here, darling. You've really made us proud. The Reestablishment is so grateful for the sacrifices you've made."

"Who are you?" I say, searching for the voice.

And then I see them, a man and a woman kneeling in front of me, and it's only then that I realize I'm lying on the ground, paralyzed. My arms and legs are bound by pulsing, electric wires. I try to fight against them and I can't.

My powers have been extinguished.

I look up at these strangers, eyes wide and terrified. "Who are you?" I say again, still raging against my restraints. "What do you want from me?"

"I'm the supreme commander of Oceania," the woman says to me, smiling. "Your father and I have come to take you home."

WARNER

JULIETTE

Why don't you just kill yourself? someone at school asked me once.

I think it was the kind of question intended to be cruel, but it was the first time I'd ever contemplated the possibility. I didn't know what to say. Maybe I was crazy to consider it, but I'd always hoped that if I were a good enough girl—if I did everything right, if I said the right things or said nothing at all—I thought my parents would change their minds. I thought they would finally listen when I tried to talk. I thought they would give me a chance. I thought they might finally love me.

I always had that ~~stupid~~ hope.

—AN EXCERPT FROM JULIETTE'S JOURNALS IN THE ASYLUM

When I open my eyes, I see stars.

Dozens of them. Little plastic stars stuck to the ceiling. They glow, faintly, in the dim light, and I sit up, head pounding, as I try to orient myself. There's a window on my right; a sheer, gauzy curtain filters sunset oranges and blues into the room at odd angles. I'm sitting on a small bed. I look up, look around.

Everything is pink.

Pink blanket, pink pillows. Pink rug on the floor.

I get to my feet and spin around, confused, to find that there's another, identical bed in here, but its sheets are purple. The pillows are purple.

The room is divided by an imaginary line, each half a mirror image of the other. Two desks; one pink, one purple. Two chairs; one pink, one purple. Two dressers, two mirrors. Pink, purple. Painted flowers on the walls. A small table and chairs off to one side. A rack of fluffy costume dresses. A box of tiaras on the floor. A little chalkboard easel in the corner. A bin under the window, full to the brim with dolls and stuffed animals.

This is a child's bedroom.

I feel my heart racing. My skin goes hot and cold.

I can still feel a loss inside of me—an inherent knowledge that my powers aren't working—and I realize only then that there are glowing, electric cuffs clamped around my wrists and ankles. I yank at them, use every bit of my strength to tear them open, and they don't budge.

I'm growing more panicked by the moment.

I run to the window, desperate for some sense of place—for some explanation of where I am, for proof that this isn't some kind of hallucination—and I'm disappointed; the view out the window only confuses me. I see a stunning vista. Endless, rolling hills. Mountains in the distance. A massive, glittering lake reflecting the colors of the sunset. It's *beautiful*.

I step back, feeling suddenly more terrified.

My eyes move instead to the pink desk and chair, scanning their surfaces for clues. There are only stacks of colorful notebooks. A porcelain cup full of markers and glitter pens. Several pages of fluorescent stickers.

My hand shakes as I pull open the desk drawer.

Inside are stacks of old letters and Polaroids.

At first, I can only stare at them. My heartbeats echo in my head, throbbing so hard I can almost feel them in my throat. My breaths come in faster, the inhalations shallow. I feel my head spin and I blink once, twice, forcing myself to be steady. To be brave.

Slowly, very slowly, I pick up the stack of letters.

All I have to do is look at the mailing addresses to know that these letters predate The Reestablishment. They've all been sent to the attention of Evie and Maximillian Sommers. To a street in Glenorchy, New Zealand.

New Zealand.

And then I remember, with a sudden gasp, the faces of the man and woman who carried me out of the symposium.

I'm the supreme commander of Oceania, she'd said. *Your father and I have come to take you home.*

I close my eyes and stars explode in the blackness behind my eyelids, leaving me faint. Breathless. I blink my eyes open. My fingers feel loose, clumsy as I open the letter at the top of the stack.

The note is brief. It's dated twelve years ago.

M & E—
All is well. We've found her a suitable family. No sign of powers yet, but we'll keep a close eye on her. Still, I must advise you to put her out of your mind. She and Emmaline have had their memories expunged. They no longer ask about you. This will be my last update.
P. Anderson.

P. Anderson.

Paris Anderson. Warner's father.

I look around the bedroom with new eyes, feeling a terrible chill creep up my spine as the impossible pieces of this new insanity come together in my mind.

Vomit threatens. I swallow it back.

I'm staring now at the stack of Polaroids, untouched,

inside the open desk drawer. I think I've lost feeling in parts of my face. Still, I force myself to pick up the stack.

The first is a picture of two little girls in matching yellow dresses. They're both brown-haired and a little skinny, holding hands in a garden path. One of them looks at the camera, the other one looks at her feet.

I flip the photo over.

Ella's first day of school

The stack of photos falls out of my trembling hands, scattering as they go. My every instinct is shrieking at me, sounding alarm bells, begging me to run.

Get out, I try to scream at myself. *Get out of here.*

But my curiosity won't let me go.

A few of the photos have landed face-up on the desk, and I can't stop staring at them, my heart pounding in my ears. Carefully, I pick them up.

Three little brown-haired girls stand next to bikes that are slightly too big for them. They're all looking at each other, laughing at something.

I flip the photo over.

Ella, Emmaline, and Nazeera. No more training wheels.

I gasp, the sound choking me as it leaves my chest. I feel my lungs squeeze and I reach out, catch the desk with one hand to steady myself. I feel like I'm floating, unhinged.

Caught in a nightmare.

I flip through the photos with a desperation now, my mind working faster than my hands as I fumble, trying and failing to make sense of what I'm seeing.

The next photo is of a little girl holding the hand of an older man.

Emmaline and Papa, it says on the back.

Another photo, this one of both girls climbing a tree.

The day Ella twisted her ankle

Another one, blurred faces, cupcakes and candles—

Emmaline's 5th birthday

Another, this time a picture of a handsome couple—

Paris and Leila, visiting for Christmas

And I freeze

stunned

feel the air leave my body.

I'm holding only one photo now, and I have to force myself, beg myself to look at it, the square Polaroid shaking in my trembling hand.

It's a picture of a little boy standing next to a little girl. She's sitting in a stairwell. He looks at her as she eats a piece of cake.

I flip it over.

Aaron and Ella

is all it says.

I trip backward, stumbling, and collapse onto the floor. My whole body is seizing, shaking with terror, with confusion, with impossibility.

Suddenly, as if on cue, there's a knock at my door. A woman—the woman from before; an older version of the woman in the pictures—pops her head inside, smiles at me and says, "Ella, honey, don't you want to come outside? Your dinner is getting cold."

And I'm certain I'm going to be sick.

The room tilts around me.
I see spots
feel myself sway
and then—
all at once

The world goes black.

The brand new YA fantasy romance series from the author of *TikTok* sensation, **Shatter Me**